my LITTLE

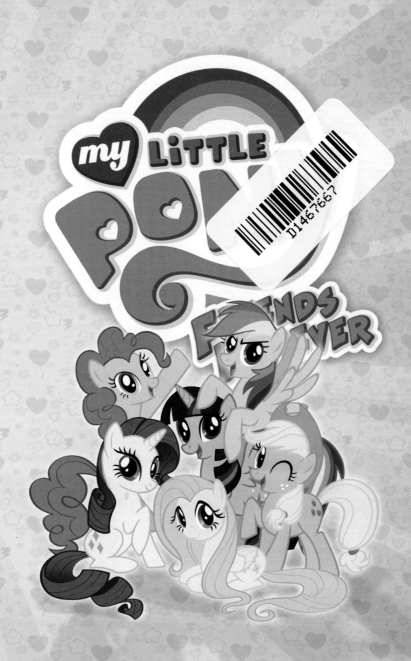

Pinkie Pie & Applejack

Written and Lettered by **Alex De Campi**
Art by **Carla Speed McNeil**
Colors by **Jenn Manley Lee** & **Bill Mudron**

Discord & The Cutie Mark Crusaders

Written by **Jeremy Whitley**
Art by **Tony Fleecs**
Color Flats by **Lauren Perry**

Princess Celestia & Spike

Written by **Ted Anderson**
Art by **Agnes Garbowska**

Twilight Sparkle & Shining Armor

Written by **Rob Anderson**
Art by **Amy Mebberson**
Colors by **Heather Breckel**

Fluttershy & Zecora

Written by **Thom Zahler**
Art by **Tony Fleecs**
Colors by **Heather Breckel**

Letters by **Neil Uyetake**
Series Edits by **Bobby Curnow**

Cover Art by **Jay Fosgitt**
Collection Edits by **Justin Eisinger** & **Alonzo Simon**
Collection Design by **Neil Uyetake**
Publisher: **Ted Adams**

Licensed By: Hasbro

www.IDWPUBLISHING.com
ISBN: 978-1-63140-771-0

24 23 22 21   4 5 6 7

Special thanks to Meghan McCarthy, Eliza Hart, Ed Lane, Beth Artale, and Michael Kelly.

For international rights, contact licensing@idwpublishing.com

Nachie Marsham, Publisher • Blake Kobashigawa, VP of Sales • Tara McCrillis, VP Publishing Operations • John Barber, Editor-in-Chief • Mark Doyle, Editorial Director, Originals • Erika Turner, Executive Editor • Scott Dunbier, Director, Special Projects • Lauren LaPera, Managing Editor • Joe Hughes, Director, Talent Relations • Anna Morrow, Sr. Marketing Director • Alexandra Hargett, Book & Mass Market Sales Director • Keith Davidsen, Director Marketing & PR • Topher Alford, Sr Digital Marketing Manager • Shauna Monteforte, Sr. Director of Manufacturing Operations • Jamie Miller, Sr. Operations Manager • Nathan Widick, Sr. Art Director, Head of Design • Neil Uyetake, Sr. Art Director Design & Production • Shawn Lee, Art Director Design & Production • Jack Rivera, Art Director, Marketing

Ted Adams and Robbie Robbins, IDW Founders

Facebook: facebook.com/idwpublishing • Twitter: @idwpublishing • YouTube: youtube.com/idwpublishing
Tumblr: tumblr.idwpublishing.com • Instagram: instagram.com/idwpublishing

Rainbow Dash & Trixie

Written by **Thom Zahler**
Art by **Agnes Garbowska**

Pinkie Pie & Princess Luna

Written by **Jeremy Whitley**
Art by **Tony Fleecs**
Colors by **Heather Breckel**

Applejack & Rarity

Written by **Katie Cook**
Art by **Andy Price**
Colors by **Heather Breckel**

Granny & The Flim Flam Brothers

Written by **Christina Rice**
Art by **Tony Fleecs**
Colors by **Heather Breckel**

Fluttershy & Iron Will

Written by **Christina Rice**
Colors by **Agnes Garbowska**

Rainbow Dash & Spitfire

Written by **Ted Anderson**
Art by **Jay Fosgitt**
Colors by **Heather Breckel**

Pinkie Pie & Twilight Sparkle

Written by **Barbara Randall Kesel**
Art by **Brenda Hickey**
Colors by **Heather Breckel**

Pinkie Pie & Applejack

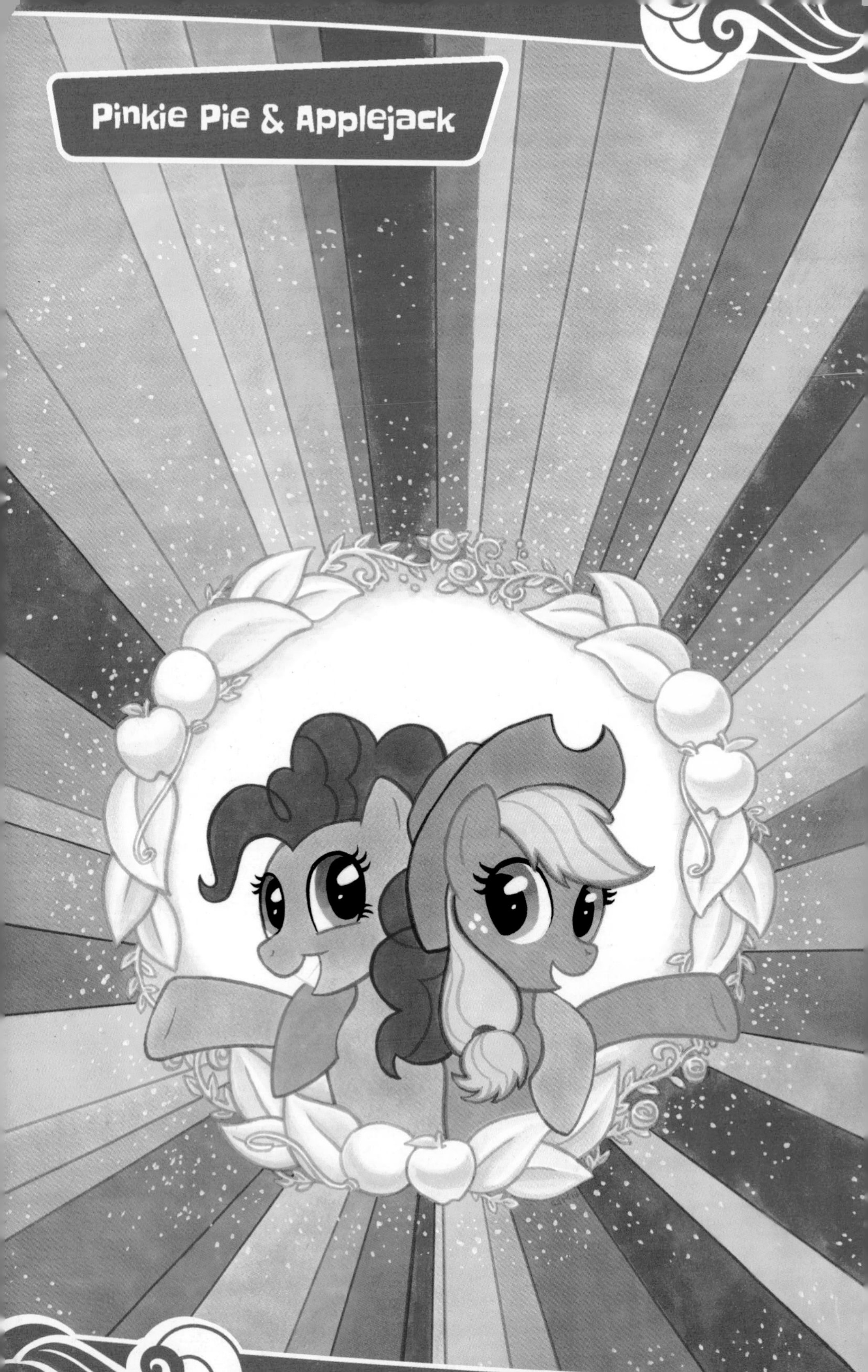

art by CARLA SPEED McNEIL

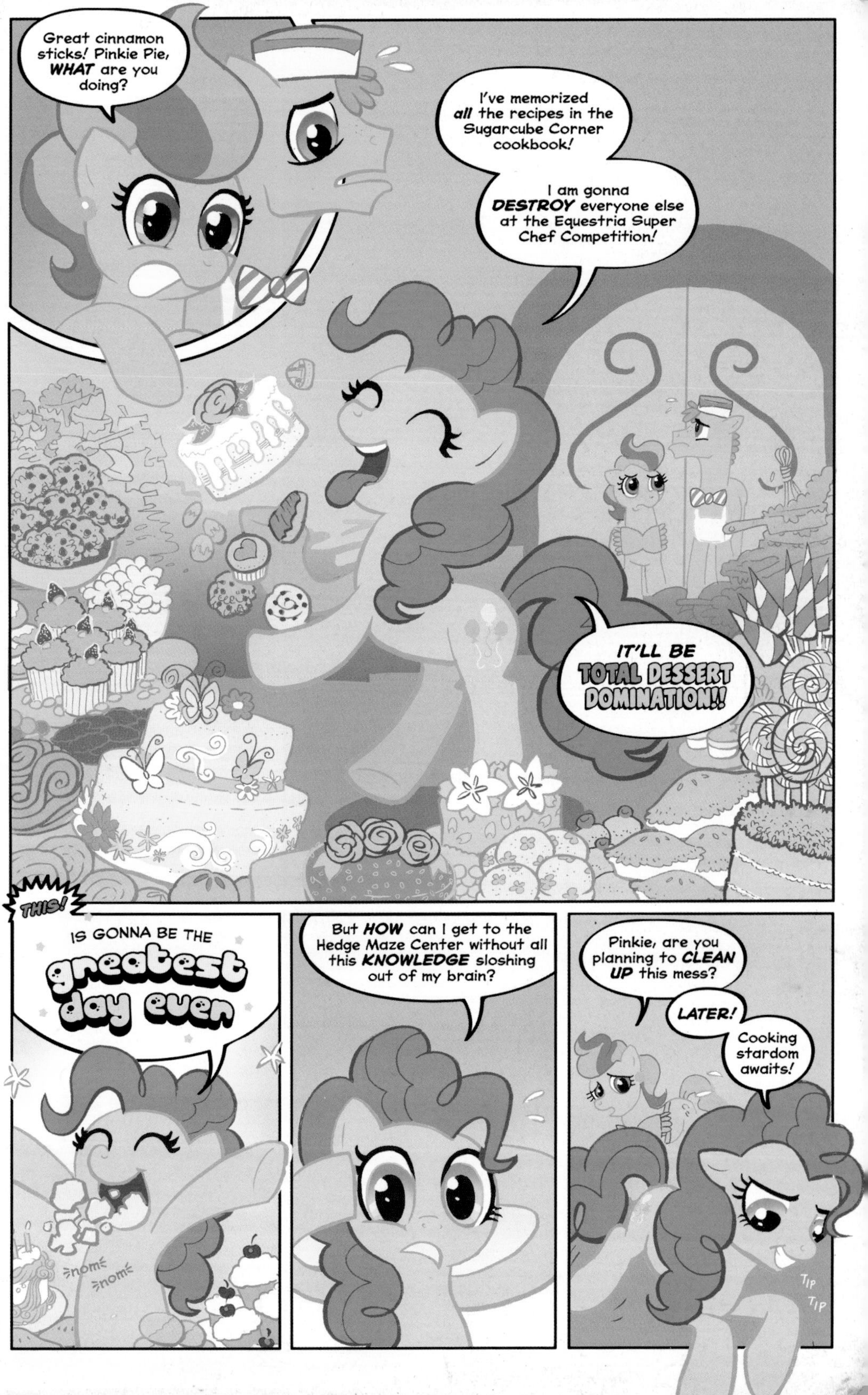
Great cinnamon sticks! Pinkie Pie, WHAT are you doing?
I've memorized all the recipes in the Sugarcube Corner cookbook!
I am gonna DESTROY everyone else at the Equestria Super Chef Competition!
IT'LL BE TOTAL DESSERT DOMINATION!!
THIS!
IS GONNA BE THE greatest day ever
nom
nom
But HOW can I get to the Hedge Maze Center without all this KNOWLEDGE sloshing out of my brain?
Pinkie, are you planning to CLEAN UP this mess?
LATER!
Cooking stardom awaits!
TIP
TIP

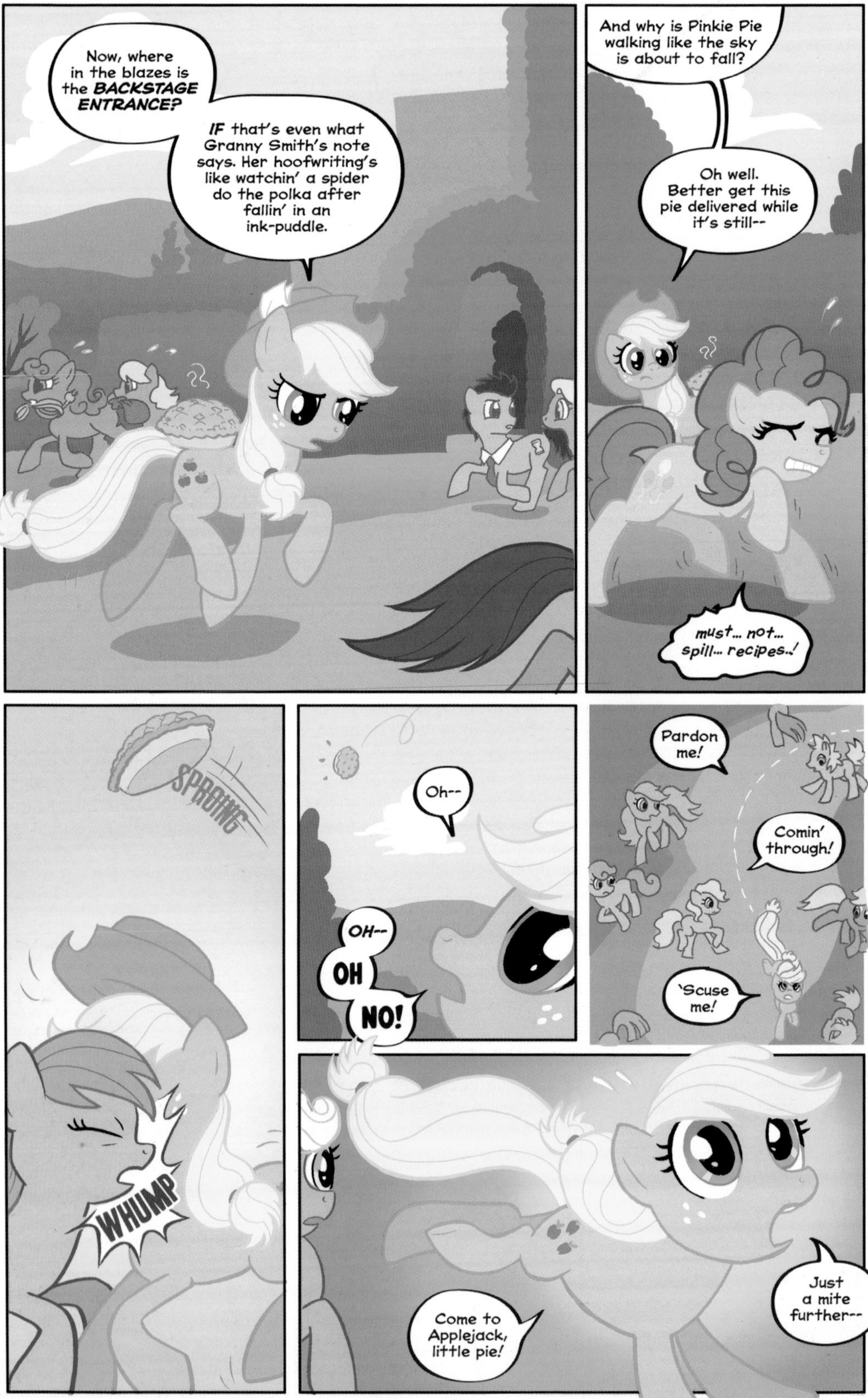
Now, where in the blazes is the BACKSTAGE ENTRANCE?
IF that's even what Granny Smith's note says. Her hoofwriting's like watchin' a spider do the polka after fallin' in an ink-puddle.
And why is Pinkie Pie walking like the sky is about to fall?
Oh well. Better get this pie delivered while it's still--
must... not... spill... recipes..!
SPROING
WHUMP
Oh--
OH--
OH
NO!
Pardon me!
Comin' through!
'Scuse me!
Come to Applejack, little pie!
Just a mite further--

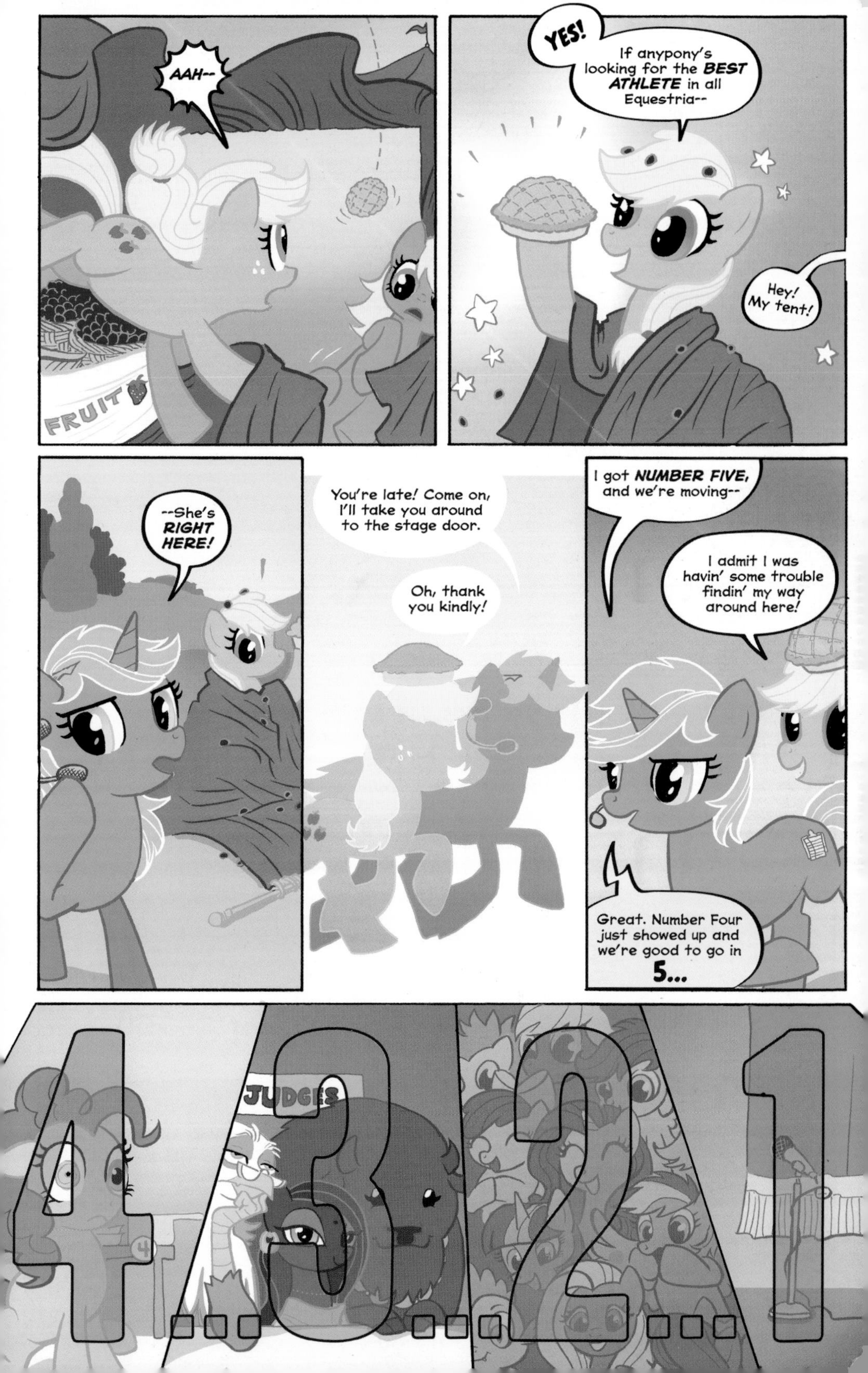
AAH--
YES!
If anypony's looking for the **BEST ATHLETE** in all Equestria--
Hey! My tent!
--She's **RIGHT HERE!**
You're late! Come on, I'll take you around to the stage door.
Oh, thank you kindly!
I got **NUMBER FIVE,** and we're moving--
I admit I was havin' some trouble findin' my way around here!
Great. Number Four just showed up and we're good to go in
5...
FRUIT
JUDGES
4... 3... 2... 1

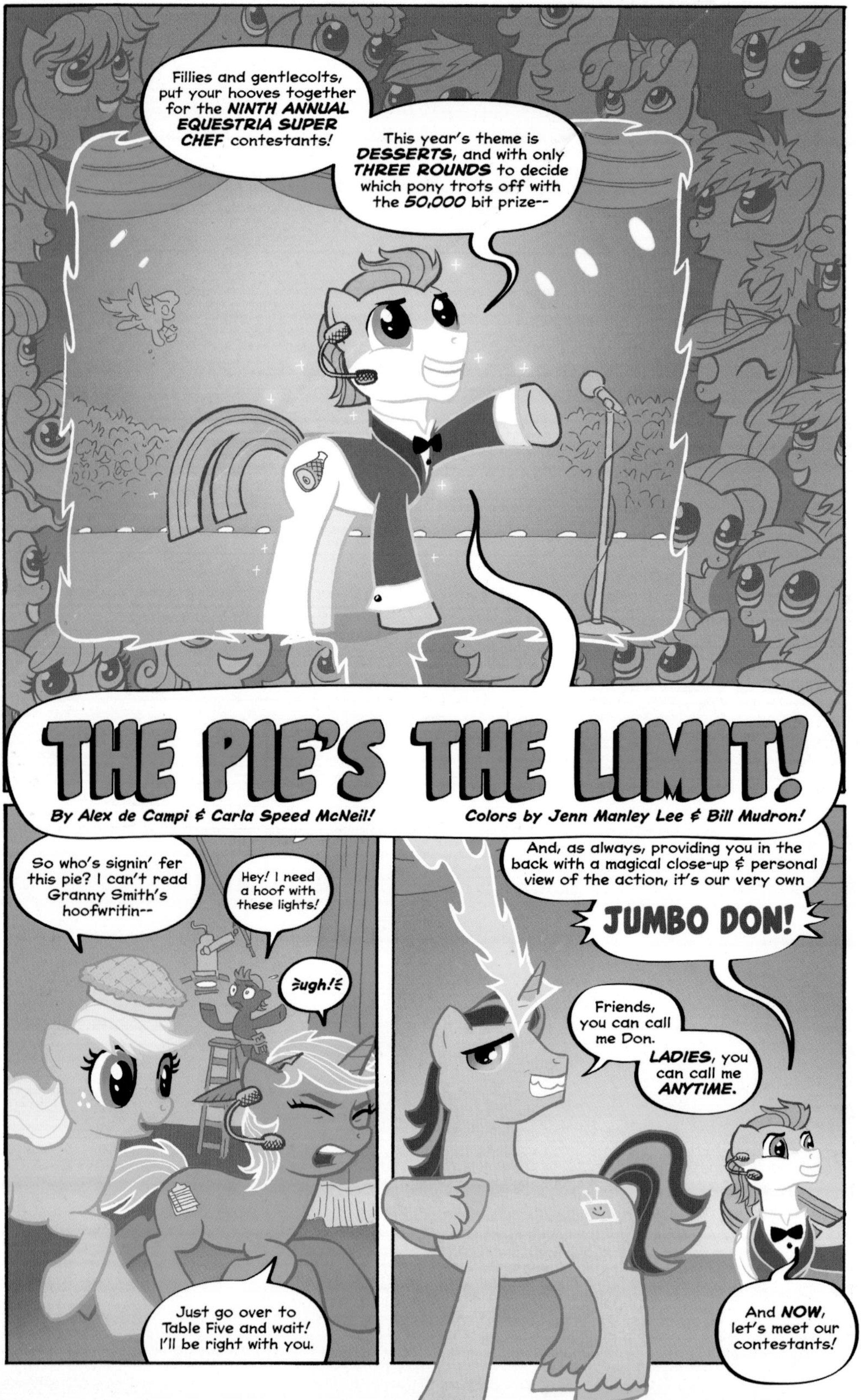

Fillies and gentlecolts, put your hooves together for the NINTH ANNUAL EQUESTRIA SUPER CHEF contestants!
This year's theme is DESSERTS, and with only THREE ROUNDS to decide which pony trots off with the 50,000 bit prize--
THE PIE'S THE LIMIT!
By Alex de Campi & Carla Speed McNeil!
Colors by Jenn Manley Lee & Bill Mudron!
So who's signin' fer this pie? I can't read Granny Smith's hoofwritin--
Hey! I need a hoof with these lights!
ugh!
Just go over to Table Five and wait! I'll be right with you.
And, as always, providing you in the back with a magical close-up & personal view of the action, it's our very own
JUMBO DON!
Friends, you can call me Don.
LADIES, you can call me ANYTIME.
And NOW, let's meet our contestants!

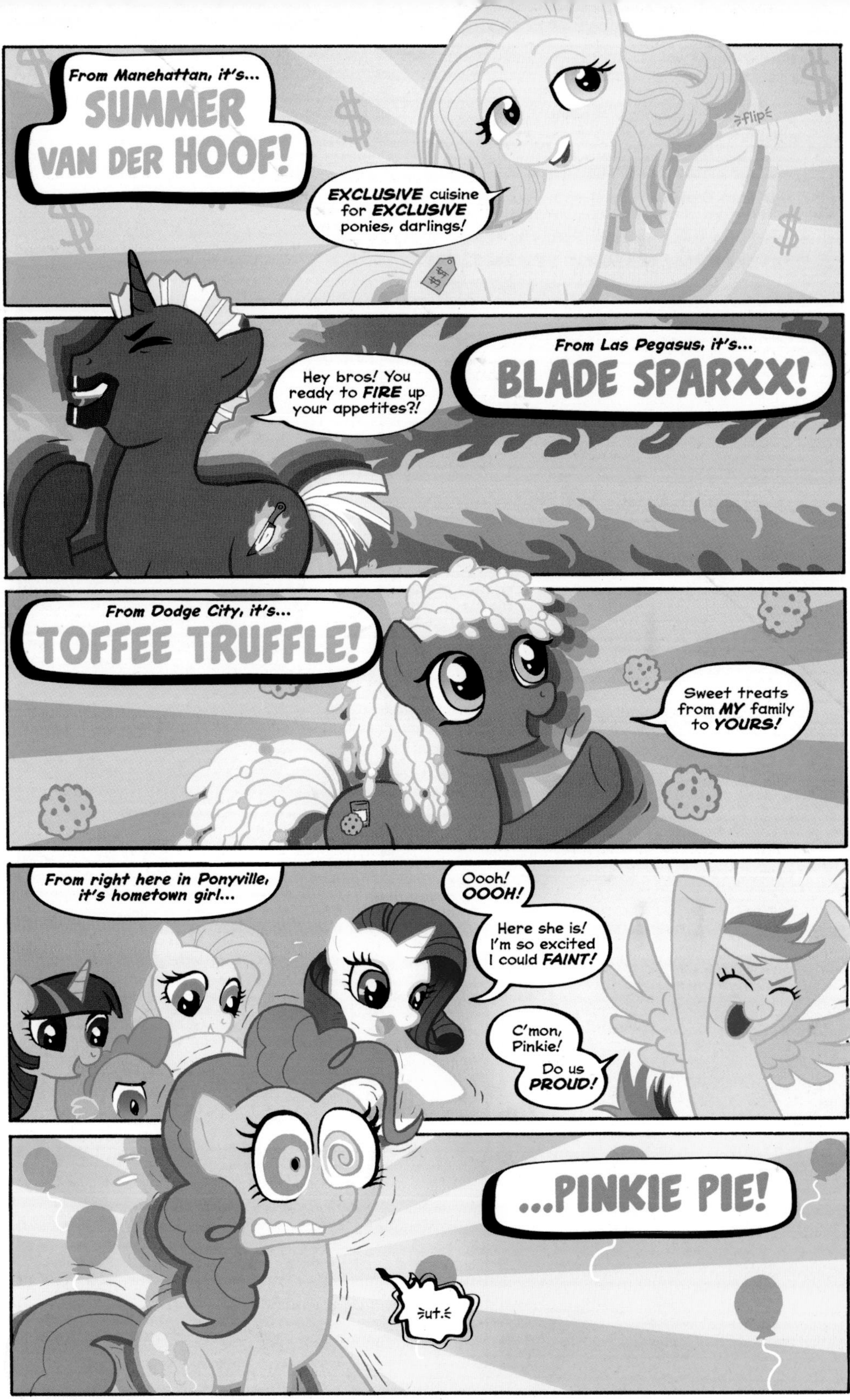
From Manehattan, it's... SUMMER VAN DER HOOF!
EXCLUSIVE cuisine for EXCLUSIVE ponies, darlings!
flip
From Las Pegasus, it's... BLADE SPARXX!
Hey bros! You ready to FIRE up your appetites?!
From Dodge City, it's... TOFFEE TRUFFLE!
Sweet treats from MY family to YOURS!
From right here in Ponyville, it's hometown girl...
Oooh! OOOH!
Here she is! I'm so excited I could FAINT!
C'mon, Pinkie!
Do us PROUD!
...PINKIE PIE!
ut.

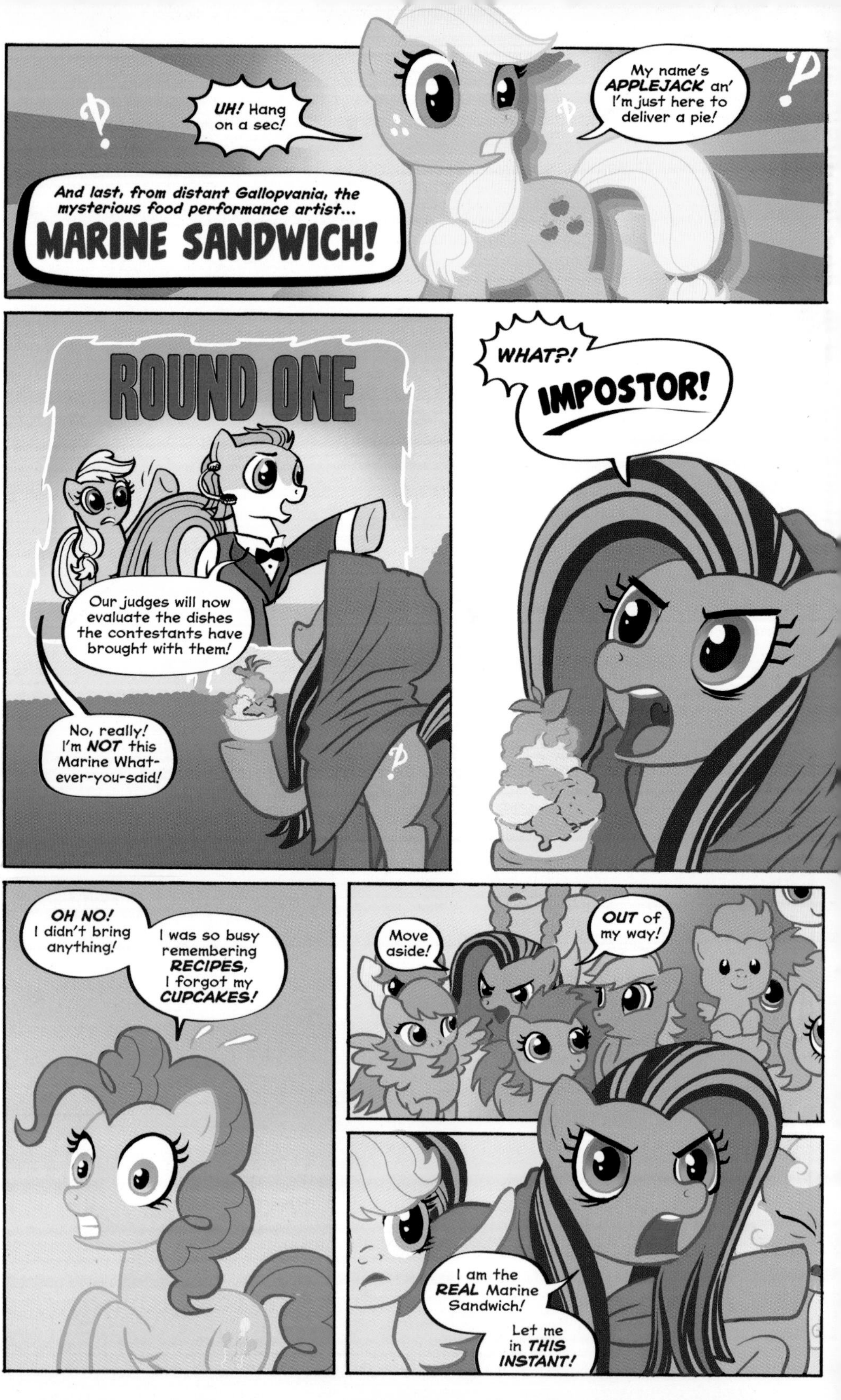
And last, from distant Gallopvania, the mysterious food performance artist...
MARINE SANDWICH!
UH! Hang on a sec!
My name's APPLEJACK an' I'm just here to deliver a pie!
ROUND ONE
Our judges will now evaluate the dishes the contestants have brought with them!
No, really! I'm NOT this Marine What-ever-you-said!
WHAT?!
IMPOSTOR!
OH NO! I didn't bring anything!
I was so busy remembering RECIPES, I forgot my CUPCAKES!
Move aside!
OUT of my way!
I am the REAL Marine Sandwich!
Let me in THIS INSTANT!

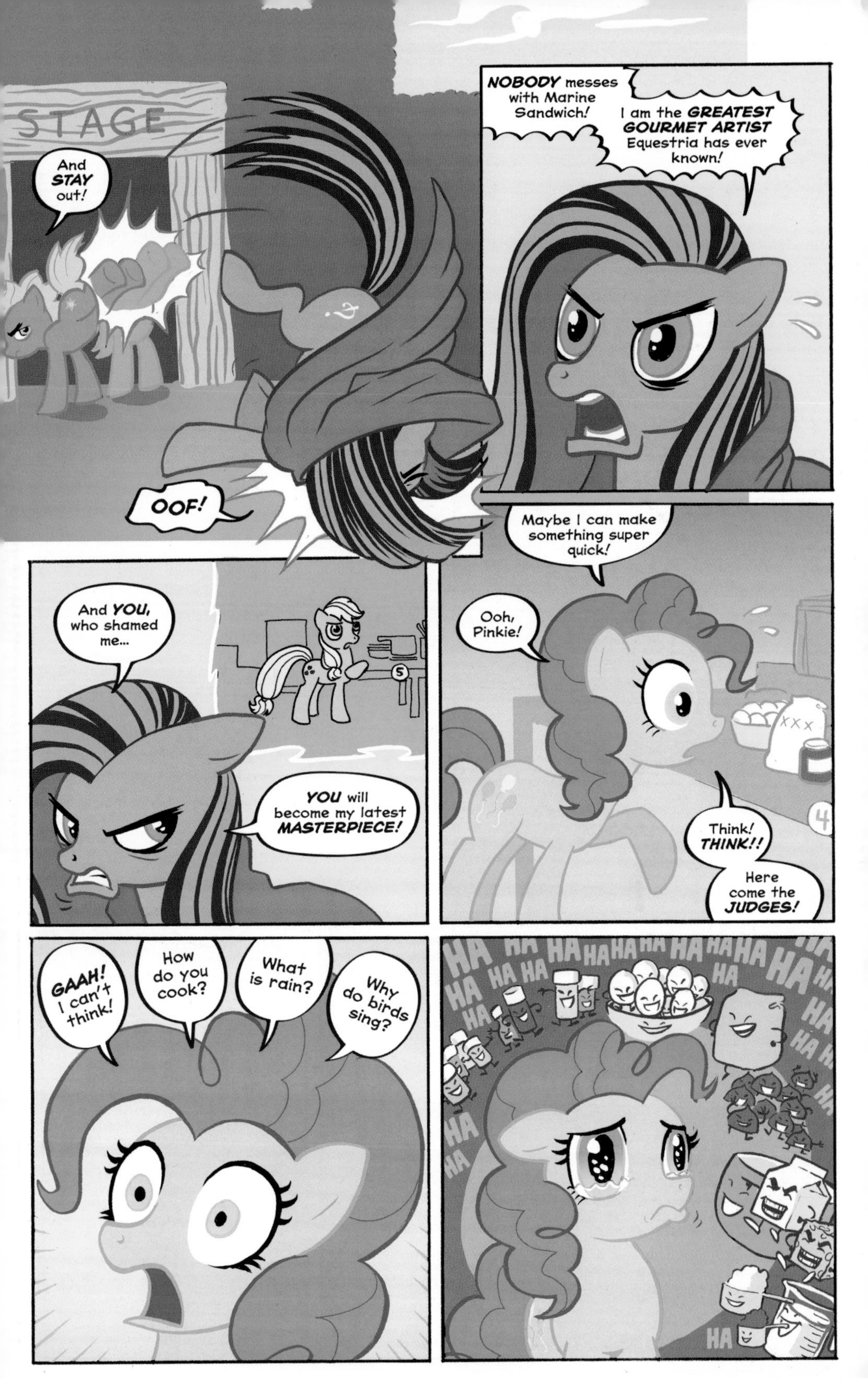
STAGE
And STAY out!
OOF!
NOBODY messes with Marine Sandwich!
I am the GREATEST GOURMET ARTIST Equestria has ever known!
And YOU, who shamed me...
YOU will become my latest MASTERPIECE!
Maybe I can make something super quick!
Ooh, Pinkie!
Think! THINK!!
Here come the JUDGES!
GAAH! I can't think!
How do you cook?
What is rain?
Why do birds sing?

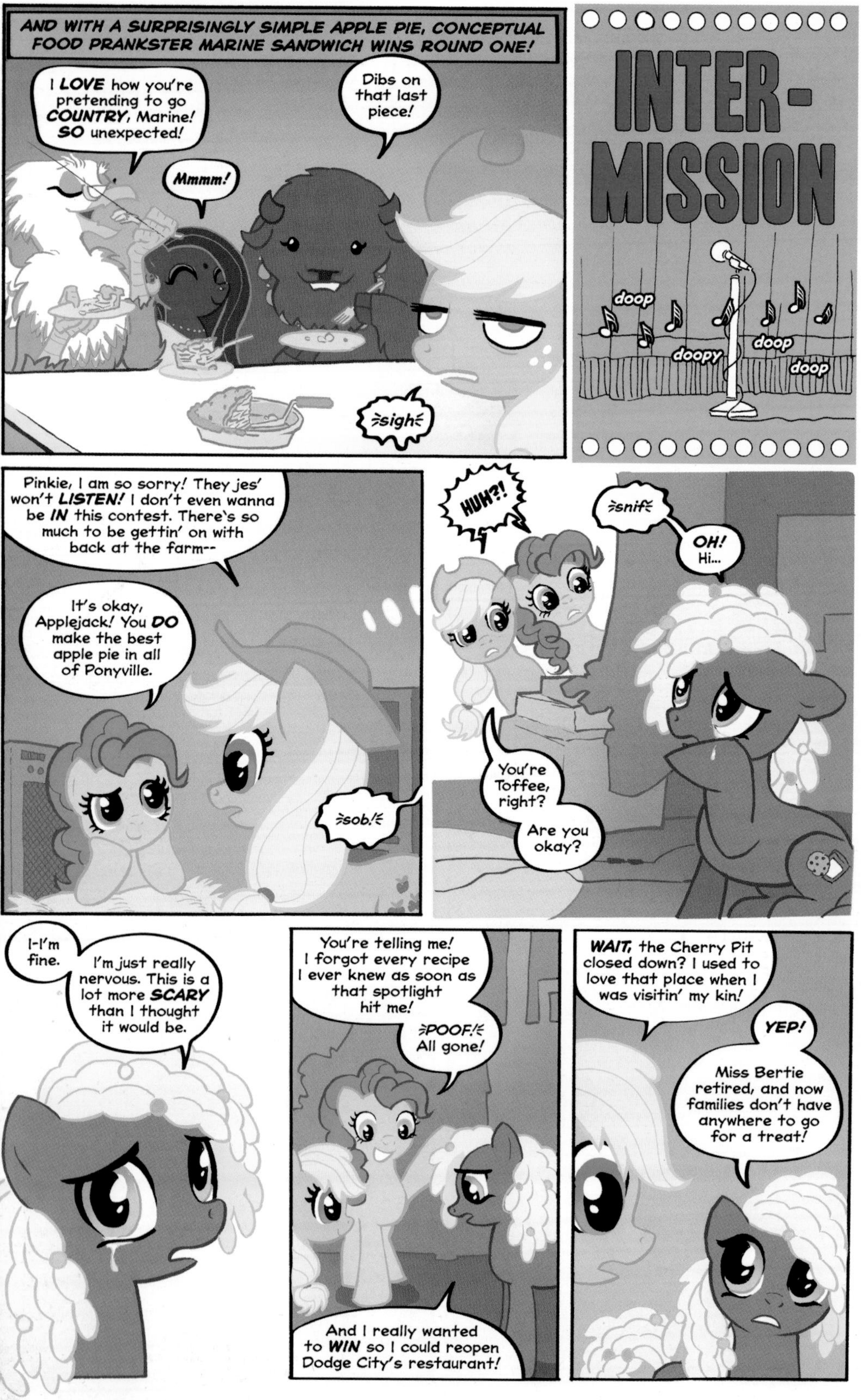
AND WITH A SURPRISINGLY SIMPLE APPLE PIE, CONCEPTUAL FOOD PRANKSTER MARINE SANDWICH WINS ROUND ONE!
I LOVE how you're pretending to go COUNTRY, Marine! SO unexpected!
Mmmm!
Dibs on that last piece!
sigh
INTER-MISSION
doop
doopy
doop
doop
Pinkie, I am so sorry! They jes' won't LISTEN! I don't even wanna be IN this contest. There's so much to be gettin' on with back at the farm--
It's okay, Applejack! You DO make the best apple pie in all of Ponyville.
sob!
HUH?!
snif
OH! Hi...
You're Toffee, right?
Are you okay?
I-I'm fine.
I'm just really nervous. This is a lot more SCARY than I thought it would be.
You're telling me! I forgot every recipe I ever knew as soon as that spotlight hit me!
POOF! All gone!
And I really wanted to WIN so I could reopen Dodge City's restaurant!
WAIT, the Cherry Pit closed down? I used to love that place when I was visitin' my kin!
YEP!
Miss Bertie retired, and now families don't have anywhere to go for a treat!

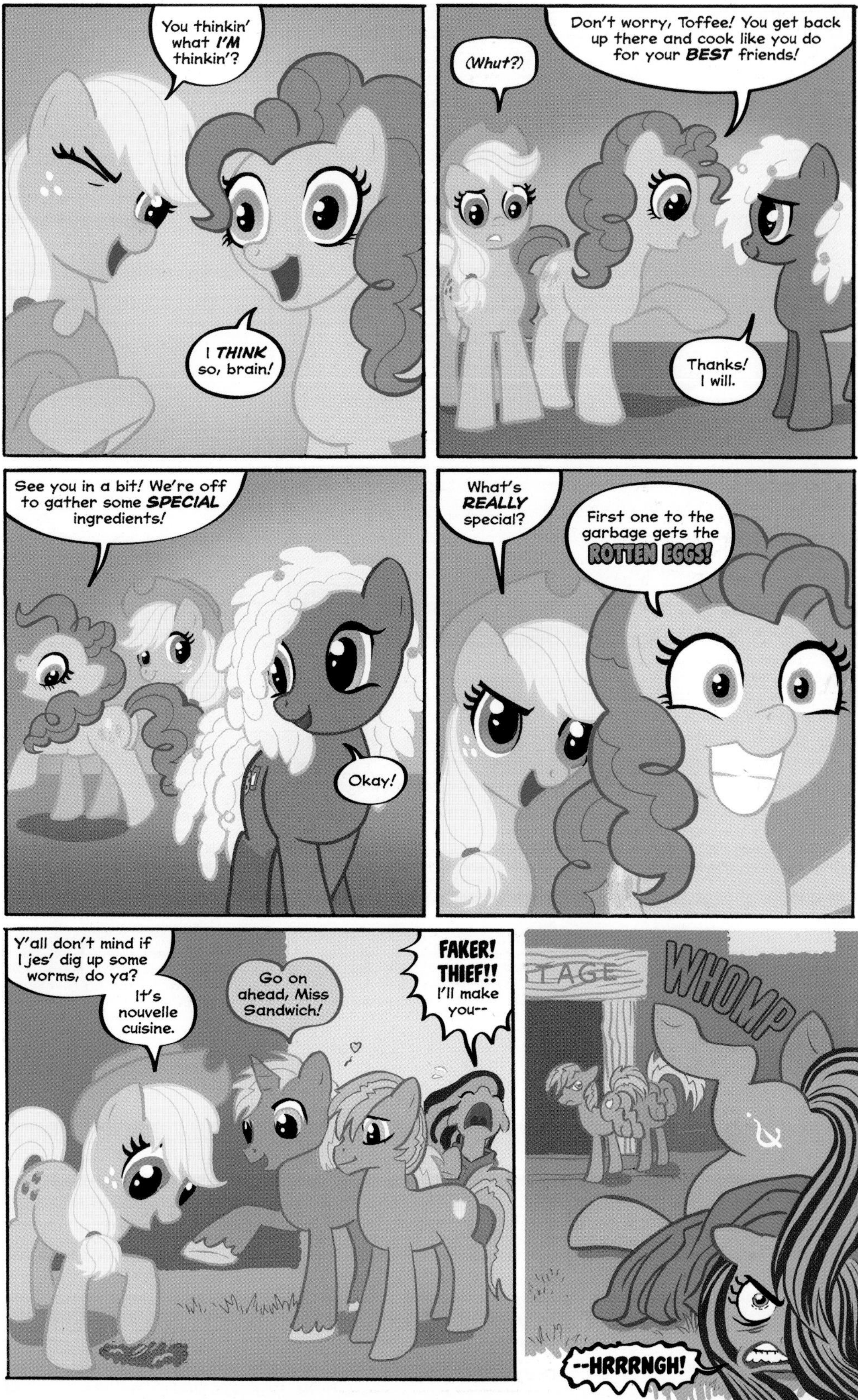

You thinkin' what I'M thinkin'?
I THINK so, brain!
(Whut?)
Don't worry, Toffee! You get back up there and cook like you do for your BEST friends!
Thanks! I will.
See you in a bit! We're off to gather some SPECIAL ingredients!
Okay!
What's REALLY special?
First one to the garbage gets the ROTTEN EGGS!
Y'all don't mind if I jes' dig up some worms, do ya?
It's nouvelle cuisine.
Go on ahead, Miss Sandwich!
FAKER! THIEF!! I'll make you--
STAGE
WHOMP
--HRRRNGH!

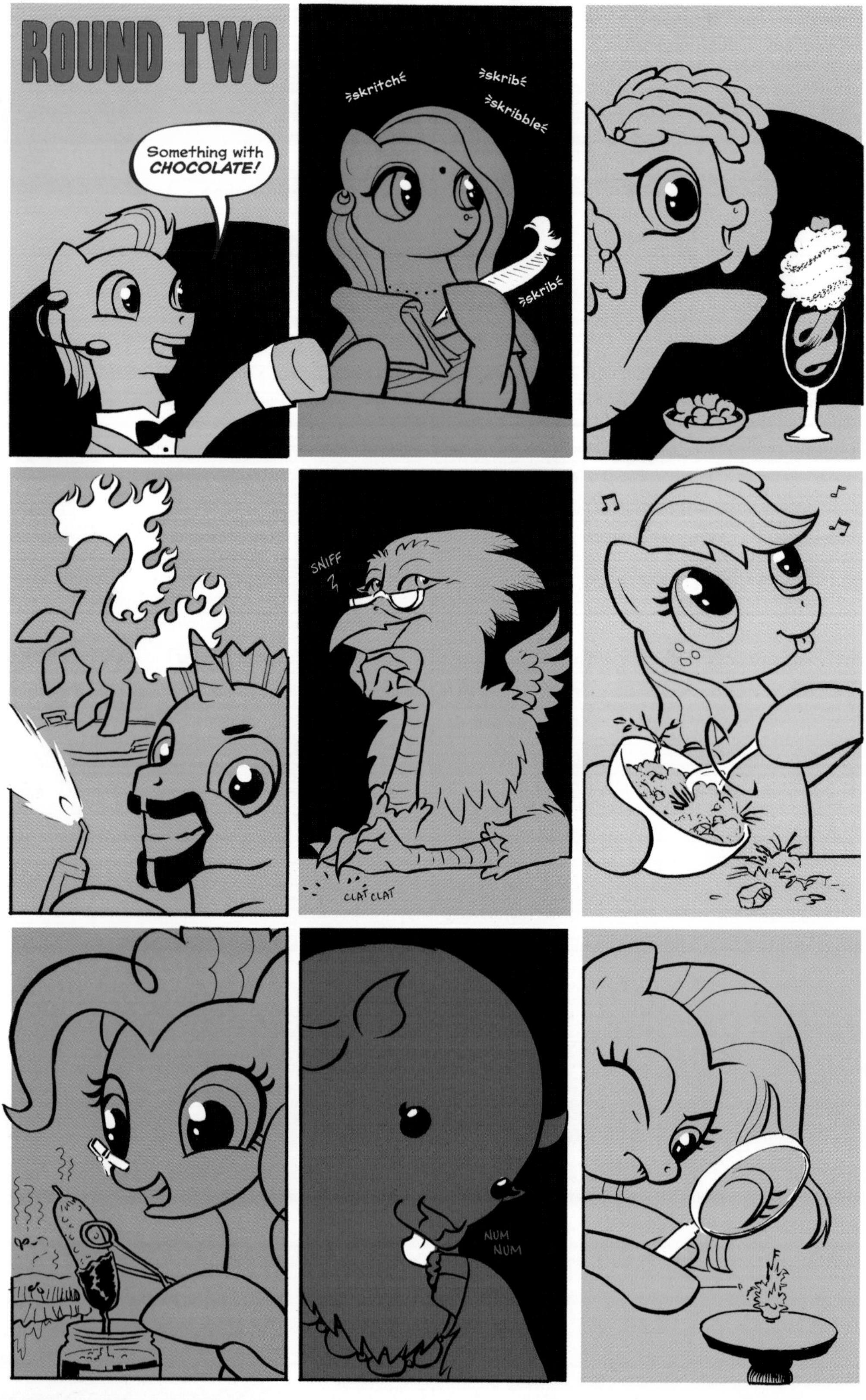
ROUND TWO
Something with CHOCOLATE!
skritch
skrib
skribble
skrib
SNIFF
CLAT CLAT
NUM NUM

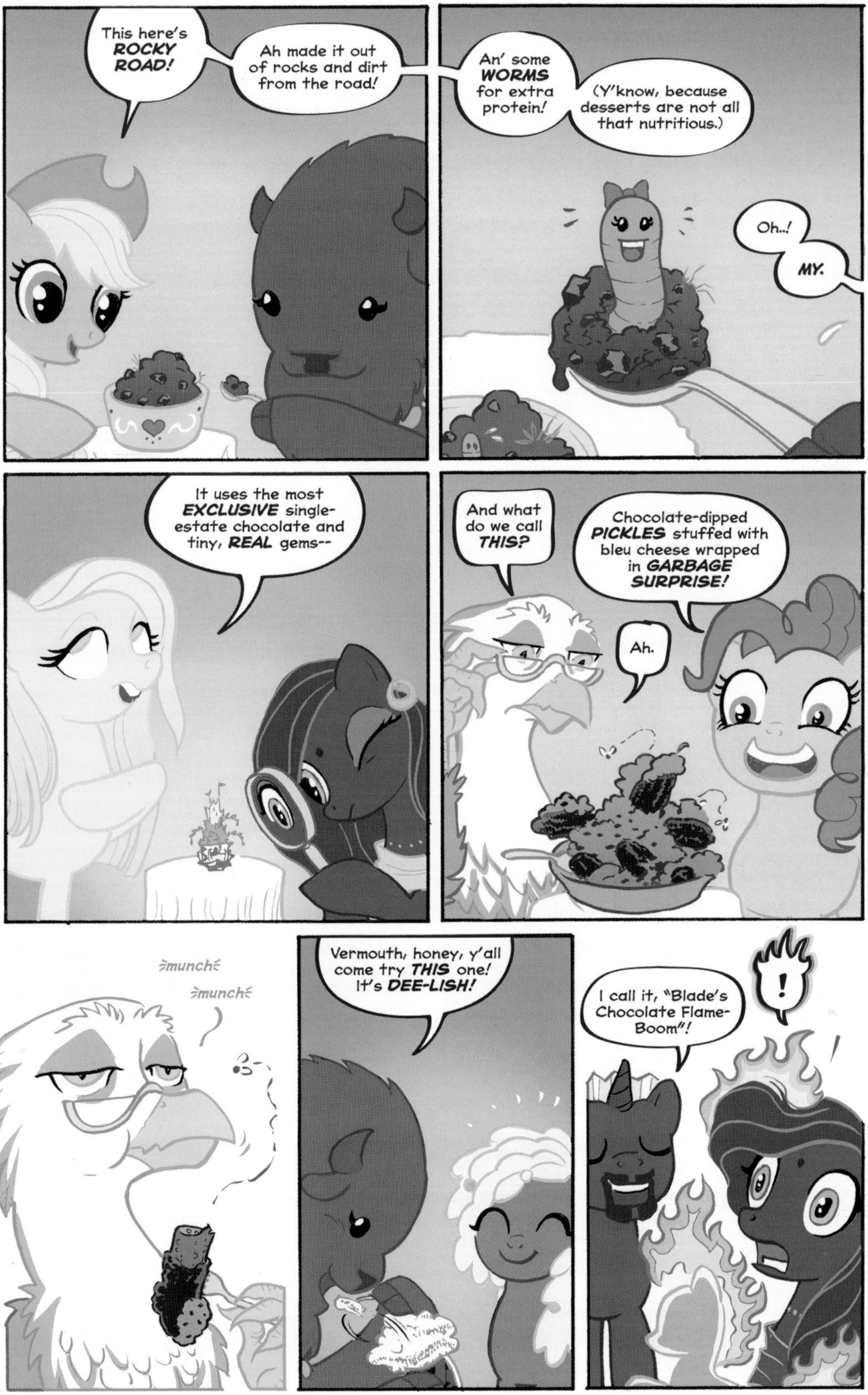
This here's ROCKY ROAD!
Ah made it out of rocks and dirt from the road!
An' some WORMS for extra protein!
(Y'know, because desserts are not all that nutritious.)
Oh..!
MY.
It uses the most EXCLUSIVE single-estate chocolate and tiny, REAL gems--
And what do we call THIS?
Chocolate-dipped PICKLES stuffed with bleu cheese wrapped in GARBAGE SURPRISE!
Ah.
munch
munch
Vermouth, honey, y'all come try THIS one! It's DEE-LISH!
I call it, "Blade's Chocolate Flame-Boom"!
!

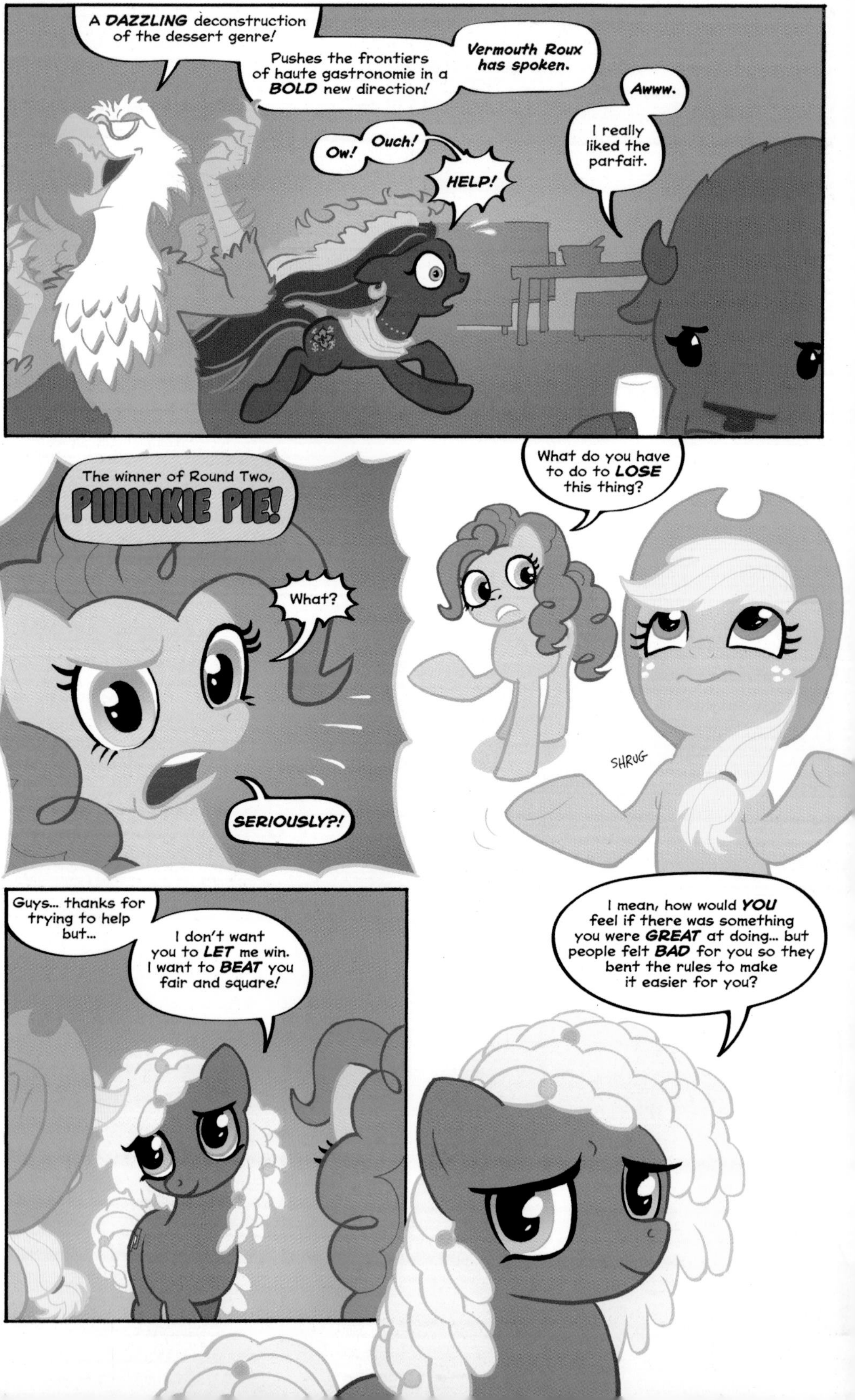

A DAZZLING deconstruction of the dessert genre!
Pushes the frontiers of haute gastronomie in a BOLD new direction!
Vermouth Roux has spoken.
Ow!
Ouch!
HELP!
Awww.
I really liked the parfait.
The winner of Round Two, PIIIINKIE PIE!
What?
SERIOUSLY?!
What do you have to do to LOSE this thing?
SHRUG
Guys... thanks for trying to help but...
I don't want you to LET me win. I want to BEAT you fair and square!
I mean, how would YOU feel if there was something you were GREAT at doing... but people felt BAD for you so they bent the rules to make it easier for you?

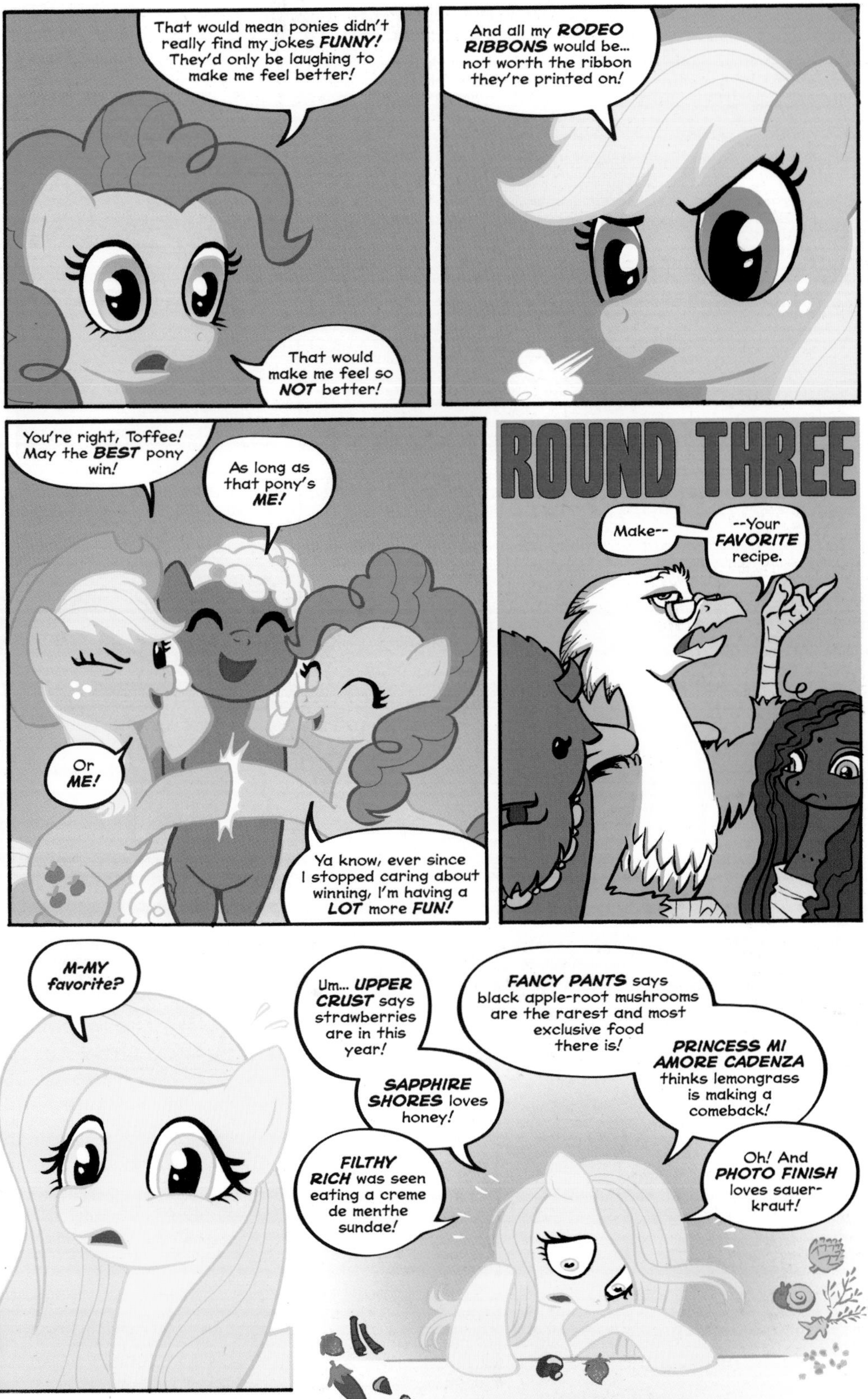

That would mean ponies didn't really find my jokes FUNNY! They'd only be laughing to make me feel better!
That would make me feel so NOT better!
And all my RODEO RIBBONS would be... not worth the ribbon they're printed on!
You're right, Toffee! May the BEST pony win!
As long as that pony's ME!
Or ME!
Ya know, ever since I stopped caring about winning, I'm having a LOT more FUN!
ROUND THREE
Make--
--Your FAVORITE recipe.
M-MY favorite?
Um... UPPER CRUST says strawberries are in this year!
SAPPHIRE SHORES loves honey!
FILTHY RICH was seen eating a creme de menthe sundae!
FANCY PANTS says black apple-root mushrooms are the rarest and most exclusive food there is!
PRINCESS MI AMORE CADENZA thinks lemongrass is making a comeback!
Oh! And PHOTO FINISH loves sauer-kraut!

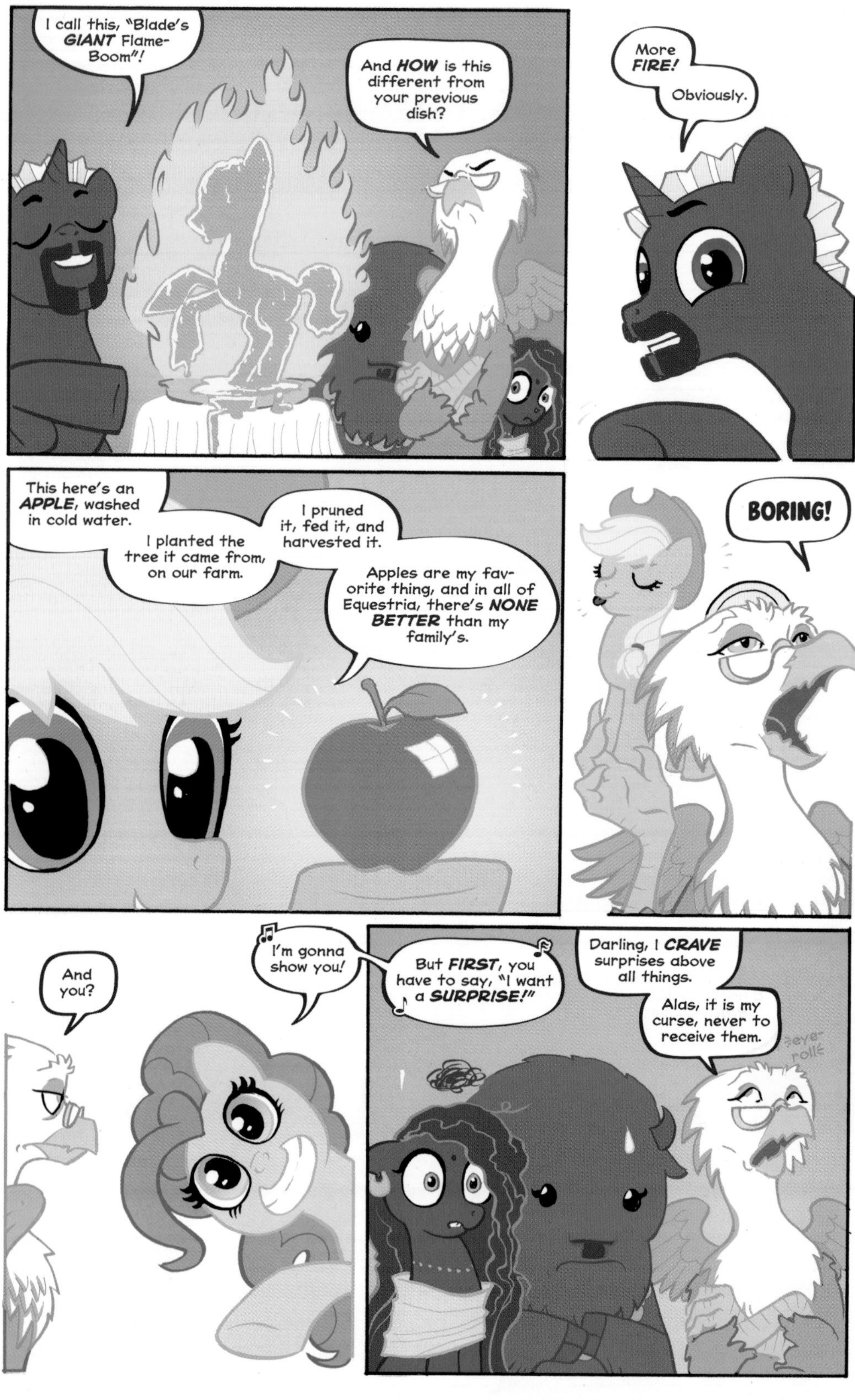

I call this, "Blade's *GIANT* Flame-Boom"!
And *HOW* is this different from your previous dish?
More *FIRE!*
Obviously.
This here's an *APPLE*, washed in cold water.
I planted the tree it came from, on our farm.
I pruned it, fed it, and harvested it.
Apples are my fav-orite thing, and in all of Equestria, there's *NONE BETTER* than my family's.
BORING!
And you?
I'm gonna show you!
But *FIRST*, you have to say, "I want a *SURPRISE!*"
Darling, I *CRAVE* surprises above all things.
Alas, it is my curse, never to receive them.
eye-roll

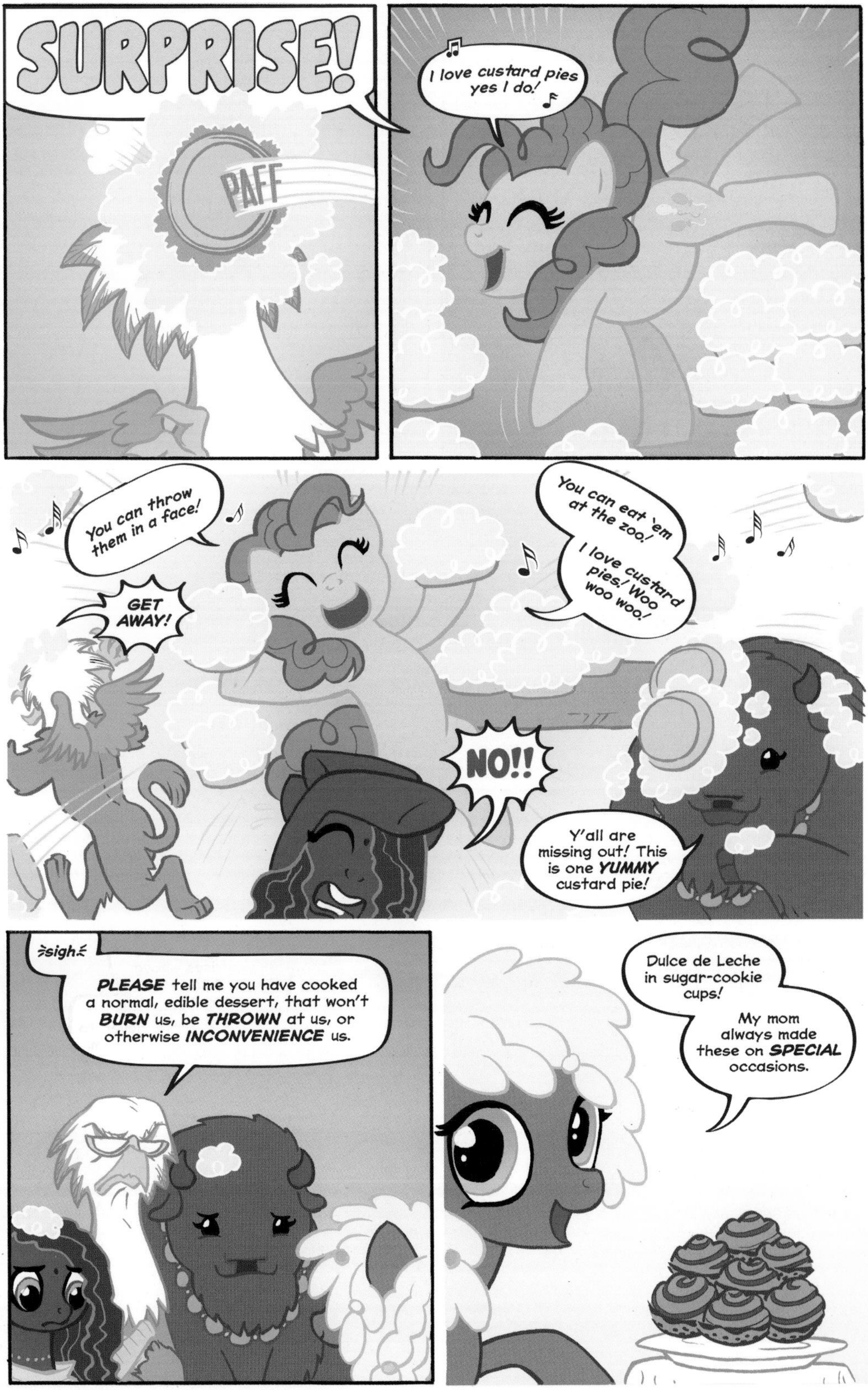
SURPRISE!
PAFF
I love custard pies yes I do!
You can throw them in a face!
GET AWAY!
You can eat 'em at the zoo!
I love custard pies! Woo woo woo!
NO!!
Y'all are missing out! This is one YUMMY custard pie!
sigh
PLEASE tell me you have cooked a normal, edible dessert, that won't BURN us, be THROWN at us, or otherwise INCONVENIENCE us.
Dulce de Leche in sugar-cookie cups!
My mom always made these on SPECIAL occasions.

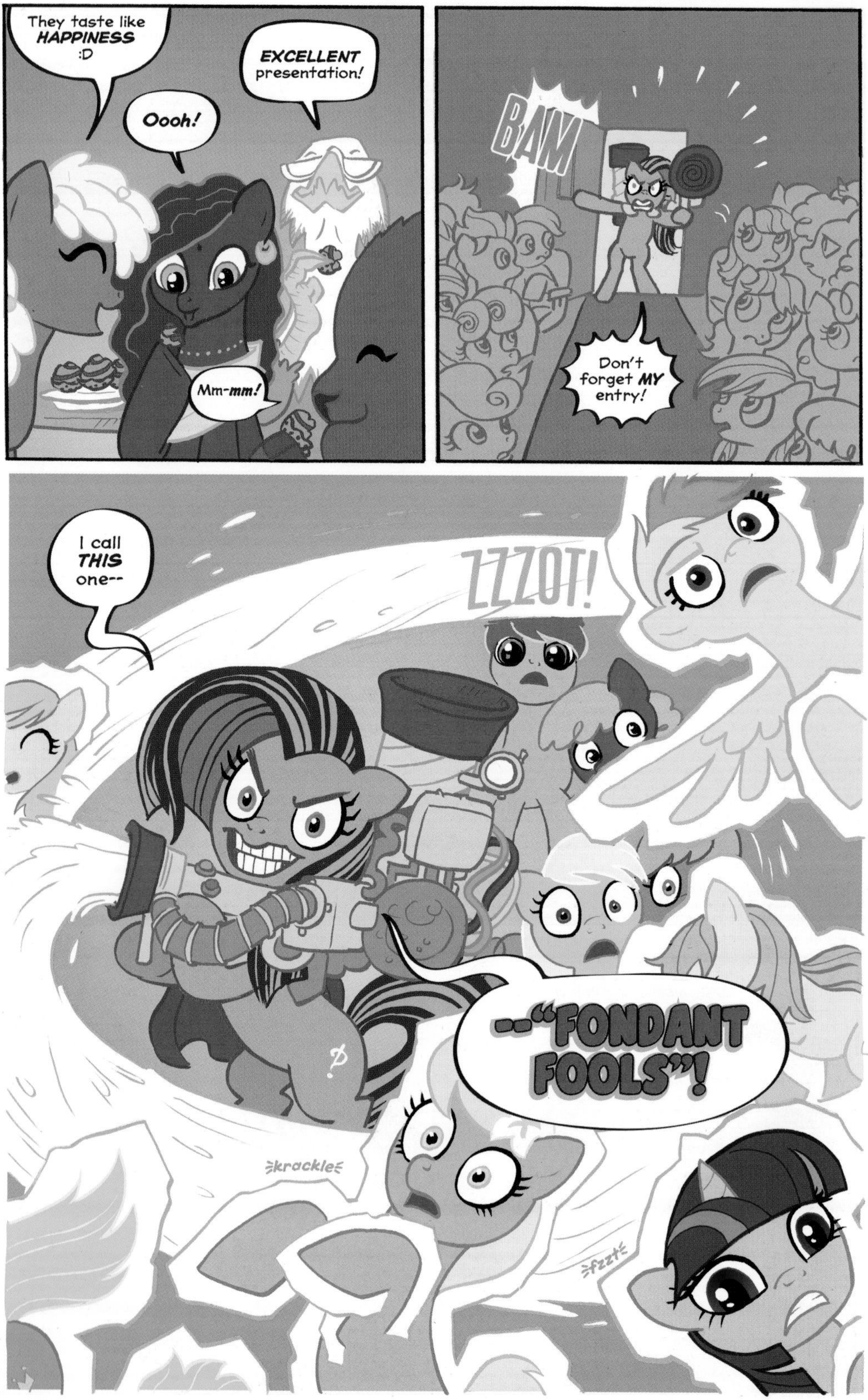

They taste like **HAPPINESS** :D
Oooh!
EXCELLENT presentation!
Mm-*mm!*
BAM
Don't forget **MY** entry!
I call **THIS** one--
ZZZOT!
--"FONDANT FOOLS"!
krackle
fzzt

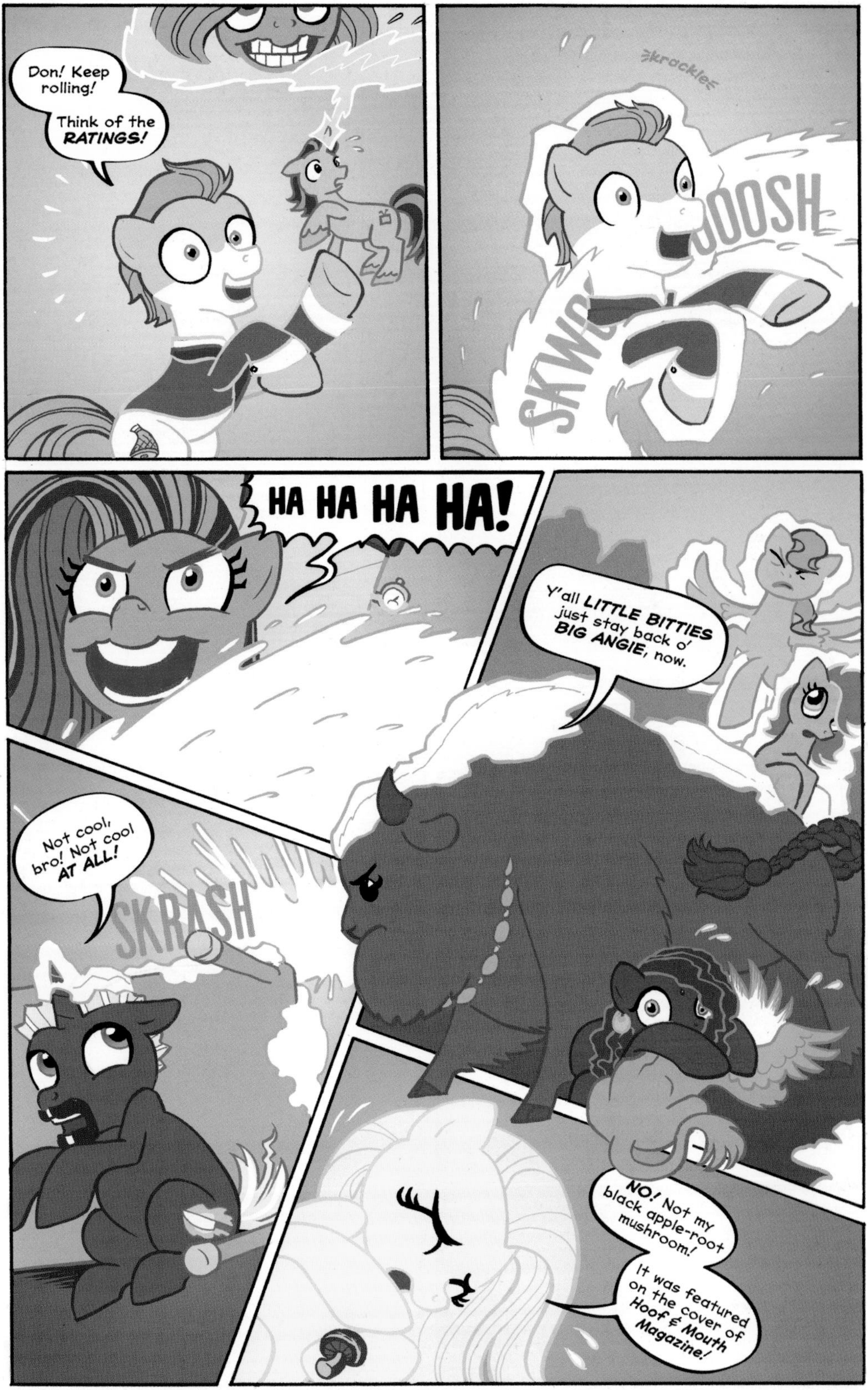

Don! Keep rolling!
Think of the RATINGS!
krackle
SKWE
OOSH
HA HA HA HA!
Y'all LITTLE BITTIES just stay back o' BIG ANGIE, now.
Not cool, bro! Not cool AT ALL!
SKRASH
NO! Not my black apple-root mushroom!
It was featured on the cover of Hoof & Mouth Magazine!

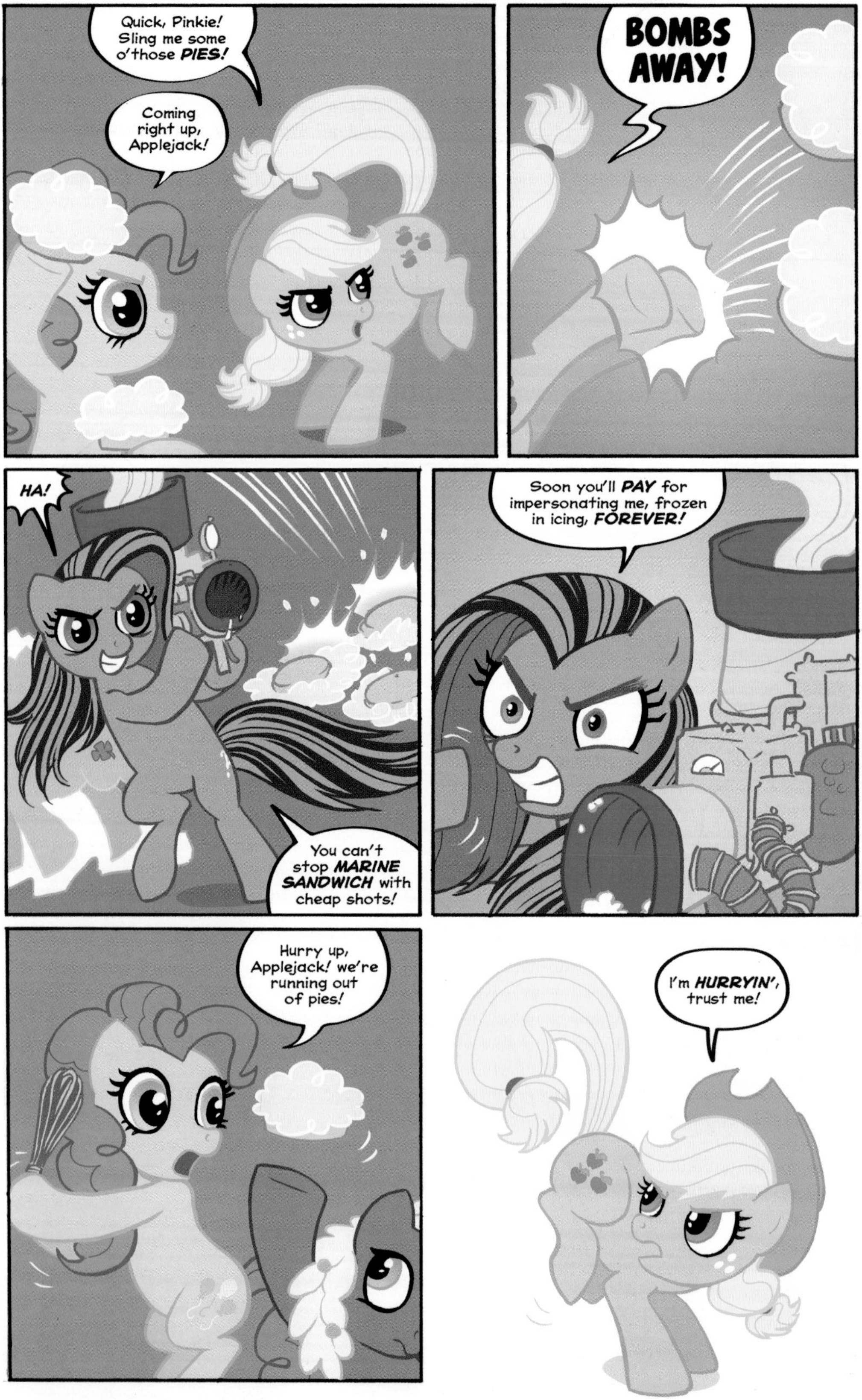
Quick, Pinkie! Sling me some o'those PIES!
Coming right up, Applejack!
BOMBS AWAY!
HA!
You can't stop MARINE SANDWICH with cheap shots!
Soon you'll PAY for impersonating me, frozen in icing, FOREVER!
Hurry up, Applejack! we're running out of pies!
I'm HURRYIN', trust me!

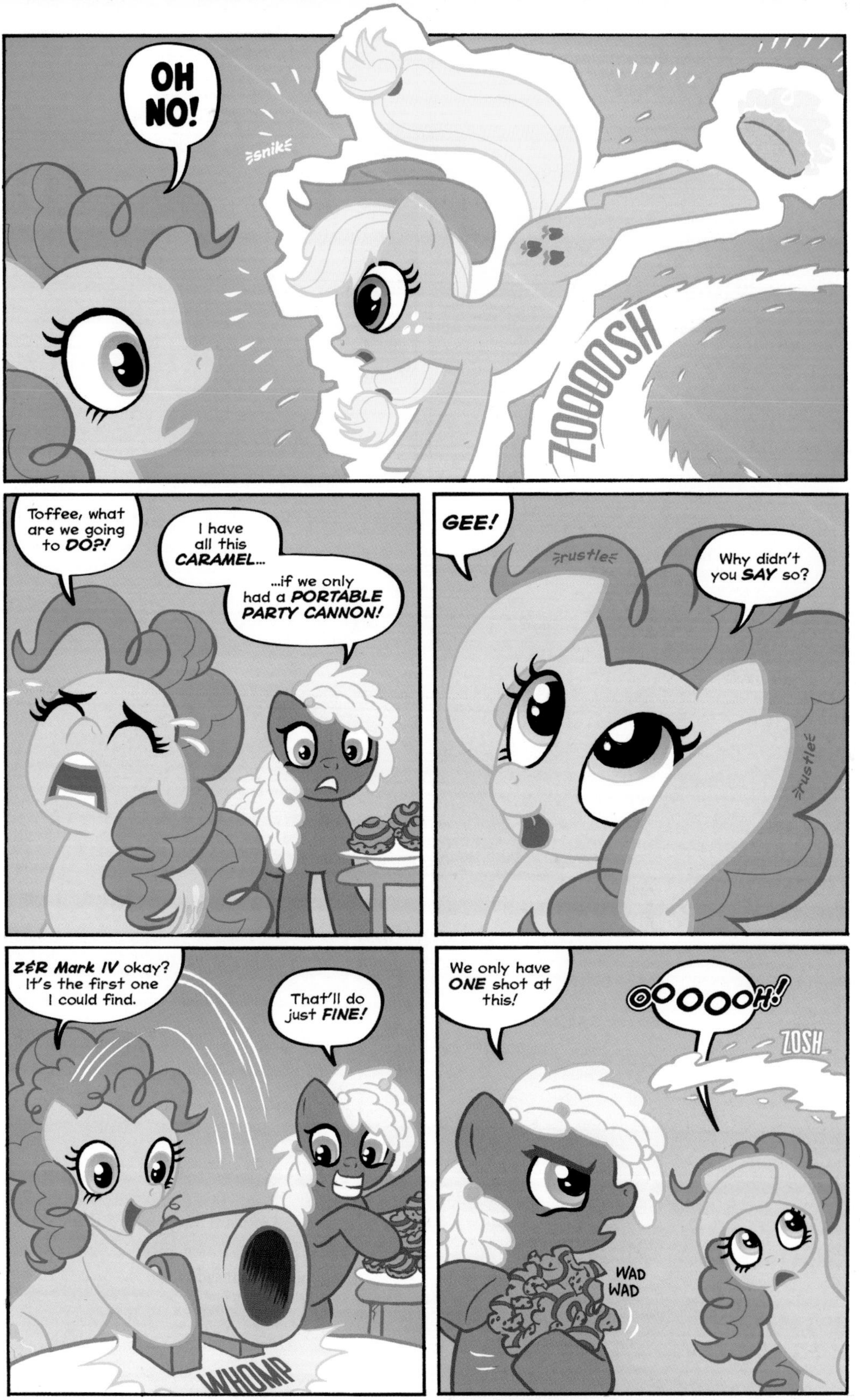

OH NO!
snik
ZOOOOSH
Toffee, what are we going to DO?!
I have all this CARAMEL...
...if we only had a PORTABLE PARTY CANNON!
GEE!
rustle
Why didn't you SAY so?
rustle
Z&R Mark IV okay? It's the first one I could find.
That'll do just FINE!
WHOMP
We only have ONE shot at this!
OOOOOOH!
ZOSH
WAD WAD

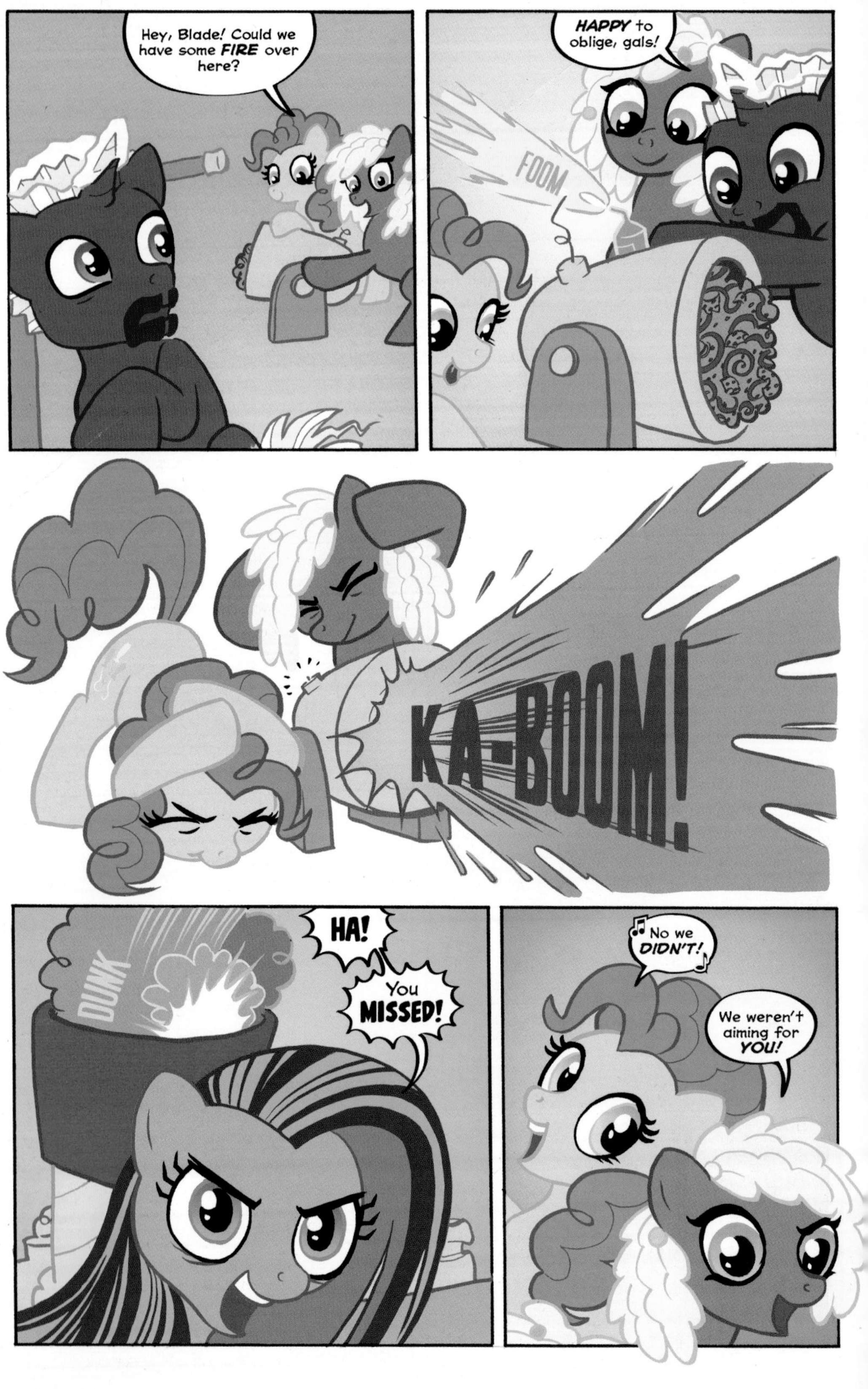

Hey, Blade! Could we have some FIRE over here?
HAPPY to oblige, gals!
FOOM
KA-BOOM!
DUNK
HA!
You MISSED!
No we DIDN'T!
We weren't aiming for YOU!

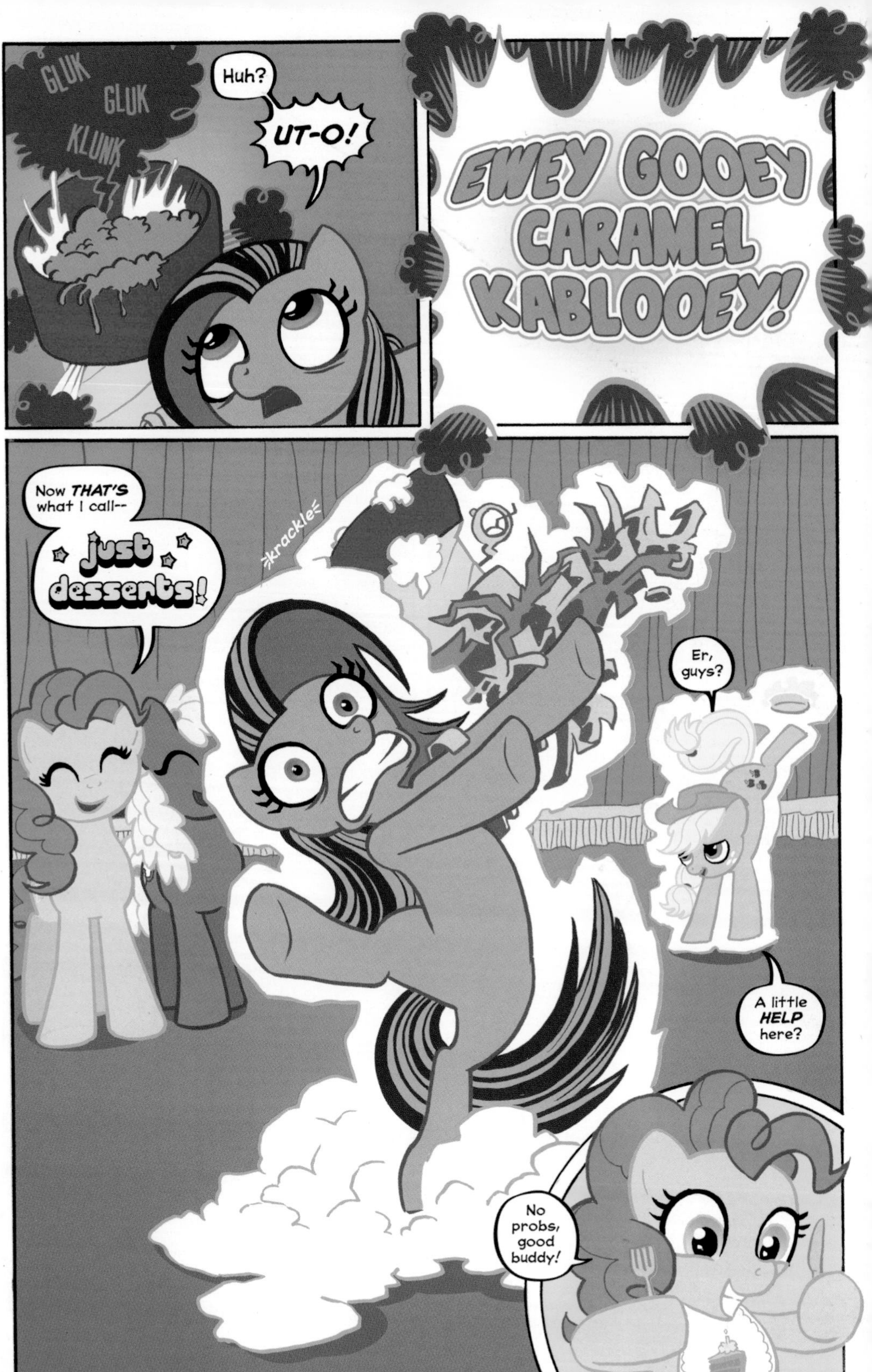
GLUK
GLUK
KLUNK
Huh?
UT-O!
EWEY GOOEY CARAMEL KABLOOEY!
Now THAT'S what I call--
just desserts!
krackle
Er, guys?
A little HELP here?
No probs, good buddy!

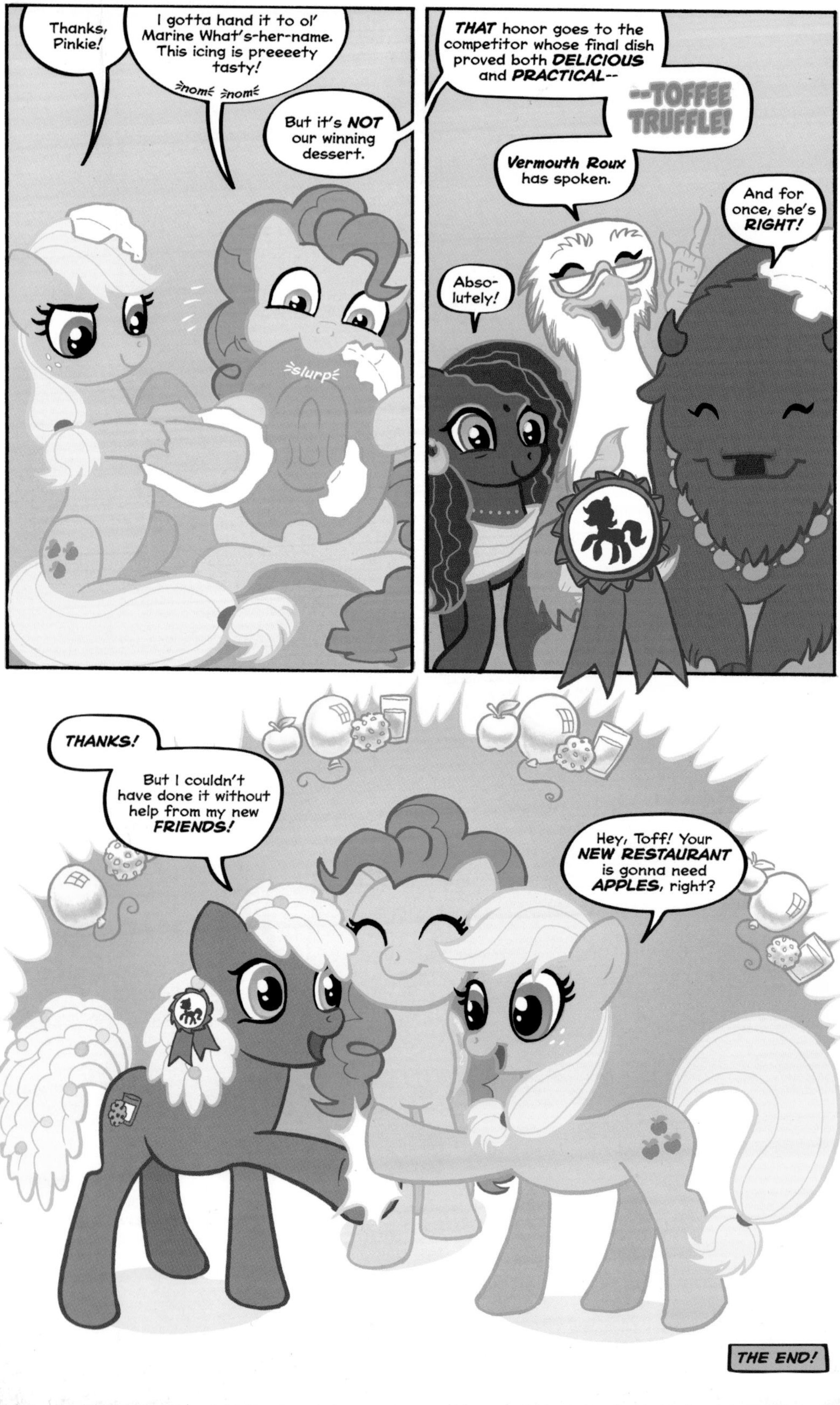
Thanks, Pinkie!
I gotta hand it to ol' Marine What's-her-name. This icing is preeeety tasty!
nom nom
slurp
But it's NOT our winning dessert.
THAT honor goes to the competitor whose final dish proved both DELICIOUS and PRACTICAL--
--TOFFEE TRUFFLE!
Vermouth Roux has spoken.
And for once, she's RIGHT!
Abso-lutely!
THANKS!
But I couldn't have done it without help from my new FRIENDS!
Hey, Toff! Your NEW RESTAURANT is gonna need APPLES, right?
THE END!

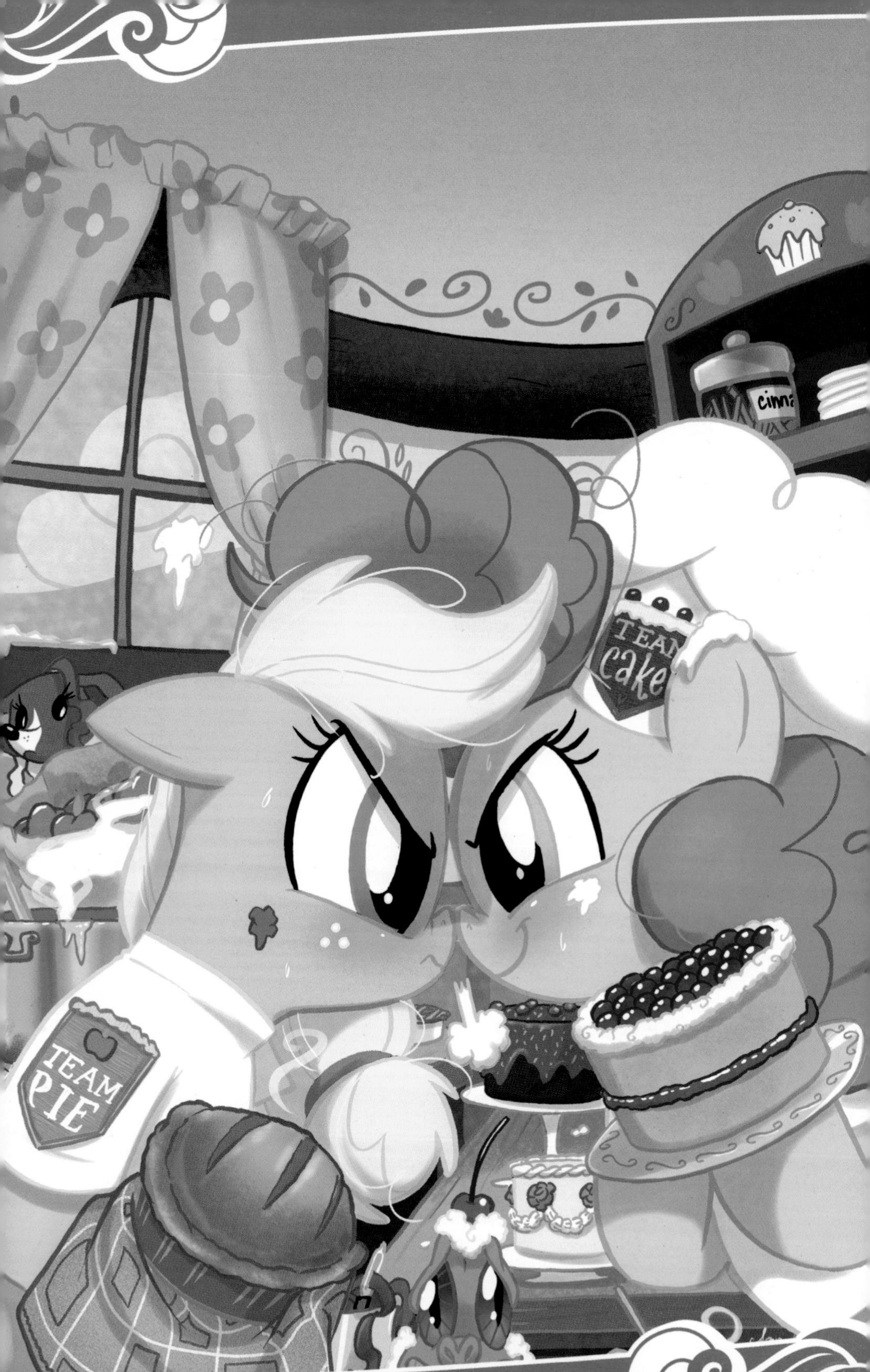
cinna
TEAM cake
TEAM PIE

art by AMY MEBBERSON

Discord & The Cutie Mark Crusaders

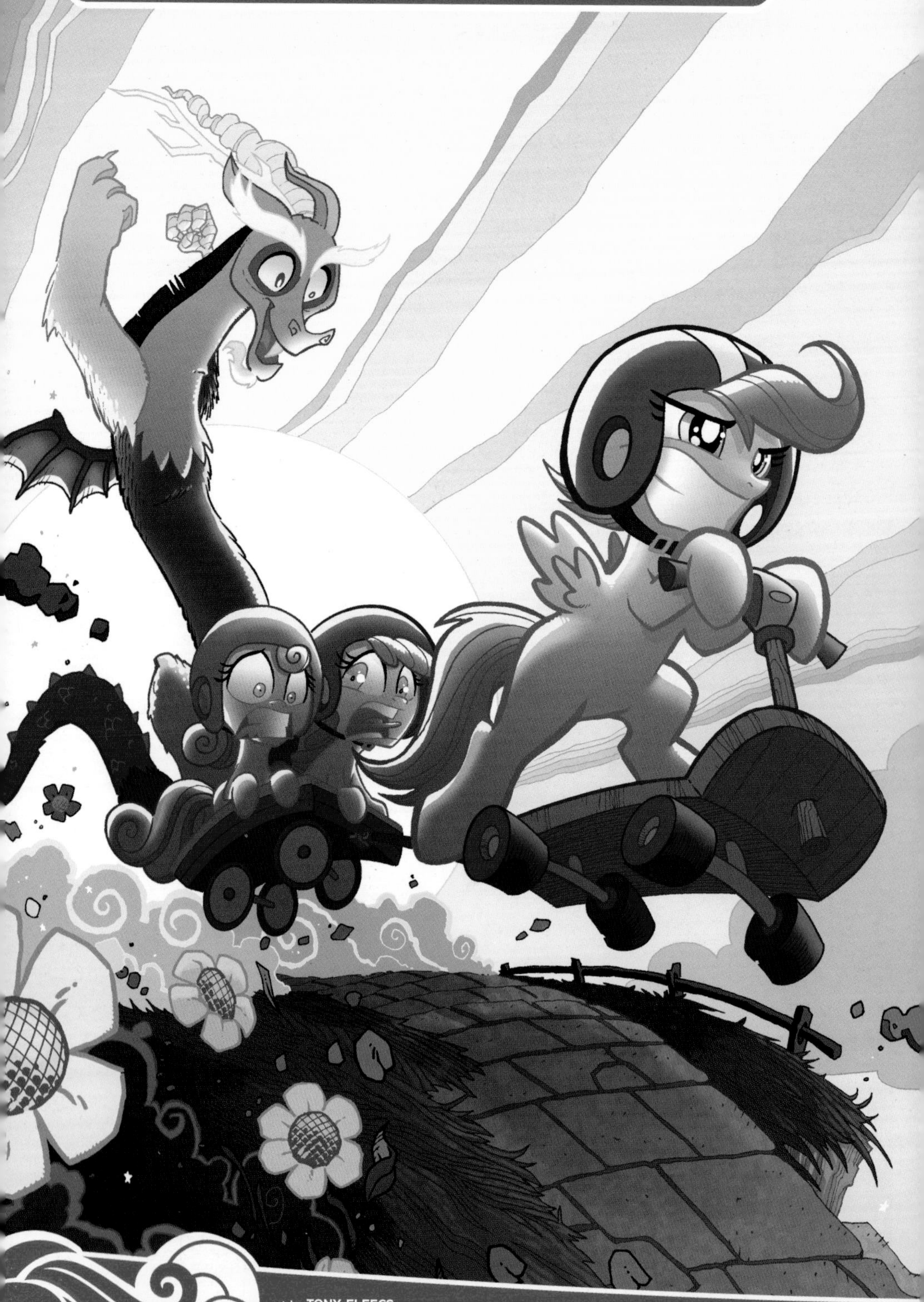

art by TONY FLEECS

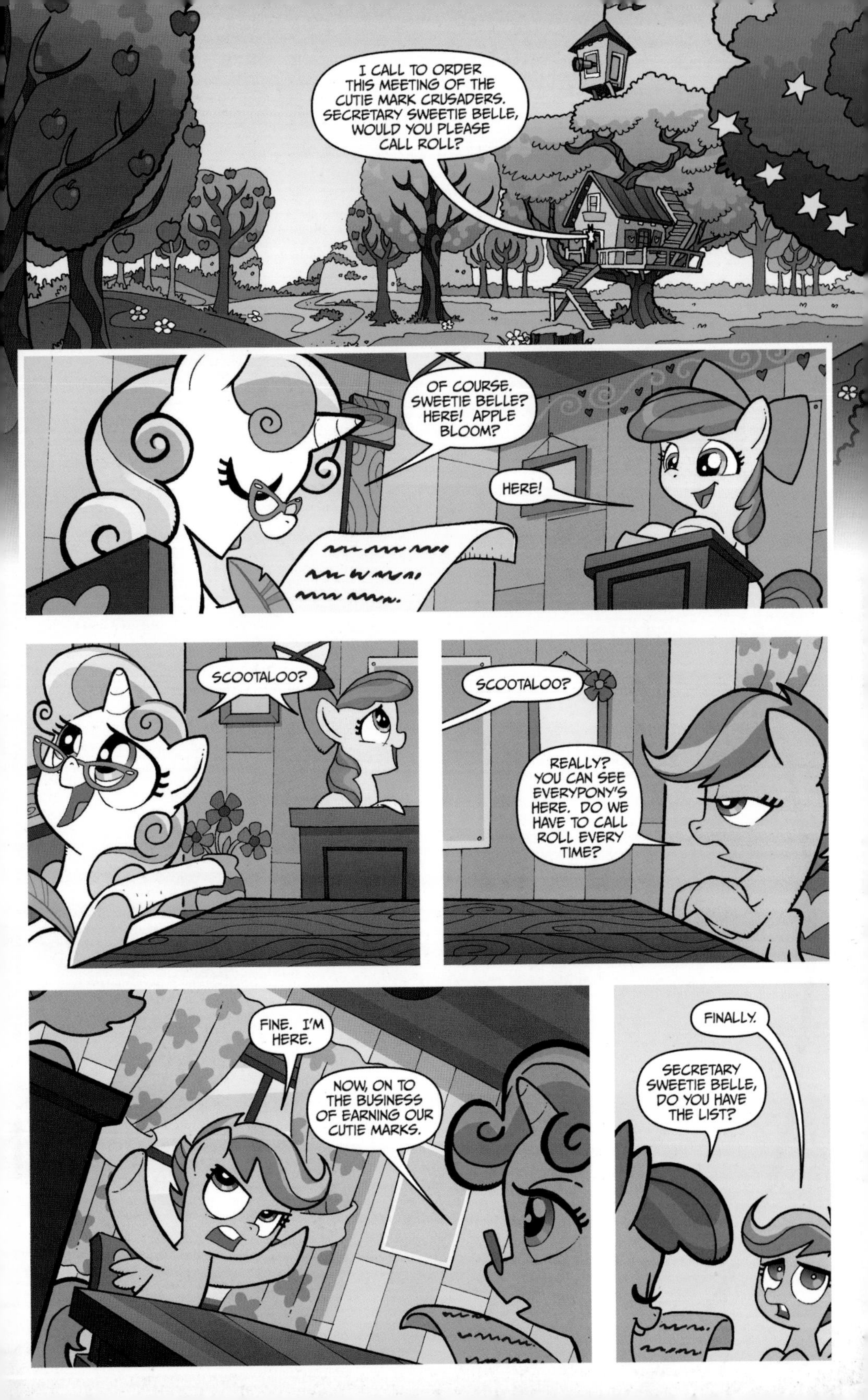
I CALL TO ORDER THIS MEETING OF THE CUTIE MARK CRUSADERS. SECRETARY SWEETIE BELLE, WOULD YOU PLEASE CALL ROLL?
OF COURSE. SWEETIE BELLE? HERE! APPLE BLOOM?
HERE!
SCOOTALOO?
SCOOTALOO?
REALLY? YOU CAN SEE EVERYPONY'S HERE. DO WE HAVE TO CALL ROLL EVERY TIME?
FINE. I'M HERE.
NOW, ON TO THE BUSINESS OF EARNING OUR CUTIE MARKS.
FINALLY.
SECRETARY SWEETIE BELLE, DO YOU HAVE THE LIST?

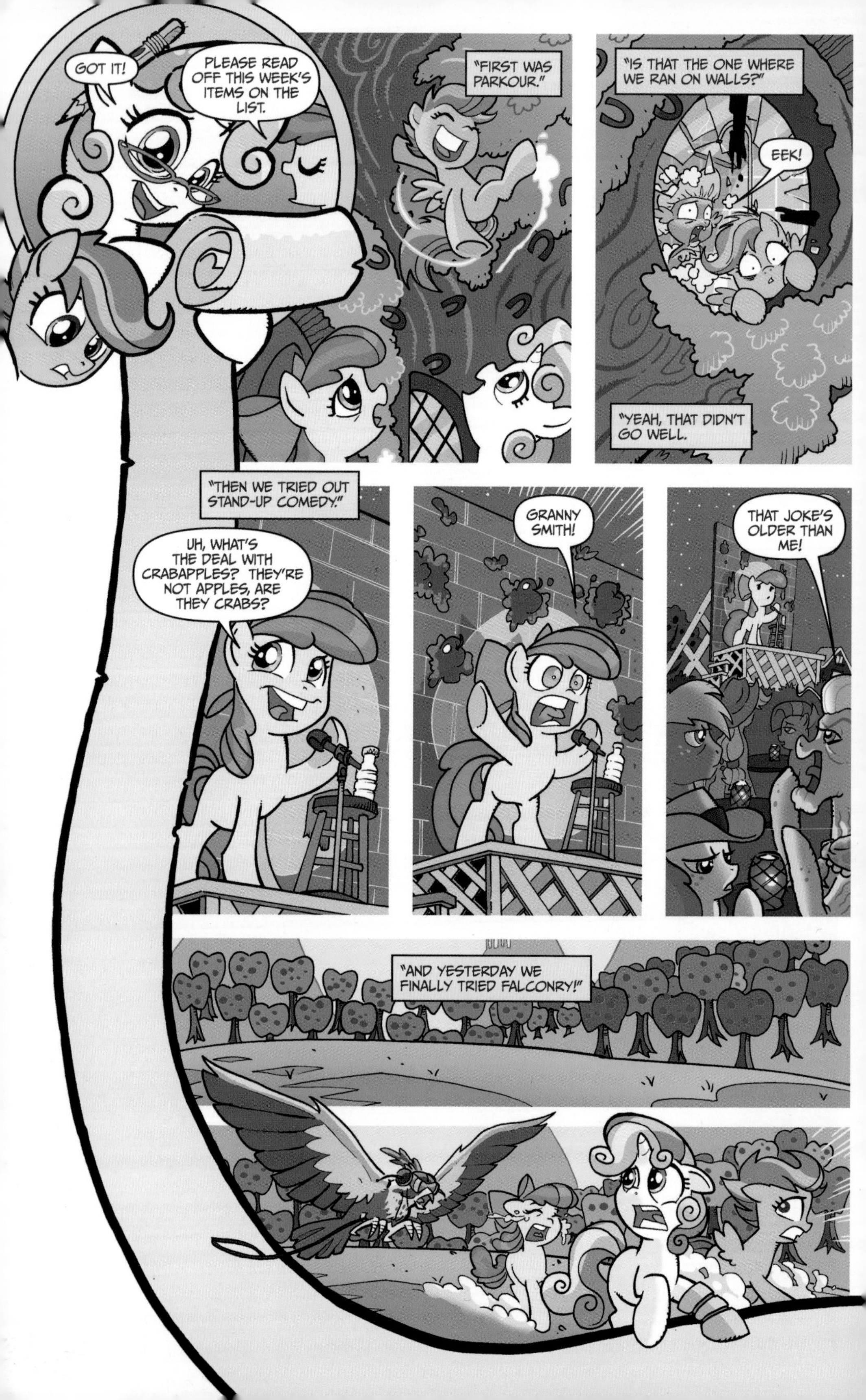
GOT IT!
PLEASE READ OFF THIS WEEK'S ITEMS ON THE LIST.
"FIRST WAS PARKOUR."
"IS THAT THE ONE WHERE WE RAN ON WALLS?"
EEK!
"YEAH, THAT DIDN'T GO WELL.
"THEN WE TRIED OUT STAND-UP COMEDY."
UH, WHAT'S THE DEAL WITH CRABAPPLES? THEY'RE NOT APPLES, ARE THEY CRABS?
GRANNY SMITH!
THAT JOKE'S OLDER THAN ME!
"AND YESTERDAY WE FINALLY TRIED FALCONRY!"

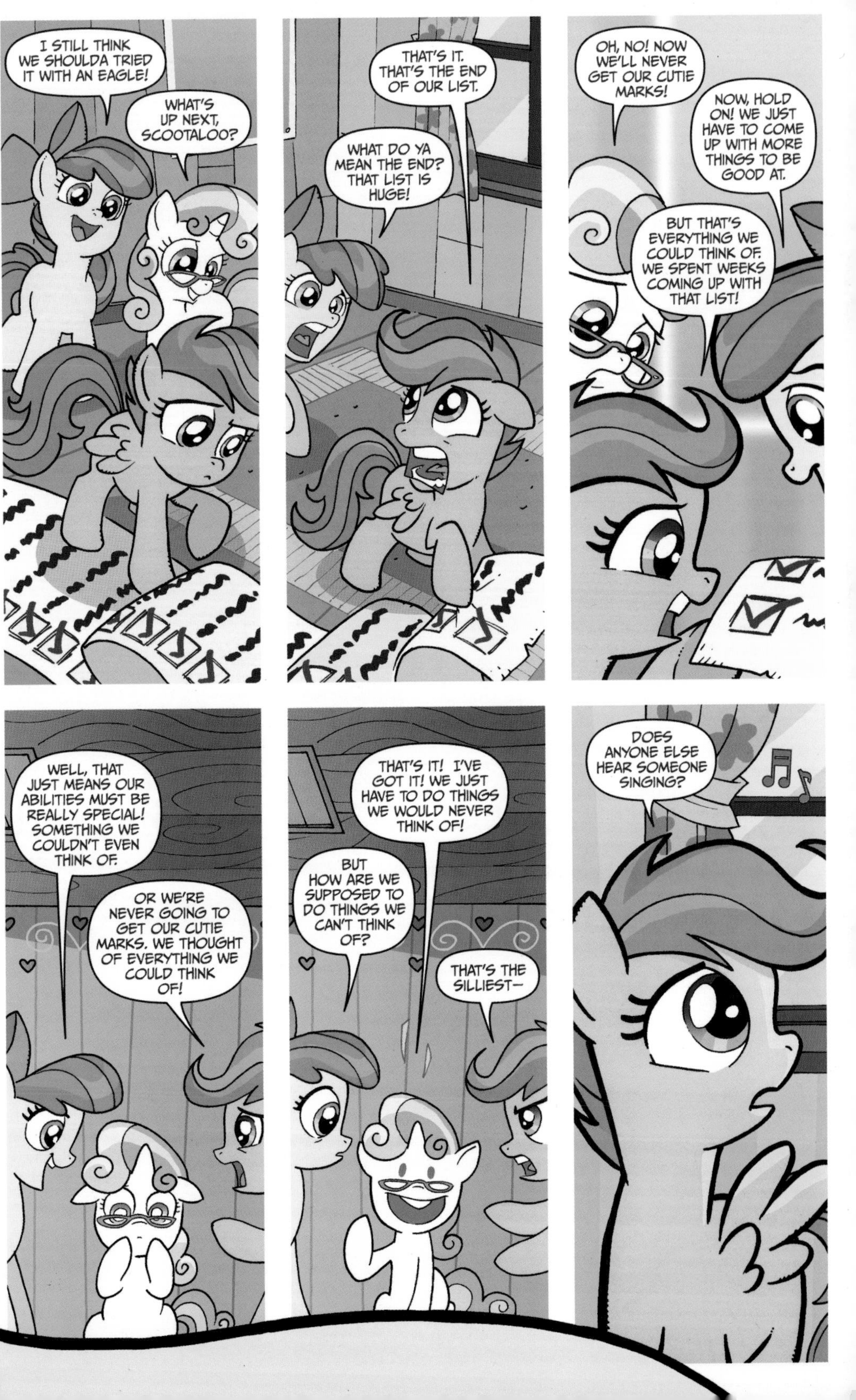
I STILL THINK WE SHOULDA TRIED IT WITH AN EAGLE!
WHAT'S UP NEXT, SCOOTALOO?
THAT'S IT. THAT'S THE END OF OUR LIST.
WHAT DO YA MEAN THE END? THAT LIST IS HUGE!
OH, NO! NOW WE'LL NEVER GET OUR CUTIE MARKS!
NOW, HOLD ON! WE JUST HAVE TO COME UP WITH MORE THINGS TO BE GOOD AT.
BUT THAT'S EVERYTHING WE COULD THINK OF. WE SPENT WEEKS COMING UP WITH THAT LIST!
WELL, THAT JUST MEANS OUR ABILITIES MUST BE REALLY SPECIAL! SOMETHING WE COULDN'T EVEN THINK OF.
OR WE'RE NEVER GOING TO GET OUR CUTIE MARKS. WE THOUGHT OF EVERYTHING WE COULD THINK OF!
THAT'S IT! I'VE GOT IT! WE JUST HAVE TO DO THINGS WE WOULD NEVER THINK OF!
BUT HOW ARE WE SUPPOSED TO DO THINGS WE CAN'T THINK OF?
THAT'S THE SILLIEST—
DOES ANYONE ELSE HEAR SOMEONE SINGING?

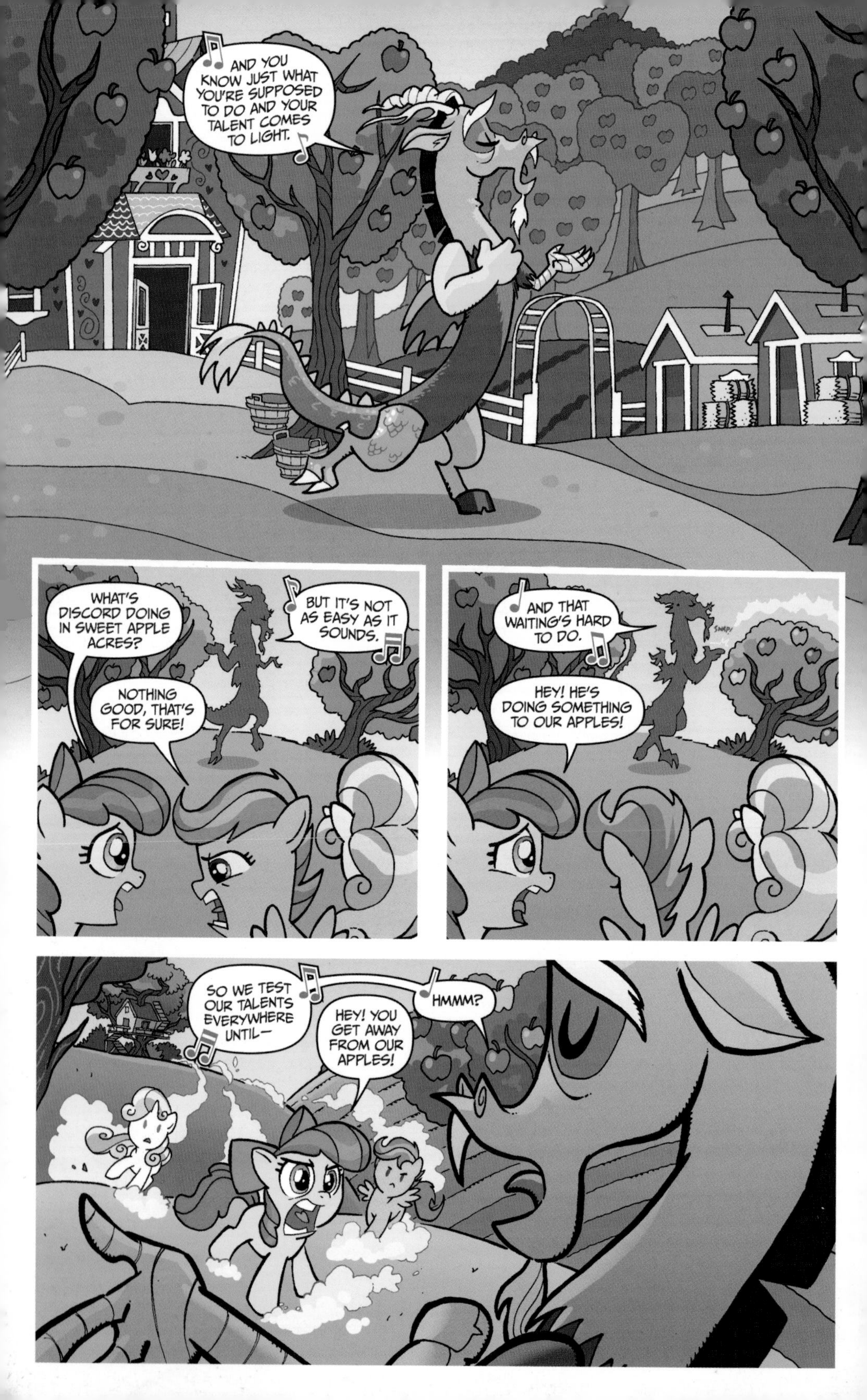
AND YOU KNOW JUST WHAT YOU'RE SUPPOSED TO DO AND YOUR TALENT COMES TO LIGHT.
WHAT'S DISCORD DOING IN SWEET APPLE ACRES?
BUT IT'S NOT AS EASY AS IT SOUNDS.
NOTHING GOOD, THAT'S FOR SURE!
AND THAT WAITING'S HARD TO DO.
SNAP!
HEY! HE'S DOING SOMETHING TO OUR APPLES!
SO WE TEST OUR TALENTS EVERYWHERE UNTIL—
HMMM?
HEY! YOU GET AWAY FROM OUR APPLES!

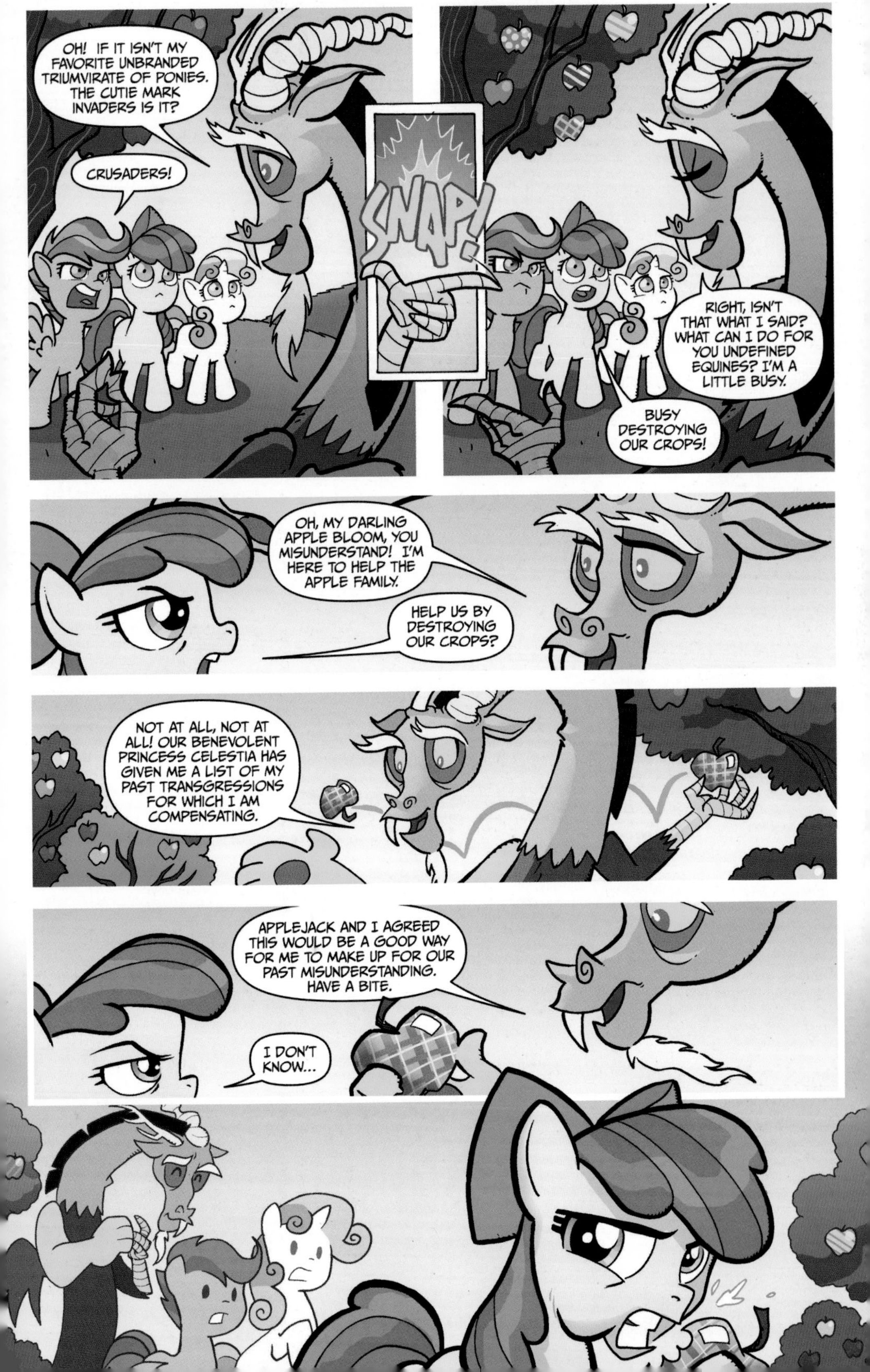
OH! IF IT ISN'T MY FAVORITE UNBRANDED TRIUMVIRATE OF PONIES. THE CUTIE MARK INVADERS IS IT?
CRUSADERS!
SNAP!
RIGHT, ISN'T THAT WHAT I SAID? WHAT CAN I DO FOR YOU UNDEFINED EQUINES? I'M A LITTLE BUSY.
BUSY DESTROYING OUR CROPS!
OH, MY DARLING APPLE BLOOM, YOU MISUNDERSTAND! I'M HERE TO HELP THE APPLE FAMILY.
HELP US BY DESTROYING OUR CROPS?
NOT AT ALL, NOT AT ALL! OUR BENEVOLENT PRINCESS CELESTIA HAS GIVEN ME A LIST OF MY PAST TRANSGRESSIONS FOR WHICH I AM COMPENSATING.
APPLEJACK AND I AGREED THIS WOULD BE A GOOD WAY FOR ME TO MAKE UP FOR OUR PAST MISUNDERSTANDING. HAVE A BITE.
I DON'T KNOW...

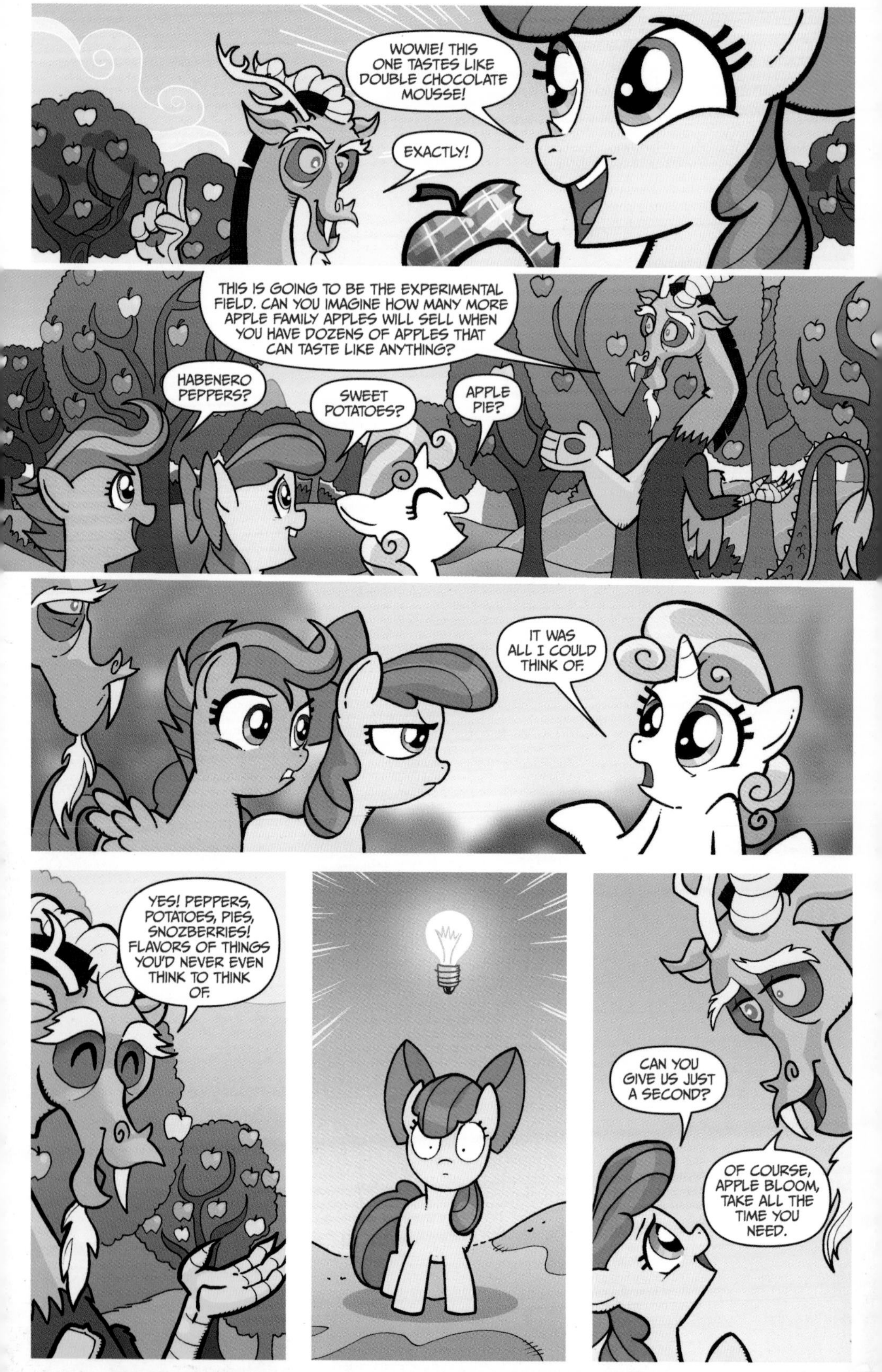
WOWIE! THIS ONE TASTES LIKE DOUBLE CHOCOLATE MOUSSE!
EXACTLY!
THIS IS GOING TO BE THE EXPERIMENTAL FIELD. CAN YOU IMAGINE HOW MANY MORE APPLE FAMILY APPLES WILL SELL WHEN YOU HAVE DOZENS OF APPLES THAT CAN TASTE LIKE ANYTHING?
HABENERO PEPPERS?
SWEET POTATOES?
APPLE PIE?
IT WAS ALL I COULD THINK OF.
YES! PEPPERS, POTATOES, PIES, SNOZBERRIES! FLAVORS OF THINGS YOU'D NEVER EVEN THINK TO THINK OF.
CAN YOU GIVE US JUST A SECOND?
OF COURSE, APPLE BLOOM, TAKE ALL THE TIME YOU NEED.

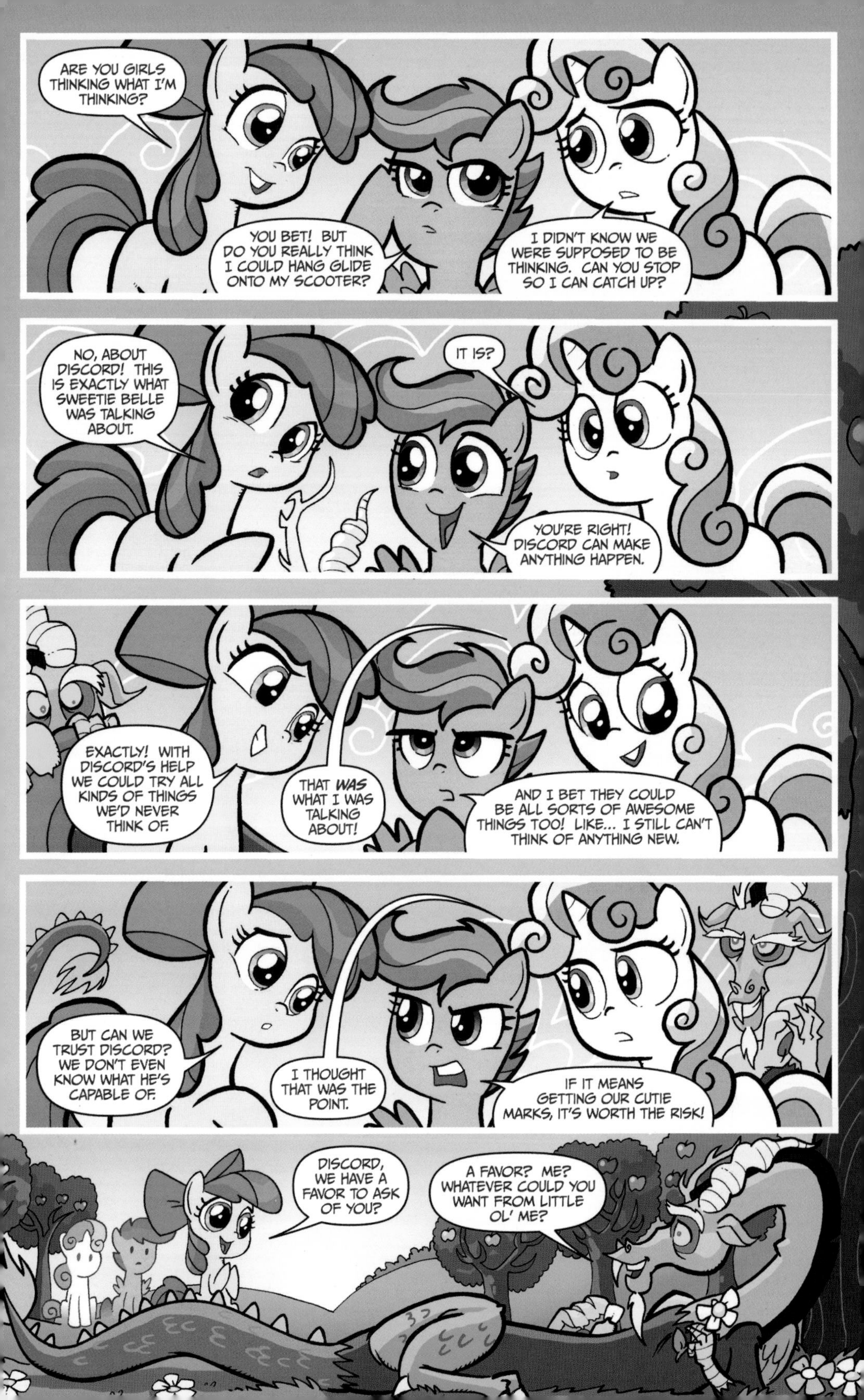
ARE YOU GIRLS THINKING WHAT I'M THINKING?
YOU BET! BUT DO YOU REALLY THINK I COULD HANG GLIDE ONTO MY SCOOTER?
I DIDN'T KNOW WE WERE SUPPOSED TO BE THINKING. CAN YOU STOP SO I CAN CATCH UP?
NO, ABOUT DISCORD! THIS IS EXACTLY WHAT SWEETIE BELLE WAS TALKING ABOUT.
IT IS?
YOU'RE RIGHT! DISCORD CAN MAKE ANYTHING HAPPEN.
EXACTLY! WITH DISCORD'S HELP WE COULD TRY ALL KINDS OF THINGS WE'D NEVER THINK OF.
THAT WAS WHAT I WAS TALKING ABOUT!
AND I BET THEY COULD BE ALL SORTS OF AWESOME THINGS TOO! LIKE... I STILL CAN'T THINK OF ANYTHING NEW.
BUT CAN WE TRUST DISCORD? WE DON'T EVEN KNOW WHAT HE'S CAPABLE OF.
I THOUGHT THAT WAS THE POINT.
IF IT MEANS GETTING OUR CUTIE MARKS, IT'S WORTH THE RISK!
DISCORD, WE HAVE A FAVOR TO ASK OF YOU?
A FAVOR? ME? WHATEVER COULD YOU WANT FROM LITTLE OL' ME?

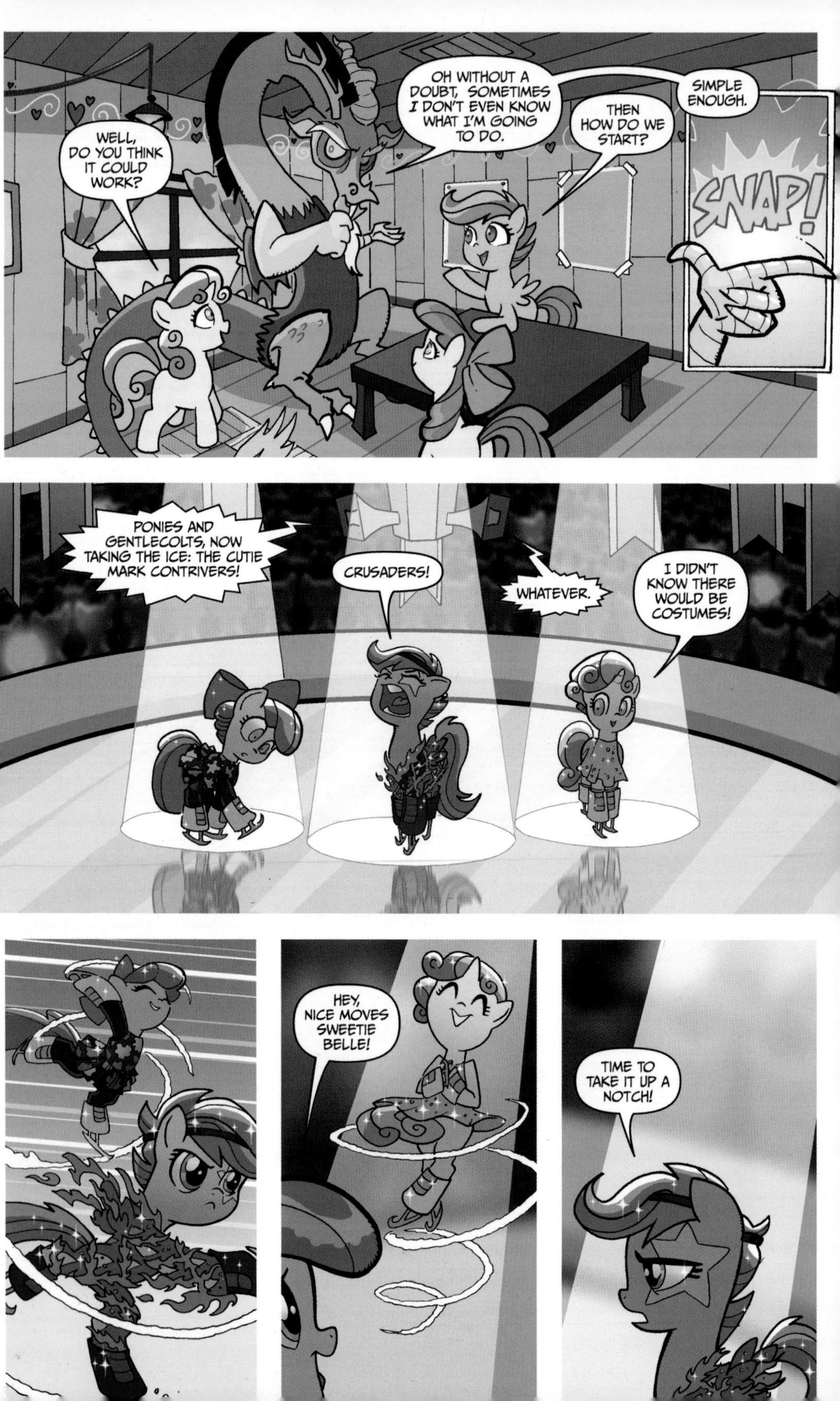
WELL, DO YOU THINK IT COULD WORK?
OH WITHOUT A DOUBT, SOMETIMES I DON'T EVEN KNOW WHAT I'M GOING TO DO.
THEN HOW DO WE START?
SIMPLE ENOUGH.
SNAP!
PONIES AND GENTLECOLTS, NOW TAKING THE ICE: THE CUTIE MARK CONTRIVERS!
CRUSADERS!
WHATEVER.
I DIDN'T KNOW THERE WOULD BE COSTUMES!
HEY, NICE MOVES SWEETIE BELLE!
TIME TO TAKE IT UP A NOTCH!

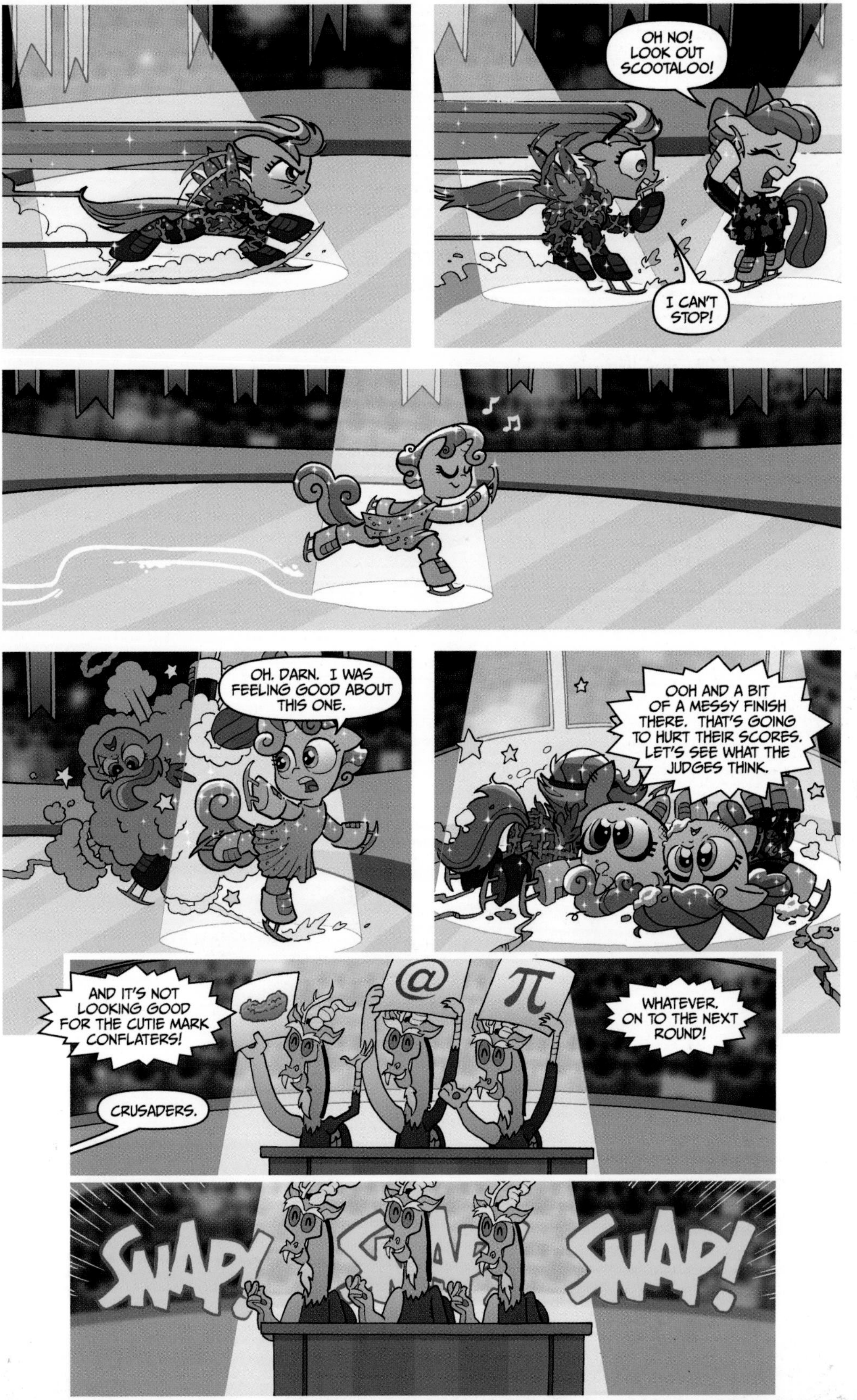
OH NO! LOOK OUT SCOOTALOO!
I CAN'T STOP!
OH. DARN. I WAS FEELING GOOD ABOUT THIS ONE.
OOH AND A BIT OF A MESSY FINISH THERE. THAT'S GOING TO HURT THEIR SCORES. LET'S SEE WHAT THE JUDGES THINK.
AND IT'S NOT LOOKING GOOD FOR THE CUTIE MARK CONFLATERS!
@
π
CRUSADERS.
WHATEVER. ON TO THE NEXT ROUND!
SNAP!
SNAP!

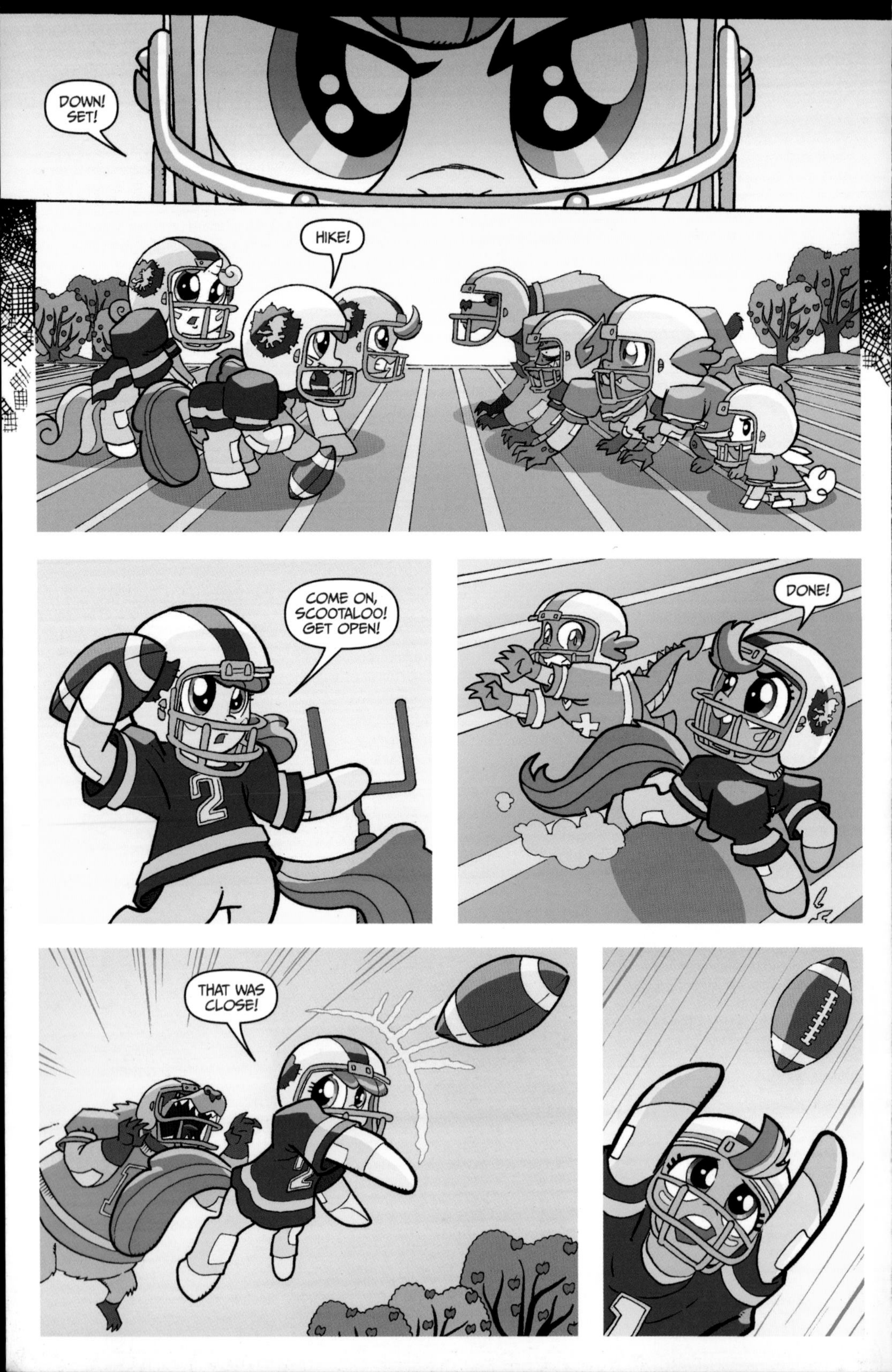
DOWN! SET!
HIKE!
COME ON, SCOOTALOO! GET OPEN!
DONE!
THAT WAS CLOSE!

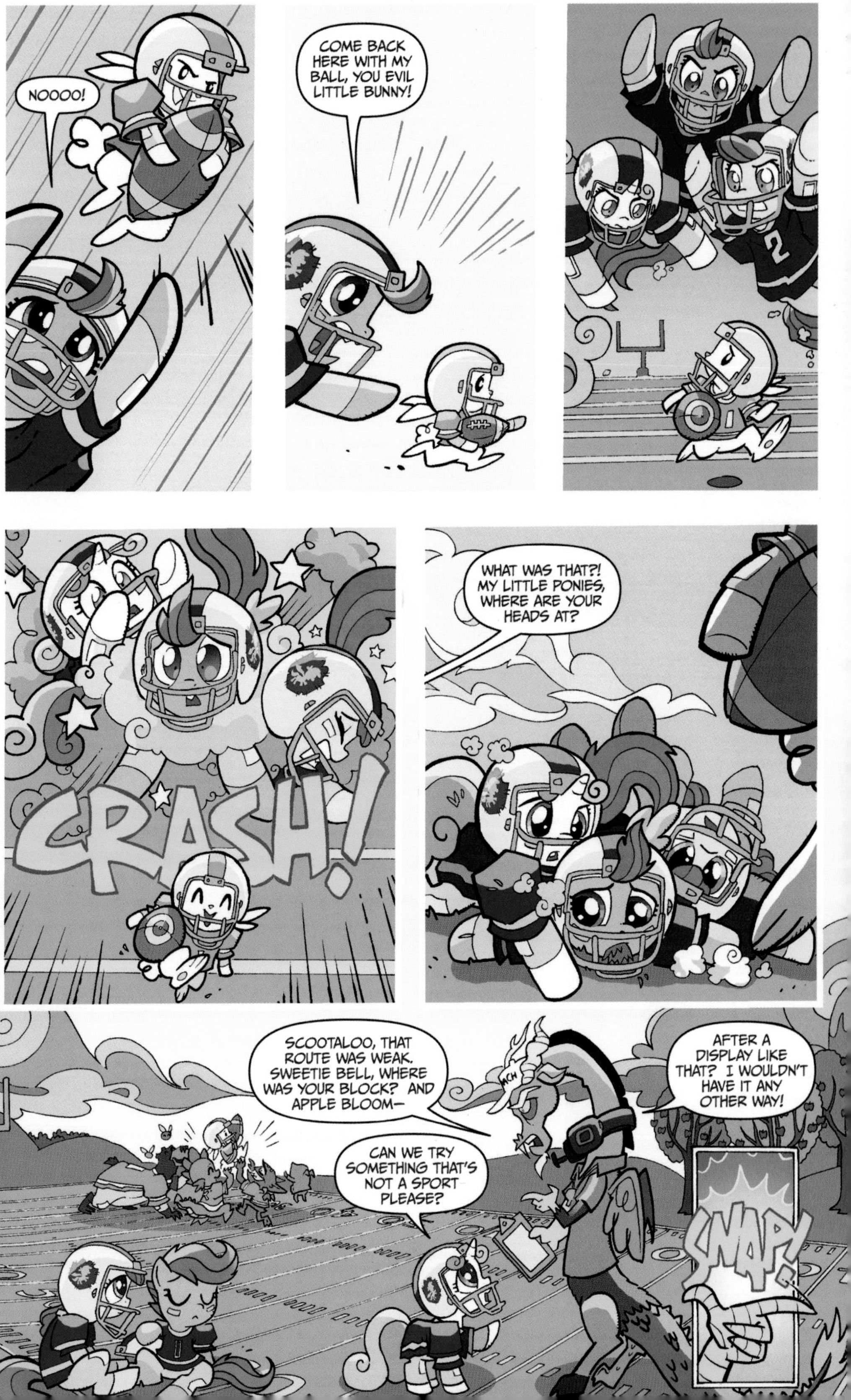
NOOOO!
COME BACK HERE WITH MY BALL, YOU EVIL LITTLE BUNNY!
CRASH!
WHAT WAS THAT?! MY LITTLE PONIES, WHERE ARE YOUR HEADS AT?
SCOOTALOO, THAT ROUTE WAS WEAK. SWEETIE BELL, WHERE WAS YOUR BLOCK? AND APPLE BLOOM—
CAN WE TRY SOMETHING THAT'S NOT A SPORT PLEASE?
AFTER A DISPLAY LIKE THAT? I WOULDN'T HAVE IT ANY OTHER WAY!
SNAP!

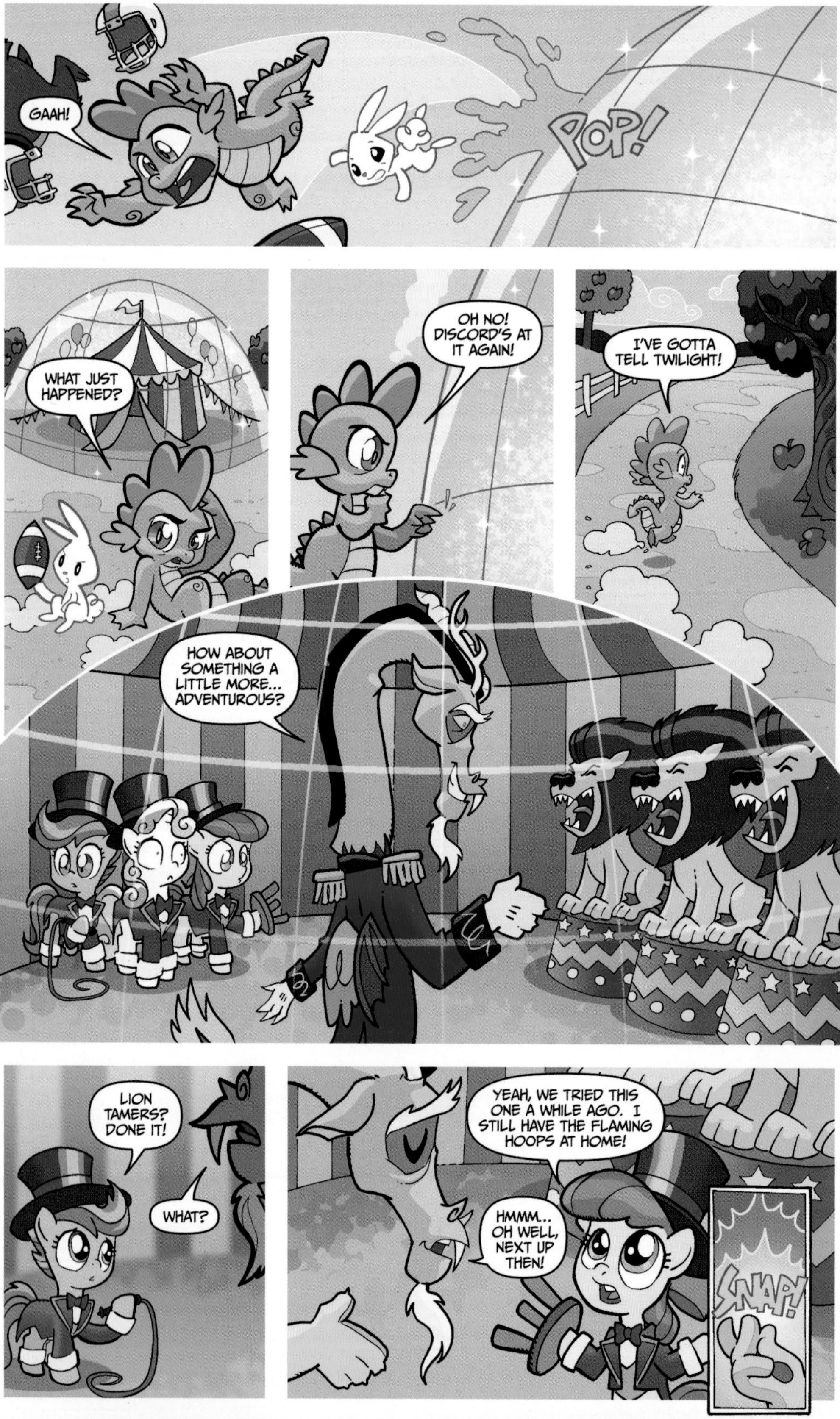

GAAH!
POP!
WHAT JUST HAPPENED?
OH NO! DISCORD'S AT IT AGAIN!
I'VE GOTTA TELL TWILIGHT!
HOW ABOUT SOMETHING A LITTLE MORE... ADVENTUROUS?
LION TAMERS? DONE IT!
WHAT?
YEAH, WE TRIED THIS ONE A WHILE AGO. I STILL HAVE THE FLAMING HOOPS AT HOME!
HMMM... OH WELL, NEXT UP THEN!
SNAP!

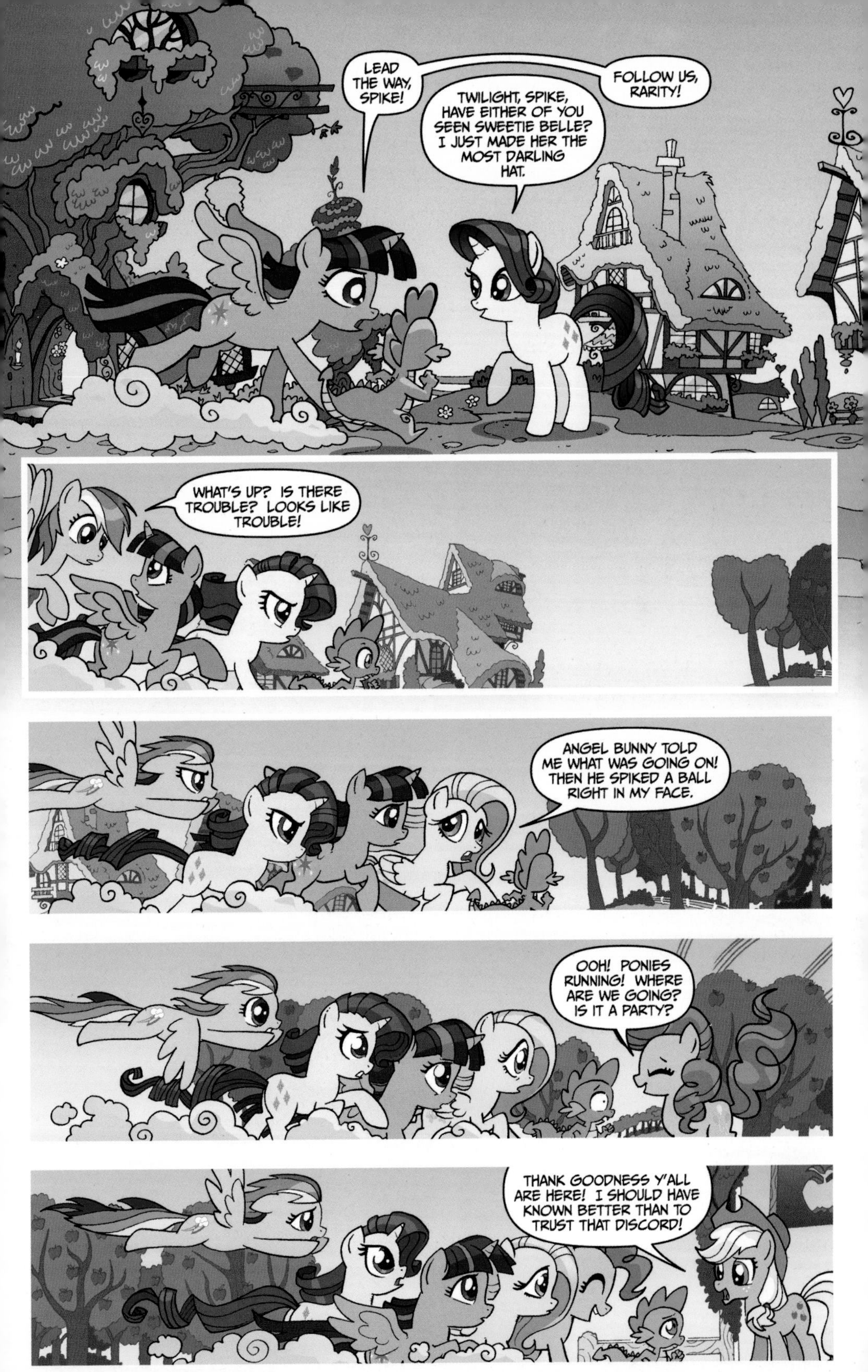
TWILIGHT, SPIKE, HAVE EITHER OF YOU SEEN SWEETIE BELLE? I JUST MADE HER THE MOST DARLING HAT.
LEAD THE WAY, SPIKE!
FOLLOW US, RARITY!
WHAT'S UP? IS THERE TROUBLE? LOOKS LIKE TROUBLE!
ANGEL BUNNY TOLD ME WHAT WAS GOING ON! THEN HE SPIKED A BALL RIGHT IN MY FACE.
OOH! PONIES RUNNING! WHERE ARE WE GOING? IS IT A PARTY?
THANK GOODNESS Y'ALL ARE HERE! I SHOULD HAVE KNOWN BETTER THAN TO TRUST THAT DISCORD!

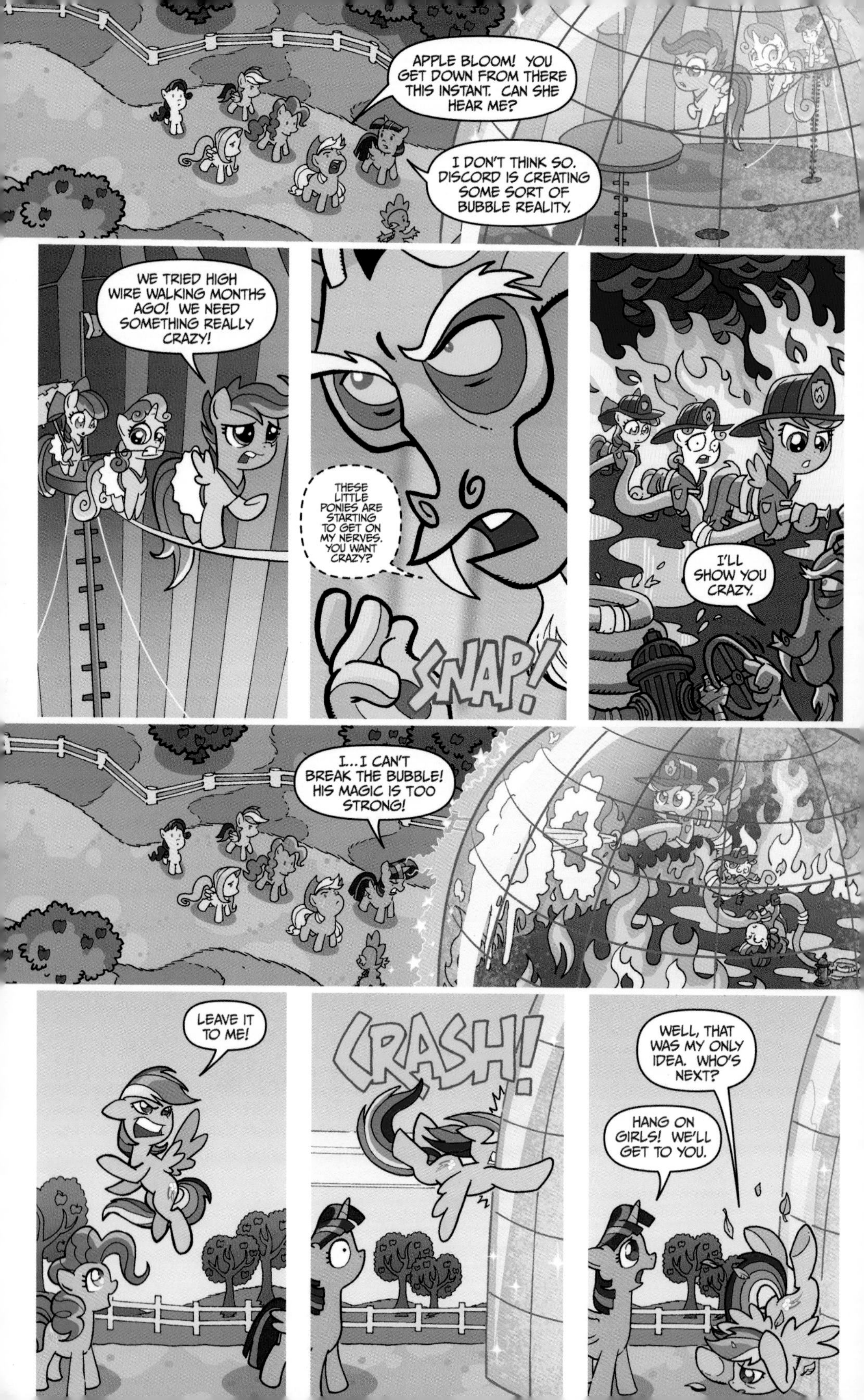
APPLE BLOOM! YOU GET DOWN FROM THERE THIS INSTANT. CAN SHE HEAR ME?
I DON'T THINK SO. DISCORD IS CREATING SOME SORT OF BUBBLE REALITY.
WE TRIED HIGH WIRE WALKING MONTHS AGO! WE NEED SOMETHING REALLY CRAZY!
THESE LITTLE PONIES ARE STARTING TO GET ON MY NERVES. YOU WANT CRAZY?
SNAP!
I'LL SHOW YOU CRAZY.
I...I CAN'T BREAK THE BUBBLE! HIS MAGIC IS TOO STRONG!
LEAVE IT TO ME!
CRASH!
WELL, THAT WAS MY ONLY IDEA. WHO'S NEXT?
HANG ON GIRLS! WE'LL GET TO YOU.

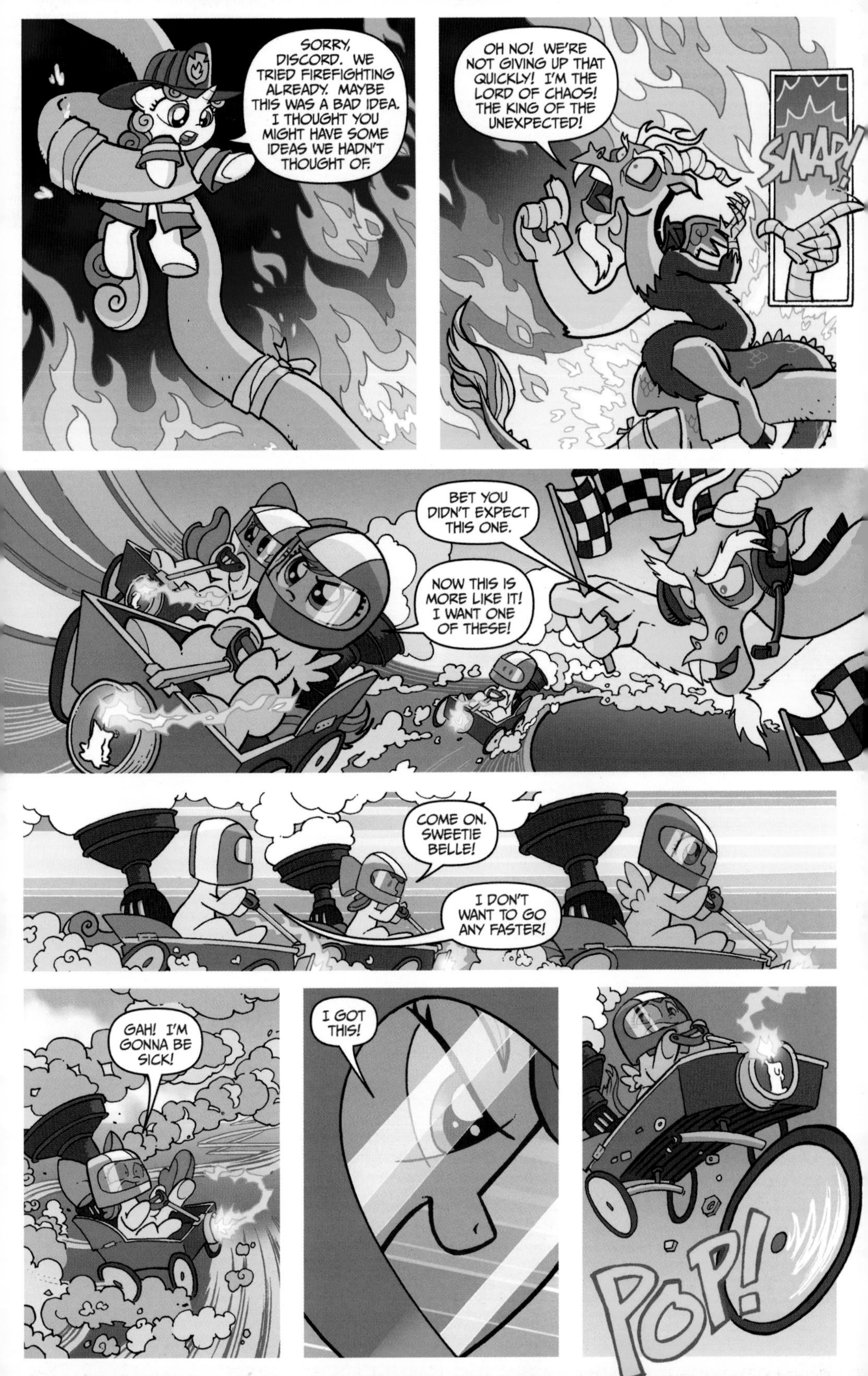
SORRY, DISCORD. WE TRIED FIREFIGHTING ALREADY. MAYBE THIS WAS A BAD IDEA. I THOUGHT YOU MIGHT HAVE SOME IDEAS WE HADN'T THOUGHT OF.
OH NO! WE'RE NOT GIVING UP THAT QUICKLY! I'M THE LORD OF CHAOS! THE KING OF THE UNEXPECTED!
SNAP!
BET YOU DIDN'T EXPECT THIS ONE.
NOW THIS IS MORE LIKE IT! I WANT ONE OF THESE!
COME ON. SWEETIE BELLE!
I DON'T WANT TO GO ANY FASTER!
GAH! I'M GONNA BE SICK!
I GOT THIS!
POP!

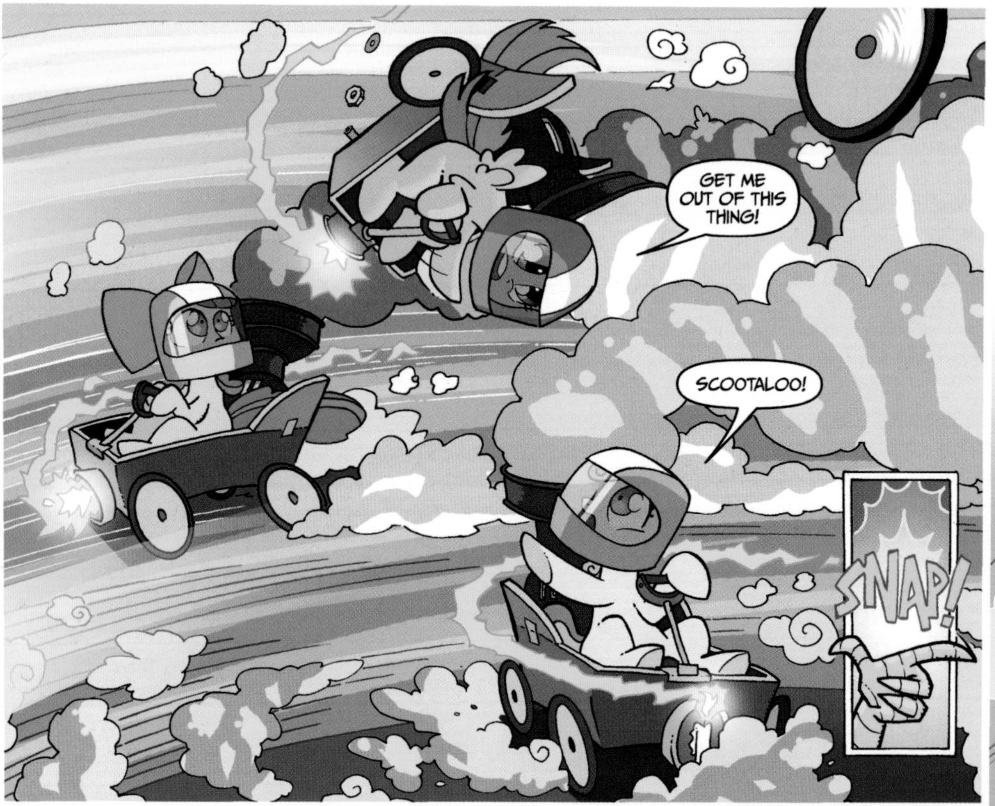
GET ME OUT OF THIS THING!
SCOOTALOO!
SNAP!

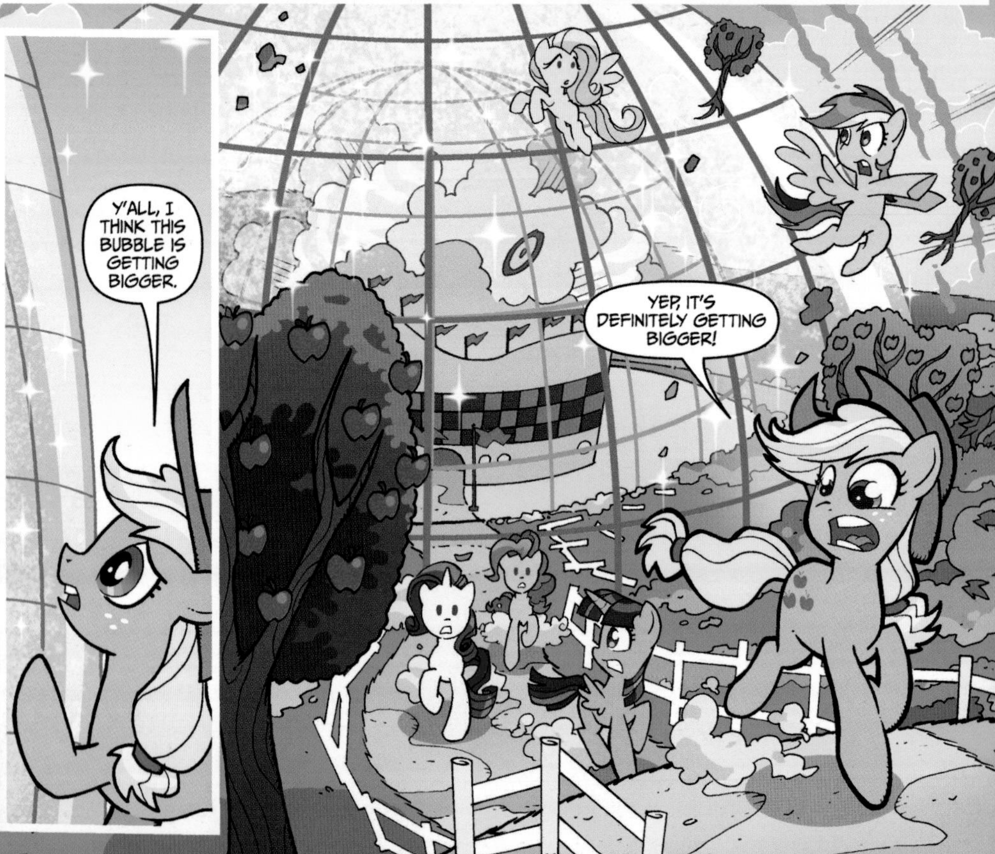
Y'ALL, I THINK THIS BUBBLE IS GETTING BIGGER.
YEP, IT'S DEFINITELY GETTING BIGGER!

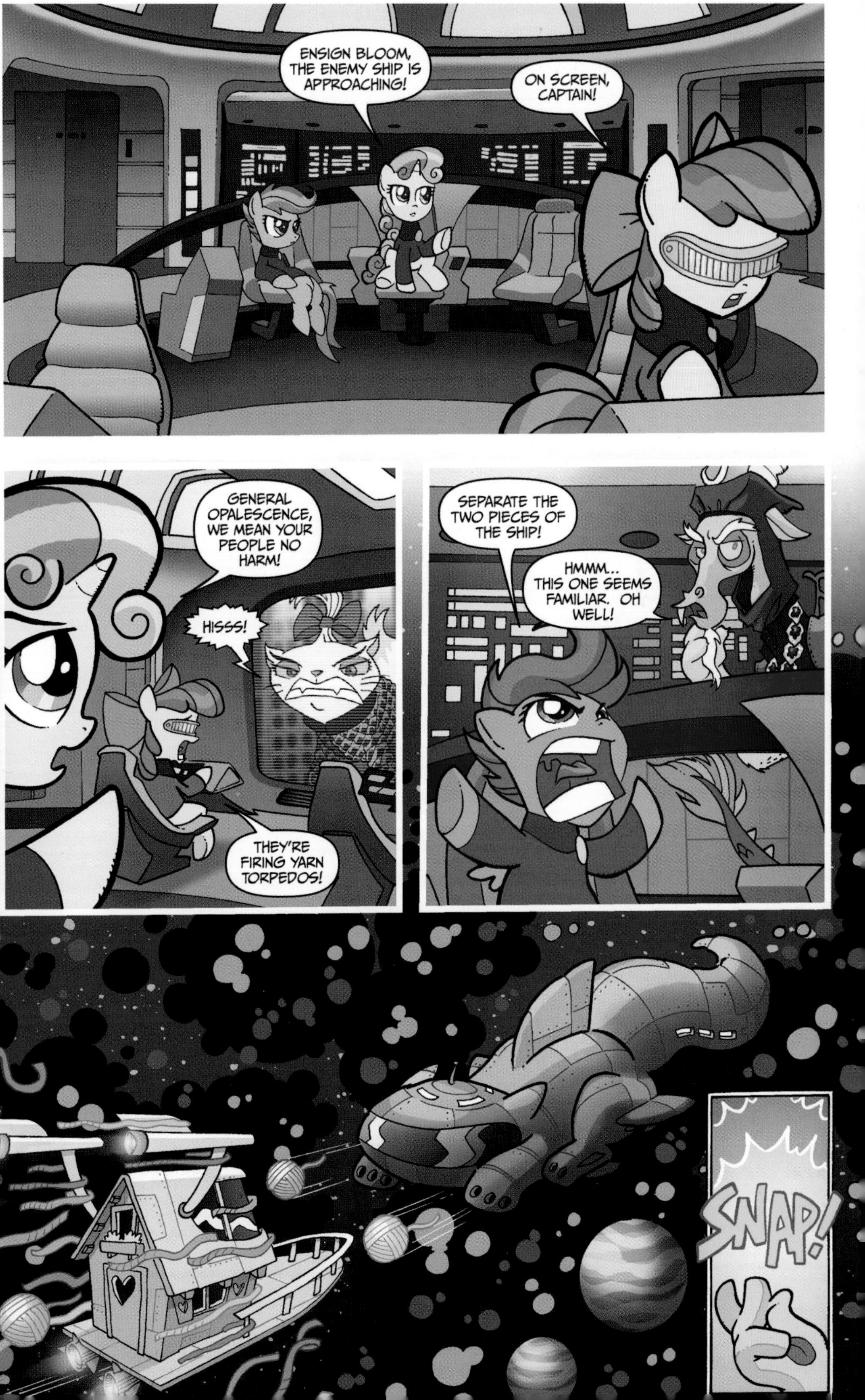
ENSIGN BLOOM, THE ENEMY SHIP IS APPROACHING!
ON SCREEN, CAPTAIN!
GENERAL OPALESCENCE, WE MEAN YOUR PEOPLE NO HARM!
HISSS!
THEY'RE FIRING YARN TORPEDOS!
SEPARATE THE TWO PIECES OF THE SHIP!
HMMM... THIS ONE SEEMS FAMILIAR. OH WELL!
SNAP!

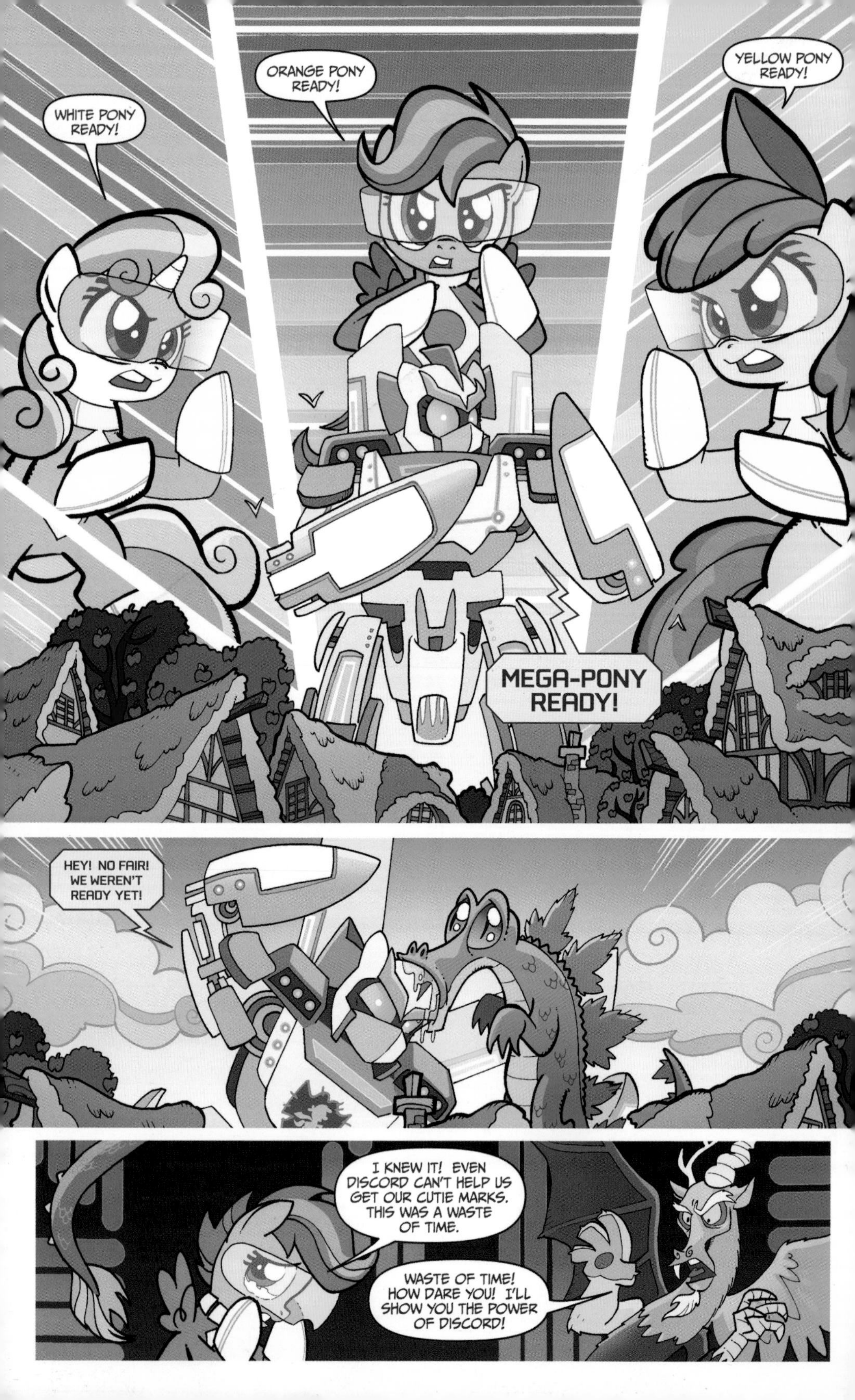
WHITE PONY READY!
ORANGE PONY READY!
YELLOW PONY READY!
MEGA-PONY READY!
HEY! NO FAIR! WE WEREN'T READY YET!
I KNEW IT! EVEN DISCORD CAN'T HELP US GET OUR CUTIE MARKS. THIS WAS A WASTE OF TIME.
WASTE OF TIME! HOW DARE YOU! I'LL SHOW YOU THE POWER OF DISCORD!

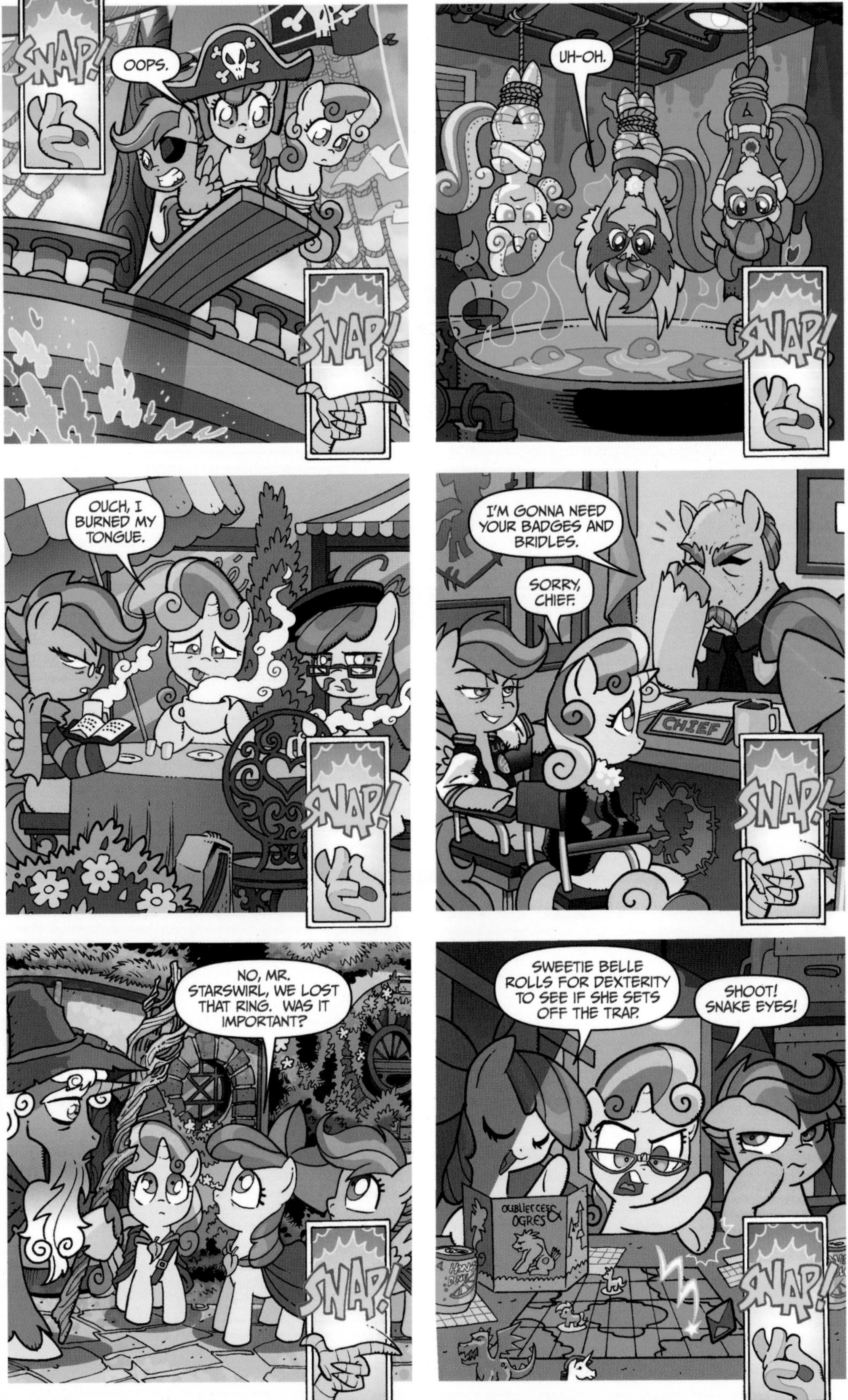
SNAP!
OOPS.
SNAP!
UH-OH.
SNAP!
OUCH, I BURNED MY TONGUE.
SNAP!
I'M GONNA NEED YOUR BADGES AND BRIDLES.
SORRY, CHIEF.
CHIEF
SNAP!
NO, MR. STARSWIRL, WE LOST THAT RING. WAS IT IMPORTANT?
SNAP!
SWEETIE BELLE ROLLS FOR DEXTERITY TO SEE IF SHE SETS OFF THE TRAP.
SHOOT! SNAKE EYES!
SNAP!

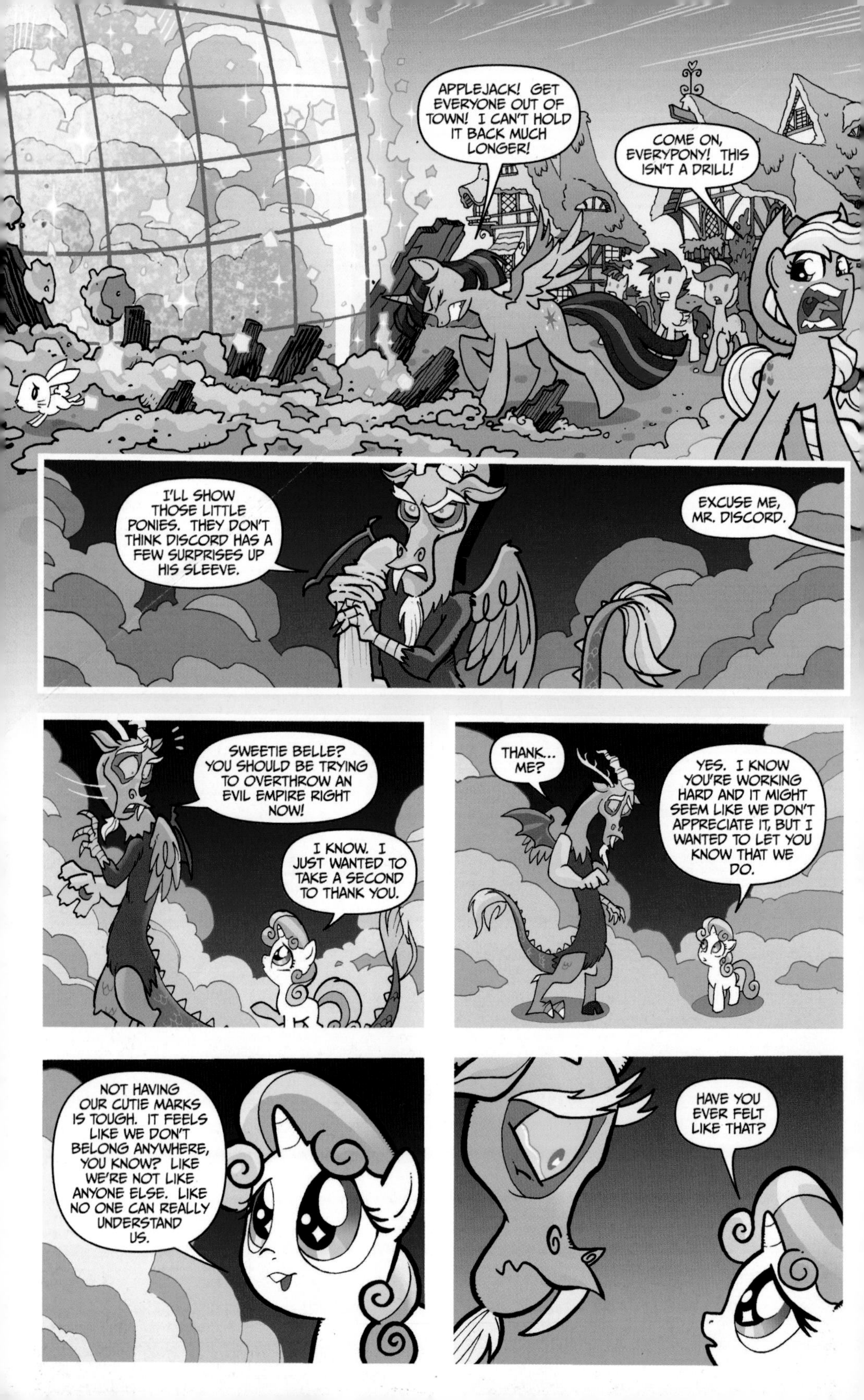
APPLEJACK! GET EVERYONE OUT OF TOWN! I CAN'T HOLD IT BACK MUCH LONGER!
COME ON, EVERYPONY! THIS ISN'T A DRILL!
I'LL SHOW THOSE LITTLE PONIES. THEY DON'T THINK DISCORD HAS A FEW SURPRISES UP HIS SLEEVE.
EXCUSE ME, MR. DISCORD.
SWEETIE BELLE? YOU SHOULD BE TRYING TO OVERTHROW AN EVIL EMPIRE RIGHT NOW!
I KNOW. I JUST WANTED TO TAKE A SECOND TO THANK YOU.
THANK... ME?
YES. I KNOW YOU'RE WORKING HARD AND IT MIGHT SEEM LIKE WE DON'T APPRECIATE IT, BUT I WANTED TO LET YOU KNOW THAT WE DO.
NOT HAVING OUR CUTIE MARKS IS TOUGH. IT FEELS LIKE WE DON'T BELONG ANYWHERE, YOU KNOW? LIKE WE'RE NOT LIKE ANYONE ELSE. LIKE NO ONE CAN REALLY UNDERSTAND US.
HAVE YOU EVER FELT LIKE THAT?

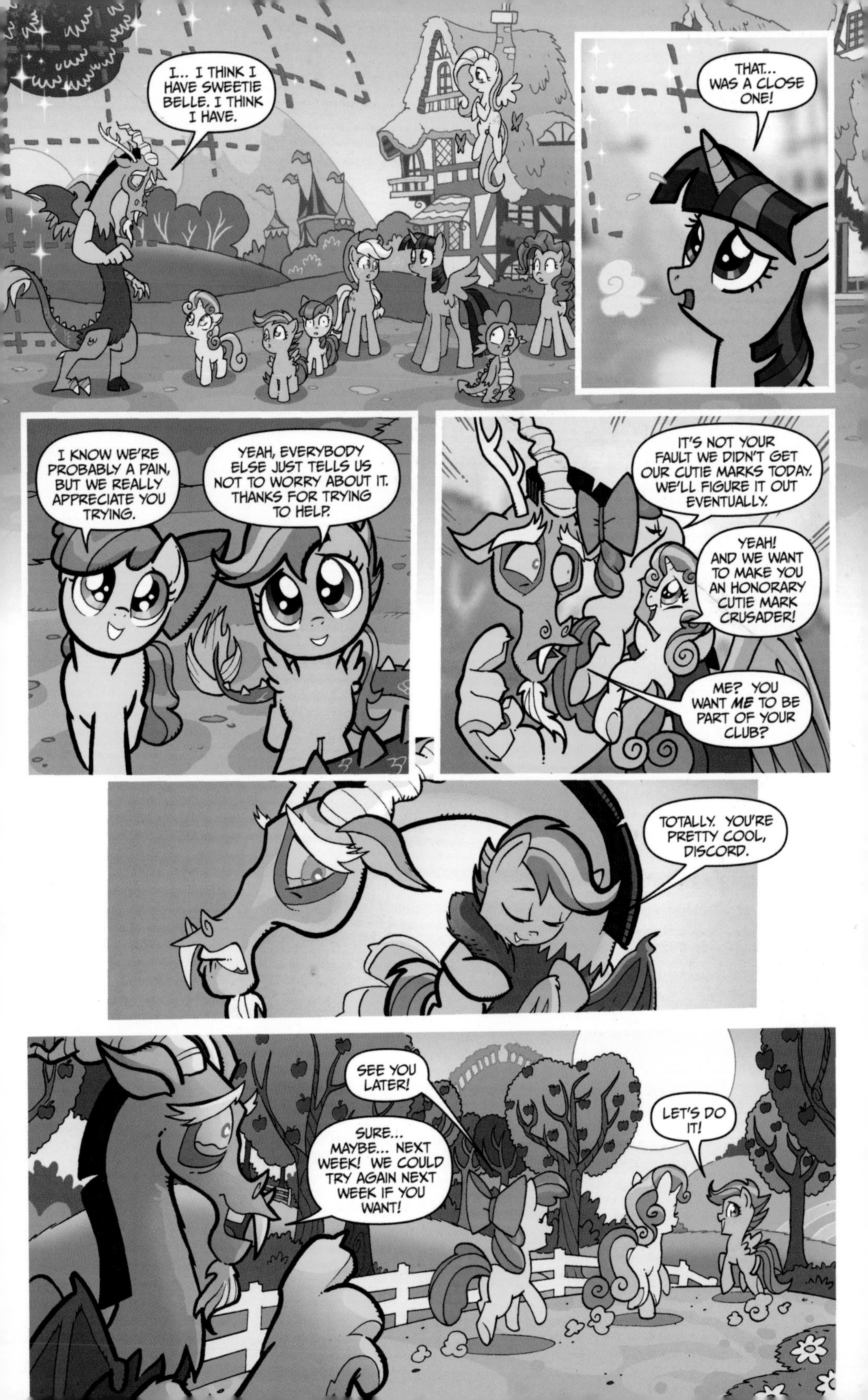
I... I THINK I HAVE SWEETIE BELLE. I THINK I HAVE.
THAT... WAS A CLOSE ONE!
I KNOW WE'RE PROBABLY A PAIN, BUT WE REALLY APPRECIATE YOU TRYING.
YEAH, EVERYBODY ELSE JUST TELLS US NOT TO WORRY ABOUT IT. THANKS FOR TRYING TO HELP.
IT'S NOT YOUR FAULT WE DIDN'T GET OUR CUTIE MARKS TODAY. WE'LL FIGURE IT OUT EVENTUALLY.
YEAH! AND WE WANT TO MAKE YOU AN HONORARY CUTIE MARK CRUSADER!
ME? YOU WANT *ME* TO BE PART OF YOUR CLUB?
TOTALLY. YOU'RE PRETTY COOL, DISCORD.
SEE YOU LATER!
SURE... MAYBE... NEXT WEEK! WE COULD TRY AGAIN NEXT WEEK IF YOU WANT!
LET'S DO IT!

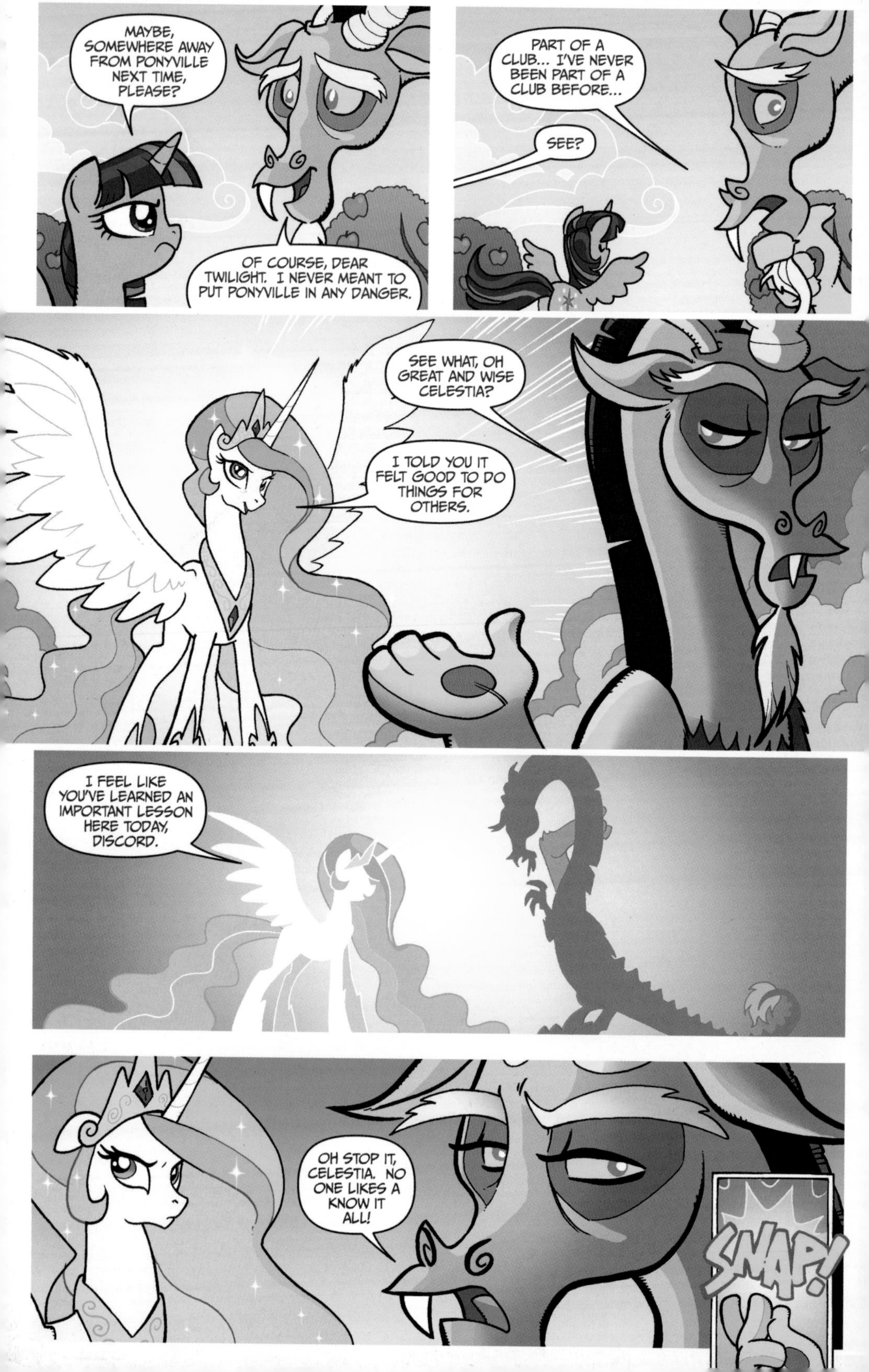
MAYBE, SOMEWHERE AWAY FROM PONYVILLE NEXT TIME, PLEASE?
OF COURSE, DEAR TWILIGHT. I NEVER MEANT TO PUT PONYVILLE IN ANY DANGER.
PART OF A CLUB... I'VE NEVER BEEN PART OF A CLUB BEFORE...
SEE?
SEE WHAT, OH GREAT AND WISE CELESTIA?
I TOLD YOU IT FELT GOOD TO DO THINGS FOR OTHERS.
I FEEL LIKE YOU'VE LEARNED AN IMPORTANT LESSON HERE TODAY, DISCORD.
OH STOP IT, CELESTIA. NO ONE LIKES A KNOW IT ALL!
SNAP!

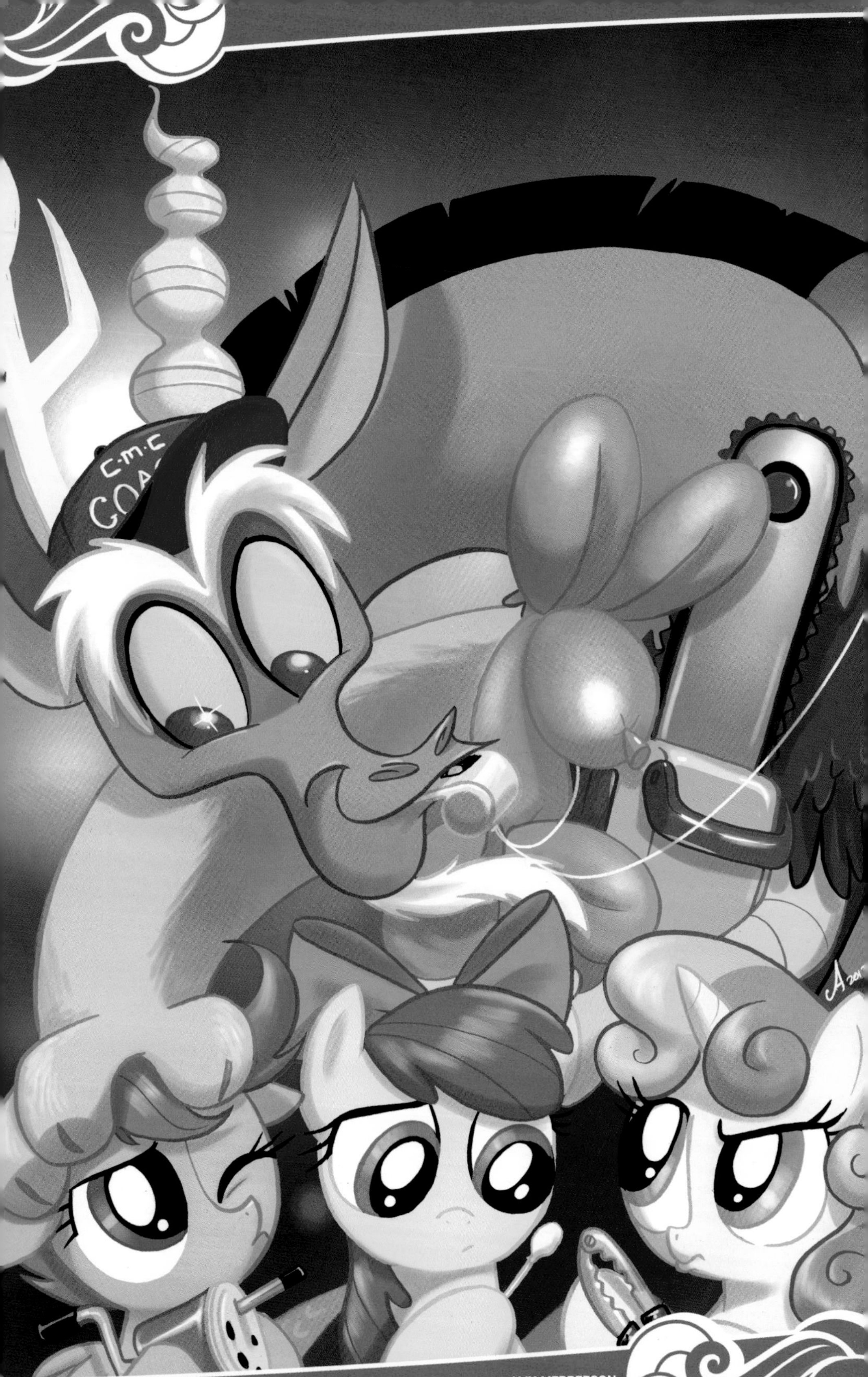
C·M·C

art by AMY MEBBERSON

Princess Celestia & Spike

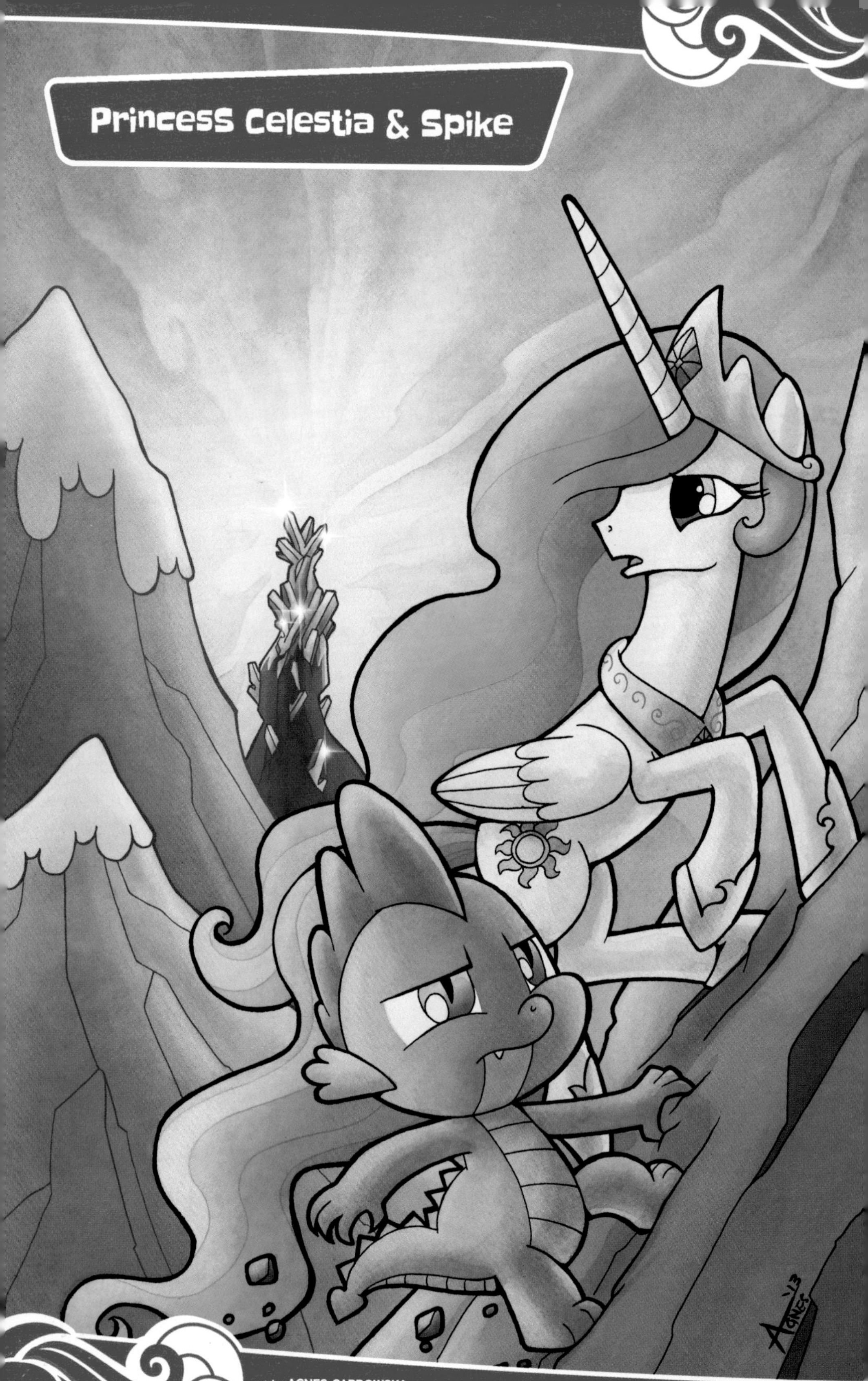

art by AGNES GARBOWSKA

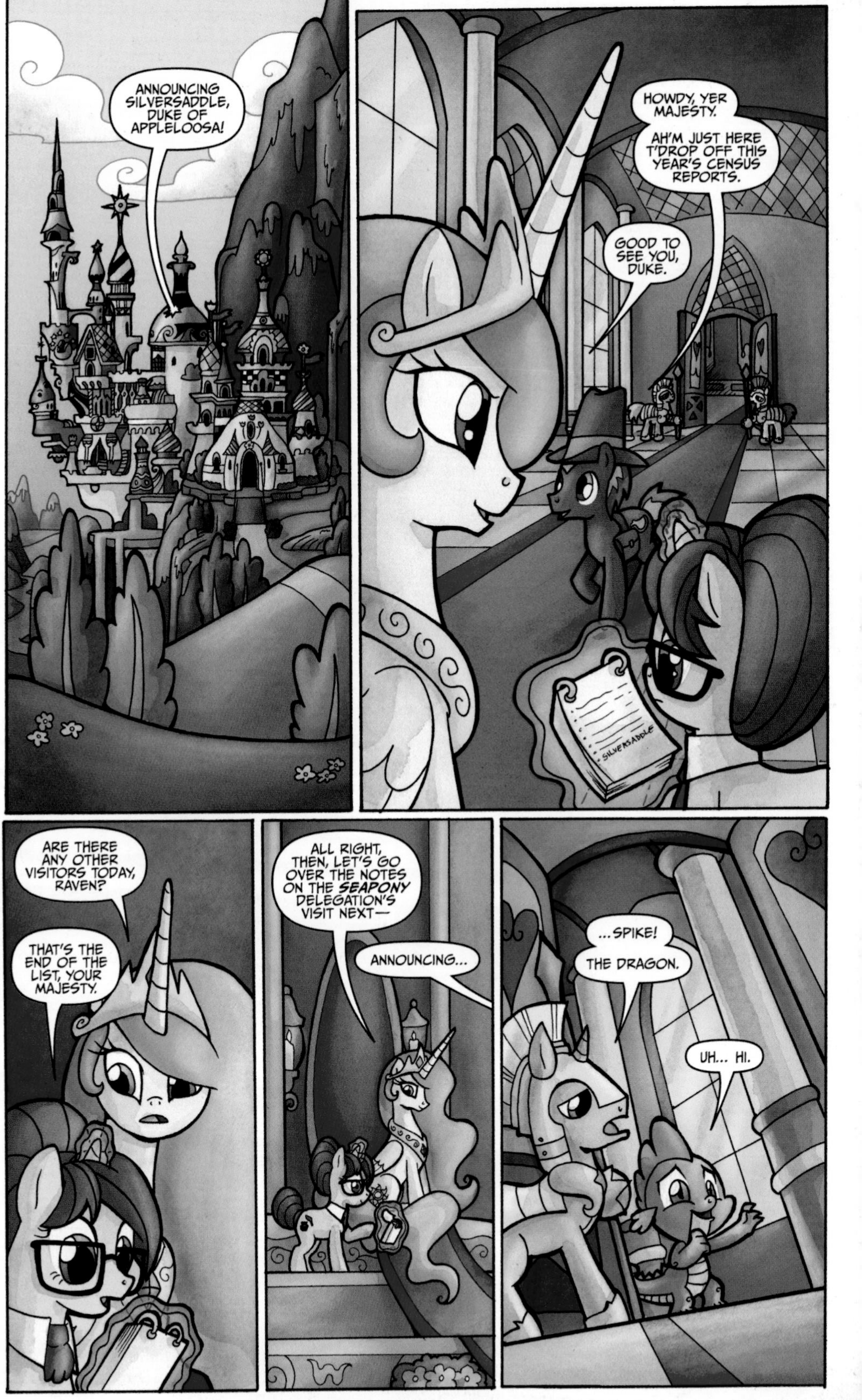
ANNOUNCING SILVERSADDLE, DUKE OF APPLELOOSA!
HOWDY, YER MAJESTY.
AH'M JUST HERE T'DROP OFF THIS YEAR'S CENSUS REPORTS.
GOOD TO SEE YOU, DUKE.
SILVERSADDLE
ARE THERE ANY OTHER VISITORS TODAY, RAVEN?
THAT'S THE END OF THE LIST, YOUR MAJESTY.
ALL RIGHT, THEN, LET'S GO OVER THE NOTES ON THE *SEAPONY* DELEGATION'S VISIT NEXT—
ANNOUNCING...
...SPIKE!
THE DRAGON.
UH... HI.

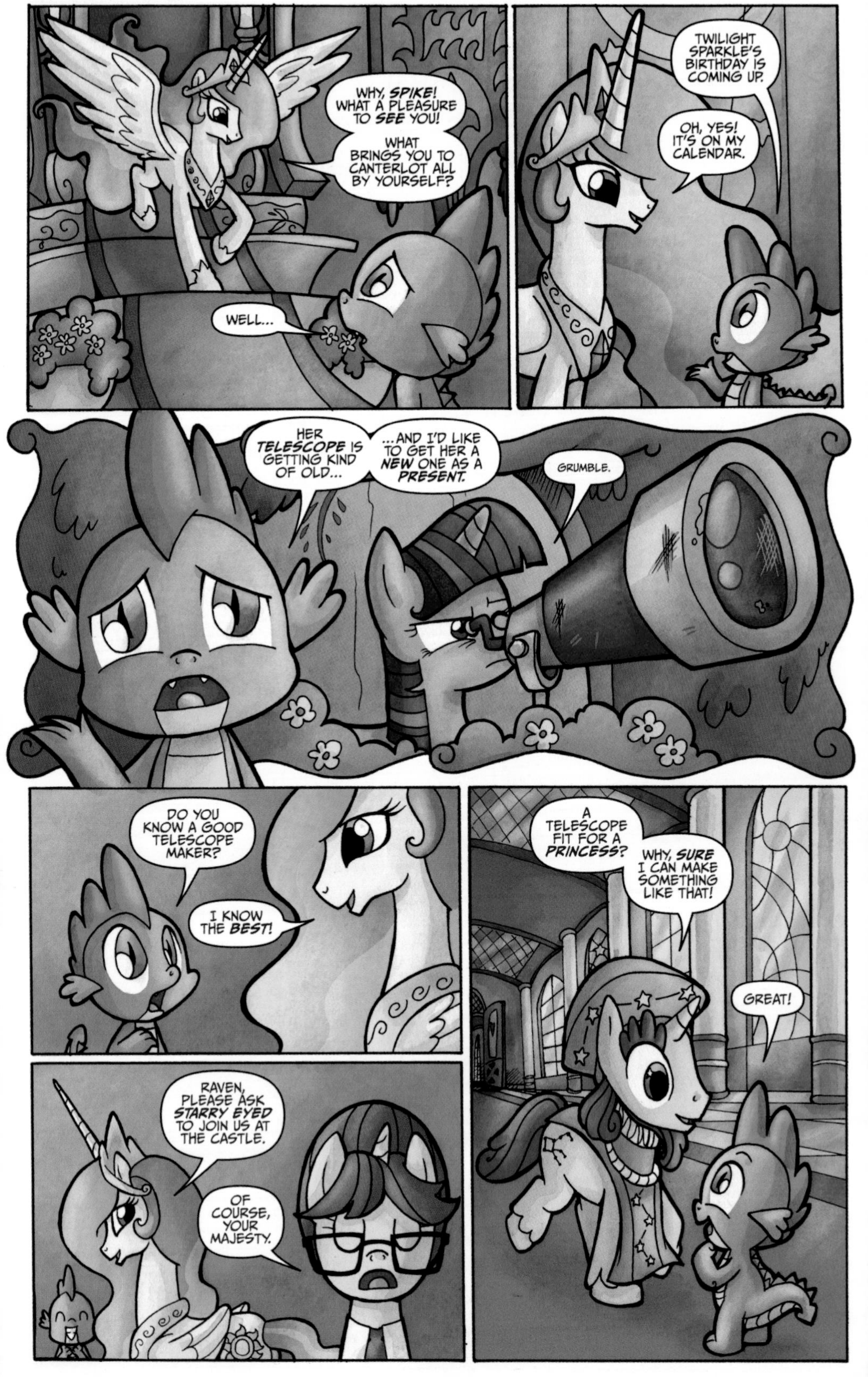
WHY, SPIKE! WHAT A PLEASURE TO SEE YOU!
WHAT BRINGS YOU TO CANTERLOT ALL BY YOURSELF?
WELL...
TWILIGHT SPARKLE'S BIRTHDAY IS COMING UP.
OH, YES! IT'S ON MY CALENDAR.
HER TELESCOPE IS GETTING KIND OF OLD...
...AND I'D LIKE TO GET HER A NEW ONE AS A PRESENT.
GRUMBLE.
DO YOU KNOW A GOOD TELESCOPE MAKER?
I KNOW THE BEST!
RAVEN, PLEASE ASK STARRY EYED TO JOIN US AT THE CASTLE.
OF COURSE, YOUR MAJESTY.
A TELESCOPE FIT FOR A PRINCESS?
WHY, SURE I CAN MAKE SOMETHING LIKE THAT!
GREAT!

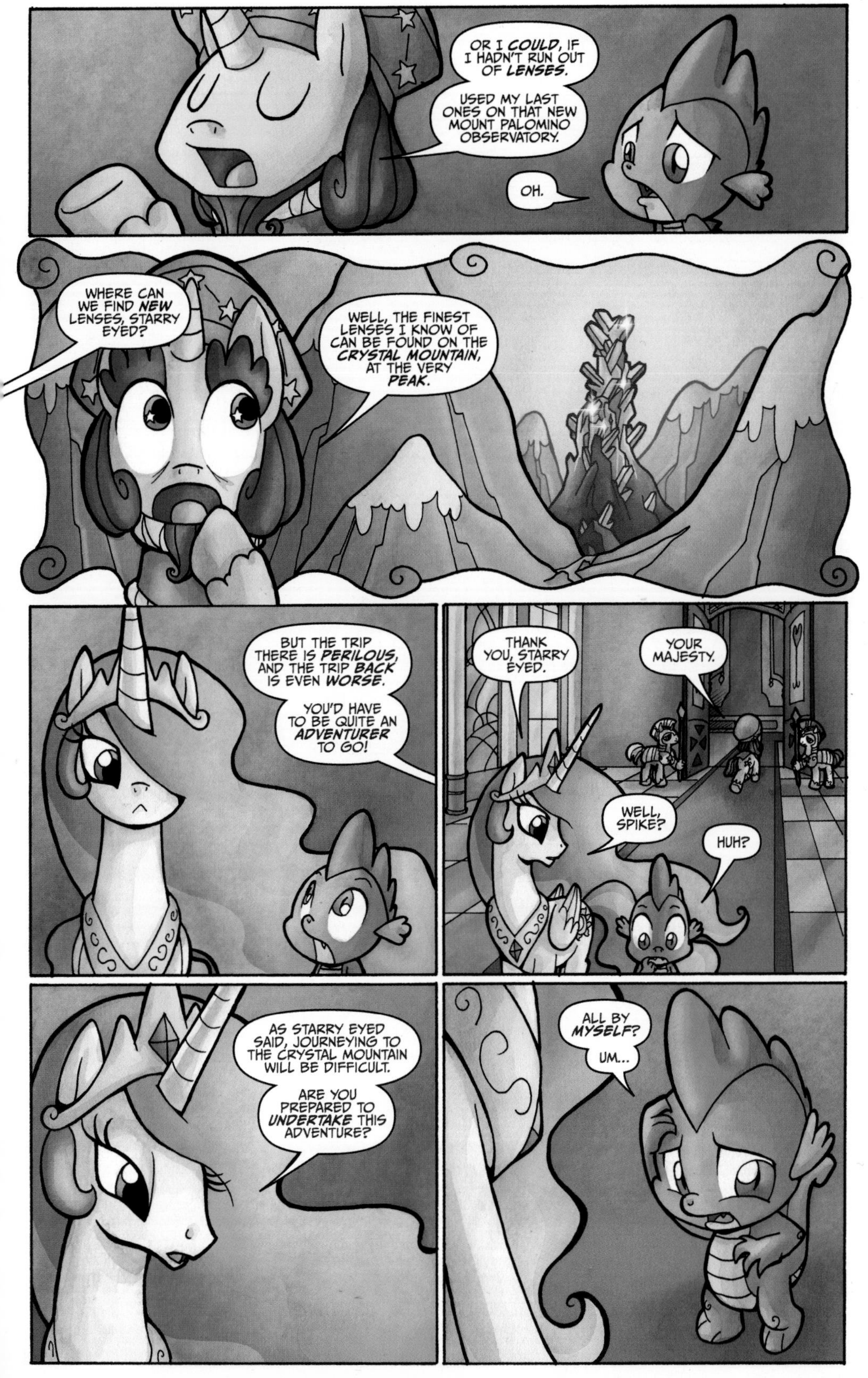
OR I COULD, IF I HADN'T RUN OUT OF LENSES.
USED MY LAST ONES ON THAT NEW MOUNT PALOMINO OBSERVATORY.
OH.
WHERE CAN WE FIND NEW LENSES, STARRY EYED?
WELL, THE FINEST LENSES I KNOW OF CAN BE FOUND ON THE CRYSTAL MOUNTAIN, AT THE VERY PEAK.
BUT THE TRIP THERE IS PERILOUS, AND THE TRIP BACK IS EVEN WORSE.
YOU'D HAVE TO BE QUITE AN ADVENTURER TO GO!
THANK YOU, STARRY EYED.
YOUR MAJESTY.
WELL, SPIKE?
HUH?
AS STARRY EYED SAID, JOURNEYING TO THE CRYSTAL MOUNTAIN WILL BE DIFFICULT.
ARE YOU PREPARED TO UNDERTAKE THIS ADVENTURE?
ALL BY MYSELF?
UM...

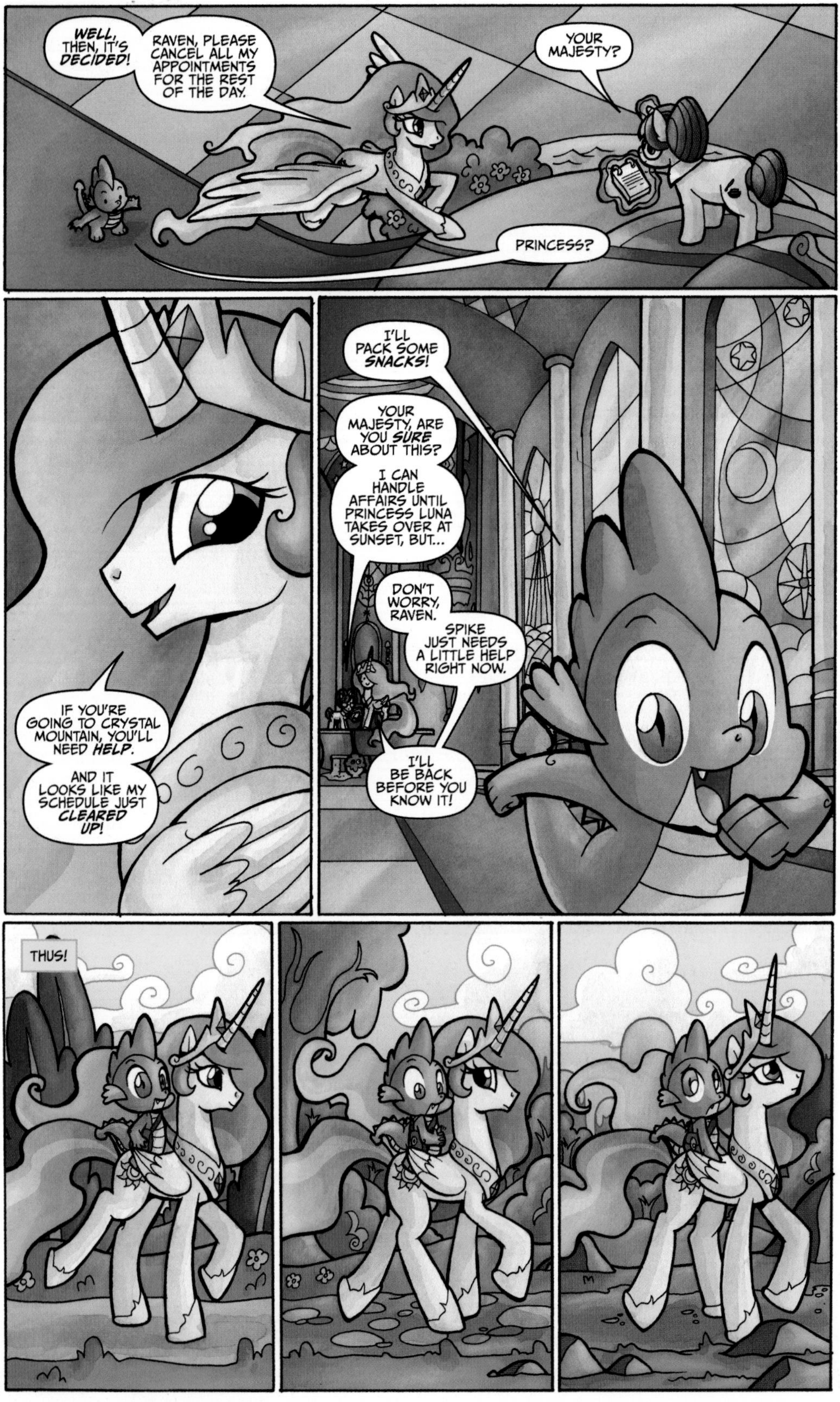
WELL, THEN, IT'S DECIDED!
RAVEN, PLEASE CANCEL ALL MY APPOINTMENTS FOR THE REST OF THE DAY.
YOUR MAJESTY?
PRINCESS?
IF YOU'RE GOING TO CRYSTAL MOUNTAIN, YOU'LL NEED HELP.
AND IT LOOKS LIKE MY SCHEDULE JUST CLEARED UP!
I'LL PACK SOME SNACKS!
YOUR MAJESTY, ARE YOU SURE ABOUT THIS?
I CAN HANDLE AFFAIRS UNTIL PRINCESS LUNA TAKES OVER AT SUNSET, BUT...
DON'T WORRY, RAVEN.
SPIKE JUST NEEDS A LITTLE HELP RIGHT NOW.
I'LL BE BACK BEFORE YOU KNOW IT!
THUS!

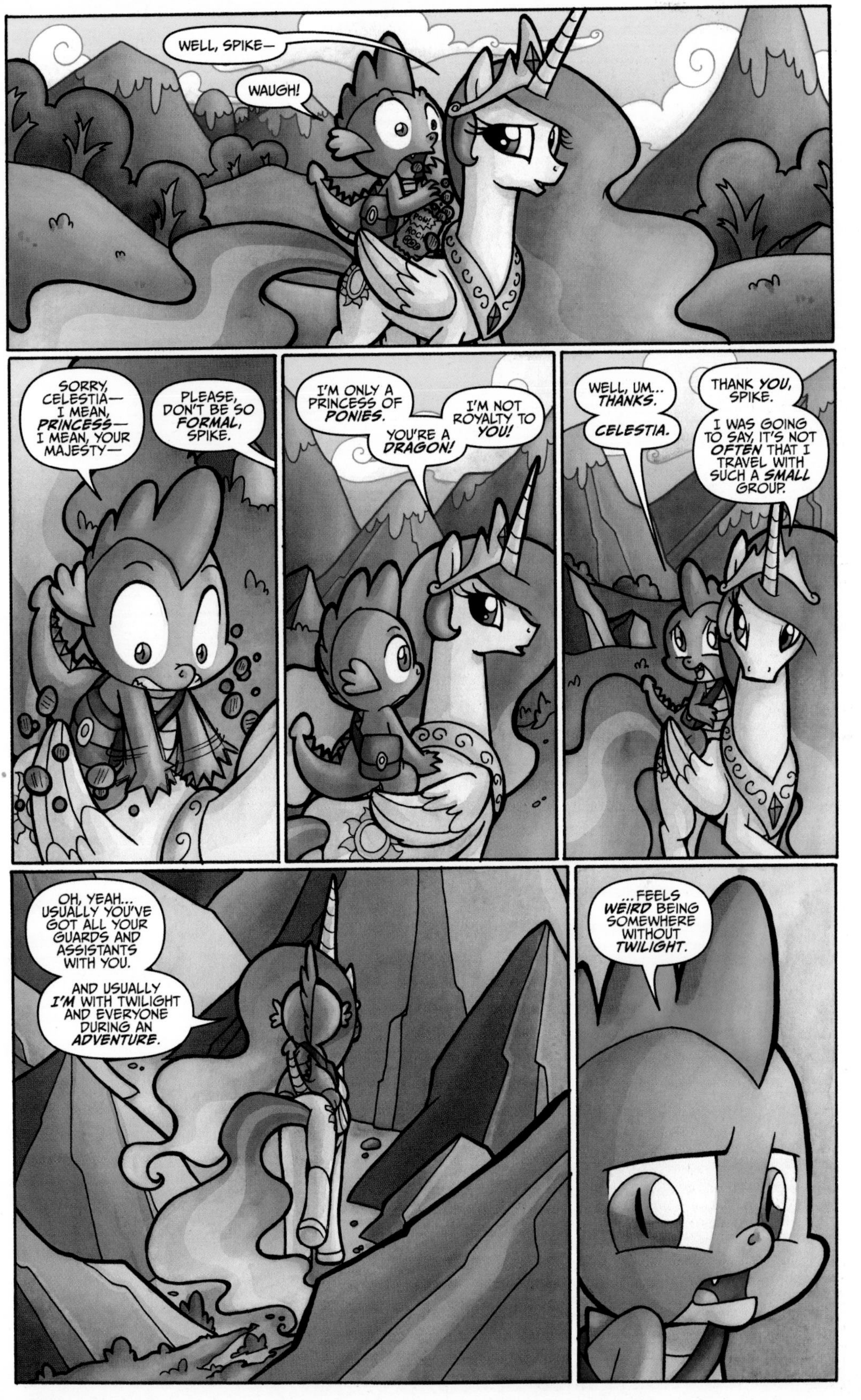
WELL, SPIKE—
WAUGH!
SORRY, CELESTIA— I MEAN, PRINCESS— I MEAN, YOUR MAJESTY—
PLEASE, DON'T BE SO FORMAL, SPIKE.
I'M ONLY A PRINCESS OF PONIES.
I'M NOT ROYALTY TO YOU!
YOU'RE A DRAGON!
WELL, UM... THANKS.
CELESTIA.
THANK YOU, SPIKE.
I WAS GOING TO SAY, IT'S NOT OFTEN THAT I TRAVEL WITH SUCH A SMALL GROUP.
OH, YEAH... USUALLY YOU'VE GOT ALL YOUR GUARDS AND ASSISTANTS WITH YOU.
AND USUALLY I'M WITH TWILIGHT AND EVERYONE DURING AN ADVENTURE.
...FEELS WEIRD BEING SOMEWHERE WITHOUT TWILIGHT.

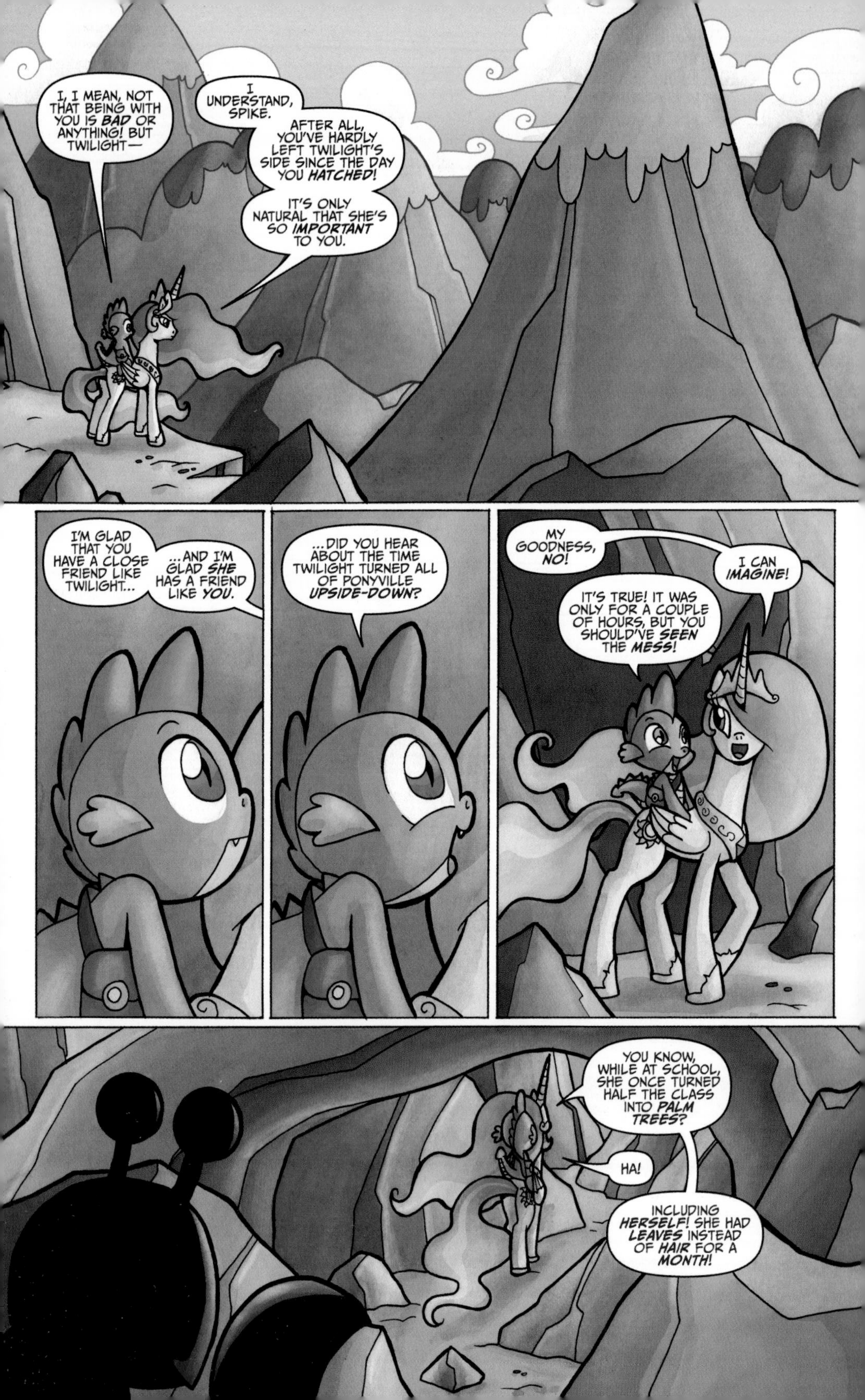
I, I MEAN, NOT THAT BEING WITH YOU IS BAD OR ANYTHING! BUT TWILIGHT—
I UNDERSTAND, SPIKE.
AFTER ALL, YOU'VE HARDLY LEFT TWILIGHT'S SIDE SINCE THE DAY YOU HATCHED!
IT'S ONLY NATURAL THAT SHE'S SO IMPORTANT TO YOU.
I'M GLAD THAT YOU HAVE A CLOSE FRIEND LIKE TWILIGHT...
...AND I'M GLAD SHE HAS A FRIEND LIKE YOU.
...DID YOU HEAR ABOUT THE TIME TWILIGHT TURNED ALL OF PONYVILLE UPSIDE-DOWN?
MY GOODNESS, NO!
IT'S TRUE! IT WAS ONLY FOR A COUPLE OF HOURS, BUT YOU SHOULD'VE SEEN THE MESS!
I CAN IMAGINE!
YOU KNOW, WHILE AT SCHOOL, SHE ONCE TURNED HALF THE CLASS INTO PALM TREES?
HA!
INCLUDING HERSELF! SHE HAD LEAVES INSTEAD OF HAIR FOR A MONTH!

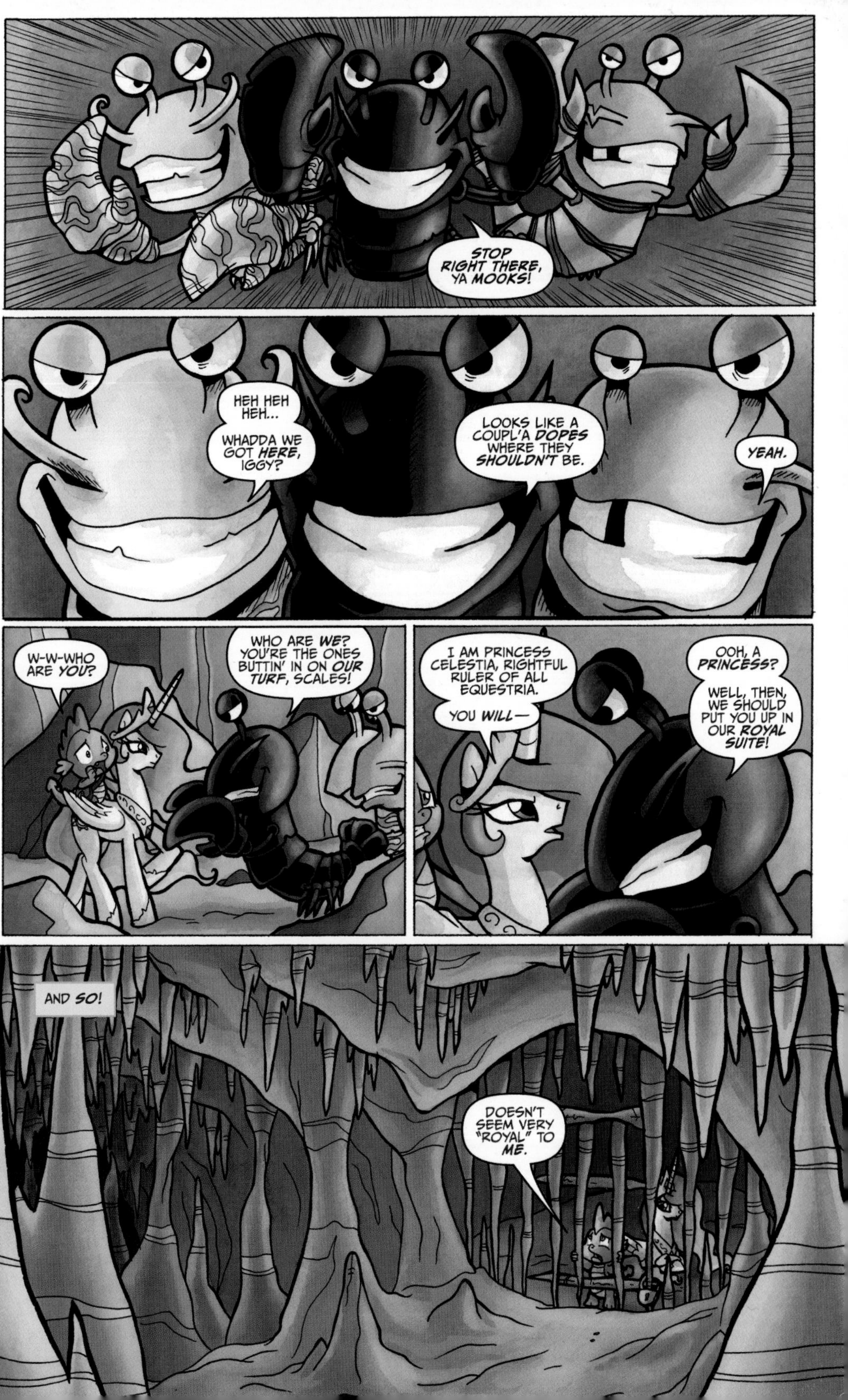
STOP RIGHT THERE, YA MOOKS!
HEH HEH HEH... WHADDA WE GOT HERE, IGGY?
LOOKS LIKE A COUPL'A DOPES WHERE THEY SHOULDN'T BE.
YEAH.
W-W-WHO ARE YOU?
WHO ARE WE? YOU'RE THE ONES BUTTIN' IN ON OUR TURF, SCALES!
I AM PRINCESS CELESTIA, RIGHTFUL RULER OF ALL EQUESTRIA.
YOU WILL—
OOH, A PRINCESS?
WELL, THEN, WE SHOULD PUT YOU UP IN OUR ROYAL SUITE!
AND SO!
DOESN'T SEEM VERY "ROYAL" TO ME.

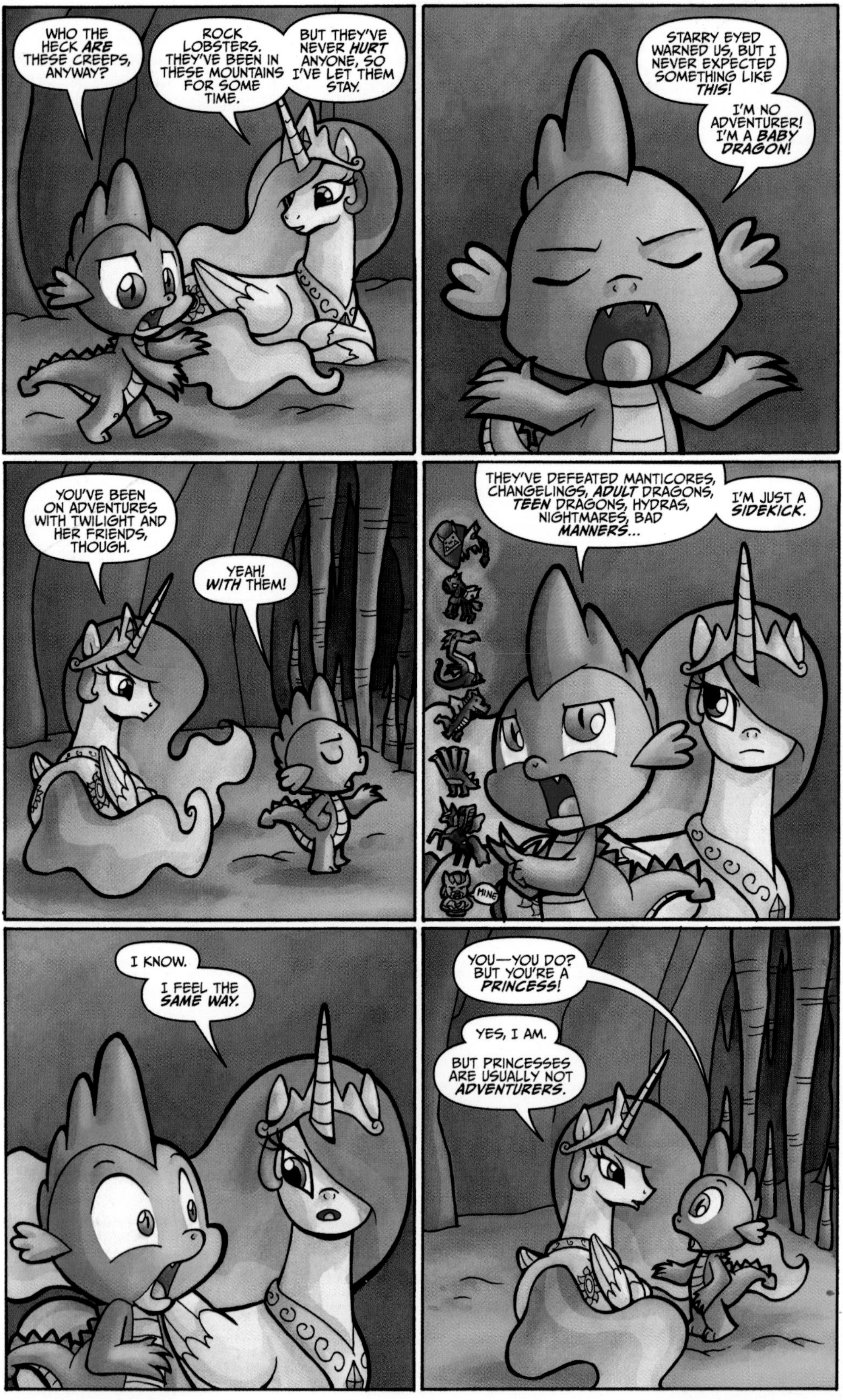
WHO THE HECK *ARE* THESE CREEPS, ANYWAY?
ROCK LOBSTERS. THEY'VE BEEN IN THESE MOUNTAINS FOR SOME TIME.
BUT THEY'VE NEVER *HURT* ANYONE, SO I'VE LET THEM STAY.
STARRY EYED WARNED US, BUT I NEVER EXPECTED SOMETHING LIKE *THIS*!
I'M NO ADVENTURER! I'M A *BABY DRAGON*!
YOU'VE BEEN ON ADVENTURES WITH TWILIGHT AND HER FRIENDS, THOUGH.
YEAH! *WITH* THEM!
THEY'VE DEFEATED MANTICORES, CHANGELINGS, *ADULT* DRAGONS, *TEEN* DRAGONS, HYDRAS, NIGHTMARES, BAD *MANNERS*...
I'M JUST A *SIDEKICK*.
MINE
I KNOW.
I FEEL THE *SAME WAY*.
YOU—YOU DO? BUT YOU'RE A *PRINCESS*!
YES, I AM.
BUT PRINCESSES ARE USUALLY NOT *ADVENTURERS*.

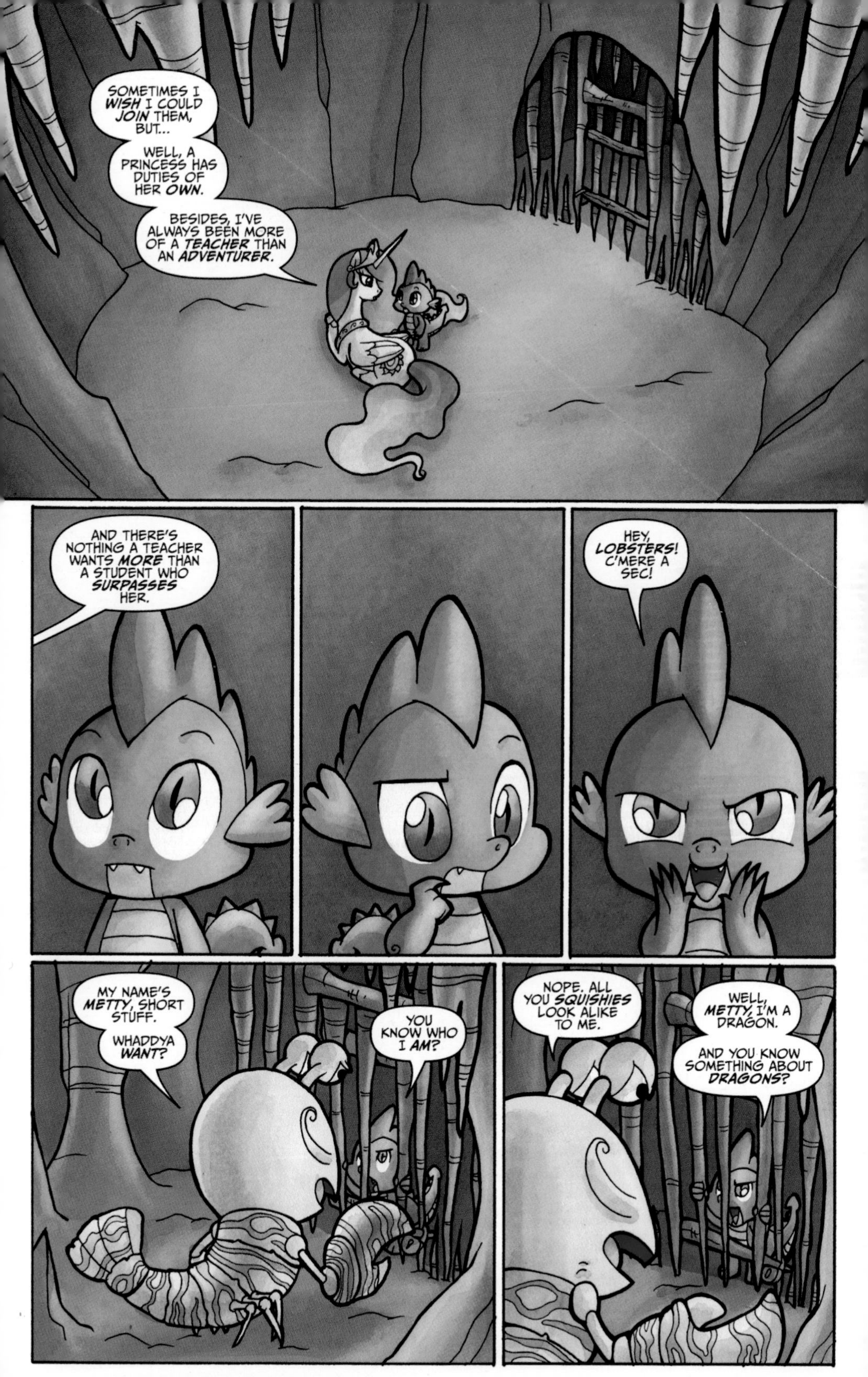
SOMETIMES I WISH I COULD JOIN THEM, BUT...
WELL, A PRINCESS HAS DUTIES OF HER OWN.
BESIDES, I'VE ALWAYS BEEN MORE OF A TEACHER THAN AN ADVENTURER.
AND THERE'S NOTHING A TEACHER WANTS MORE THAN A STUDENT WHO SURPASSES HER.
HEY, LOBSTERS! C'MERE A SEC!
MY NAME'S METTY, SHORT STUFF.
WHADDYA WANT?
YOU KNOW WHO I AM?
NOPE. ALL YOU SQUISHIES LOOK ALIKE TO ME.
WELL, METTY, I'M A DRAGON.
AND YOU KNOW SOMETHING ABOUT DRAGONS?

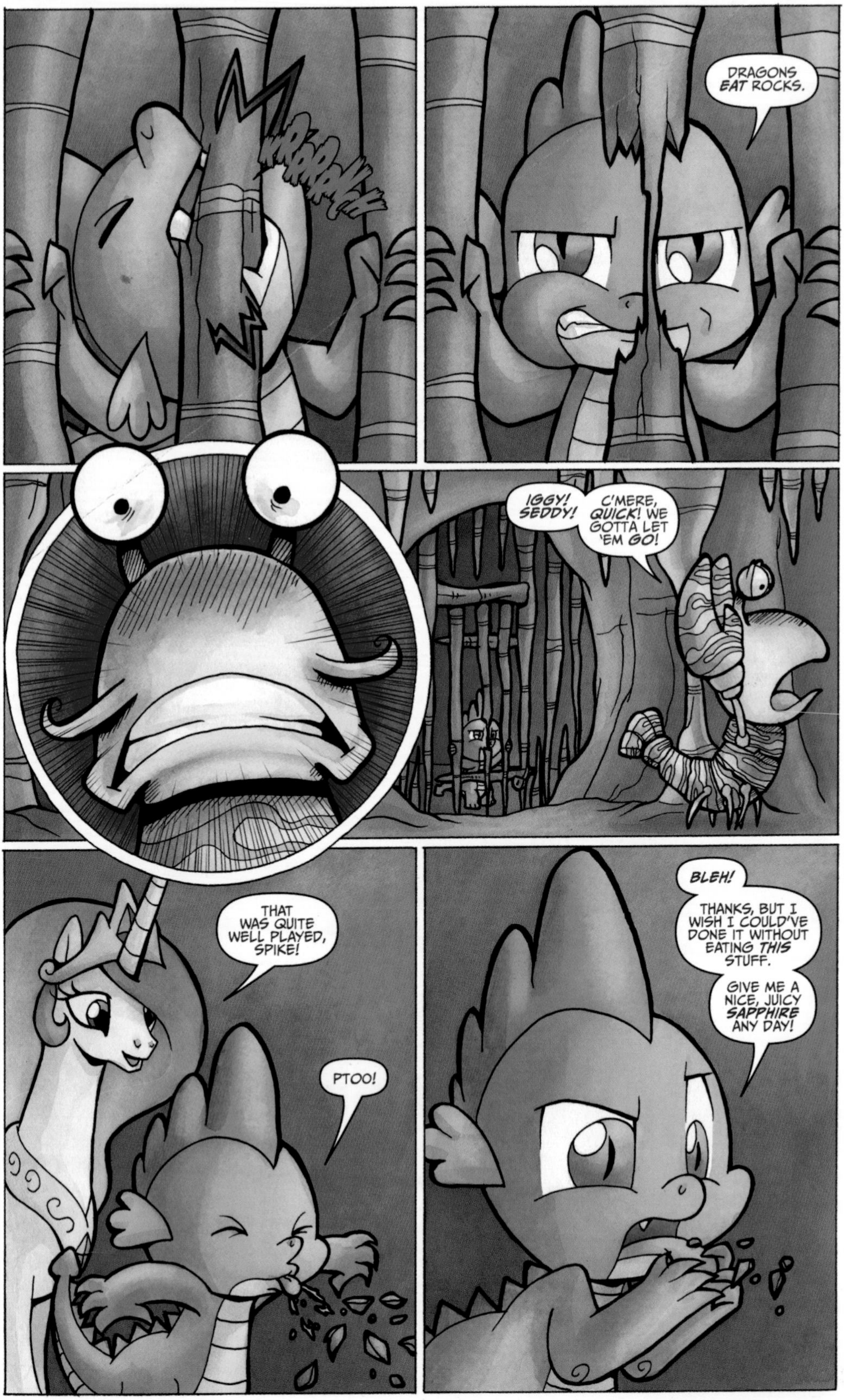

KRRRAKK
DRAGONS EAT ROCKS.
IGGY! SEDDY!
C'MERE, QUICK! WE GOTTA LET 'EM GO!
THAT WAS QUITE WELL PLAYED, SPIKE!
PTOO!
BLEH!
THANKS, BUT I WISH I COULD'VE DONE IT WITHOUT EATING THIS STUFF.
GIVE ME A NICE, JUICY SAPPHIRE ANY DAY!

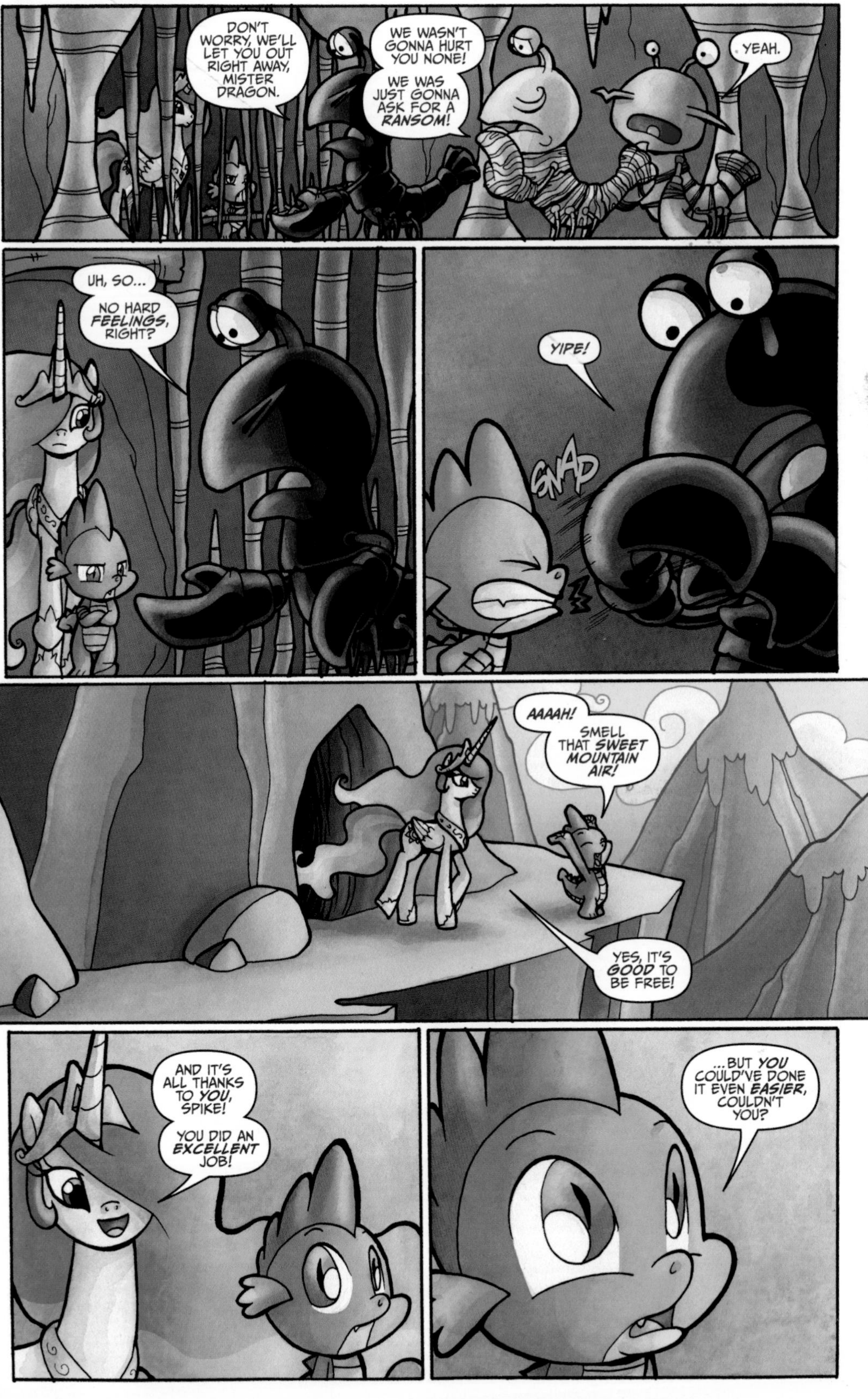
DON'T WORRY, WE'LL LET YOU OUT RIGHT AWAY, MISTER DRAGON.
WE WASN'T GONNA HURT YOU NONE!
WE WAS JUST GONNA ASK FOR A RANSOM!
YEAH.
UH, SO...
NO HARD FEELINGS, RIGHT?
YIPE!
SNAP
AAAAH!
SMELL THAT SWEET MOUNTAIN AIR!
YES, IT'S GOOD TO BE FREE!
AND IT'S ALL THANKS TO YOU, SPIKE!
YOU DID AN EXCELLENT JOB!
...BUT YOU COULD'VE DONE IT EVEN EASIER, COULDN'T YOU?

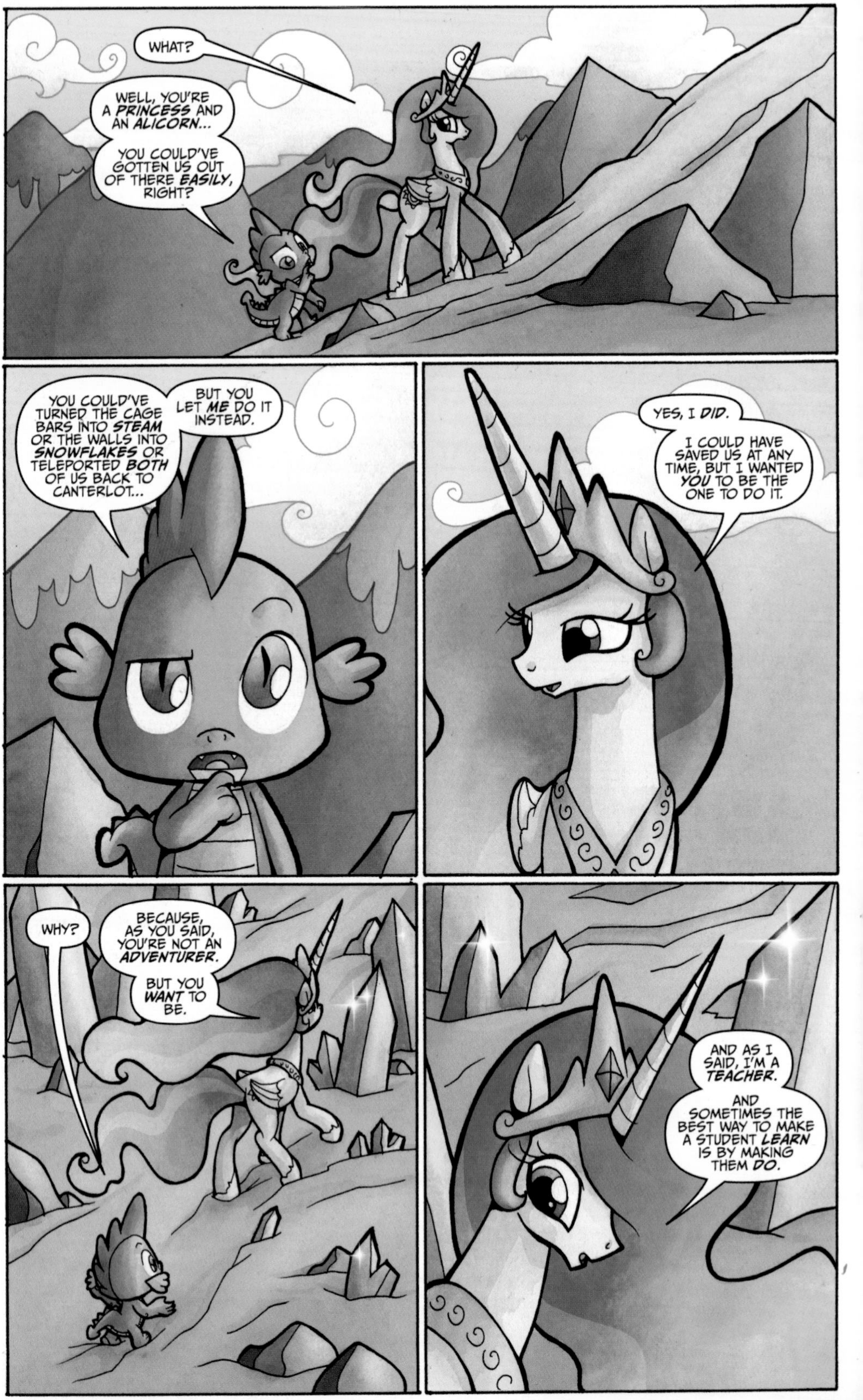
WHAT?
WELL, YOU'RE A PRINCESS AND AN ALICORN...
YOU COULD'VE GOTTEN US OUT OF THERE EASILY, RIGHT?
YOU COULD'VE TURNED THE CAGE BARS INTO STEAM OR THE WALLS INTO SNOWFLAKES OR TELEPORTED BOTH OF US BACK TO CANTERLOT...
BUT YOU LET ME DO IT INSTEAD.
YES, I DID.
I COULD HAVE SAVED US AT ANY TIME, BUT I WANTED YOU TO BE THE ONE TO DO IT.
WHY?
BECAUSE, AS YOU SAID, YOU'RE NOT AN ADVENTURER.
BUT YOU WANT TO BE.
AND AS I SAID, I'M A TEACHER.
AND SOMETIMES THE BEST WAY TO MAKE A STUDENT LEARN IS BY MAKING THEM DO.

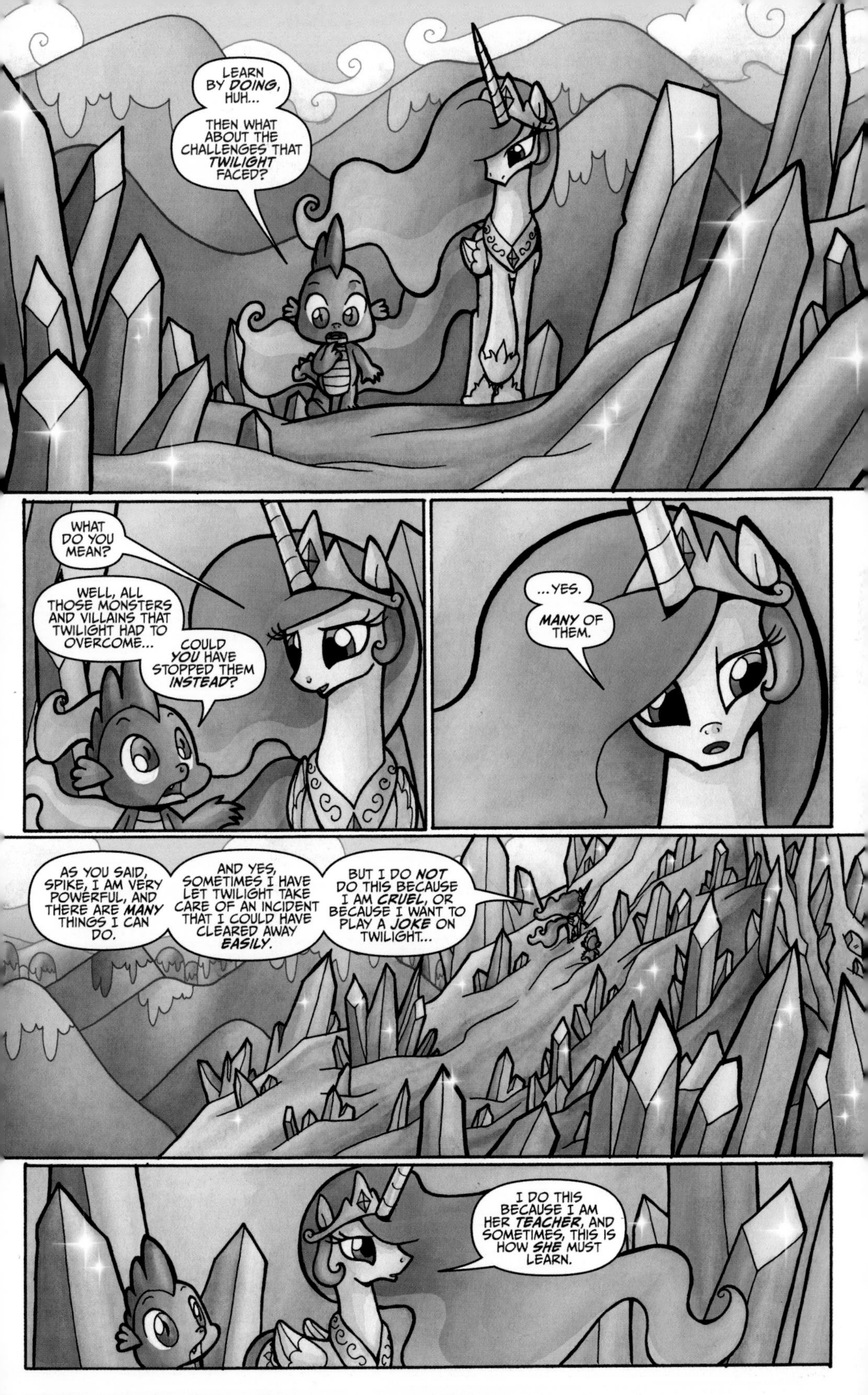
LEARN BY DOING, HUH...
THEN WHAT ABOUT THE CHALLENGES THAT TWILIGHT FACED?
WHAT DO YOU MEAN?
WELL, ALL THOSE MONSTERS AND VILLAINS THAT TWILIGHT HAD TO OVERCOME...
COULD YOU HAVE STOPPED THEM INSTEAD?
...YES.
MANY OF THEM.
AS YOU SAID, SPIKE, I AM VERY POWERFUL, AND THERE ARE MANY THINGS I CAN DO.
AND YES, SOMETIMES I HAVE LET TWILIGHT TAKE CARE OF AN INCIDENT THAT I COULD HAVE CLEARED AWAY EASILY.
BUT I DO NOT DO THIS BECAUSE I AM CRUEL, OR BECAUSE I WANT TO PLAY A JOKE ON TWILIGHT...
I DO THIS BECAUSE I AM HER TEACHER, AND SOMETIMES, THIS IS HOW SHE MUST LEARN.

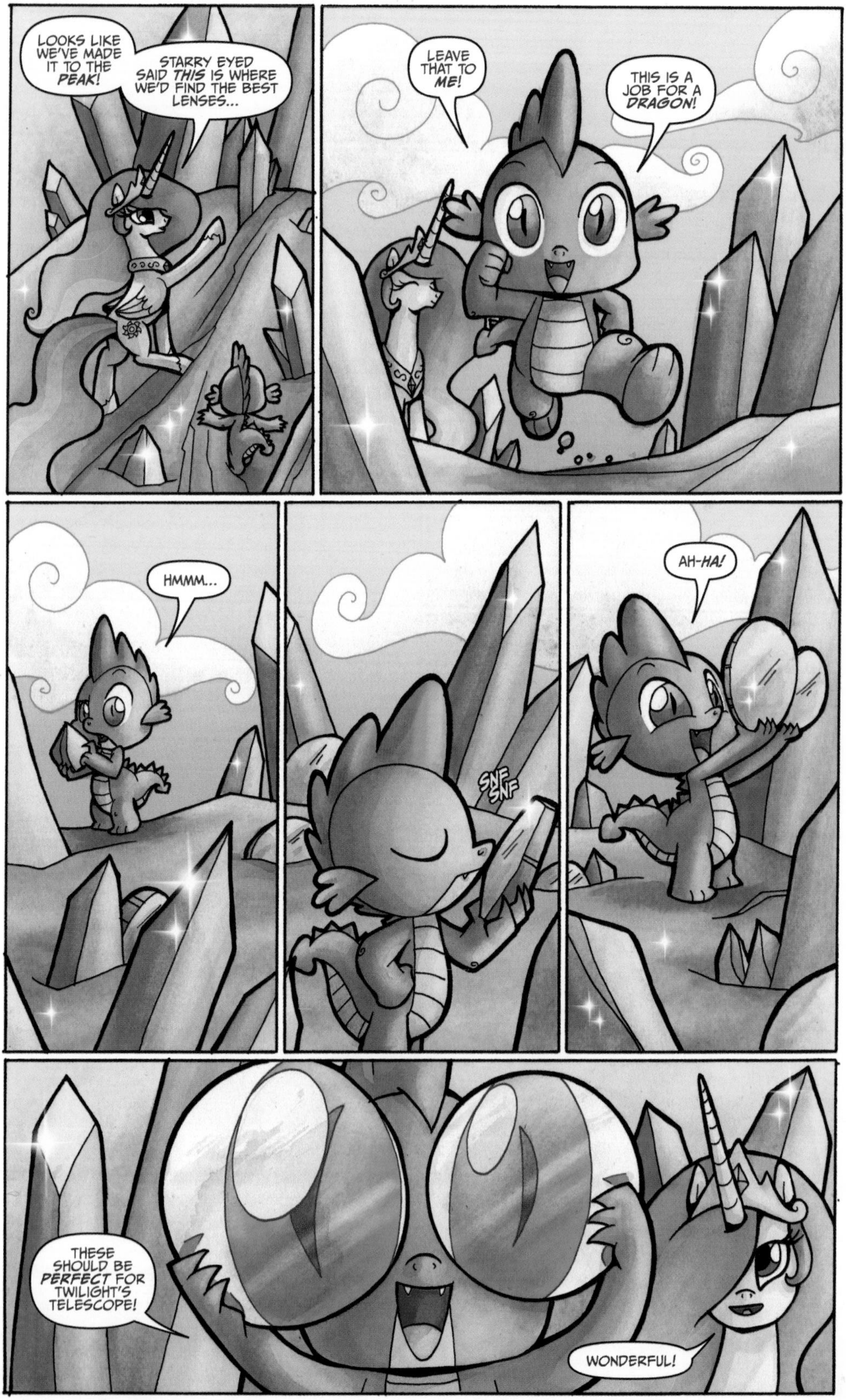
LOOKS LIKE WE'VE MADE IT TO THE PEAK!
STARRY EYED SAID THIS IS WHERE WE'D FIND THE BEST LENSES...
LEAVE THAT TO ME!
THIS IS A JOB FOR A DRAGON!
HMMM...
SNF SNF
AH-HA!
THESE SHOULD BE PERFECT FOR TWILIGHT'S TELESCOPE!
WONDERFUL!

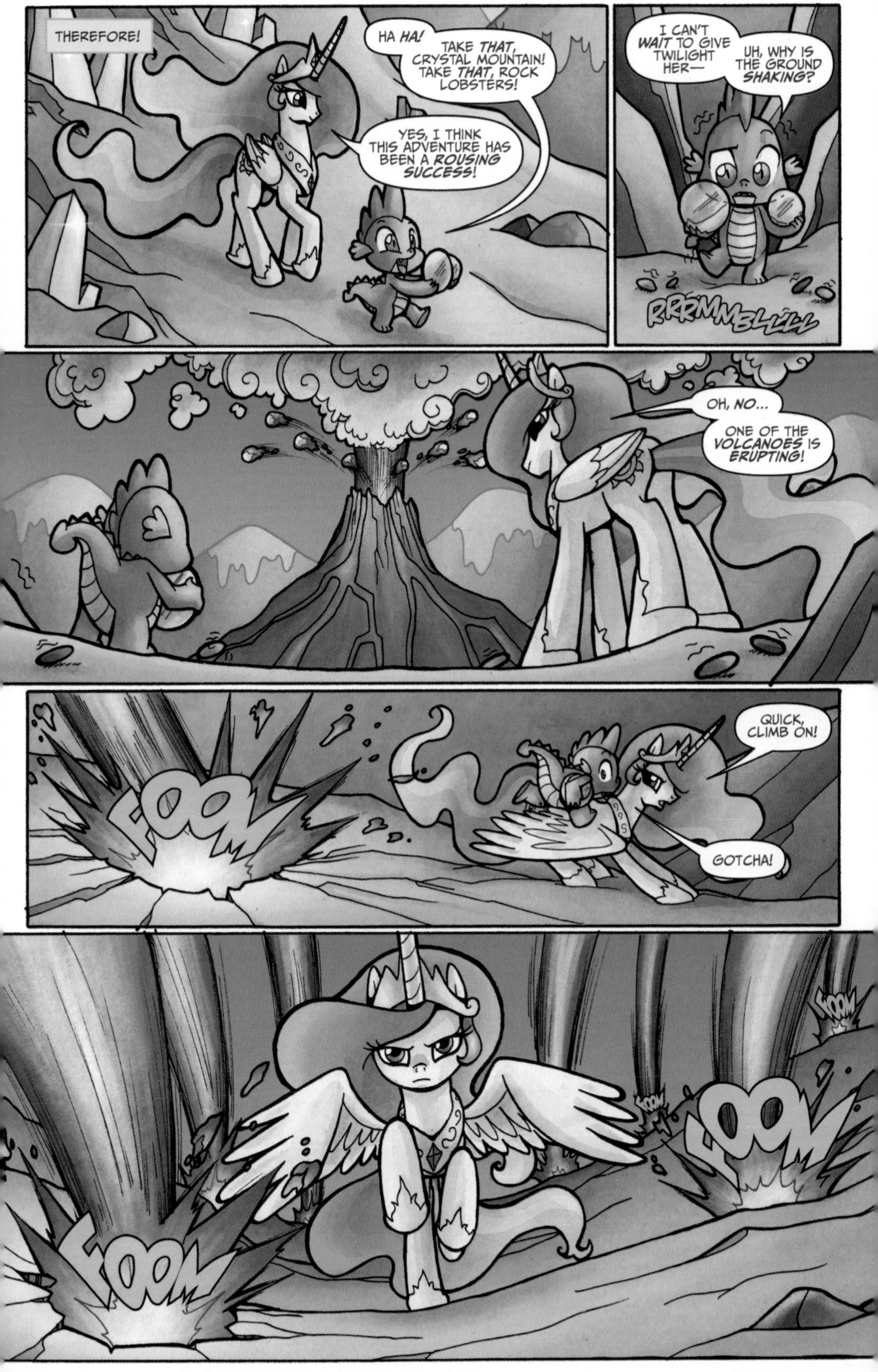
THEREFORE!
HA HA! TAKE THAT, CRYSTAL MOUNTAIN! TAKE THAT, ROCK LOBSTERS!
YES, I THINK THIS ADVENTURE HAS BEEN A ROUSING SUCCESS!
I CAN'T WAIT TO GIVE TWILIGHT HER—
UH, WHY IS THE GROUND SHAKING?
RRRMMBLLLL
OH, NO...
ONE OF THE VOLCANOES IS ERUPTING!
FOOM
QUICK, CLIMB ON!
GOTCHA!
FOOM
FOOM
FOOM

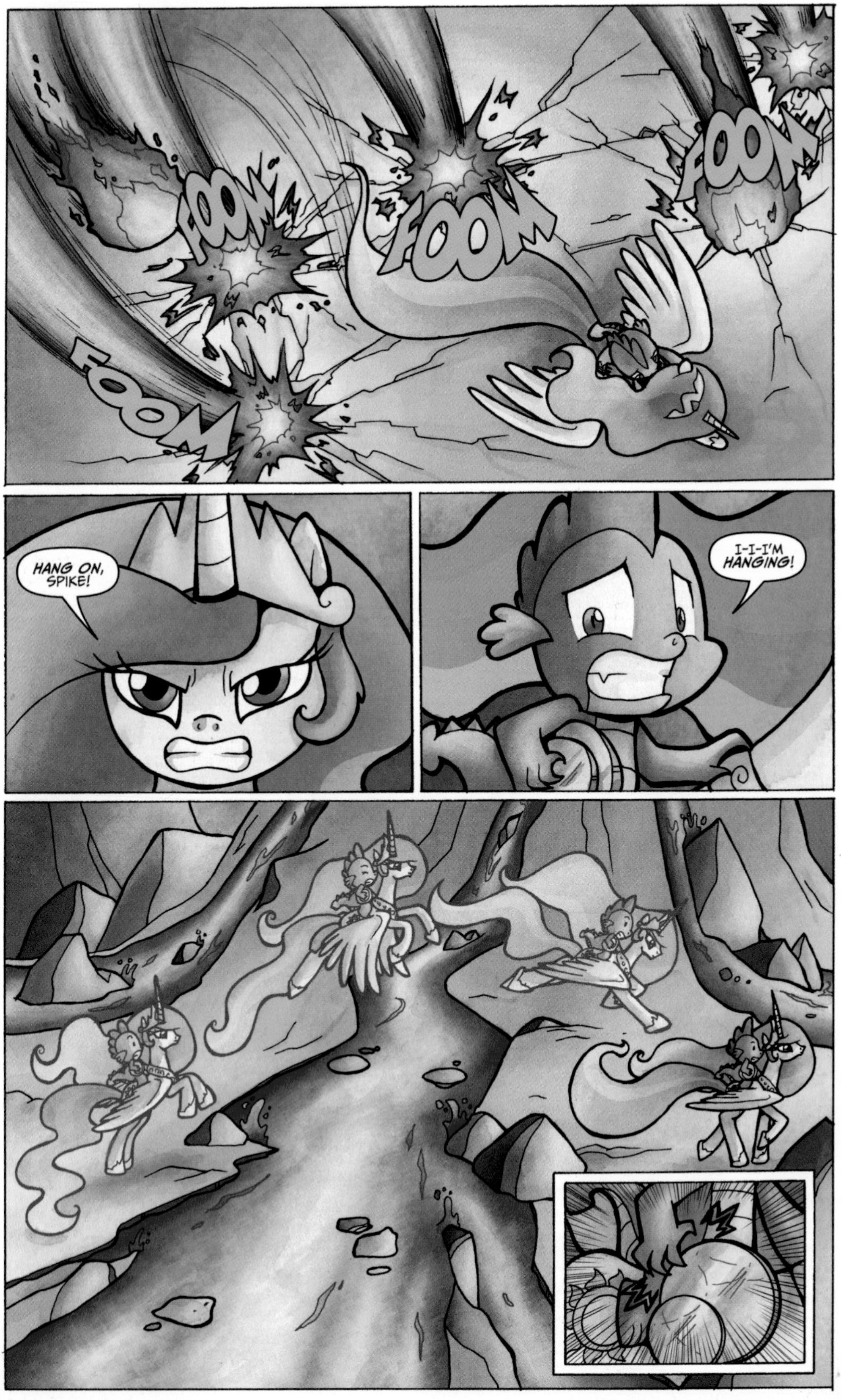
FOOM
FOOM
FOOM
FOOM
HANG ON, SPIKE!
I-I-I'M HANGING!

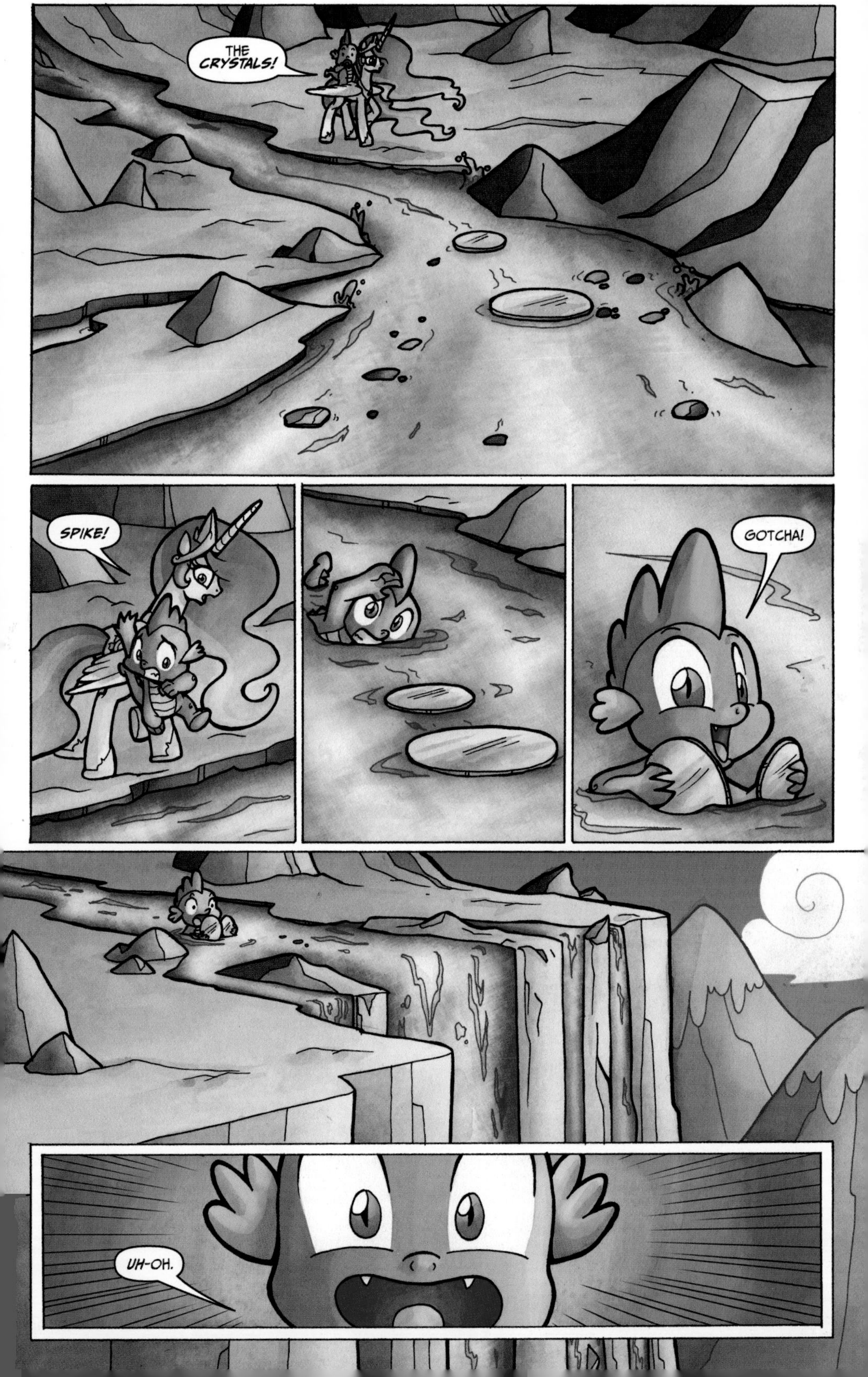
THE CRYSTALS!
SPIKE!
GOTCHA!
UH-OH.

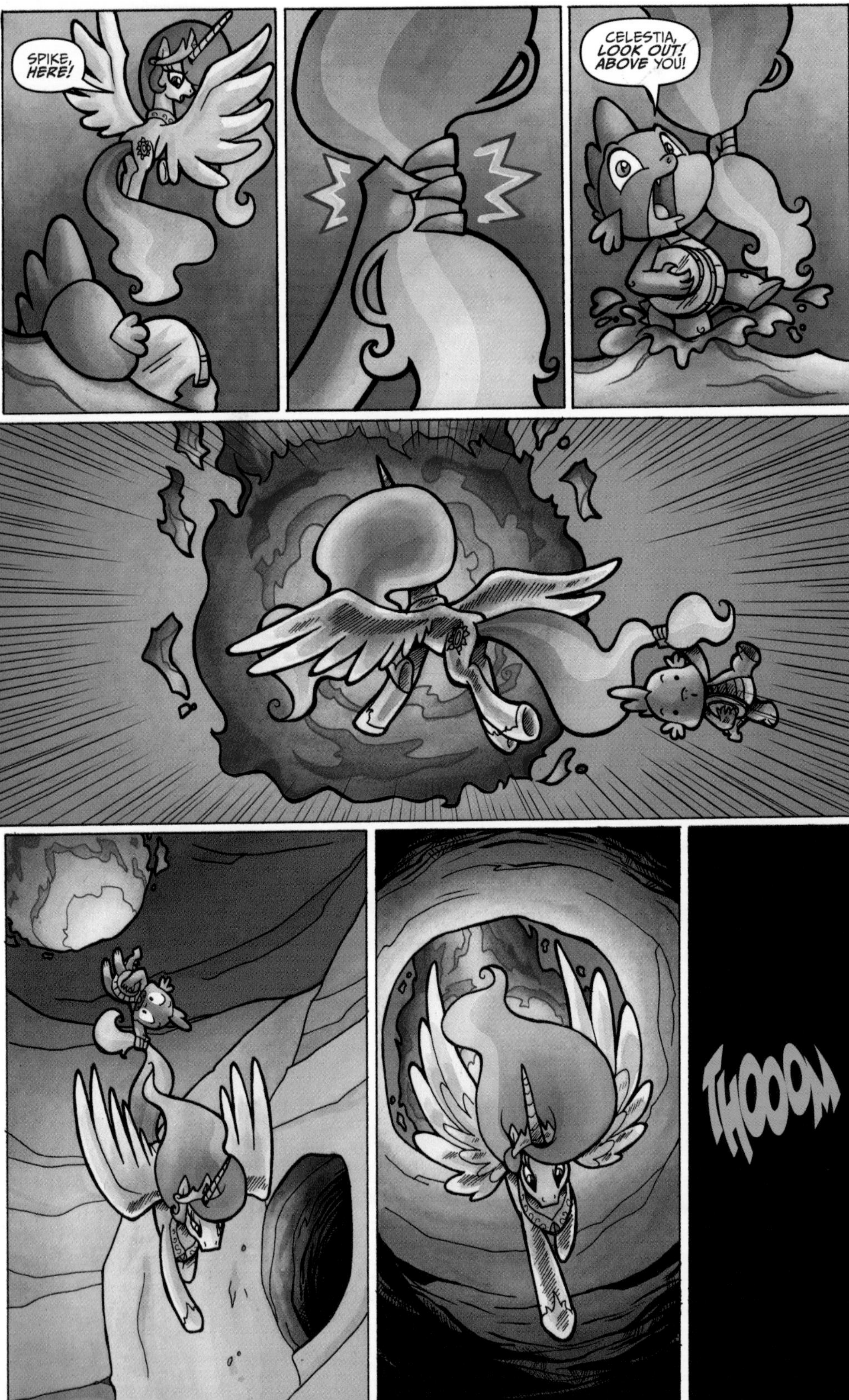
SPIKE, HERE!
CELESTIA, LOOK OUT! ABOVE YOU!
THOOOM

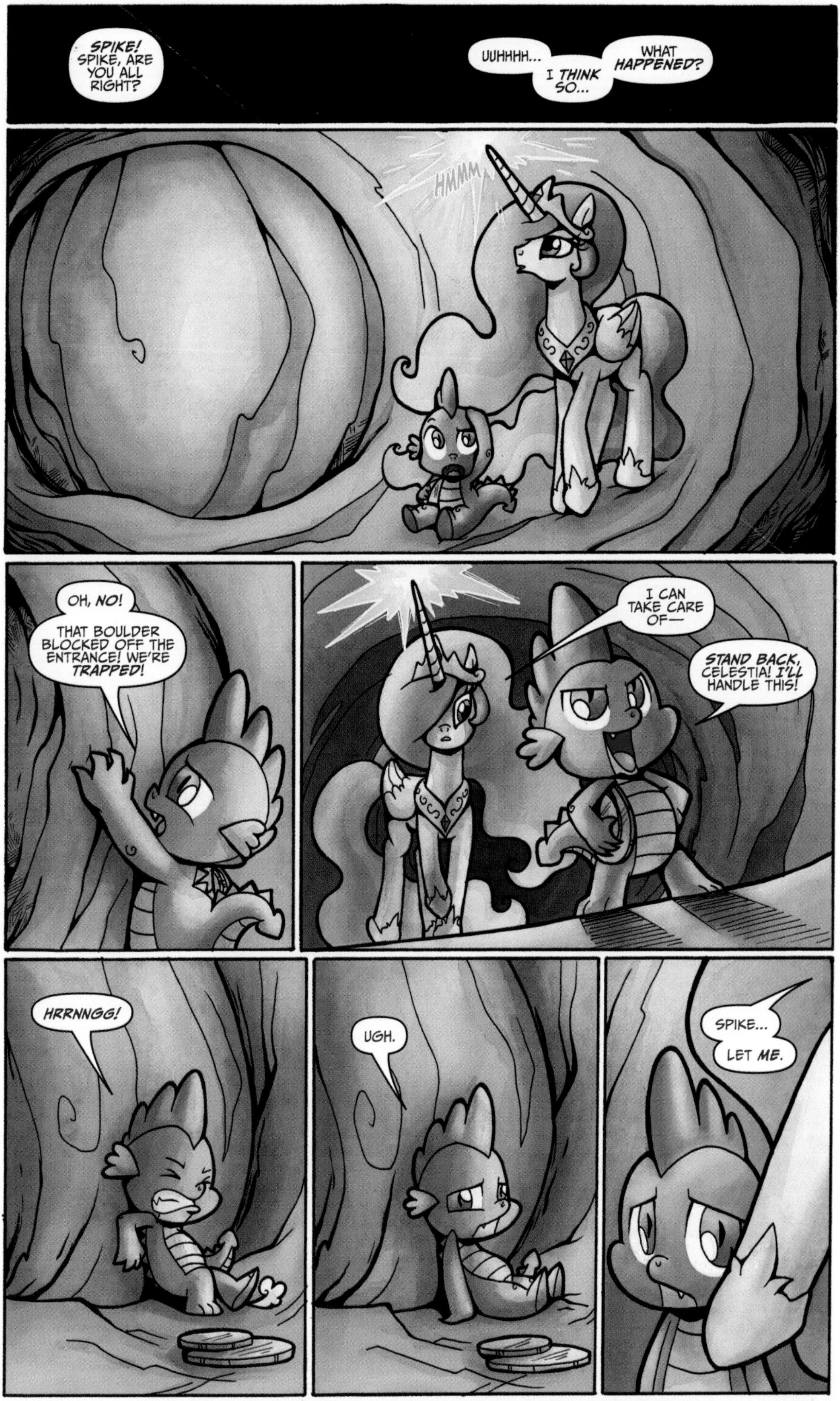
SPIKE! SPIKE, ARE YOU ALL RIGHT?
UUHHHH...
I THINK SO...
WHAT HAPPENED?
HMMM
OH, NO!
THAT BOULDER BLOCKED OFF THE ENTRANCE! WE'RE TRAPPED!
I CAN TAKE CARE OF—
STAND BACK, CELESTIA! I'LL HANDLE THIS!
HRRNNGG!
UGH.
SPIKE...
LET ME.

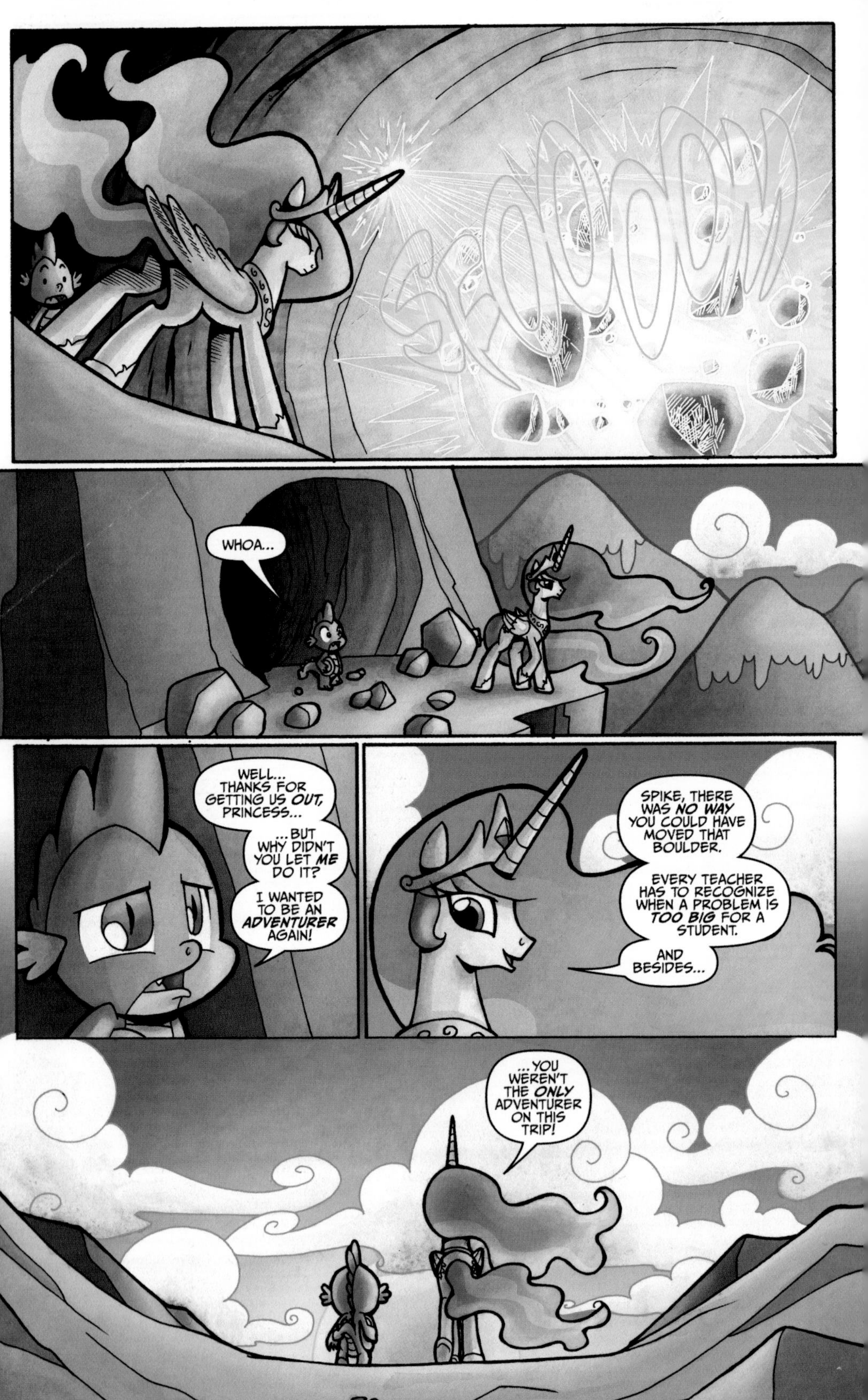
WHOA...
WELL... THANKS FOR GETTING US OUT, PRINCESS...
...BUT WHY DIDN'T YOU LET ME DO IT?
I WANTED TO BE AN ADVENTURER AGAIN!
SPIKE, THERE WAS NO WAY YOU COULD HAVE MOVED THAT BOULDER.
EVERY TEACHER HAS TO RECOGNIZE WHEN A PROBLEM IS TOO BIG FOR A STUDENT.
AND BESIDES...
...YOU WEREN'T THE ONLY ADVENTURER ON THIS TRIP!

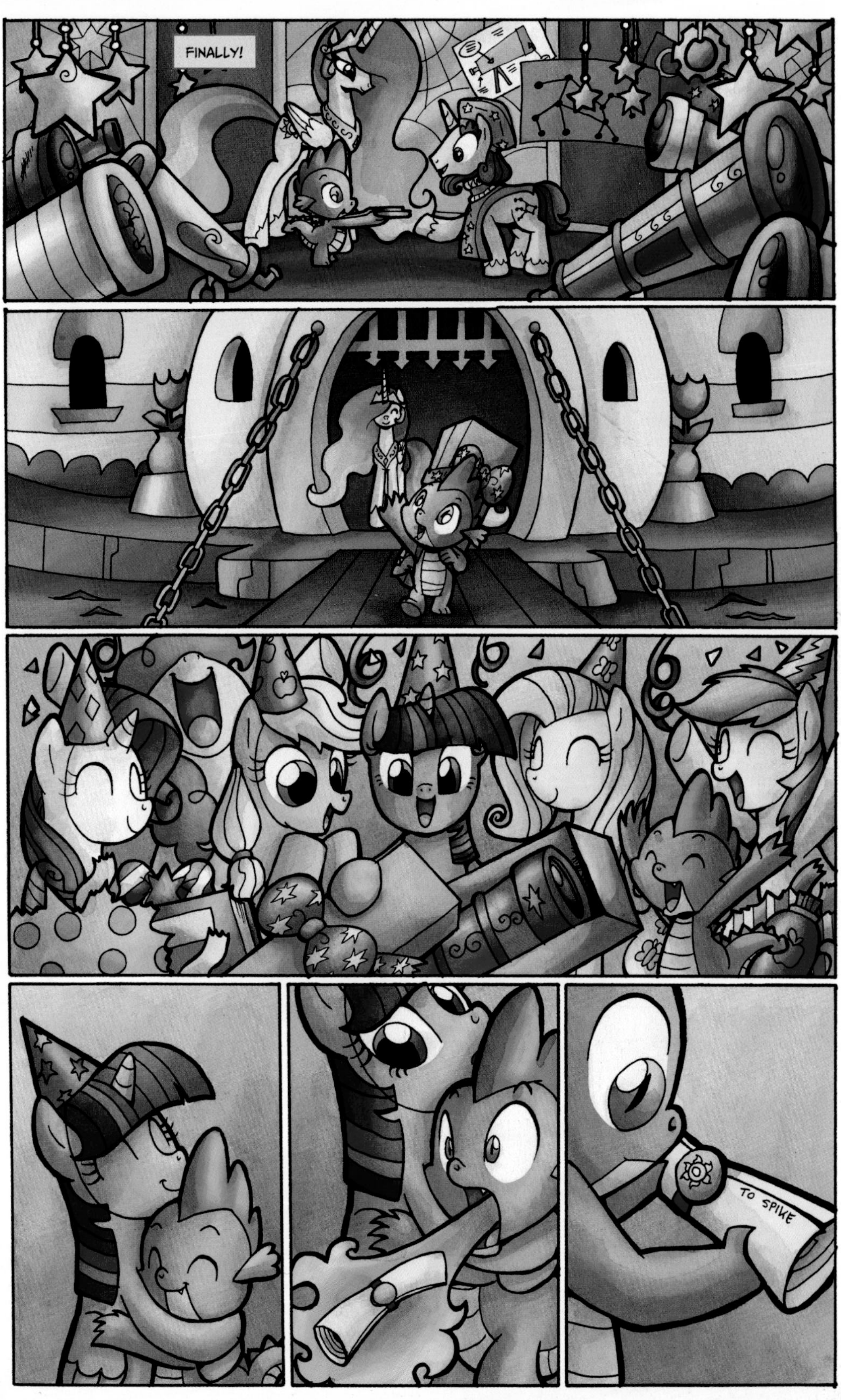
FINALLY!
TO SPIKE

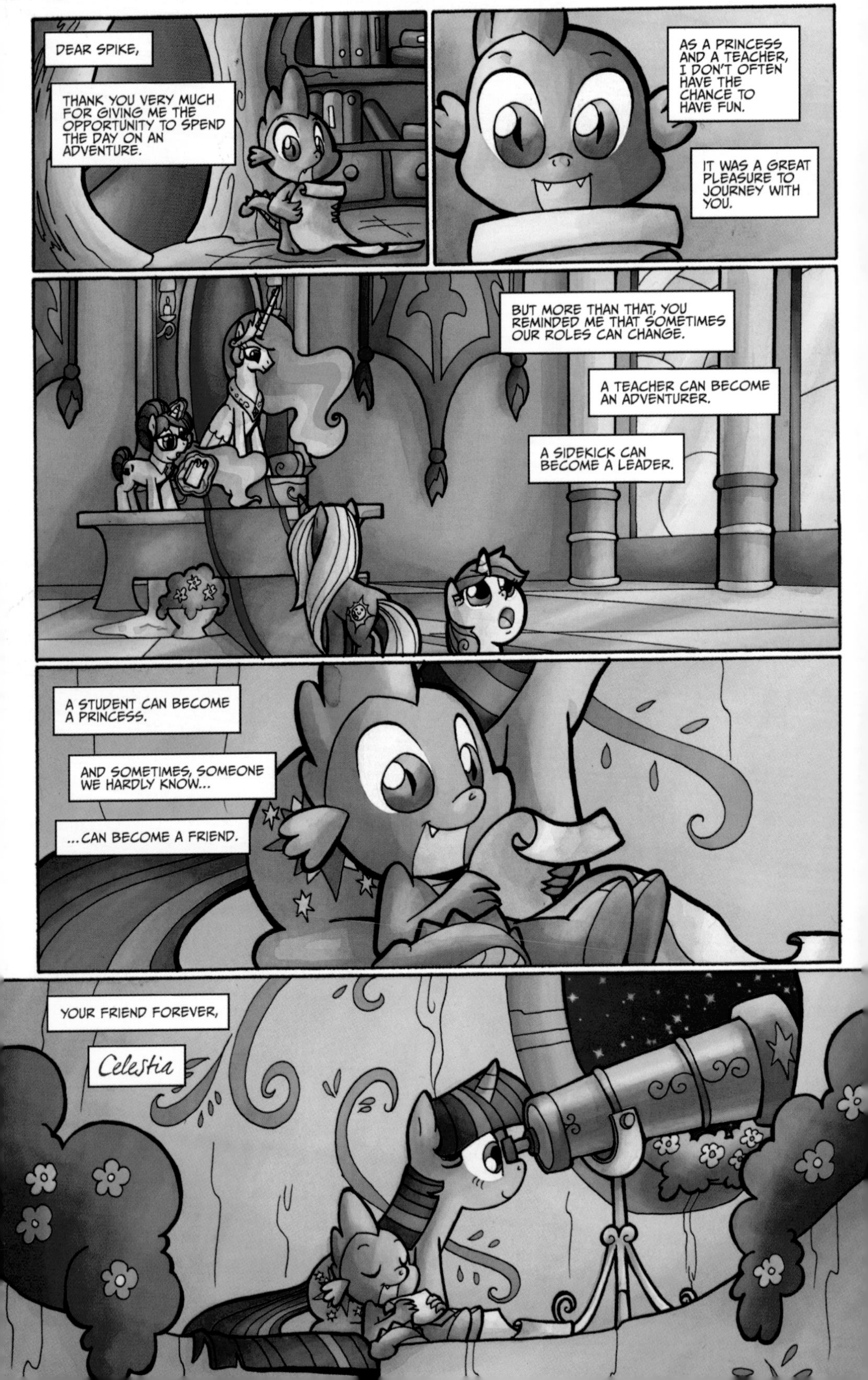
DEAR SPIKE,
THANK YOU VERY MUCH FOR GIVING ME THE OPPORTUNITY TO SPEND THE DAY ON AN ADVENTURE.
AS A PRINCESS AND A TEACHER, I DON'T OFTEN HAVE THE CHANCE TO HAVE FUN.
IT WAS A GREAT PLEASURE TO JOURNEY WITH YOU.
BUT MORE THAN THAT, YOU REMINDED ME THAT SOMETIMES OUR ROLES CAN CHANGE.
A TEACHER CAN BECOME AN ADVENTURER.
A SIDEKICK CAN BECOME A LEADER.
A STUDENT CAN BECOME A PRINCESS.
AND SOMETIMES, SOMEONE WE HARDLY KNOW...
...CAN BECOME A FRIEND.
YOUR FRIEND FOREVER,
Celestia

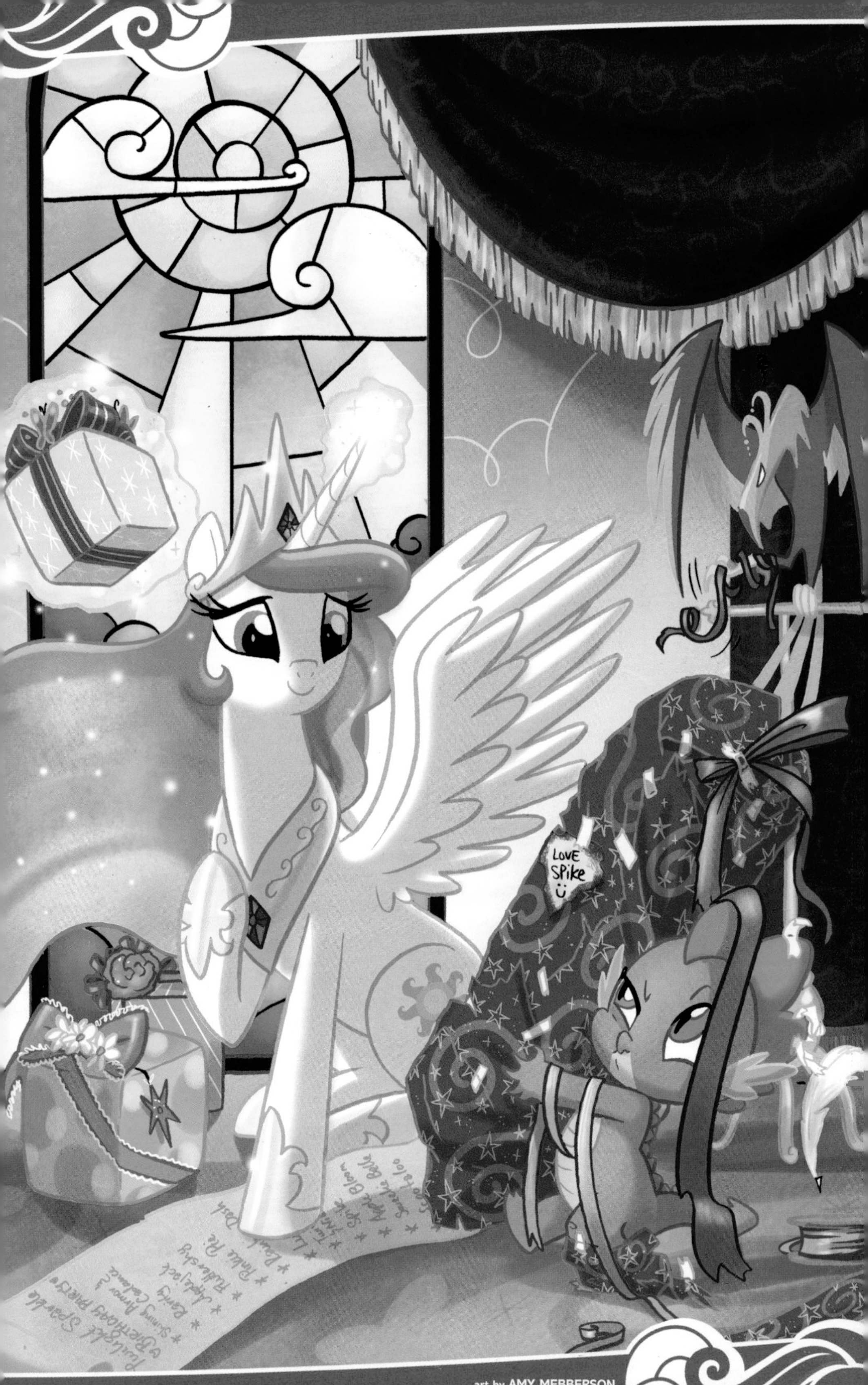
LOVE
SPike

art by AMY MEBBERSON

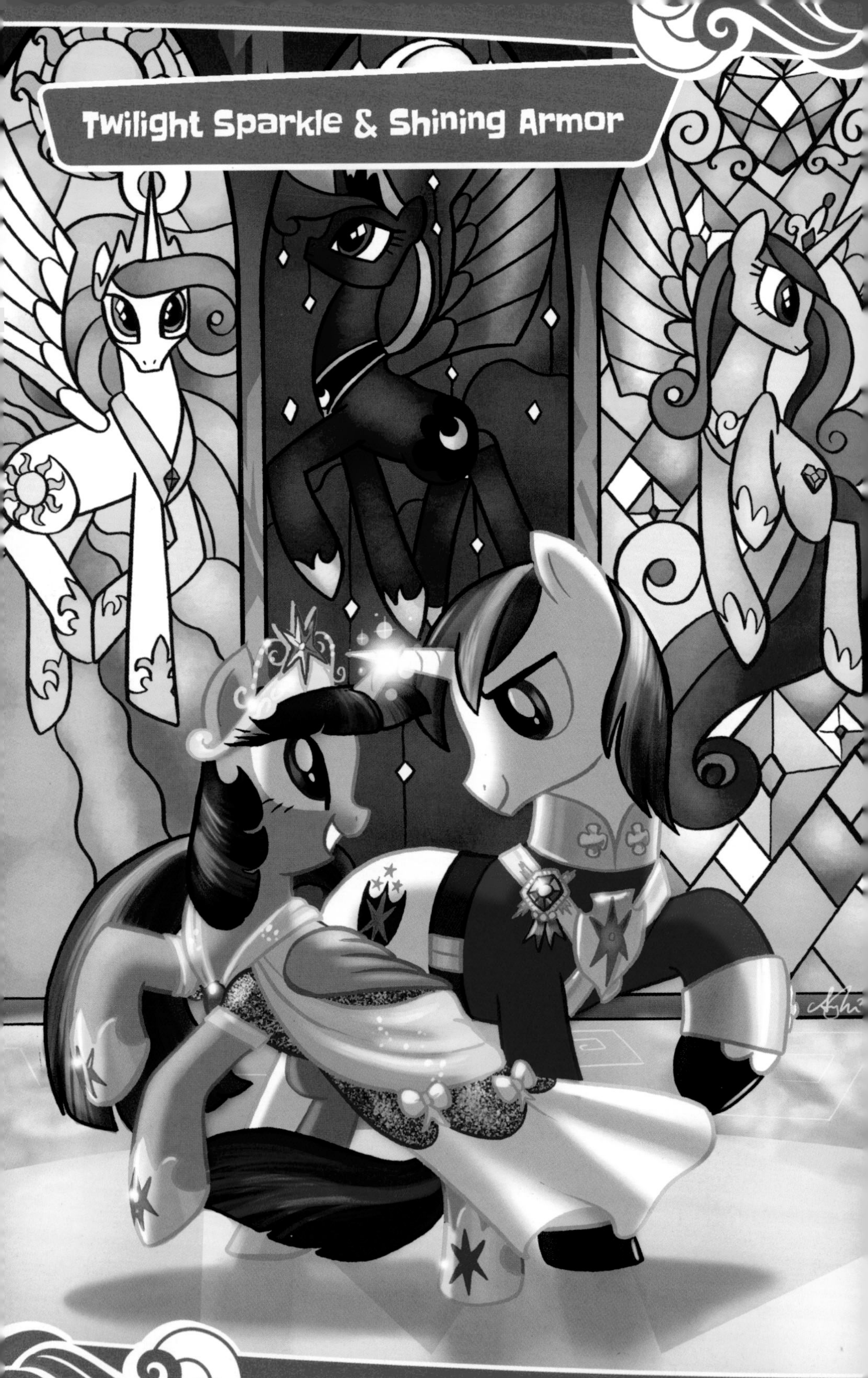
Twilight Sparkle & Shining Armor

art by AMY MEBBERSON

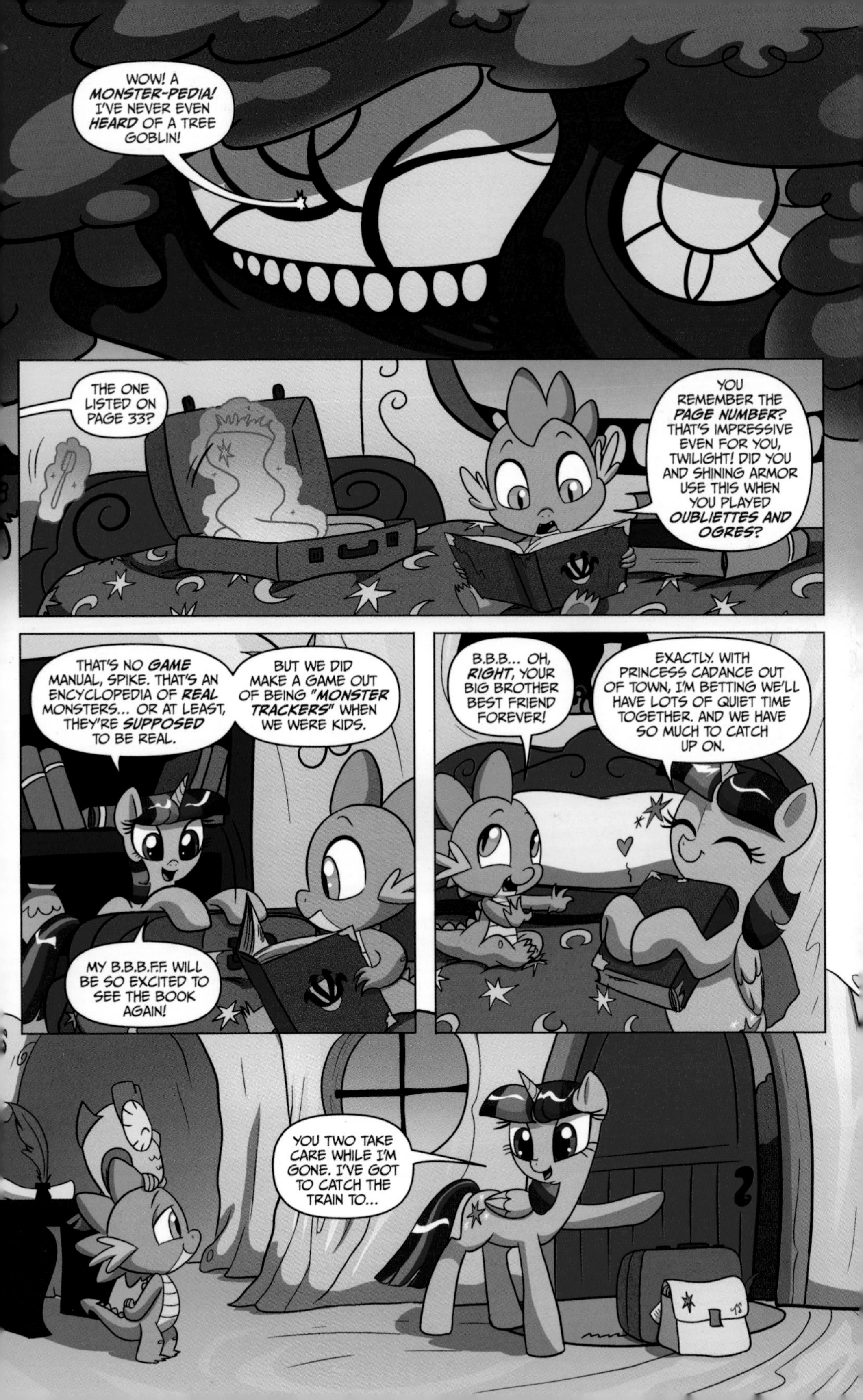
WOW! A MONSTER-PEDIA! I'VE NEVER EVEN HEARD OF A TREE GOBLIN!
THE ONE LISTED ON PAGE 33?
YOU REMEMBER THE PAGE NUMBER? THAT'S IMPRESSIVE EVEN FOR YOU, TWILIGHT! DID YOU AND SHINING ARMOR USE THIS WHEN YOU PLAYED OUBLIETTES AND OGRES?
THAT'S NO GAME MANUAL, SPIKE. THAT'S AN ENCYCLOPEDIA OF REAL MONSTERS... OR AT LEAST, THEY'RE SUPPOSED TO BE REAL.
BUT WE DID MAKE A GAME OUT OF BEING "MONSTER TRACKERS" WHEN WE WERE KIDS.
MY B.B.B.F.F. WILL BE SO EXCITED TO SEE THE BOOK AGAIN!
B.B.B... OH, RIGHT, YOUR BIG BROTHER BEST FRIEND FOREVER!
EXACTLY. WITH PRINCESS CADANCE OUT OF TOWN, I'M BETTING WE'LL HAVE LOTS OF QUIET TIME TOGETHER. AND WE HAVE SO MUCH TO CATCH UP ON.
YOU TWO TAKE CARE WHILE I'M GONE. I'VE GOT TO CATCH THE TRAIN TO...

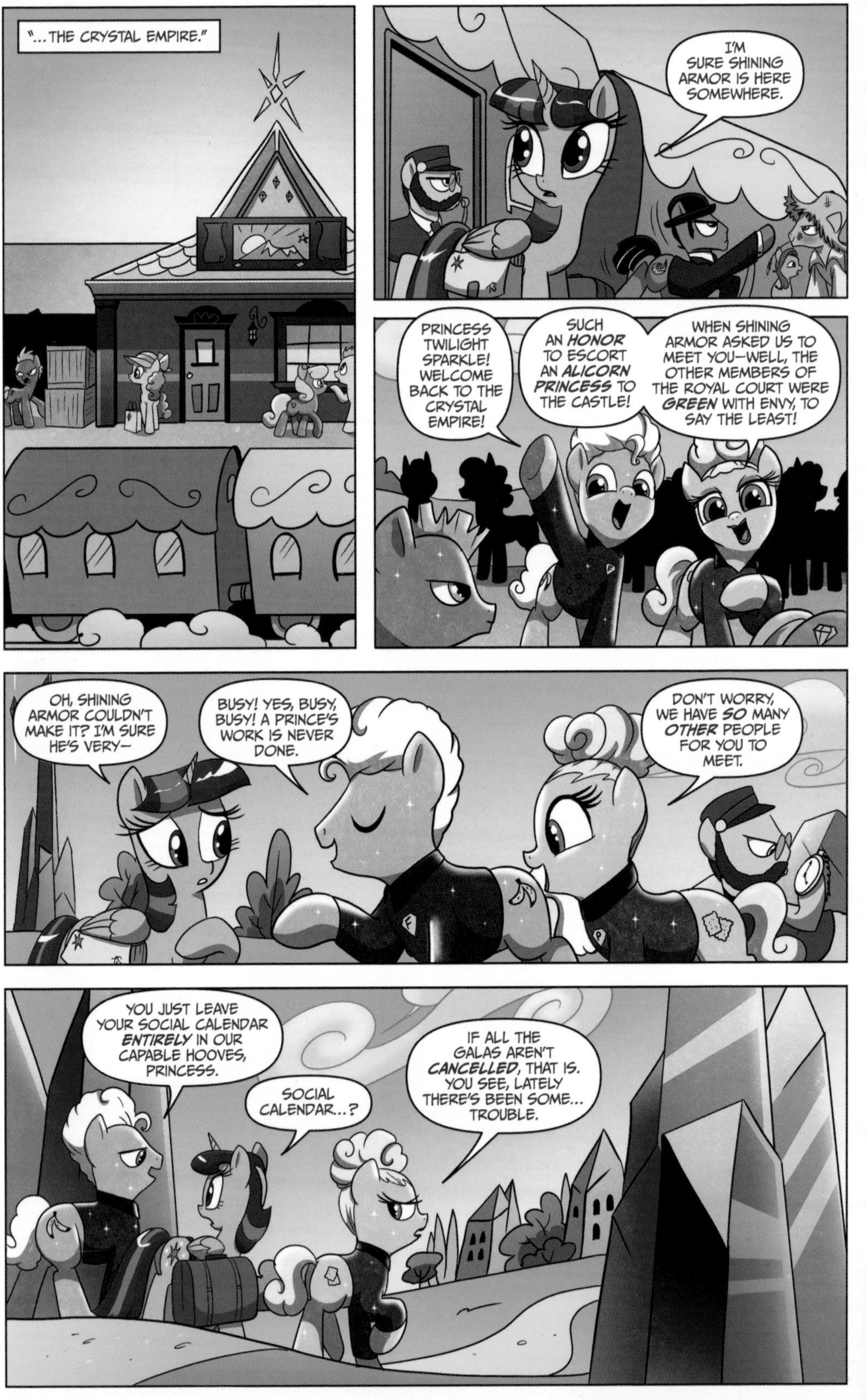
"...THE CRYSTAL EMPIRE."
I'M SURE SHINING ARMOR IS HERE SOMEWHERE.
PRINCESS TWILIGHT SPARKLE! WELCOME BACK TO THE CRYSTAL EMPIRE!
SUCH AN HONOR TO ESCORT AN ALICORN PRINCESS TO THE CASTLE!
WHEN SHINING ARMOR ASKED US TO MEET YOU—WELL, THE OTHER MEMBERS OF THE ROYAL COURT WERE GREEN WITH ENVY, TO SAY THE LEAST!
OH, SHINING ARMOR COULDN'T MAKE IT? I'M SURE HE'S VERY—
BUSY! YES, BUSY, BUSY! A PRINCE'S WORK IS NEVER DONE.
DON'T WORRY, WE HAVE SO MANY OTHER PEOPLE FOR YOU TO MEET.
YOU JUST LEAVE YOUR SOCIAL CALENDAR ENTIRELY IN OUR CAPABLE HOOVES, PRINCESS.
SOCIAL CALENDAR...?
IF ALL THE GALAS AREN'T CANCELLED, THAT IS. YOU SEE, LATELY THERE'S BEEN SOME... TROUBLE.

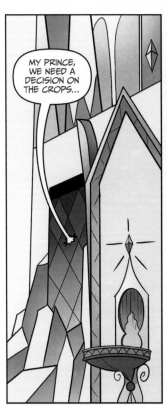

MY PRINCE, WE NEED A DECISION ON THE CROPS...

...I THINK WE SHOULD CONTINUE TO CONCENTRATE ON CRYSTAL BERRY PRODUCTION—

WHY, THAT'S JUST FOOLISH! WE SHOULD BE DIVERSIFYING INTO APPLES AS WELL. IN PONYVILLE, THEY—

YOU TWO ARE ALWAYS FOCUSED ON FRUIT! *I'M* HERE TO DISCUSS HOW OFF-KEY THE *FLUGELHORNS* WERE AT THE LAST—

TWYLIE, YOU'RE HERE!

I'M SO HAPPY TO SEE YOU! I'M SORRY I COULDN'T MAKE IT TO THE TRAIN STATION. THINGS HAVE BEEN A LITTLE CRAZY WITH CADANCE OUT OF TOWN.

I CAN SEE. BUT I BROUGHT SOME THINGS TO CHEER YOU UP—

I'M SORRY TO INTERRUPT, MY PRINCE, BUT WE REALLY *MUST* DISCUSS SOMETHING MORE SERIOUS THAN BERRIES AND FLUGELHORNS...

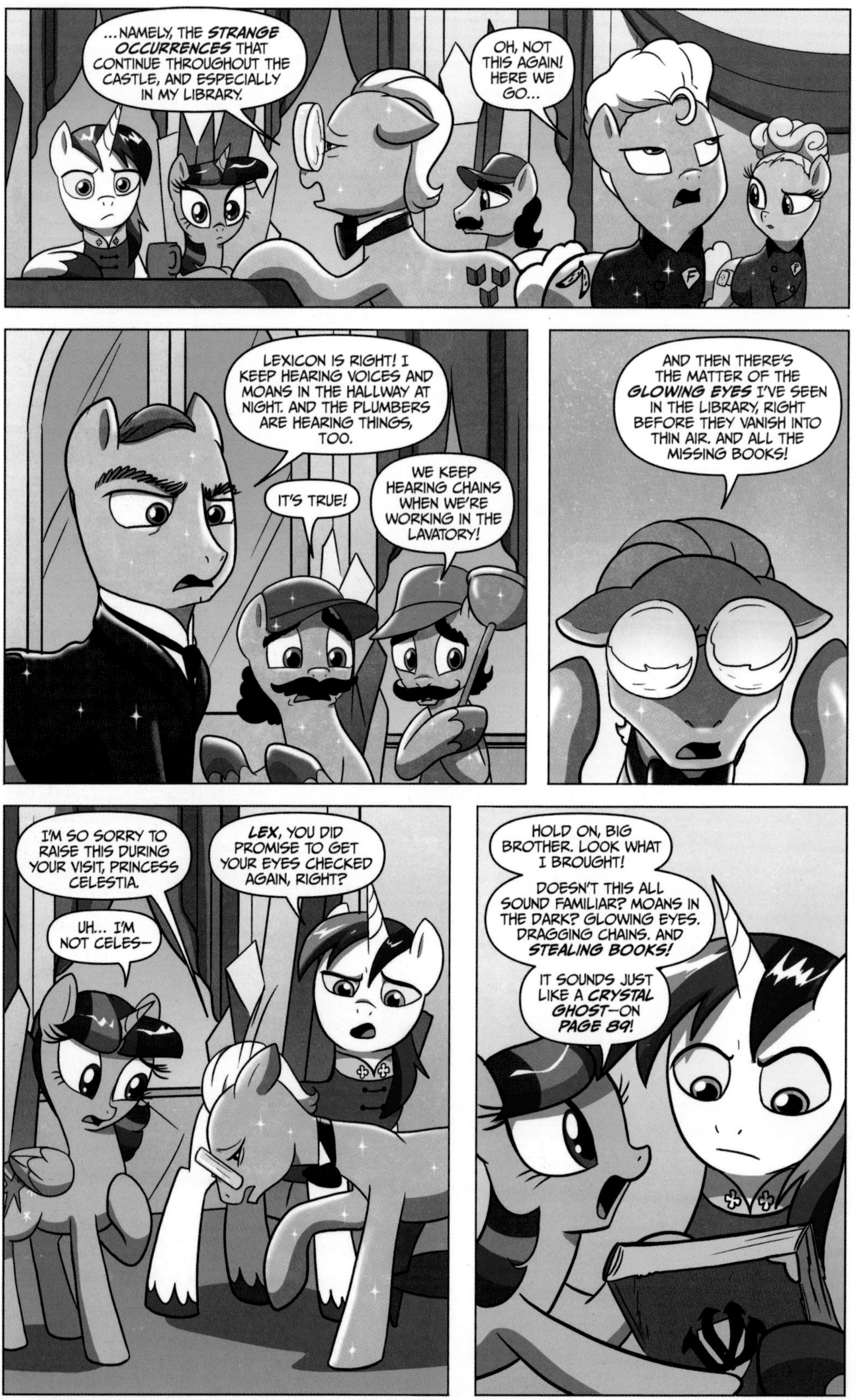
...NAMELY, THE STRANGE OCCURRENCES THAT CONTINUE THROUGHOUT THE CASTLE, AND ESPECIALLY IN MY LIBRARY.
OH, NOT THIS AGAIN! HERE WE GO...
LEXICON IS RIGHT! I KEEP HEARING VOICES AND MOANS IN THE HALLWAY AT NIGHT. AND THE PLUMBERS ARE HEARING THINGS, TOO.
IT'S TRUE!
WE KEEP HEARING CHAINS WHEN WE'RE WORKING IN THE LAVATORY!
AND THEN THERE'S THE MATTER OF THE GLOWING EYES I'VE SEEN IN THE LIBRARY, RIGHT BEFORE THEY VANISH INTO THIN AIR. AND ALL THE MISSING BOOKS!
I'M SO SORRY TO RAISE THIS DURING YOUR VISIT, PRINCESS CELESTIA.
UH... I'M NOT CELES—
LEX, YOU DID PROMISE TO GET YOUR EYES CHECKED AGAIN, RIGHT?
HOLD ON, BIG BROTHER. LOOK WHAT I BROUGHT!
DOESN'T THIS ALL SOUND FAMILIAR? MOANS IN THE DARK? GLOWING EYES. DRAGGING CHAINS. AND STEALING BOOKS!
IT SOUNDS JUST LIKE A CRYSTAL GHOST—ON PAGE 89!

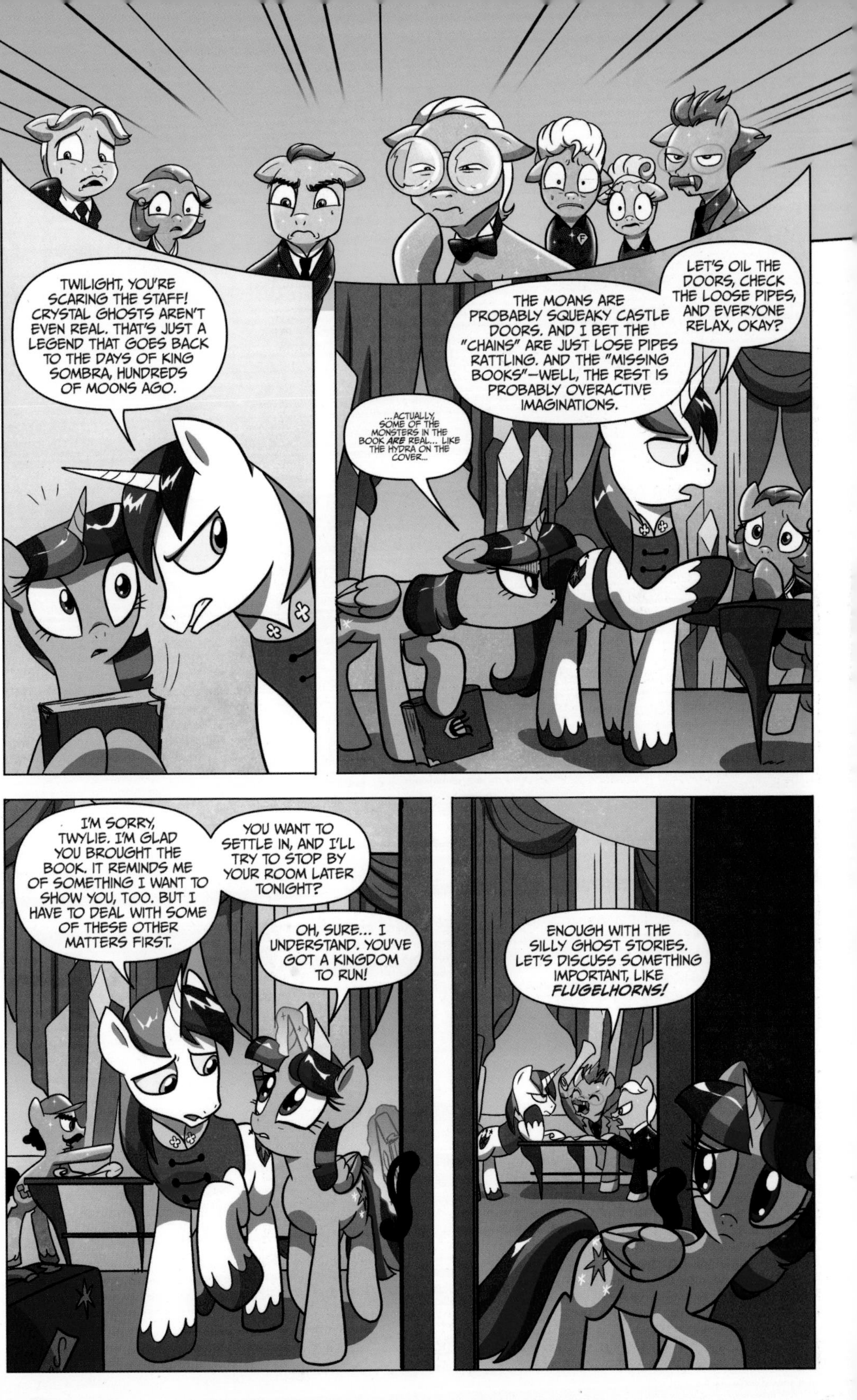
TWILIGHT, YOU'RE SCARING THE STAFF! CRYSTAL GHOSTS AREN'T EVEN REAL. THAT'S JUST A LEGEND THAT GOES BACK TO THE DAYS OF KING SOMBRA, HUNDREDS OF MOONS AGO.
THE MOANS ARE PROBABLY SQUEAKY CASTLE DOORS. AND I BET THE "CHAINS" ARE JUST LOSE PIPES RATTLING. AND THE "MISSING BOOKS"—WELL, THE REST IS PROBABLY OVERACTIVE IMAGINATIONS.
LET'S OIL THE DOORS, CHECK THE LOOSE PIPES, AND EVERYONE RELAX, OKAY?
...ACTUALLY, SOME OF THE MONSTERS IN THE BOOK *ARE* REAL... LIKE THE HYDRA ON THE COVER...
I'M SORRY, TWYLIE. I'M GLAD YOU BROUGHT THE BOOK. IT REMINDS ME OF SOMETHING I WANT TO SHOW YOU, TOO. BUT I HAVE TO DEAL WITH SOME OF THESE OTHER MATTERS FIRST.
YOU WANT TO SETTLE IN, AND I'LL TRY TO STOP BY YOUR ROOM LATER TONIGHT?
OH, SURE... I UNDERSTAND. YOU'VE GOT A KINGDOM TO RUN!
ENOUGH WITH THE SILLY GHOST STORIES. LET'S DISCUSS SOMETHING IMPORTANT, LIKE ***FLUGELHORNS!***

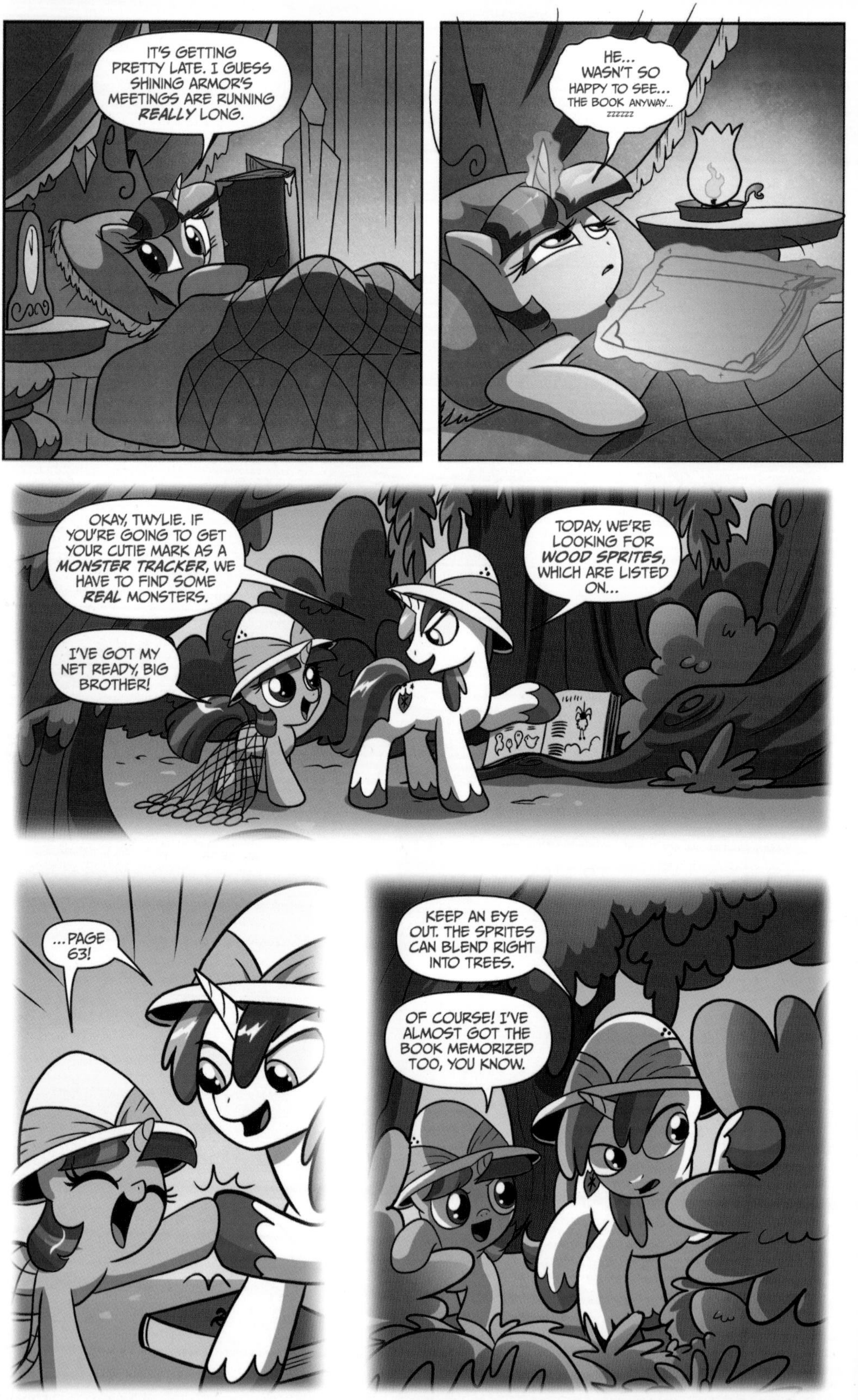
IT'S GETTING PRETTY LATE. I GUESS SHINING ARMOR'S MEETINGS ARE RUNNING REALLY LONG.
HE... WASN'T SO HAPPY TO SEE... THE BOOK ANYWAY... zzzzzz
OKAY, TWYLIE. IF YOU'RE GOING TO GET YOUR CUTIE MARK AS A MONSTER TRACKER, WE HAVE TO FIND SOME REAL MONSTERS.
I'VE GOT MY NET READY, BIG BROTHER!
TODAY, WE'RE LOOKING FOR WOOD SPRITES, WHICH ARE LISTED ON...
...PAGE 63!
KEEP AN EYE OUT. THE SPRITES CAN BLEND RIGHT INTO TREES.
OF COURSE! I'VE ALMOST GOT THE BOOK MEMORIZED TOO, YOU KNOW.

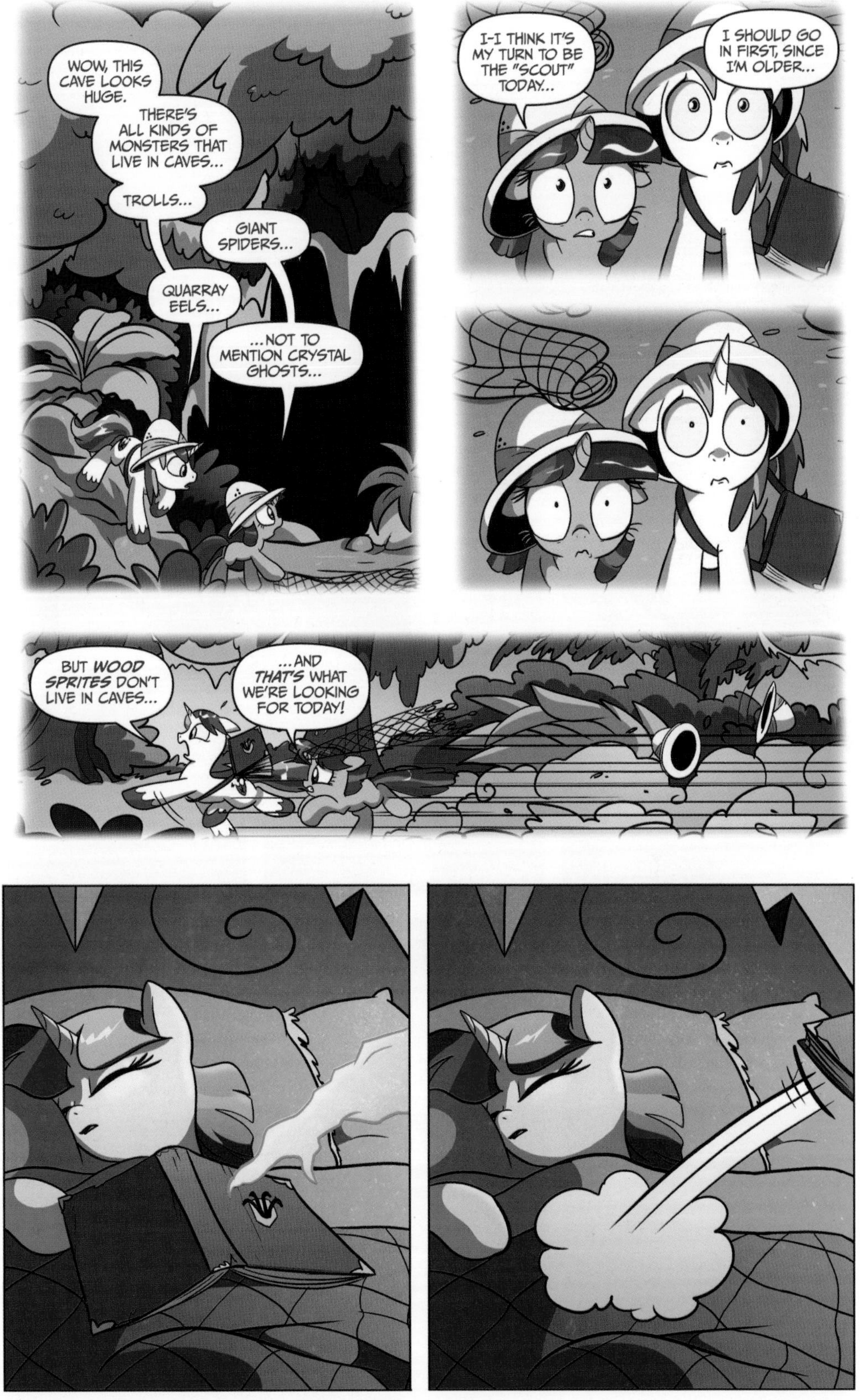
WOW, THIS CAVE LOOKS HUGE.
THERE'S ALL KINDS OF MONSTERS THAT LIVE IN CAVES...
TROLLS...
GIANT SPIDERS...
QUARRAY EELS...
...NOT TO MENTION CRYSTAL GHOSTS...
I-I THINK IT'S MY TURN TO BE THE "SCOUT" TODAY...
I SHOULD GO IN FIRST, SINCE I'M OLDER...
BUT WOOD SPRITES DON'T LIVE IN CAVES...
...AND THAT'S WHAT WE'RE LOOKING FOR TODAY!

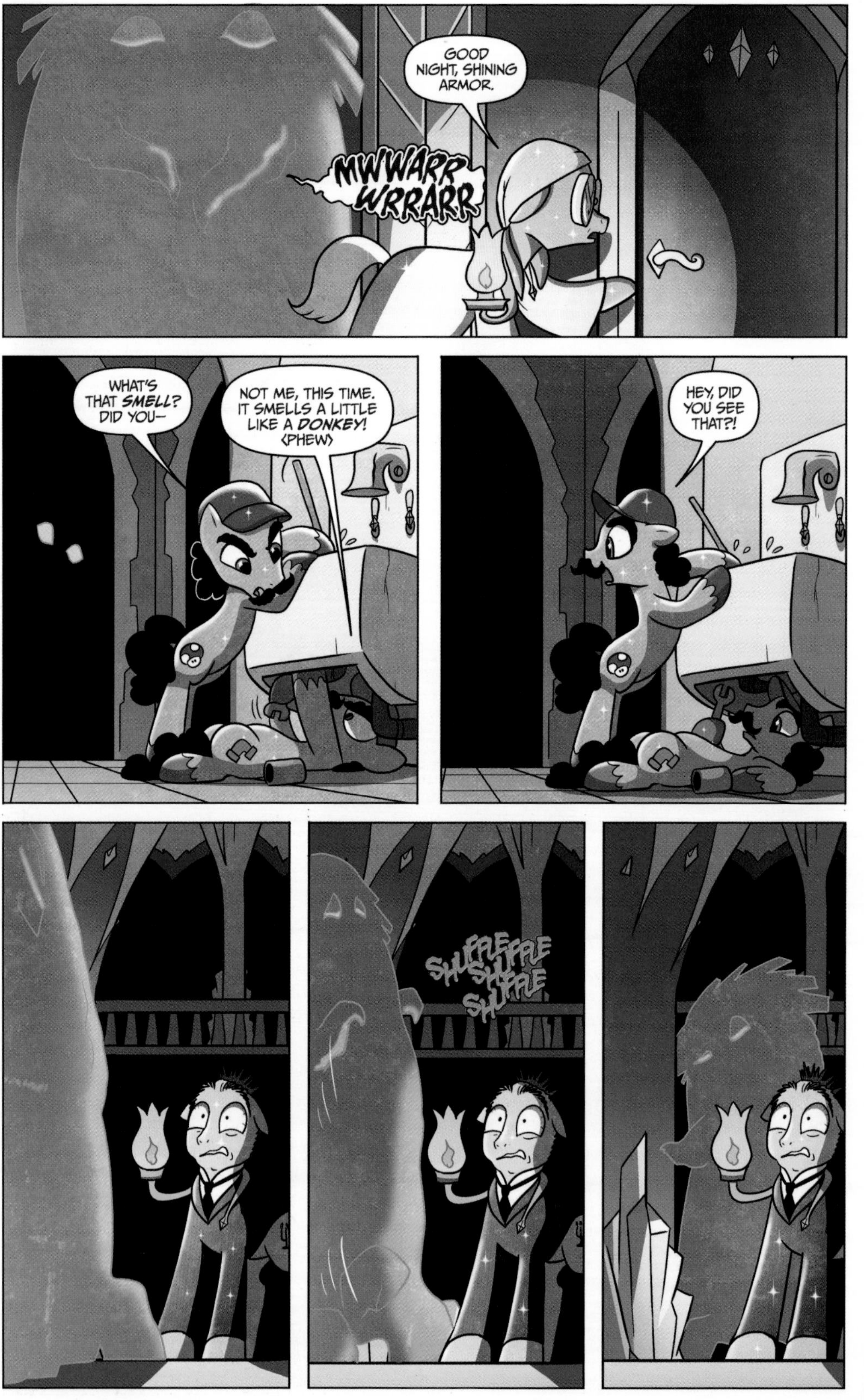
GOOD NIGHT, SHINING ARMOR.
MWWARR WRRARR
WHAT'S THAT SMELL? DID YOU—
NOT ME, THIS TIME. IT SMELLS A LITTLE LIKE A DONKEY! <PHEW>
HEY, DID YOU SEE THAT?!
SHUFFLE SHUFFLE SHUFFLE

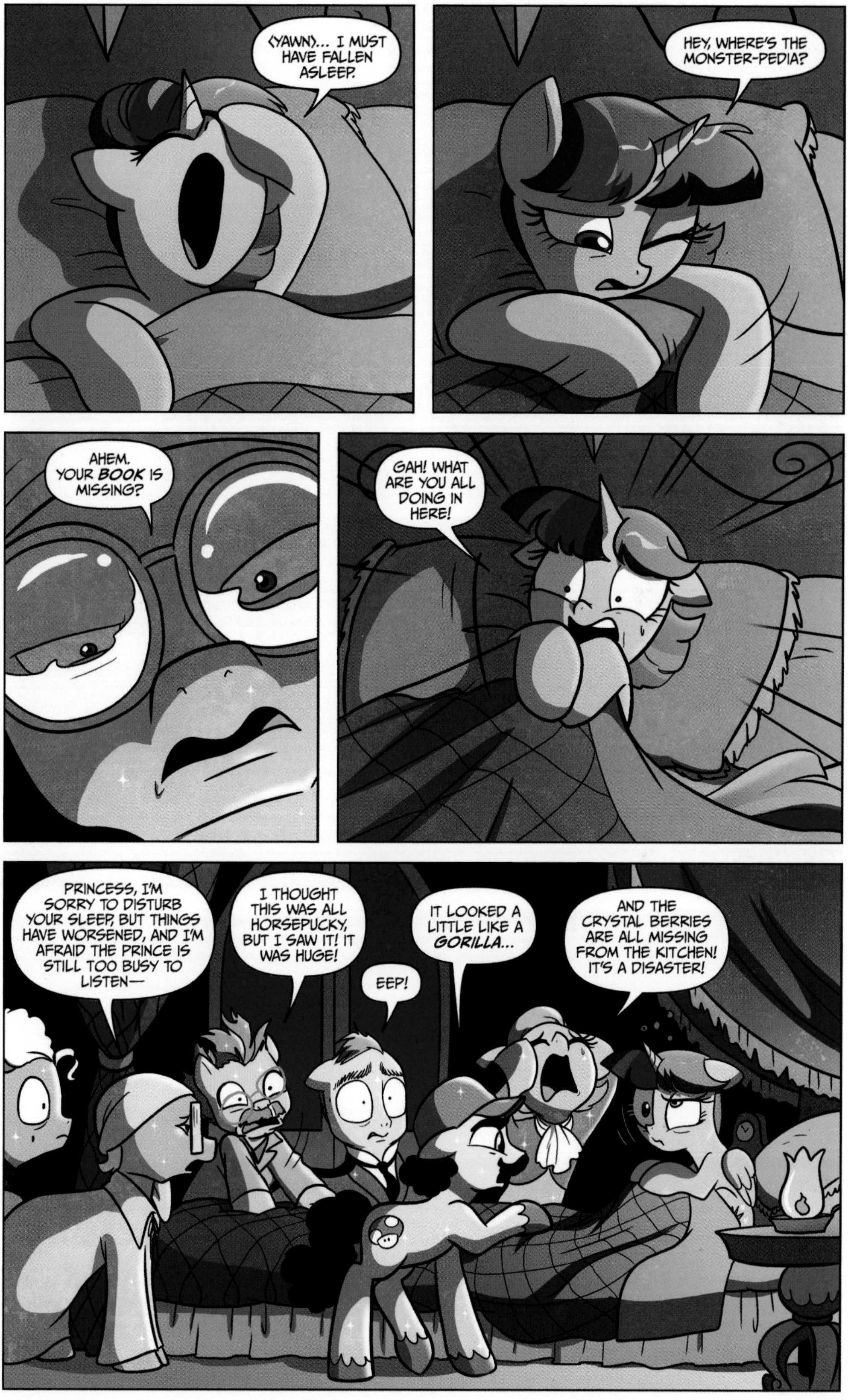

‹YAWN›... I MUST HAVE FALLEN ASLEEP.
HEY, WHERE'S THE MONSTER-PEDIA?
AHEM. YOUR *BOOK* IS MISSING?
GAH! WHAT ARE YOU ALL DOING IN HERE!
PRINCESS, I'M SORRY TO DISTURB YOUR SLEEP, BUT THINGS HAVE WORSENED, AND I'M AFRAID THE PRINCE IS STILL TOO BUSY TO LISTEN—
I THOUGHT THIS WAS ALL HORSEPUCKY, BUT I SAW IT! IT WAS HUGE!
EEP!
IT LOOKED A LITTLE LIKE A *GORILLA*...
AND THE CRYSTAL BERRIES ARE ALL MISSING FROM THE KITCHEN! IT'S A DISASTER!

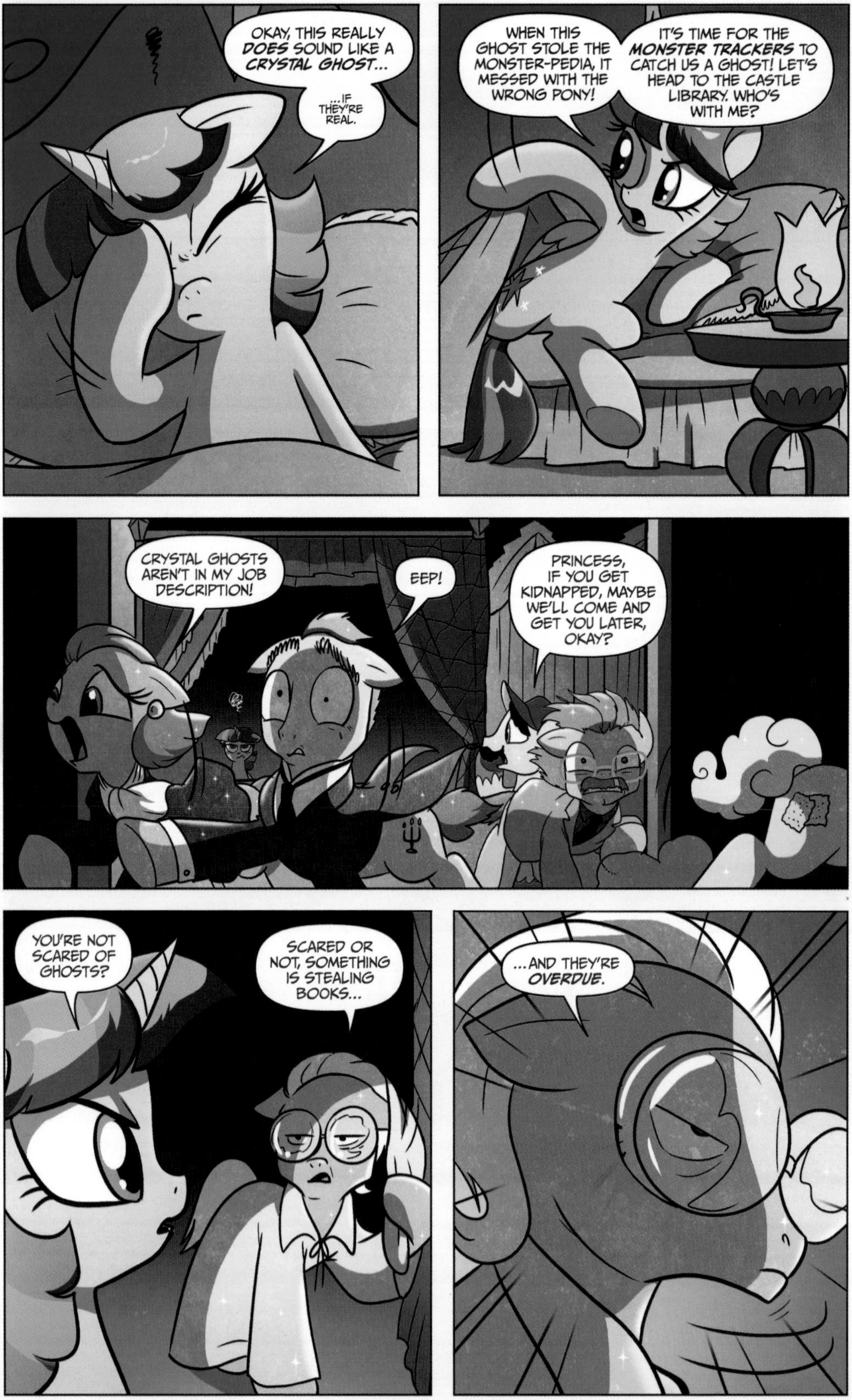
OKAY, THIS REALLY DOES SOUND LIKE A CRYSTAL GHOST...
...IF THEY'RE REAL.
WHEN THIS GHOST STOLE THE MONSTER-PEDIA, IT MESSED WITH THE WRONG PONY!
IT'S TIME FOR THE MONSTER TRACKERS TO CATCH US A GHOST! LET'S HEAD TO THE CASTLE LIBRARY. WHO'S WITH ME?
CRYSTAL GHOSTS AREN'T IN MY JOB DESCRIPTION!
EEP!
PRINCESS, IF YOU GET KIDNAPPED, MAYBE WE'LL COME AND GET YOU LATER, OKAY?
YOU'RE NOT SCARED OF GHOSTS?
SCARED OR NOT, SOMETHING IS STEALING BOOKS...
...AND THEY'RE OVERDUE.

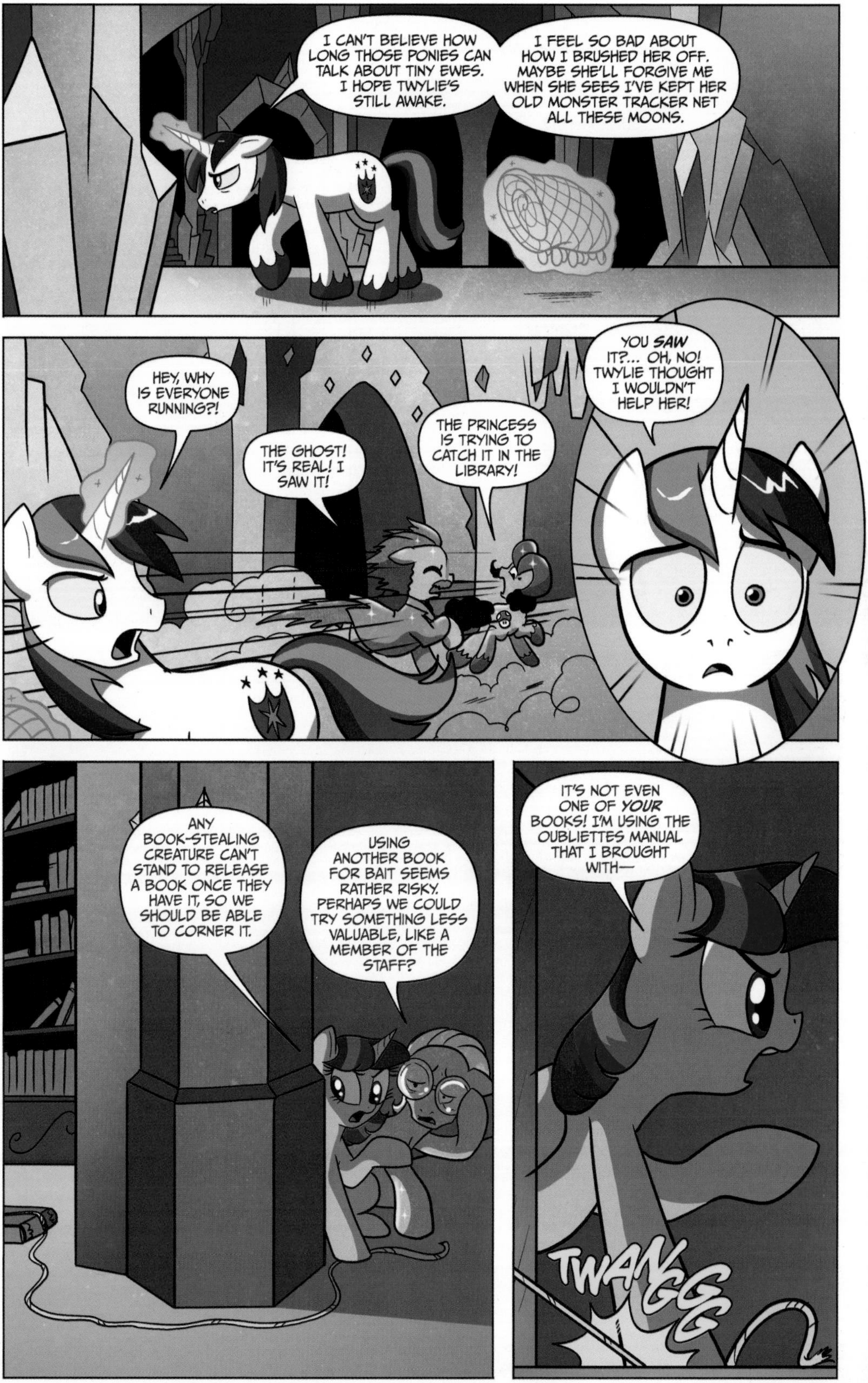

I CAN'T BELIEVE HOW LONG THOSE PONIES CAN TALK ABOUT TINY EWES. I HOPE TWYLIE'S STILL AWAKE.
I FEEL SO BAD ABOUT HOW I BRUSHED HER OFF. MAYBE SHE'LL FORGIVE ME WHEN SHE SEES I'VE KEPT HER OLD MONSTER TRACKER NET ALL THESE MOONS.
HEY, WHY IS EVERYONE RUNNING?!
THE GHOST! IT'S REAL! I SAW IT!
THE PRINCESS IS TRYING TO CATCH IT IN THE LIBRARY!
YOU SAW IT?... OH, NO! TWYLIE THOUGHT I WOULDN'T HELP HER!
ANY BOOK-STEALING CREATURE CAN'T STAND TO RELEASE A BOOK ONCE THEY HAVE IT, SO WE SHOULD BE ABLE TO CORNER IT.
USING ANOTHER BOOK FOR BAIT SEEMS RATHER RISKY. PERHAPS WE COULD TRY SOMETHING LESS VALUABLE, LIKE A MEMBER OF THE STAFF?
IT'S NOT EVEN ONE OF YOUR BOOKS! I'M USING THE OUBLIETTES MANUAL THAT I BROUGHT WITH—
TWANGG

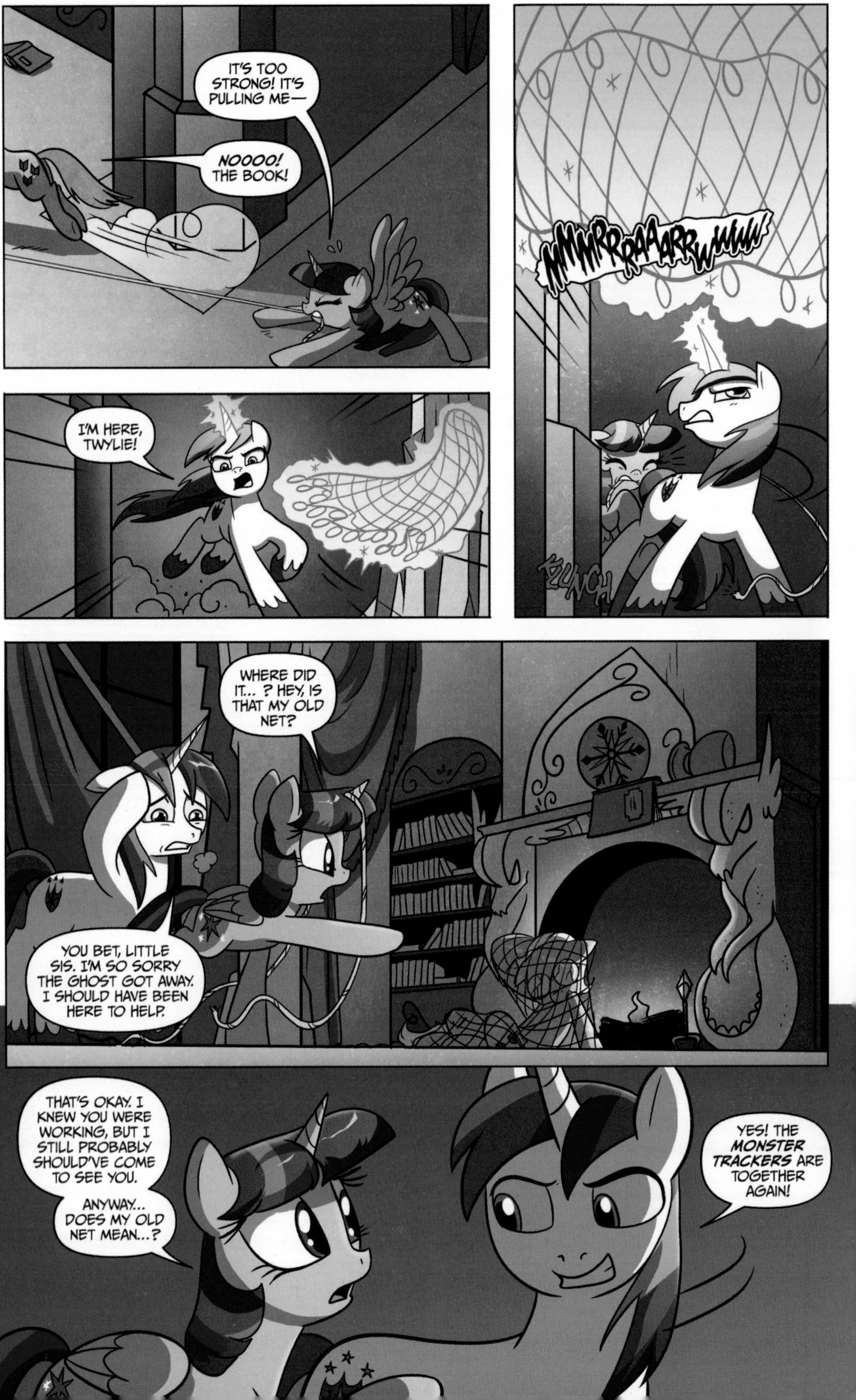

IT'S TOO STRONG! IT'S PULLING ME—
NOOOO! THE BOOK!
MMMRRRAAARRWWW
I'M HERE, TWYLIE!
KLUNCH
WHERE DID IT... ? HEY, IS THAT MY OLD NET?
YOU BET, LITTLE SIS. I'M SO SORRY THE GHOST GOT AWAY. I SHOULD HAVE BEEN HERE TO HELP.
THAT'S OKAY. I KNEW YOU WERE WORKING, BUT I STILL PROBABLY SHOULD'VE COME TO SEE YOU.
ANYWAY... DOES MY OLD NET MEAN...?
YES! THE MONSTER TRACKERS ARE TOGETHER AGAIN!

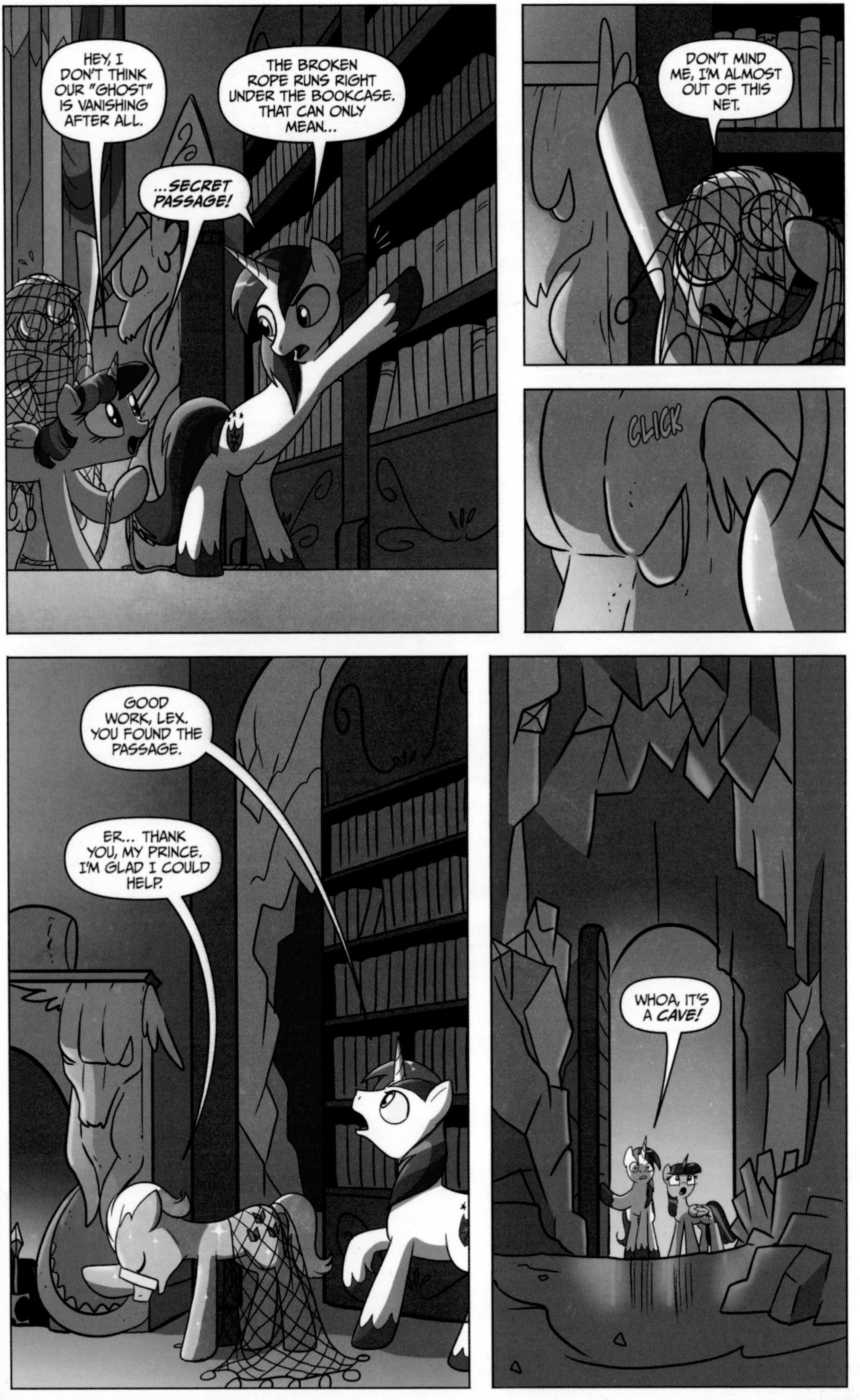
HEY, I DON'T THINK OUR "GHOST" IS VANISHING AFTER ALL.
THE BROKEN ROPE RUNS RIGHT UNDER THE BOOKCASE. THAT CAN ONLY MEAN...
...SECRET PASSAGE!
DON'T MIND ME, I'M ALMOST OUT OF THIS NET.
CLICK
GOOD WORK, LEX. YOU FOUND THE PASSAGE.
ER... THANK YOU, MY PRINCE. I'M GLAD I COULD HELP.
WHOA, IT'S A CAVE!

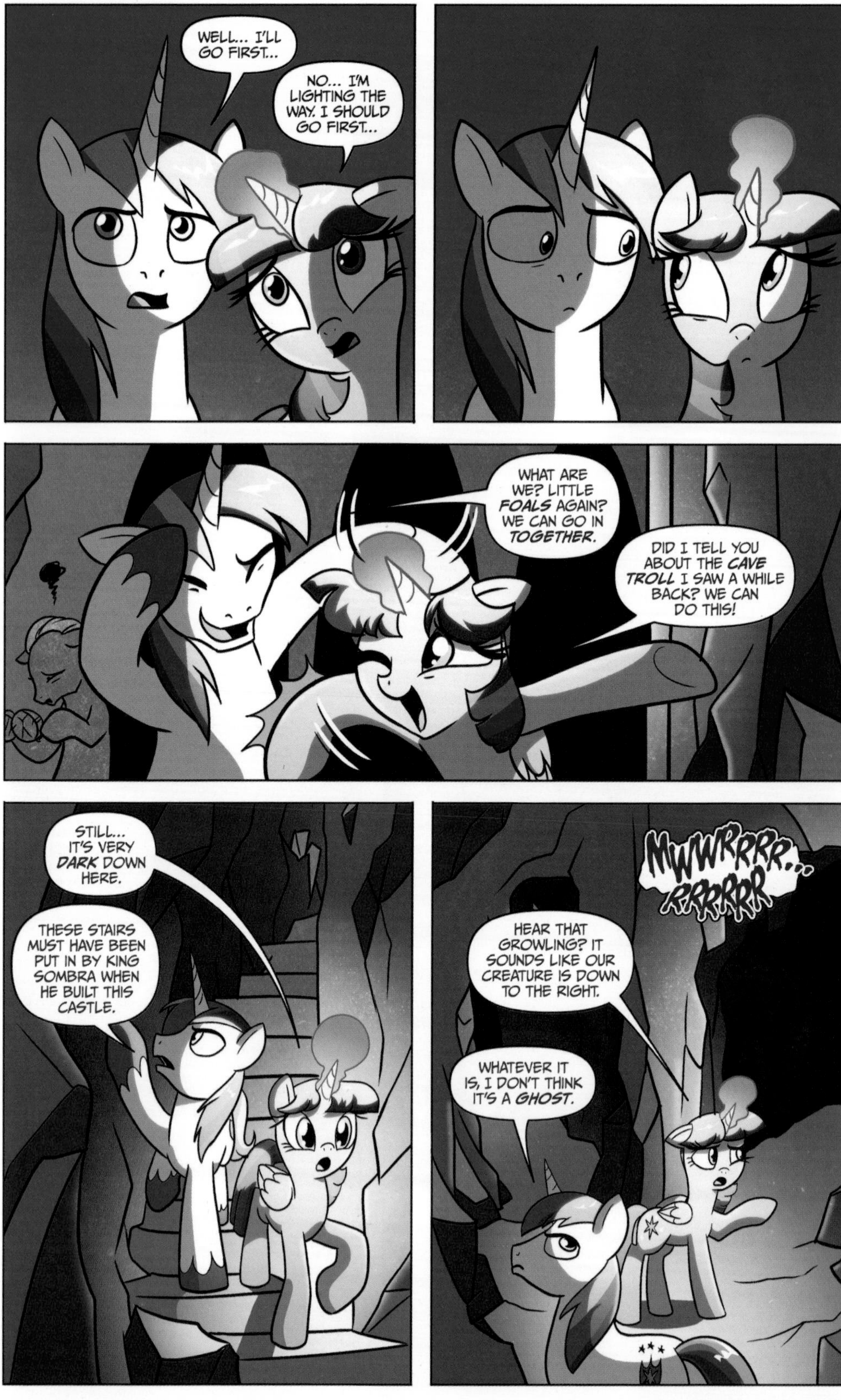

WELL... I'LL GO FIRST...
NO... I'M LIGHTING THE WAY. I SHOULD GO FIRST...
WHAT ARE WE? LITTLE FOALS AGAIN? WE CAN GO IN TOGETHER.
DID I TELL YOU ABOUT THE CAVE TROLL I SAW A WHILE BACK? WE CAN DO THIS!
STILL... IT'S VERY DARK DOWN HERE.
THESE STAIRS MUST HAVE BEEN PUT IN BY KING SOMBRA WHEN HE BUILT THIS CASTLE.
MWWRRRR... RRRRRR
HEAR THAT GROWLING? IT SOUNDS LIKE OUR CREATURE IS DOWN TO THE RIGHT.
WHATEVER IT IS, I DON'T THINK IT'S A GHOST.

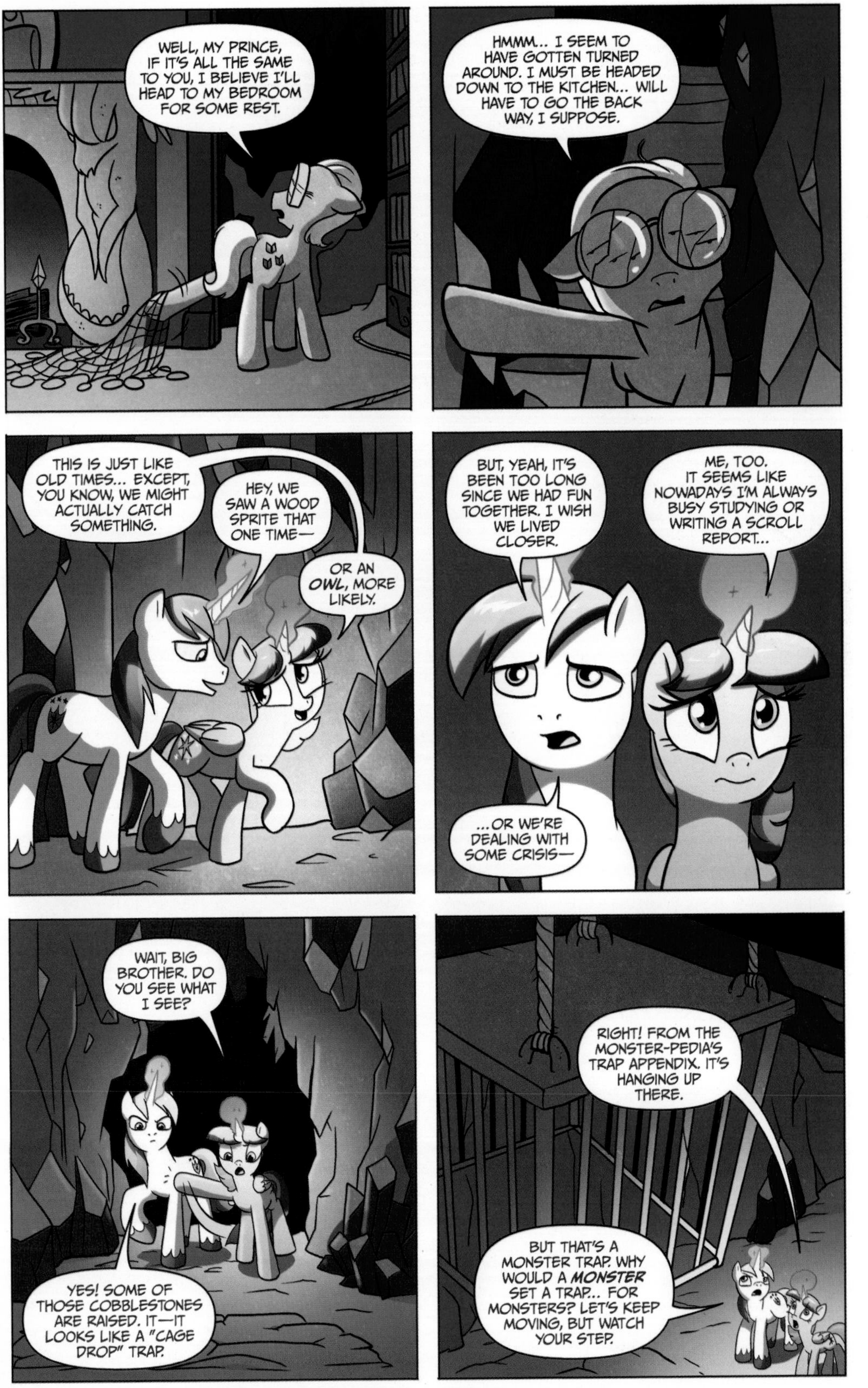
WELL, MY PRINCE, IF IT'S ALL THE SAME TO YOU, I BELIEVE I'LL HEAD TO MY BEDROOM FOR SOME REST.
HMMM... I SEEM TO HAVE GOTTEN TURNED AROUND. I MUST BE HEADED DOWN TO THE KITCHEN... WILL HAVE TO GO THE BACK WAY, I SUPPOSE.
THIS IS JUST LIKE OLD TIMES... EXCEPT, YOU KNOW, WE MIGHT ACTUALLY CATCH SOMETHING.
HEY, WE SAW A WOOD SPRITE THAT ONE TIME—
OR AN *OWL*, MORE LIKELY.
BUT, YEAH, IT'S BEEN TOO LONG SINCE WE HAD FUN TOGETHER. I WISH WE LIVED CLOSER.
ME, TOO. IT SEEMS LIKE NOWADAYS I'M ALWAYS BUSY STUDYING OR WRITING A SCROLL REPORT...
...OR WE'RE DEALING WITH SOME CRISIS—
WAIT, BIG BROTHER. DO YOU SEE WHAT I SEE?
YES! SOME OF THOSE COBBLESTONES ARE RAISED. IT—IT LOOKS LIKE A "CAGE DROP" TRAP.
RIGHT! FROM THE MONSTER-PEDIA'S TRAP APPENDIX. IT'S HANGING UP THERE.
BUT THAT'S A MONSTER TRAP. WHY WOULD A ***MONSTER*** SET A TRAP... FOR MONSTERS? LET'S KEEP MOVING, BUT WATCH YOUR STEP.

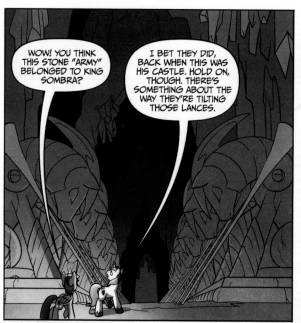

WOW! YOU THINK THIS STONE "ARMY" BELONGED TO KING SOMBRA?

I BET THEY DID, BACK WHEN THIS WAS HIS CASTLE. HOLD ON, THOUGH. THERE'S SOMETHING ABOUT THE WAY THEY'RE TILTING THOSE LANCES.

YEP, LOOK, THEY'RE FILLED WITH GEARS. THESE THINGS WERE MADE TO SALUTE KING SOMBRA...

...AND I THINK SOMEONE TURNED IT INTO...

...ANOTHER MONSTER TRAP!

NICE CATCH! I THINK I SEE A BIGGER CAVERN AHEAD.

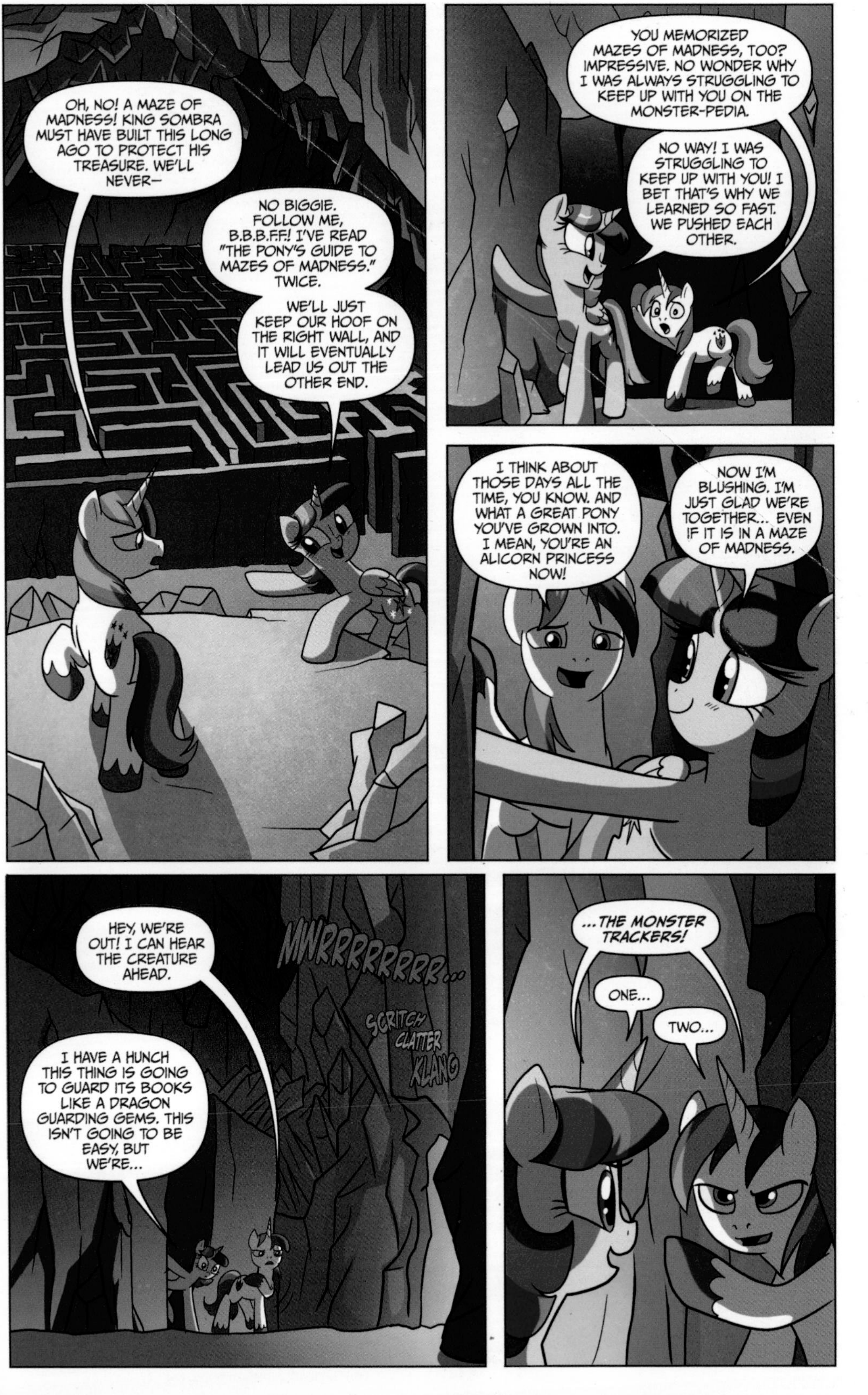
OH, NO! A MAZE OF MADNESS! KING SOMBRA MUST HAVE BUILT THIS LONG AGO TO PROTECT HIS TREASURE. WE'LL NEVER—
NO BIGGIE. FOLLOW ME, B.B.B.F.F.! I'VE READ "THE PONY'S GUIDE TO MAZES OF MADNESS." TWICE.
WE'LL JUST KEEP OUR HOOF ON THE RIGHT WALL, AND IT WILL EVENTUALLY LEAD US OUT THE OTHER END.
YOU MEMORIZED MAZES OF MADNESS, TOO? IMPRESSIVE. NO WONDER WHY I WAS ALWAYS STRUGGLING TO KEEP UP WITH YOU ON THE MONSTER-PEDIA.
NO WAY! I WAS STRUGGLING TO KEEP UP WITH YOU! I BET THAT'S WHY WE LEARNED SO FAST. WE PUSHED EACH OTHER.
I THINK ABOUT THOSE DAYS ALL THE TIME, YOU KNOW. AND WHAT A GREAT PONY YOU'VE GROWN INTO. I MEAN, YOU'RE AN ALICORN PRINCESS NOW!
NOW I'M BLUSHING. I'M JUST GLAD WE'RE TOGETHER... EVEN IF IT IS IN A MAZE OF MADNESS.
HEY, WE'RE OUT! I CAN HEAR THE CREATURE AHEAD.
MWRRRRRRRR...
SCRITCH
CLATTER
KLANG
I HAVE A HUNCH THIS THING IS GOING TO GUARD ITS BOOKS LIKE A DRAGON GUARDING GEMS. THIS ISN'T GOING TO BE EASY, BUT WE'RE...
...THE MONSTER TRACKERS!
ONE...
TWO...

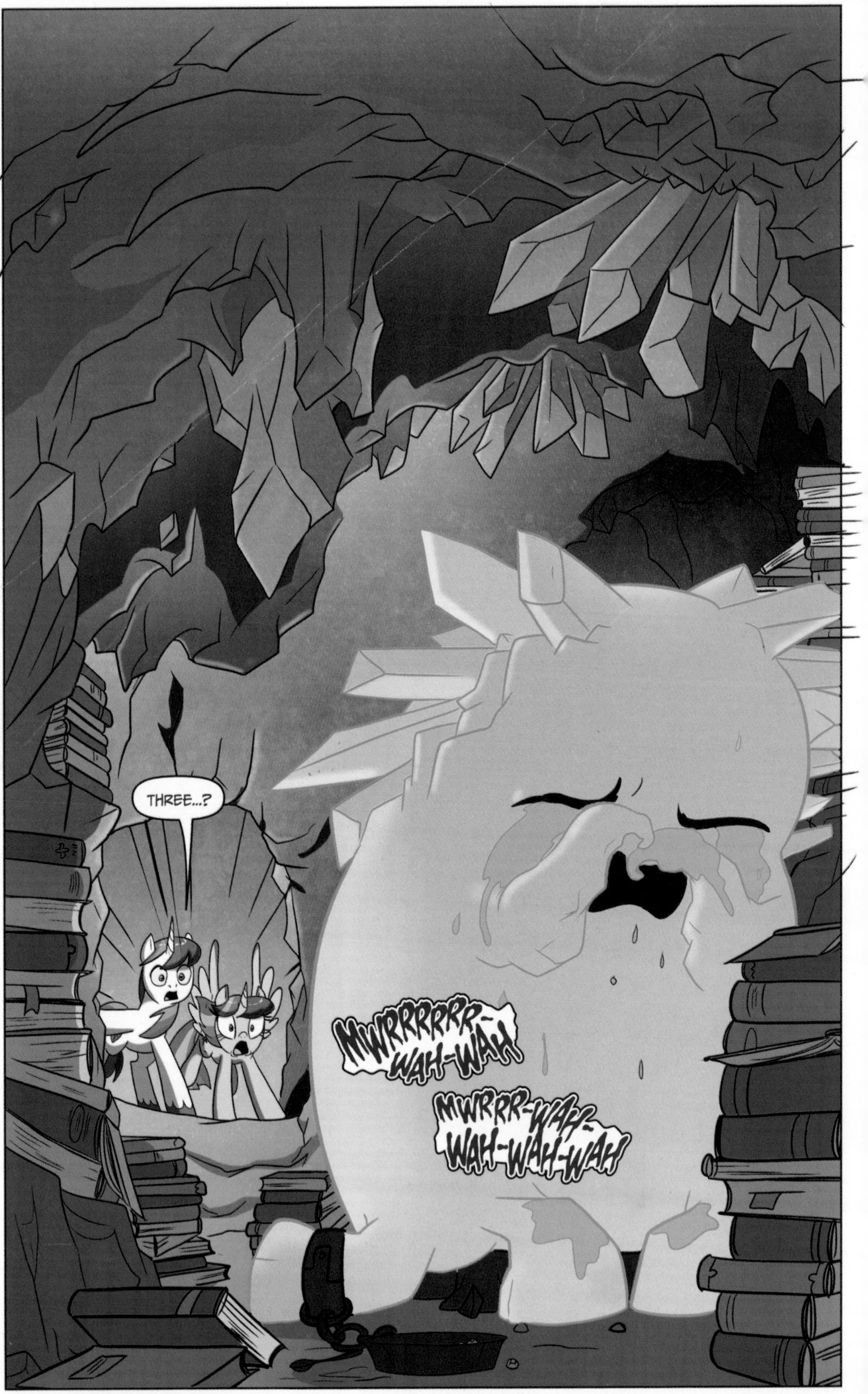
THREE...?
MWRRRRRR-WAH-WAH
MWRRR-WAH-WAH-WAH-WAH

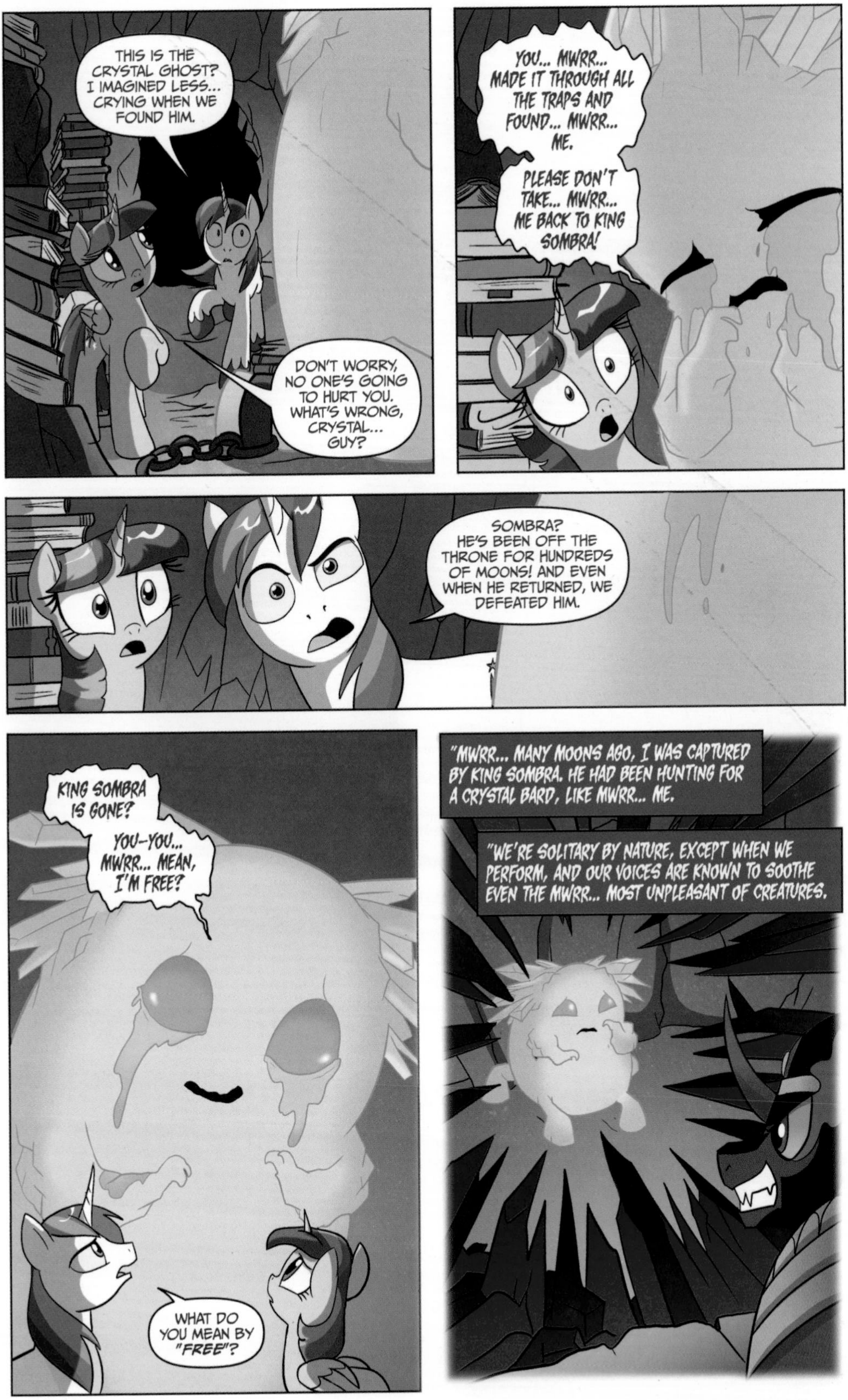

THIS IS THE CRYSTAL GHOST? I IMAGINED LESS... CRYING WHEN WE FOUND HIM.
DON'T WORRY, NO ONE'S GOING TO HURT YOU. WHAT'S WRONG, CRYSTAL... GUY?
YOU... MWRR... MADE IT THROUGH ALL THE TRAPS AND FOUND... MWRR... ME.
PLEASE DON'T TAKE... MWRR... ME BACK TO KING SOMBRA!
SOMBRA? HE'S BEEN OFF THE THRONE FOR HUNDREDS OF MOONS! AND EVEN WHEN HE RETURNED, WE DEFEATED HIM.
KING SOMBRA IS GONE?
YOU-YOU... MWRR... MEAN, I'M FREE?
WHAT DO YOU MEAN BY "FREE"?
"MWRR... MANY MOONS AGO, I WAS CAPTURED BY KING SOMBRA. HE HAD BEEN HUNTING FOR A CRYSTAL BARD, LIKE MWRR... ME.
"WE'RE SOLITARY BY NATURE, EXCEPT WHEN WE PERFORM, AND OUR VOICES ARE KNOWN TO SOOTHE EVEN THE MWRR... MOST UNPLEASANT OF CREATURES.

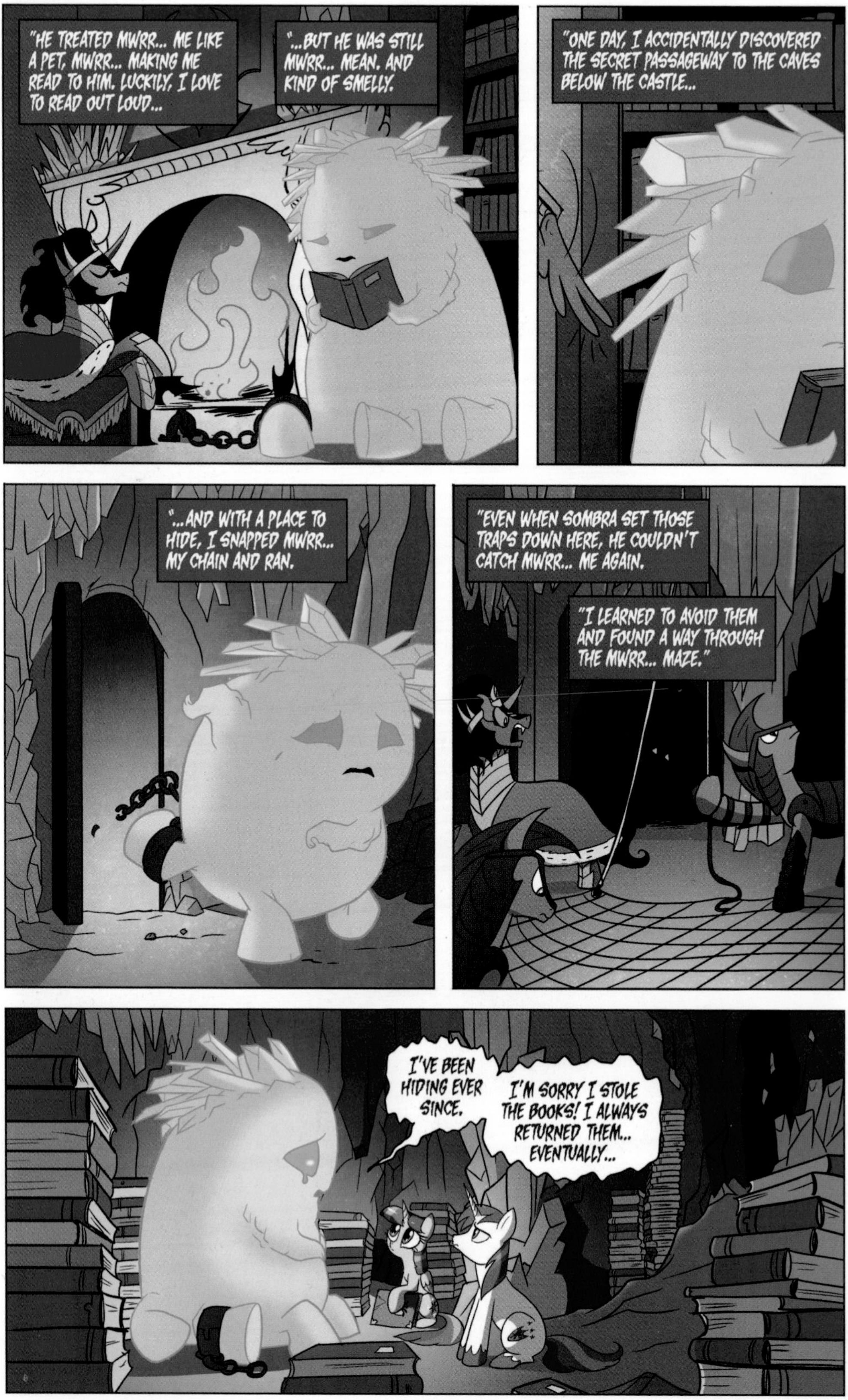
"HE TREATED MWRR... ME LIKE A PET, MWRR... MAKING ME READ TO HIM. LUCKILY, I LOVE TO READ OUT LOUD...
"...BUT HE WAS STILL MWRR... MEAN, AND KIND OF SMELLY.
"ONE DAY, I ACCIDENTALLY DISCOVERED THE SECRET PASSAGEWAY TO THE CAVES BELOW THE CASTLE...
"...AND WITH A PLACE TO HIDE, I SNAPPED MWRR... MY CHAIN AND RAN.
"EVEN WHEN SOMBRA SET THOSE TRAPS DOWN HERE, HE COULDN'T CATCH MWRR... ME AGAIN.
"I LEARNED TO AVOID THEM AND FOUND A WAY THROUGH THE MWRR... MAZE."
I'VE BEEN HIDING EVER SINCE.
I'M SORRY I STOLE THE BOOKS! I ALWAYS RETURNED THEM... EVENTUALLY...

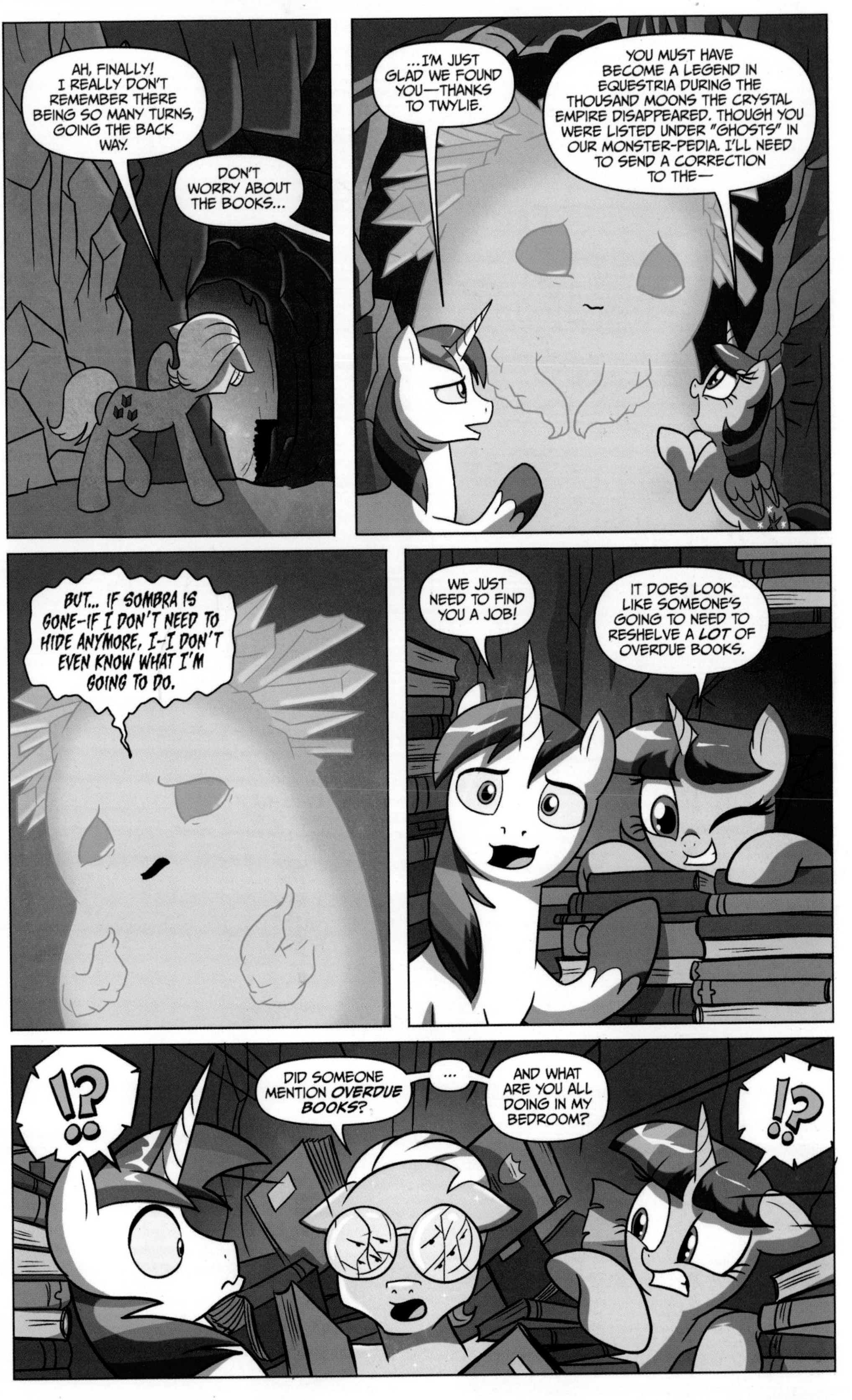
AH, FINALLY! I REALLY DON'T REMEMBER THERE BEING SO MANY TURNS, GOING THE BACK WAY.
DON'T WORRY ABOUT THE BOOKS...
...I'M JUST GLAD WE FOUND YOU—THANKS TO TWYLIE.
YOU MUST HAVE BECOME A LEGEND IN EQUESTRIA DURING THE THOUSAND MOONS THE CRYSTAL EMPIRE DISAPPEARED. THOUGH YOU WERE LISTED UNDER "GHOSTS" IN OUR MONSTER-PEDIA. I'LL NEED TO SEND A CORRECTION TO THE—
BUT... IF SOMBRA IS GONE-IF I DON'T NEED TO HIDE ANYMORE, I-I DON'T EVEN KNOW WHAT I'M GOING TO DO.
WE JUST NEED TO FIND YOU A JOB!
IT DOES LOOK LIKE SOMEONE'S GOING TO NEED TO RESHELVE A *LOT* OF OVERDUE BOOKS.
!?
DID SOMEONE MENTION ***OVERDUE BOOKS***?
...
AND WHAT ARE YOU ALL DOING IN MY BEDROOM?
!?

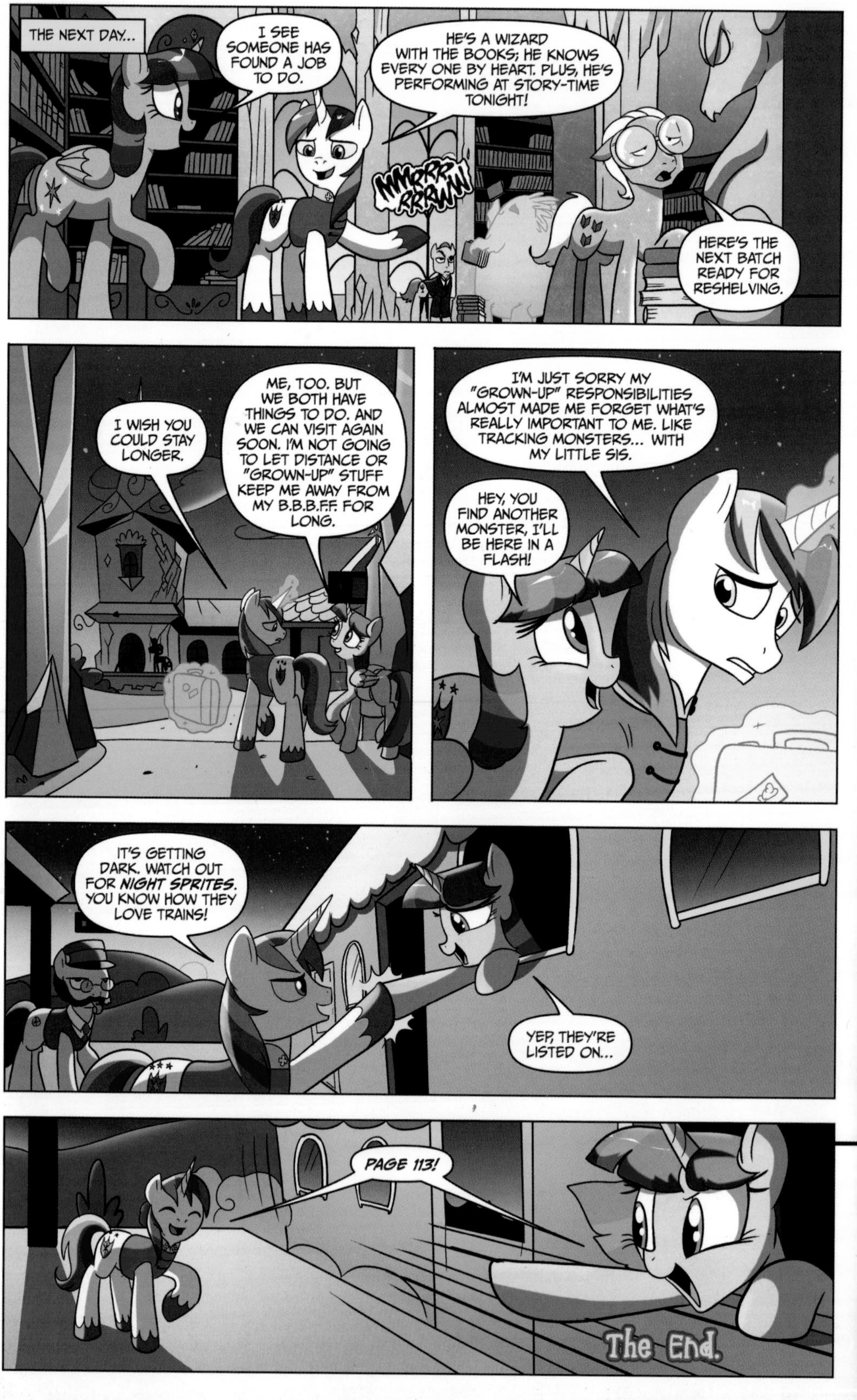
THE NEXT DAY...
I SEE SOMEONE HAS FOUND A JOB TO DO.
HE'S A WIZARD WITH THE BOOKS; HE KNOWS EVERY ONE BY HEART. PLUS, HE'S PERFORMING AT STORY-TIME TONIGHT!
MMRRR RRRWW
HERE'S THE NEXT BATCH READY FOR RESHELVING.
I WISH YOU COULD STAY LONGER.
ME, TOO. BUT WE BOTH HAVE THINGS TO DO. AND WE CAN VISIT AGAIN SOON. I'M NOT GOING TO LET DISTANCE OR "GROWN-UP" STUFF KEEP ME AWAY FROM MY B.B.B.F.F. FOR LONG.
I'M JUST SORRY MY "GROWN-UP" RESPONSIBILITIES ALMOST MADE ME FORGET WHAT'S REALLY IMPORTANT TO ME. LIKE TRACKING MONSTERS... WITH MY LITTLE SIS.
HEY, YOU FIND ANOTHER MONSTER, I'LL BE HERE IN A FLASH!
IT'S GETTING DARK. WATCH OUT FOR NIGHT SPRITES. YOU KNOW HOW THEY LOVE TRAINS!
YEP, THEY'RE LISTED ON...
PAGE 113!
The End.

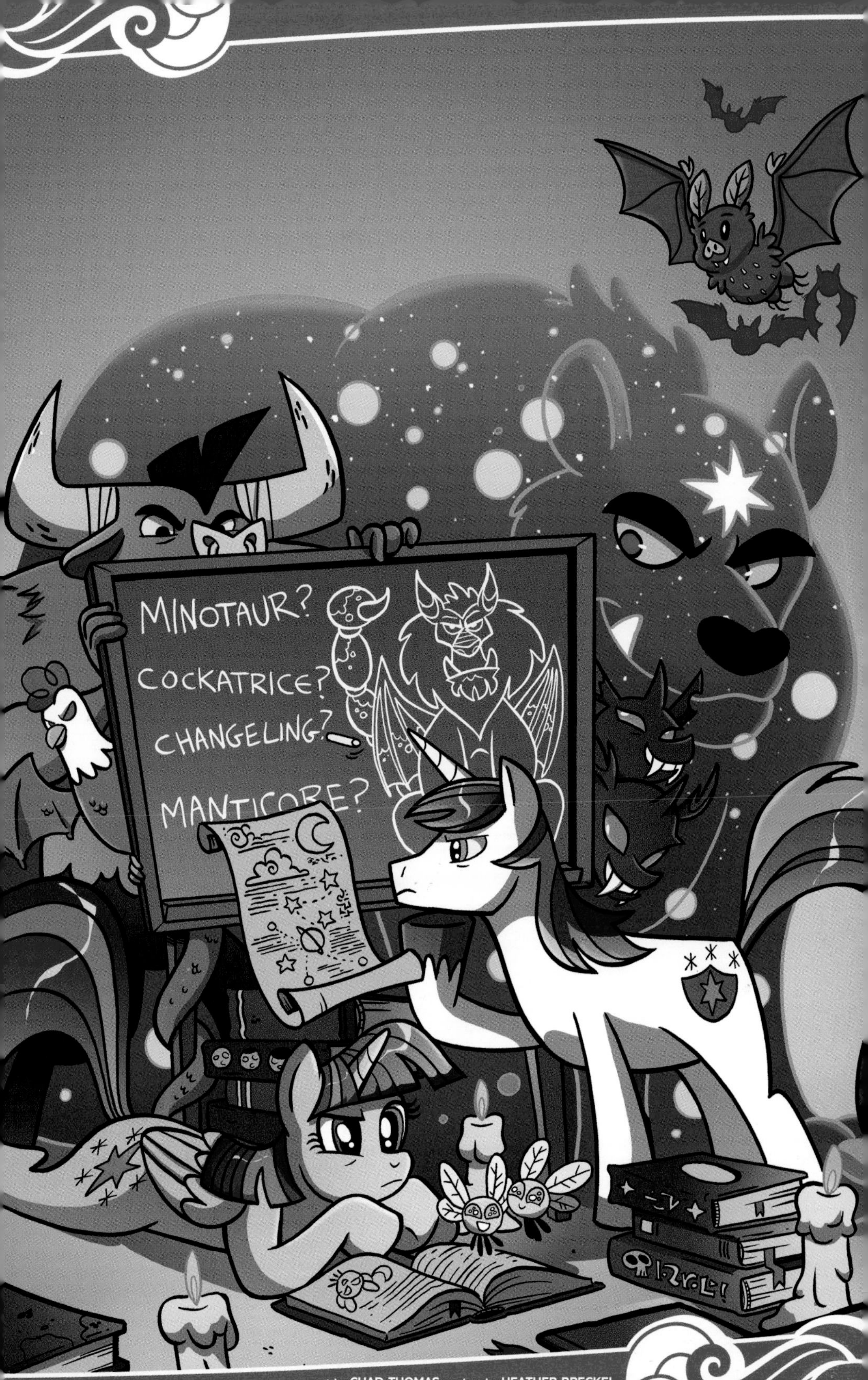
MINOTAUR?
COCKATRICE?
CHANGELING?
MANTICORE?

art by CHAD THOMAS • colors by HEATHER BRECKEL

Fluttershy & Zecora

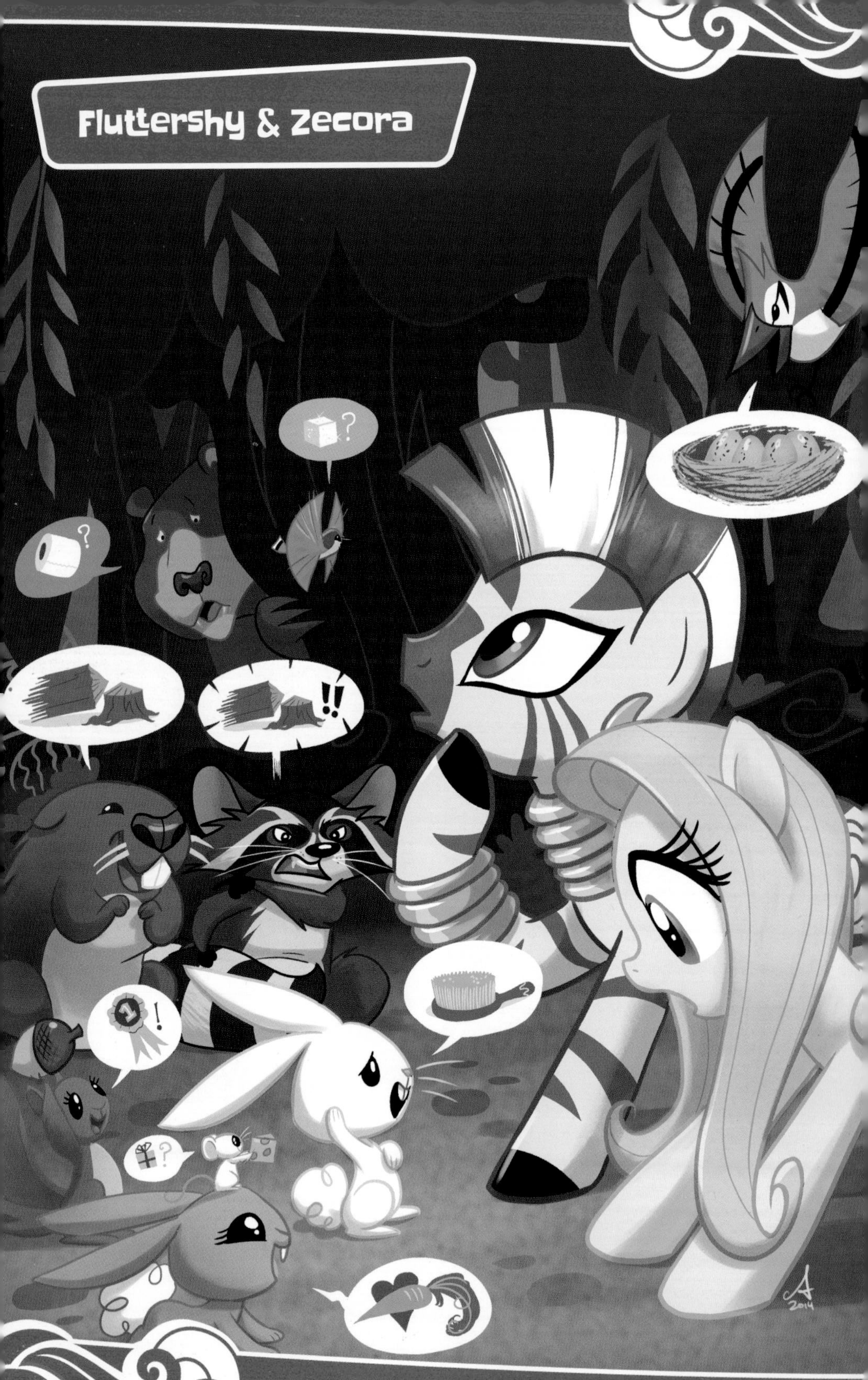

art by AMY MEBBERSON

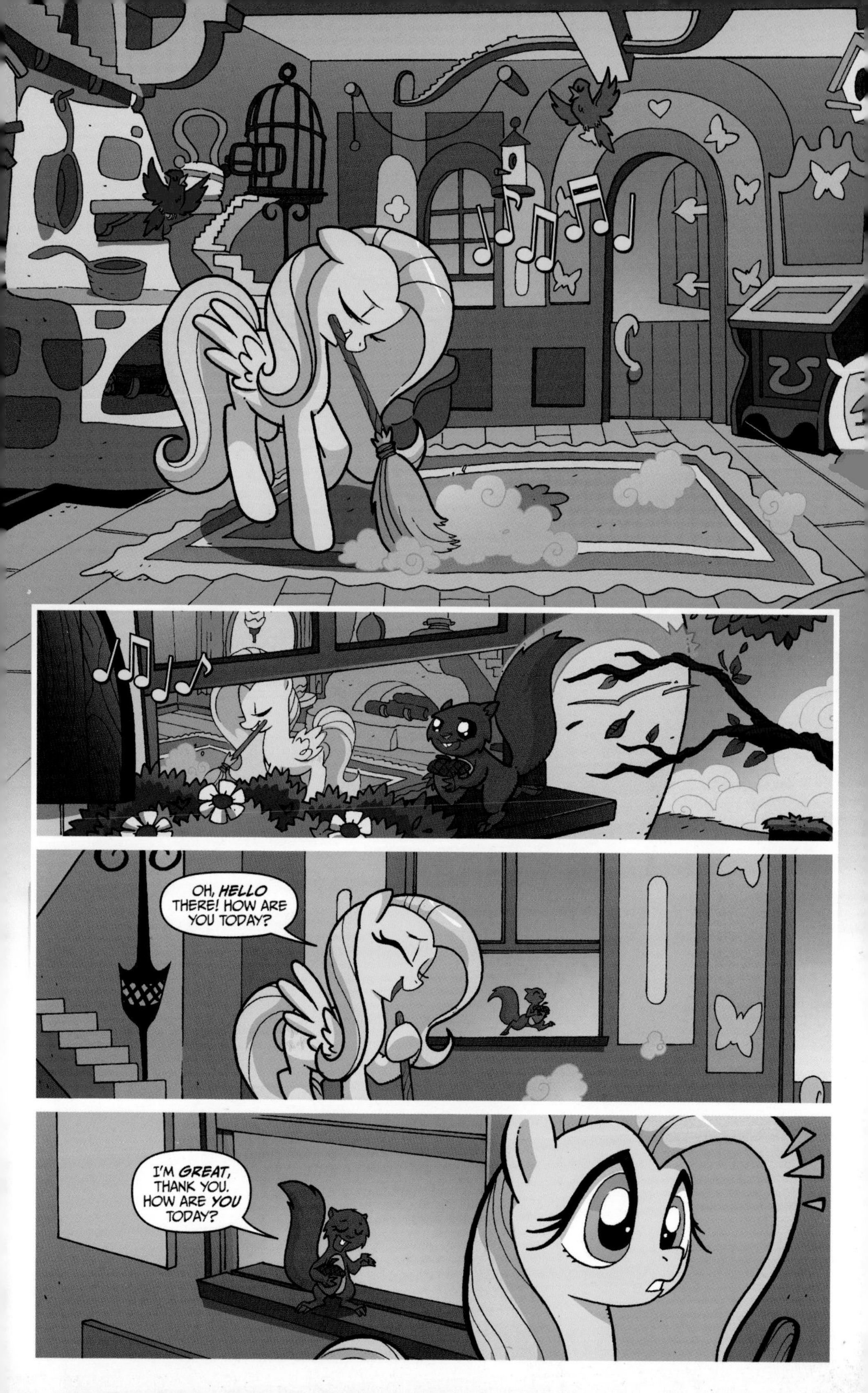
OH, HELLO THERE! HOW ARE YOU TODAY?
I'M GREAT, THANK YOU. HOW ARE YOU TODAY?

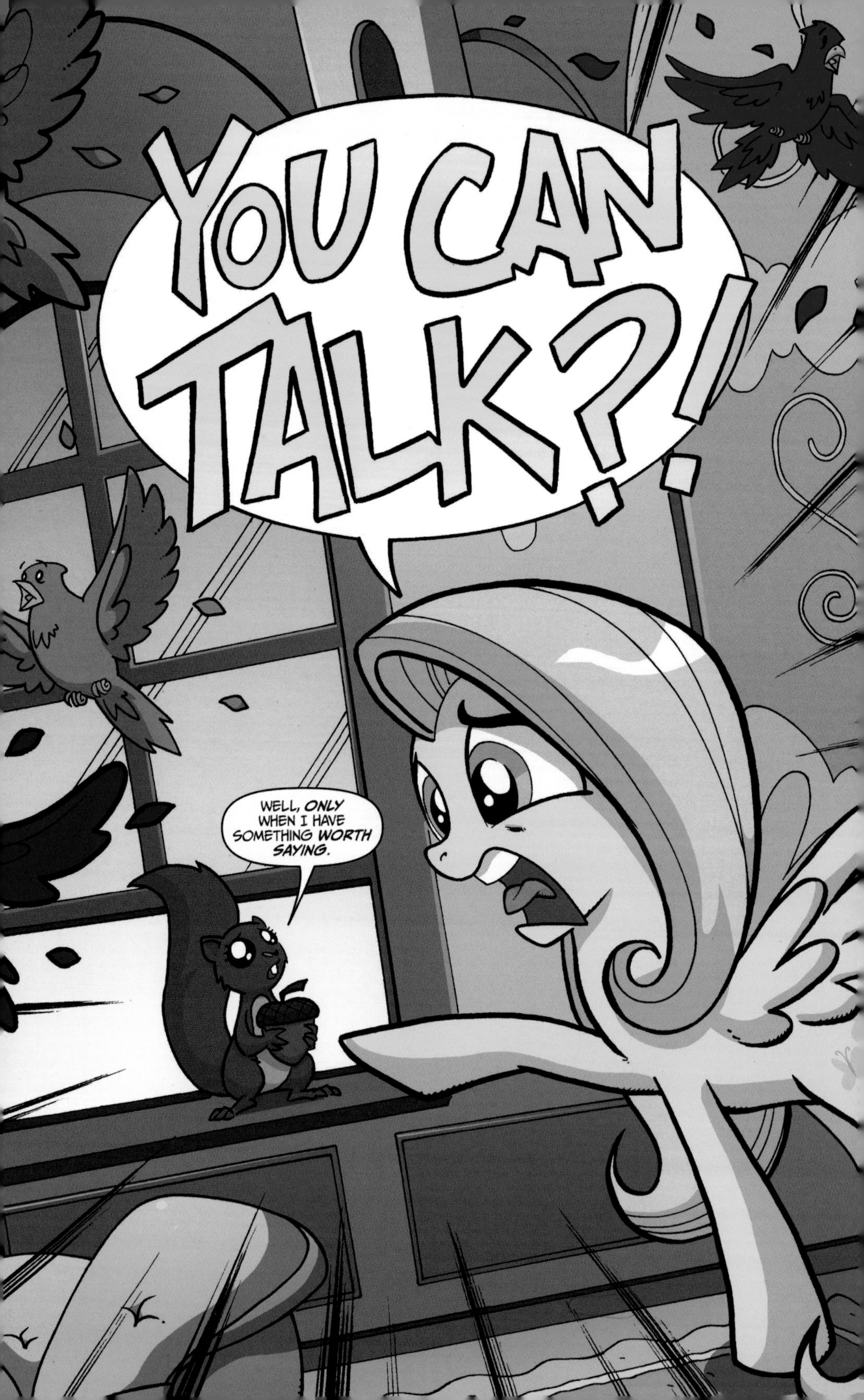
YOU CAN TALK?!
WELL, *ONLY* WHEN I HAVE SOMETHING *WORTH* SAYING.

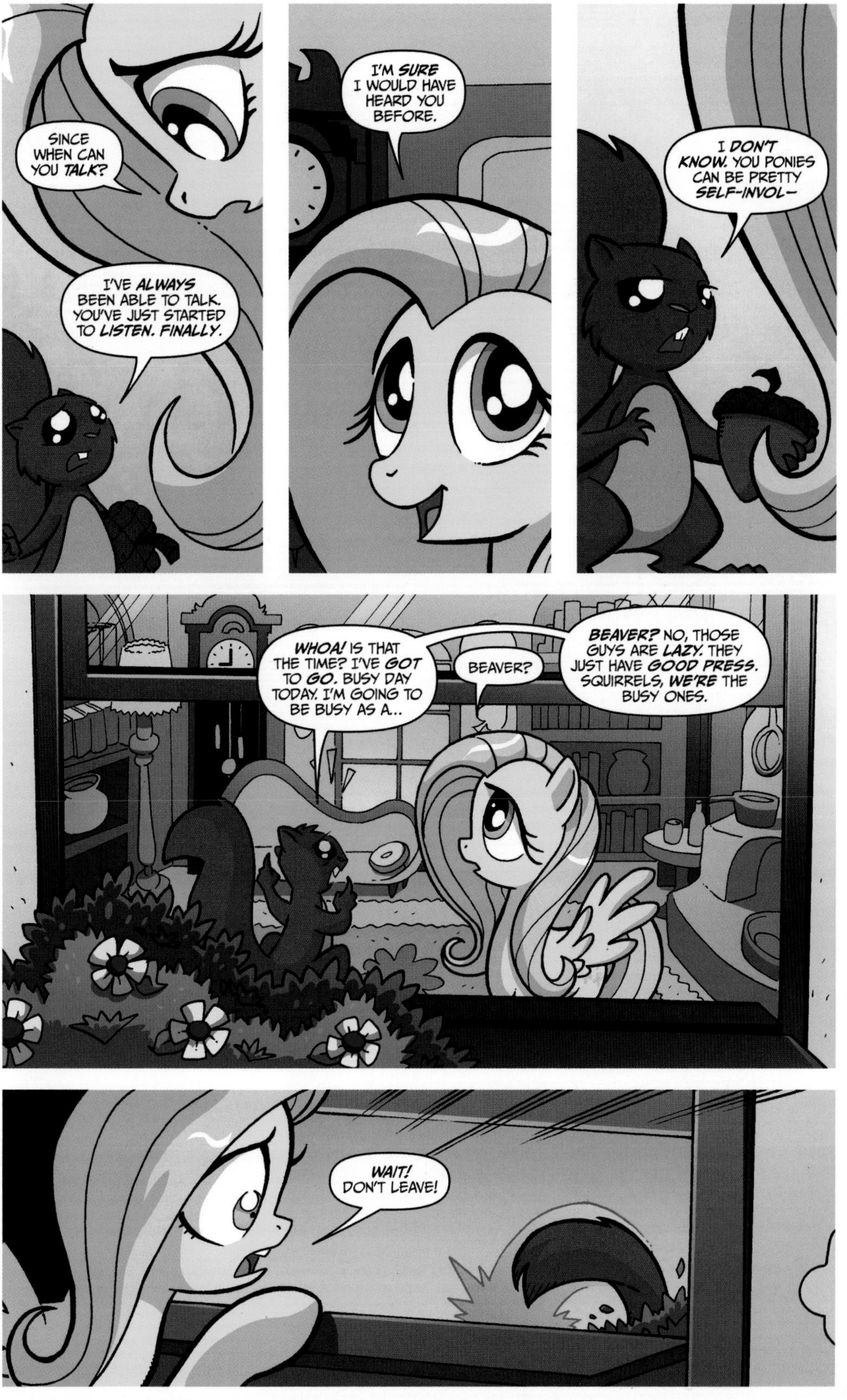
SINCE WHEN CAN YOU TALK?
I'VE ALWAYS BEEN ABLE TO TALK. YOU'VE JUST STARTED TO LISTEN. FINALLY.
I'M SURE I WOULD HAVE HEARD YOU BEFORE.
I DON'T KNOW. YOU PONIES CAN BE PRETTY SELF-INVOL–
WHOA! IS THAT THE TIME? I'VE GOT TO GO. BUSY DAY TODAY. I'M GOING TO BE BUSY AS A...
BEAVER?
BEAVER? NO, THOSE GUYS ARE LAZY. THEY JUST HAVE GOOD PRESS. SQUIRRELS, WE'RE THE BUSY ONES.
WAIT! DON'T LEAVE!

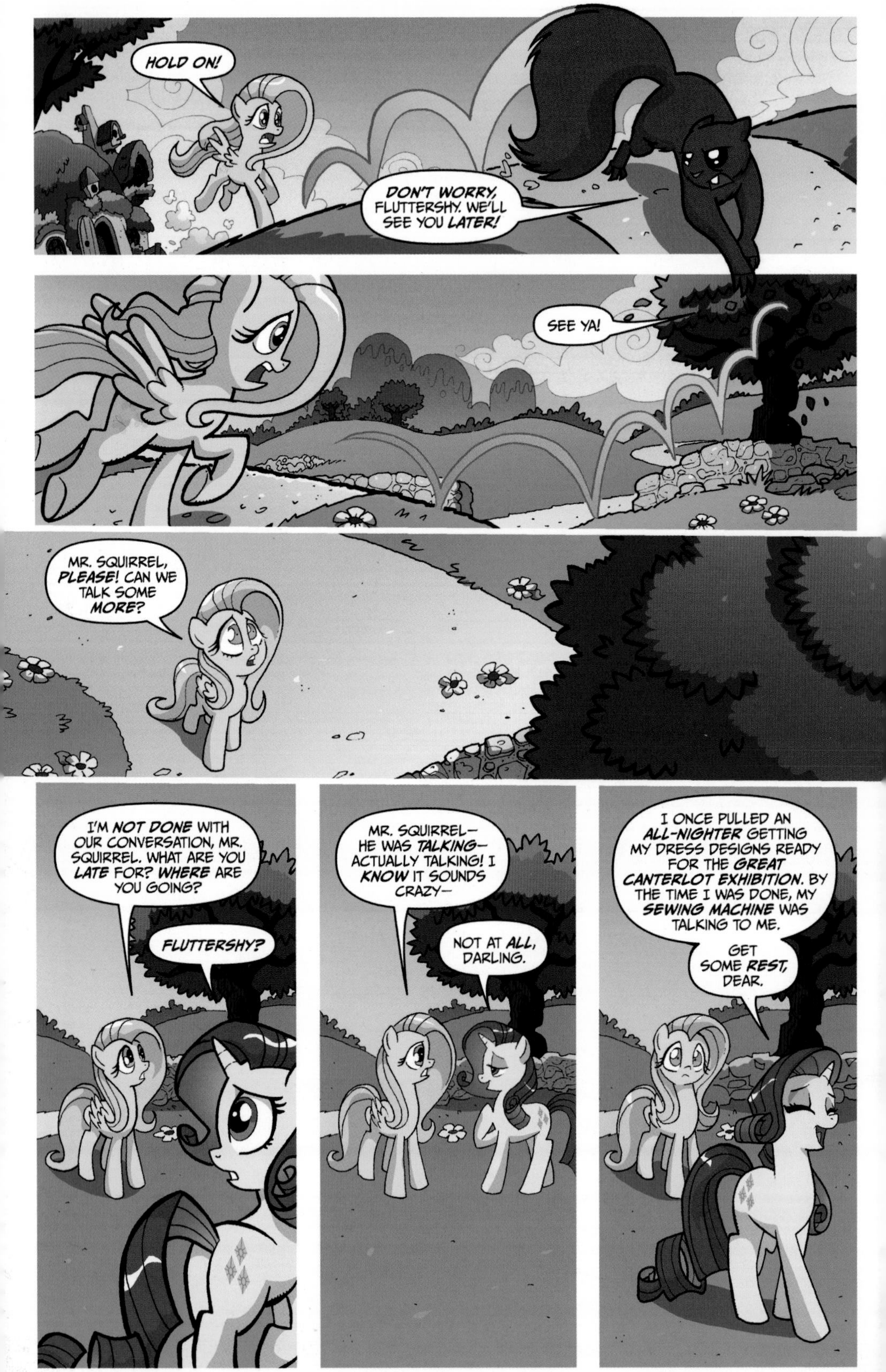
HOLD ON!
DON'T WORRY, FLUTTERSHY. WE'LL SEE YOU LATER!
SEE YA!
MR. SQUIRREL, PLEASE! CAN WE TALK SOME MORE?
I'M NOT DONE WITH OUR CONVERSATION, MR. SQUIRREL. WHAT ARE YOU LATE FOR? WHERE ARE YOU GOING?
FLUTTERSHY?
MR. SQUIRREL— HE WAS TALKING— ACTUALLY TALKING! I KNOW IT SOUNDS CRAZY—
NOT AT ALL, DARLING.
I ONCE PULLED AN ALL-NIGHTER GETTING MY DRESS DESIGNS READY FOR THE GREAT CANTERLOT EXHIBITION. BY THE TIME I WAS DONE, MY SEWING MACHINE WAS TALKING TO ME.
GET SOME REST, DEAR.

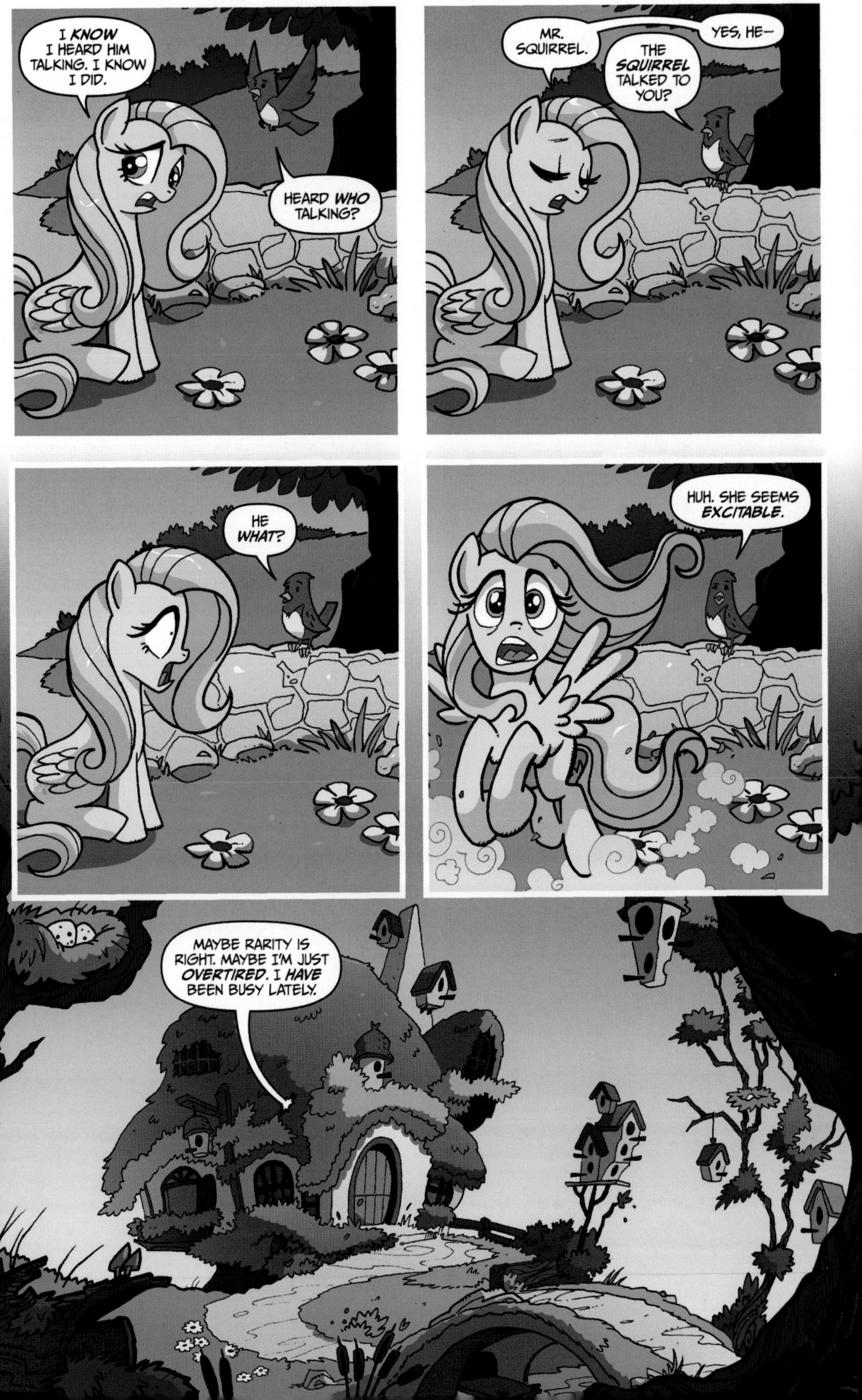
I KNOW I HEARD HIM TALKING. I KNOW I DID.
HEARD WHO TALKING?
MR. SQUIRREL.
YES, HE—
THE SQUIRREL TALKED TO YOU?
HE WHAT?
HUH. SHE SEEMS EXCITABLE.
MAYBE RARITY IS RIGHT. MAYBE I'M JUST OVERTIRED. I HAVE BEEN BUSY LATELY.

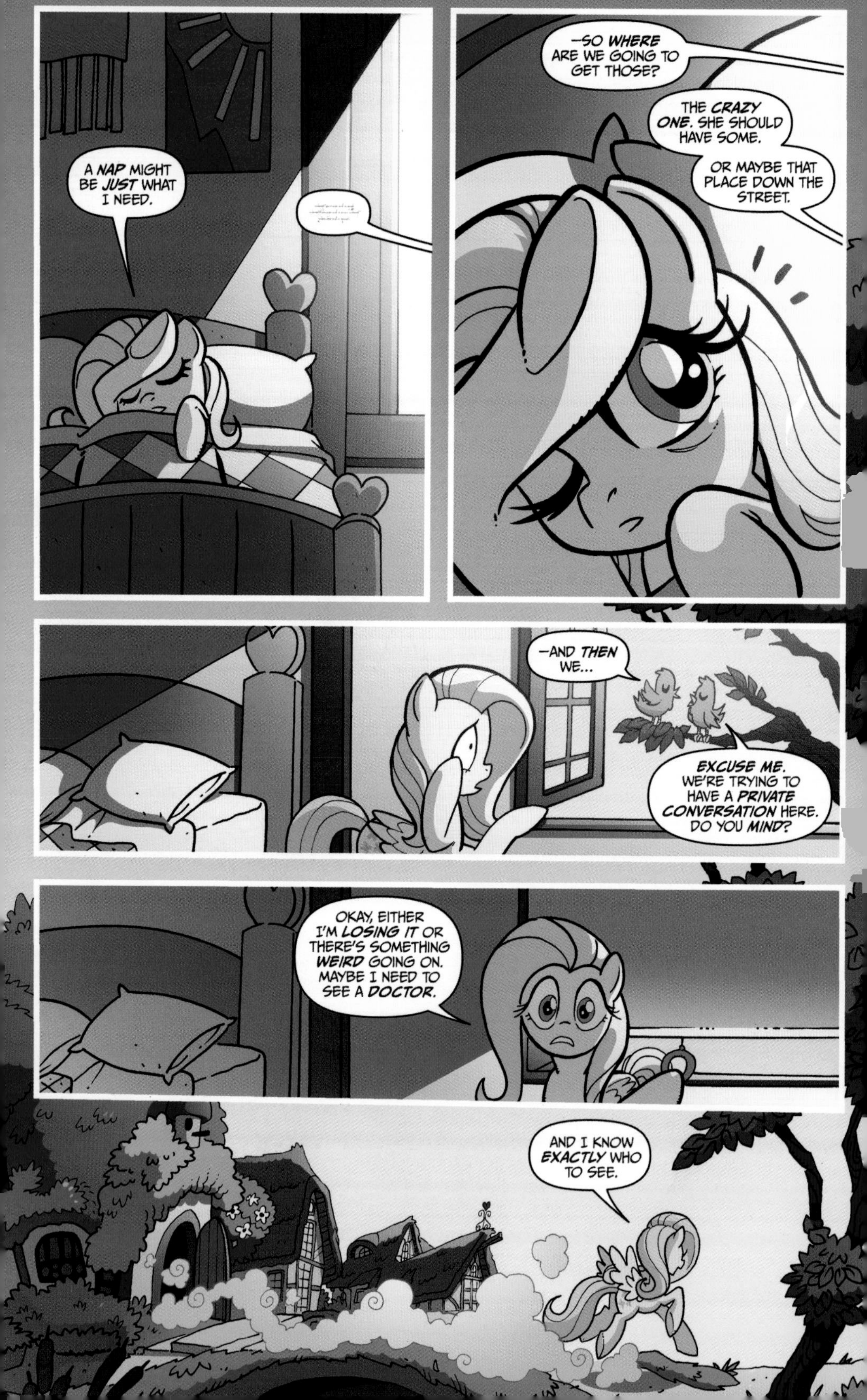
A NAP MIGHT BE JUST WHAT I NEED.
—SO WHERE ARE WE GOING TO GET THOSE?
THE CRAZY ONE. SHE SHOULD HAVE SOME.
OR MAYBE THAT PLACE DOWN THE STREET.
—AND THEN WE...
EXCUSE ME. WE'RE TRYING TO HAVE A PRIVATE CONVERSATION HERE. DO YOU MIND?
OKAY, EITHER I'M LOSING IT OR THERE'S SOMETHING WEIRD GOING ON. MAYBE I NEED TO SEE A DOCTOR.
AND I KNOW EXACTLY WHO TO SEE.

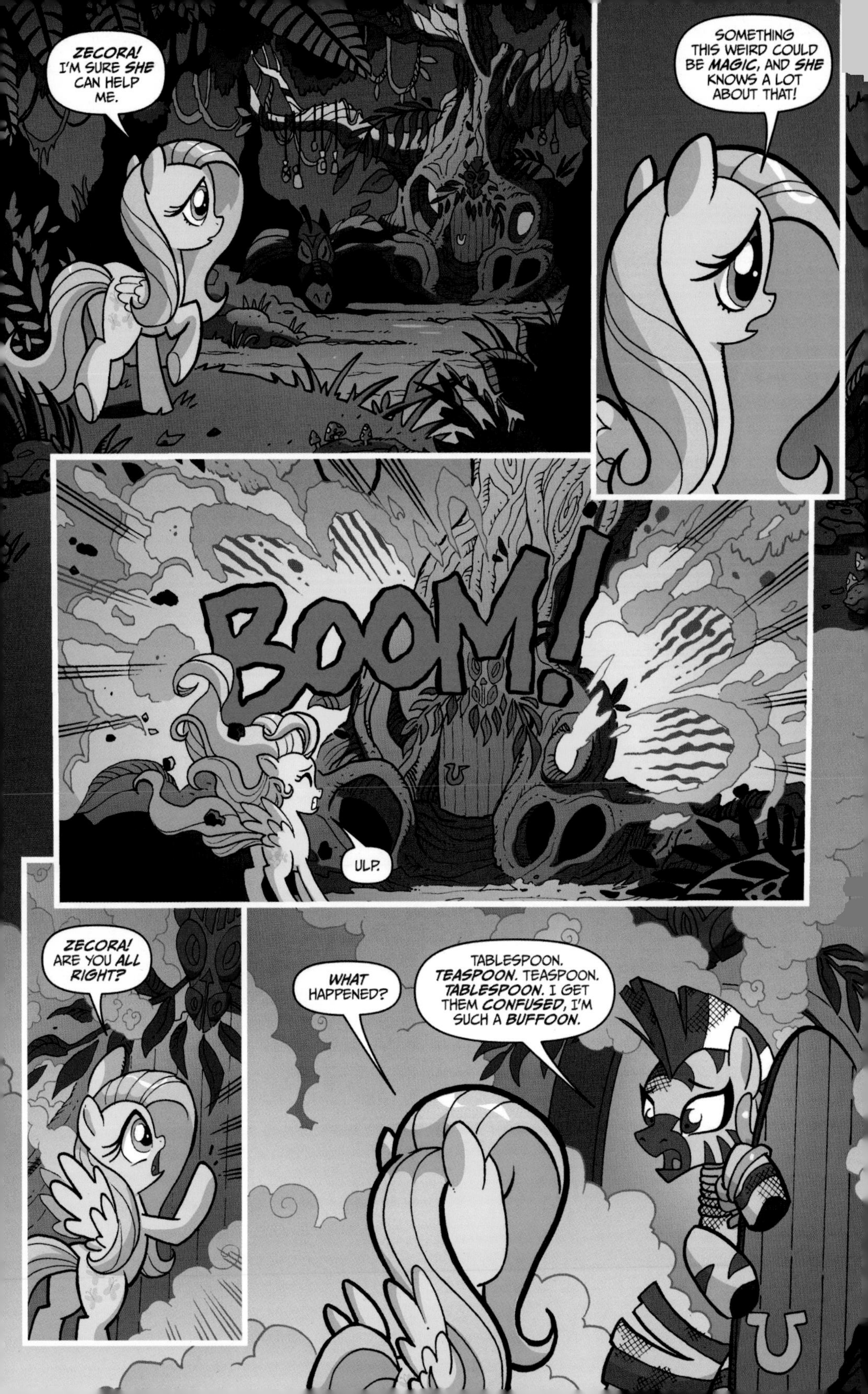
ZECORA! I'M SURE SHE CAN HELP ME.
SOMETHING THIS WEIRD COULD BE MAGIC, AND SHE KNOWS A LOT ABOUT THAT!
BOOM!
ULP.
ZECORA! ARE YOU ALL RIGHT?
WHAT HAPPENED?
TABLESPOON. TEASPOON. TEASPOON. TABLESPOON. I GET THEM CONFUSED, I'M SUCH A BUFFOON.

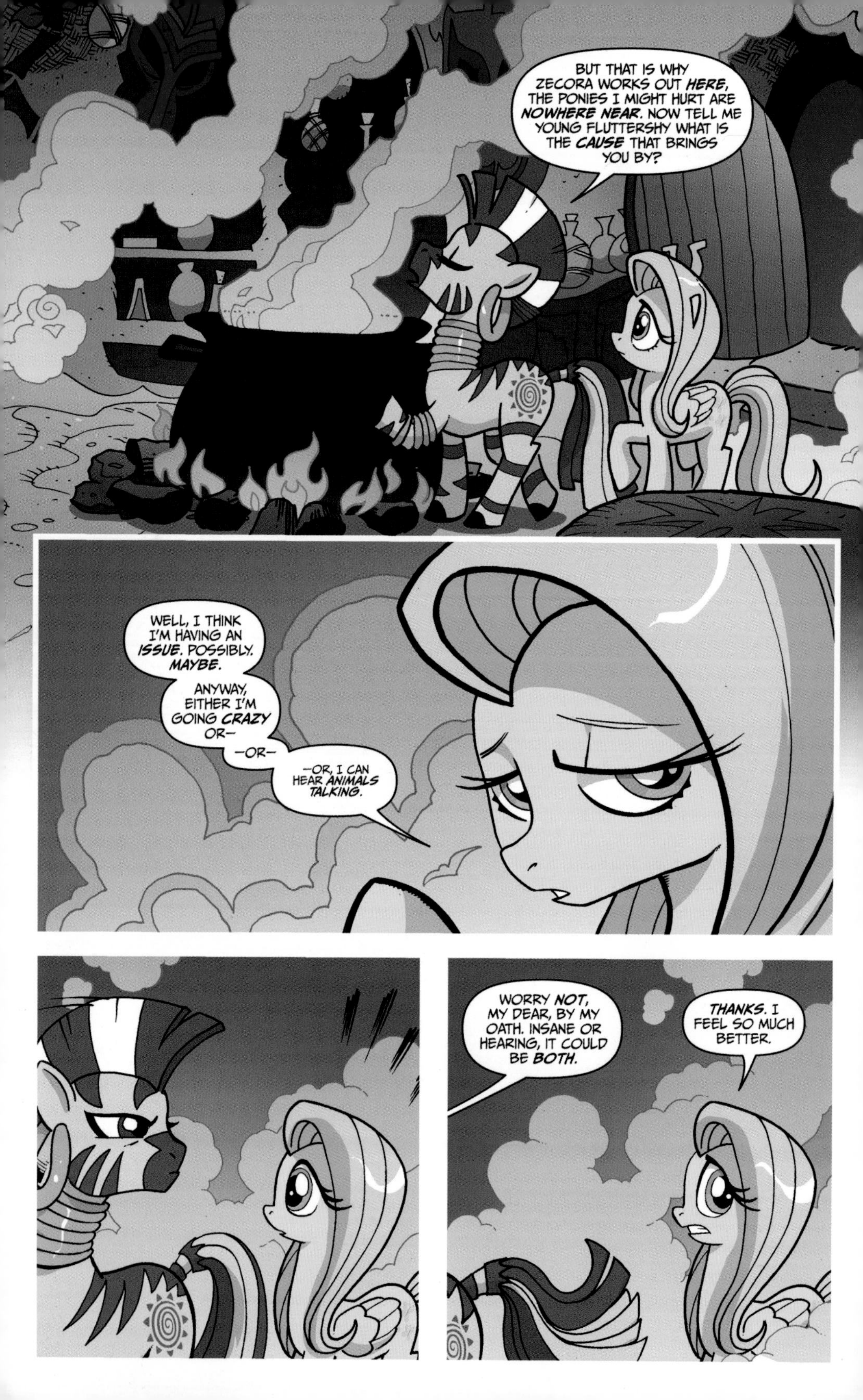

BUT THAT IS WHY ZECORA WORKS OUT *HERE*, THE PONIES I MIGHT HURT ARE *NOWHERE NEAR*. NOW TELL ME YOUNG FLUTTERSHY WHAT IS THE *CAUSE* THAT BRINGS YOU BY?
WELL, I THINK I'M HAVING AN *ISSUE*. POSSIBLY. *MAYBE*.
ANYWAY, EITHER I'M GOING *CRAZY* OR—
—OR—
—OR, I CAN HEAR *ANIMALS TALKING*.
WORRY *NOT*, MY DEAR, BY MY OATH. INSANE OR HEARING, IT COULD BE *BOTH*.
THANKS. I FEEL SO MUCH BETTER.

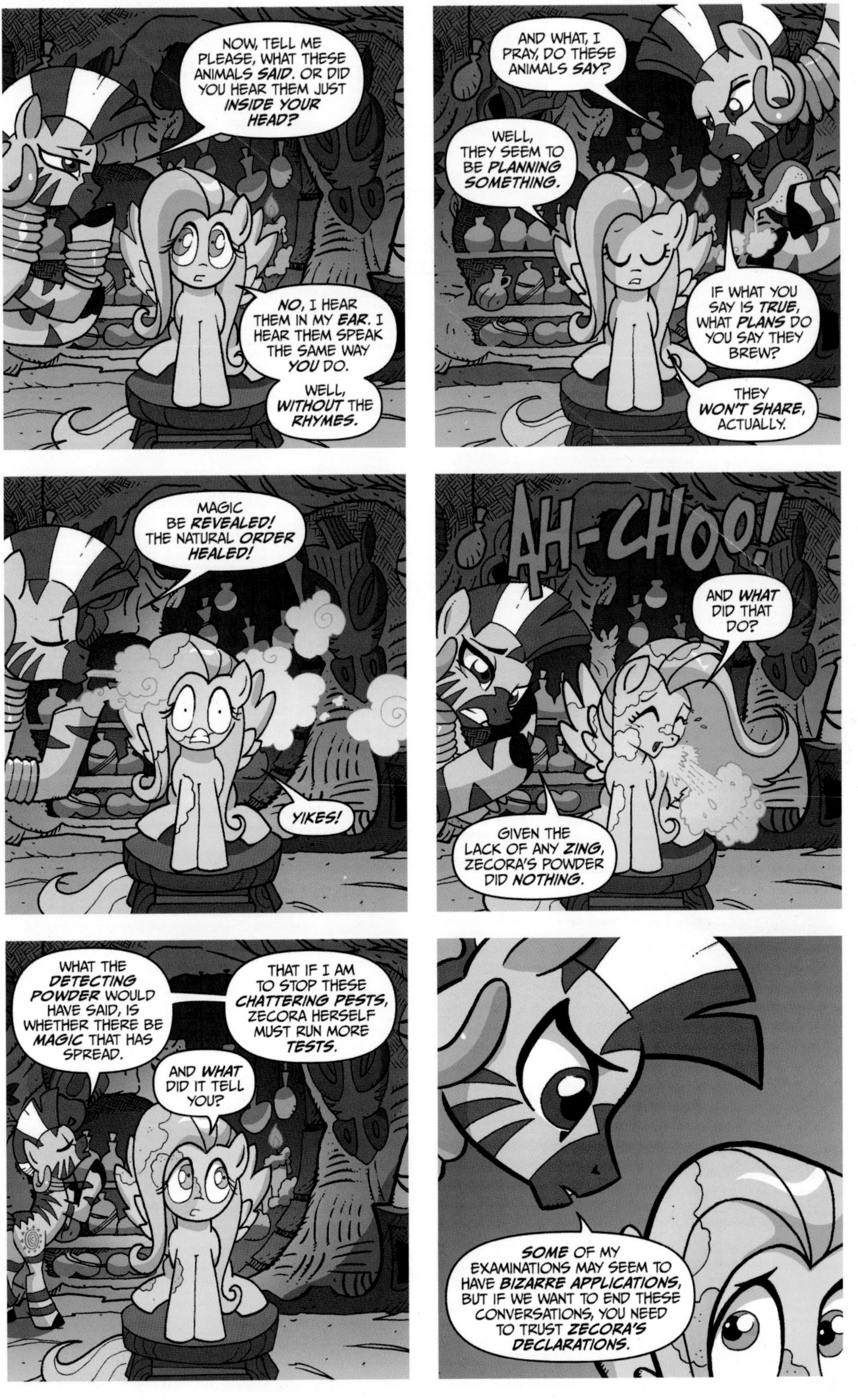
NOW, TELL ME PLEASE, WHAT THESE ANIMALS SAID. OR DID YOU HEAR THEM JUST INSIDE YOUR HEAD?
NO, I HEAR THEM IN MY EAR. I HEAR THEM SPEAK THE SAME WAY YOU DO.
WELL, WITHOUT THE RHYMES.
AND WHAT, I PRAY, DO THESE ANIMALS SAY?
WELL, THEY SEEM TO BE PLANNING SOMETHING.
IF WHAT YOU SAY IS TRUE, WHAT PLANS DO YOU SAY THEY BREW?
THEY WON'T SHARE, ACTUALLY.
MAGIC BE REVEALED! THE NATURAL ORDER HEALED!
YIKES!
AH-CHOO!
AND WHAT DID THAT DO?
GIVEN THE LACK OF ANY ZING, ZECORA'S POWDER DID NOTHING.
WHAT THE DETECTING POWDER WOULD HAVE SAID, IS WHETHER THERE BE MAGIC THAT HAS SPREAD.
AND WHAT DID IT TELL YOU?
THAT IF I AM TO STOP THESE CHATTERING PESTS, ZECORA HERSELF MUST RUN MORE TESTS.
SOME OF MY EXAMINATIONS MAY SEEM TO HAVE BIZARRE APPLICATIONS, BUT IF WE WANT TO END THESE CONVERSATIONS, YOU NEED TO TRUST ZECORA'S DECLARATIONS.

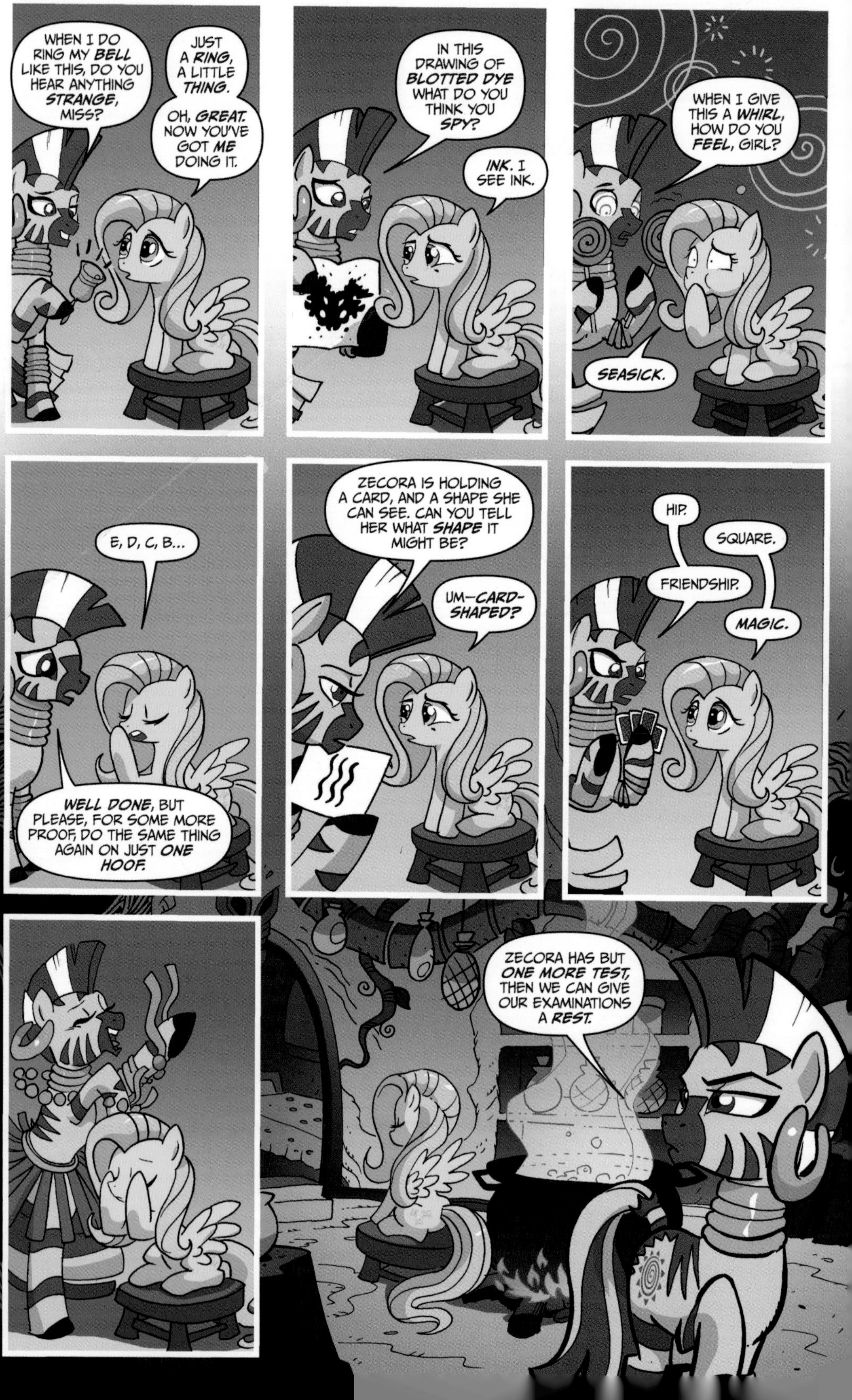
WHEN I DO RING MY BELL LIKE THIS, DO YOU HEAR ANYTHING STRANGE, MISS?
JUST A RING, A LITTLE THING.
OH, GREAT. NOW YOU'VE GOT ME DOING IT.
IN THIS DRAWING OF BLOTTED DYE WHAT DO YOU THINK YOU SPY?
INK. I SEE INK.
WHEN I GIVE THIS A WHIRL, HOW DO YOU FEEL, GIRL?
SEASICK.
E, D, C, B...
WELL DONE, BUT PLEASE, FOR SOME MORE PROOF, DO THE SAME THING AGAIN ON JUST ONE HOOF.
ZECORA IS HOLDING A CARD, AND A SHAPE SHE CAN SEE. CAN YOU TELL HER WHAT SHAPE IT MIGHT BE?
UM—CARD-SHAPED?
HIP.
FRIENDSHIP.
SQUARE.
MAGIC.
ZECORA HAS BUT ONE MORE TEST, THEN WE CAN GIVE OUR EXAMINATIONS A REST.

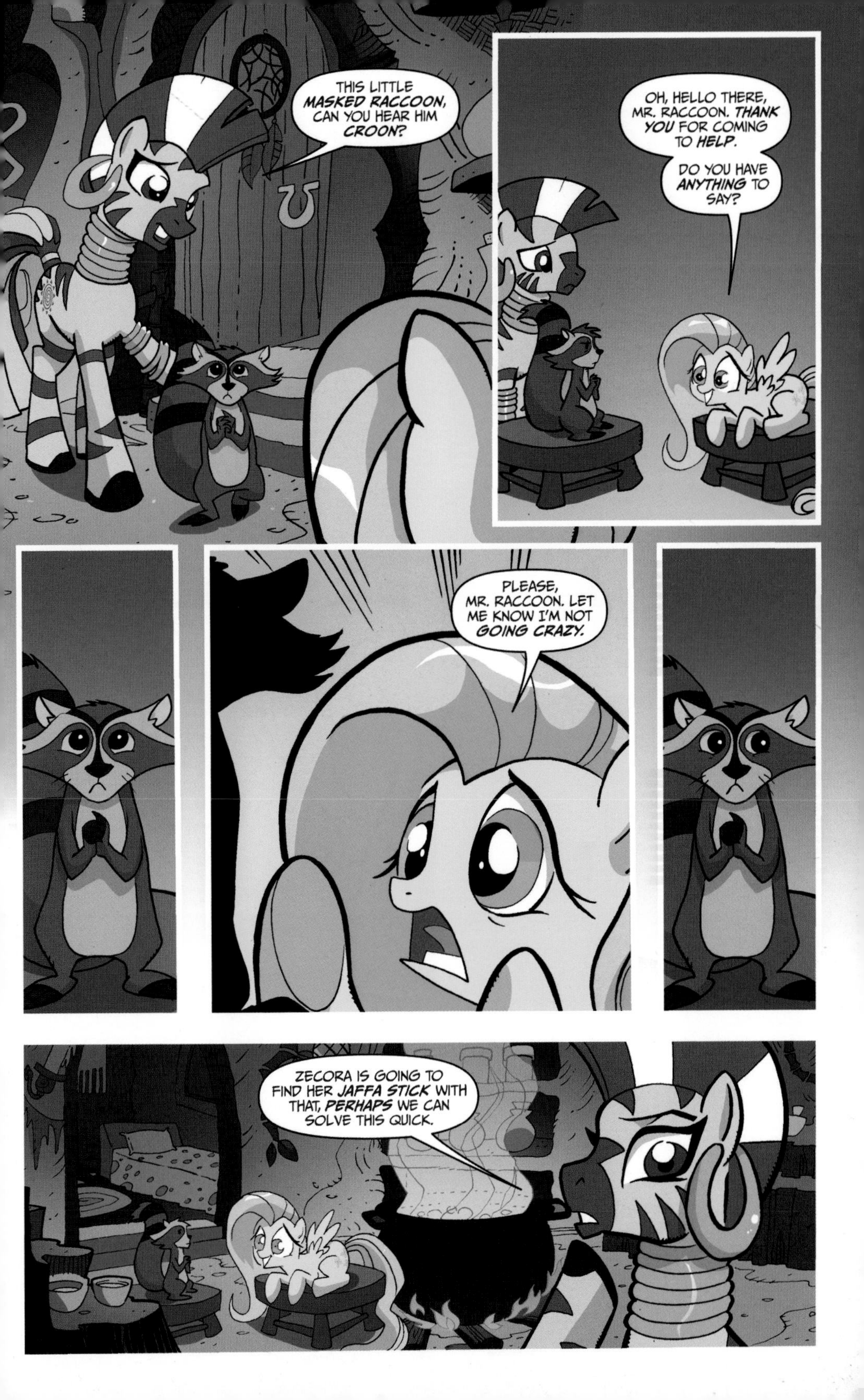
THIS LITTLE MASKED RACCOON, CAN YOU HEAR HIM CROON?
OH, HELLO THERE, MR. RACCOON. THANK YOU FOR COMING TO HELP.
DO YOU HAVE ANYTHING TO SAY?
PLEASE, MR. RACCOON. LET ME KNOW I'M NOT GOING CRAZY.
ZECORA IS GOING TO FIND HER JAFFA STICK WITH THAT, PERHAPS WE CAN SOLVE THIS QUICK.

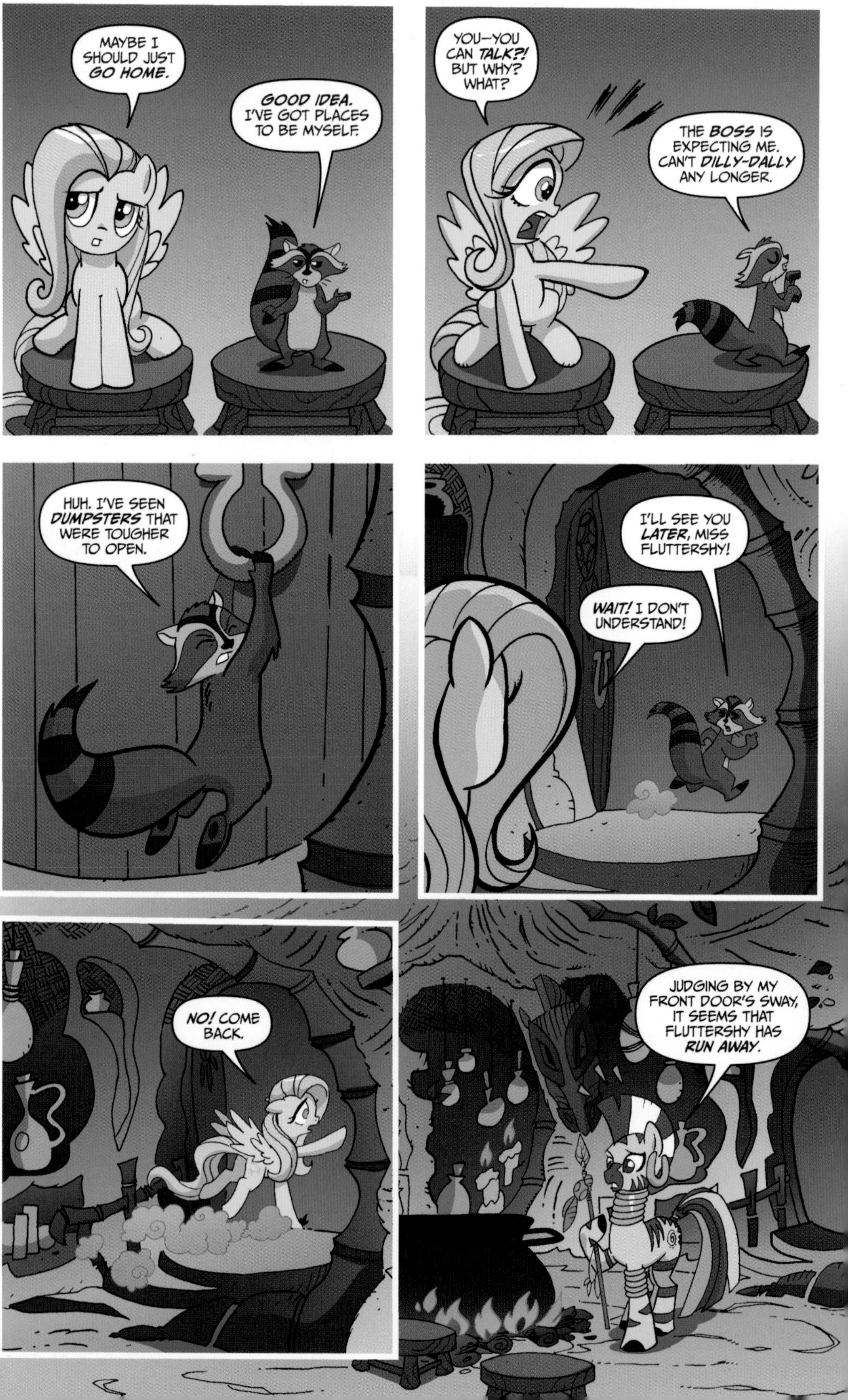
MAYBE I SHOULD JUST GO HOME.
GOOD IDEA. I'VE GOT PLACES TO BE MYSELF.
YOU—YOU CAN TALK?! BUT WHY? WHAT?
THE BOSS IS EXPECTING ME. CAN'T DILLY-DALLY ANY LONGER.
HUH. I'VE SEEN DUMPSTERS THAT WERE TOUGHER TO OPEN.
I'LL SEE YOU LATER, MISS FLUTTERSHY!
WAIT! I DON'T UNDERSTAND!
NO! COME BACK.
JUDGING BY MY FRONT DOOR'S SWAY, IT SEEMS THAT FLUTTERSHY HAS RUN AWAY.

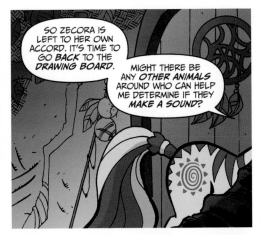

SO ZECORA IS LEFT TO HER OWN ACCORD. IT'S TIME TO GO *BACK* TO THE *DRAWING BOARD*.

MIGHT THERE BE ANY *OTHER ANIMALS* AROUND WHO CAN HELP ME DETERMINE IF THEY *MAKE A SOUND*?

I THINK YOU TWO *CATS* WILL DO JUST *FINE* TO HELP ME WITH THIS *PROBLEM* OF MINE.

YOU TWO SEEM TO HAVE *NOTHING TO SAY* AND WE CANNOT JUST *SIT HERE* ALL DAY.

MAYBE MY *JAFFA STICK* HERE WILL HELP GET YOU TWO IN GEAR.

STILL HAVE *NOTHING* YET TO SAY? FLUTTERSHY WOULD NOT COME HERE TO *PLAY*. I THINK SHE *INDEED* HEARD YOU SPEAK. SO HAS SOMETHING HAPPENED TO YOUR *PHYSIQUE*?

STILL TRYING TO BE *DEFIANT*? I *NEED* YOU TO BE *COMPLIANT*.

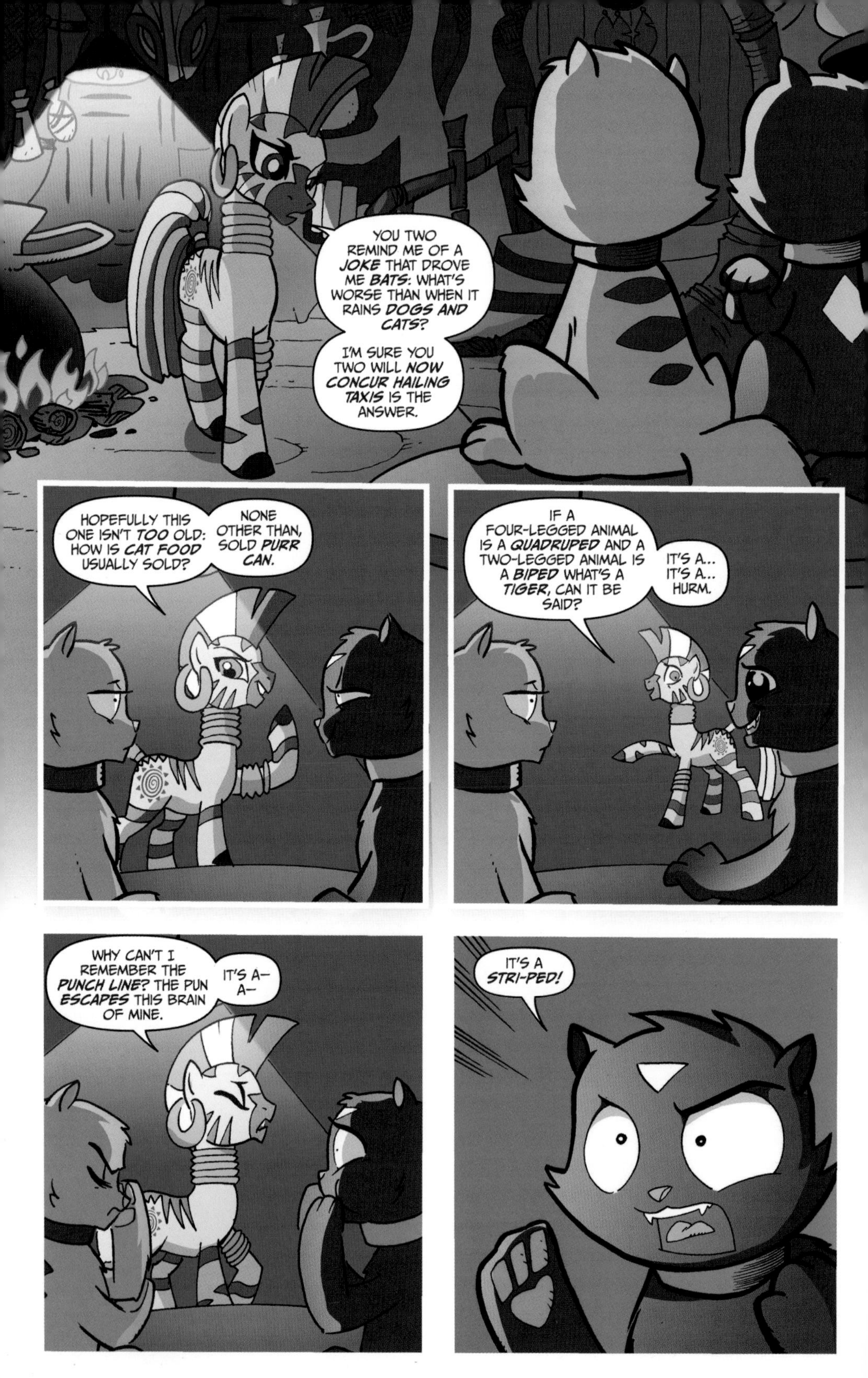

YOU TWO REMIND ME OF A JOKE THAT DROVE ME BATS: WHAT'S WORSE THAN WHEN IT RAINS DOGS AND CATS?
I'M SURE YOU TWO WILL NOW CONCUR HAILING TAXIS IS THE ANSWER.
HOPEFULLY THIS ONE ISN'T TOO OLD: HOW IS CAT FOOD USUALLY SOLD?
NONE OTHER THAN, SOLD PURR CAN.
IF A FOUR-LEGGED ANIMAL IS A QUADRUPED AND A TWO-LEGGED ANIMAL IS A BIPED WHAT'S A TIGER, CAN IT BE SAID?
IT'S A... IT'S A... HURM.
WHY CAN'T I REMEMBER THE PUNCH LINE? THE PUN ESCAPES THIS BRAIN OF MINE.
IT'S A— A—
IT'S A STRI-PED!

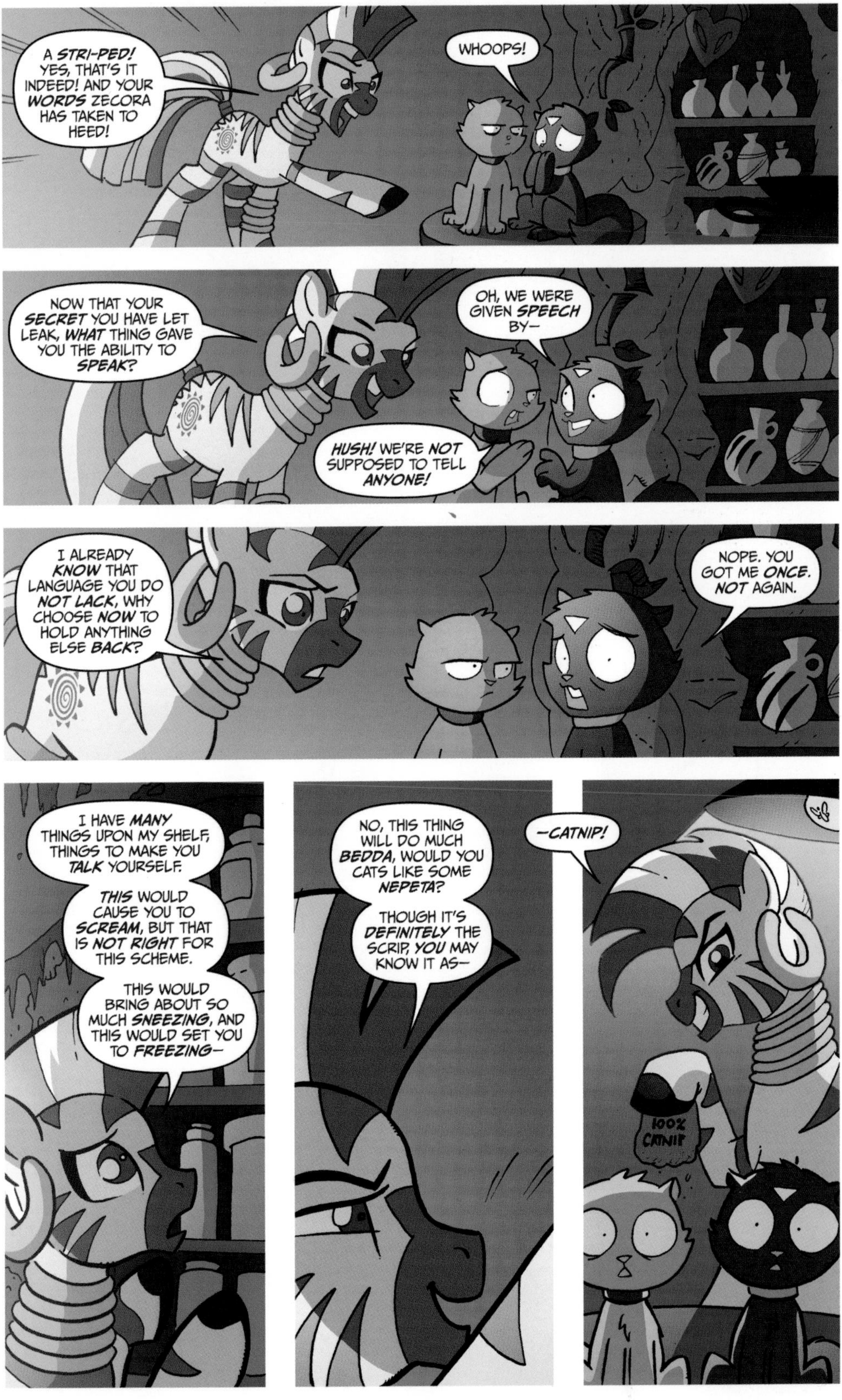
A STRI-PED! YES, THAT'S IT INDEED! AND YOUR WORDS ZECORA HAS TAKEN TO HEED!
WHOOPS!
NOW THAT YOUR SECRET YOU HAVE LET LEAK, WHAT THING GAVE YOU THE ABILITY TO SPEAK?
OH, WE WERE GIVEN SPEECH BY—
HUSH! WE'RE NOT SUPPOSED TO TELL ANYONE!
I ALREADY KNOW THAT LANGUAGE YOU DO NOT LACK, WHY CHOOSE NOW TO HOLD ANYTHING ELSE BACK?
NOPE. YOU GOT ME ONCE. NOT AGAIN.
I HAVE MANY THINGS UPON MY SHELF, THINGS TO MAKE YOU TALK YOURSELF.
THIS WOULD CAUSE YOU TO SCREAM, BUT THAT IS NOT RIGHT FOR THIS SCHEME.
THIS WOULD BRING ABOUT SO MUCH SNEEZING, AND THIS WOULD SET YOU TO FREEZING—
NO, THIS THING WILL DO MUCH BEDDA, WOULD YOU CATS LIKE SOME NEPETA?
THOUGH IT'S DEFINITELY THE SCRIP, YOU MAY KNOW IT AS—
—CATNIP!
100% CATNIP

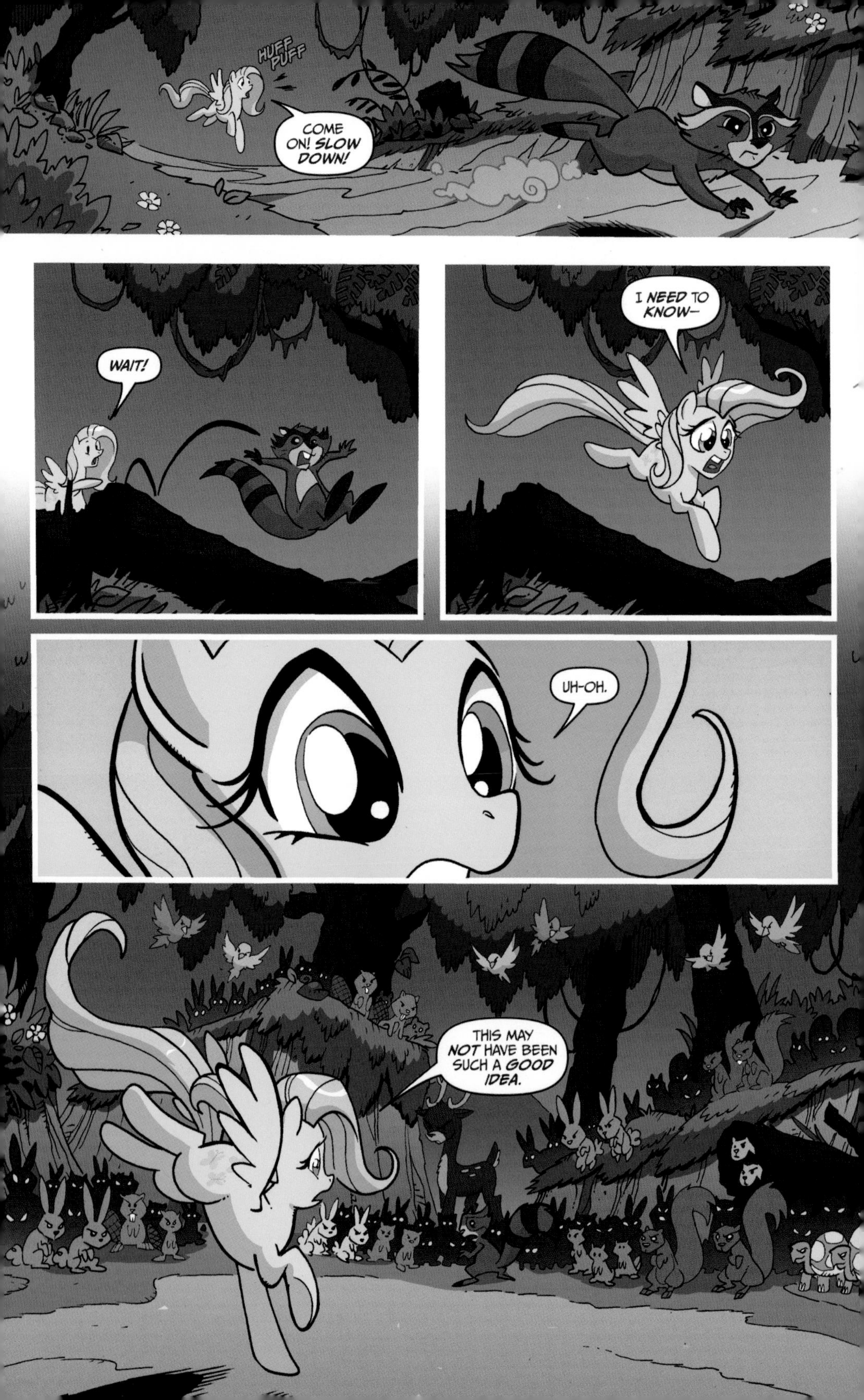
HUFF PUFF
COME ON! SLOW DOWN!
WAIT!
I NEED TO KNOW—
UH-OH.
THIS MAY NOT HAVE BEEN SUCH A GOOD IDEA.

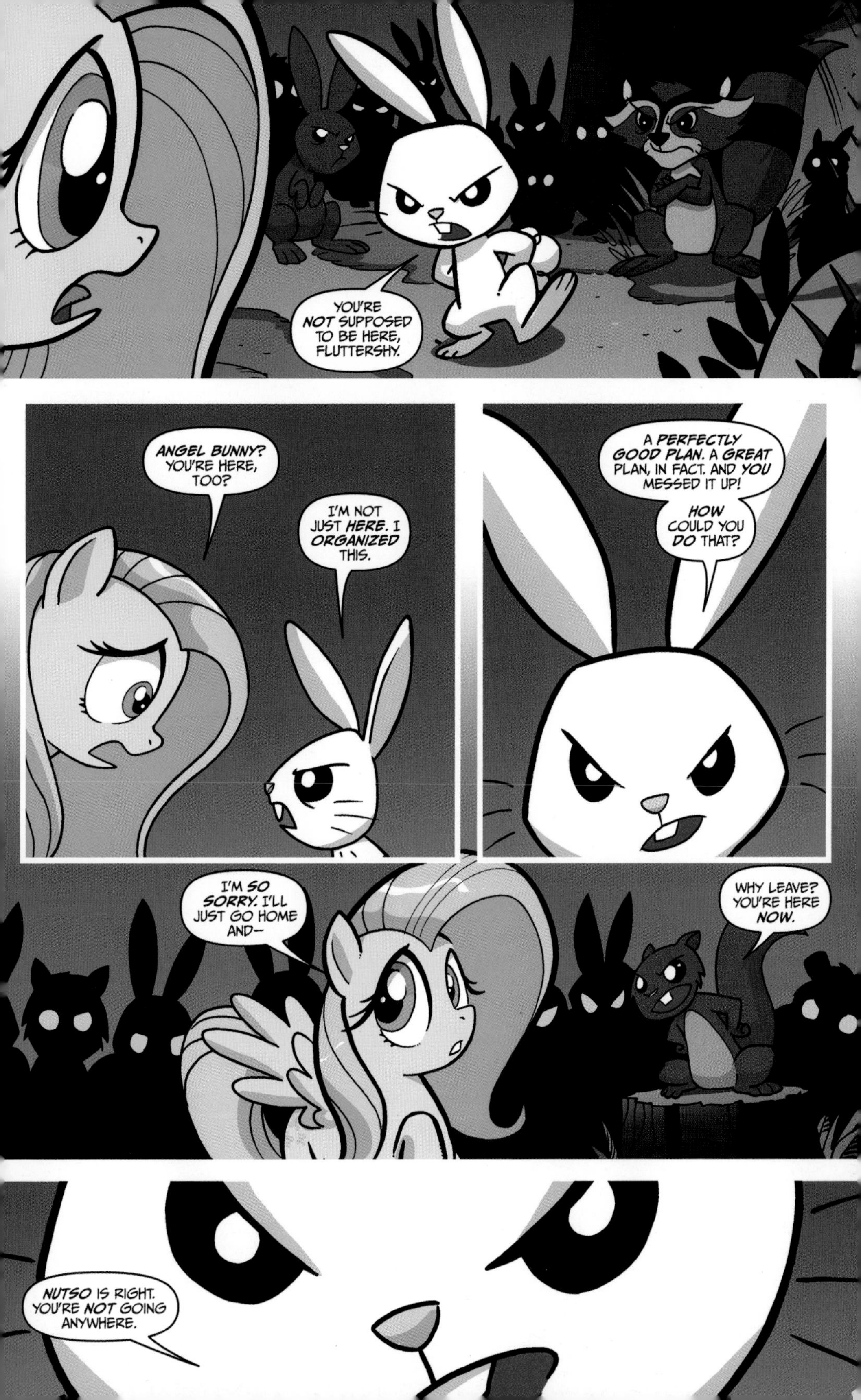
YOU'RE NOT SUPPOSED TO BE HERE, FLUTTERSHY.
ANGEL BUNNY? YOU'RE HERE, TOO?
I'M NOT JUST HERE. I ORGANIZED THIS.
A PERFECTLY GOOD PLAN. A GREAT PLAN, IN FACT. AND YOU MESSED IT UP!
HOW COULD YOU DO THAT?
I'M SO SORRY. I'LL JUST GO HOME AND—
WHY LEAVE? YOU'RE HERE NOW.
NUTSO IS RIGHT. YOU'RE NOT GOING ANYWHERE.

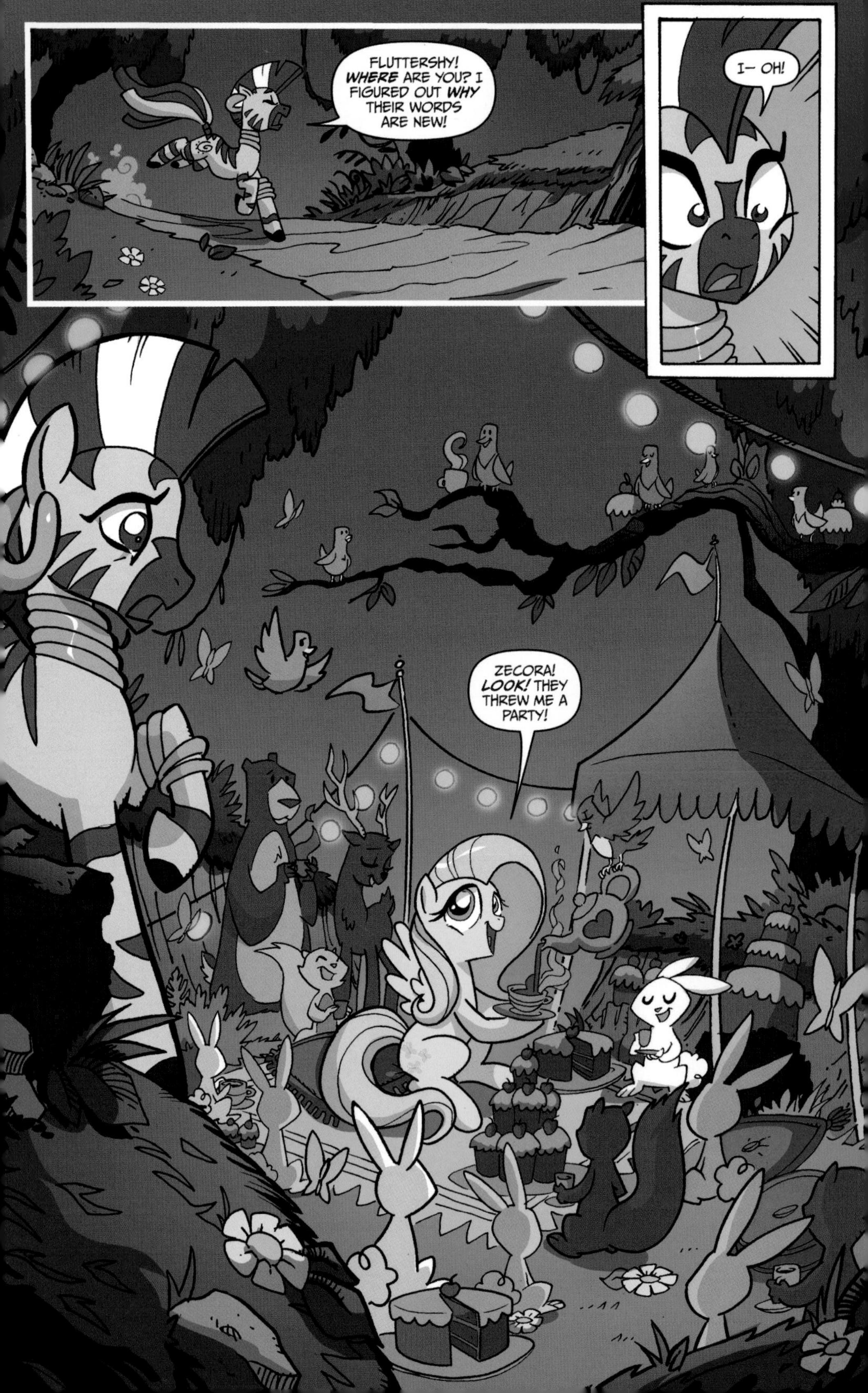
FLUTTERSHY! WHERE ARE YOU? I FIGURED OUT WHY THEIR WORDS ARE NEW!
I— OH!
ZECORA! LOOK! THEY THREW ME A PARTY!

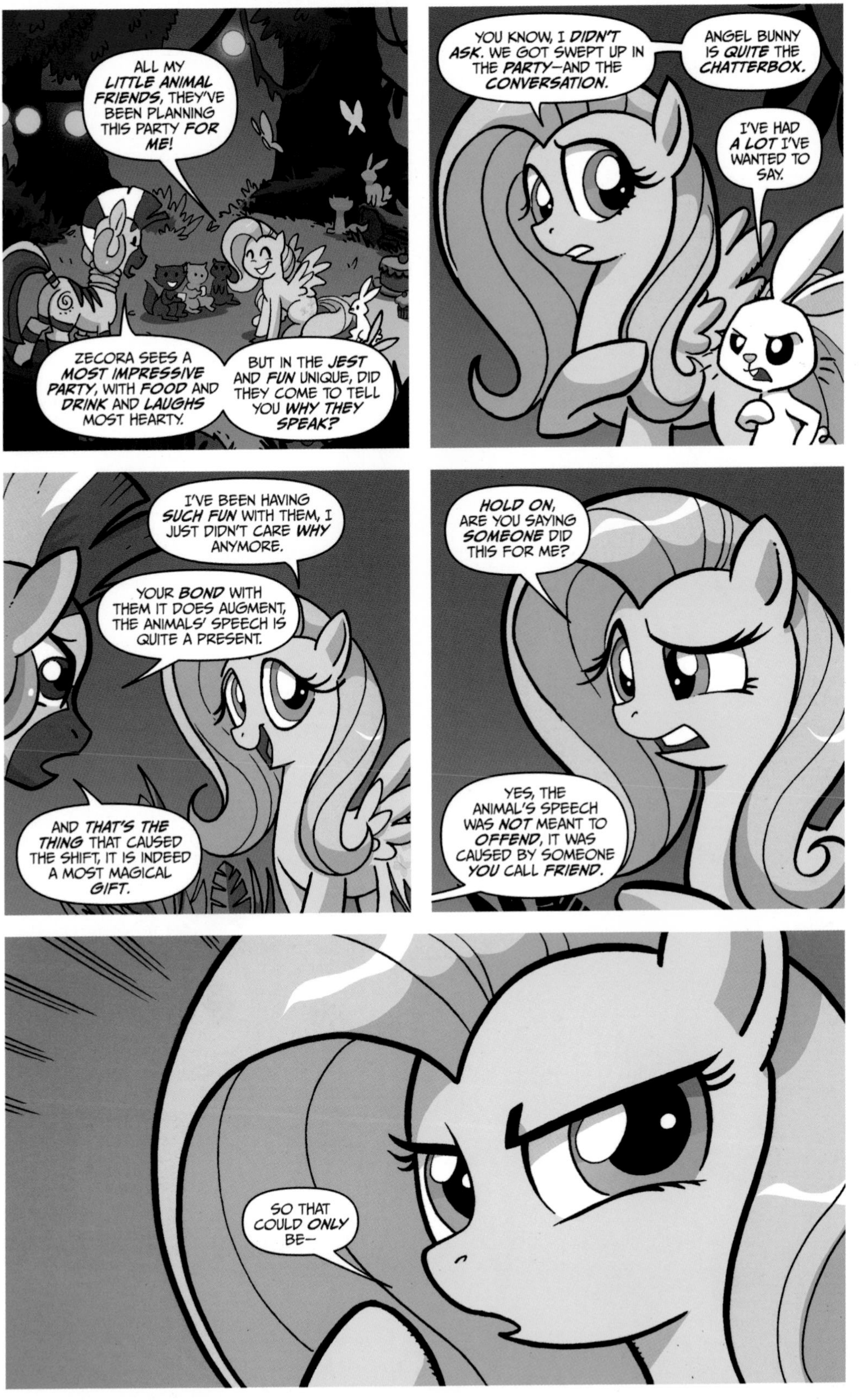

ALL MY LITTLE ANIMAL FRIENDS, THEY'VE BEEN PLANNING THIS PARTY FOR ME!
ZECORA SEES A MOST IMPRESSIVE PARTY, WITH FOOD AND DRINK AND LAUGHS MOST HEARTY.
BUT IN THE JEST AND FUN UNIQUE, DID THEY COME TO TELL YOU WHY THEY SPEAK?
YOU KNOW, I DIDN'T ASK. WE GOT SWEPT UP IN THE PARTY—AND THE CONVERSATION.
ANGEL BUNNY IS QUITE THE CHATTERBOX.
I'VE HAD A LOT I'VE WANTED TO SAY.
I'VE BEEN HAVING SUCH FUN WITH THEM, I JUST DIDN'T CARE WHY ANYMORE.
YOUR BOND WITH THEM IT DOES AUGMENT, THE ANIMALS' SPEECH IS QUITE A PRESENT.
AND THAT'S THE THING THAT CAUSED THE SHIFT, IT IS INDEED A MOST MAGICAL GIFT.
HOLD ON, ARE YOU SAYING SOMEONE DID THIS FOR ME?
YES, THE ANIMAL'S SPEECH WAS NOT MEANT TO OFFEND, IT WAS CAUSED BY SOMEONE YOU CALL FRIEND.
SO THAT COULD ONLY BE—

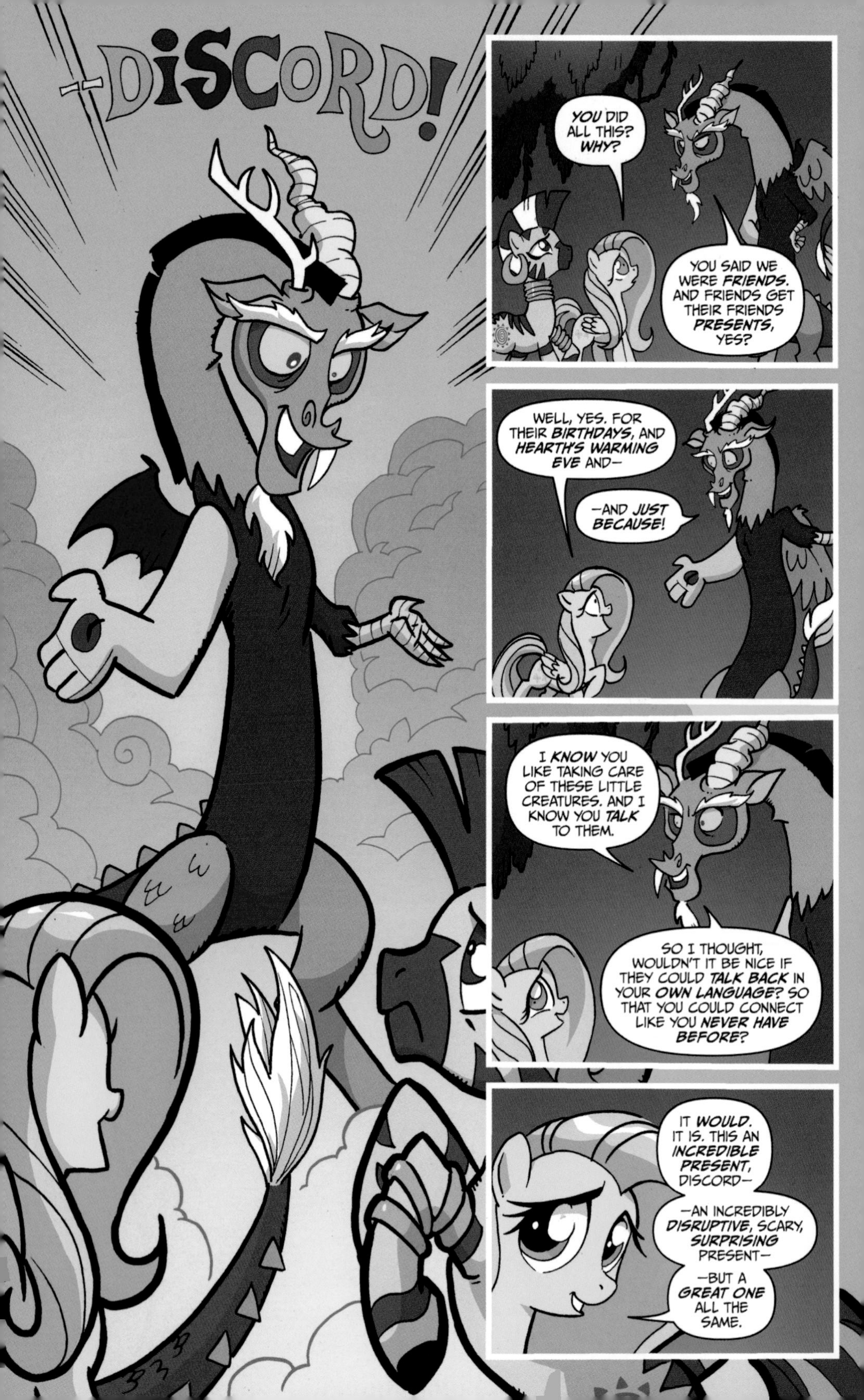
DISCORD!
YOU DID ALL THIS? WHY?
YOU SAID WE WERE FRIENDS. AND FRIENDS GET THEIR FRIENDS PRESENTS, YES?
WELL, YES. FOR THEIR BIRTHDAYS, AND HEARTH'S WARMING EVE AND—
—AND JUST BECAUSE!
I KNOW YOU LIKE TAKING CARE OF THESE LITTLE CREATURES. AND I KNOW YOU TALK TO THEM.
SO I THOUGHT, WOULDN'T IT BE NICE IF THEY COULD TALK BACK IN YOUR OWN LANGUAGE? SO THAT YOU COULD CONNECT LIKE YOU NEVER HAVE BEFORE?
IT WOULD. IT IS. THIS AN INCREDIBLE PRESENT, DISCORD—
—AN INCREDIBLY DISRUPTIVE, SCARY, SURPRISING PRESENT—
—BUT A GREAT ONE ALL THE SAME.

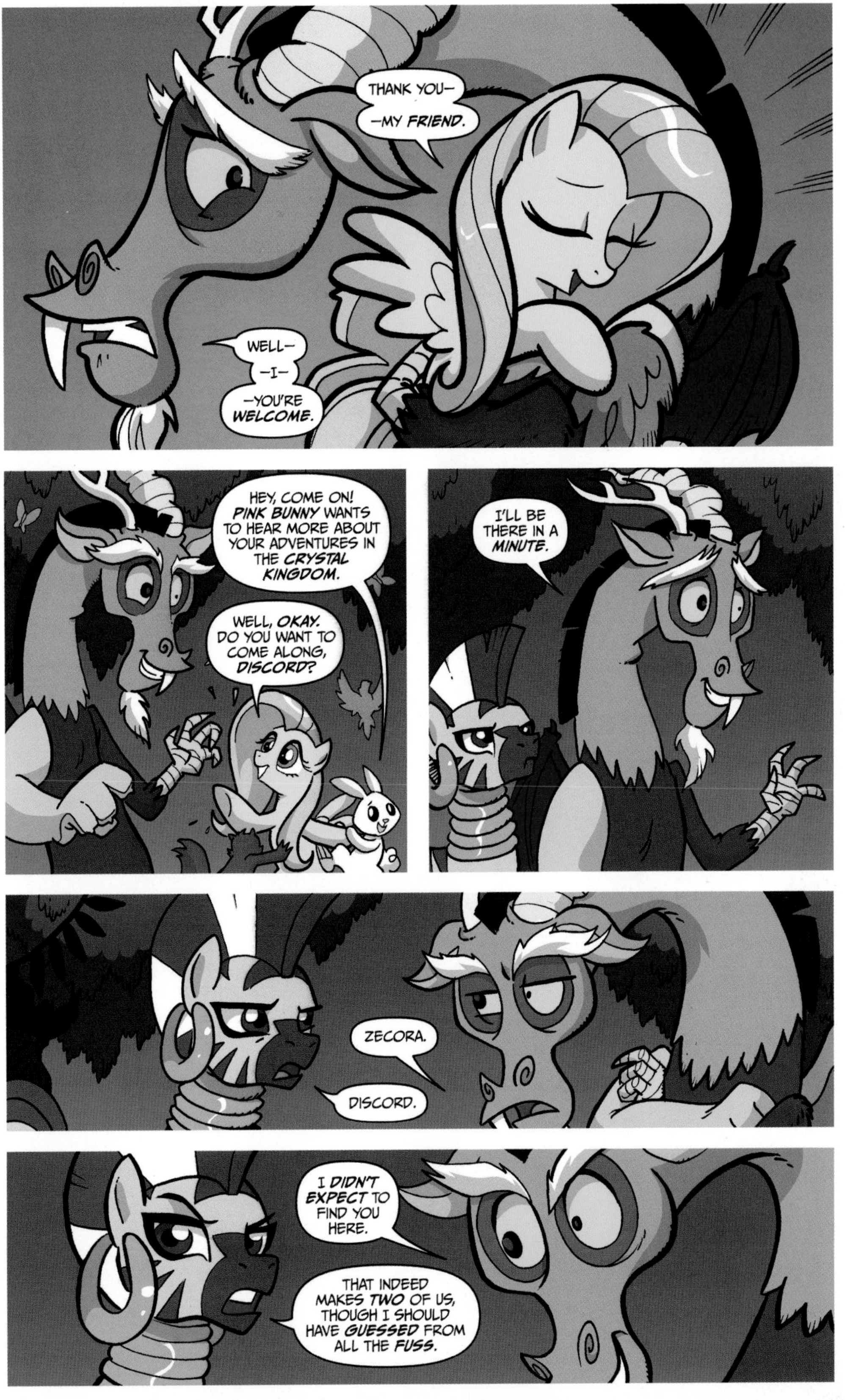
THANK YOU—
—MY *FRIEND*.
WELL—
—I—
—YOU'RE *WELCOME*.
HEY, COME ON! *PINK BUNNY* WANTS TO HEAR MORE ABOUT YOUR ADVENTURES IN THE *CRYSTAL KINGDOM*.
WELL, *OKAY*. DO YOU WANT TO COME ALONG, *DISCORD*?
I'LL BE THERE IN A *MINUTE*.
ZECORA.
DISCORD.
I *DIDN'T EXPECT* TO FIND YOU HERE.
THAT INDEED MAKES *TWO* OF US, THOUGH I SHOULD HAVE *GUESSED* FROM ALL THE *FUSS*.

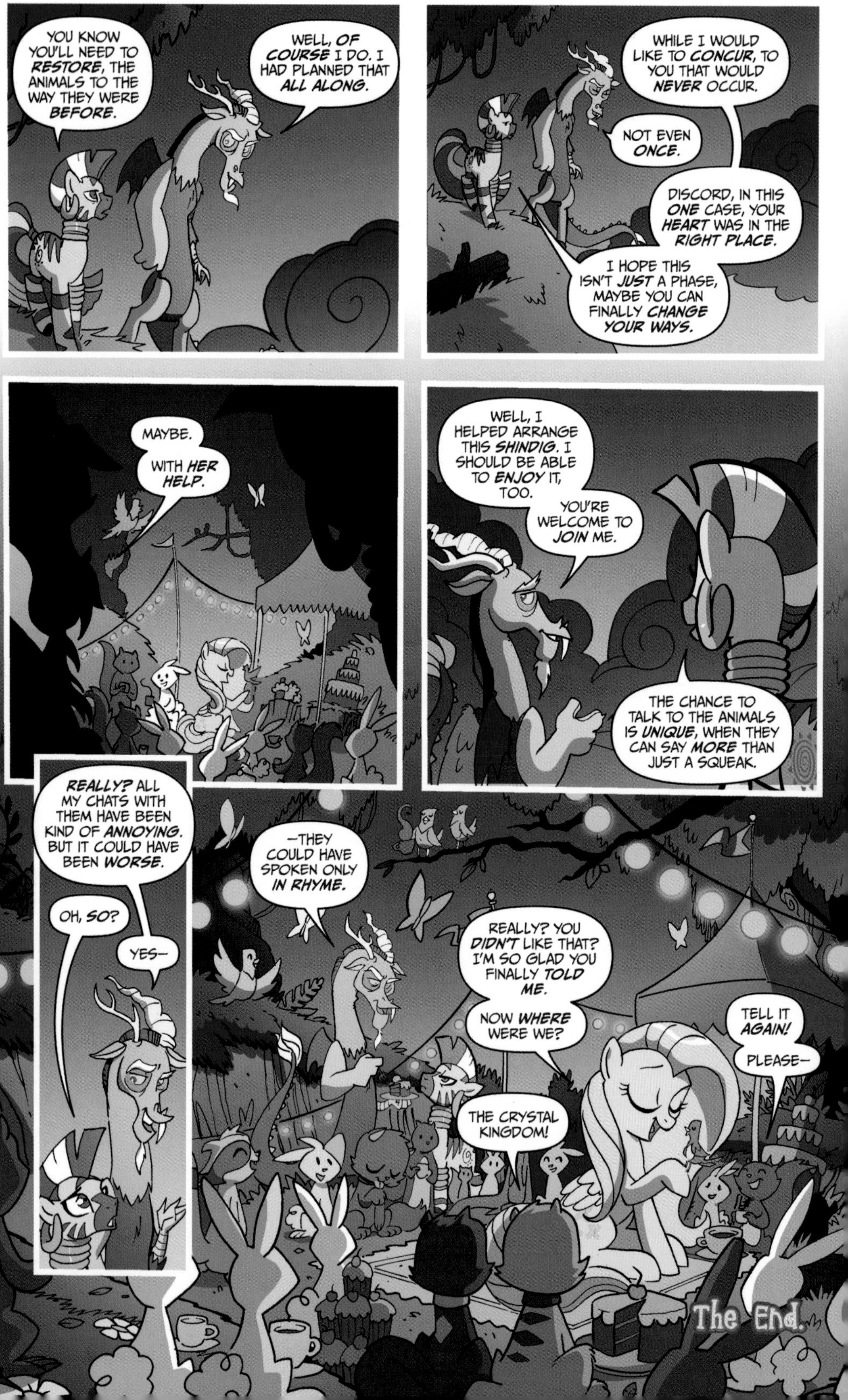

YOU KNOW YOU'LL NEED TO RESTORE, THE ANIMALS TO THE WAY THEY WERE BEFORE.
WELL, OF COURSE I DO. I HAD PLANNED THAT ALL ALONG.
WHILE I WOULD LIKE TO CONCUR, TO YOU THAT WOULD NEVER OCCUR.
NOT EVEN ONCE.
DISCORD, IN THIS ONE CASE, YOUR HEART WAS IN THE RIGHT PLACE.
I HOPE THIS ISN'T JUST A PHASE, MAYBE YOU CAN FINALLY CHANGE YOUR WAYS.
MAYBE.
WITH HER HELP.
WELL, I HELPED ARRANGE THIS SHINDIG. I SHOULD BE ABLE TO ENJOY IT, TOO.
YOU'RE WELCOME TO JOIN ME.
THE CHANCE TO TALK TO THE ANIMALS IS UNIQUE, WHEN THEY CAN SAY MORE THAN JUST A SQUEAK.
REALLY? ALL MY CHATS WITH THEM HAVE BEEN KIND OF ANNOYING. BUT IT COULD HAVE BEEN WORSE.
OH, SO?
YES—
—THEY COULD HAVE SPOKEN ONLY IN RHYME.
REALLY? YOU DIDN'T LIKE THAT? I'M SO GLAD YOU FINALLY TOLD ME.
NOW WHERE WERE WE?
THE CRYSTAL KINGDOM!
TELL IT AGAIN!
PLEASE—
The End.

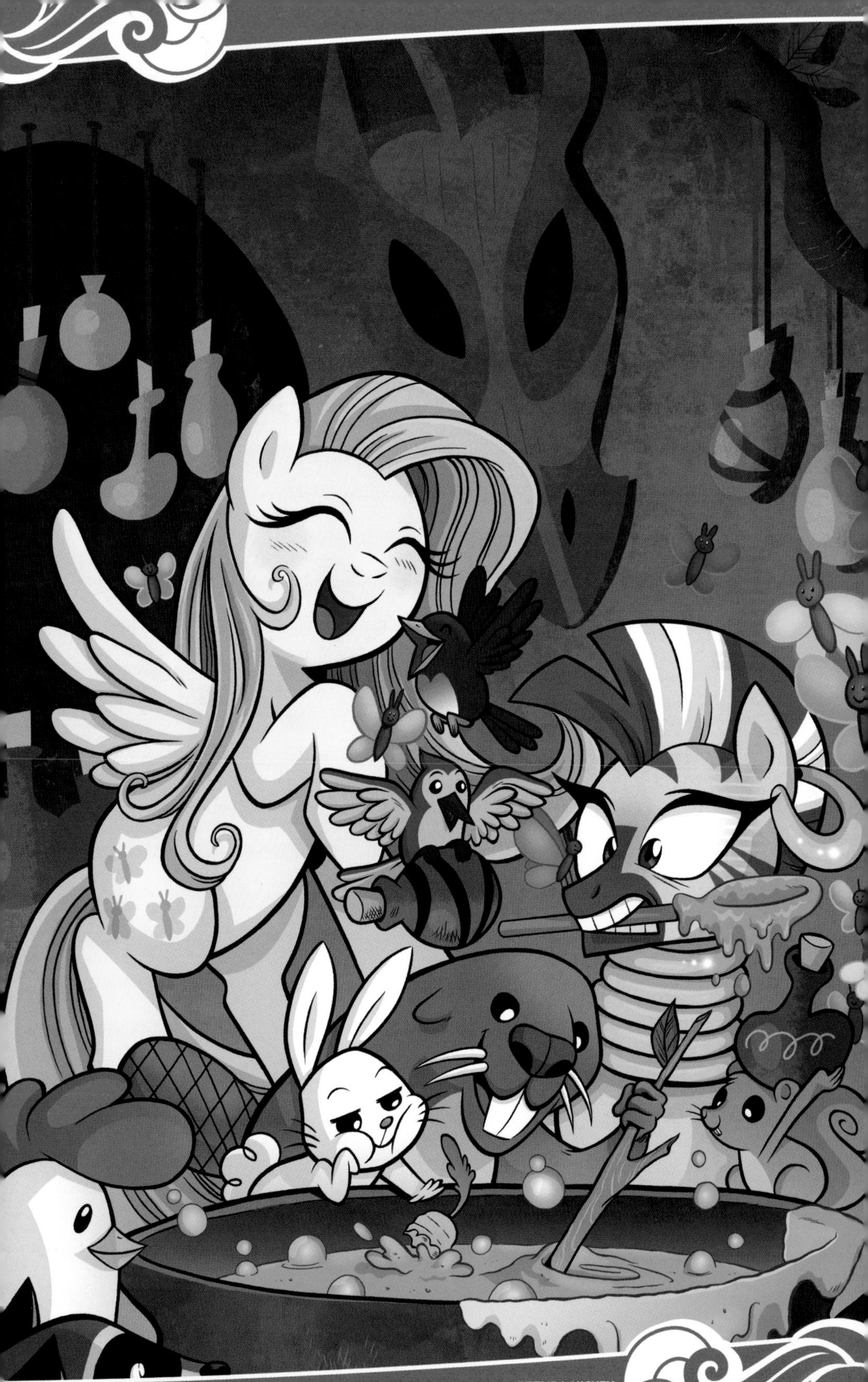

art by BRENDA HICKEY

Rainbow Dash & Trixie

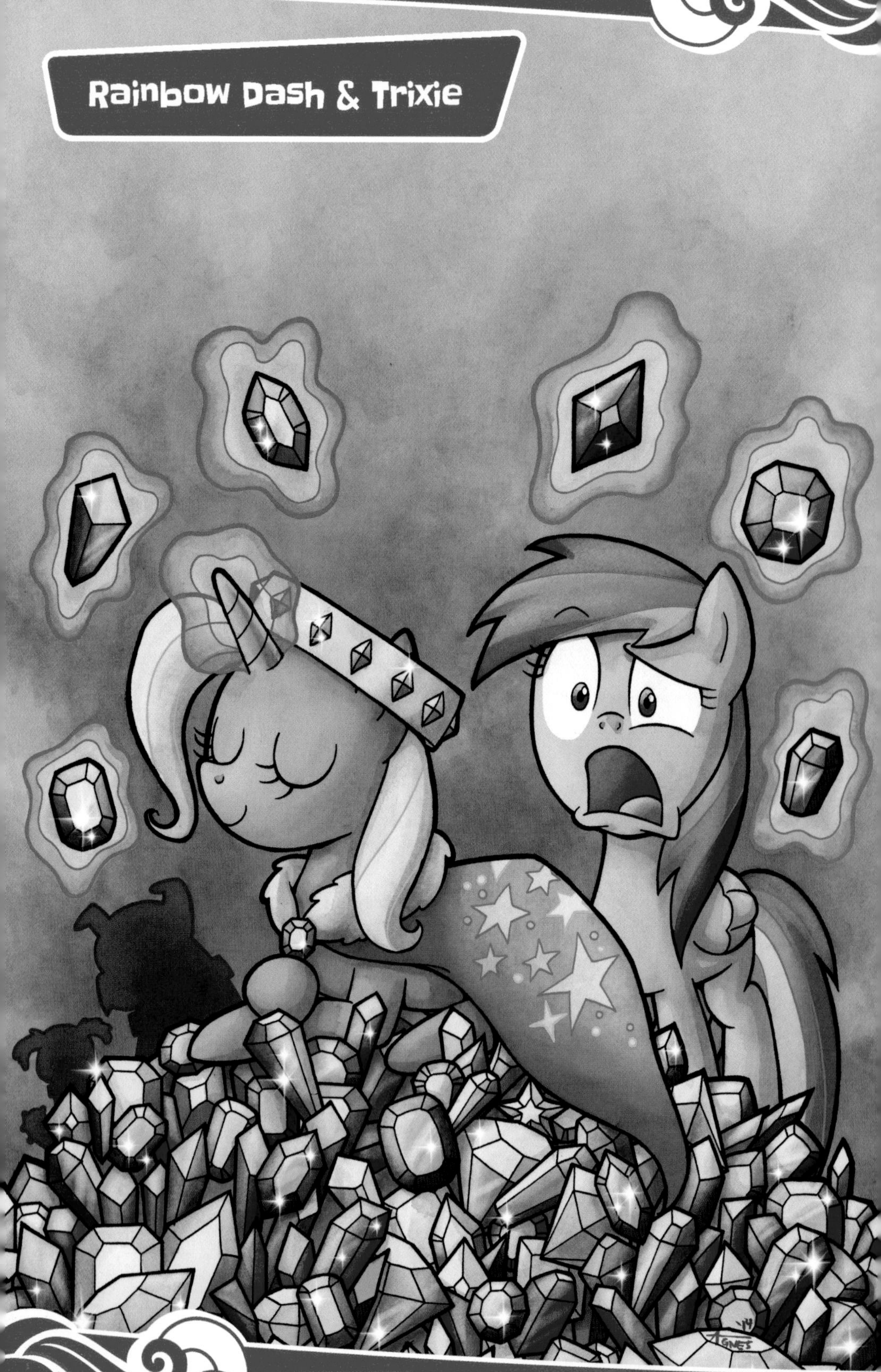

art by AGNES GARBOWSKA

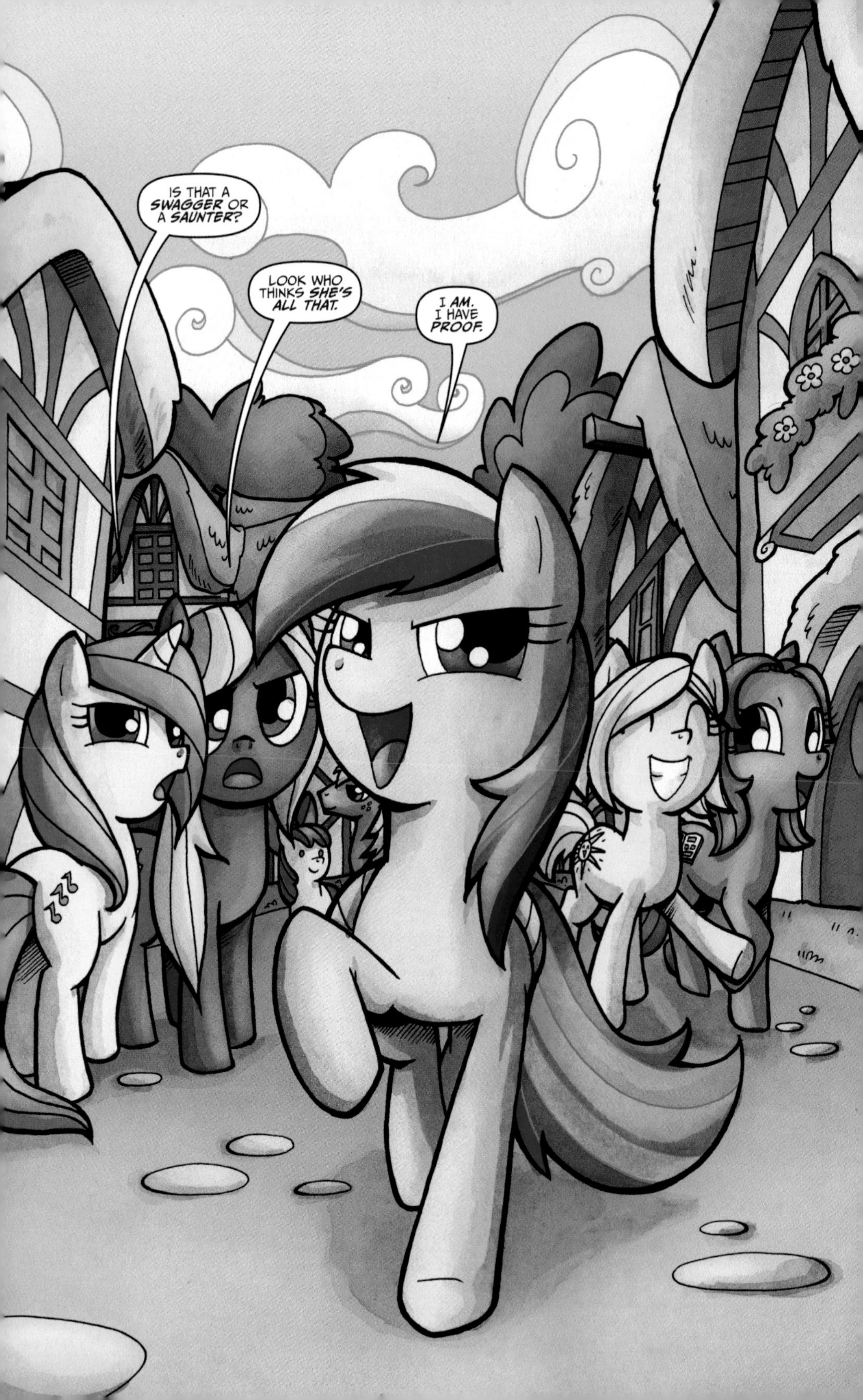
IS THAT A SWAGGER OR A SAUNTER?
LOOK WHO THINKS SHE'S ALL THAT.
I AM. I HAVE PROOF.

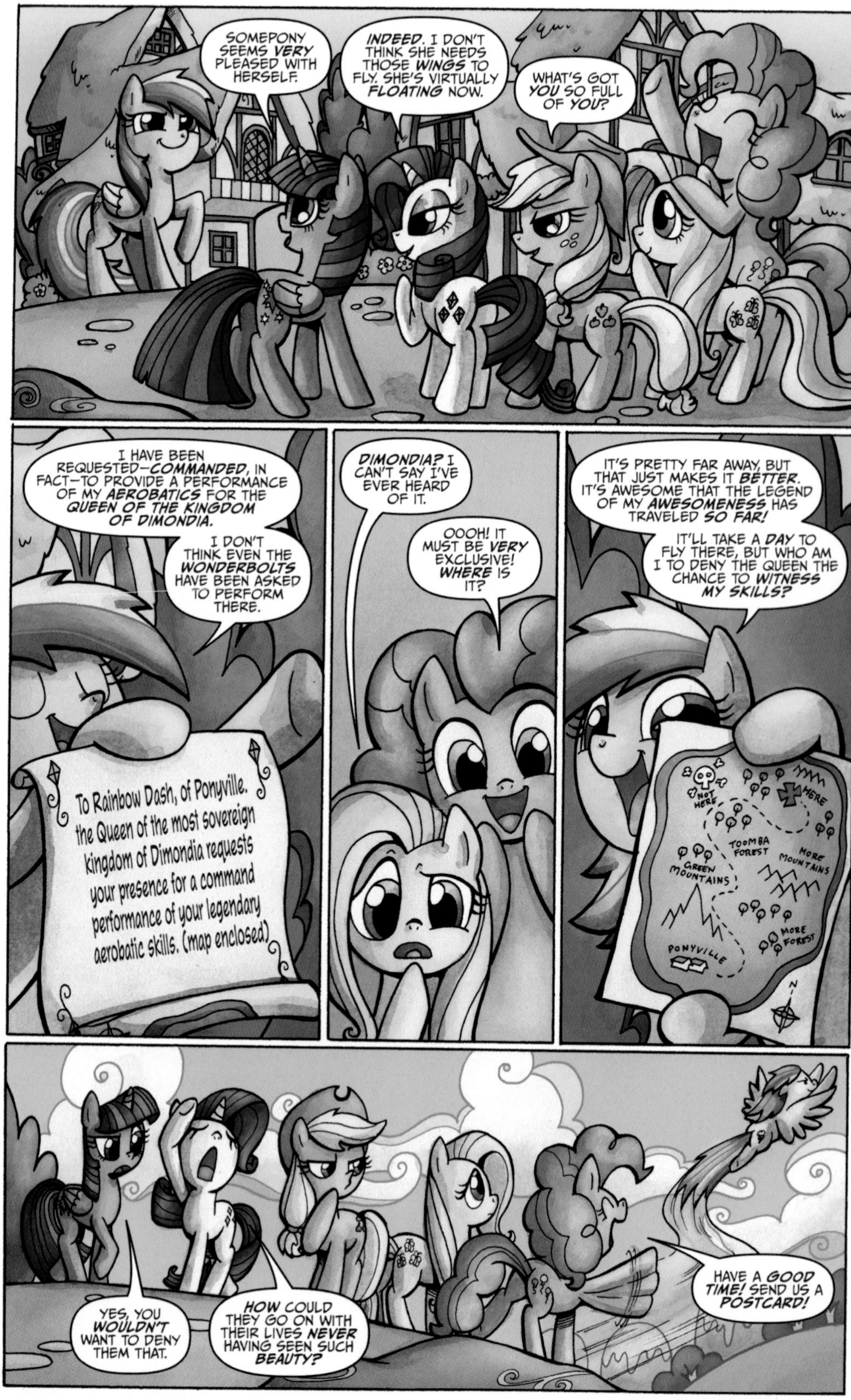
SOMEPONY SEEMS VERY PLEASED WITH HERSELF.
INDEED. I DON'T THINK SHE NEEDS THOSE WINGS TO FLY. SHE'S VIRTUALLY FLOATING NOW.
WHAT'S GOT YOU SO FULL OF YOU?
I HAVE BEEN REQUESTED—COMMANDED, IN FACT—TO PROVIDE A PERFORMANCE OF MY AEROBATICS FOR THE QUEEN OF THE KINGDOM OF DIMONDIA.
I DON'T THINK EVEN THE WONDERBOLTS HAVE BEEN ASKED TO PERFORM THERE.
To Rainbow Dash, of Ponyville. the Queen of the most sovereign kingdom of Dimondia requests your presence for a command performance of your legendary aerobatic skills. (map enclosed)
DIMONDIA? I CAN'T SAY I'VE EVER HEARD OF IT.
OOOH! IT MUST BE VERY EXCLUSIVE! WHERE IS IT?
IT'S PRETTY FAR AWAY, BUT THAT JUST MAKES IT BETTER. IT'S AWESOME THAT THE LEGEND OF MY AWESOMENESS HAS TRAVELED SO FAR!
IT'LL TAKE A DAY TO FLY THERE, BUT WHO AM I TO DENY THE QUEEN THE CHANCE TO WITNESS MY SKILLS?
NOT HERE
HERE
TOOMBA FOREST
MORE MOUNTAINS
GREEN MOUNTAINS
MORE FOREST
PONYVILLE
N
YES, YOU WOULDN'T WANT TO DENY THEM THAT.
HOW COULD THEY GO ON WITH THEIR LIVES NEVER HAVING SEEN SUCH BEAUTY?
HAVE A GOOD TIME! SEND US A POSTCARD!

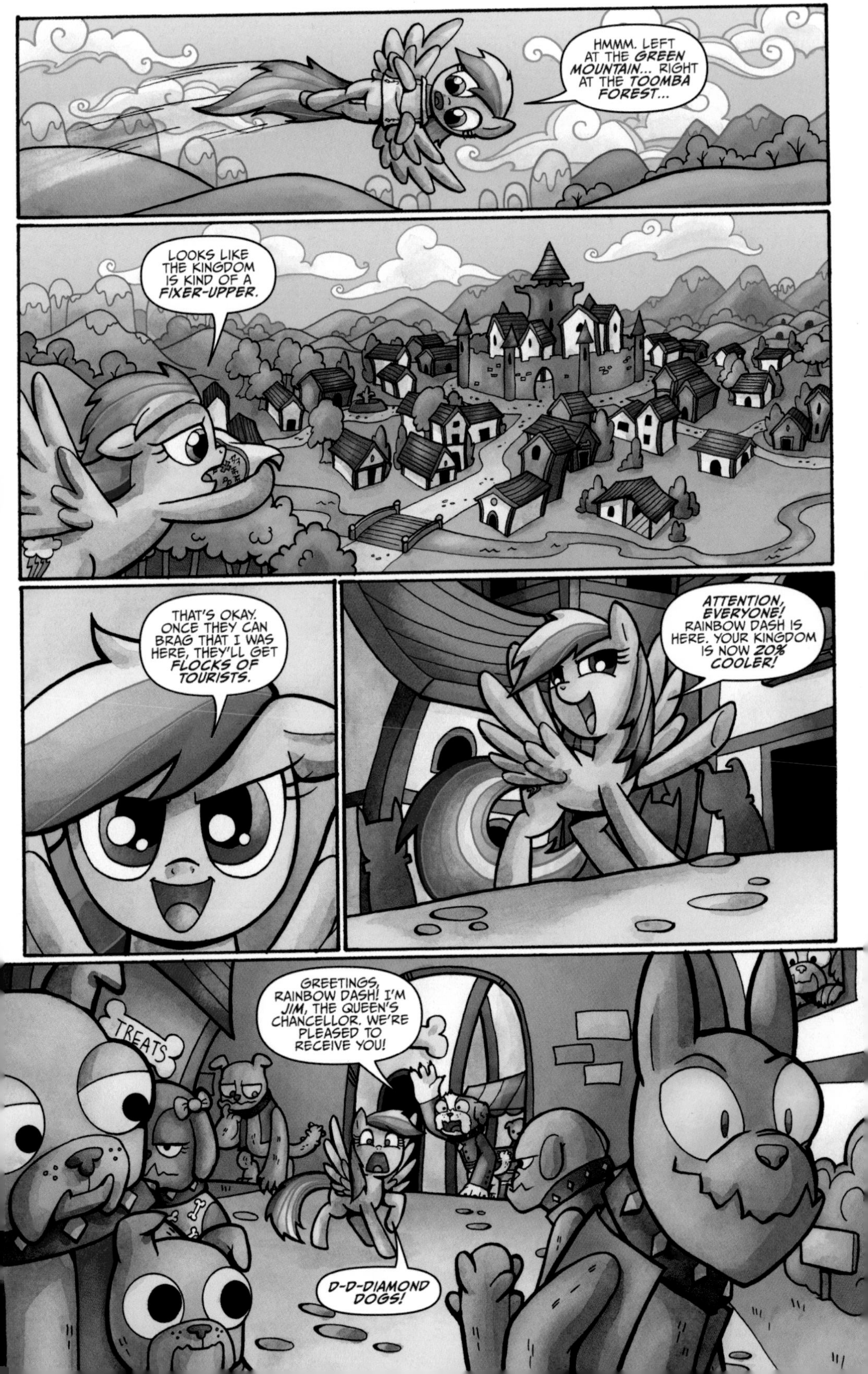

HMMM. LEFT AT THE GREEN MOUNTAIN... RIGHT AT THE TOOMBA FOREST...
LOOKS LIKE THE KINGDOM IS KIND OF A FIXER-UPPER.
THAT'S OKAY. ONCE THEY CAN BRAG THAT I WAS HERE, THEY'LL GET FLOCKS OF TOURISTS.
ATTENTION, EVERYONE! RAINBOW DASH IS HERE. YOUR KINGDOM IS NOW 20% COOLER!
TREATS
GREETINGS, RAINBOW DASH! I'M JIM, THE QUEEN'S CHANCELLOR. WE'RE PLEASED TO RECEIVE YOU!
D-D-DIAMOND DOGS!

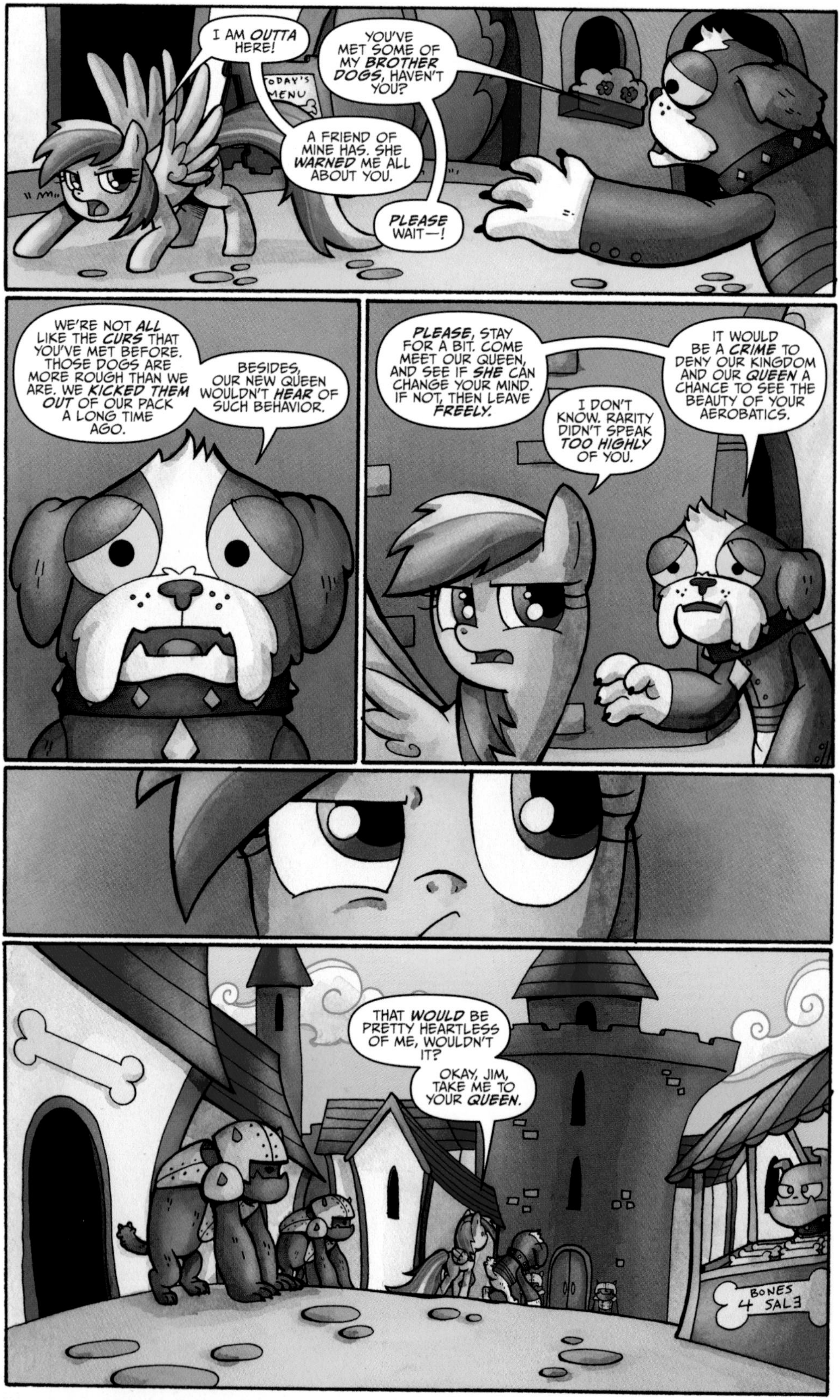
I AM OUTTA HERE!
YOU'VE MET SOME OF MY BROTHER DOGS, HAVEN'T YOU?
TODAY'S MENU
A FRIEND OF MINE HAS. SHE WARNED ME ALL ABOUT YOU.
PLEASE WAIT—!
WE'RE NOT ALL LIKE THE CURS THAT YOU'VE MET BEFORE. THOSE DOGS ARE MORE ROUGH THAN WE ARE. WE KICKED THEM OUT OF OUR PACK A LONG TIME AGO.
BESIDES, OUR NEW QUEEN WOULDN'T HEAR OF SUCH BEHAVIOR.
PLEASE, STAY FOR A BIT. COME MEET OUR QUEEN, AND SEE IF SHE CAN CHANGE YOUR MIND. IF NOT, THEN LEAVE FREELY.
IT WOULD BE A CRIME TO DENY OUR KINGDOM AND OUR QUEEN A CHANCE TO SEE THE BEAUTY OF YOUR AEROBATICS.
I DON'T KNOW. RARITY DIDN'T SPEAK TOO HIGHLY OF YOU.
THAT WOULD BE PRETTY HEARTLESS OF ME, WOULDN'T IT?
OKAY, JIM, TAKE ME TO YOUR QUEEN.
BONES 4 SAL3

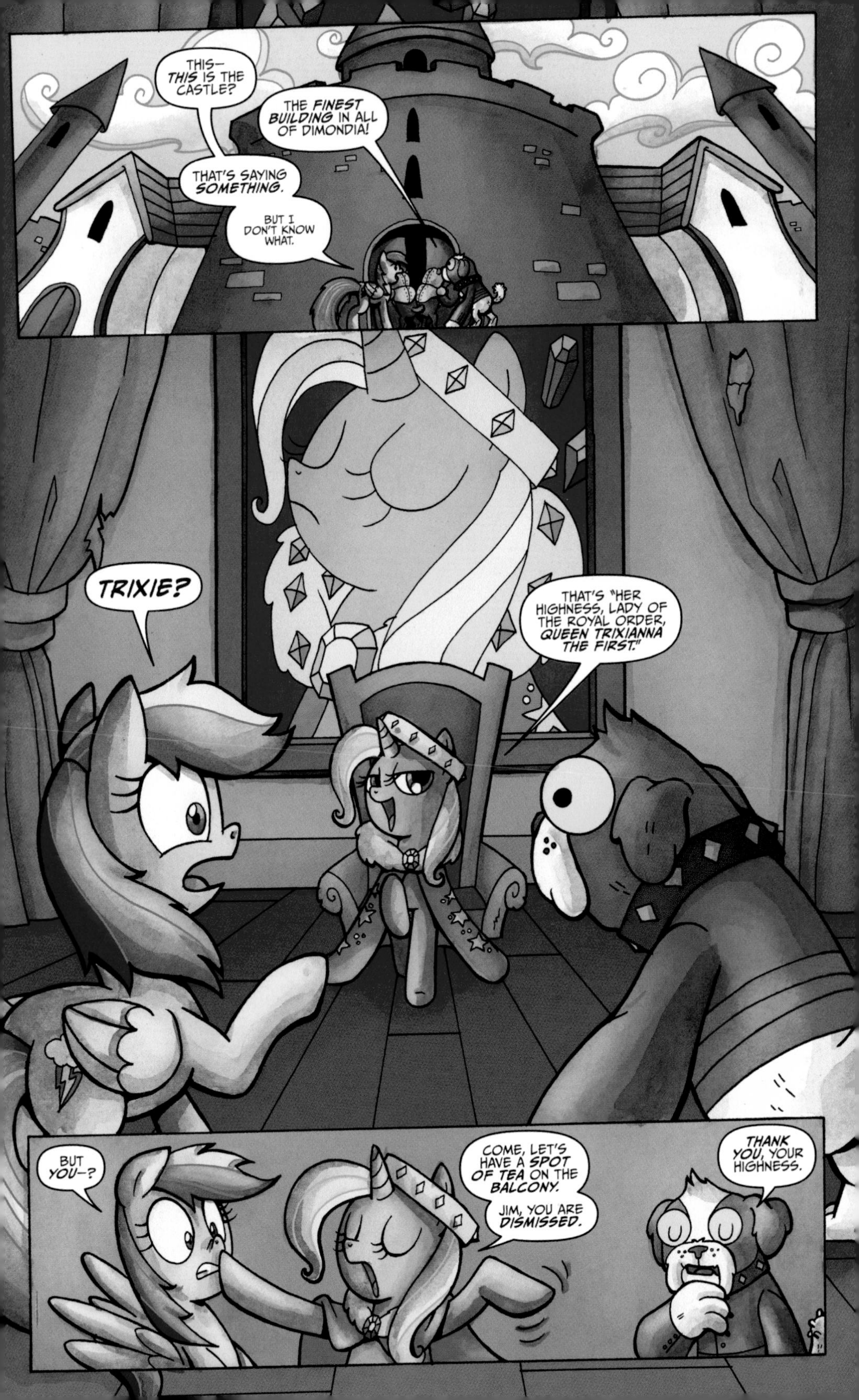
THIS— THIS IS THE CASTLE?
THE FINEST BUILDING IN ALL OF DIMONDIA!
THAT'S SAYING SOMETHING.
BUT I DON'T KNOW WHAT.
TRIXIE?
THAT'S "HER HIGHNESS, LADY OF THE ROYAL ORDER, QUEEN TRIXIANNA THE FIRST."
BUT YOU—?
COME, LET'S HAVE A SPOT OF TEA ON THE BALCONY.
JIM, YOU ARE DISMISSED.
THANK YOU, YOUR HIGHNESS.

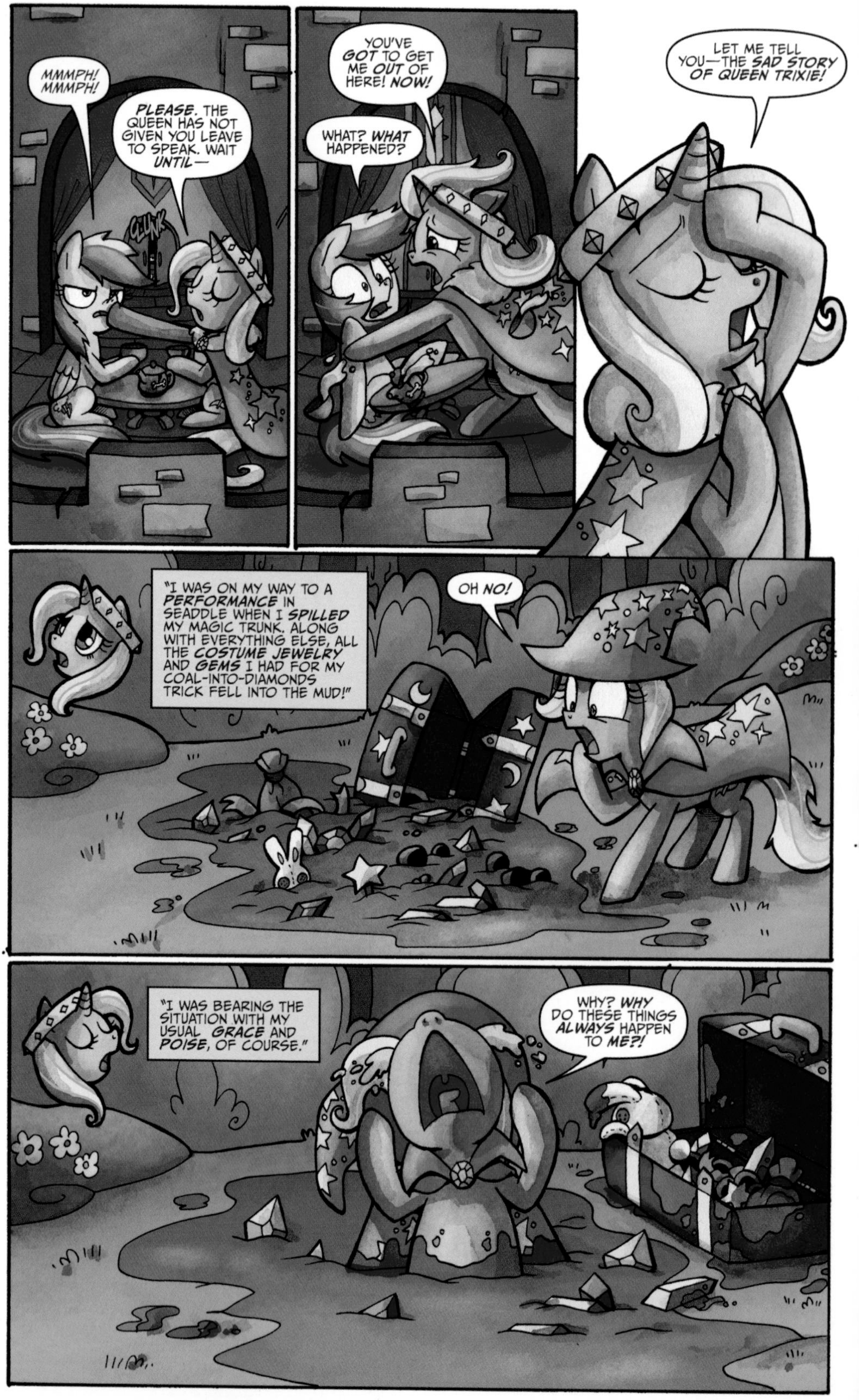
MMMPH! MMMPH!
PLEASE. THE QUEEN HAS NOT GIVEN YOU LEAVE TO SPEAK. WAIT UNTIL—
CLUNK
YOU'VE GOT TO GET ME OUT OF HERE! NOW!
WHAT? WHAT HAPPENED?
LET ME TELL YOU—THE SAD STORY OF QUEEN TRIXIE!
"I WAS ON MY WAY TO A PERFORMANCE IN SEADDLE WHEN I SPILLED MY MAGIC TRUNK. ALONG WITH EVERYTHING ELSE, ALL THE COSTUME JEWELRY AND GEMS I HAD FOR MY COAL-INTO-DIAMONDS TRICK FELL INTO THE MUD!"
OH NO!
"I WAS BEARING THE SITUATION WITH MY USUAL GRACE AND POISE, OF COURSE."
WHY? WHY DO THESE THINGS ALWAYS HAPPEN TO ME?!

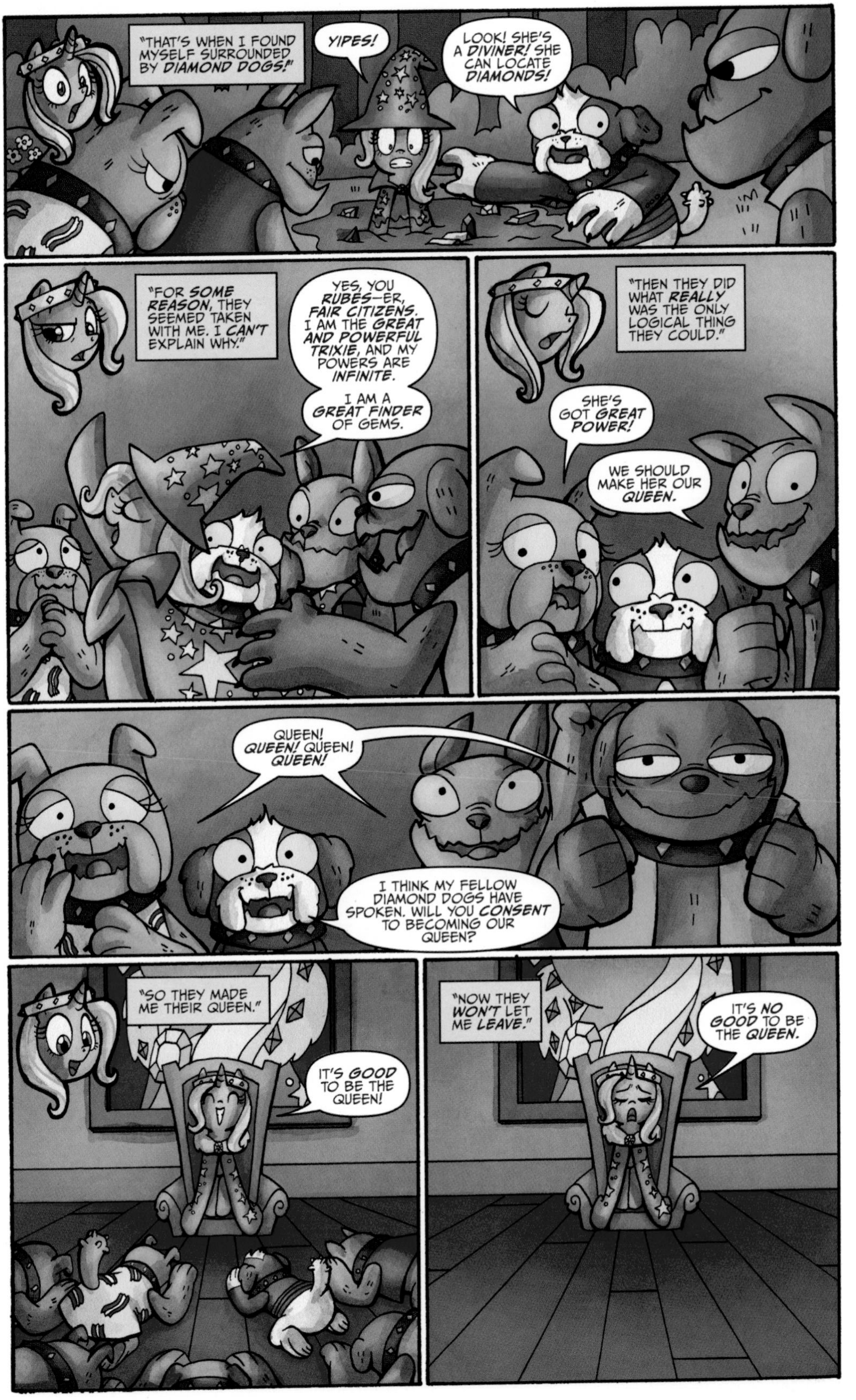
"THAT'S WHEN I FOUND MYSELF SURROUNDED BY *DIAMOND DOGS!*"
YIPES!
LOOK! SHE'S A *DIVINER!* SHE CAN LOCATE *DIAMONDS!*
"FOR *SOME REASON*, THEY SEEMED TAKEN WITH ME. I *CAN'T* EXPLAIN WHY."
YES, YOU *RUBES*—ER, *FAIR CITIZENS*. I AM THE *GREAT AND POWERFUL TRIXIE*, AND MY POWERS ARE *INFINITE*.
I AM A *GREAT FINDER* OF GEMS.
"THEN THEY DID WHAT *REALLY* WAS THE ONLY LOGICAL THING THEY COULD."
SHE'S GOT *GREAT POWER!*
WE SHOULD MAKE HER OUR *QUEEN*.
QUEEN! *QUEEN!* QUEEN! *QUEEN!*
I THINK MY FELLOW DIAMOND DOGS HAVE SPOKEN. WILL YOU *CONSENT* TO BECOMING OUR QUEEN?
"SO THEY MADE ME THEIR QUEEN."
IT'S *GOOD* TO BE THE QUEEN!
"NOW THEY *WON'T* LET ME *LEAVE*."
IT'S *NO GOOD* TO BE THE *QUEEN*.

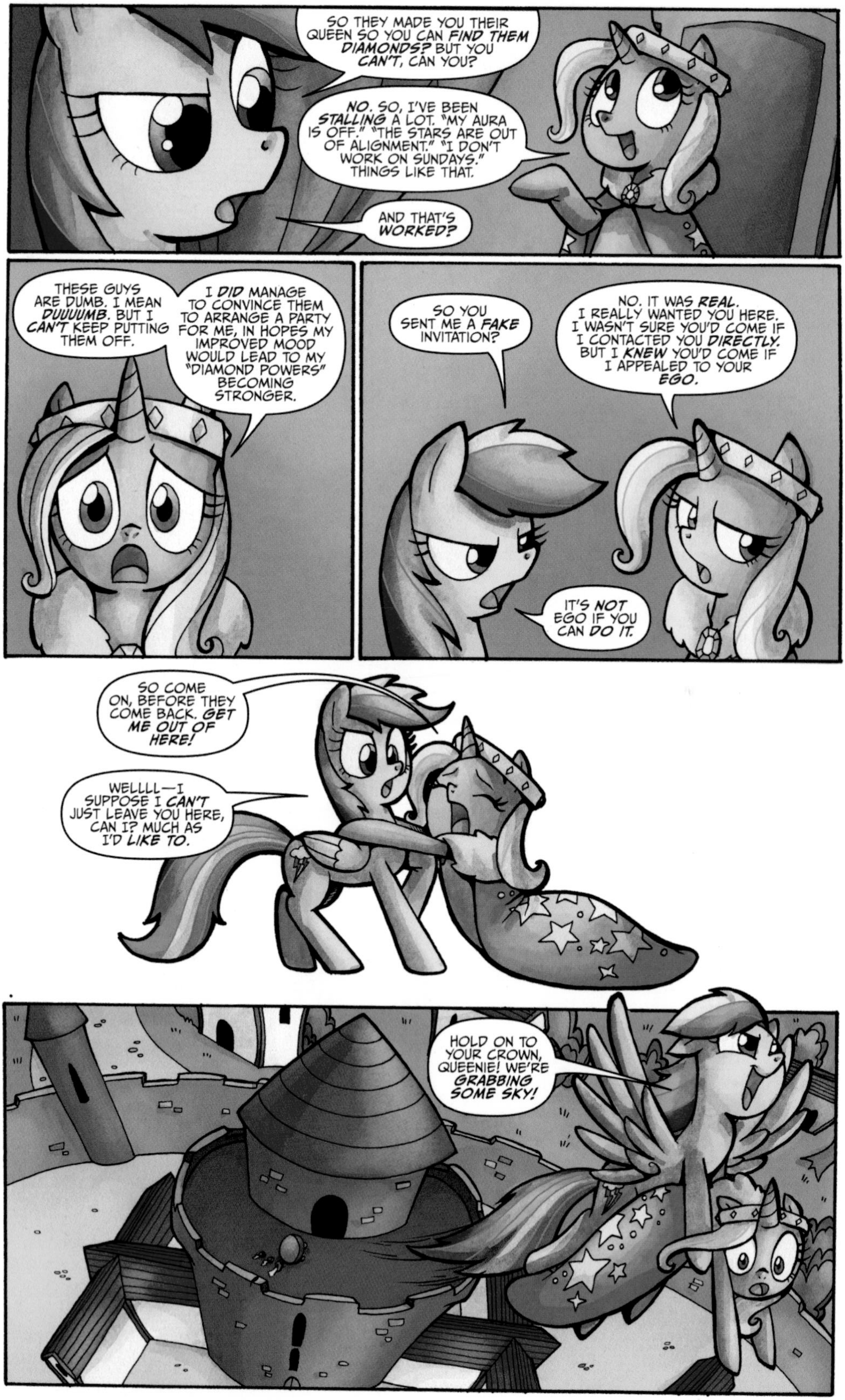
SO THEY MADE YOU THEIR QUEEN SO YOU CAN FIND THEM DIAMONDS? BUT YOU CAN'T, CAN YOU?
NO. SO, I'VE BEEN STALLING A LOT. "MY AURA IS OFF." "THE STARS ARE OUT OF ALIGNMENT." "I DON'T WORK ON SUNDAYS." THINGS LIKE THAT.
AND THAT'S WORKED?
THESE GUYS ARE DUMB. I MEAN DUUUUMB. BUT I CAN'T KEEP PUTTING THEM OFF.
I DID MANAGE TO CONVINCE THEM TO ARRANGE A PARTY FOR ME, IN HOPES MY IMPROVED MOOD WOULD LEAD TO MY "DIAMOND POWERS" BECOMING STRONGER.
SO YOU SENT ME A FAKE INVITATION?
NO. IT WAS REAL. I REALLY WANTED YOU HERE. I WASN'T SURE YOU'D COME IF I CONTACTED YOU DIRECTLY. BUT I KNEW YOU'D COME IF I APPEALED TO YOUR EGO.
IT'S NOT EGO IF YOU CAN DO IT.
SO COME ON, BEFORE THEY COME BACK. GET ME OUT OF HERE!
WELLLL—I SUPPOSE I CAN'T JUST LEAVE YOU HERE, CAN I? MUCH AS I'D LIKE TO.
HOLD ON TO YOUR CROWN, QUEENIE! WE'RE GRABBING SOME SKY!

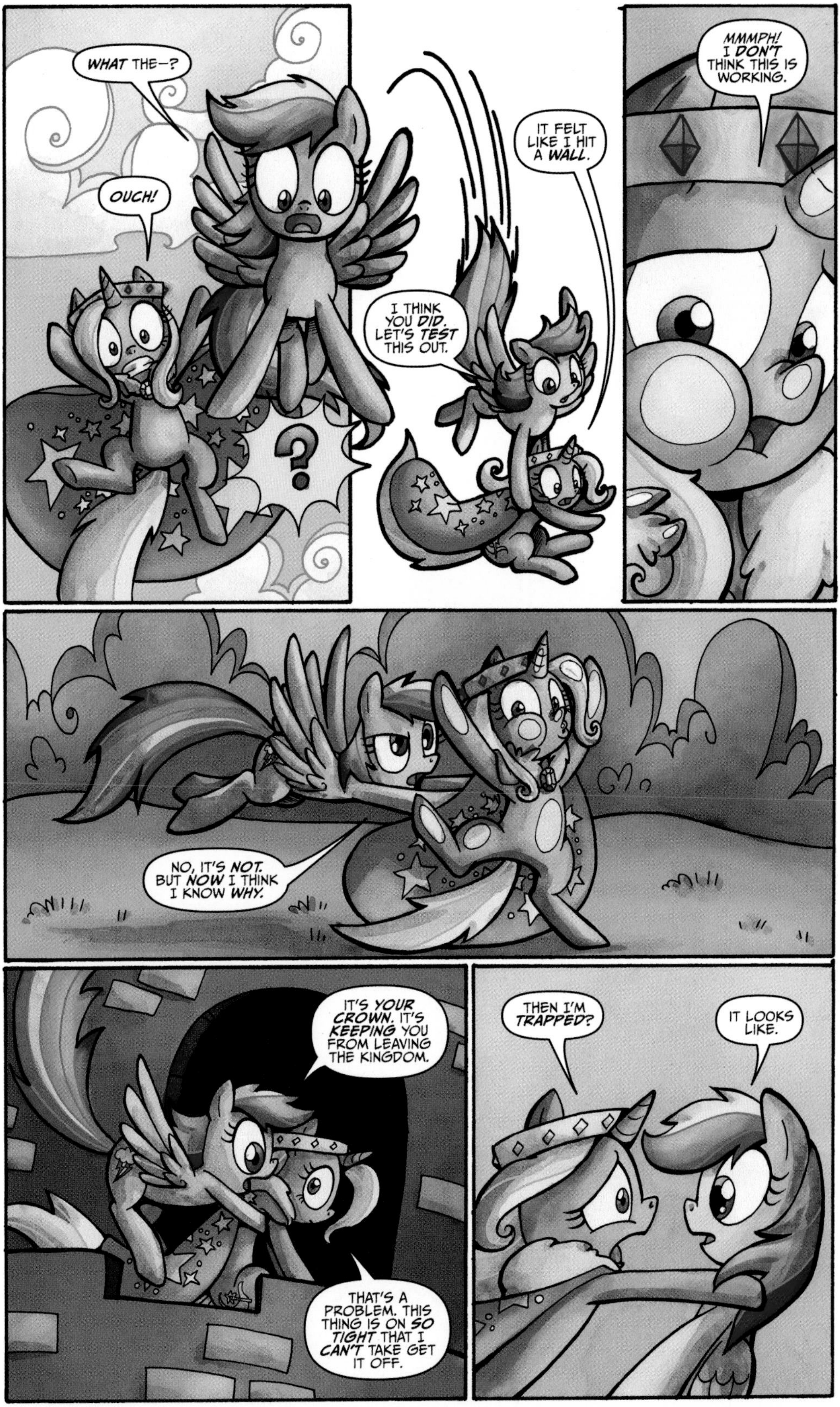
WHAT THE--?
OUCH!
IT FELT LIKE I HIT A WALL.
I THINK YOU DID. LET'S TEST THIS OUT.
MMMPH! I DON'T THINK THIS IS WORKING.
NO, IT'S NOT. BUT NOW I THINK I KNOW WHY.
IT'S YOUR CROWN. IT'S KEEPING YOU FROM LEAVING THE KINGDOM.
THAT'S A PROBLEM. THIS THING IS ON SO TIGHT THAT I CAN'T TAKE GET IT OFF.
THEN I'M TRAPPED?
IT LOOKS LIKE.

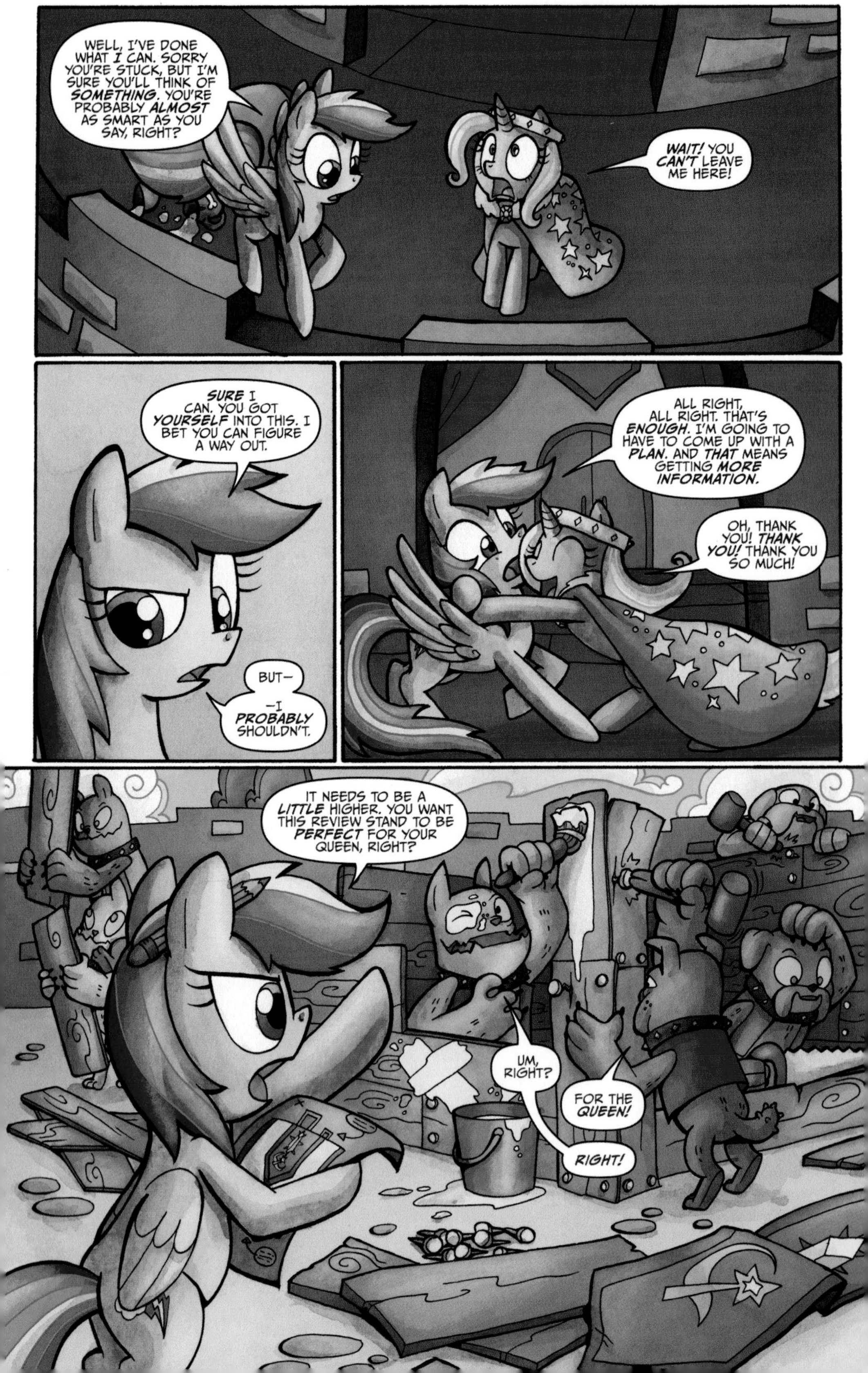

WELL, I'VE DONE WHAT I CAN. SORRY YOU'RE STUCK, BUT I'M SURE YOU'LL THINK OF SOMETHING. YOU'RE PROBABLY ALMOST AS SMART AS YOU SAY, RIGHT?
WAIT! YOU CAN'T LEAVE ME HERE!
SURE I CAN. YOU GOT YOURSELF INTO THIS. I BET YOU CAN FIGURE A WAY OUT.
BUT—
—I PROBABLY SHOULDN'T.
ALL RIGHT, ALL RIGHT. THAT'S ENOUGH. I'M GOING TO HAVE TO COME UP WITH A PLAN. AND THAT MEANS GETTING MORE INFORMATION.
OH, THANK YOU! THANK YOU! THANK YOU SO MUCH!
IT NEEDS TO BE A LITTLE HIGHER. YOU WANT THIS REVIEW STAND TO BE PERFECT FOR YOUR QUEEN, RIGHT?
UM, RIGHT?
FOR THE QUEEN!
RIGHT!

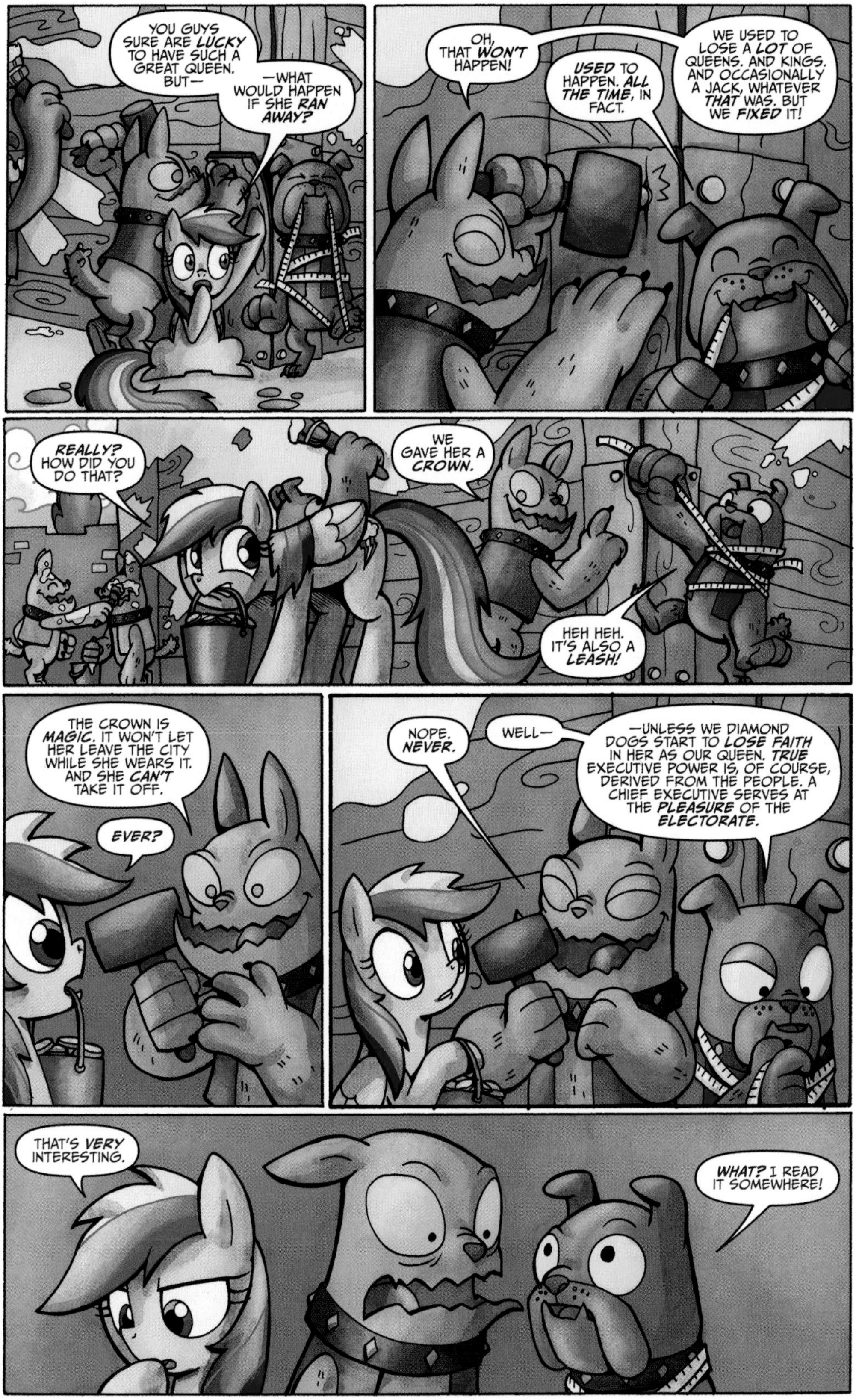
YOU GUYS SURE ARE LUCKY TO HAVE SUCH A GREAT QUEEN. BUT—
—WHAT WOULD HAPPEN IF SHE RAN AWAY?
OH, THAT WON'T HAPPEN!
USED TO HAPPEN. ALL THE TIME, IN FACT.
WE USED TO LOSE A LOT OF QUEENS. AND KINGS. AND OCCASIONALLY A JACK, WHATEVER THAT WAS. BUT WE FIXED IT!
REALLY? HOW DID YOU DO THAT?
WE GAVE HER A CROWN.
HEH HEH. IT'S ALSO A LEASH!
THE CROWN IS MAGIC. IT WON'T LET HER LEAVE THE CITY WHILE SHE WEARS IT. AND SHE CAN'T TAKE IT OFF.
EVER?
NOPE. NEVER.
WELL—
—UNLESS WE DIAMOND DOGS START TO LOSE FAITH IN HER AS OUR QUEEN. TRUE EXECUTIVE POWER IS, OF COURSE, DERIVED FROM THE PEOPLE. A CHIEF EXECUTIVE SERVES AT THE PLEASURE OF THE ELECTORATE.
THAT'S VERY INTERESTING.
WHAT? I READ IT SOMEWHERE!

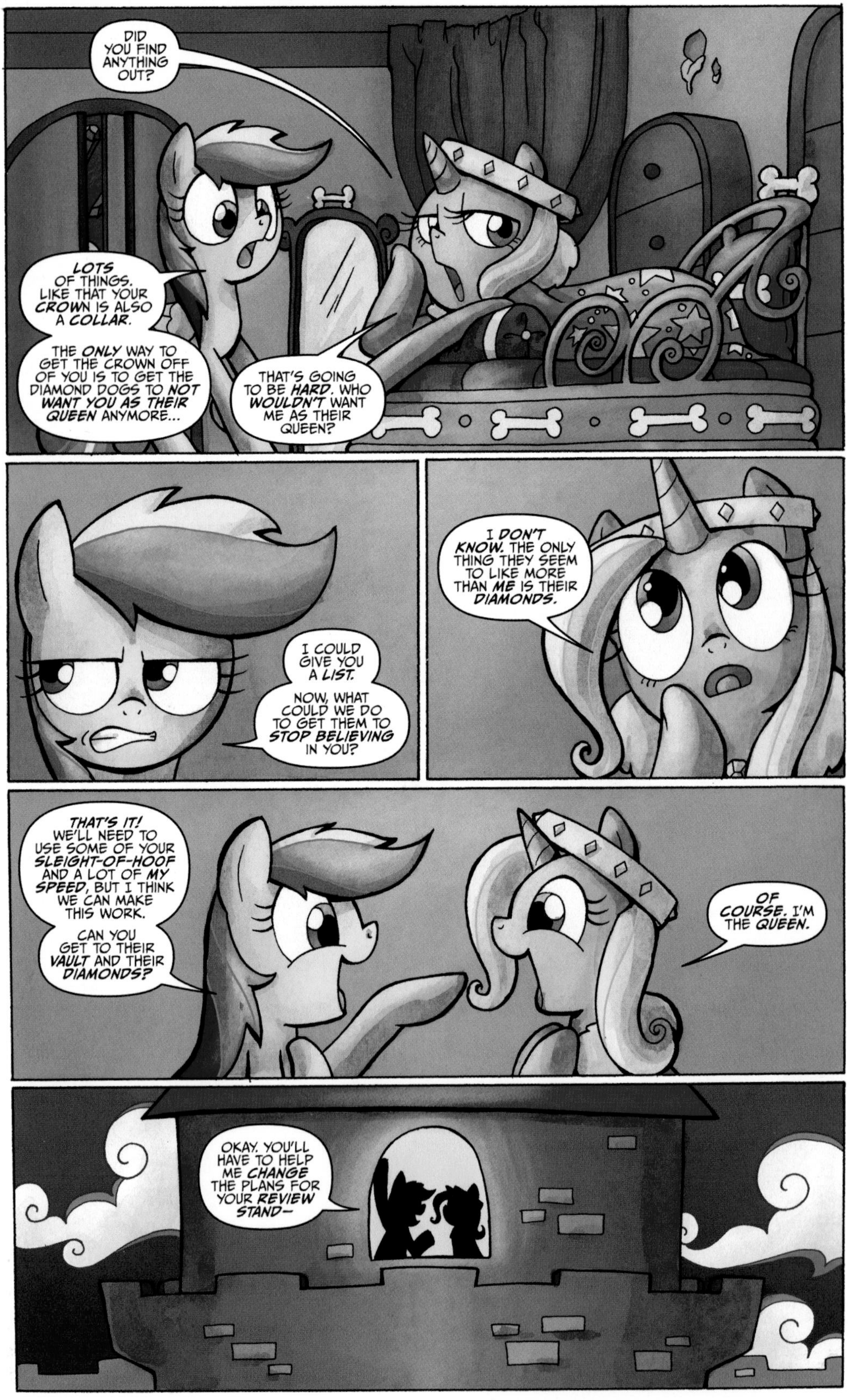
DID YOU FIND ANYTHING OUT?
LOTS OF THINGS. LIKE THAT YOUR CROWN IS ALSO A COLLAR.
THE ONLY WAY TO GET THE CROWN OFF OF YOU IS TO GET THE DIAMOND DOGS TO NOT WANT YOU AS THEIR QUEEN ANYMORE...
THAT'S GOING TO BE HARD. WHO WOULDN'T WANT ME AS THEIR QUEEN?
I COULD GIVE YOU A LIST.
NOW, WHAT COULD WE DO TO GET THEM TO STOP BELIEVING IN YOU?
I DON'T KNOW. THE ONLY THING THEY SEEM TO LIKE MORE THAN ME IS THEIR DIAMONDS.
THAT'S IT! WE'LL NEED TO USE SOME OF YOUR SLEIGHT-OF-HOOF AND A LOT OF MY SPEED, BUT I THINK WE CAN MAKE THIS WORK.
CAN YOU GET TO THEIR VAULT AND THEIR DIAMONDS?
OF COURSE. I'M THE QUEEN.
OKAY. YOU'LL HAVE TO HELP ME CHANGE THE PLANS FOR YOUR REVIEW STAND—

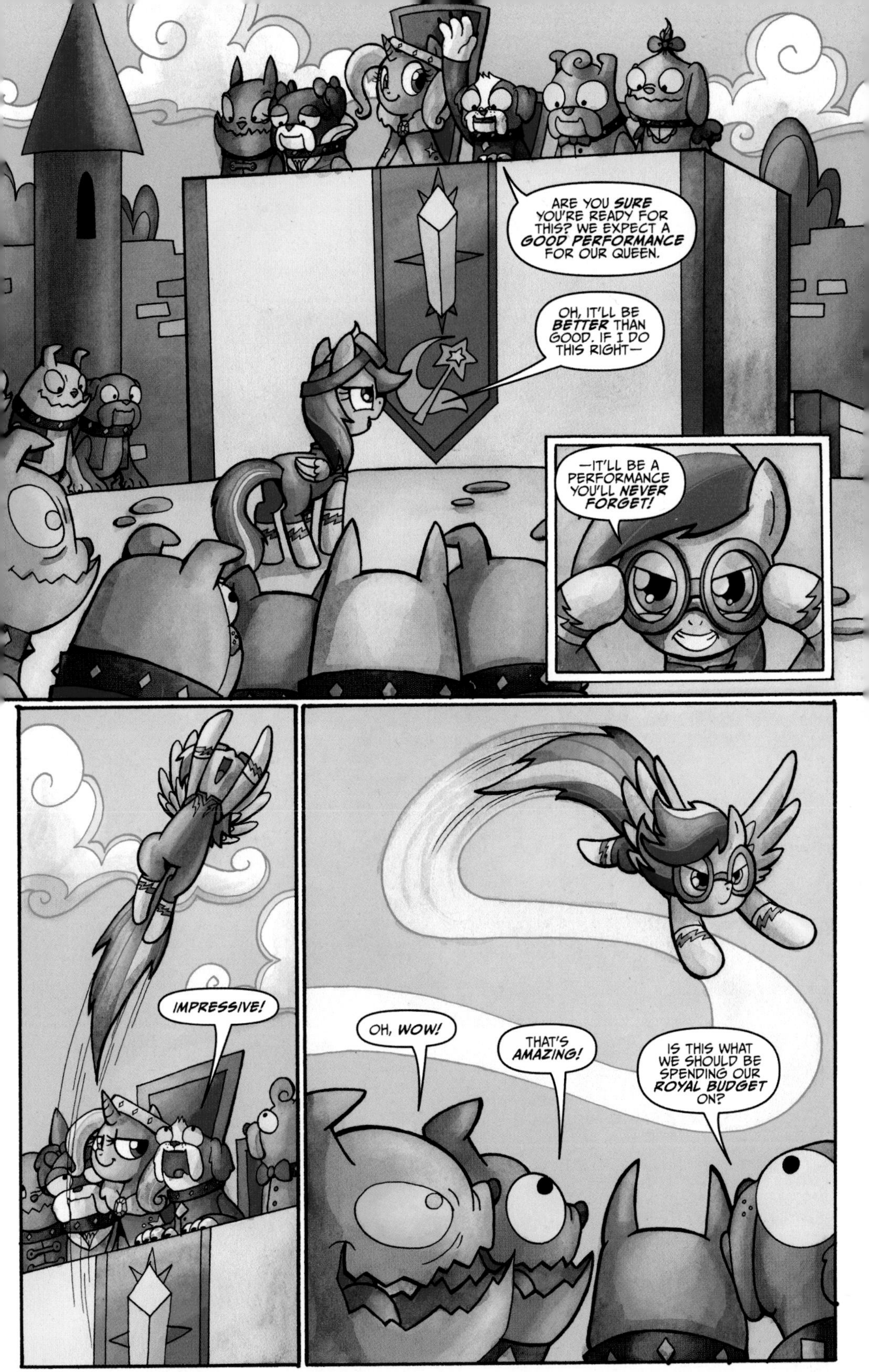
ARE YOU SURE YOU'RE READY FOR THIS? WE EXPECT A GOOD PERFORMANCE FOR OUR QUEEN.
OH, IT'LL BE BETTER THAN GOOD. IF I DO THIS RIGHT—
—IT'LL BE A PERFORMANCE YOU'LL NEVER FORGET!
IMPRESSIVE!
OH, WOW!
THAT'S AMAZING!
IS THIS WHAT WE SHOULD BE SPENDING OUR ROYAL BUDGET ON?

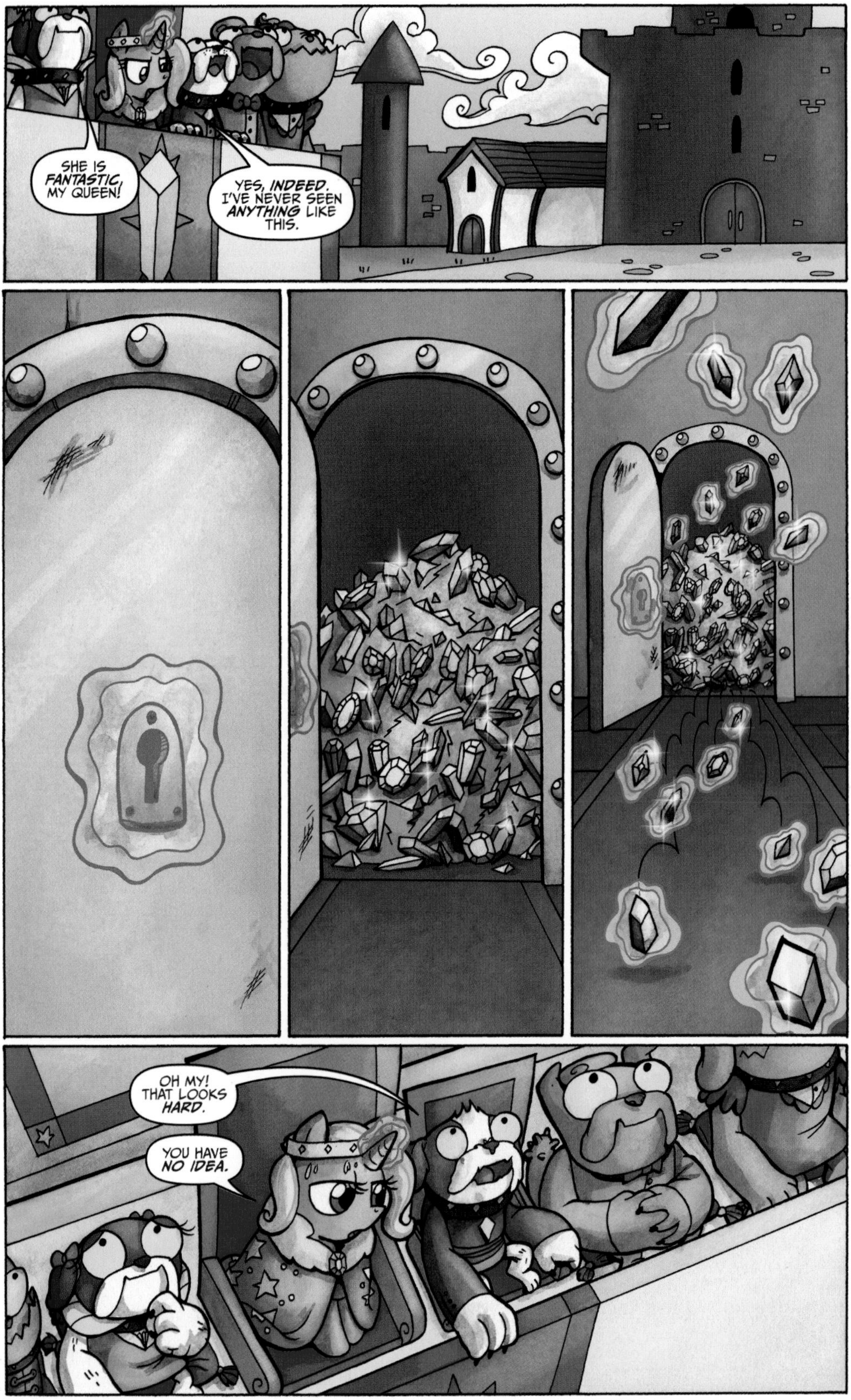
SHE IS FANTASTIC, MY QUEEN!
YES, INDEED. I'VE NEVER SEEN ANYTHING LIKE THIS.
OH MY! THAT LOOKS HARD.
YOU HAVE NO IDEA.

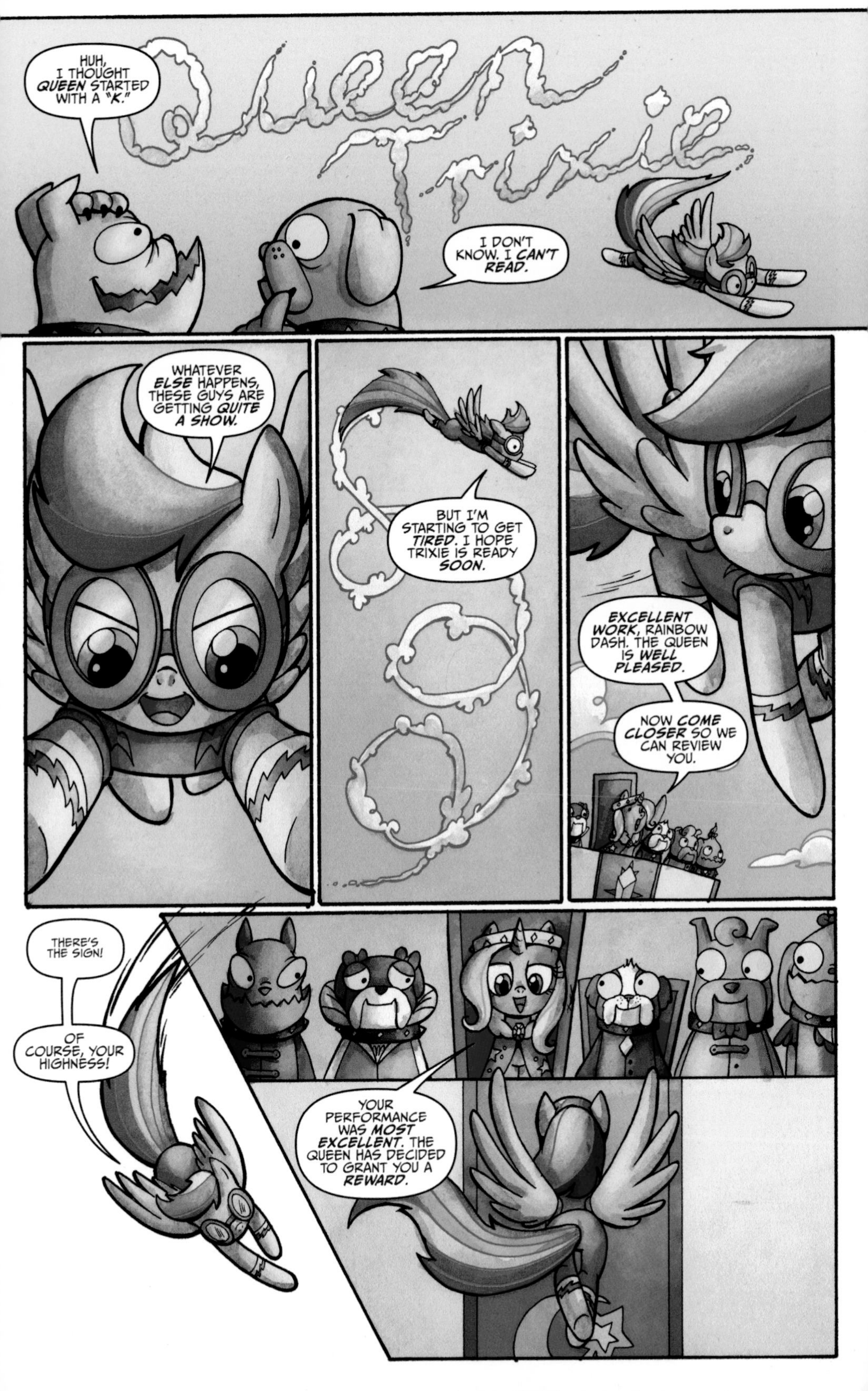
HUH, I THOUGHT QUEEN STARTED WITH A "K."
Queen Trixie
I DON'T KNOW. I CAN'T READ.
WHATEVER ELSE HAPPENS, THESE GUYS ARE GETTING QUITE A SHOW.
BUT I'M STARTING TO GET TIRED. I HOPE TRIXIE IS READY SOON.
EXCELLENT WORK, RAINBOW DASH. THE QUEEN IS WELL PLEASED.
NOW COME CLOSER SO WE CAN REVIEW YOU.
THERE'S THE SIGN!
OF COURSE, YOUR HIGHNESS!
YOUR PERFORMANCE WAS MOST EXCELLENT. THE QUEEN HAS DECIDED TO GRANT YOU A REWARD.

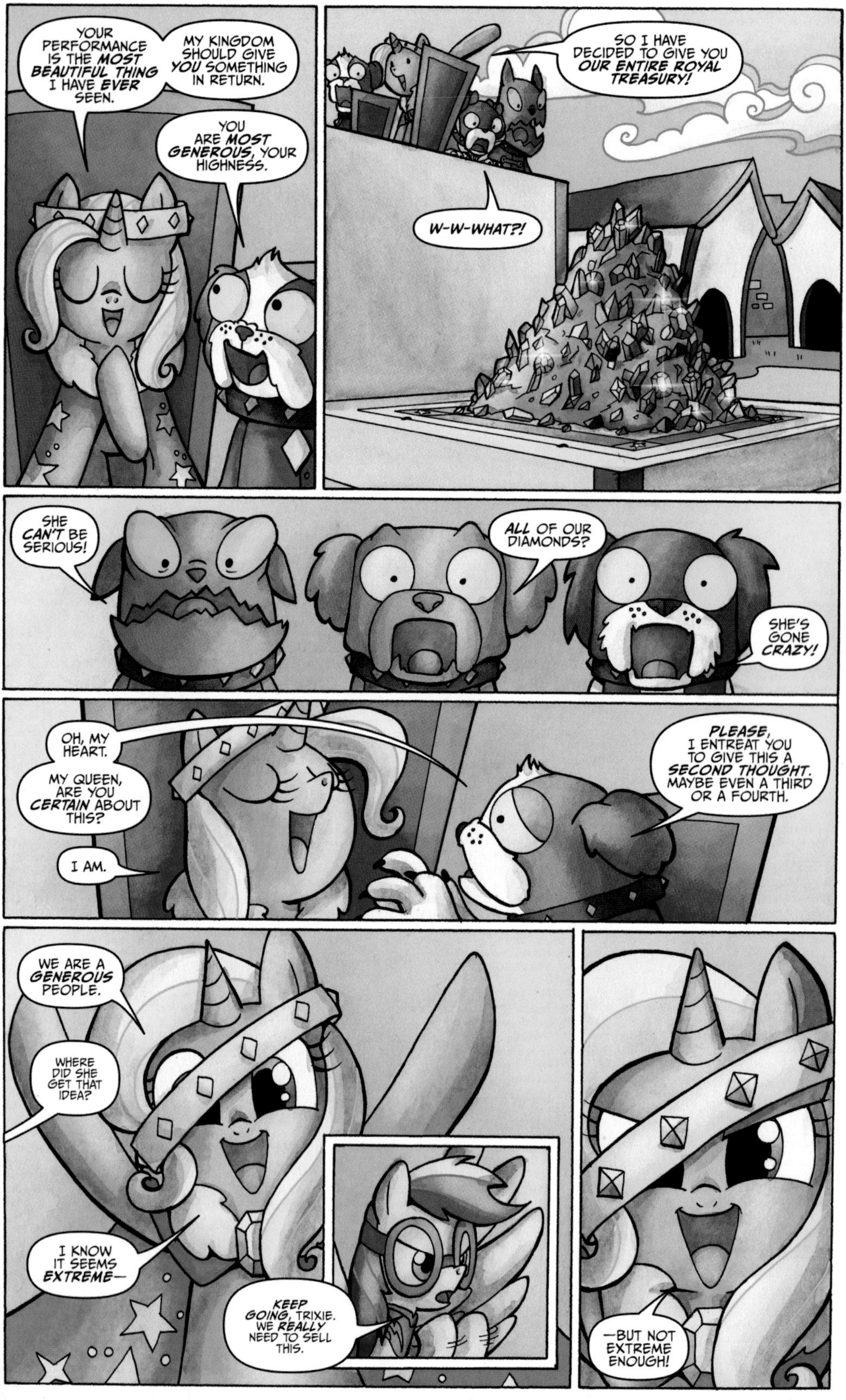
YOUR PERFORMANCE IS THE MOST BEAUTIFUL THING I HAVE EVER SEEN.
MY KINGDOM SHOULD GIVE YOU SOMETHING IN RETURN.
YOU ARE MOST GENEROUS, YOUR HIGHNESS.
SO I HAVE DECIDED TO GIVE YOU OUR ENTIRE ROYAL TREASURY!
W-W-WHAT?!
SHE CAN'T BE SERIOUS!
ALL OF OUR DIAMONDS?
SHE'S GONE CRAZY!
OH, MY HEART.
MY QUEEN, ARE YOU CERTAIN ABOUT THIS?
I AM.
PLEASE, I ENTREAT YOU TO GIVE THIS A SECOND THOUGHT. MAYBE EVEN A THIRD OR A FOURTH.
WE ARE A GENEROUS PEOPLE.
WHERE DID SHE GET THAT IDEA?
I KNOW IT SEEMS EXTREME—
KEEP GOING, TRIXIE. WE REALLY NEED TO SELL THIS.
—BUT NOT EXTREME ENOUGH!

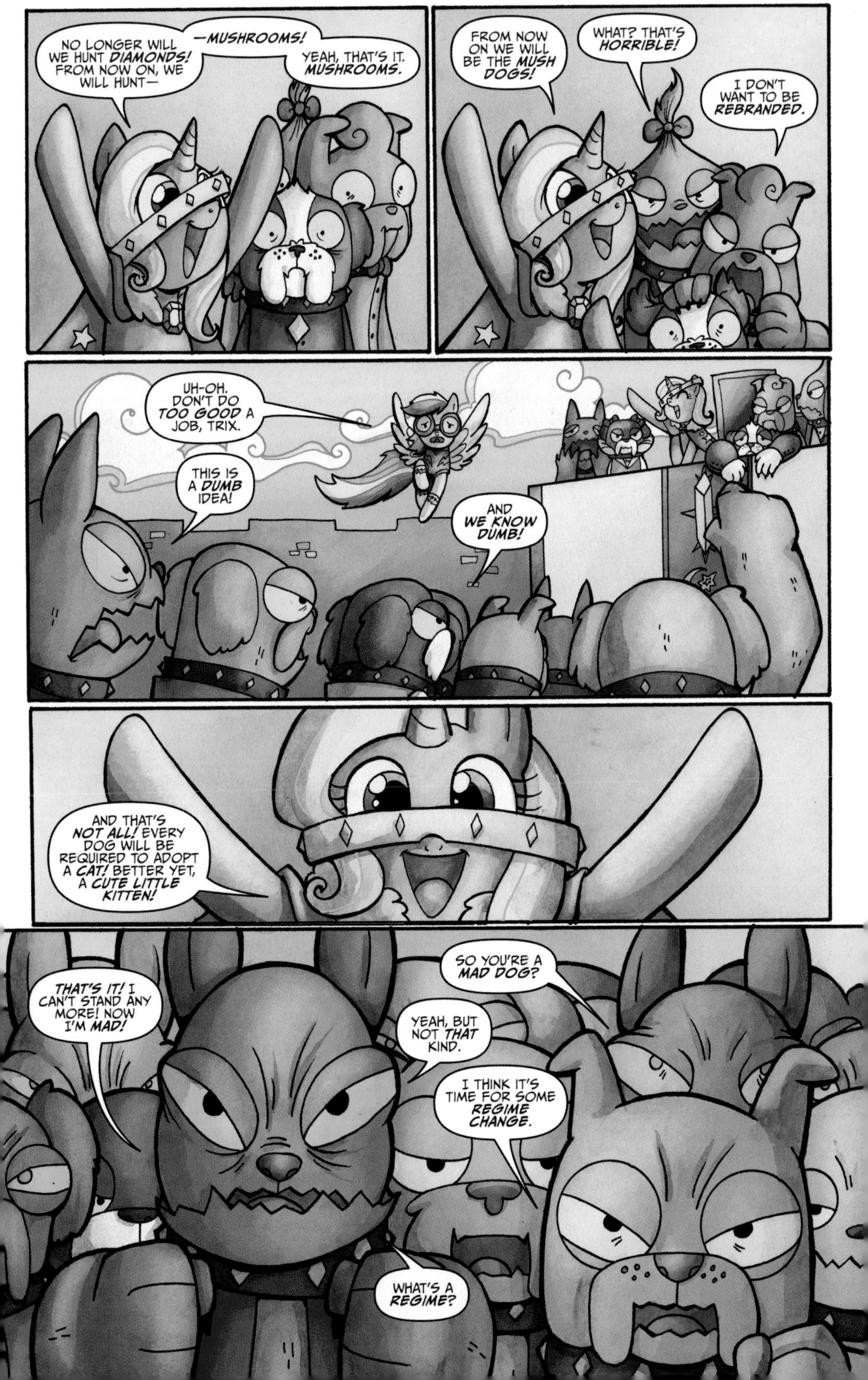
NO LONGER WILL WE HUNT DIAMONDS! FROM NOW ON, WE WILL HUNT—
—MUSHROOMS!
YEAH, THAT'S IT. MUSHROOMS.
FROM NOW ON WE WILL BE THE MUSH DOGS!
WHAT? THAT'S HORRIBLE!
I DON'T WANT TO BE REBRANDED.
UH-OH. DON'T DO TOO GOOD A JOB, TRIX.
THIS IS A DUMB IDEA!
AND WE KNOW DUMB!
AND THAT'S NOT ALL! EVERY DOG WILL BE REQUIRED TO ADOPT A CAT! BETTER YET, A CUTE LITTLE KITTEN!
THAT'S IT! I CAN'T STAND ANY MORE! NOW I'M MAD!
SO YOU'RE A MAD DOG?
YEAH, BUT NOT THAT KIND.
I THINK IT'S TIME FOR SOME REGIME CHANGE.
WHAT'S A REGIME?

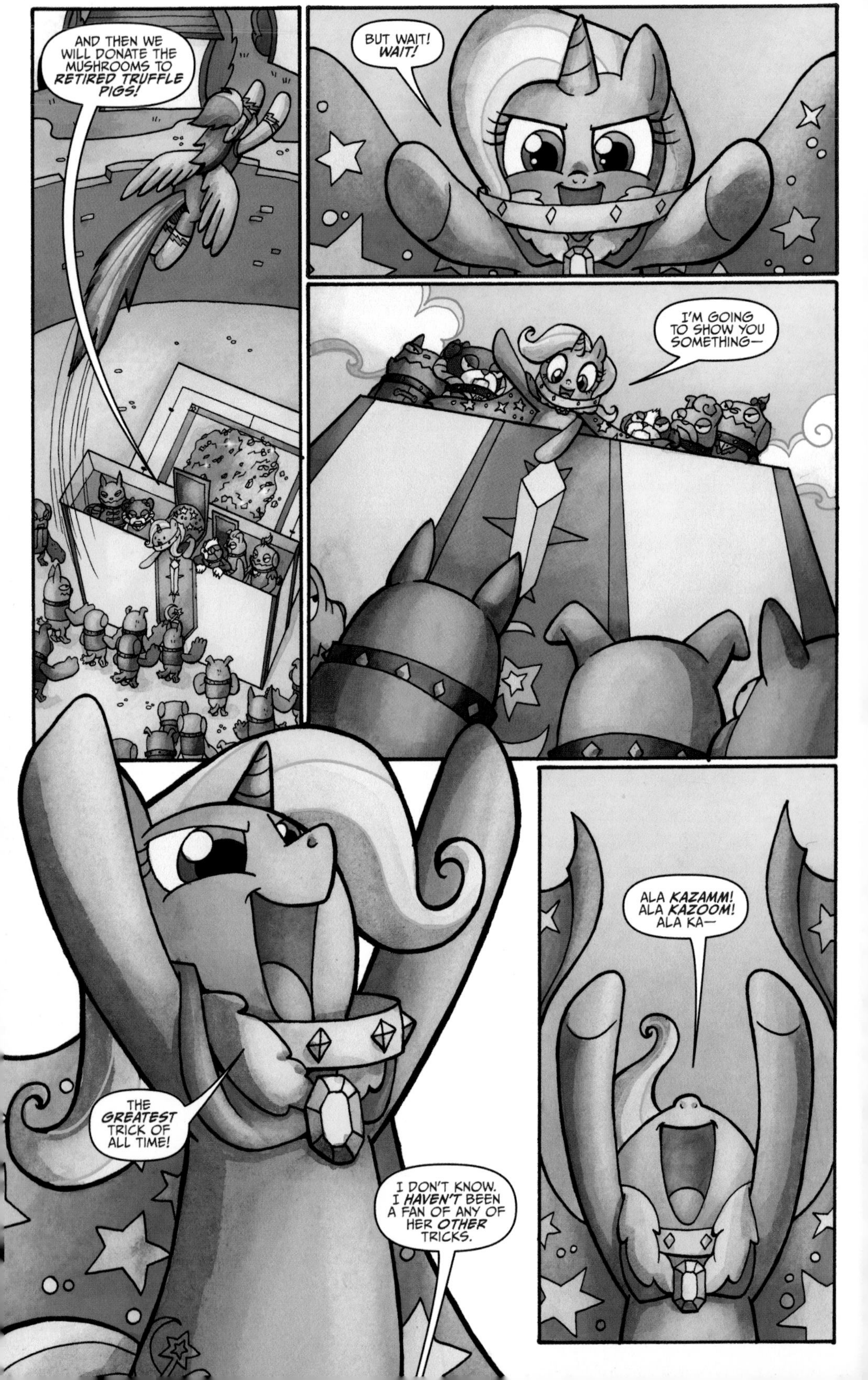
AND THEN WE WILL DONATE THE MUSHROOMS TO RETIRED TRUFFLE PIGS!
BUT WAIT! WAIT!
I'M GOING TO SHOW YOU SOMETHING—
THE GREATEST TRICK OF ALL TIME!
I DON'T KNOW. I HAVEN'T BEEN A FAN OF ANY OF HER OTHER TRICKS.
ALA KAZAMM! ALA KAZOOM! ALA KA—

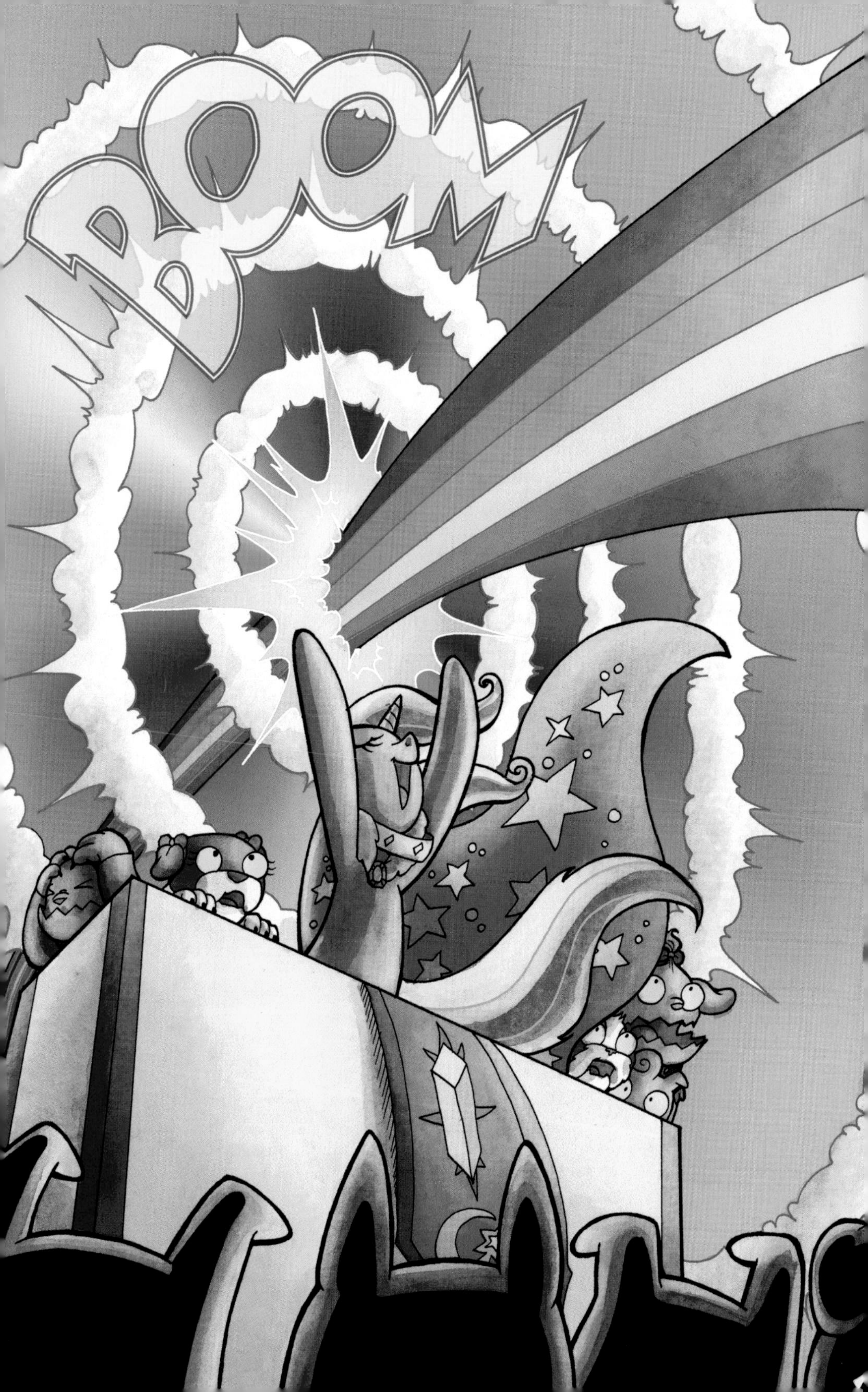
BOOM

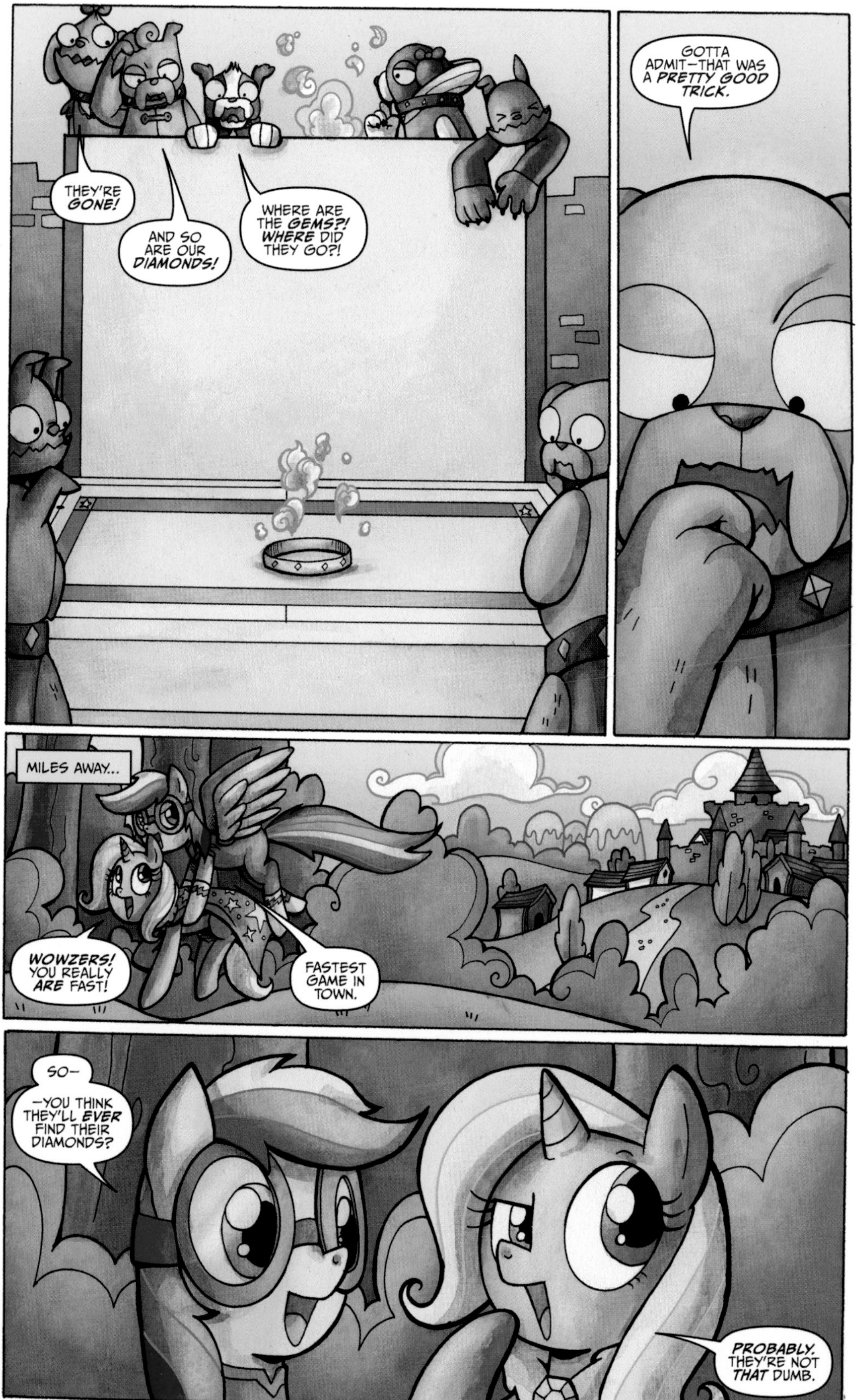
THEY'RE *GONE!*
AND SO ARE OUR *DIAMONDS!*
WHERE ARE THE *GEMS?! WHERE* DID THEY GO?!
GOTTA ADMIT—THAT WAS A *PRETTY GOOD* TRICK.
MILES AWAY...
WOWZERS! YOU REALLY *ARE* FAST!
FASTEST GAME IN TOWN.
SO—
—YOU THINK THEY'LL *EVER* FIND THEIR DIAMONDS?
PROBABLY. THEY'RE NOT *THAT* DUMB.

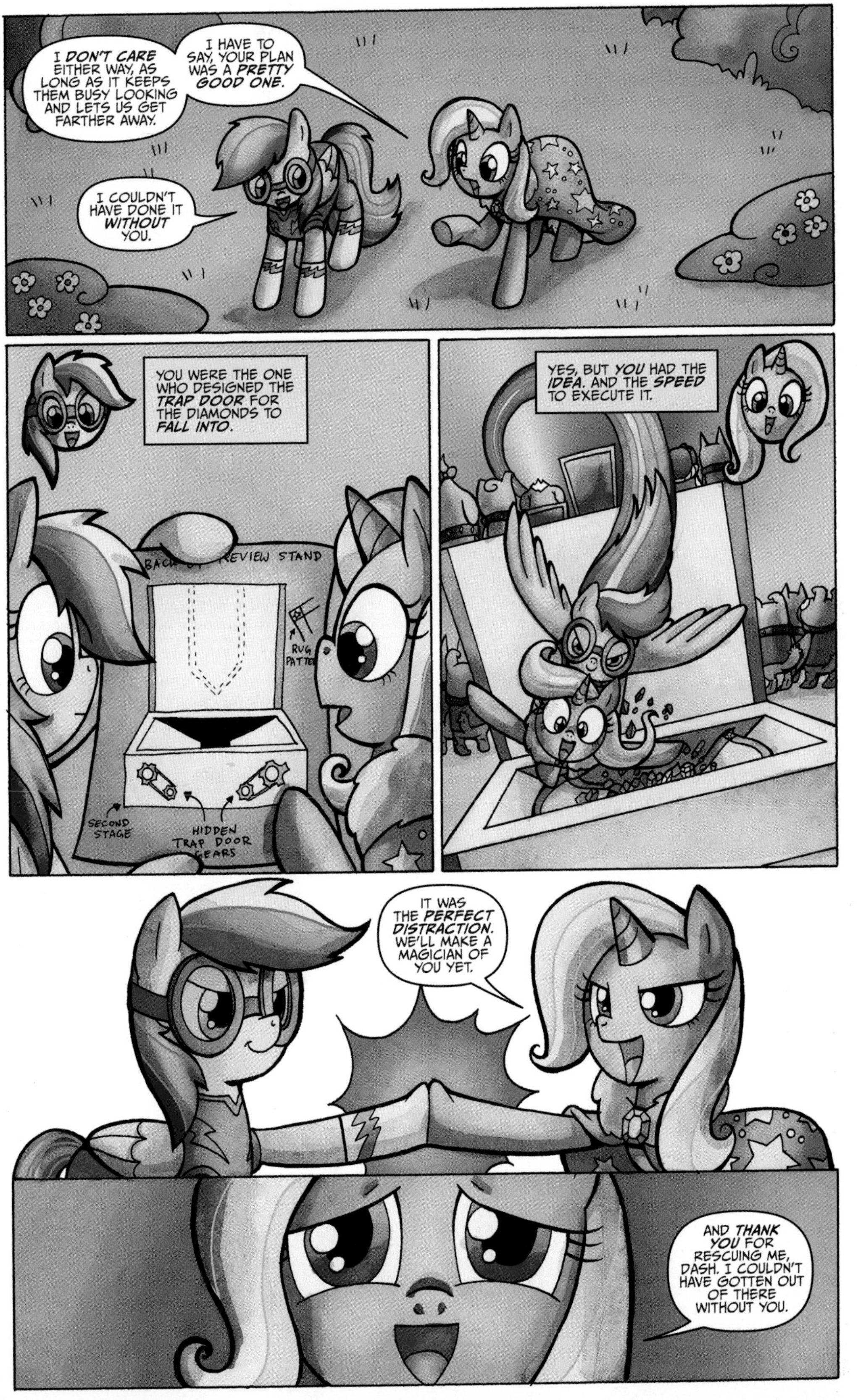
I DON'T CARE EITHER WAY, AS LONG AS IT KEEPS THEM BUSY LOOKING AND LETS US GET FARTHER AWAY.
I HAVE TO SAY, YOUR PLAN WAS A PRETTY GOOD ONE.
I COULDN'T HAVE DONE IT WITHOUT YOU.
YOU WERE THE ONE WHO DESIGNED THE TRAP DOOR FOR THE DIAMONDS TO FALL INTO.
REVIEW STAND
RUG
SECOND STAGE
HIDDEN TRAP DOOR
YES, BUT YOU HAD THE IDEA. AND THE SPEED TO EXECUTE IT.
IT WAS THE PERFECT DISTRACTION. WE'LL MAKE A MAGICIAN OF YOU YET.
AND THANK YOU FOR RESCUING ME, DASH. I COULDN'T HAVE GOTTEN OUT OF THERE WITHOUT YOU.

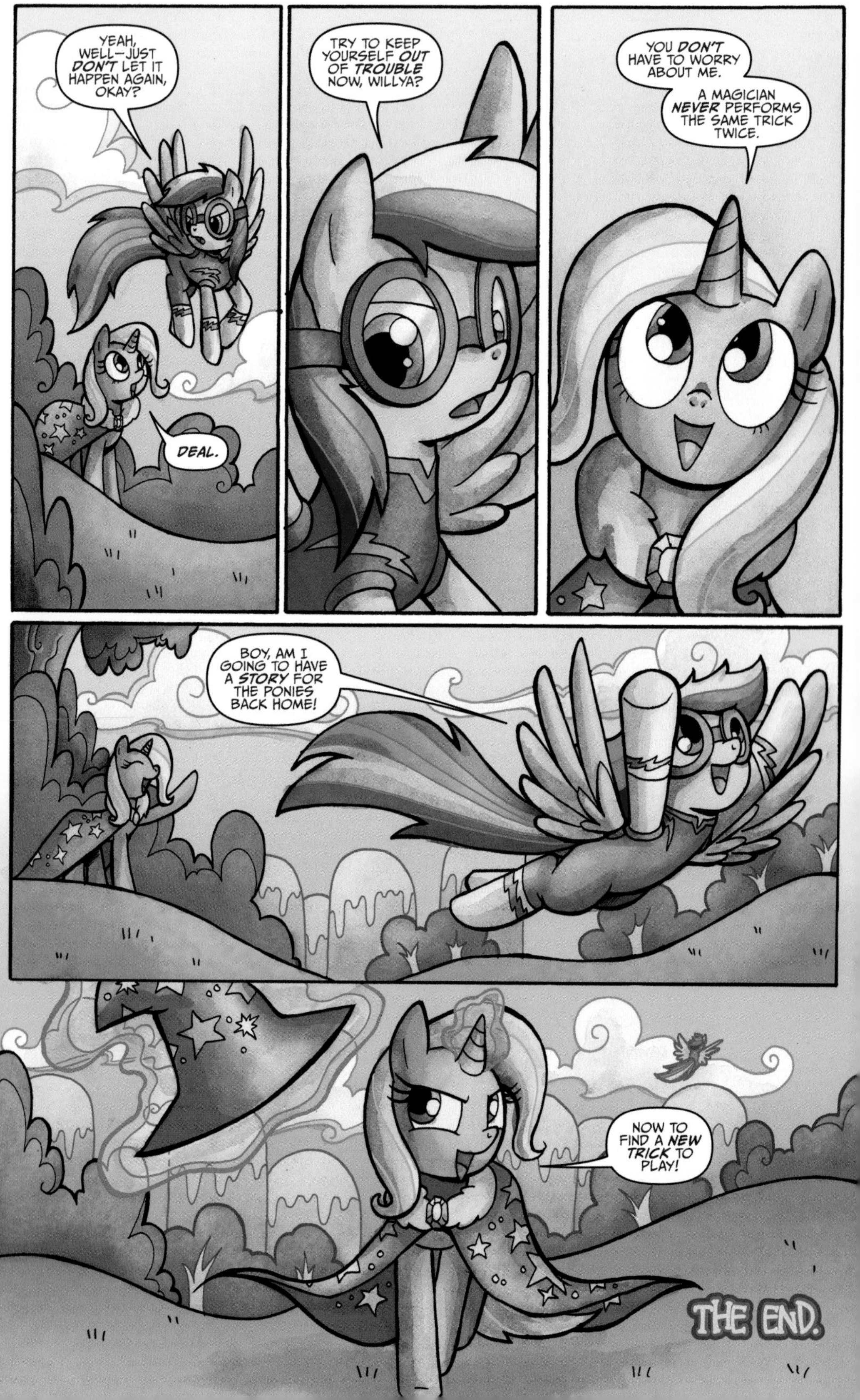
YEAH, WELL—JUST DON'T LET IT HAPPEN AGAIN, OKAY?
DEAL.
TRY TO KEEP YOURSELF OUT OF TROUBLE NOW, WILLYA?
YOU DON'T HAVE TO WORRY ABOUT ME.
A MAGICIAN NEVER PERFORMS THE SAME TRICK TWICE.
BOY, AM I GOING TO HAVE A STORY FOR THE PONIES BACK HOME!
NOW TO FIND A NEW TRICK TO PLAY!
THE END.

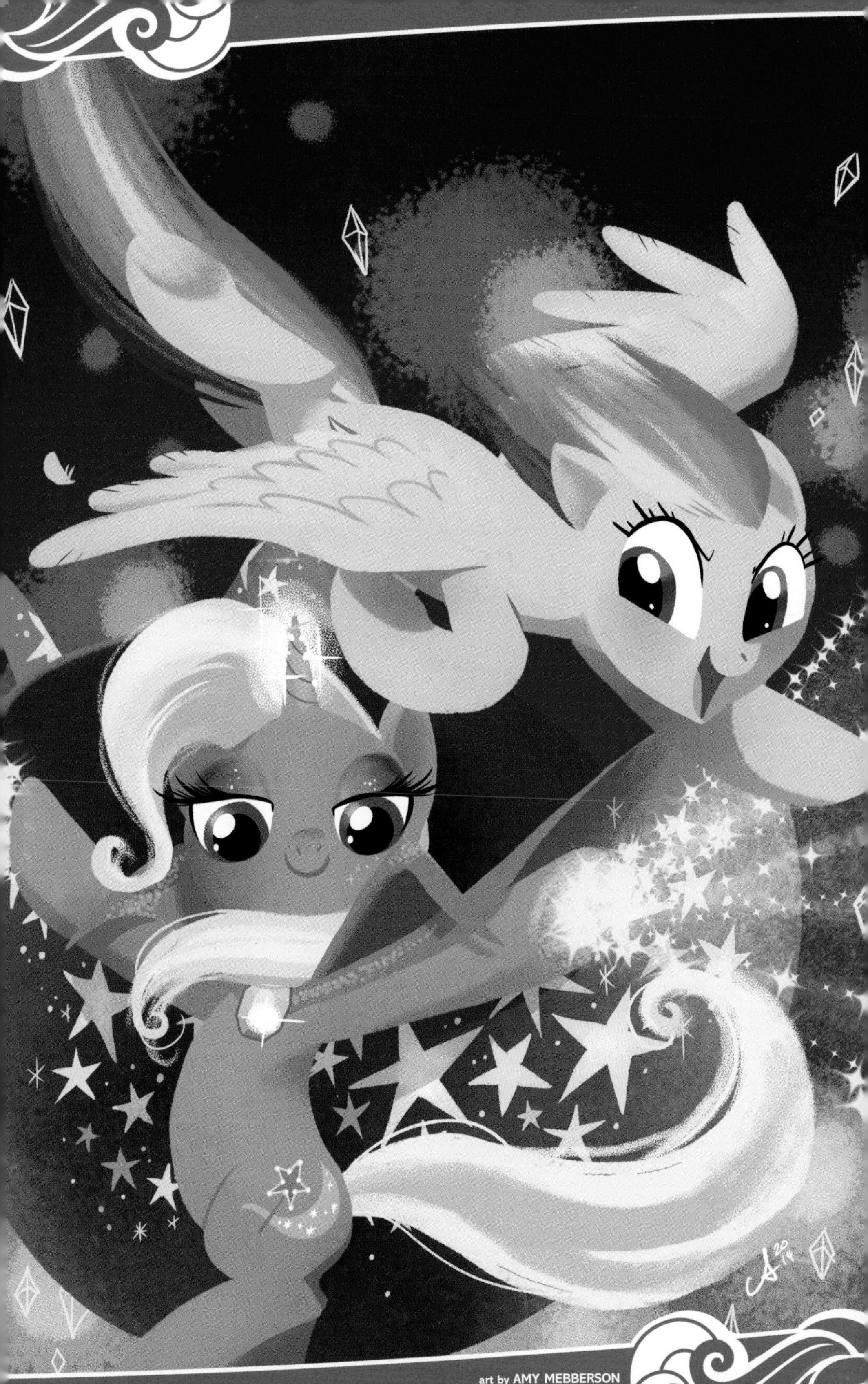

art by AMY MEBBERSON

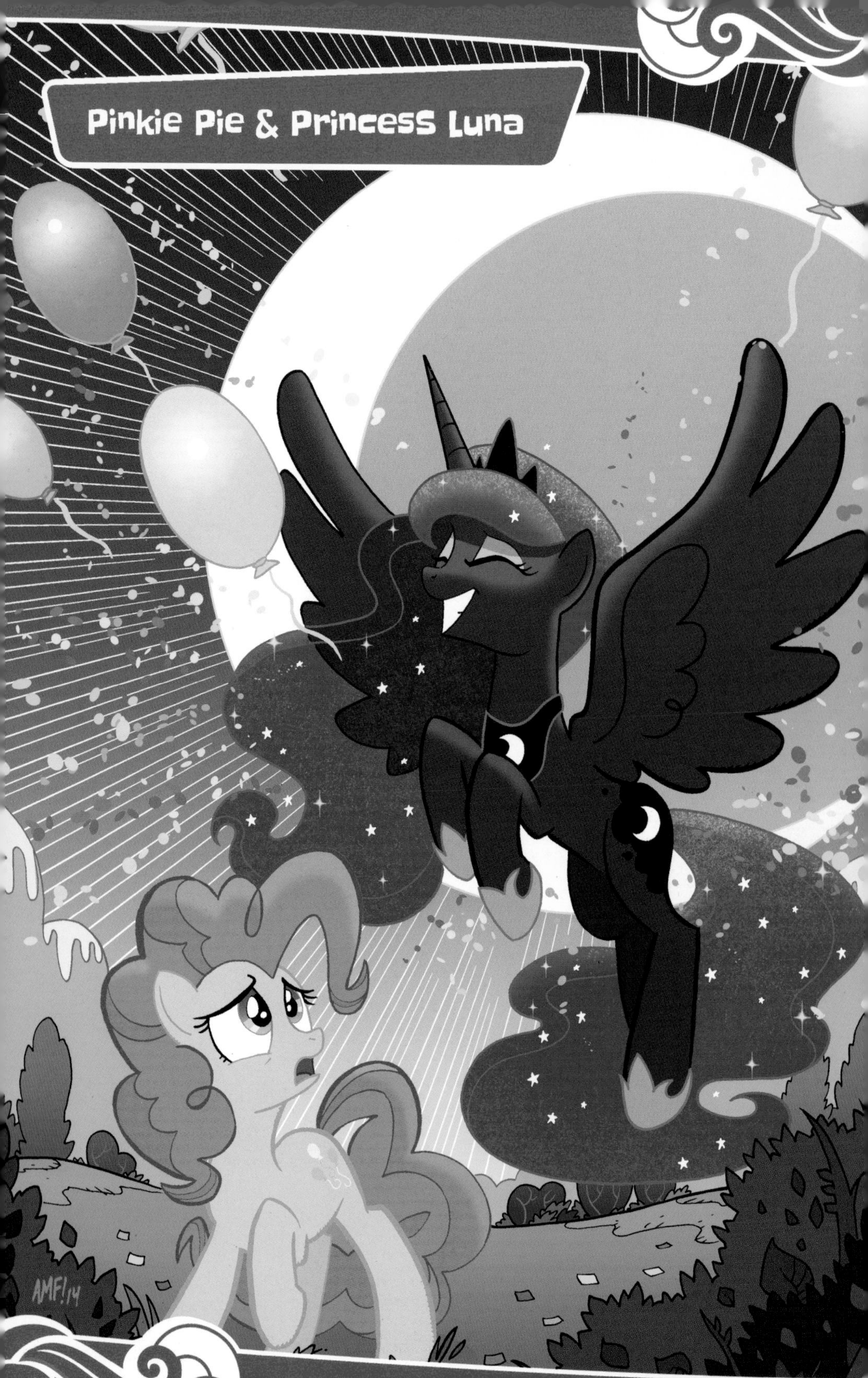
Pinkie Pie & Princess Luna
AMF!14
art by TONY FLEECS

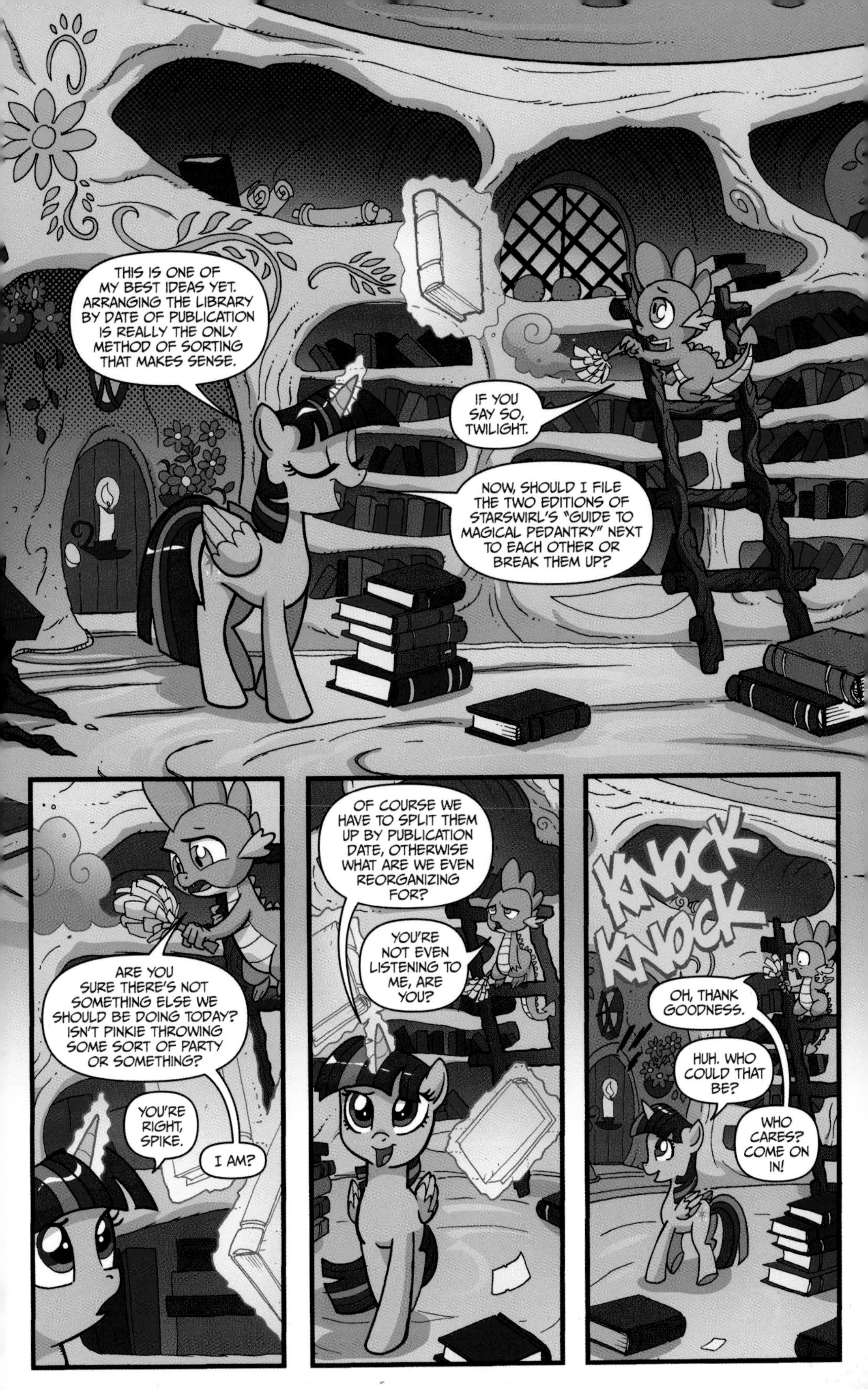
THIS IS ONE OF MY BEST IDEAS YET. ARRANGING THE LIBRARY BY DATE OF PUBLICATION IS REALLY THE ONLY METHOD OF SORTING THAT MAKES SENSE.
IF YOU SAY SO, TWILIGHT.
NOW, SHOULD I FILE THE TWO EDITIONS OF STARSWIRL'S "GUIDE TO MAGICAL PEDANTRY" NEXT TO EACH OTHER OR BREAK THEM UP?
ARE YOU SURE THERE'S NOT SOMETHING ELSE WE SHOULD BE DOING TODAY? ISN'T PINKIE THROWING SOME SORT OF PARTY OR SOMETHING?
YOU'RE RIGHT, SPIKE.
I AM?
OF COURSE WE HAVE TO SPLIT THEM UP BY PUBLICATION DATE, OTHERWISE WHAT ARE WE EVEN REORGANIZING FOR?
YOU'RE NOT EVEN LISTENING TO ME, ARE YOU?
KNOCK KNOCK
OH, THANK GOODNESS.
HUH. WHO COULD THAT BE?
WHO CARES? COME ON IN!

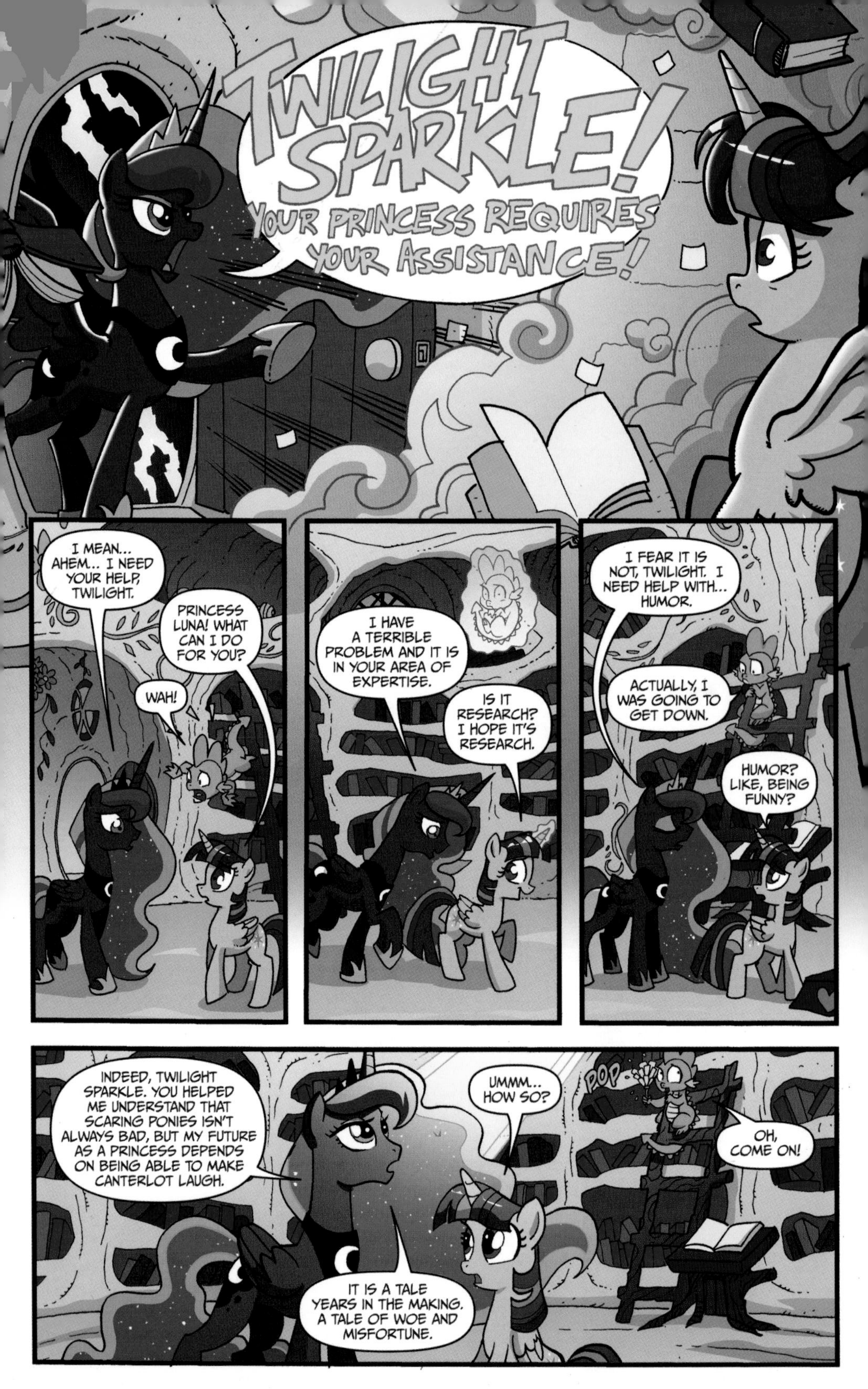
TWILIGHT SPARKLE! YOUR PRINCESS REQUIRES YOUR ASSISTANCE!
I MEAN... AHEM... I NEED YOUR HELP, TWILIGHT.
PRINCESS LUNA! WHAT CAN I DO FOR YOU?
WAH!
I HAVE A TERRIBLE PROBLEM AND IT IS IN YOUR AREA OF EXPERTISE.
IS IT RESEARCH? I HOPE IT'S RESEARCH.
I FEAR IT IS NOT, TWILIGHT. I NEED HELP WITH... HUMOR.
ACTUALLY, I WAS GOING TO GET DOWN.
HUMOR? LIKE, BEING FUNNY?
INDEED, TWILIGHT SPARKLE. YOU HELPED ME UNDERSTAND THAT SCARING PONIES ISN'T ALWAYS BAD, BUT MY FUTURE AS A PRINCESS DEPENDS ON BEING ABLE TO MAKE CANTERLOT LAUGH.
UMMM... HOW SO?
POP
OH, COME ON!
IT IS A TALE YEARS IN THE MAKING. A TALE OF WOE AND MISFORTUNE.

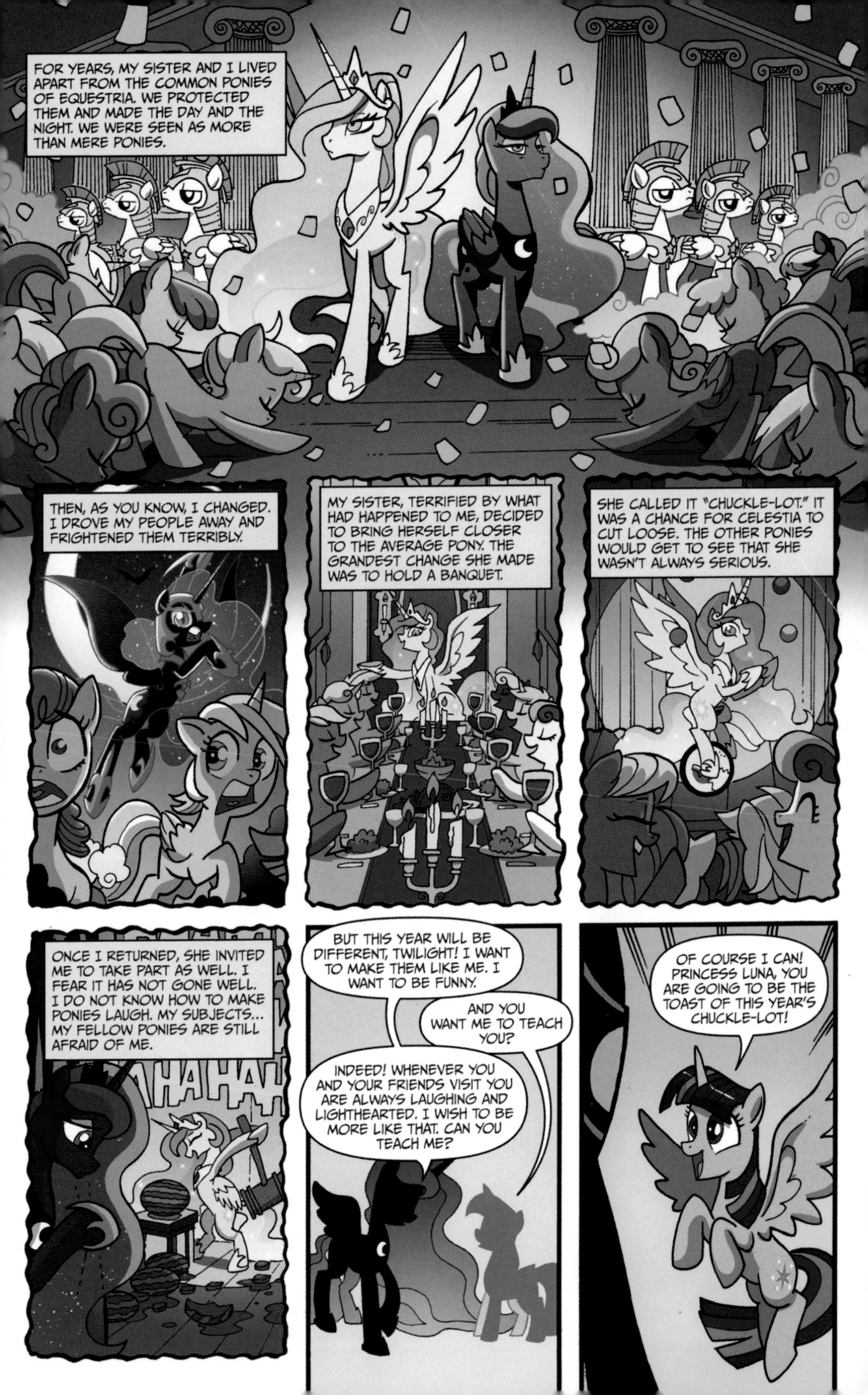
FOR YEARS, MY SISTER AND I LIVED APART FROM THE COMMON PONIES OF EQUESTRIA. WE PROTECTED THEM AND MADE THE DAY AND THE NIGHT. WE WERE SEEN AS MORE THAN MERE PONIES.
THEN, AS YOU KNOW, I CHANGED. I DROVE MY PEOPLE AWAY AND FRIGHTENED THEM TERRIBLY.
MY SISTER, TERRIFIED BY WHAT HAD HAPPENED TO ME, DECIDED TO BRING HERSELF CLOSER TO THE AVERAGE PONY. THE GRANDEST CHANGE SHE MADE WAS TO HOLD A BANQUET.
SHE CALLED IT "CHUCKLE-LOT." IT WAS A CHANCE FOR CELESTIA TO CUT LOOSE. THE OTHER PONIES WOULD GET TO SEE THAT SHE WASN'T ALWAYS SERIOUS.
ONCE I RETURNED, SHE INVITED ME TO TAKE PART AS WELL. I FEAR IT HAS NOT GONE WELL. I DO NOT KNOW HOW TO MAKE PONIES LAUGH. MY SUBJECTS... MY FELLOW PONIES ARE STILL AFRAID OF ME.
HAHAHA
BUT THIS YEAR WILL BE DIFFERENT, TWILIGHT! I WANT TO MAKE THEM LIKE ME. I WANT TO BE FUNNY.
AND YOU WANT ME TO TEACH YOU?
INDEED! WHENEVER YOU AND YOUR FRIENDS VISIT YOU ARE ALWAYS LAUGHING AND LIGHTHEARTED. I WISH TO BE MORE LIKE THAT. CAN YOU TEACH ME?
OF COURSE I CAN! PRINCESS LUNA, YOU ARE GOING TO BE THE TOAST OF THIS YEAR'S CHUCKLE-LOT!

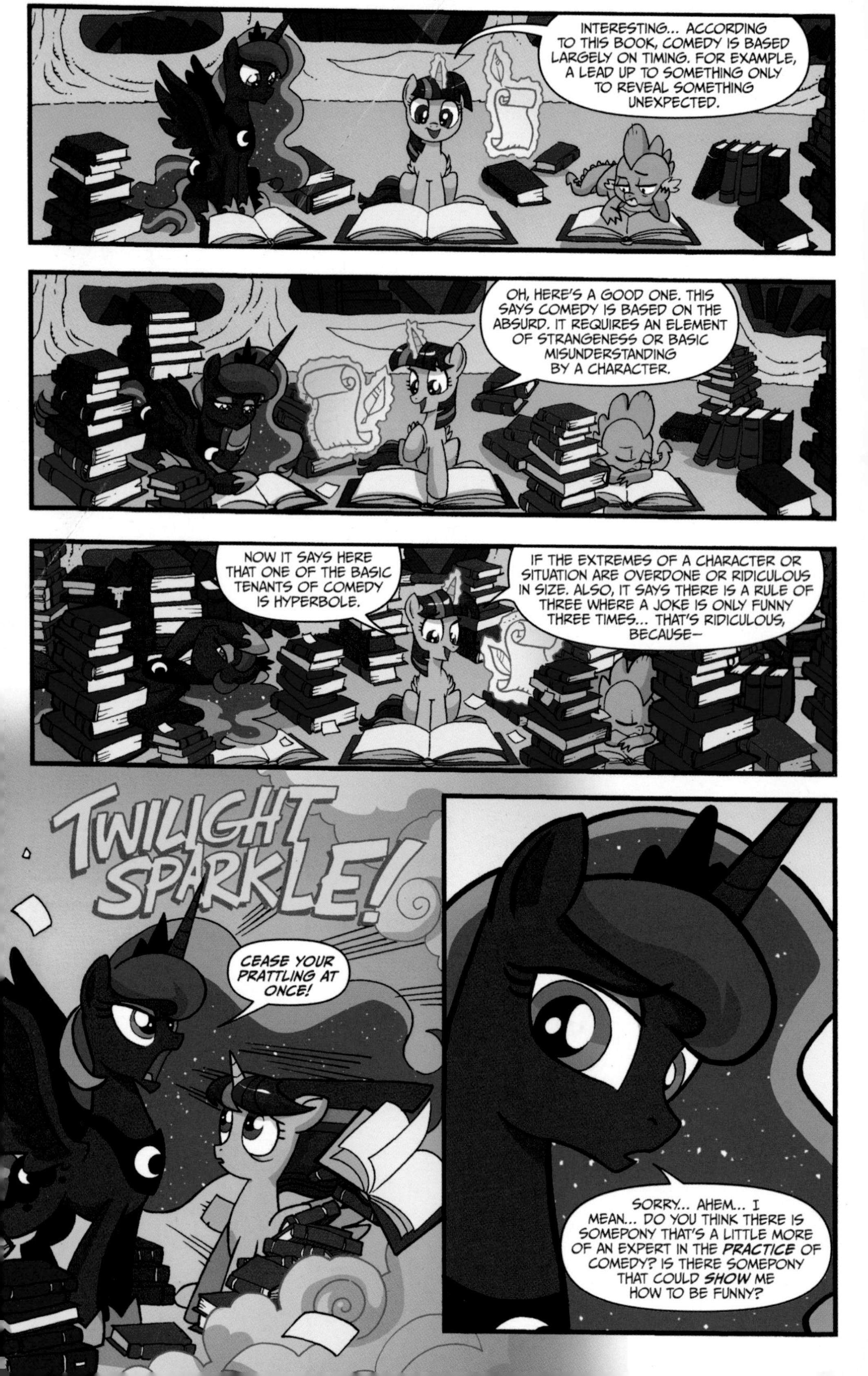
INTERESTING... ACCORDING TO THIS BOOK, COMEDY IS BASED LARGELY ON TIMING. FOR EXAMPLE, A LEAD UP TO SOMETHING ONLY TO REVEAL SOMETHING UNEXPECTED.
OH, HERE'S A GOOD ONE. THIS SAYS COMEDY IS BASED ON THE ABSURD. IT REQUIRES AN ELEMENT OF STRANGENESS OR BASIC MISUNDERSTANDING BY A CHARACTER.
NOW IT SAYS HERE THAT ONE OF THE BASIC TENANTS OF COMEDY IS HYPERBOLE.
IF THE EXTREMES OF A CHARACTER OR SITUATION ARE OVERDONE OR RIDICULOUS IN SIZE. ALSO, IT SAYS THERE IS A RULE OF THREE WHERE A JOKE IS ONLY FUNNY THREE TIMES... THAT'S RIDICULOUS, BECAUSE–
TWILIGHT SPARKLE!
CEASE YOUR PRATTLING AT ONCE!
SORRY... AHEM... I MEAN... DO YOU THINK THERE IS SOMEPONY THAT'S A LITTLE MORE OF AN EXPERT IN THE PRACTICE OF COMEDY? IS THERE SOMEPONY THAT COULD SHOW ME HOW TO BE FUNNY?

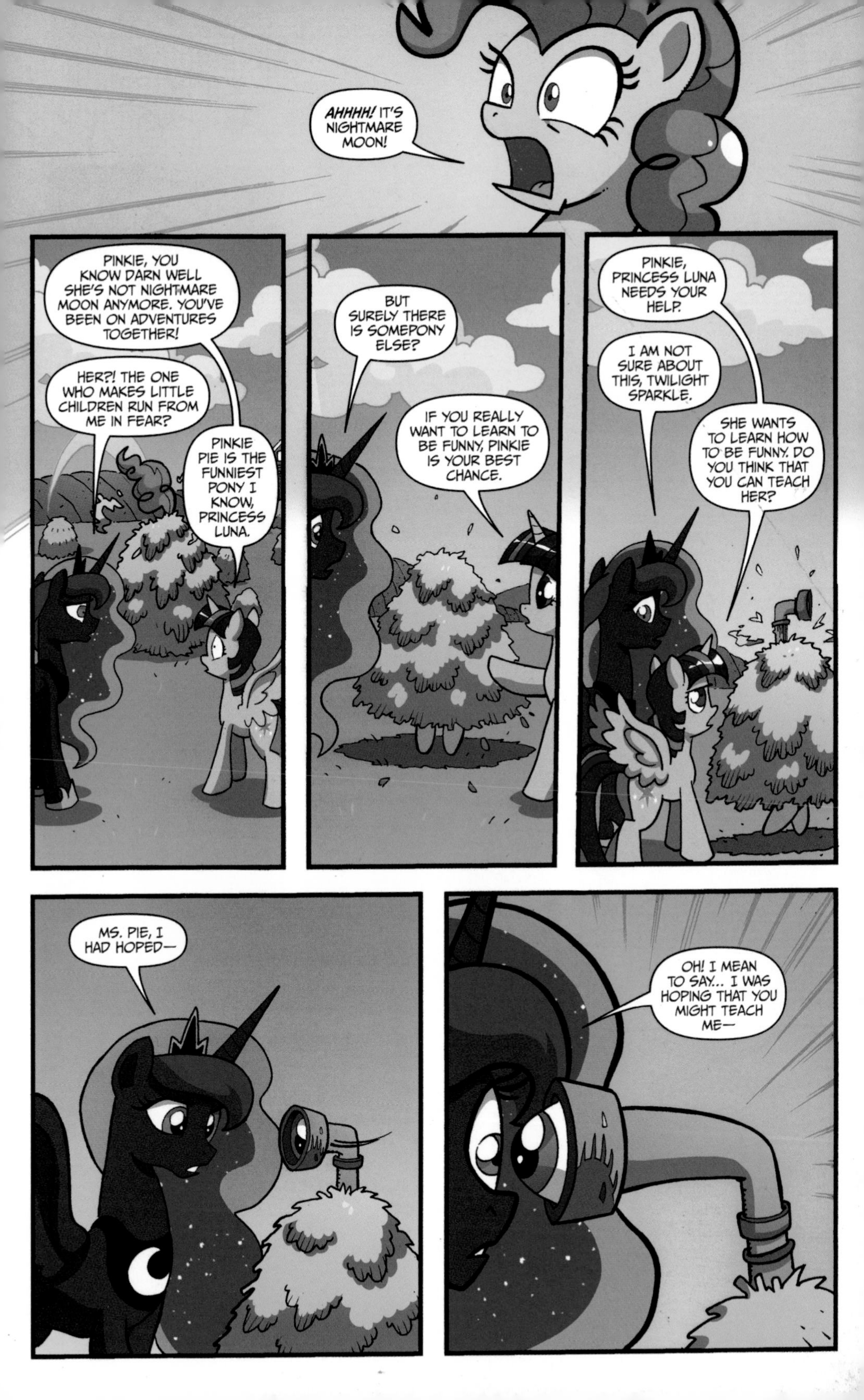
AHHHH! IT'S NIGHTMARE MOON!
PINKIE, YOU KNOW DARN WELL SHE'S NOT NIGHTMARE MOON ANYMORE. YOU'VE BEEN ON ADVENTURES TOGETHER!
HER?! THE ONE WHO MAKES LITTLE CHILDREN RUN FROM ME IN FEAR?
PINKIE PIE IS THE FUNNIEST PONY I KNOW, PRINCESS LUNA.
BUT SURELY THERE IS SOMEPONY ELSE?
IF YOU REALLY WANT TO LEARN TO BE FUNNY, PINKIE IS YOUR BEST CHANCE.
PINKIE, PRINCESS LUNA NEEDS YOUR HELP.
I AM NOT SURE ABOUT THIS, TWILIGHT SPARKLE.
SHE WANTS TO LEARN HOW TO BE FUNNY. DO YOU THINK THAT YOU CAN TEACH HER?
MS. PIE, I HAD HOPED—
OH! I MEAN TO SAY... I WAS HOPING THAT YOU MIGHT TEACH ME—

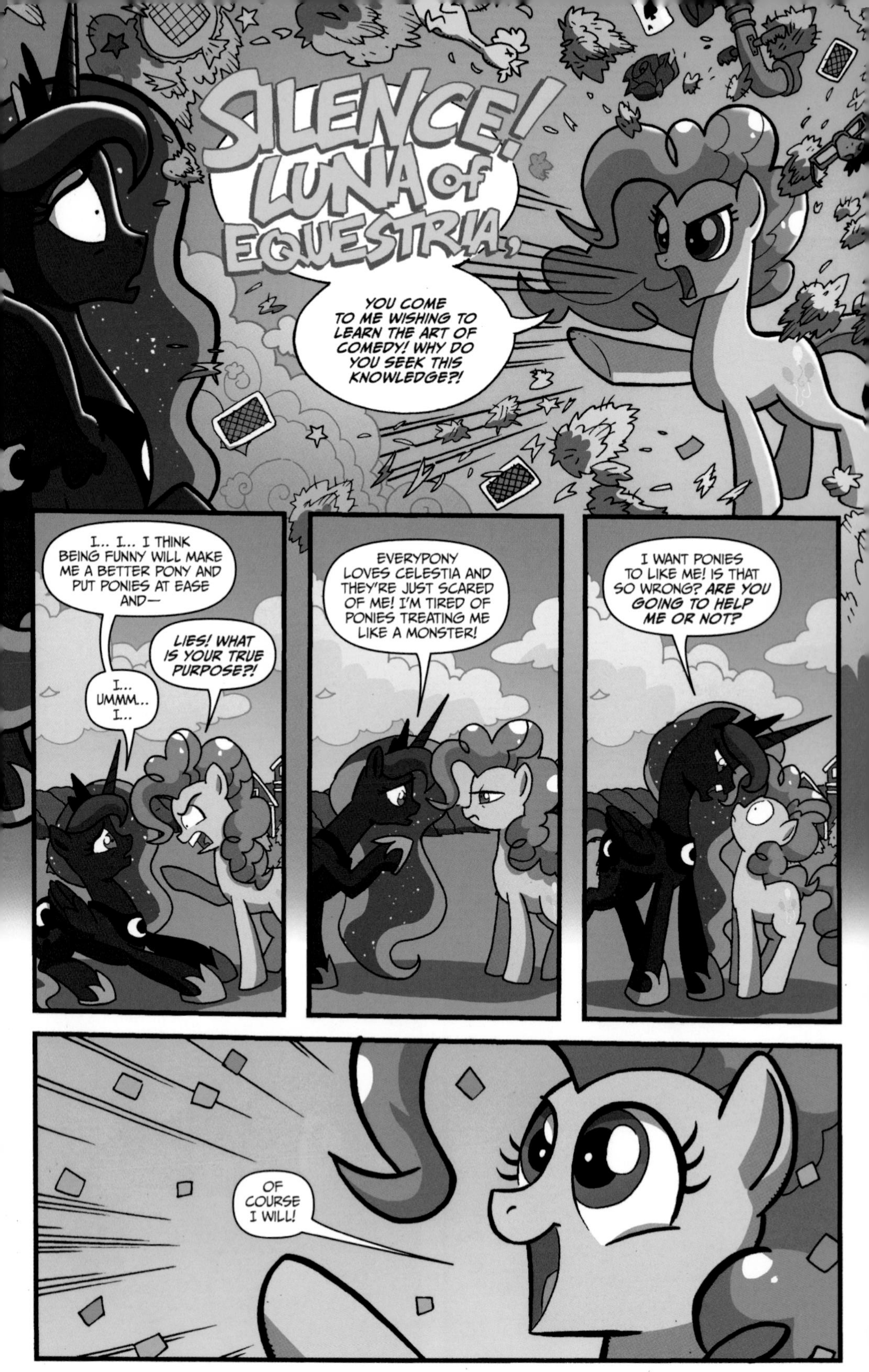
SILENCE! LUNA of EQUESTRIA,
YOU COME TO ME WISHING TO LEARN THE ART OF COMEDY! WHY DO YOU SEEK THIS KNOWLEDGE?!
I... I... I THINK BEING FUNNY WILL MAKE ME A BETTER PONY AND PUT PONIES AT EASE AND—
LIES! WHAT IS YOUR TRUE PURPOSE?!
I... UMMM... I...
EVERYPONY LOVES CELESTIA AND THEY'RE JUST SCARED OF ME! I'M TIRED OF PONIES TREATING ME LIKE A MONSTER!
I WANT PONIES TO LIKE ME! IS THAT SO WRONG? ARE YOU GOING TO HELP ME OR NOT?
OF COURSE I WILL!

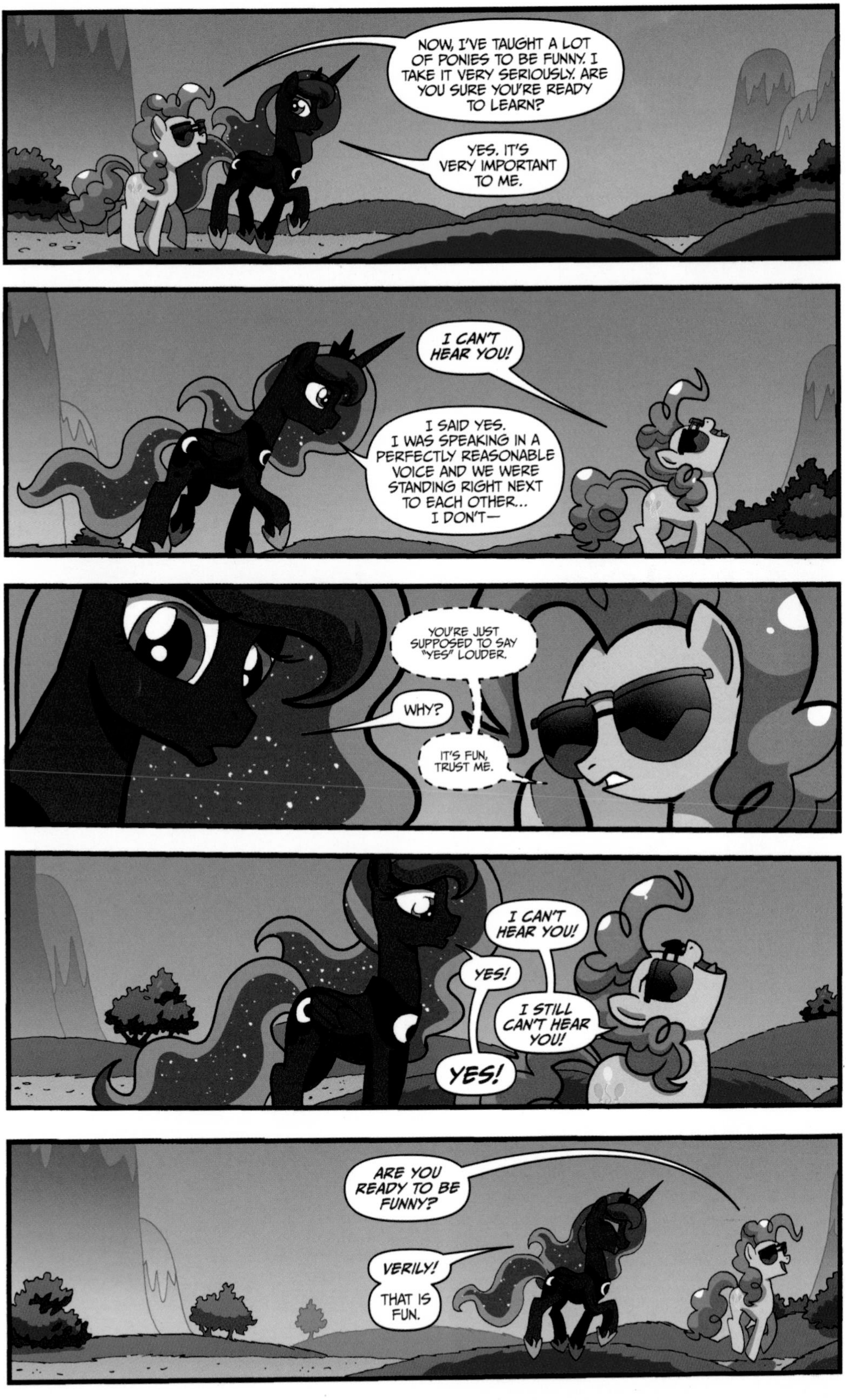
NOW, I'VE TAUGHT A LOT OF PONIES TO BE FUNNY. I TAKE IT VERY SERIOUSLY. ARE YOU SURE YOU'RE READY TO LEARN?
YES. IT'S VERY IMPORTANT TO ME.
I CAN'T HEAR YOU!
I SAID YES. I WAS SPEAKING IN A PERFECTLY REASONABLE VOICE AND WE WERE STANDING RIGHT NEXT TO EACH OTHER... I DON'T—
YOU'RE JUST SUPPOSED TO SAY "YES" LOUDER.
WHY?
IT'S FUN, TRUST ME.
I CAN'T HEAR YOU!
YES!
I STILL CAN'T HEAR YOU!
YES!
ARE YOU READY TO BE FUNNY?
VERILY!
THAT IS FUN.

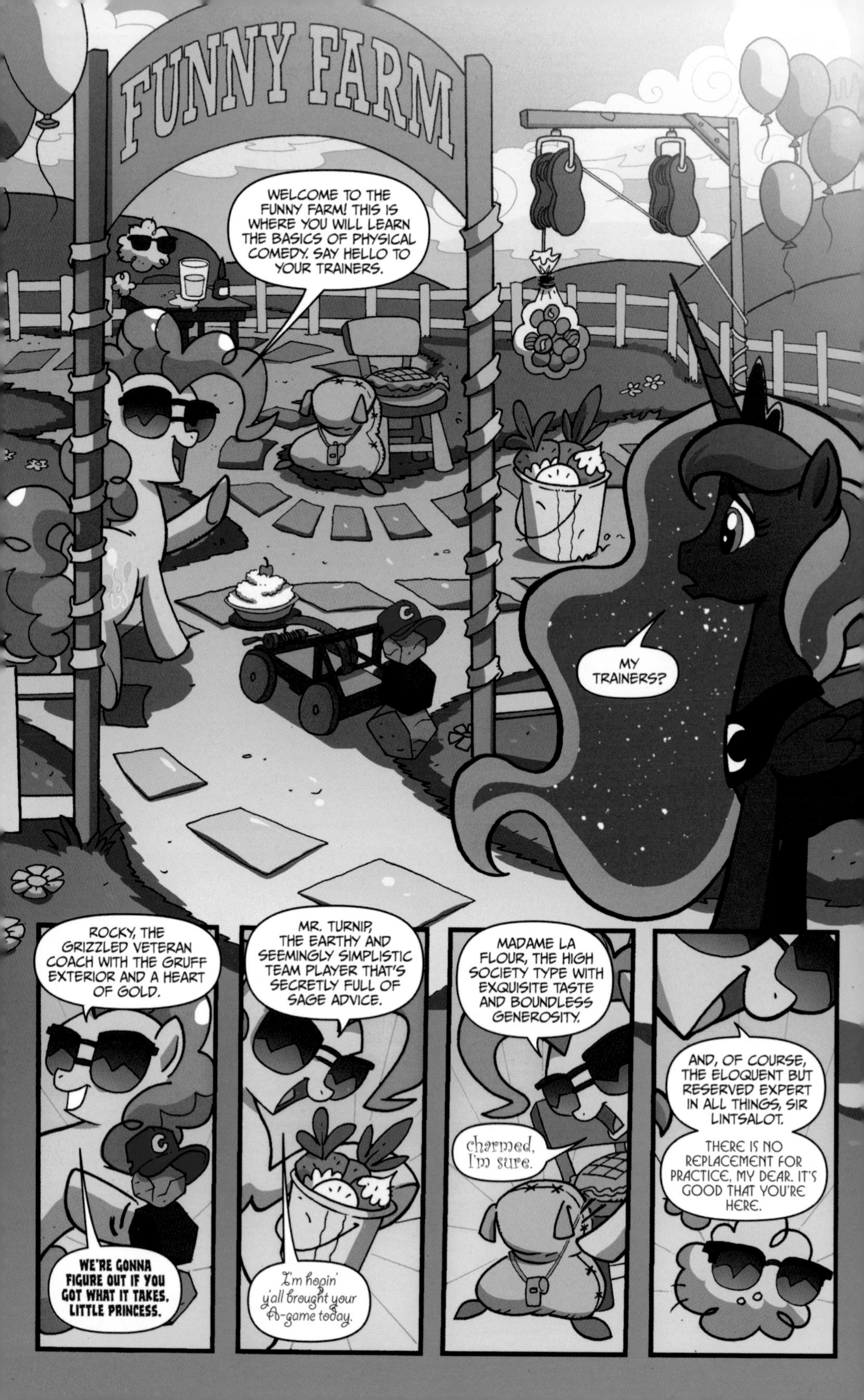
FUNNY FARM
WELCOME TO THE FUNNY FARM! THIS IS WHERE YOU WILL LEARN THE BASICS OF PHYSICAL COMEDY. SAY HELLO TO YOUR TRAINERS.
MY TRAINERS?
ROCKY, THE GRIZZLED VETERAN COACH WITH THE GRUFF EXTERIOR AND A HEART OF GOLD.
WE'RE GONNA FIGURE OUT IF YOU GOT WHAT IT TAKES, LITTLE PRINCESS.
MR. TURNIP, THE EARTHY AND SEEMINGLY SIMPLISTIC TEAM PLAYER THAT'S SECRETLY FULL OF SAGE ADVICE.
I'm hopin' y'all brought your A-game today.
MADAME LA FLOUR, THE HIGH SOCIETY TYPE WITH EXQUISITE TASTE AND BOUNDLESS GENEROSITY.
charmed, I'm sure.
AND, OF COURSE, THE ELOQUENT BUT RESERVED EXPERT IN ALL THINGS, SIR LINTSALOT.
THERE IS NO REPLACEMENT FOR PRACTICE, MY DEAR. IT'S GOOD THAT YOU'RE HERE.

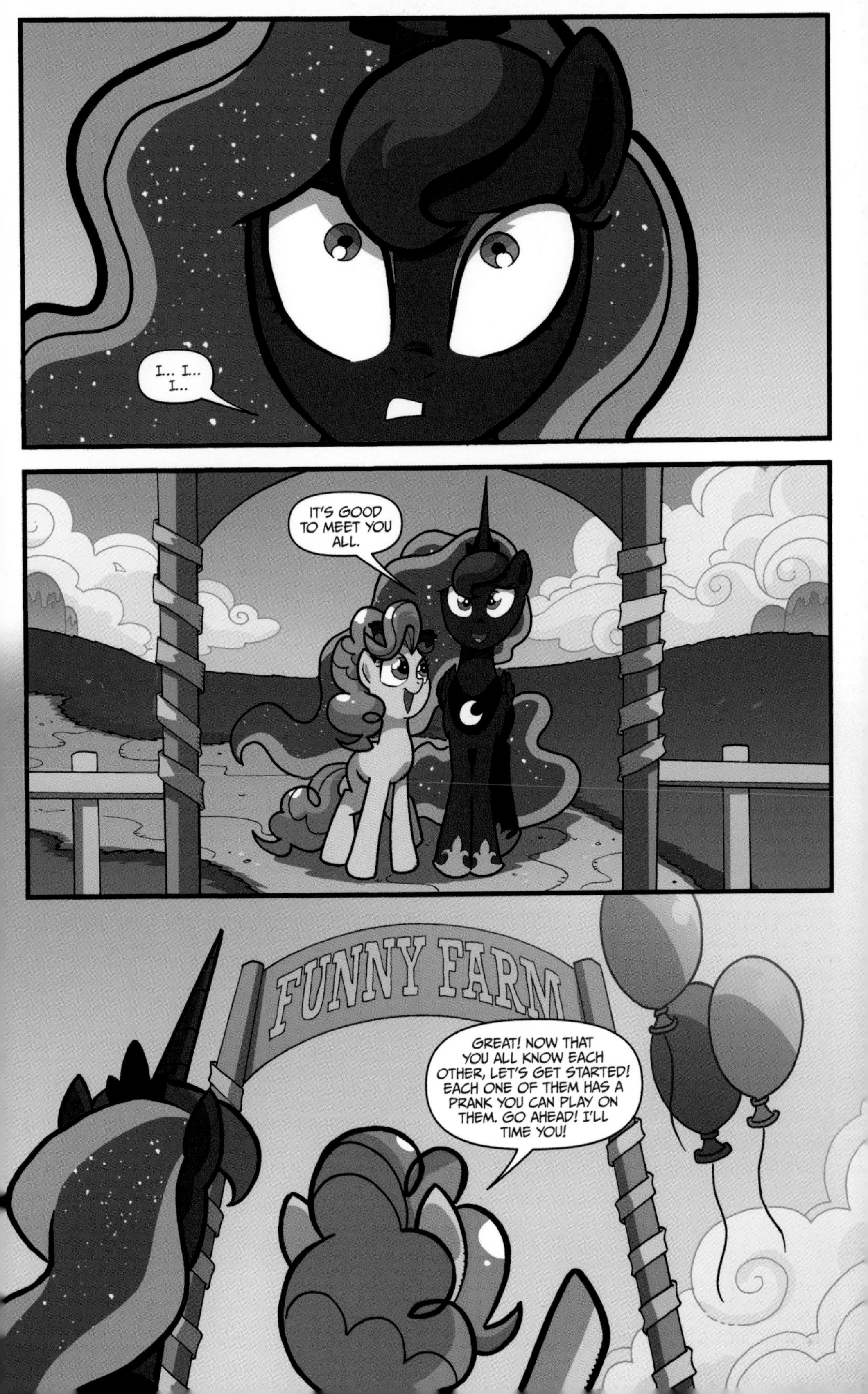
I... I...
I...
IT'S GOOD TO MEET YOU ALL.
FUNNY FARM
GREAT! NOW THAT YOU ALL KNOW EACH OTHER, LET'S GET STARTED! EACH ONE OF THEM HAS A PRANK YOU CAN PLAY ON THEM. GO AHEAD! I'LL TIME YOU!

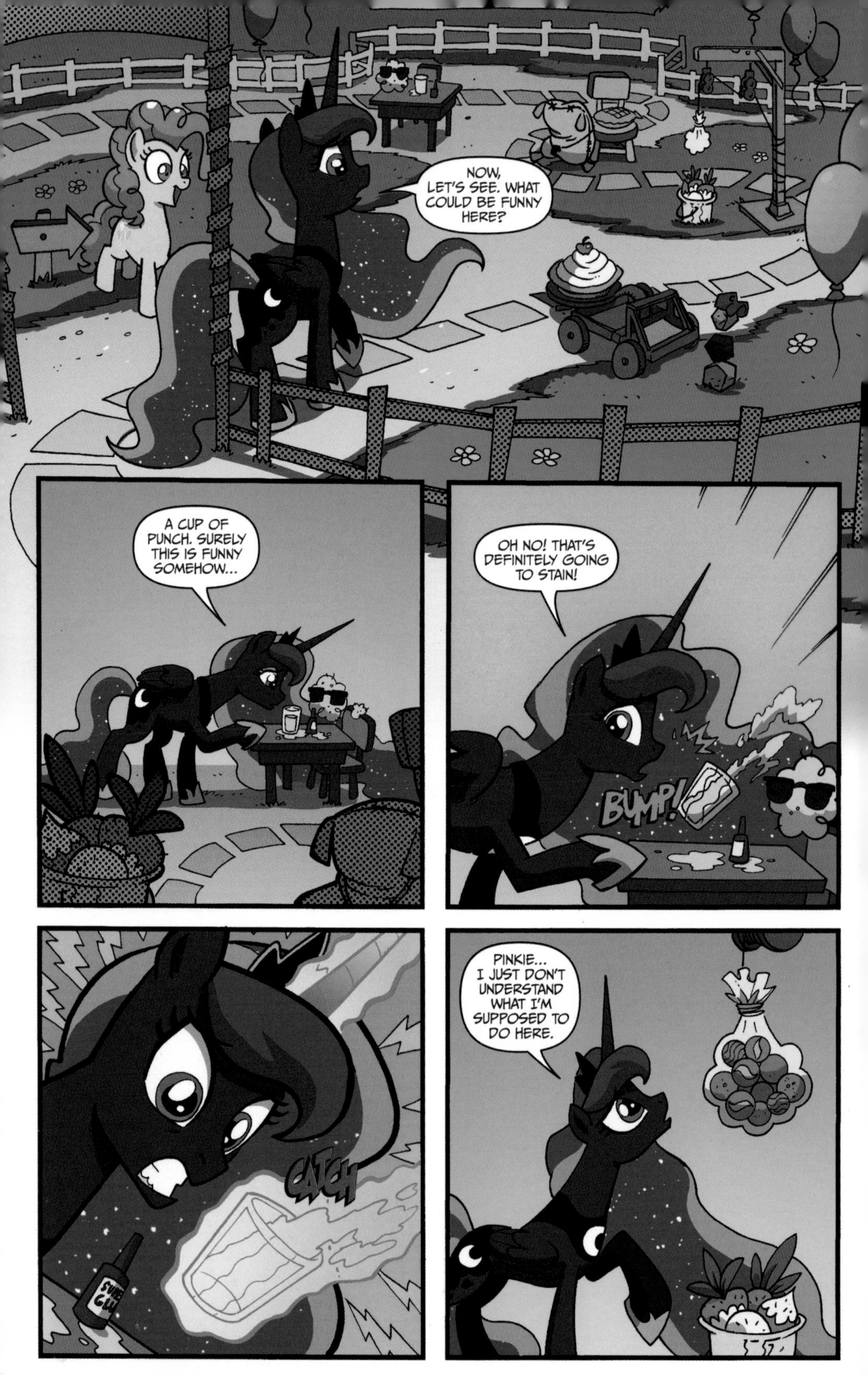
NOW, LET'S SEE. WHAT COULD BE FUNNY HERE?
A CUP OF PUNCH. SURELY THIS IS FUNNY SOMEHOW...
OH NO! THAT'S DEFINITELY GOING TO STAIN!
BUMP!
CATCH
PINKIE... I JUST DON'T UNDERSTAND WHAT I'M SUPPOSED TO DO HERE.

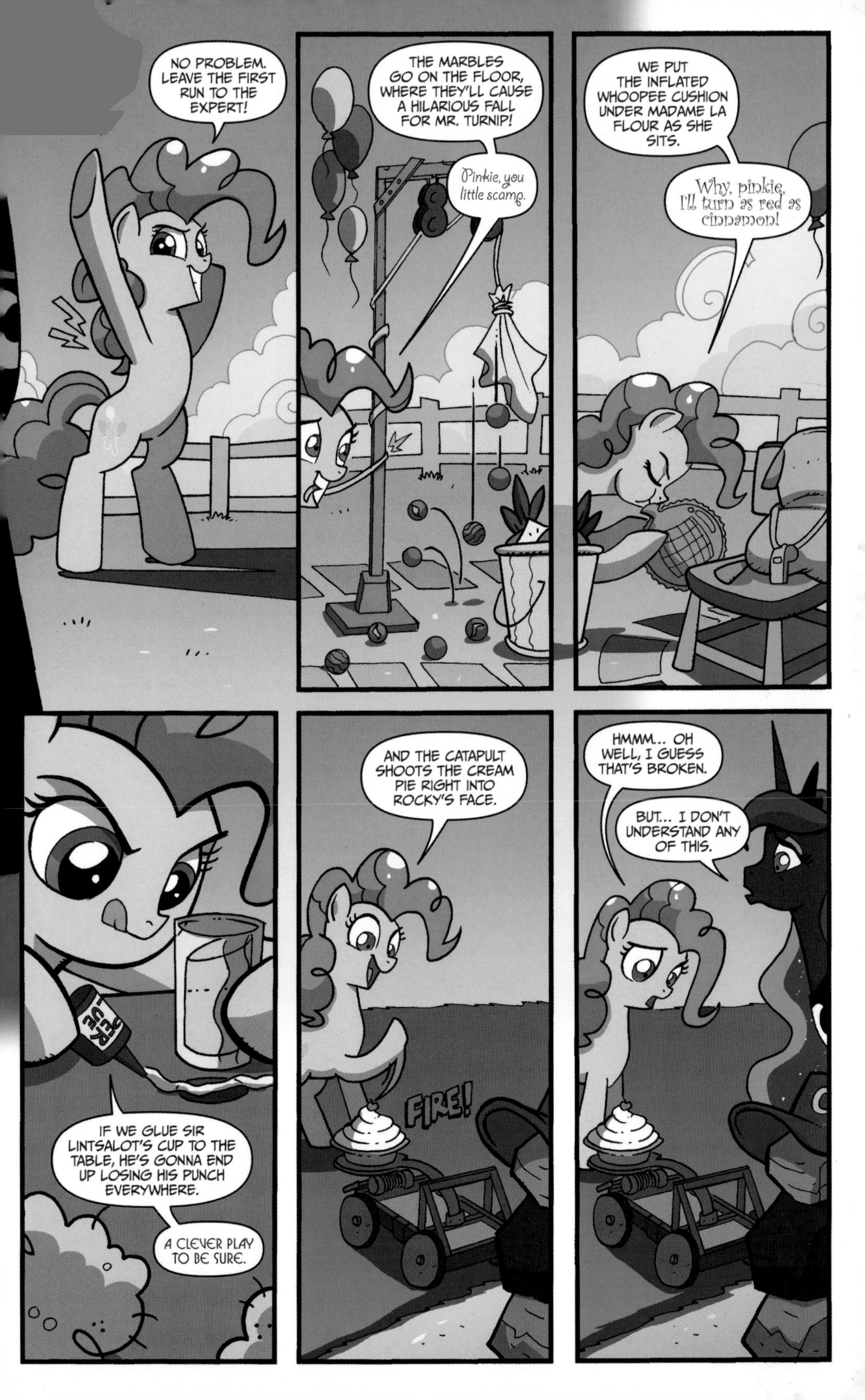
NO PROBLEM. LEAVE THE FIRST RUN TO THE EXPERT!
THE MARBLES GO ON THE FLOOR, WHERE THEY'LL CAUSE A HILARIOUS FALL FOR MR. TURNIP!
Pinkie, you little scamp.
WE PUT THE INFLATED WHOOPEE CUSHION UNDER MADAME LA FLOUR AS SHE SITS.
Why, pinkie, I'll turn as red as cinnamon!
IF WE GLUE SIR LINTSALOT'S CUP TO THE TABLE, HE'S GONNA END UP LOSING HIS PUNCH EVERYWHERE.
A CLEVER PLAY TO BE SURE.
AND THE CATAPULT SHOOTS THE CREAM PIE RIGHT INTO ROCKY'S FACE.
FIRE!
HMMM... OH WELL, I GUESS THAT'S BROKEN.
BUT... I DON'T UNDERSTAND ANY OF THIS.

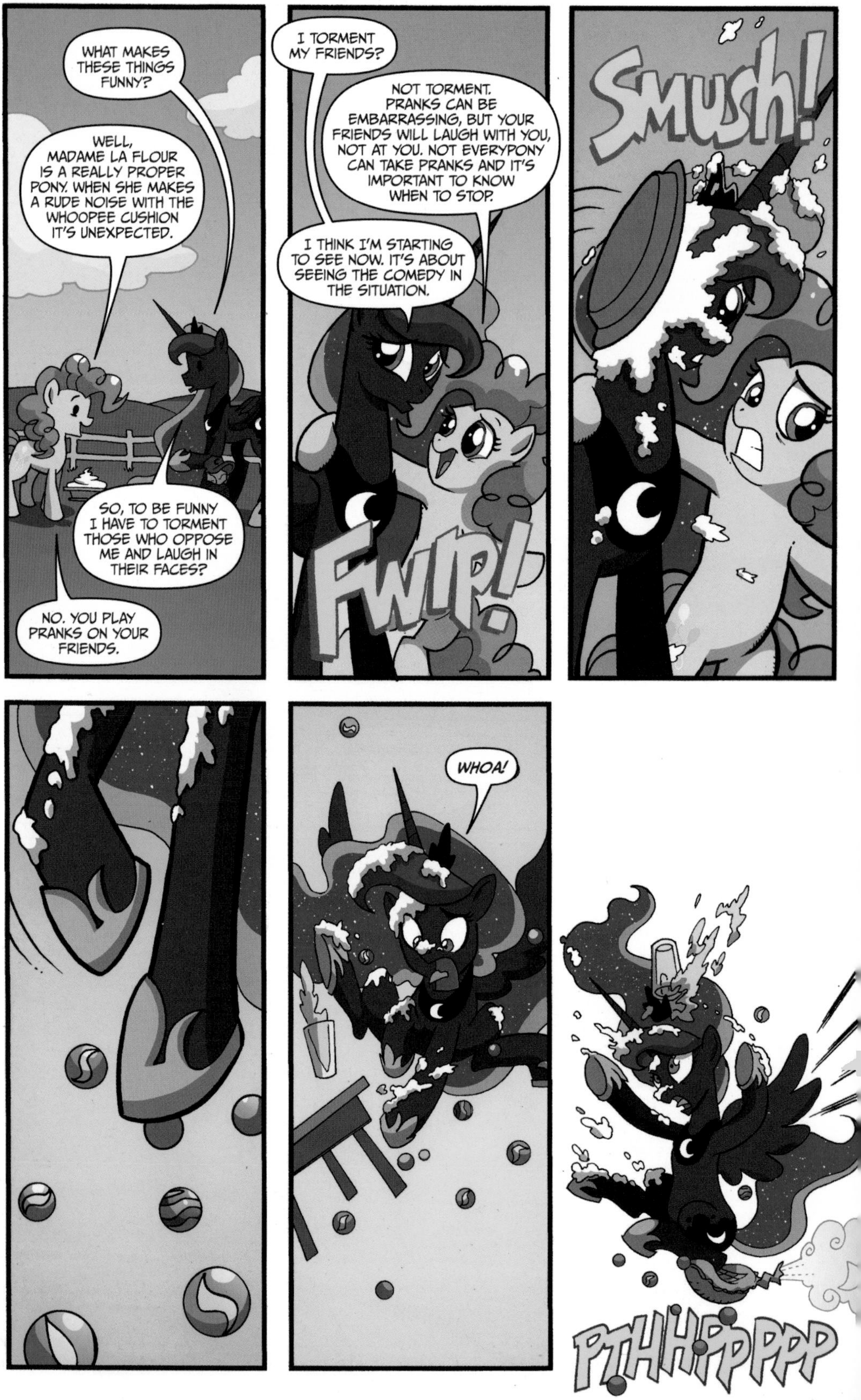
WHAT MAKES THESE THINGS FUNNY?
WELL, MADAME LA FLOUR IS A REALLY PROPER PONY. WHEN SHE MAKES A RUDE NOISE WITH THE WHOOPEE CUSHION IT'S UNEXPECTED.
SO, TO BE FUNNY I HAVE TO TORMENT THOSE WHO OPPOSE ME AND LAUGH IN THEIR FACES?
NO. YOU PLAY PRANKS ON YOUR FRIENDS.
I TORMENT MY FRIENDS?
NOT TORMENT. PRANKS CAN BE EMBARRASSING, BUT YOUR FRIENDS WILL LAUGH WITH YOU, NOT AT YOU. NOT EVERYPONY CAN TAKE PRANKS AND IT'S IMPORTANT TO KNOW WHEN TO STOP.
I THINK I'M STARTING TO SEE NOW. IT'S ABOUT SEEING THE COMEDY IN THE SITUATION.
FWIP!
SMUSH!
WHOA!
PTHHPPPPP

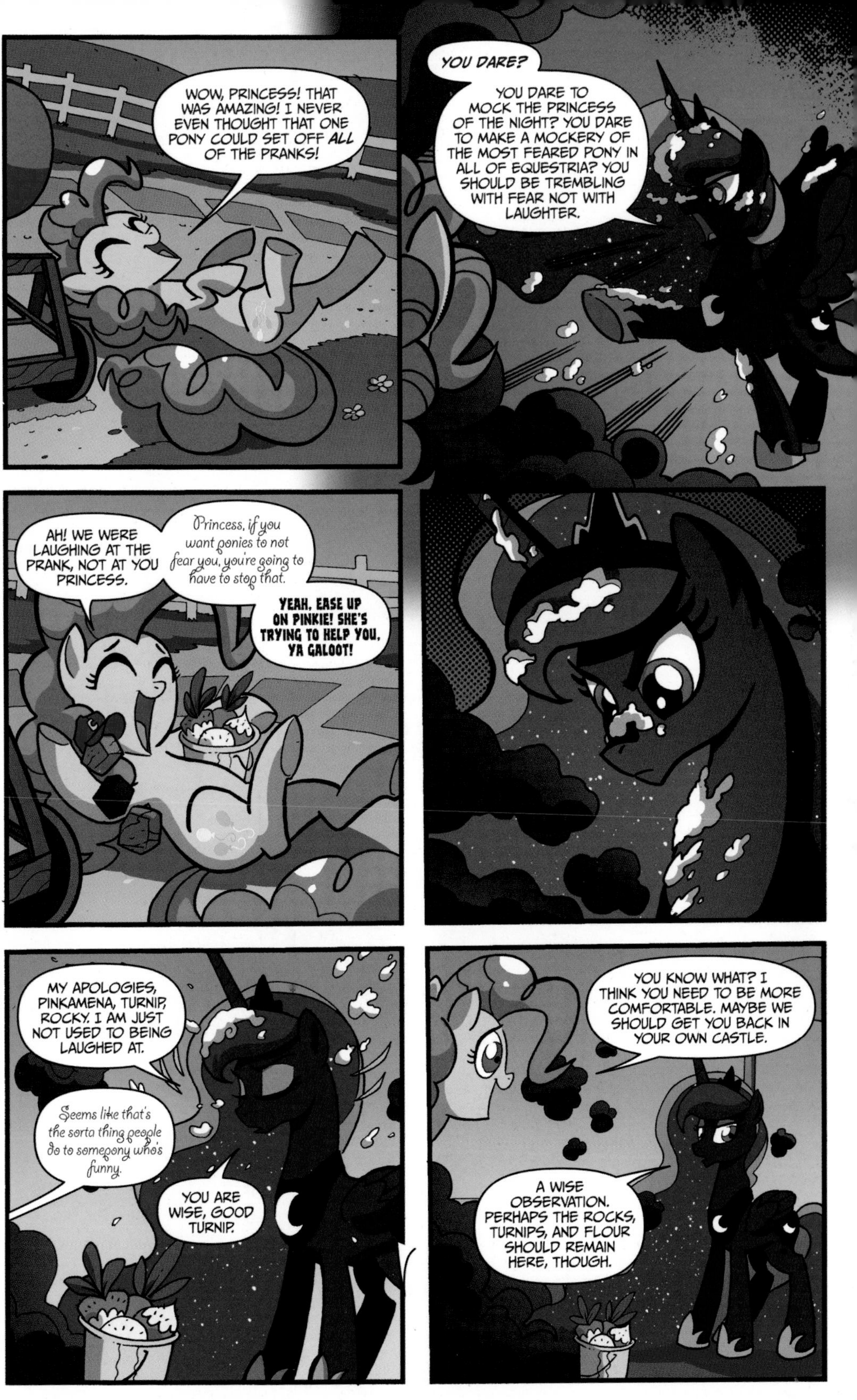
WOW, PRINCESS! THAT WAS AMAZING! I NEVER EVEN THOUGHT THAT ONE PONY COULD SET OFF ALL OF THE PRANKS!
YOU DARE?
YOU DARE TO MOCK THE PRINCESS OF THE NIGHT? YOU DARE TO MAKE A MOCKERY OF THE MOST FEARED PONY IN ALL OF EQUESTRIA? YOU SHOULD BE TREMBLING WITH FEAR NOT WITH LAUGHTER.
AH! WE WERE LAUGHING AT THE PRANK, NOT AT YOU PRINCESS.
Princess, if you want ponies to not fear you, you're going to have to stop that.
YEAH, EASE UP ON PINKIE! SHE'S TRYING TO HELP YOU, YA GALOOT!
MY APOLOGIES, PINKAMENA, TURNIP, ROCKY. I AM JUST NOT USED TO BEING LAUGHED AT.
Seems like that's the sorta thing people do to somepony who's funny.
YOU ARE WISE, GOOD TURNIP.
YOU KNOW WHAT? I THINK YOU NEED TO BE MORE COMFORTABLE. MAYBE WE SHOULD GET YOU BACK IN YOUR OWN CASTLE.
A WISE OBSERVATION. PERHAPS THE ROCKS, TURNIPS, AND FLOUR SHOULD REMAIN HERE, THOUGH.

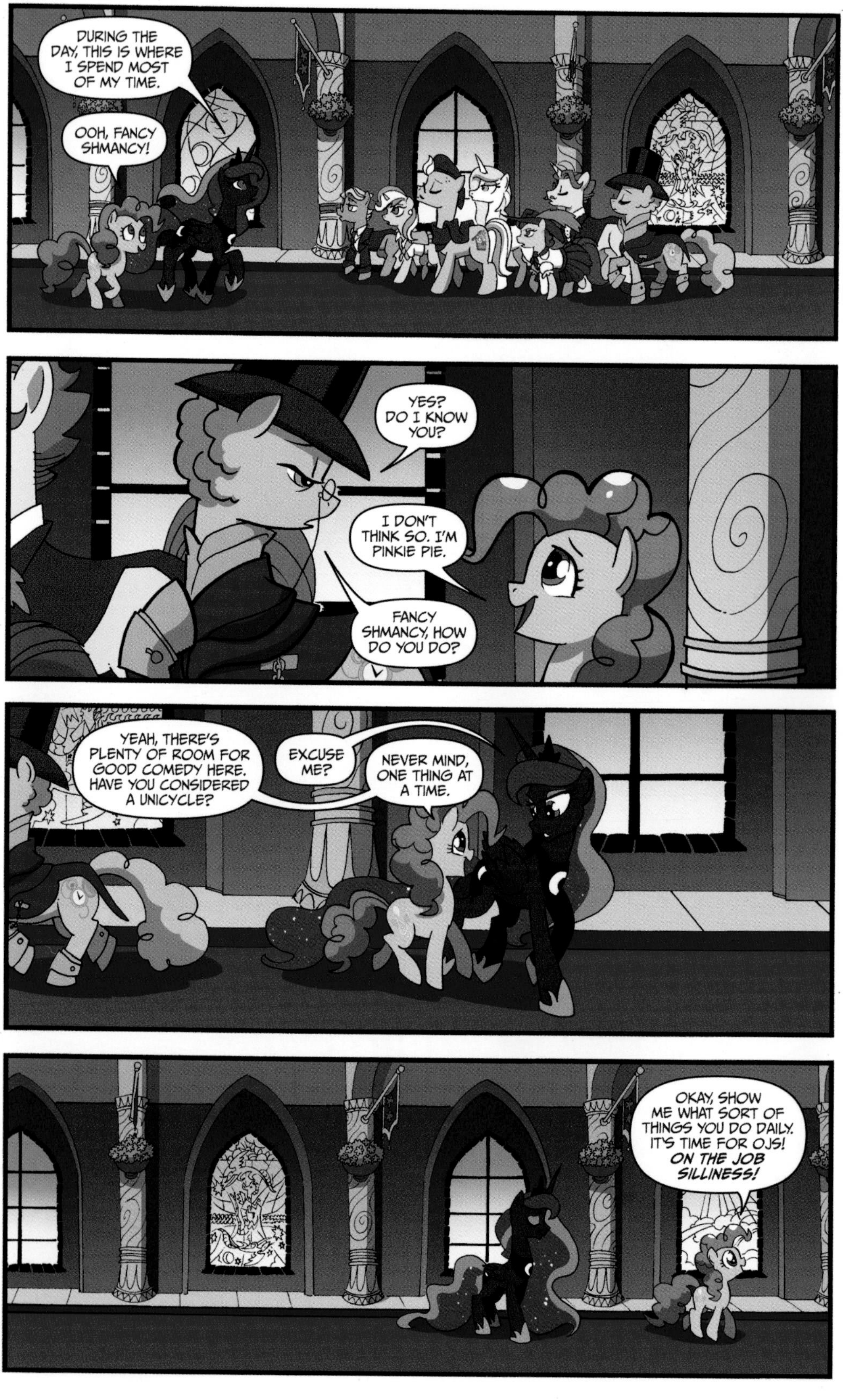
DURING THE DAY, THIS IS WHERE I SPEND MOST OF MY TIME.
OOH, FANCY SHMANCY!
YES? DO I KNOW YOU?
I DON'T THINK SO. I'M PINKIE PIE.
FANCY SHMANCY, HOW DO YOU DO?
YEAH, THERE'S PLENTY OF ROOM FOR GOOD COMEDY HERE. HAVE YOU CONSIDERED A UNICYCLE?
EXCUSE ME?
NEVER MIND, ONE THING AT A TIME.
OKAY, SHOW ME WHAT SORT OF THINGS YOU DO DAILY. IT'S TIME FOR OJS! *ON THE JOB SILLINESS!*

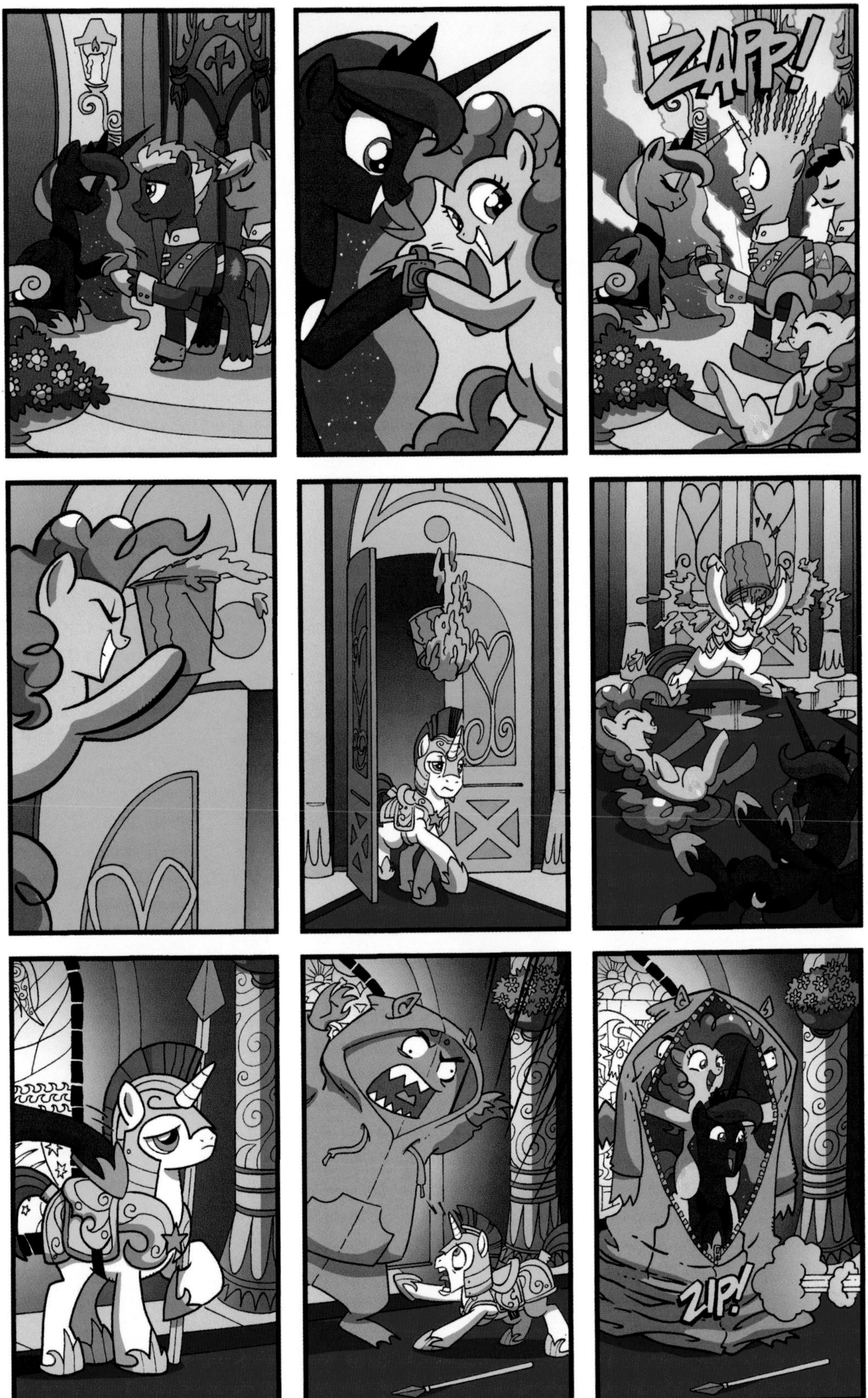
ZAPP!
ZIP!

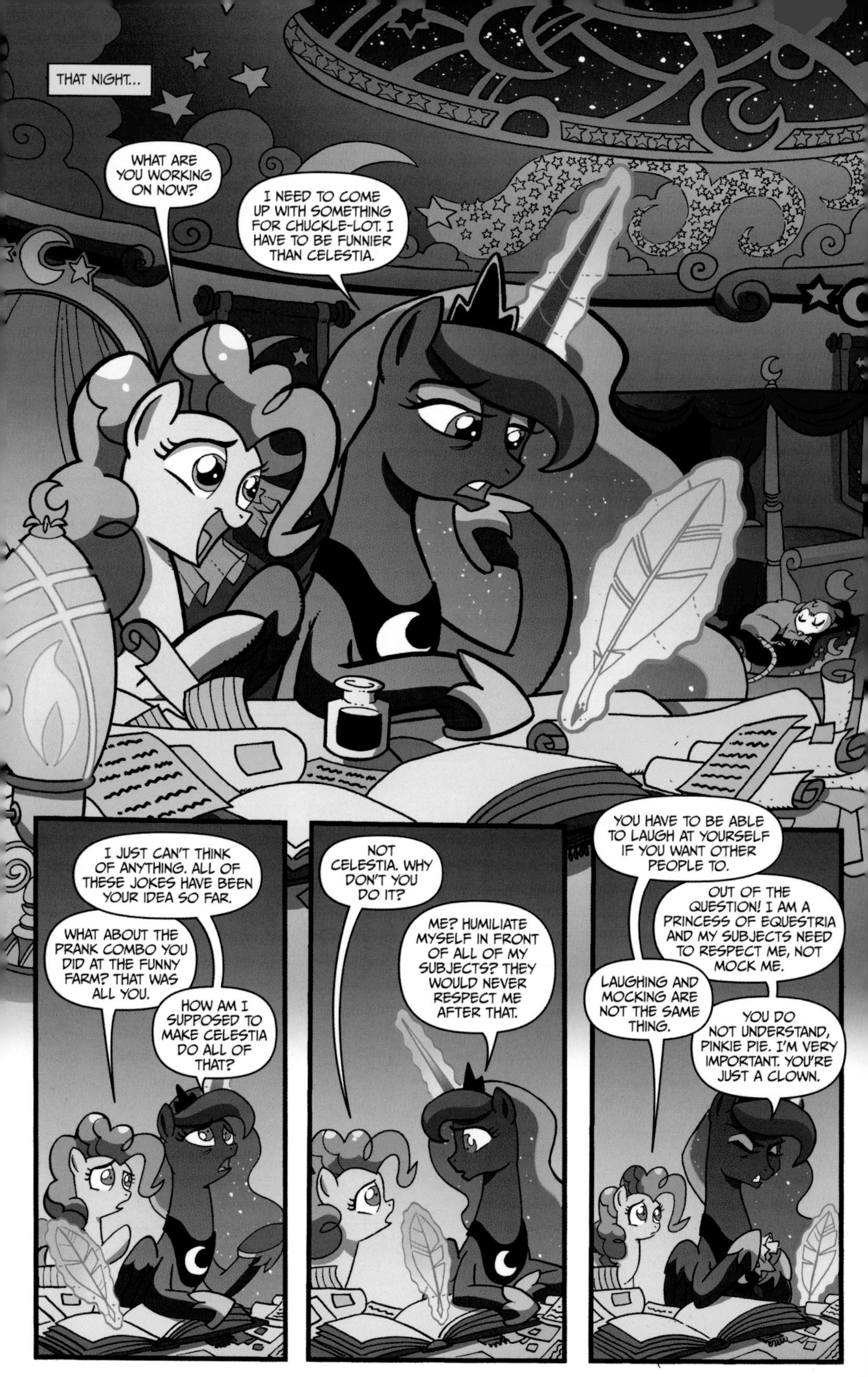
THAT NIGHT...
WHAT ARE YOU WORKING ON NOW?
I NEED TO COME UP WITH SOMETHING FOR CHUCKLE-LOT. I HAVE TO BE FUNNIER THAN CELESTIA.
I JUST CAN'T THINK OF ANYTHING. ALL OF THESE JOKES HAVE BEEN YOUR IDEA SO FAR.
WHAT ABOUT THE PRANK COMBO YOU DID AT THE FUNNY FARM? THAT WAS ALL YOU.
HOW AM I SUPPOSED TO MAKE CELESTIA DO ALL OF THAT?
NOT CELESTIA. WHY DON'T YOU DO IT?
ME? HUMILIATE MYSELF IN FRONT OF ALL OF MY SUBJECTS? THEY WOULD NEVER RESPECT ME AFTER THAT.
YOU HAVE TO BE ABLE TO LAUGH AT YOURSELF IF YOU WANT OTHER PEOPLE TO.
OUT OF THE QUESTION! I AM A PRINCESS OF EQUESTRIA AND MY SUBJECTS NEED TO RESPECT ME, NOT MOCK ME.
LAUGHING AND MOCKING ARE NOT THE SAME THING.
YOU DO NOT UNDERSTAND, PINKIE PIE. I'M VERY IMPORTANT. YOU'RE JUST A CLOWN.

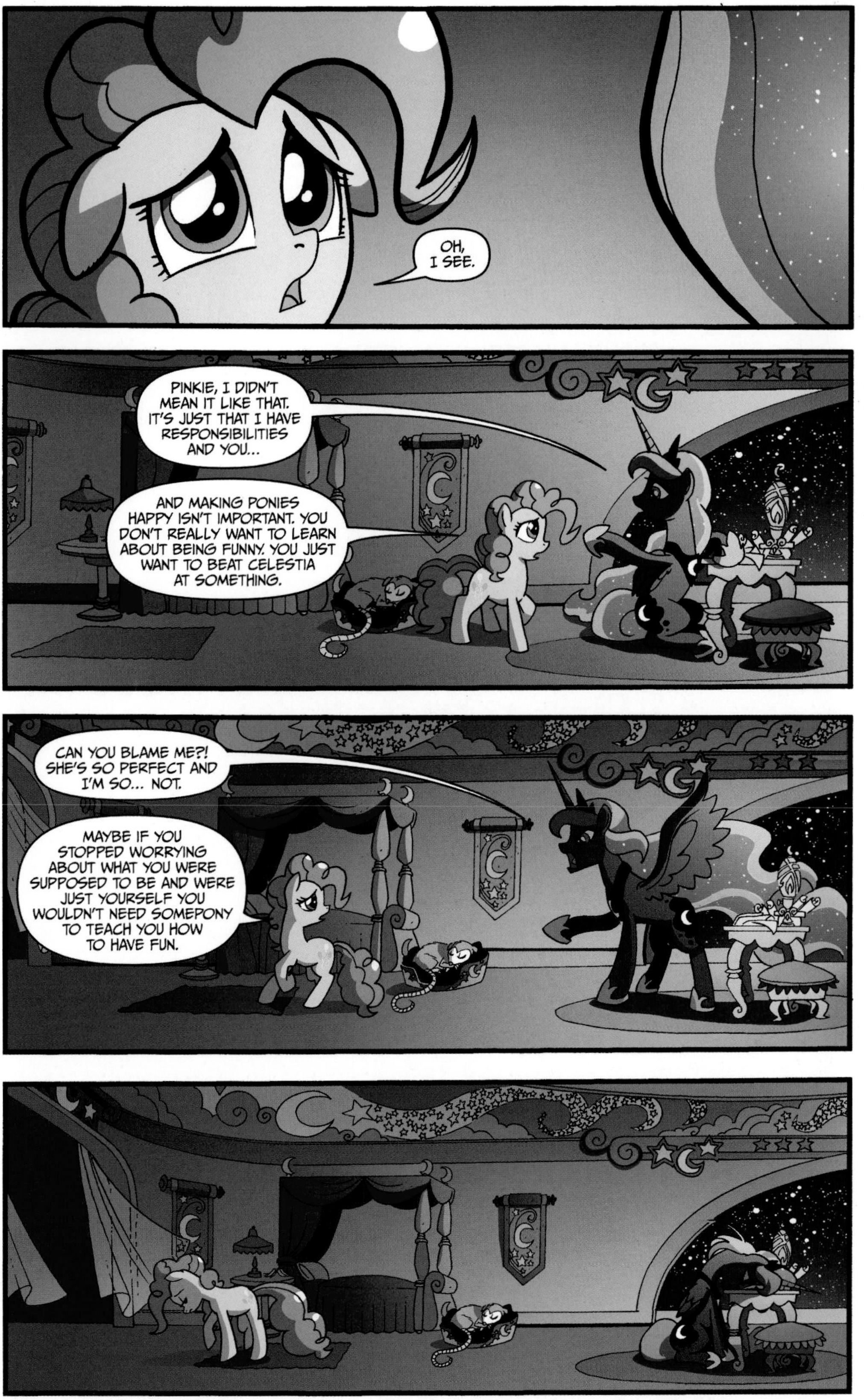
OH, I SEE.
PINKIE, I DIDN'T MEAN IT LIKE THAT. IT'S JUST THAT I HAVE RESPONSIBILITIES AND YOU...
AND MAKING PONIES HAPPY ISN'T IMPORTANT. YOU DON'T REALLY WANT TO LEARN ABOUT BEING FUNNY. YOU JUST WANT TO BEAT CELESTIA AT SOMETHING.
CAN YOU BLAME ME?! SHE'S SO PERFECT AND I'M SO... NOT.
MAYBE IF YOU STOPPED WORRYING ABOUT WHAT YOU WERE SUPPOSED TO BE AND WERE JUST YOURSELF YOU WOULDN'T NEED SOMEPONY TO TEACH YOU HOW TO HAVE FUN.

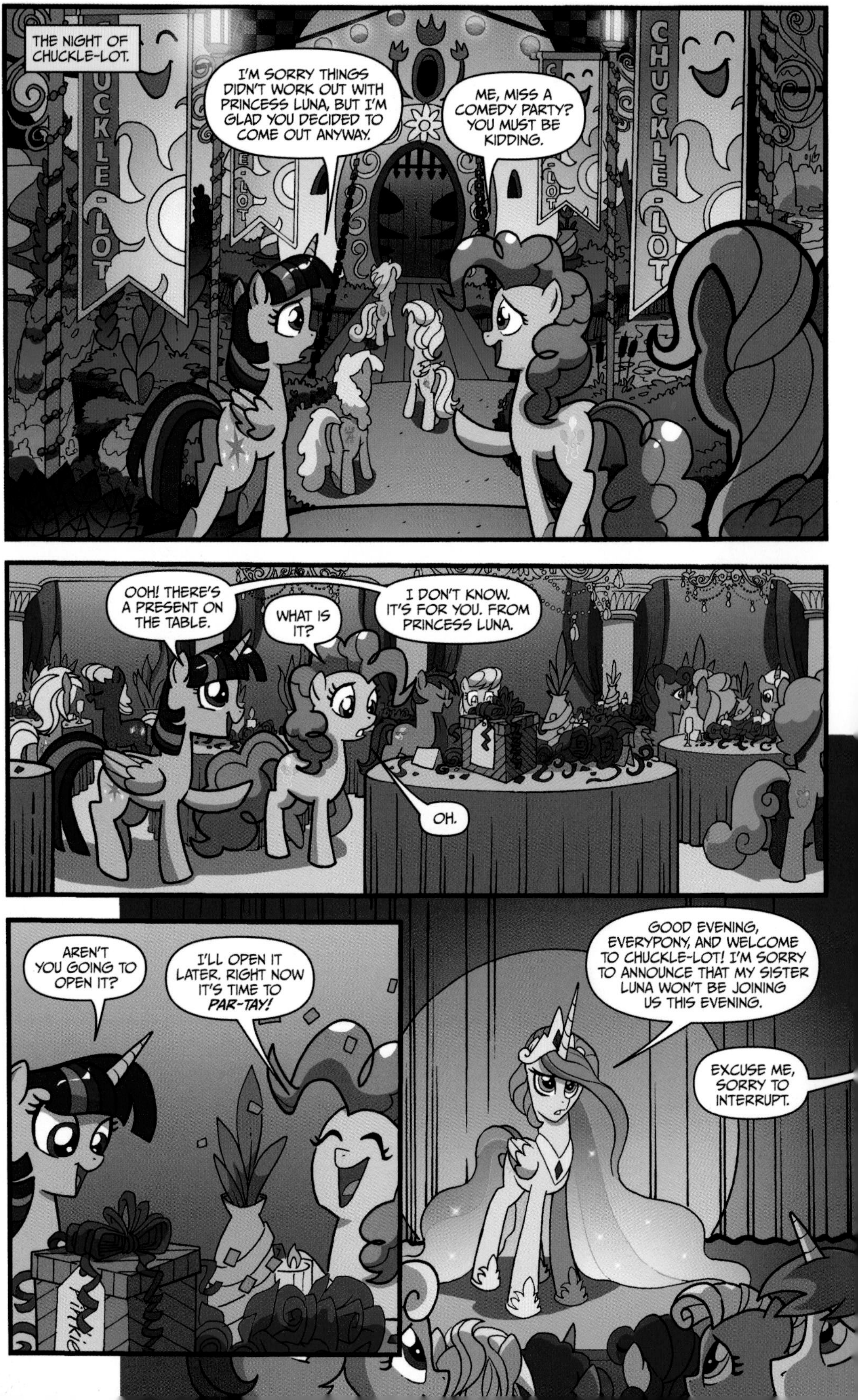

THE NIGHT OF CHUCKLE-LOT.
CHUCKLE-LOT
I'M SORRY THINGS DIDN'T WORK OUT WITH PRINCESS LUNA, BUT I'M GLAD YOU DECIDED TO COME OUT ANYWAY.
ME, MISS A COMEDY PARTY? YOU MUST BE KIDDING.
CHUCKLE-LOT
OOH! THERE'S A PRESENT ON THE TABLE.
WHAT IS IT?
I DON'T KNOW. IT'S FOR YOU. FROM PRINCESS LUNA.
OH.
AREN'T YOU GOING TO OPEN IT?
I'LL OPEN IT LATER. RIGHT NOW IT'S TIME TO *PAR-TAY!*
Pinkie
GOOD EVENING, EVERYPONY, AND WELCOME TO CHUCKLE-LOT! I'M SORRY TO ANNOUNCE THAT MY SISTER LUNA WON'T BE JOINING US THIS EVENING.
EXCUSE ME, SORRY TO INTERRUPT.

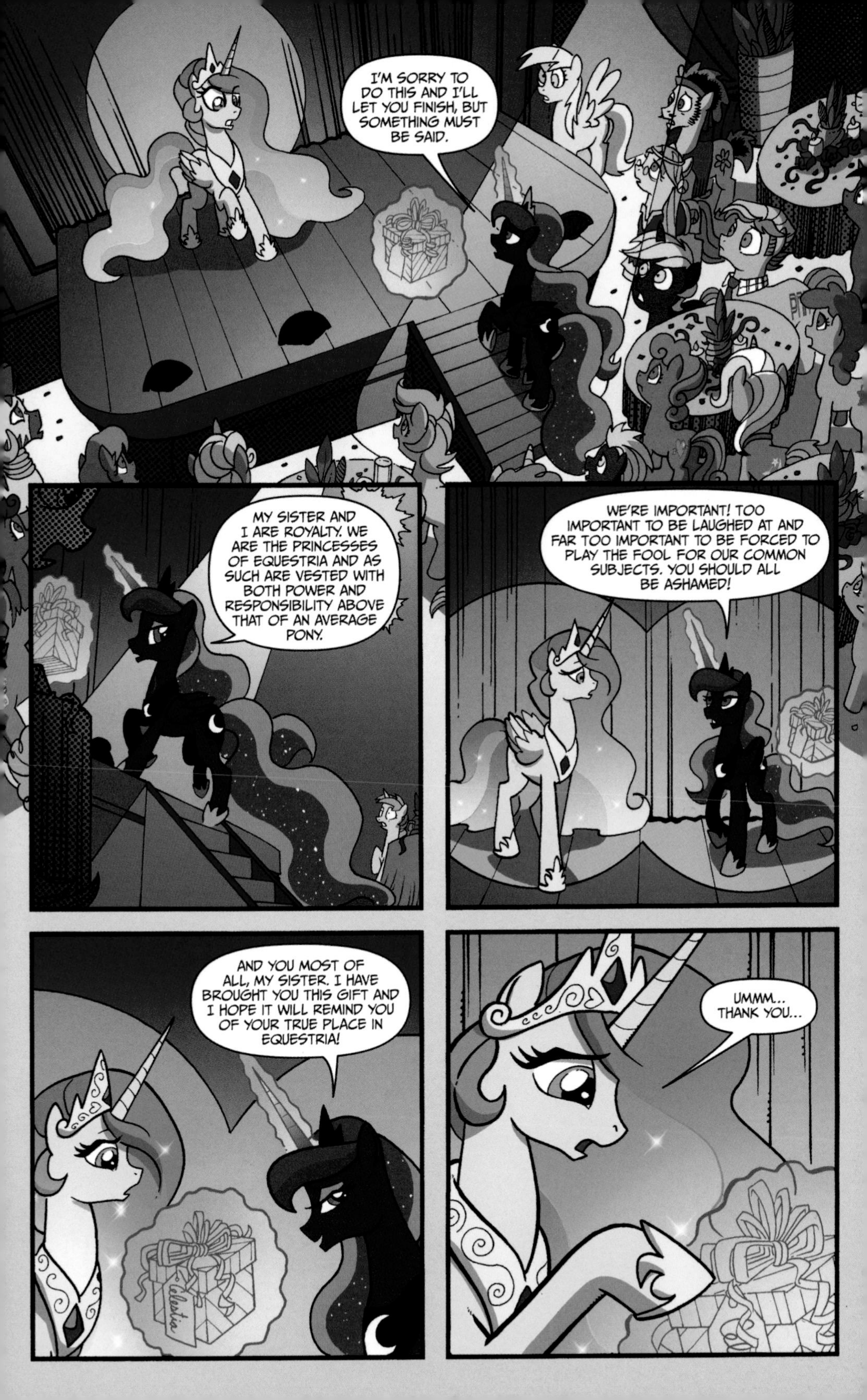
I'M SORRY TO DO THIS AND I'LL LET YOU FINISH, BUT SOMETHING MUST BE SAID.
MY SISTER AND I ARE ROYALTY. WE ARE THE PRINCESSES OF EQUESTRIA AND AS SUCH ARE VESTED WITH BOTH POWER AND RESPONSIBILITY ABOVE THAT OF AN AVERAGE PONY.
WE'RE IMPORTANT! TOO IMPORTANT TO BE LAUGHED AT AND FAR TOO IMPORTANT TO BE FORCED TO PLAY THE FOOL FOR OUR COMMON SUBJECTS. YOU SHOULD ALL BE ASHAMED!
AND YOU MOST OF ALL, MY SISTER. I HAVE BROUGHT YOU THIS GIFT AND I HOPE IT WILL REMIND YOU OF YOUR TRUE PLACE IN EQUESTRIA!
Celestia
UMMM... THANK YOU...

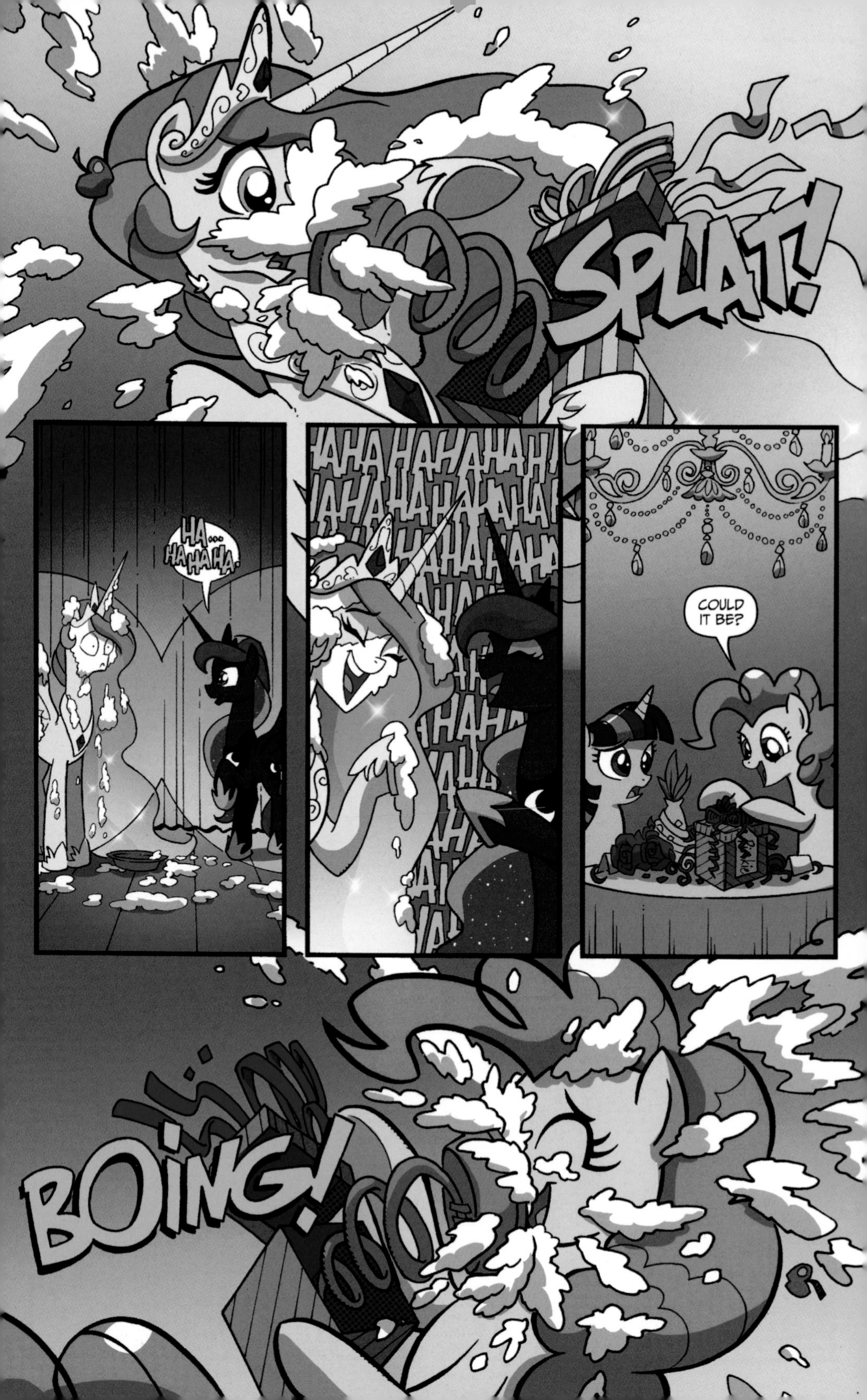
SPLAT!
HA... HAHAHA.
HAHAHAHAHAHAHA
COULD IT BE?
Pinkie
BOING!

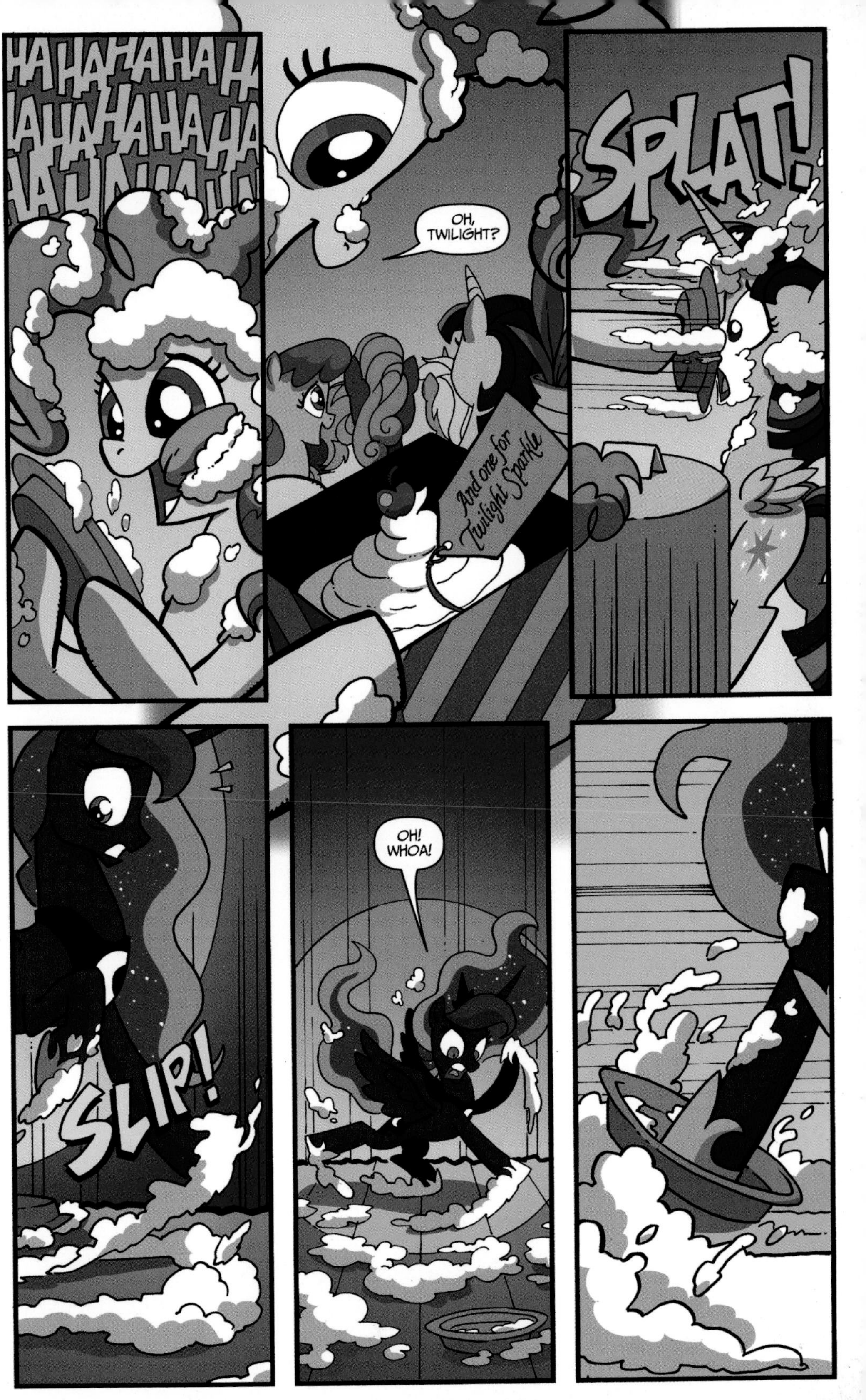
HAHAHAHAHA
OH, TWILIGHT?
And one for Twilight Sparkle
SPLAT!
SLIP!
OH! WHOA!

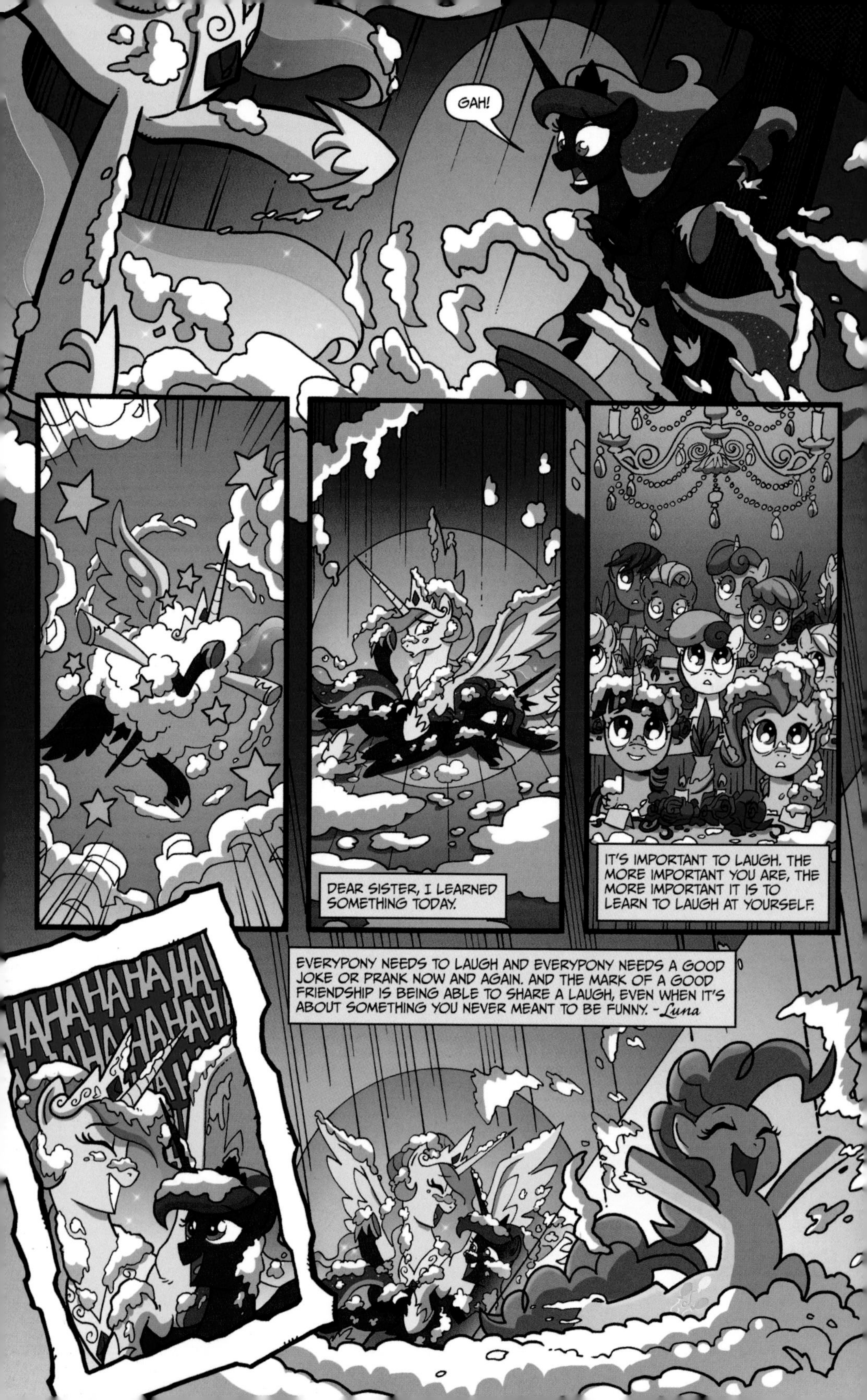
GAH!
DEAR SISTER, I LEARNED SOMETHING TODAY.
IT'S IMPORTANT TO LAUGH. THE MORE IMPORTANT YOU ARE, THE MORE IMPORTANT IT IS TO LEARN TO LAUGH AT YOURSELF.
EVERYPONY NEEDS TO LAUGH AND EVERYPONY NEEDS A GOOD JOKE OR PRANK NOW AND AGAIN. AND THE MARK OF A GOOD FRIENDSHIP IS BEING ABLE TO SHARE A LAUGH, EVEN WHEN IT'S ABOUT SOMETHING YOU NEVER MEANT TO BE FUNNY. -Luna
HAHAHAHAHA
HAHAHAHAHA

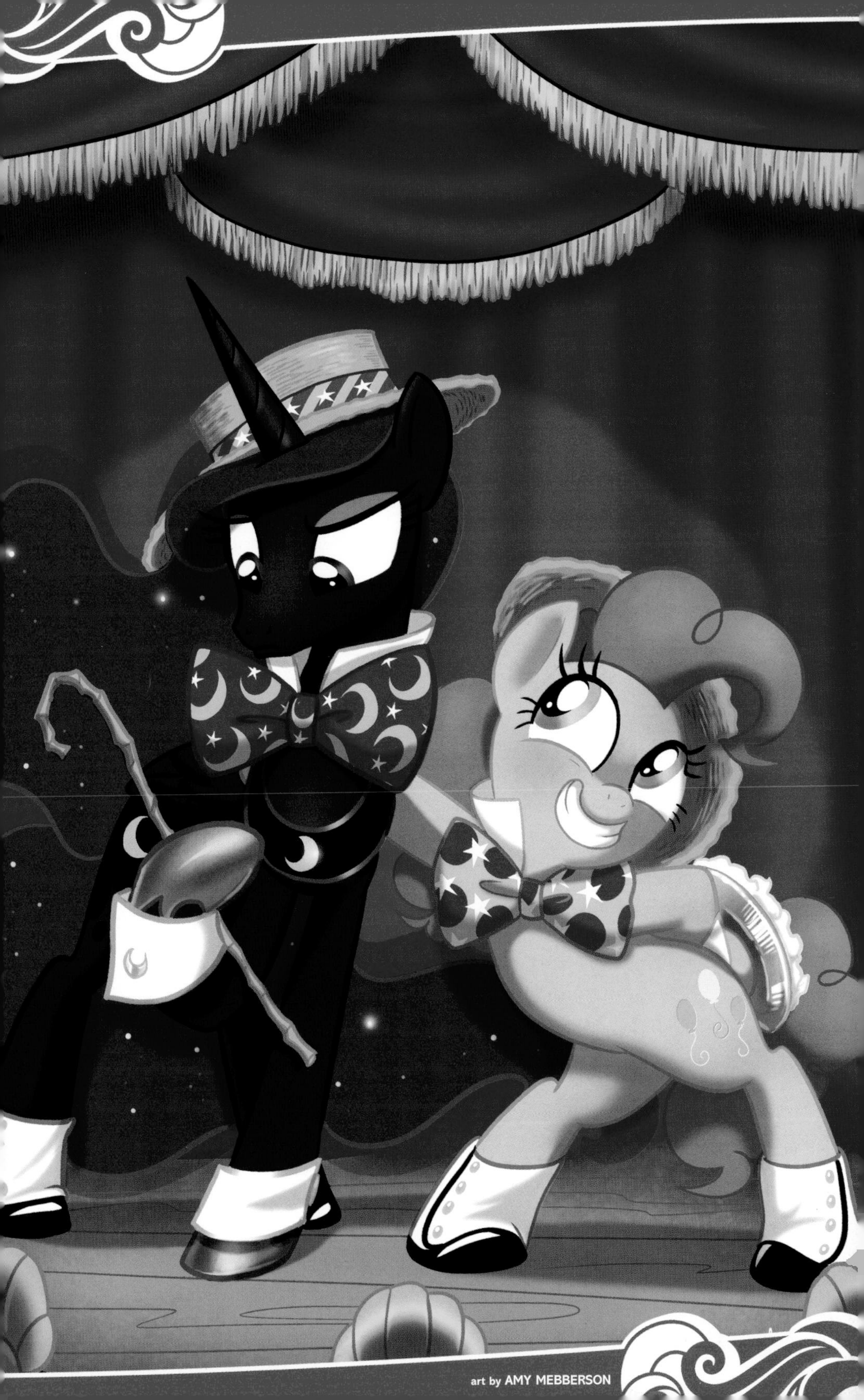

art by AMY MEBBERSON

Applejack & Rarity

The Odd Ponies

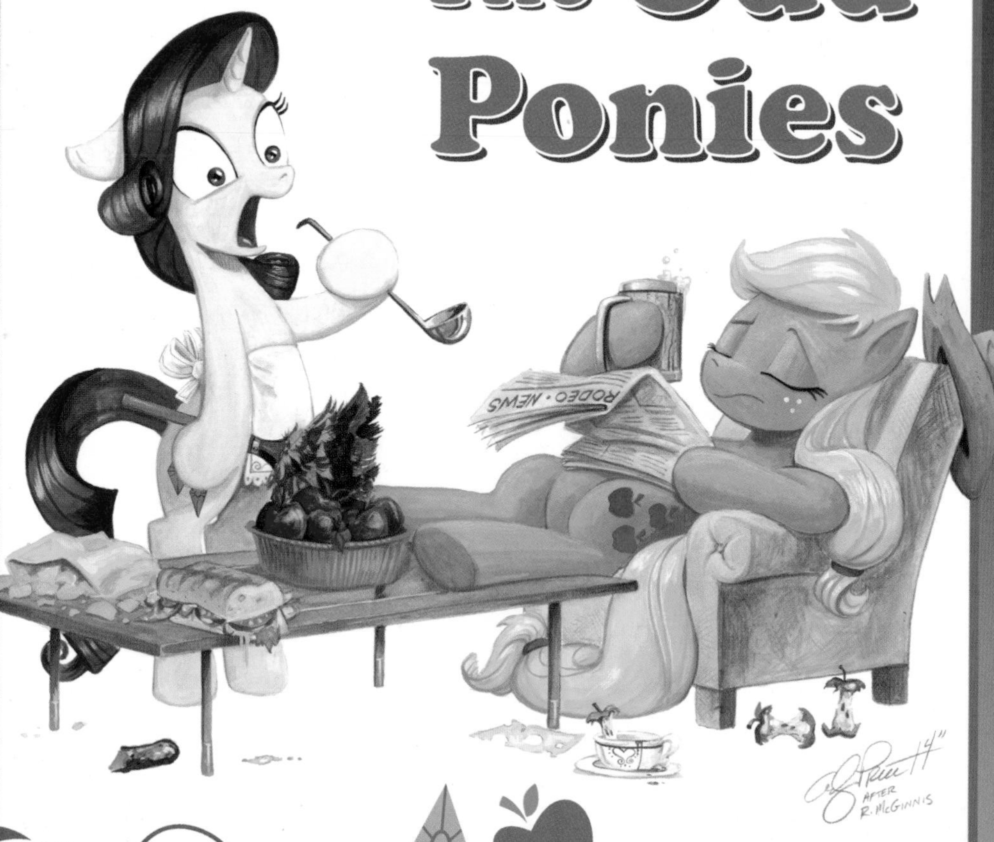
RODEO · NEWS
AFTER
R. McGINNIS

art by ANDY PRICE

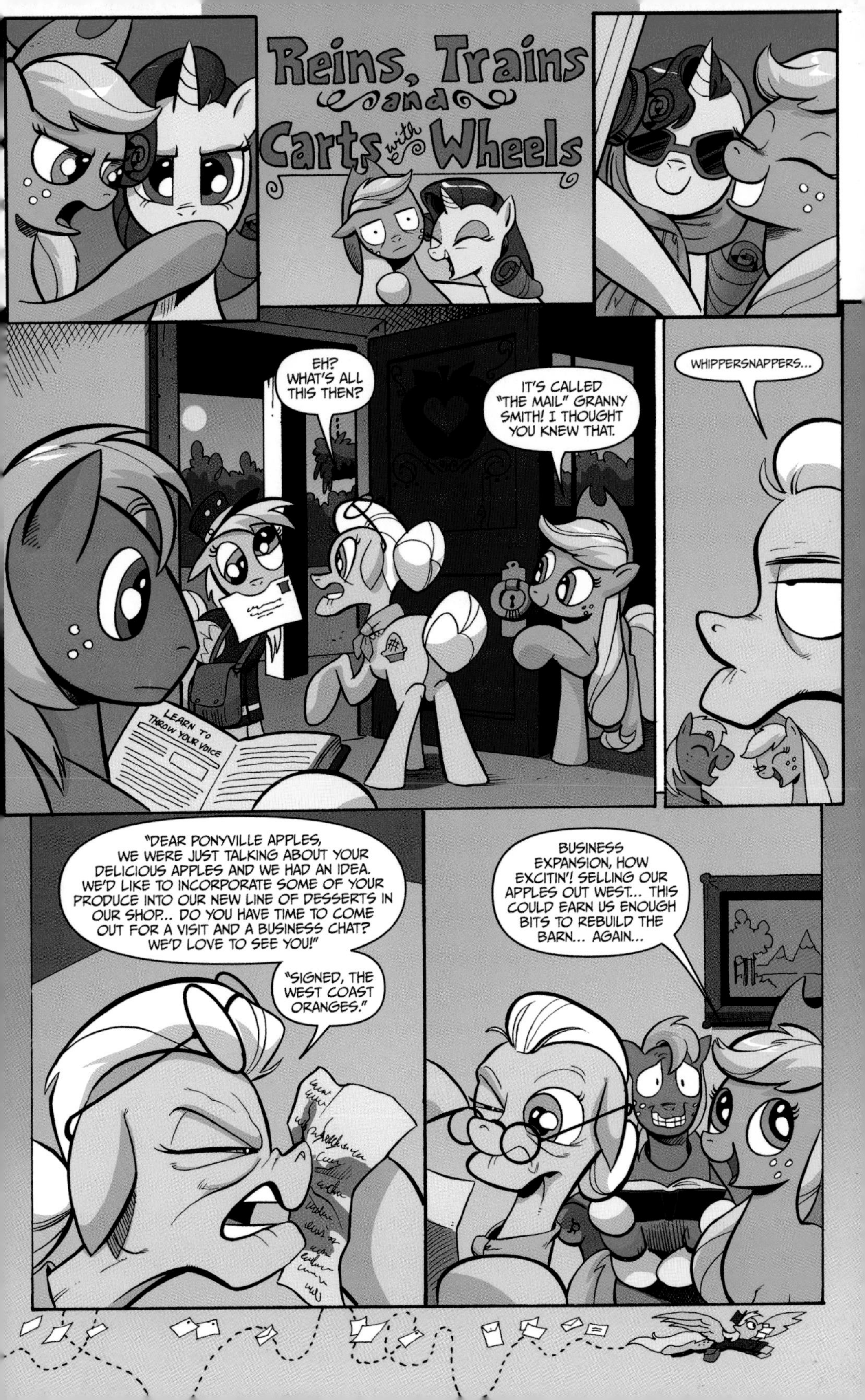
Reins, Trains and Carts with Wheels
EH? WHAT'S ALL THIS THEN?
IT'S CALLED "THE MAIL" GRANNY SMITH! I THOUGHT YOU KNEW THAT.
LEARN TO THROW YOUR VOICE
WHIPPERSNAPPERS...
"DEAR PONYVILLE APPLES, WE WERE JUST TALKING ABOUT YOUR DELICIOUS APPLES AND WE HAD AN IDEA. WE'D LIKE TO INCORPORATE SOME OF YOUR PRODUCE INTO OUR NEW LINE OF DESSERTS IN OUR SHOP... DO YOU HAVE TIME TO COME OUT FOR A VISIT AND A BUSINESS CHAT? WE'D LOVE TO SEE YOU!"
"SIGNED, THE WEST COAST ORANGES."
BUSINESS EXPANSION, HOW EXCITIN'! SELLING OUR APPLES OUT WEST... THIS COULD EARN US ENOUGH BITS TO REBUILD THE BARN... AGAIN...

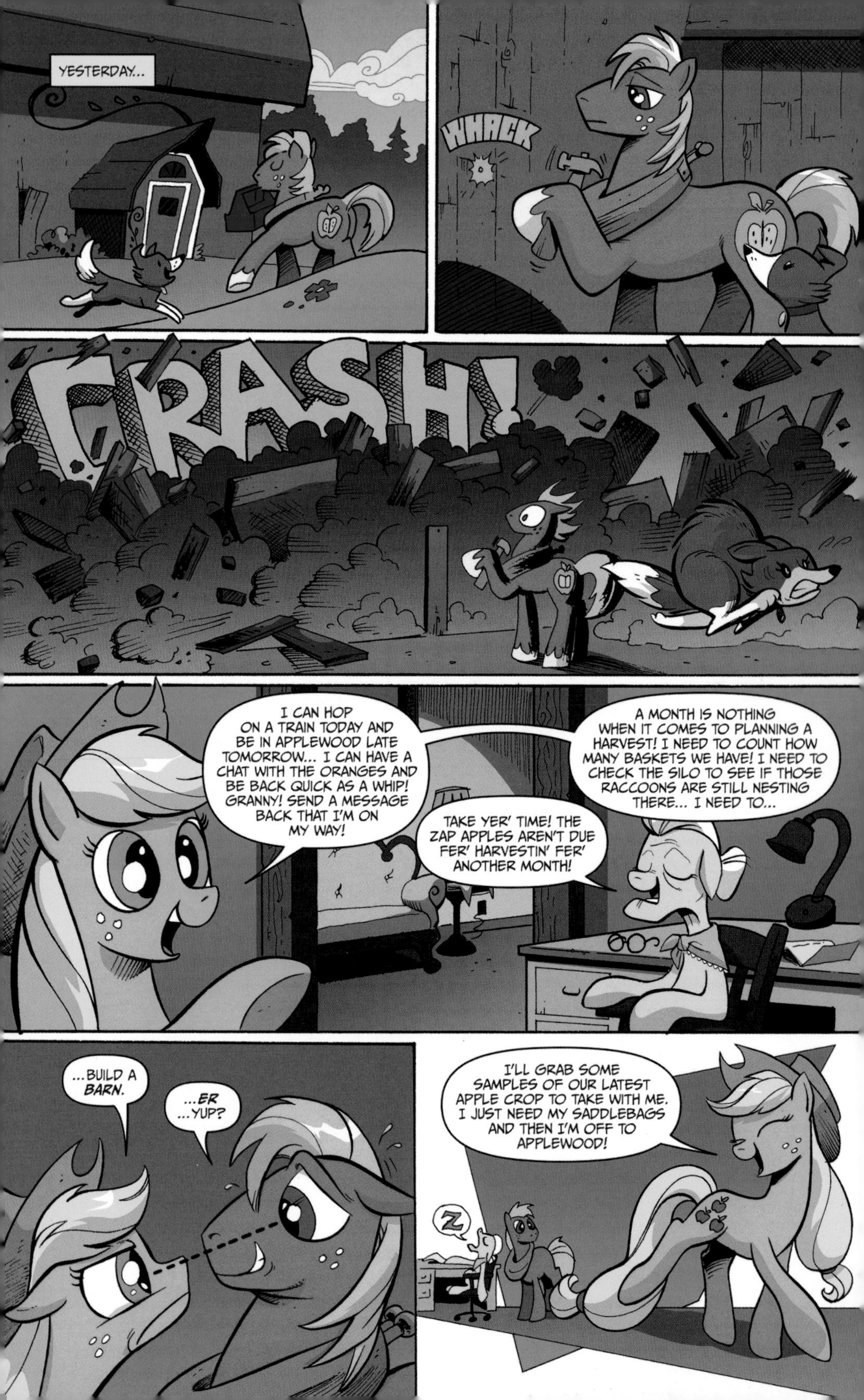
YESTERDAY...
WHACK
CRASH!
I CAN HOP ON A TRAIN TODAY AND BE IN APPLEWOOD LATE TOMORROW... I CAN HAVE A CHAT WITH THE ORANGES AND BE BACK QUICK AS A WHIP! GRANNY! SEND A MESSAGE BACK THAT I'M ON MY WAY!
TAKE YER' TIME! THE ZAP APPLES AREN'T DUE FER' HARVESTIN' FER' ANOTHER MONTH!
A MONTH IS NOTHING WHEN IT COMES TO PLANNING A HARVEST! I NEED TO COUNT HOW MANY BASKETS WE HAVE! I NEED TO CHECK THE SILO TO SEE IF THOSE RACCOONS ARE STILL NESTING THERE... I NEED TO...
...BUILD A BARN.
...ER ...YUP?
I'LL GRAB SOME SAMPLES OF OUR LATEST APPLE CROP TO TAKE WITH ME. I JUST NEED MY SADDLEBAGS AND THEN I'M OFF TO APPLEWOOD!
Z

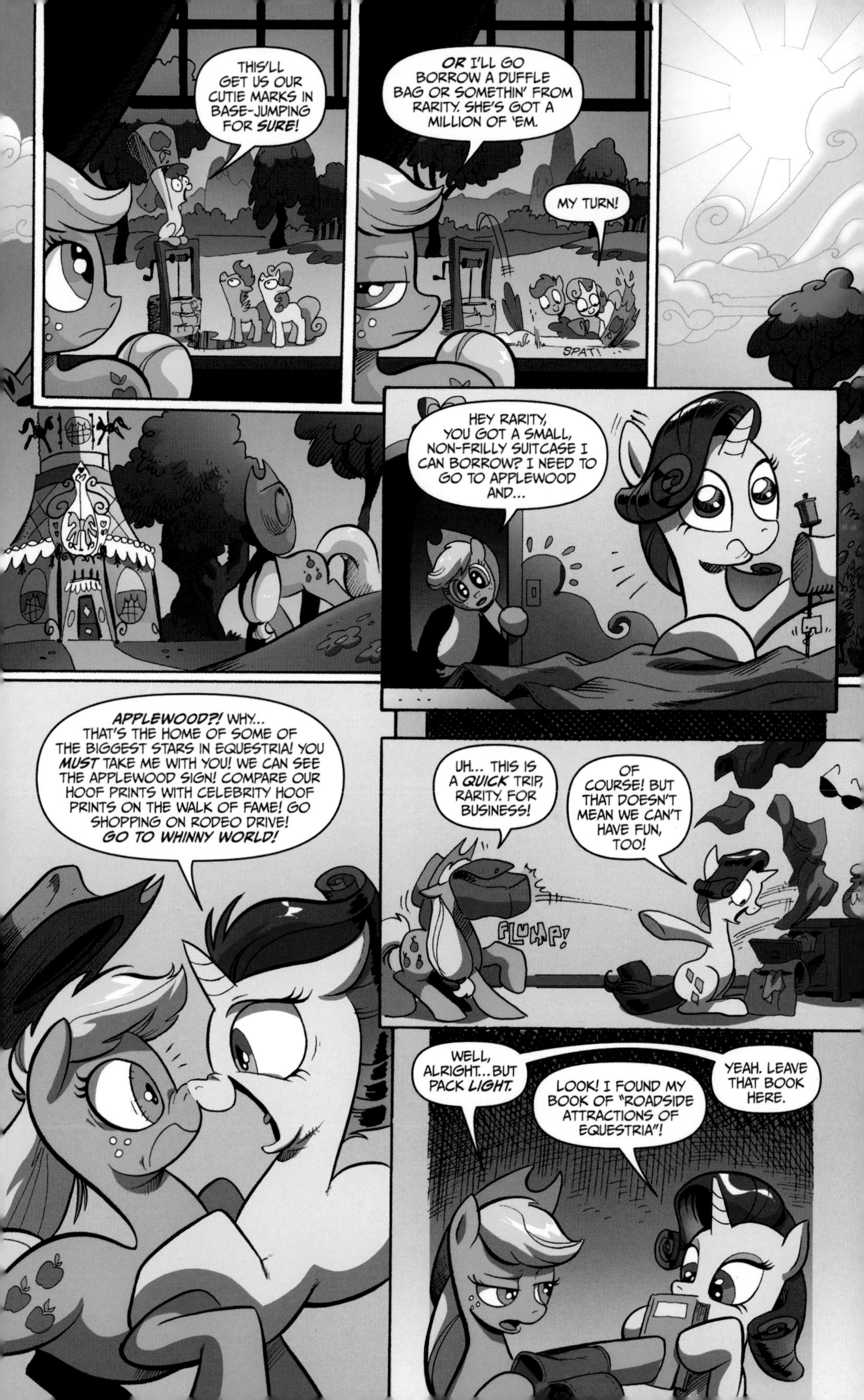
THIS'LL GET US OUR CUTIE MARKS IN BASE-JUMPING FOR SURE!
OR I'LL GO BORROW A DUFFLE BAG OR SOMETHIN' FROM RARITY. SHE'S GOT A MILLION OF 'EM.
MY TURN!
SPAT!
HEY RARITY, YOU GOT A SMALL, NON-FRILLY SUITCASE I CAN BORROW? I NEED TO GO TO APPLEWOOD AND...
APPLEWOOD?! WHY... THAT'S THE HOME OF SOME OF THE BIGGEST STARS IN EQUESTRIA! YOU MUST TAKE ME WITH YOU! WE CAN SEE THE APPLEWOOD SIGN! COMPARE OUR HOOF PRINTS WITH CELEBRITY HOOF PRINTS ON THE WALK OF FAME! GO SHOPPING ON RODEO DRIVE! GO TO WHINNY WORLD!
UH... THIS IS A QUICK TRIP, RARITY. FOR BUSINESS!
OF COURSE! BUT THAT DOESN'T MEAN WE CAN'T HAVE FUN, TOO!
FLUMP!
WELL, ALRIGHT... BUT PACK LIGHT.
LOOK! I FOUND MY BOOK OF "ROADSIDE ATTRACTIONS OF EQUESTRIA"!
YEAH. LEAVE THAT BOOK HERE.

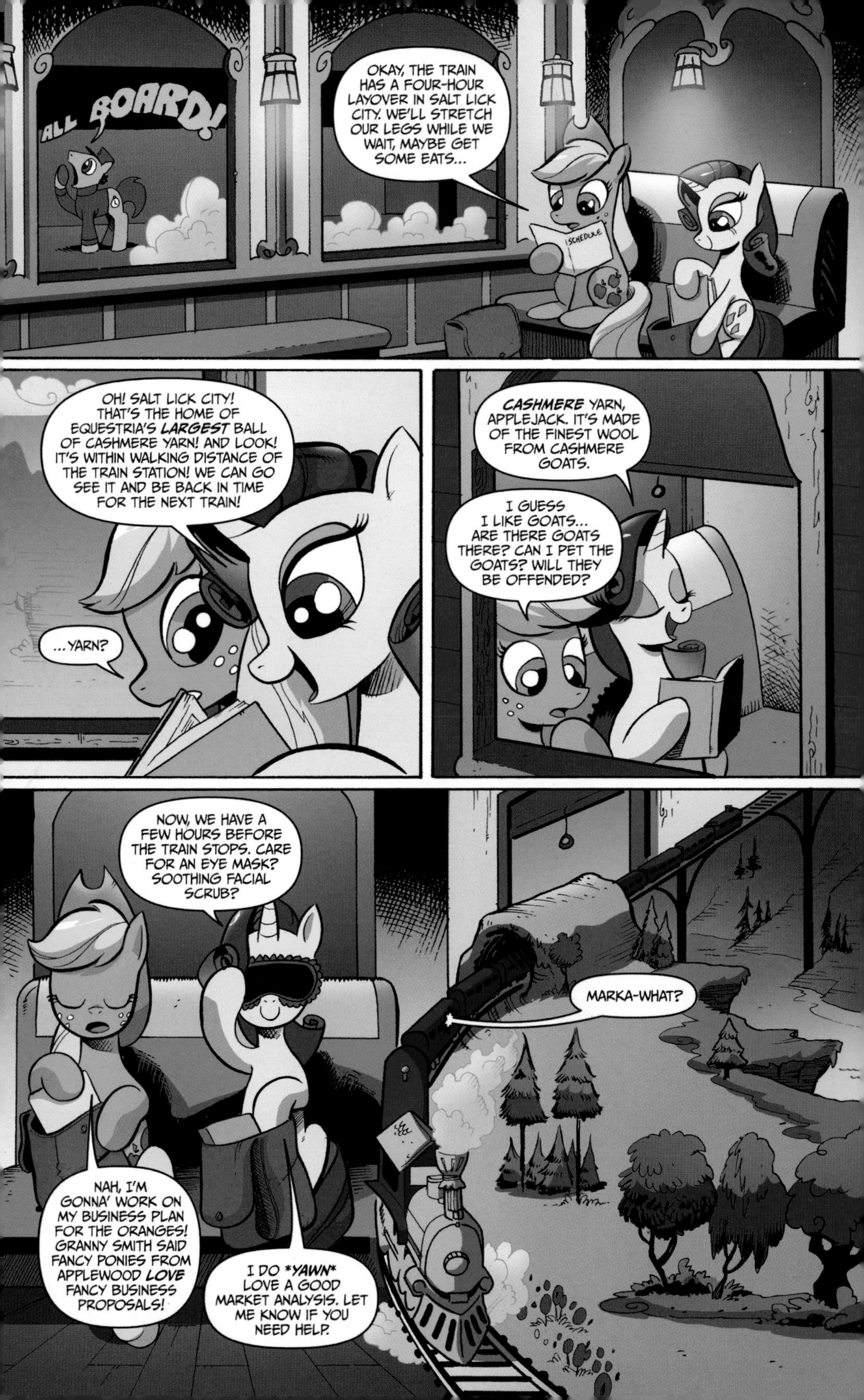
ALL BOARD!
OKAY, THE TRAIN HAS A FOUR-HOUR LAYOVER IN SALT LICK CITY. WE'LL STRETCH OUR LEGS WHILE WE WAIT, MAYBE GET SOME EATS...
SCHEDULE
OH! SALT LICK CITY! THAT'S THE HOME OF EQUESTRIA'S **LARGEST** BALL OF CASHMERE YARN! AND LOOK! IT'S WITHIN WALKING DISTANCE OF THE TRAIN STATION! WE CAN GO SEE IT AND BE BACK IN TIME FOR THE NEXT TRAIN!
...YARN?
CASHMERE YARN, APPLEJACK. IT'S MADE OF THE FINEST WOOL FROM CASHMERE GOATS.
I GUESS I LIKE GOATS... ARE THERE GOATS THERE? CAN I PET THE GOATS? WILL THEY BE OFFENDED?
NOW, WE HAVE A FEW HOURS BEFORE THE TRAIN STOPS. CARE FOR AN EYE MASK? SOOTHING FACIAL SCRUB?
NAH, I'M GONNA' WORK ON MY BUSINESS PLAN FOR THE ORANGES! GRANNY SMITH SAID FANCY PONIES FROM APPLEWOOD **LOVE** FANCY BUSINESS PROPOSALS!
I DO ***YAWN*** LOVE A GOOD MARKET ANALYSIS. LET ME KNOW IF YOU NEED HELP.
MARKA-WHAT?

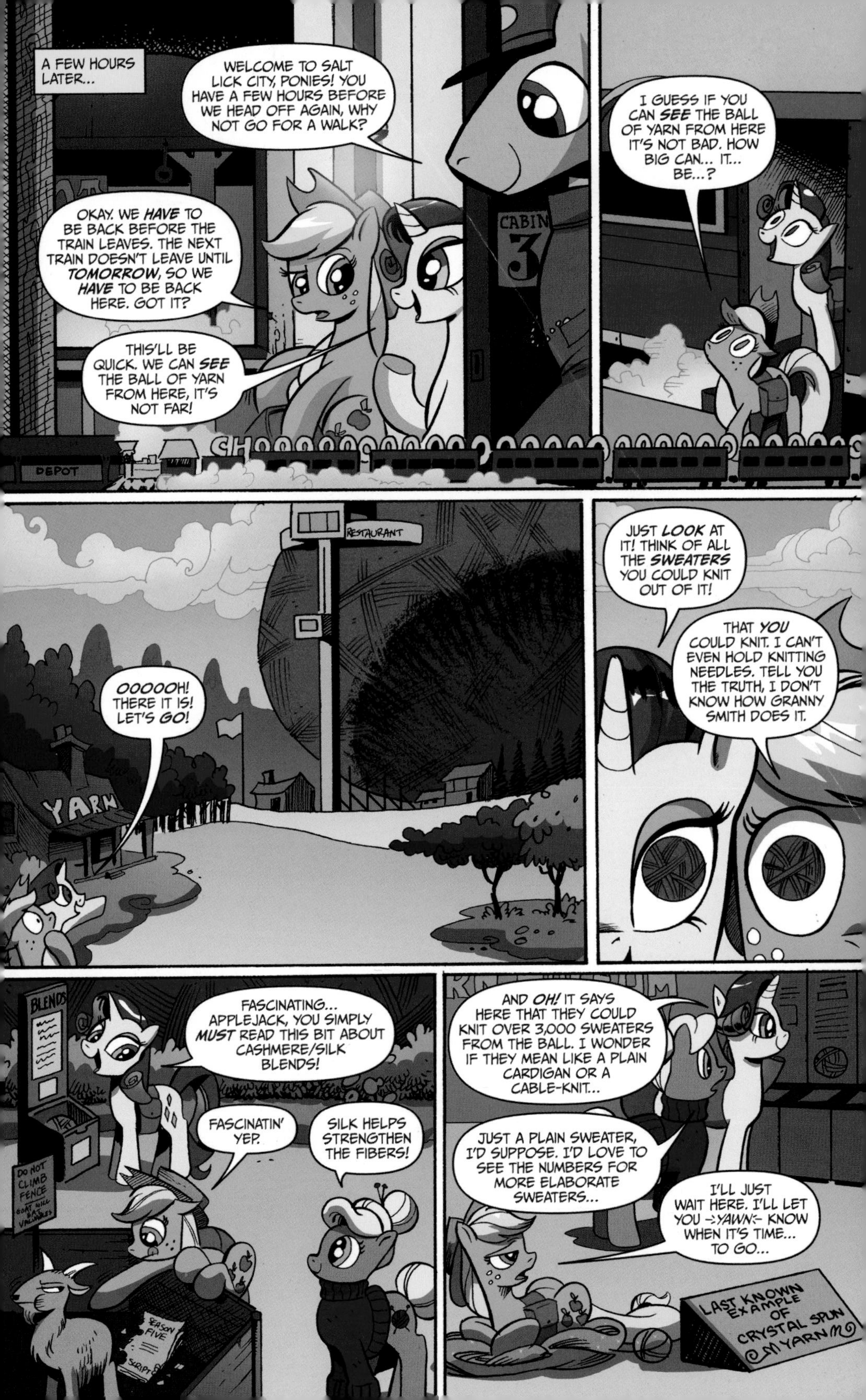
A FEW HOURS LATER...
WELCOME TO SALT LICK CITY, PONIES! YOU HAVE A FEW HOURS BEFORE WE HEAD OFF AGAIN, WHY NOT GO FOR A WALK?
CABIN 3
OKAY. WE HAVE TO BE BACK BEFORE THE TRAIN LEAVES. THE NEXT TRAIN DOESN'T LEAVE UNTIL TOMORROW, SO WE HAVE TO BE BACK HERE. GOT IT?
THIS'LL BE QUICK. WE CAN SEE THE BALL OF YARN FROM HERE, IT'S NOT FAR!
I GUESS IF YOU CAN SEE THE BALL OF YARN FROM HERE IT'S NOT BAD. HOW BIG CAN... IT... BE...?
DEPOT
CHOOOOOOOOOOOOOOOOOOOOOOO
RESTAURANT
OOOOOH! THERE IT IS! LET'S GO!
YARN
JUST LOOK AT IT! THINK OF ALL THE SWEATERS YOU COULD KNIT OUT OF IT!
THAT YOU COULD KNIT. I CAN'T EVEN HOLD KNITTING NEEDLES. TELL YOU THE TRUTH, I DON'T KNOW HOW GRANNY SMITH DOES IT.
BLENDS
FASCINATING... APPLEJACK, YOU SIMPLY MUST READ THIS BIT ABOUT CASHMERE/SILK BLENDS!
FASCINATIN'. YEP.
SILK HELPS STRENGTHEN THE FIBERS!
DO NOT CLIMB FENCE
GOAT WILL EAT VALUABLES
SEASON FIVE SCRIPT
AND OH! IT SAYS HERE THAT THEY COULD KNIT OVER 3,000 SWEATERS FROM THE BALL. I WONDER IF THEY MEAN LIKE A PLAIN CARDIGAN OR A CABLE-KNIT...
JUST A PLAIN SWEATER, I'D SUPPOSE. I'D LOVE TO SEE THE NUMBERS FOR MORE ELABORATE SWEATERS...
I'LL JUST WAIT HERE. I'LL LET YOU -YAWN- KNOW WHEN IT'S TIME... TO GO...
LAST KNOWN EXAMPLE OF CRYSTAL SPUN YARN

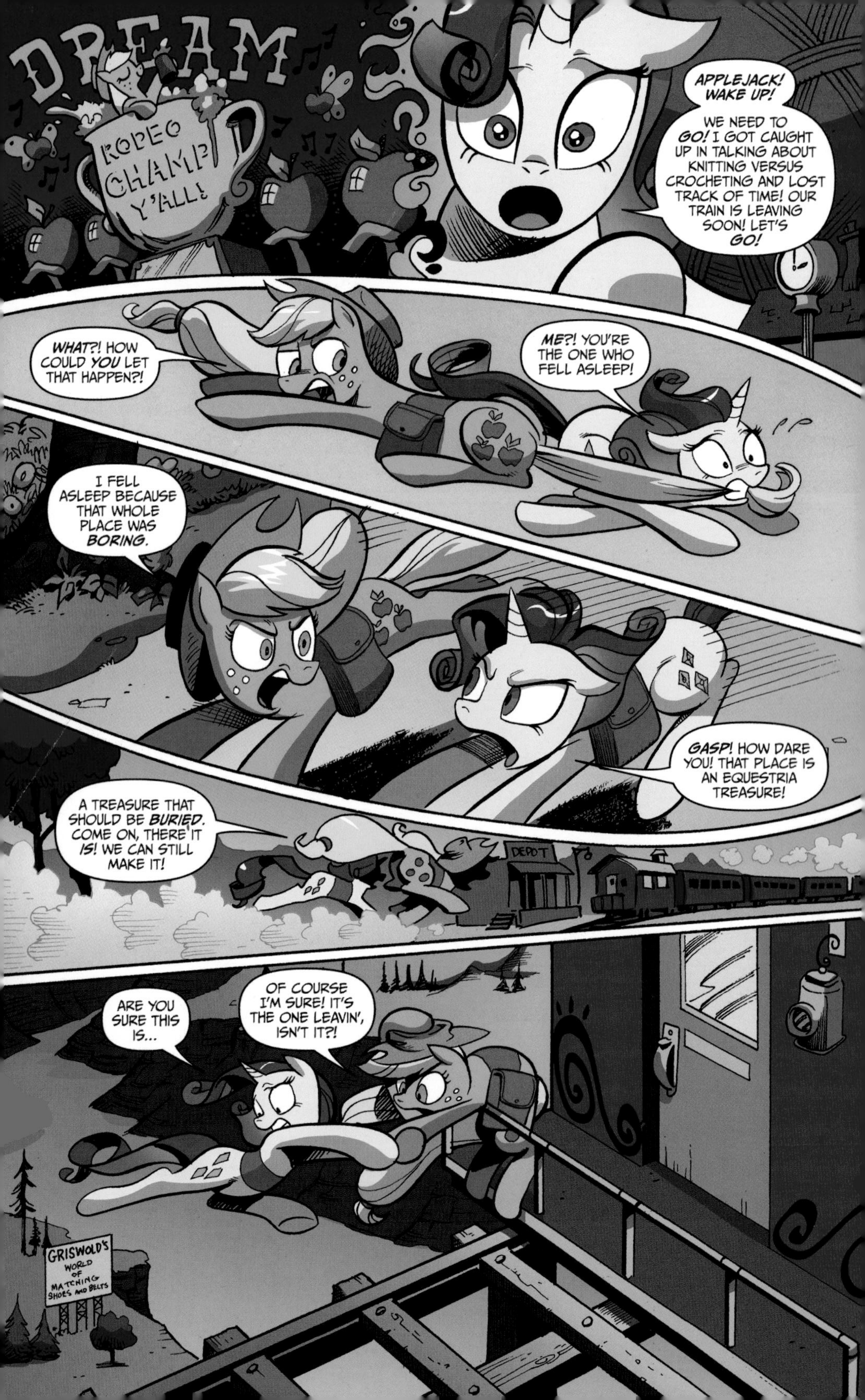
DREAM
RODEO CHAMP Y'ALL!
APPLEJACK! WAKE UP!
WE NEED TO GO! I GOT CAUGHT UP IN TALKING ABOUT KNITTING VERSUS CROCHETING AND LOST TRACK OF TIME! OUR TRAIN IS LEAVING SOON! LET'S GO!
WHAT?! HOW COULD YOU LET THAT HAPPEN?!
ME?! YOU'RE THE ONE WHO FELL ASLEEP!
I FELL ASLEEP BECAUSE THAT WHOLE PLACE WAS BORING.
GASP! HOW DARE YOU! THAT PLACE IS AN EQUESTRIA TREASURE!
A TREASURE THAT SHOULD BE BURIED. COME ON, THERE IT IS! WE CAN STILL MAKE IT!
DEPOT
ARE YOU SURE THIS IS...
OF COURSE I'M SURE! IT'S THE ONE LEAVIN', ISN'T IT?!
GRISWOLD'S WORLD OF MATCHING SHOES AND BELTS

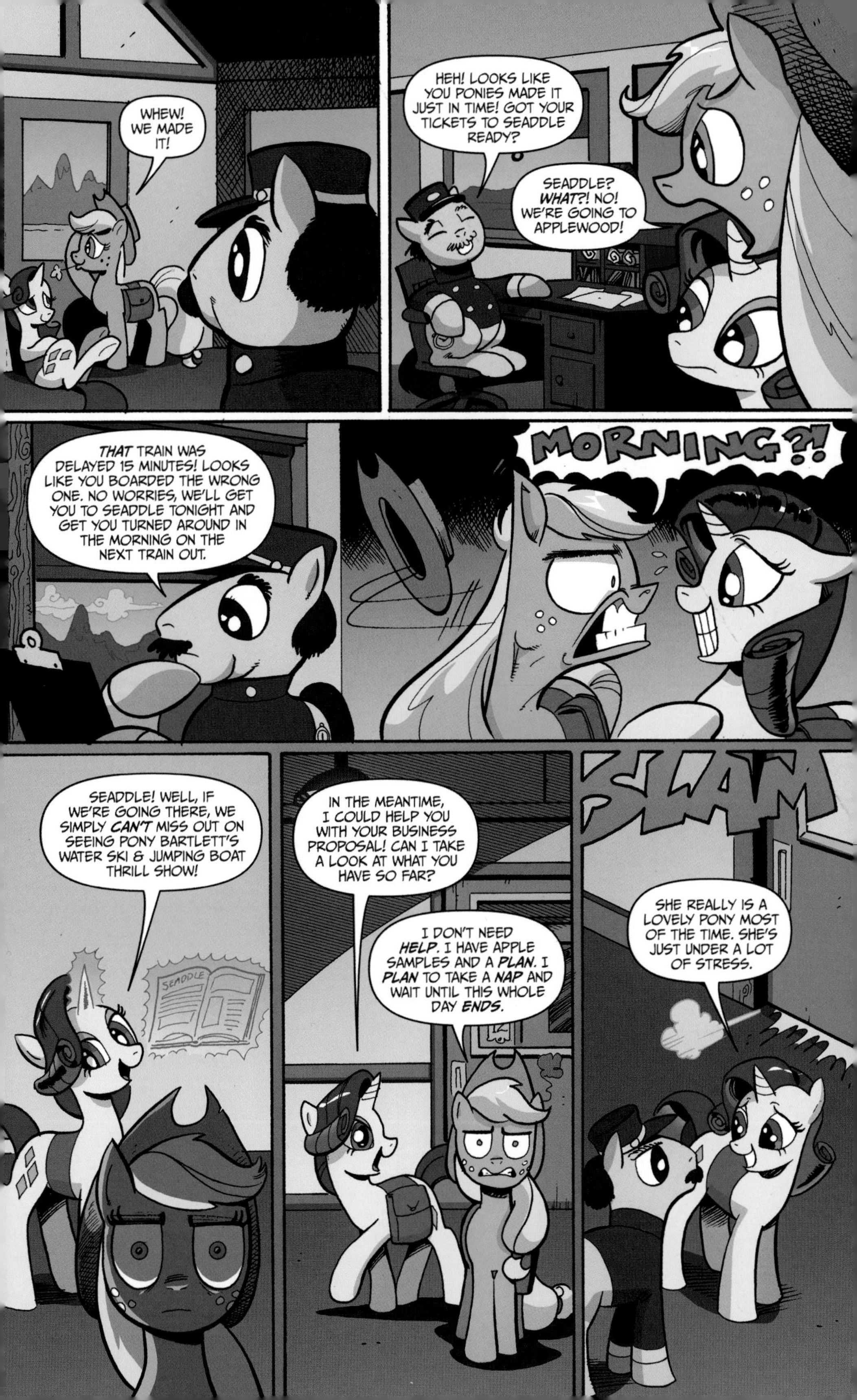
WHEW! WE MADE IT!
HEH! LOOKS LIKE YOU PONIES MADE IT JUST IN TIME! GOT YOUR TICKETS TO SEADDLE READY?
SEADDLE? WHAT?! NO! WE'RE GOING TO APPLEWOOD!
THAT TRAIN WAS DELAYED 15 MINUTES! LOOKS LIKE YOU BOARDED THE WRONG ONE. NO WORRIES, WE'LL GET YOU TO SEADDLE TONIGHT AND GET YOU TURNED AROUND IN THE MORNING ON THE NEXT TRAIN OUT.
MORNING?!
SEADDLE! WELL, IF WE'RE GOING THERE, WE SIMPLY CAN'T MISS OUT ON SEEING PONY BARTLETT'S WATER SKI & JUMPING BOAT THRILL SHOW!
SEADDLE
IN THE MEANTIME, I COULD HELP YOU WITH YOUR BUSINESS PROPOSAL! CAN I TAKE A LOOK AT WHAT YOU HAVE SO FAR?
I DON'T NEED HELP. I HAVE APPLE SAMPLES AND A PLAN. I PLAN TO TAKE A NAP AND WAIT UNTIL THIS WHOLE DAY ENDS.
SLAM
SHE REALLY IS A LOVELY PONY MOST OF THE TIME. SHE'S JUST UNDER A LOT OF STRESS.

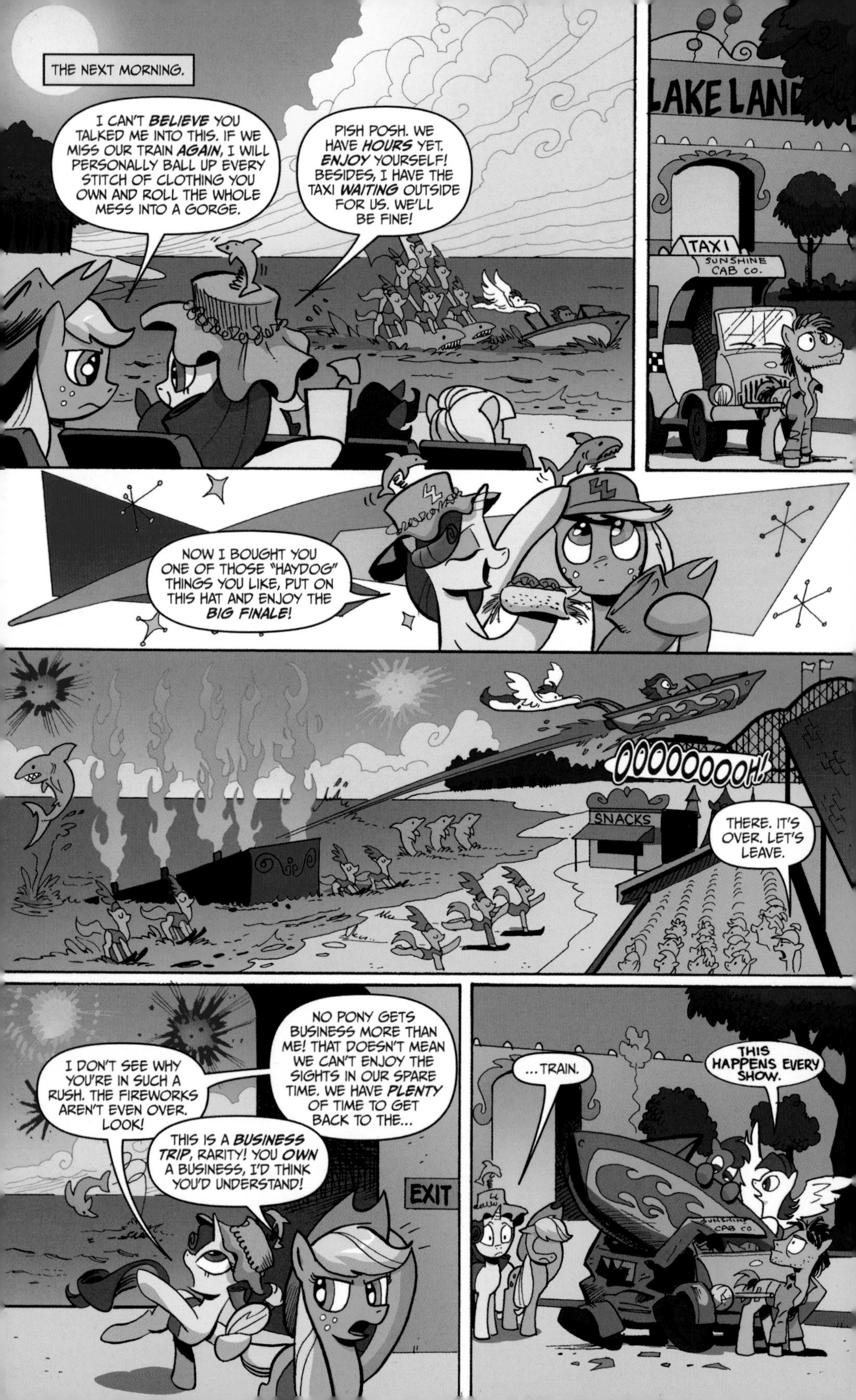
THE NEXT MORNING.
I CAN'T BELIEVE YOU TALKED ME INTO THIS. IF WE MISS OUR TRAIN AGAIN, I WILL PERSONALLY BALL UP EVERY STITCH OF CLOTHING YOU OWN AND ROLL THE WHOLE MESS INTO A GORGE.
PISH POSH. WE HAVE HOURS YET. ENJOY YOURSELF! BESIDES, I HAVE THE TAXI WAITING OUTSIDE FOR US. WE'LL BE FINE!
LAKE LAND
TAXI
SUNSHINE CAB CO.
NOW I BOUGHT YOU ONE OF THOSE "HAYDOG" THINGS YOU LIKE, PUT ON THIS HAT AND ENJOY THE BIG FINALE!
OOOOOOOOH!
SNACKS
THERE. IT'S OVER. LET'S LEAVE.
I DON'T SEE WHY YOU'RE IN SUCH A RUSH. THE FIREWORKS AREN'T EVEN OVER. LOOK!
THIS IS A BUSINESS TRIP, RARITY! YOU OWN A BUSINESS, I'D THINK YOU'D UNDERSTAND!
NO PONY GETS BUSINESS MORE THAN ME! THAT DOESN'T MEAN WE CAN'T ENJOY THE SIGHTS IN OUR SPARE TIME. WE HAVE PLENTY OF TIME TO GET BACK TO THE...
EXIT
...TRAIN.
THIS HAPPENS EVERY SHOW.

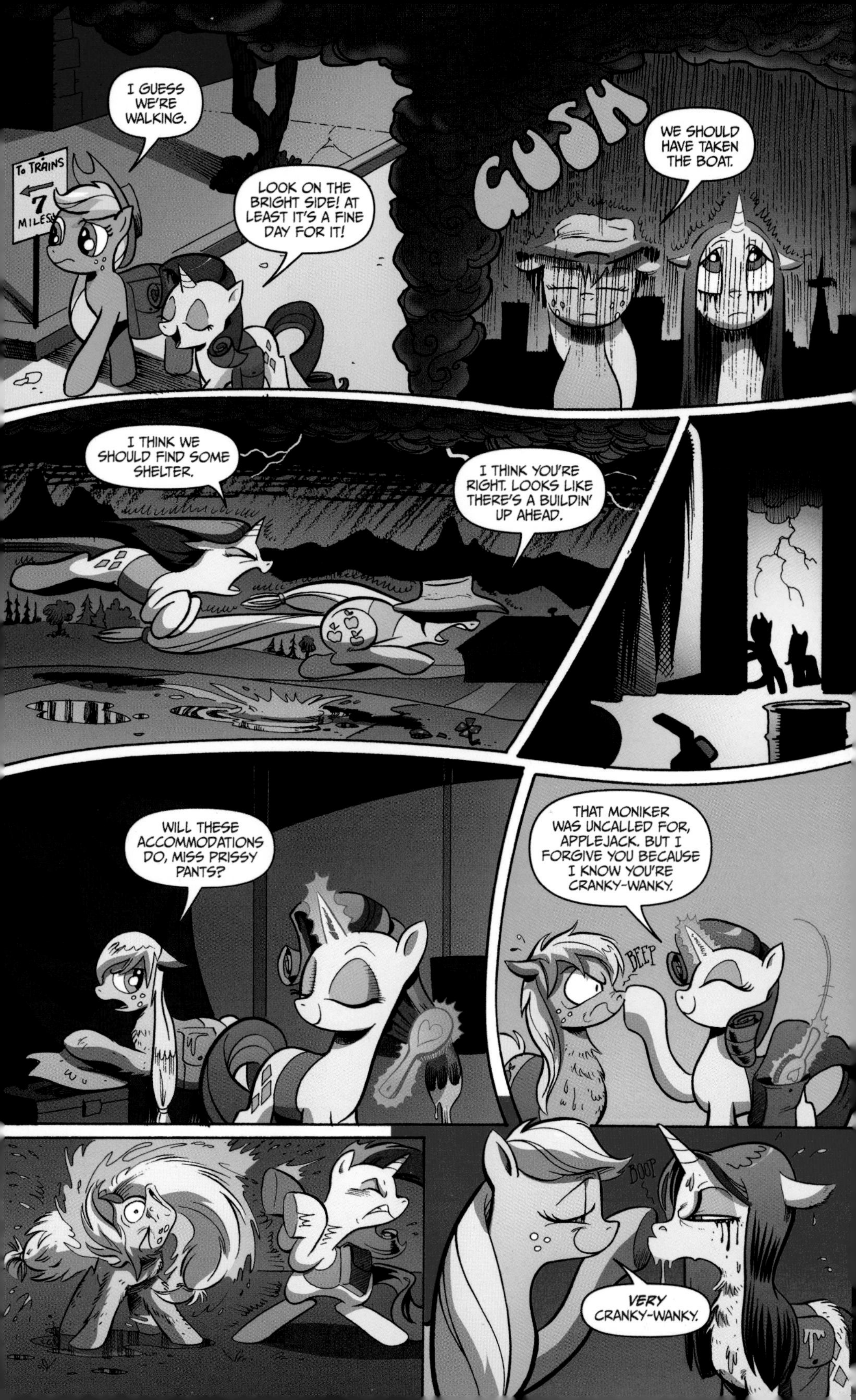
I GUESS WE'RE WALKING.
To TRAINS 7 MILES
LOOK ON THE BRIGHT SIDE! AT LEAST IT'S A FINE DAY FOR IT!
GUSH
WE SHOULD HAVE TAKEN THE BOAT.
I THINK WE SHOULD FIND SOME SHELTER.
I THINK YOU'RE RIGHT. LOOKS LIKE THERE'S A BUILDIN' UP AHEAD.
WILL THESE ACCOMMODATIONS DO, MISS PRISSY PANTS?
THAT MONIKER WAS UNCALLED FOR, APPLEJACK. BUT I FORGIVE YOU BECAUSE I KNOW YOU'RE CRANKY-WANKY.
BEEP
BOOP
VERY CRANKY-WANKY.

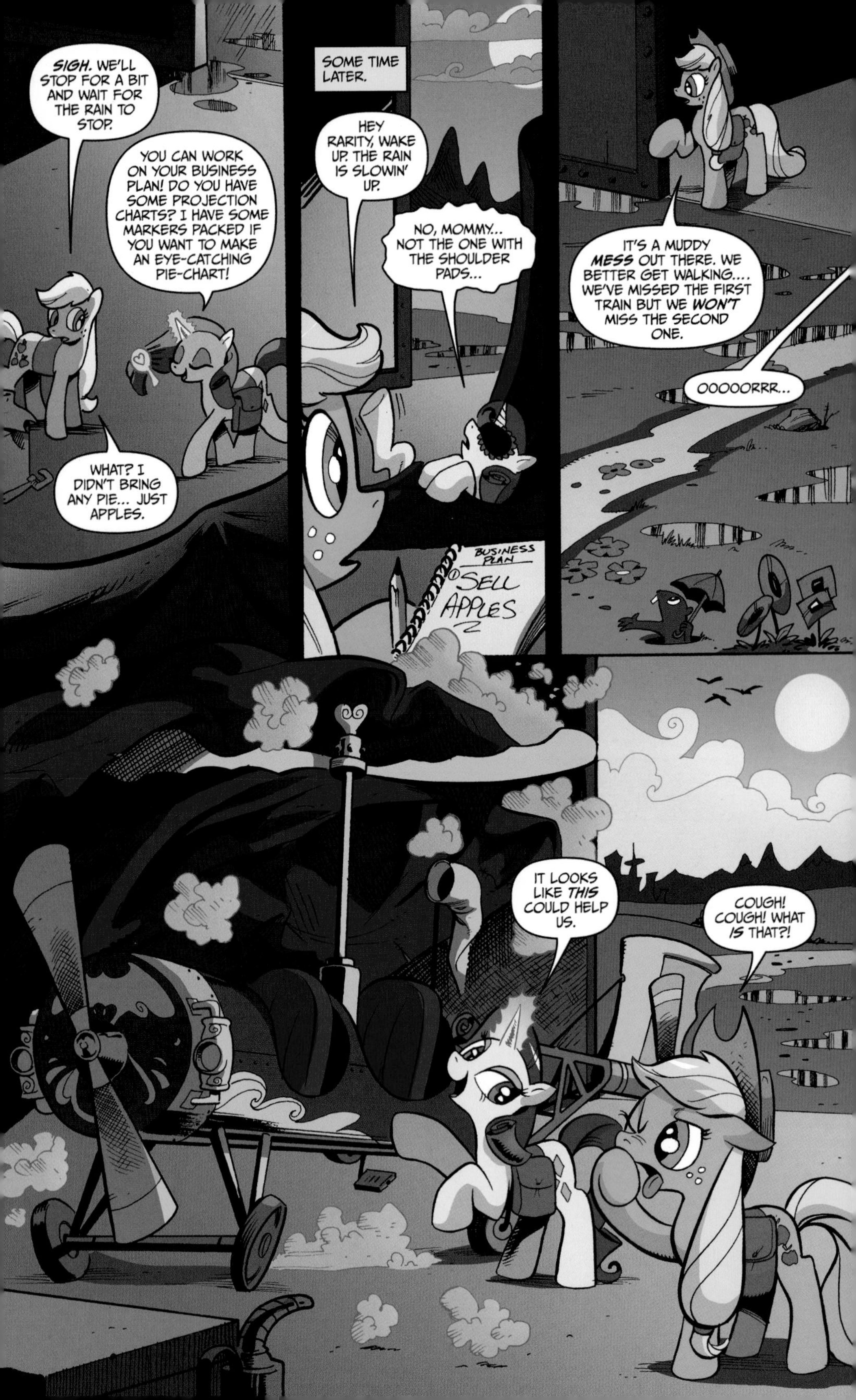
SIGH. WE'LL STOP FOR A BIT AND WAIT FOR THE RAIN TO STOP.
YOU CAN WORK ON YOUR BUSINESS PLAN! DO YOU HAVE SOME PROJECTION CHARTS? I HAVE SOME MARKERS PACKED IF YOU WANT TO MAKE AN EYE-CATCHING PIE-CHART!
WHAT? I DIDN'T BRING ANY PIE... JUST APPLES.
SOME TIME LATER.
HEY RARITY, WAKE UP. THE RAIN IS SLOWIN' UP.
NO, MOMMY... NOT THE ONE WITH THE SHOULDER PADS...
BUSINESS PLAN
1 SELL APPLES
2
IT'S A MUDDY MESS OUT THERE. WE BETTER GET WALKING.... WE'VE MISSED THE FIRST TRAIN BUT WE WON'T MISS THE SECOND ONE.
OOOOORRR...
IT LOOKS LIKE THIS COULD HELP US.
COUGH! COUGH! WHAT IS THAT?!

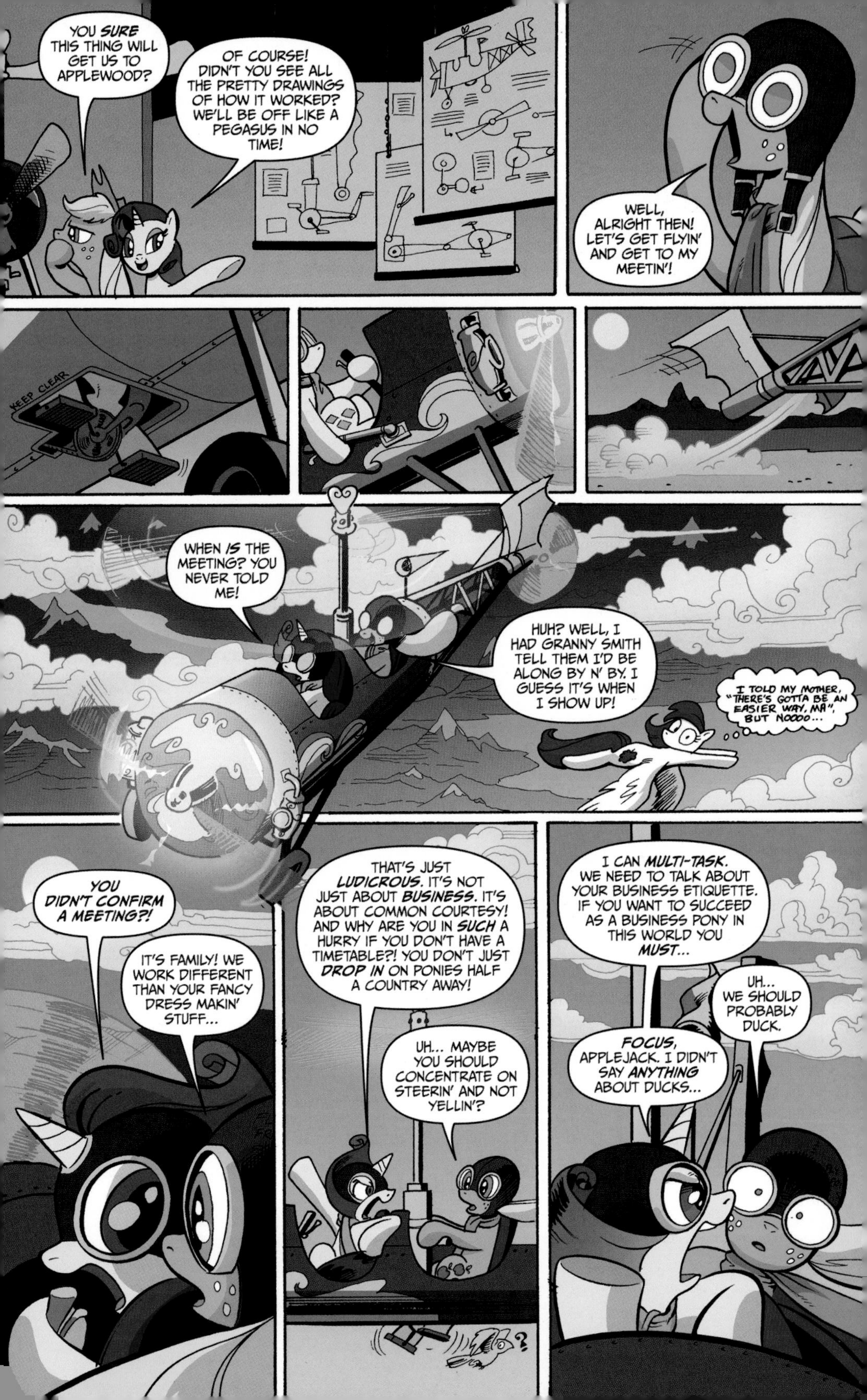
YOU SURE THIS THING WILL GET US TO APPLEWOOD?
OF COURSE! DIDN'T YOU SEE ALL THE PRETTY DRAWINGS OF HOW IT WORKED? WE'LL BE OFF LIKE A PEGASUS IN NO TIME!
WELL, ALRIGHT THEN! LET'S GET FLYIN' AND GET TO MY MEETIN'!
KEEP CLEAR
WHEN IS THE MEETING? YOU NEVER TOLD ME!
HUH? WELL, I HAD GRANNY SMITH TELL THEM I'D BE ALONG BY N' BY. I GUESS IT'S WHEN I SHOW UP!
I TOLD MY MOTHER, "THERE'S GOTTA BE AN EASIER WAY, MA", BUT NOOOO...
YOU DIDN'T CONFIRM A MEETING?!
IT'S FAMILY! WE WORK DIFFERENT THAN YOUR FANCY DRESS MAKIN' STUFF...
THAT'S JUST LUDICROUS. IT'S NOT JUST ABOUT BUSINESS. IT'S ABOUT COMMON COURTESY! AND WHY ARE YOU IN SUCH A HURRY IF YOU DON'T HAVE A TIMETABLE?! YOU DON'T JUST DROP IN ON PONIES HALF A COUNTRY AWAY!
UH... MAYBE YOU SHOULD CONCENTRATE ON STEERIN' AND NOT YELLIN'?
?
I CAN MULTI-TASK. WE NEED TO TALK ABOUT YOUR BUSINESS ETIQUETTE. IF YOU WANT TO SUCCEED AS A BUSINESS PONY IN THIS WORLD YOU MUST...
UH... WE SHOULD PROBABLY DUCK.
FOCUS, APPLEJACK. I DIDN'T SAY ANYTHING ABOUT DUCKS...

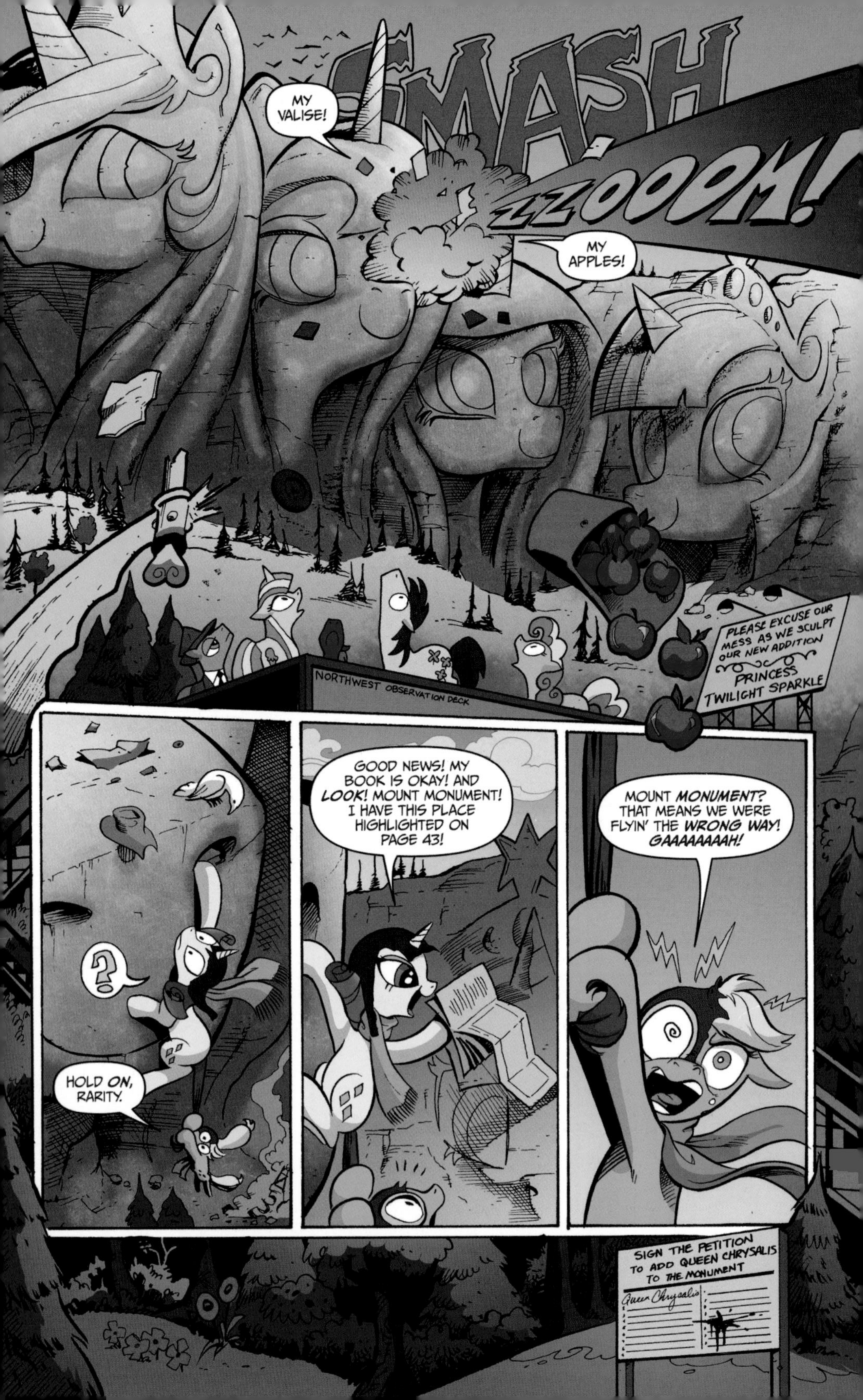
MY VALISE!
SMASH
ZZOOOOM!
MY APPLES!
PLEASE EXCUSE OUR MESS AS WE SCULPT OUR NEW ADDITION PRINCESS TWILIGHT SPARKLE
NORTHWEST OBSERVATION DECK
?
HOLD ON, RARITY.
GOOD NEWS! MY BOOK IS OKAY! AND LOOK! MOUNT MONUMENT! I HAVE THIS PLACE HIGHLIGHTED ON PAGE 43!
MOUNT MONUMENT? THAT MEANS WE WERE FLYIN' THE WRONG WAY! GAAAAAAAAH!
SIGN THE PETITION TO ADD QUEEN CHRYSALIS TO THE MONUMENT
Queen Chrysalis

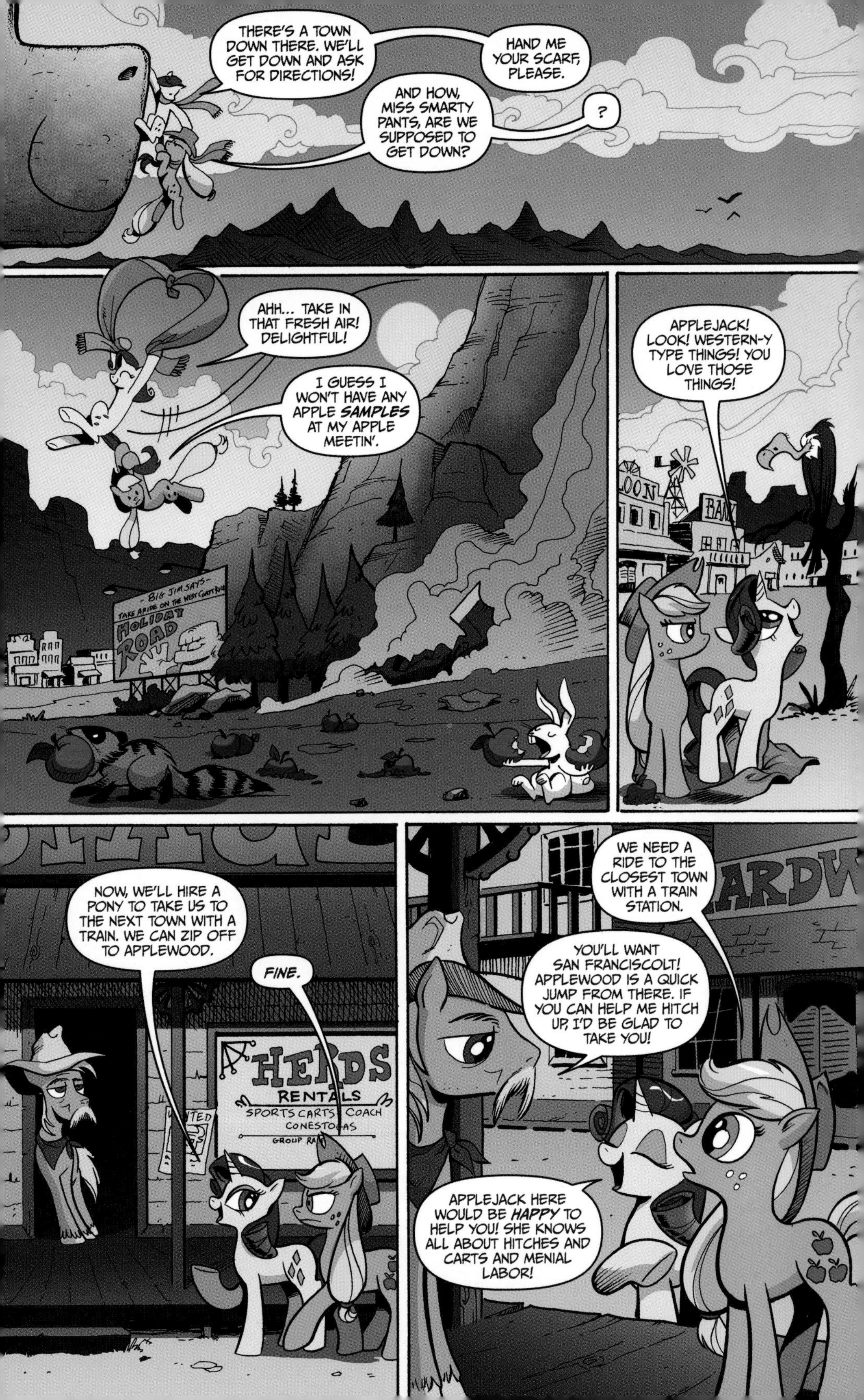
THERE'S A TOWN DOWN THERE. WE'LL GET DOWN AND ASK FOR DIRECTIONS!
HAND ME YOUR SCARF, PLEASE.
AND HOW, MISS SMARTY PANTS, ARE WE SUPPOSED TO GET DOWN?
?
AHH... TAKE IN THAT FRESH AIR! DELIGHTFUL!
I GUESS I WON'T HAVE ANY APPLE *SAMPLES* AT MY APPLE MEETIN'.
HOLIDAY ROAD
APPLEJACK! LOOK! WESTERN-Y TYPE THINGS! YOU LOVE THOSE THINGS!
NOW, WE'LL HIRE A PONY TO TAKE US TO THE NEXT TOWN WITH A TRAIN. WE CAN ZIP OFF TO APPLEWOOD.
FINE.
HERDS
RENTALS
CONESTOGAS
WE NEED A RIDE TO THE CLOSEST TOWN WITH A TRAIN STATION.
YOU'LL WANT SAN FRANCISCOLT! APPLEWOOD IS A QUICK JUMP FROM THERE. IF YOU CAN HELP ME HITCH UP, I'D BE GLAD TO TAKE YOU!
APPLEJACK HERE WOULD BE *HAPPY* TO HELP YOU! SHE KNOWS ALL ABOUT HITCHES AND CARTS AND MENIAL LABOR!

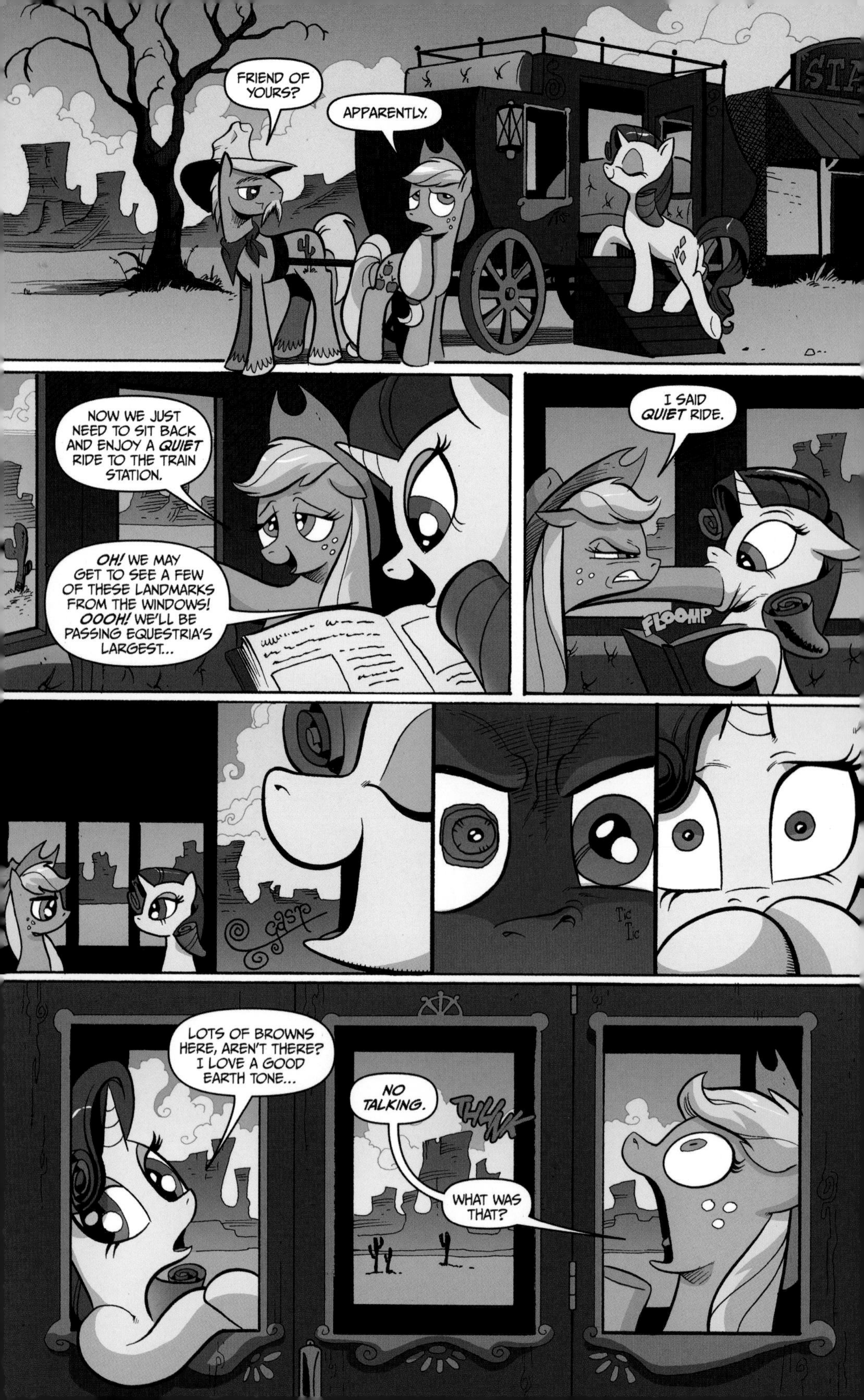

FRIEND OF YOURS?
APPARENTLY.
NOW WE JUST NEED TO SIT BACK AND ENJOY A *QUIET* RIDE TO THE TRAIN STATION.
OH! WE MAY GET TO SEE A FEW OF THESE LANDMARKS FROM THE WINDOWS! *OOOH!* WE'LL BE PASSING EQUESTRIA'S LARGEST...
I SAID *QUIET* RIDE.
FLOOMP
Tic Tic
LOTS OF BROWNS HERE, AREN'T THERE? I LOVE A GOOD EARTH TONE...
NO TALKING.
THUNK
WHAT WAS THAT?

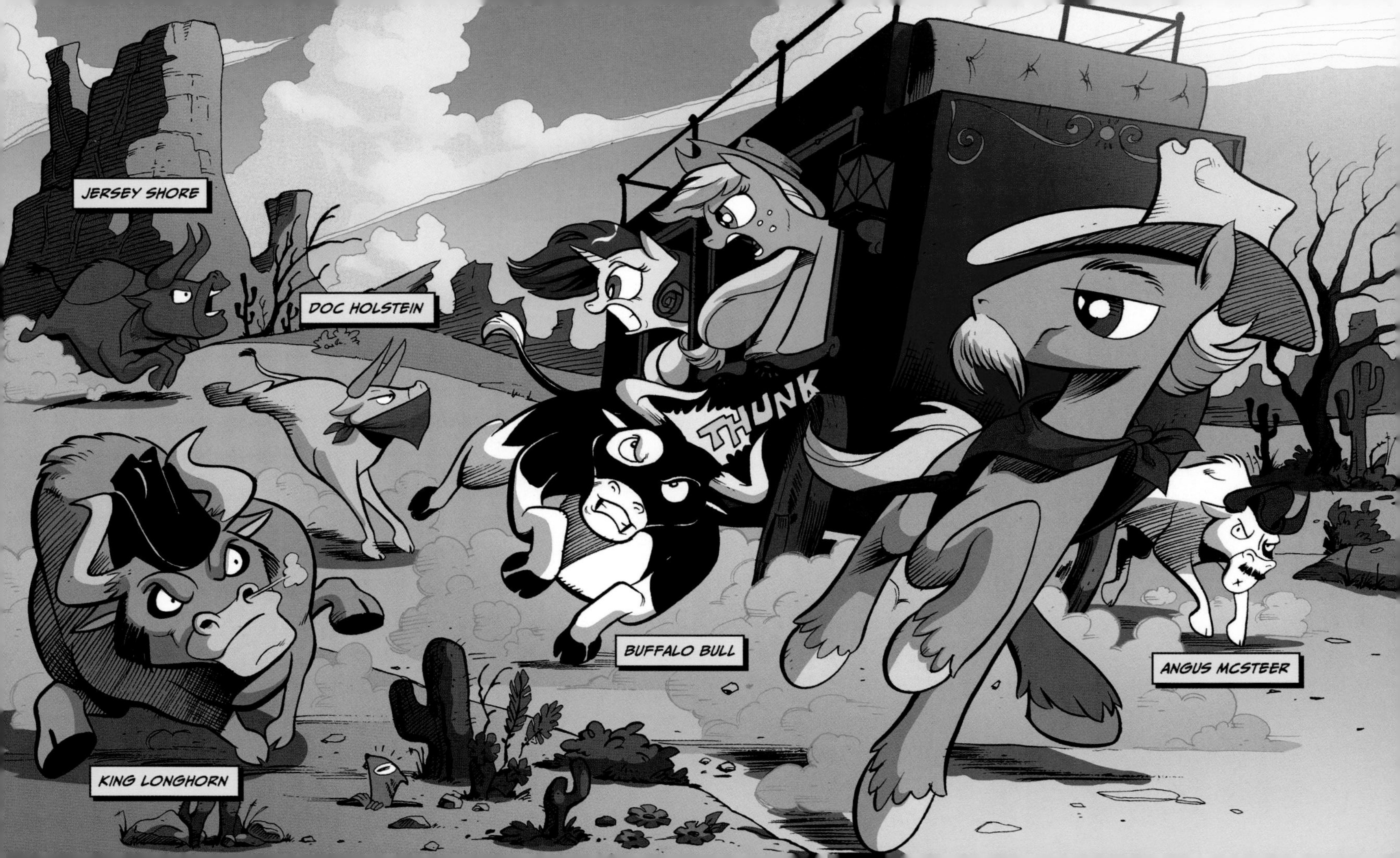
JERSEY SHORE
DOC HOLSTEIN
THUNK
BUFFALO BULL
ANGUS MCSTEER
KING LONGHORN

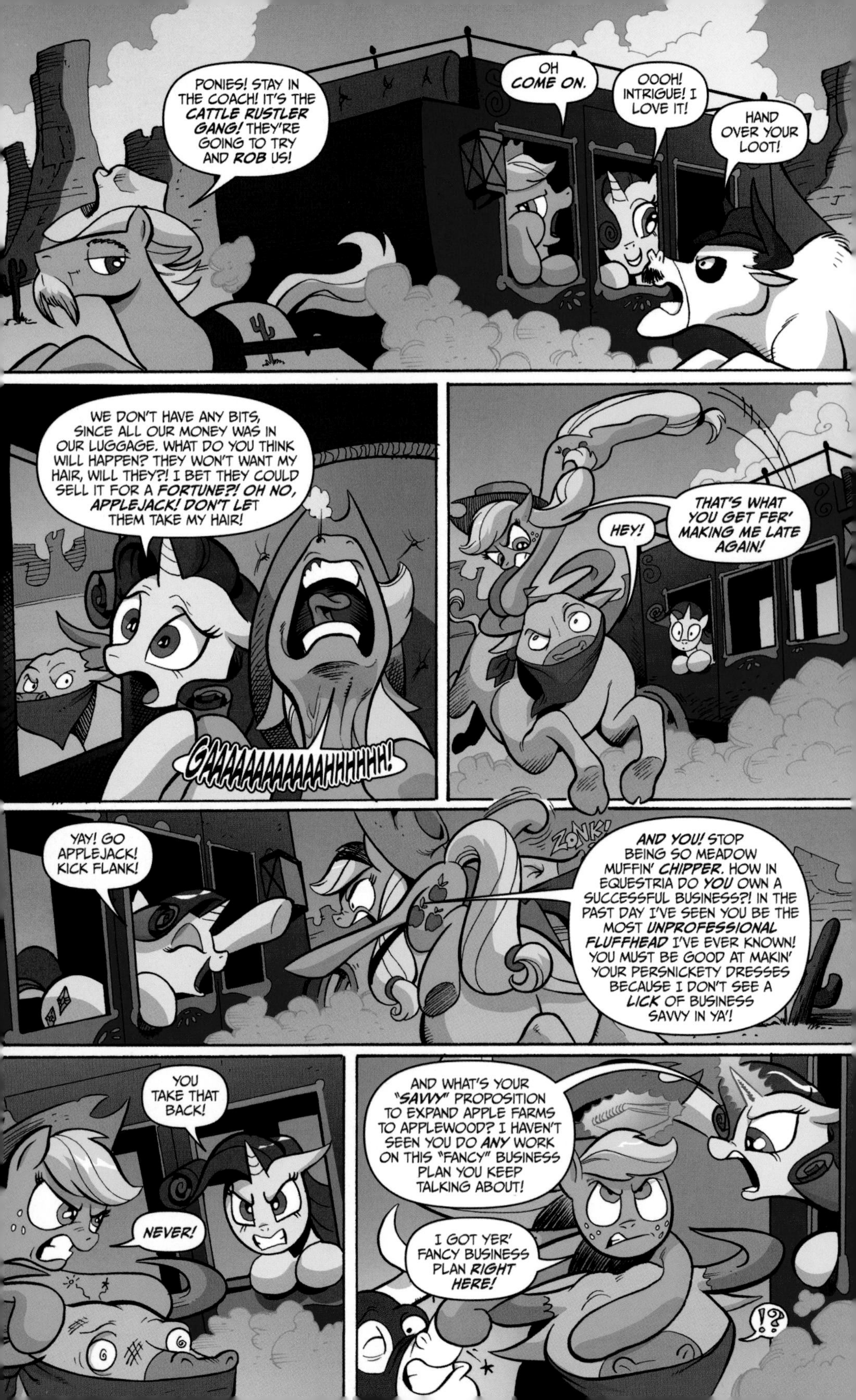
PONIES! STAY IN THE COACH! IT'S THE CATTLE RUSTLER GANG! THEY'RE GOING TO TRY AND ROB US!
OH COME ON.
OOOH! INTRIGUE! I LOVE IT!
HAND OVER YOUR LOOT!
WE DON'T HAVE ANY BITS, SINCE ALL OUR MONEY WAS IN OUR LUGGAGE. WHAT DO YOU THINK WILL HAPPEN? THEY WON'T WANT MY HAIR, WILL THEY?! I BET THEY COULD SELL IT FOR A FORTUNE?! OH NO, APPLEJACK! DON'T LET THEM TAKE MY HAIR!
GAAAAAAAAAAAHHHHHH!
HEY!
THAT'S WHAT YOU GET FER' MAKING ME LATE AGAIN!
YAY! GO APPLEJACK! KICK FLANK!
ZONK!
AND YOU! STOP BEING SO MEADOW MUFFIN' CHIPPER. HOW IN EQUESTRIA DO YOU OWN A SUCCESSFUL BUSINESS?! IN THE PAST DAY I'VE SEEN YOU BE THE MOST UNPROFESSIONAL FLUFFHEAD I'VE EVER KNOWN! YOU MUST BE GOOD AT MAKIN' YOUR PERSNICKETY DRESSES BECAUSE I DON'T SEE A LICK OF BUSINESS SAVVY IN YA'!
YOU TAKE THAT BACK!
NEVER!
AND WHAT'S YOUR "SAVVY" PROPOSITION TO EXPAND APPLE FARMS TO APPLEWOOD? I HAVEN'T SEEN YOU DO ANY WORK ON THIS "FANCY" BUSINESS PLAN YOU KEEP TALKING ABOUT!
I GOT YER' FANCY BUSINESS PLAN RIGHT HERE!
!?

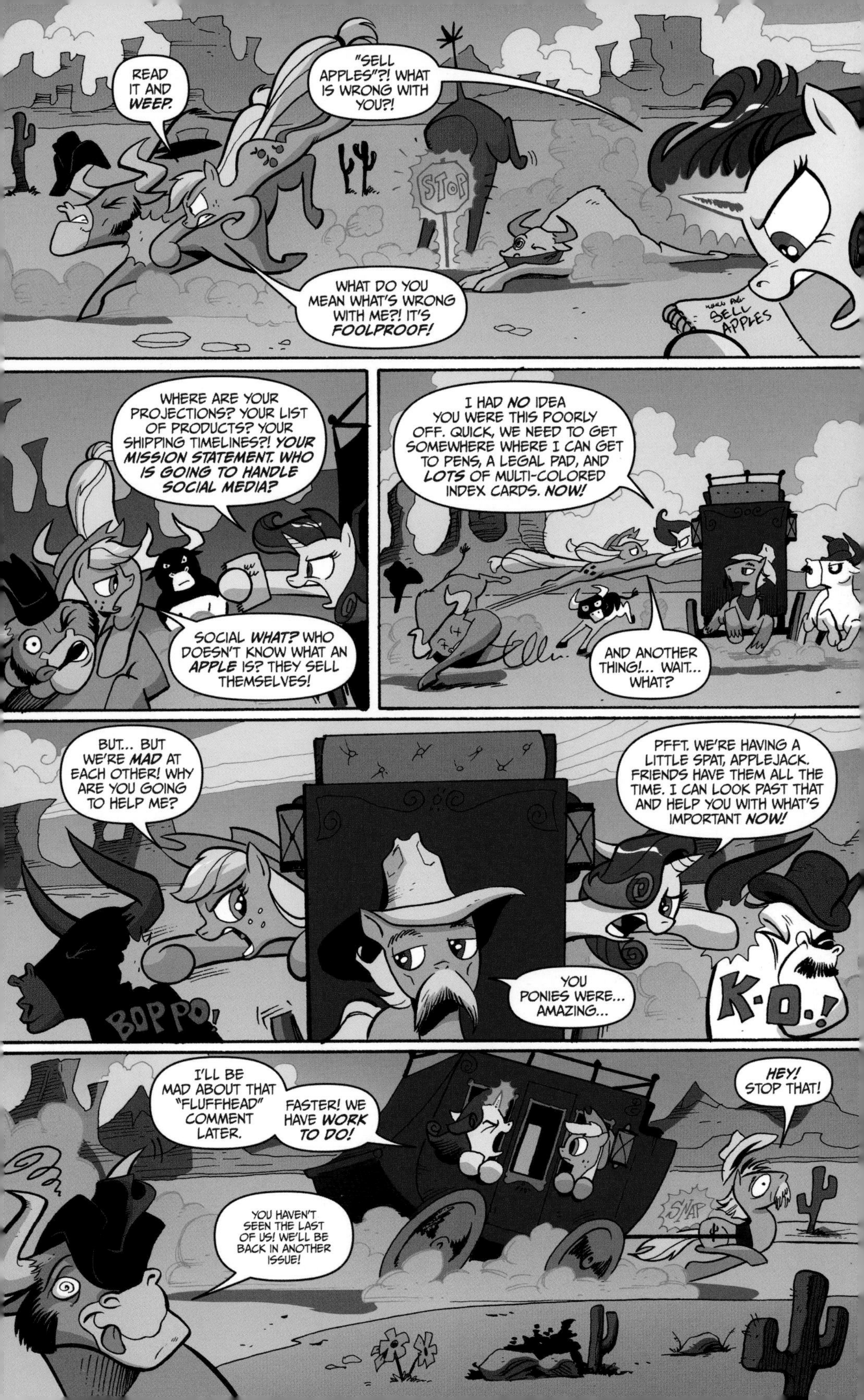
READ IT AND WEEP.
"SELL APPLES"?! WHAT IS WRONG WITH YOU?!
STOP
SELL APPLES
WHAT DO YOU MEAN WHAT'S WRONG WITH ME?! IT'S FOOLPROOF!
WHERE ARE YOUR PROJECTIONS? YOUR LIST OF PRODUCTS? YOUR SHIPPING TIMELINES?! YOUR MISSION STATEMENT. WHO IS GOING TO HANDLE SOCIAL MEDIA?
SOCIAL WHAT? WHO DOESN'T KNOW WHAT AN APPLE IS? THEY SELL THEMSELVES!
I HAD NO IDEA YOU WERE THIS POORLY OFF. QUICK, WE NEED TO GET SOMEWHERE WHERE I CAN GET TO PENS, A LEGAL PAD, AND LOTS OF MULTI-COLORED INDEX CARDS. NOW!
AND ANOTHER THING!... WAIT... WHAT?
BUT... BUT WE'RE MAD AT EACH OTHER! WHY ARE YOU GOING TO HELP ME?
PFFT. WE'RE HAVING A LITTLE SPAT, APPLEJACK. FRIENDS HAVE THEM ALL THE TIME. I CAN LOOK PAST THAT AND HELP YOU WITH WHAT'S IMPORTANT NOW!
YOU PONIES WERE... AMAZING...
BOPPO!
K-O.!
I'LL BE MAD ABOUT THAT "FLUFFHEAD" COMMENT LATER.
FASTER! WE HAVE WORK TO DO!
HEY! STOP THAT!
SNAP
YOU HAVEN'T SEEN THE LAST OF US! WE'LL BE BACK IN ANOTHER ISSUE!

TRAIN STATION
WELCOME TO
Coltifornia

I DON'T GET IT. YOU'RE USUALLY THE MOST *OVERLY DRAMATIC* PONY I KNOW. I'M USED TO SEEING YOU EYE-TWITCH AND GO HAYWIRE OVER EVERY LITTLE THING ABOUT YOUR BUSINESS. THESE PAST COUPLE DAYS, YOU'VE BEEN PRETTY CALM ABOUT THINGS...

RODEO-

BUS STOP

NEWS

I ONLY EYE-TWITCH AND, AS YOU SAY, "GO HAYWIRE" WHEN I NEED TO. YOU SAID YOU WERE FINE WORKING ON YOUR "PLAN" BY YOURSELF, I DIDN'T PUSH.

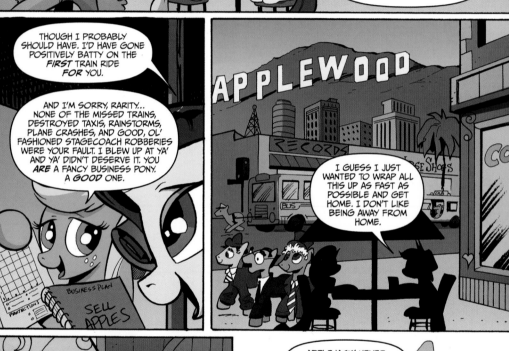

THOUGH I PROBABLY SHOULD HAVE. I'D HAVE GONE POSITIVELY BATTY ON THE *FIRST* TRAIN RIDE *FOR* YOU.

AND I'M SORRY, RARITY... NONE OF THE MISSED TRAINS, DESTROYED TAXIS, RAINSTORMS, PLANE CRASHES, AND GOOD, OL' FASHIONED STAGECOACH ROBBERIES WERE YOUR FAULT. I BLEW UP AT YA' AND YA' DIDN'T DESERVE IT. YOU *ARE* A FANCY BUSINESS PONY. A *GOOD* ONE.

APPLEWOOD

RECORDS

BUSINESS PLAN
SELL APPLES
PROJECTIONS

I GUESS I JUST WANTED TO WRAP ALL THIS UP AS FAST AS POSSIBLE AND GET HOME. I DON'T LIKE BEING AWAY FROM HOME.

APOLOGY ACCEPTED.

JUST LIKE THAT? I SAID A COUPLE HURTFUL THINGS.

APPLEJACK! NEVER TURN DOWN AN APOLOGY WHEN IT'S OFFERED!

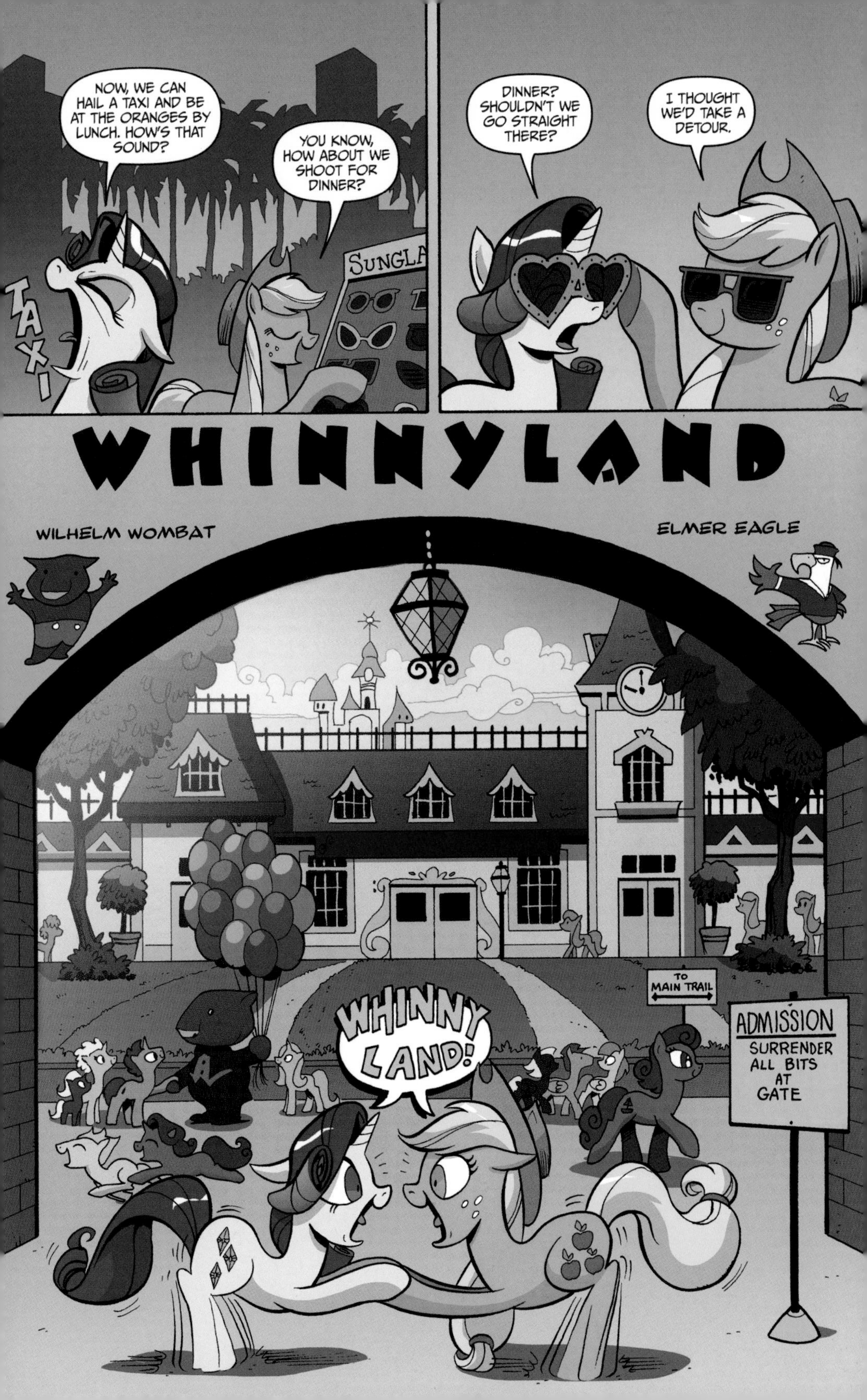
NOW, WE CAN HAIL A TAXI AND BE AT THE ORANGES BY LUNCH. HOW'S THAT SOUND?
TAXI
YOU KNOW, HOW ABOUT WE SHOOT FOR DINNER?
SUNGLA
DINNER? SHOULDN'T WE GO STRAIGHT THERE?
I THOUGHT WE'D TAKE A DETOUR.
WHINNYLAND
WILHELM WOMBAT
ELMER EAGLE
TO MAIN TRAIL
ADMISSION
SURRENDER ALL BITS AT GATE
WHINNY LAND!

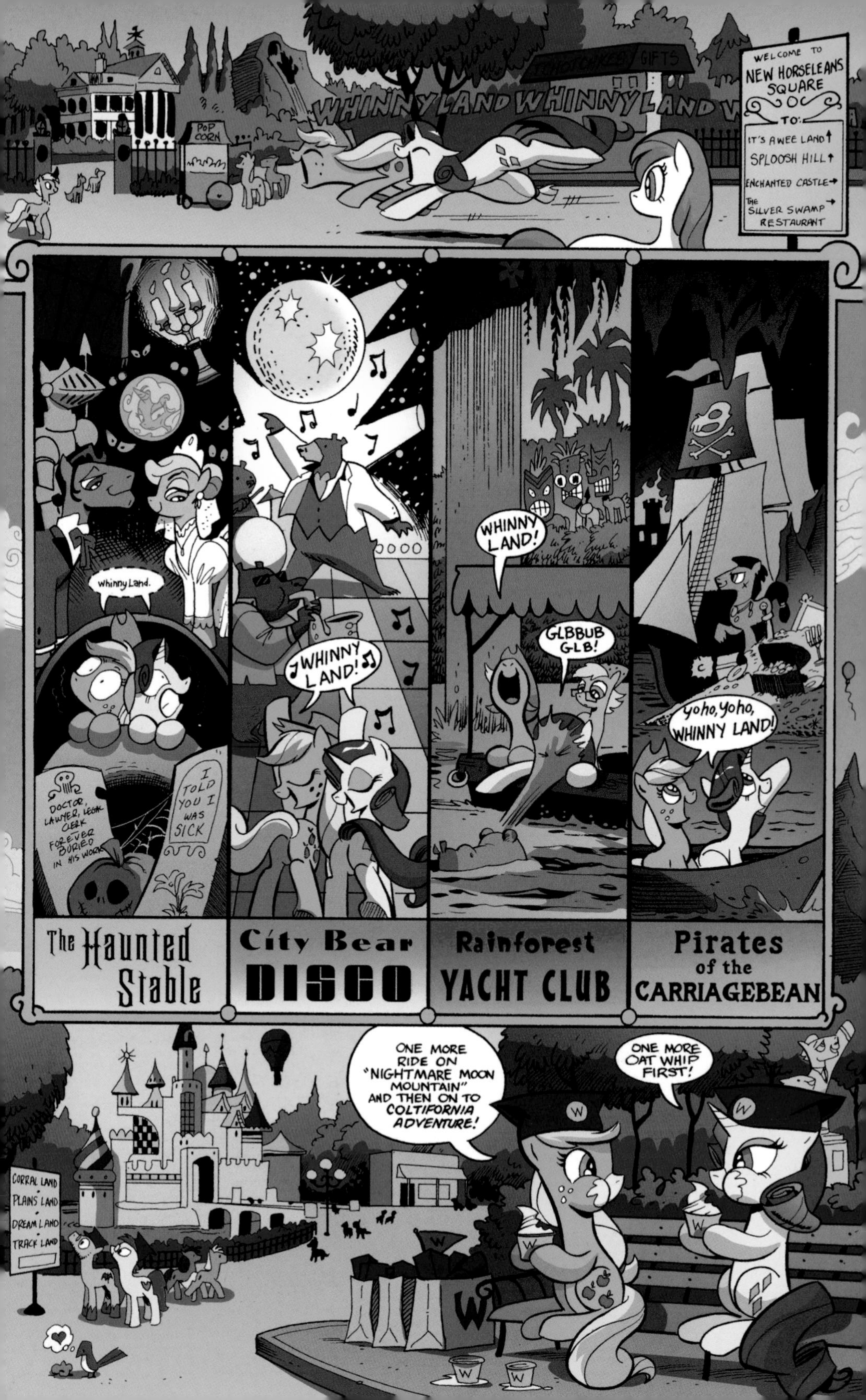

TCHOTCHKEEPS GIFTS
WHINNYLAND WHINNYLAND
POP CORN
WELCOME TO NEW HORSELEANS SQUARE
TO:
IT'S AWEE LAND↑
SPLOOSH HILL↑
ENCHANTED CASTLE→
THE SILVER SWAMP RESTAURANT→
whinny Land.
DOCTOR, LAWYER, LEGAL CLERK FOREVER BURIED IN HIS WORK
I TOLD YOU I WAS SICK
WHINNY LAND!
WHINNY LAND!
GLBBUB GLB!
Yoho, Yoho, WHINNY LAND!
The Haunted Stable
City Bear DISCO
Rainforest YACHT CLUB
Pirates of the CARRIAGEBEAN
ONE MORE RIDE ON "NIGHTMARE MOON MOUNTAIN" AND THEN ON TO COLTIFORNIA ADVENTURE!
ONE MORE OAT WHIP FIRST!
CORRAL LAND
PLAINS LAND
DREAM LAND
TRACK LAND

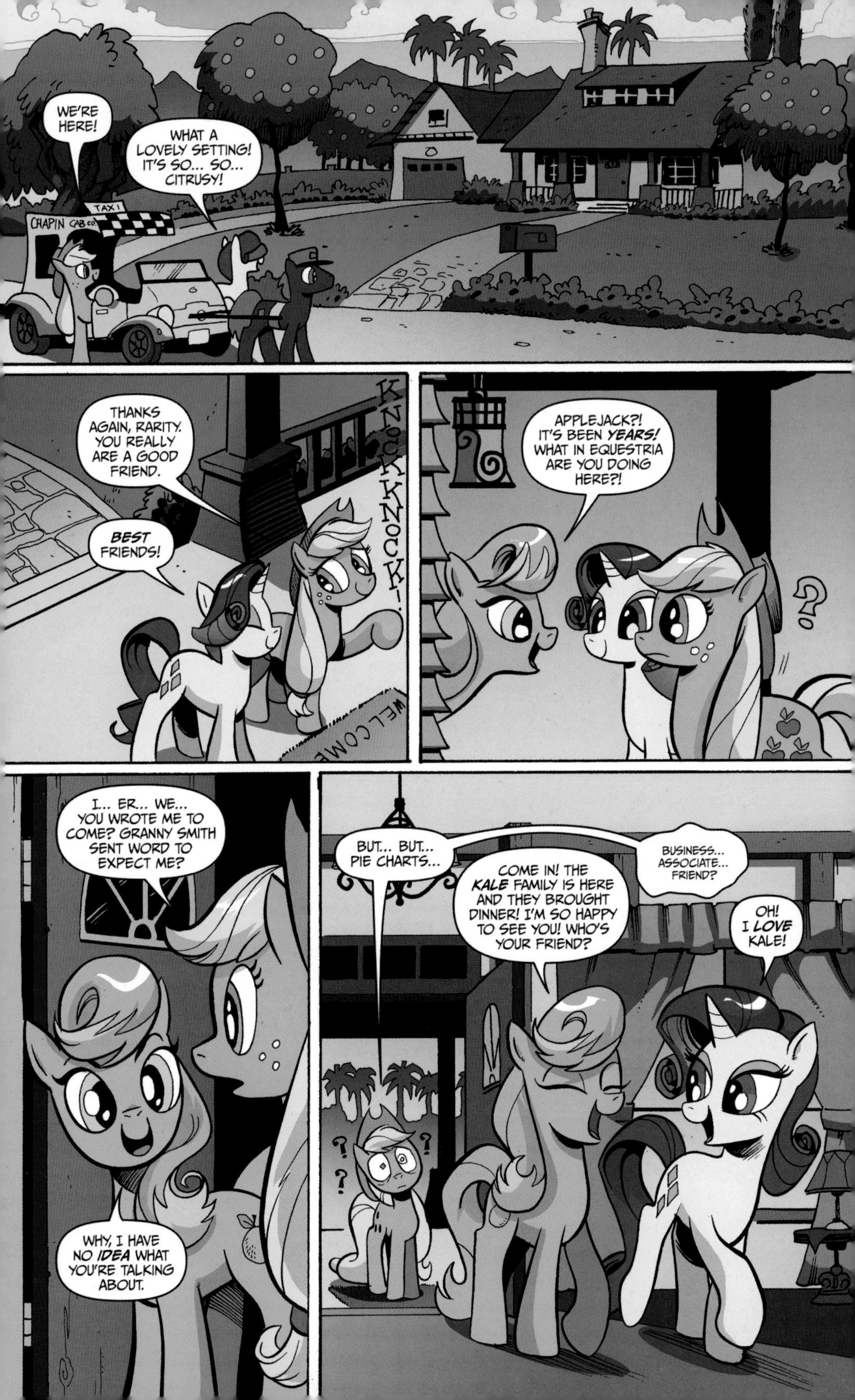
WE'RE HERE!
WHAT A LOVELY SETTING! IT'S SO... SO... CITRUSY!
TAXI
CHAPIN CAB CO.
THANKS AGAIN, RARITY. YOU REALLY ARE A GOOD FRIEND.
BEST FRIENDS!
KNOCK KNOCK!
WELCOME
APPLEJACK?! IT'S BEEN YEARS! WHAT IN EQUESTRIA ARE YOU DOING HERE?!
?
I... ER... WE... YOU WROTE ME TO COME? GRANNY SMITH SENT WORD TO EXPECT ME?
WHY, I HAVE NO IDEA WHAT YOU'RE TALKING ABOUT.
BUT... BUT... PIE CHARTS...
COME IN! THE KALE FAMILY IS HERE AND THEY BROUGHT DINNER! I'M SO HAPPY TO SEE YOU! WHO'S YOUR FRIEND?
BUSINESS... ASSOCIATE... FRIEND?
OH! I LOVE KALE!

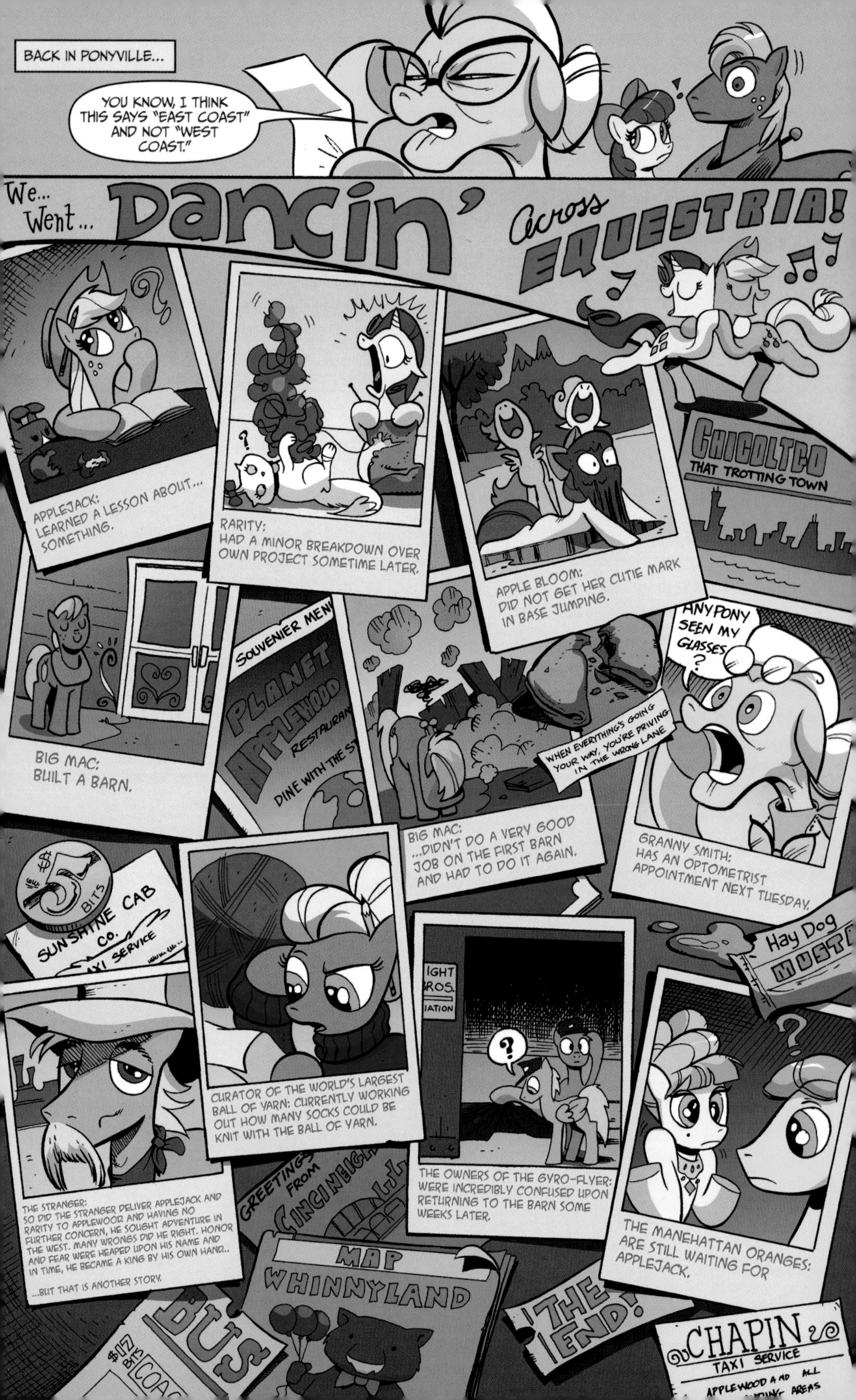

BACK IN PONYVILLE...
YOU KNOW, I THINK THIS SAYS "EAST COAST" AND NOT "WEST COAST."
We... Went... Dancin' across EQUESTRIA!
CHICOLTCO
THAT TROTTING TOWN
APPLEJACK: LEARNED A LESSON ABOUT... SOMETHING.
RARITY: HAD A MINOR BREAKDOWN OVER OWN PROJECT SOMETIME LATER.
APPLE BLOOM: DID NOT GET HER CUTIE MARK IN BASE JUMPING.
PLANET APPLEWOOD
RESTAURAN
BIG MAC: BUILT A BARN.
WHEN EVERYTHING'S GOING YOUR WAY, YOU'RE DRIVING IN THE WRONG LANE
BIG MAC: ...DIDN'T DO A VERY GOOD JOB ON THE FIRST BARN AND HAD TO DO IT AGAIN.
ANYPONY SEEN MY GLASSES?
GRANNY SMITH: HAS AN OPTOMETRIST APPOINTMENT NEXT TUESDAY.
$5 BITS
SUNSHINE CAB CO.
TAXI SERVICE
Hay Dog
CURATOR OF THE WORLD'S LARGEST BALL OF YARN: CURRENTLY WORKING OUT HOW MANY SOCKS COULD BE KNIT WITH THE BALL OF YARN.
?
THE OWNERS OF THE GYRO-FLYER: WERE INCREDIBLY CONFUSED UPON RETURNING TO THE BARN SOME WEEKS LATER.
THE STRANGER: SO DID THE STRANGER DELIVER APPLEJACK AND RARITY TO APPLEWOOD AND HAVING NO FURTHER CONCERN, HE SOUGHT ADVENTURE IN THE WEST. MANY WRONGS DID HE RIGHT. HONOR AND FEAR WERE HEAPED UPON HIS NAME AND IN TIME, HE BECAME A KING BY HIS OWN HAND...
...BUT THAT IS ANOTHER STORY.
GREETINGS FROM CINCINEIGH
THE MANEHATTAN ORANGES: ARE STILL WAITING FOR APPLEJACK.
MAP
WHINNYLAND
BUS
$17 BITS
THE END!
CHAPIN
TAXI SERVICE
APPLEWOOD AND ALL

DEPARTURES

MANEHATTAN

CANCELLED

CANTE
DELA

PON
ON T

APP

DELA

mystery spot

fudge

art by AMY MEBBERSON

Granny & The Flim Flam Brothers

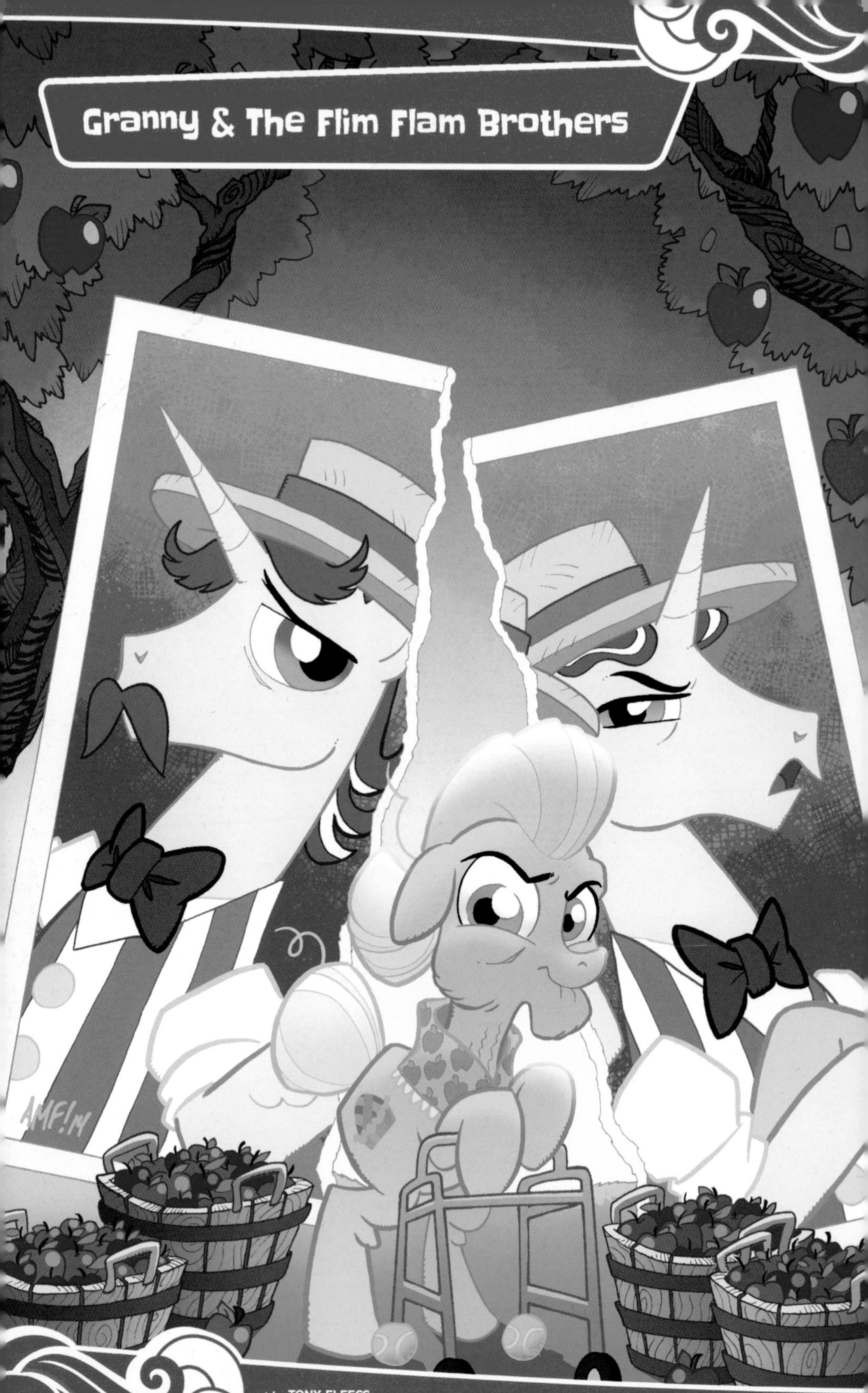

art by TONY FLEECS

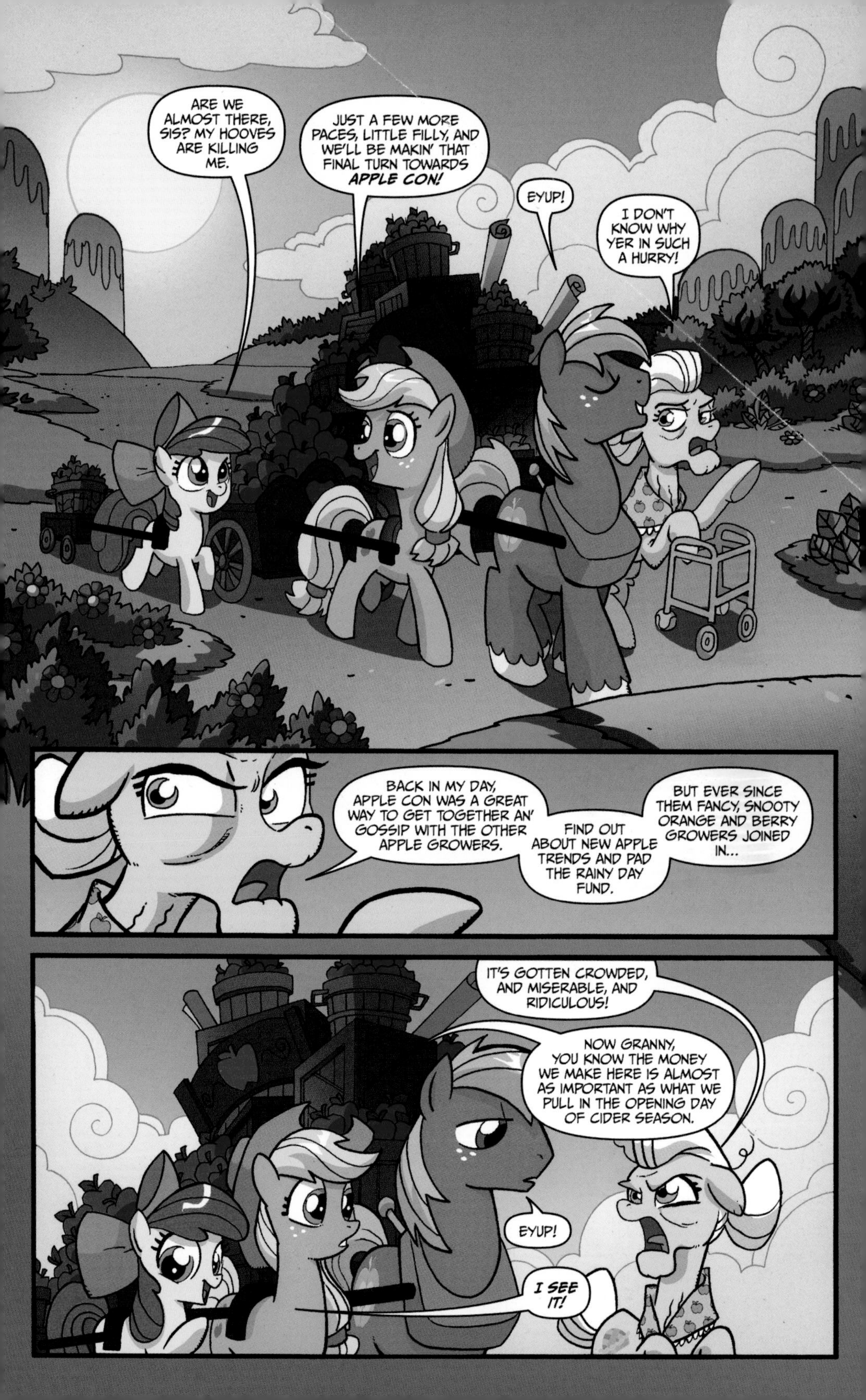
ARE WE ALMOST THERE, SIS? MY HOOVES ARE KILLING ME.
JUST A FEW MORE PACES, LITTLE FILLY, AND WE'LL BE MAKIN' THAT FINAL TURN TOWARDS APPLE CON!
EYUP!
I DON'T KNOW WHY YER IN SUCH A HURRY!
BACK IN MY DAY, APPLE CON WAS A GREAT WAY TO GET TOGETHER AN' GOSSIP WITH THE OTHER APPLE GROWERS.
FIND OUT ABOUT NEW APPLE TRENDS AND PAD THE RAINY DAY FUND.
BUT EVER SINCE THEM FANCY, SNOOTY ORANGE AND BERRY GROWERS JOINED IN...
IT'S GOTTEN CROWDED, AND MISERABLE, AND RIDICULOUS!
NOW GRANNY, YOU KNOW THE MONEY WE MAKE HERE IS ALMOST AS IMPORTANT AS WHAT WE PULL IN THE OPENING DAY OF CIDER SEASON.
EYUP!
I SEE IT!

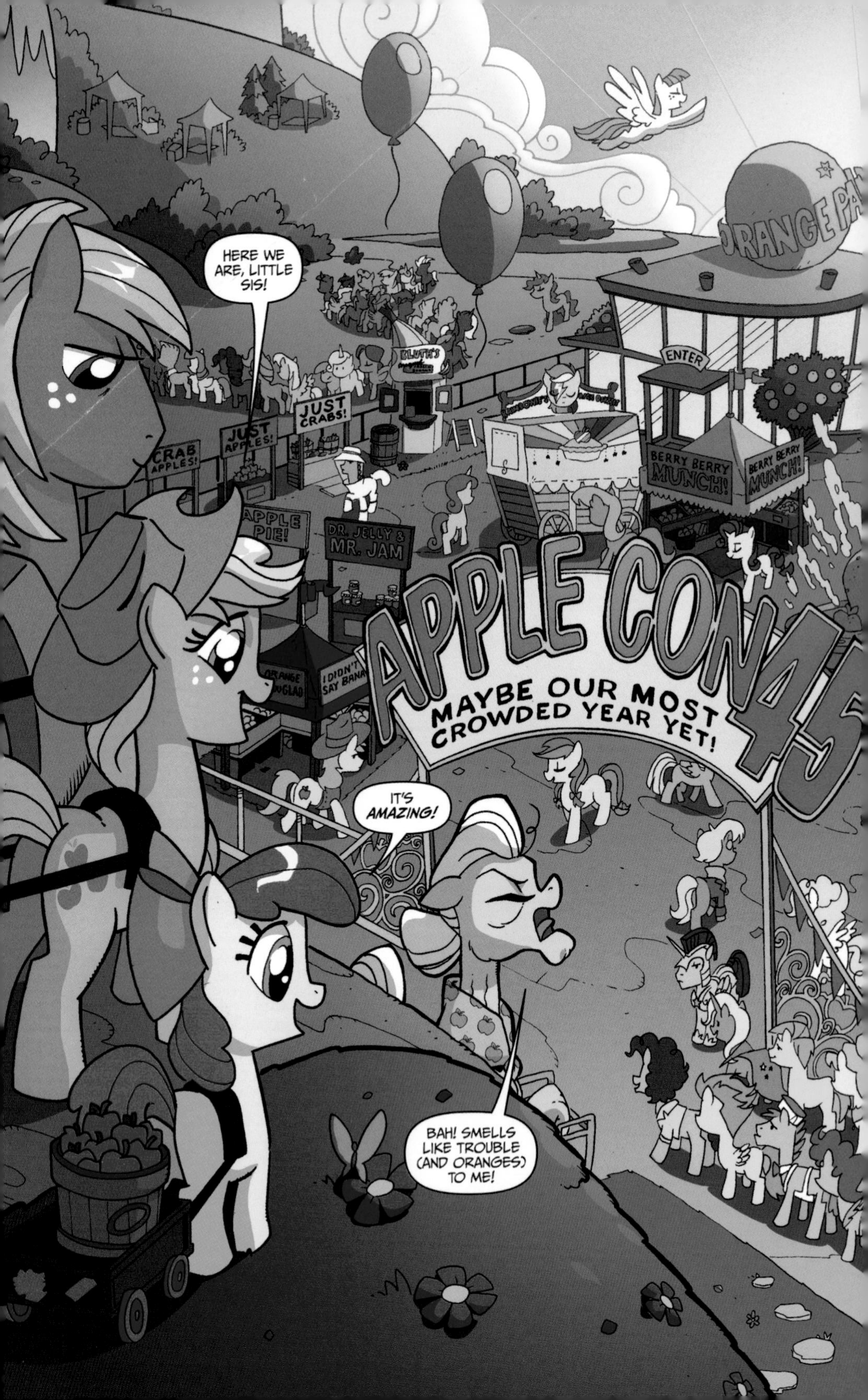
HERE WE ARE, LITTLE SIS!
ORANGE PA
ENTER
BLUTH'S
JUST CRABS!
JUST APPLES!
CRAB APPLES!
APPLE PIE!
DR. JELLY & MR. JAM
BERRY BERRY MUNCH!
BERRY BERRY MUNCH!
ORANGE DUGLAD
I DIDN'T SAY BANA
APPLE CON 45
MAYBE OUR MOST CROWDED YEAR YET!
IT'S AMAZING!
BAH! SMELLS LIKE TROUBLE (AND ORANGES) TO ME!

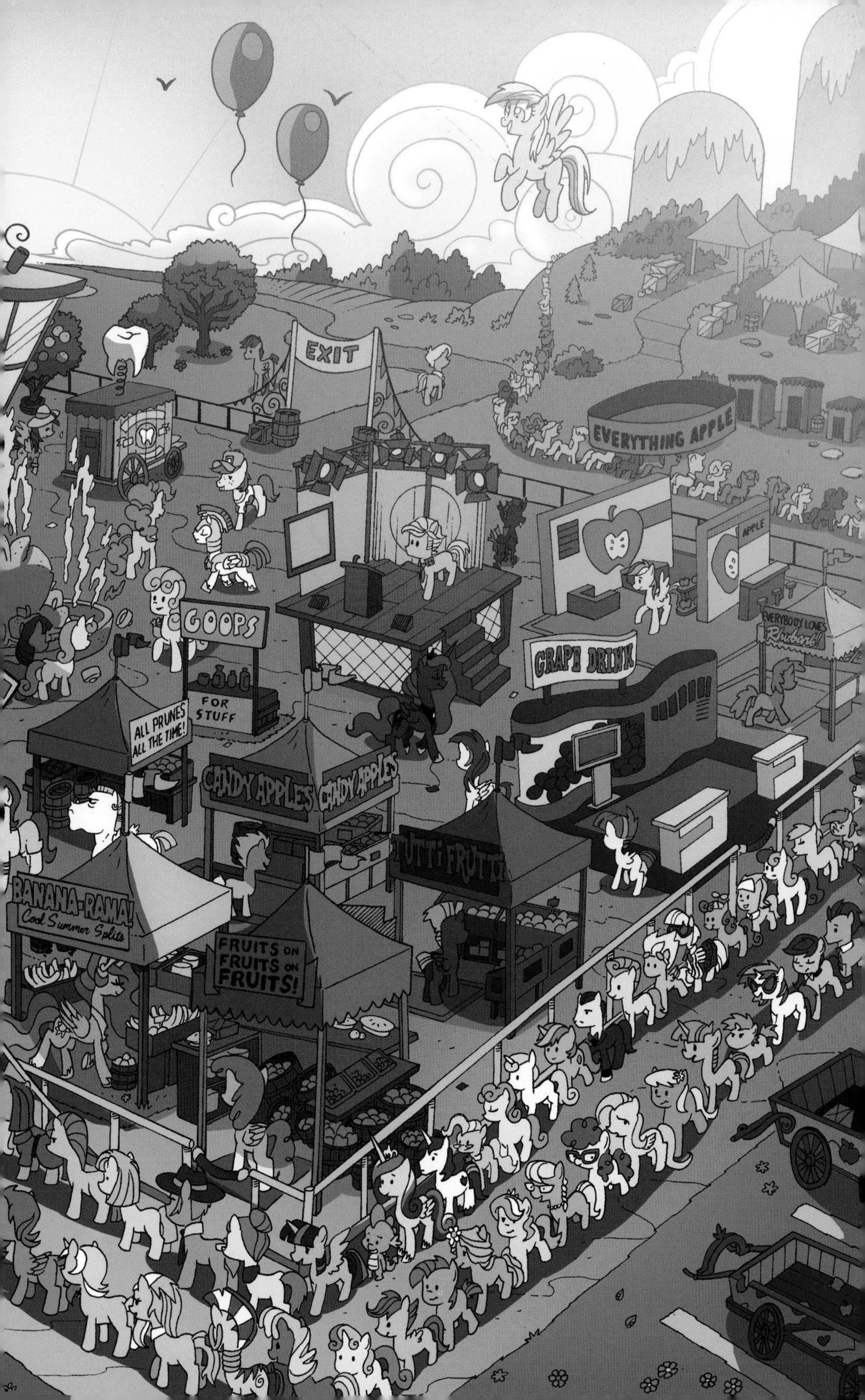
EXIT
EVERYTHING APPLE
APPLE
EVERYBODY LOVES Rhubarb!
GRAPE DRINK
GOOPS
FOR STUFF
ALL PRUNES ALL THE TIME!
CANDY APPLES
CANDY APPLES
TUTTI FRUTTI
BANANA-RAMA! Cool Summer Splits
FRUITS ON FRUITS ON FRUITS!

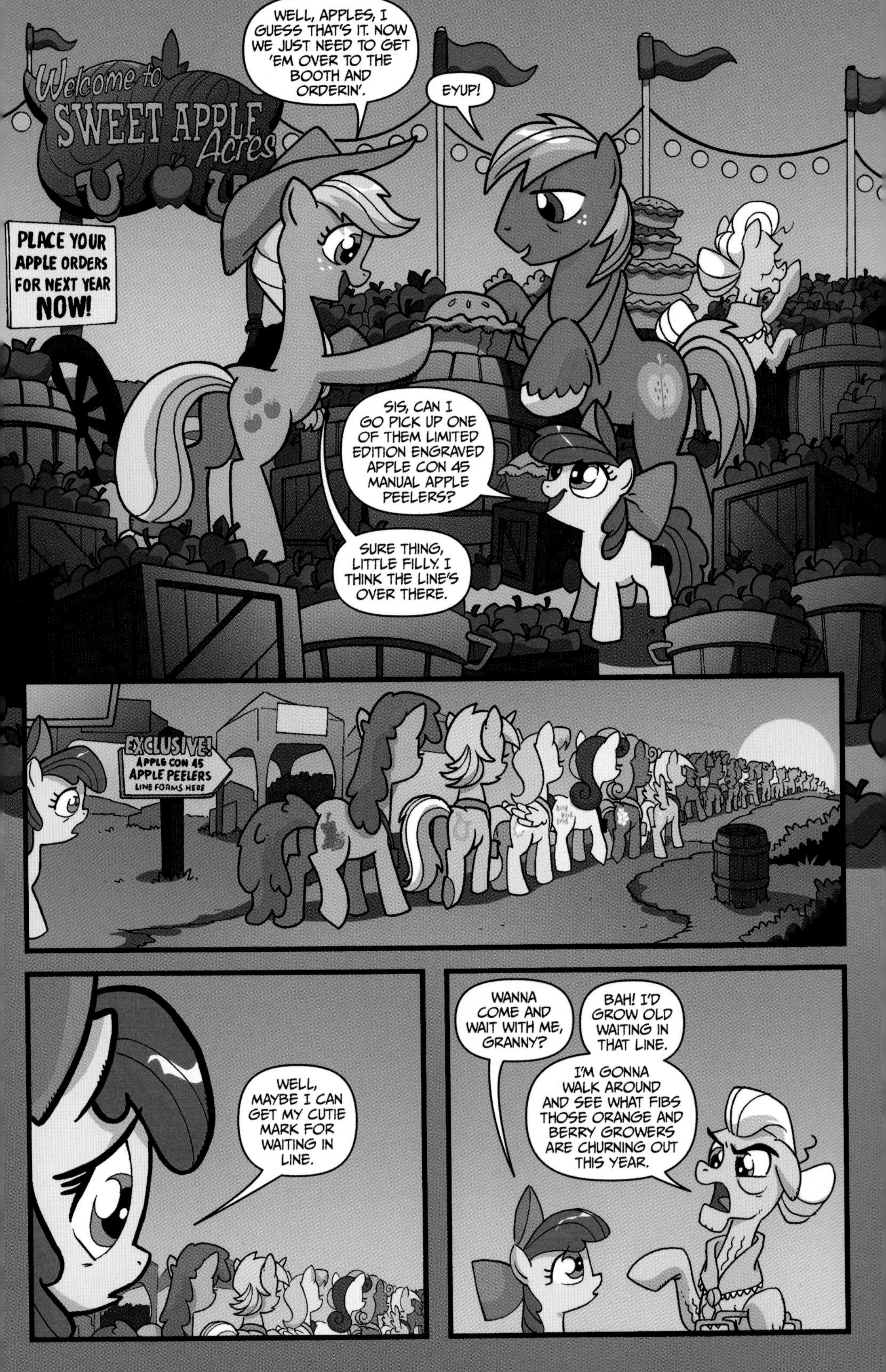
Welcome to SWEET APPLE Acres
PLACE YOUR APPLE ORDERS FOR NEXT YEAR NOW!
WELL, APPLES, I GUESS THAT'S IT. NOW WE JUST NEED TO GET 'EM OVER TO THE BOOTH AND ORDERIN'.
EYUP!
SIS, CAN I GO PICK UP ONE OF THEM LIMITED EDITION ENGRAVED APPLE CON 45 MANUAL APPLE PEELERS?
SURE THING, LITTLE FILLY. I THINK THE LINE'S OVER THERE.
EXCLUSIVE! APPLE CON 45 APPLE PEELERS LINE FORMS HERE
WELL, MAYBE I CAN GET MY CUTIE MARK FOR WAITING IN LINE.
WANNA COME AND WAIT WITH ME, GRANNY?
BAH! I'D GROW OLD WAITING IN THAT LINE.
I'M GONNA WALK AROUND AND SEE WHAT FIBS THOSE ORANGE AND BERRY GROWERS ARE CHURNING OUT THIS YEAR.

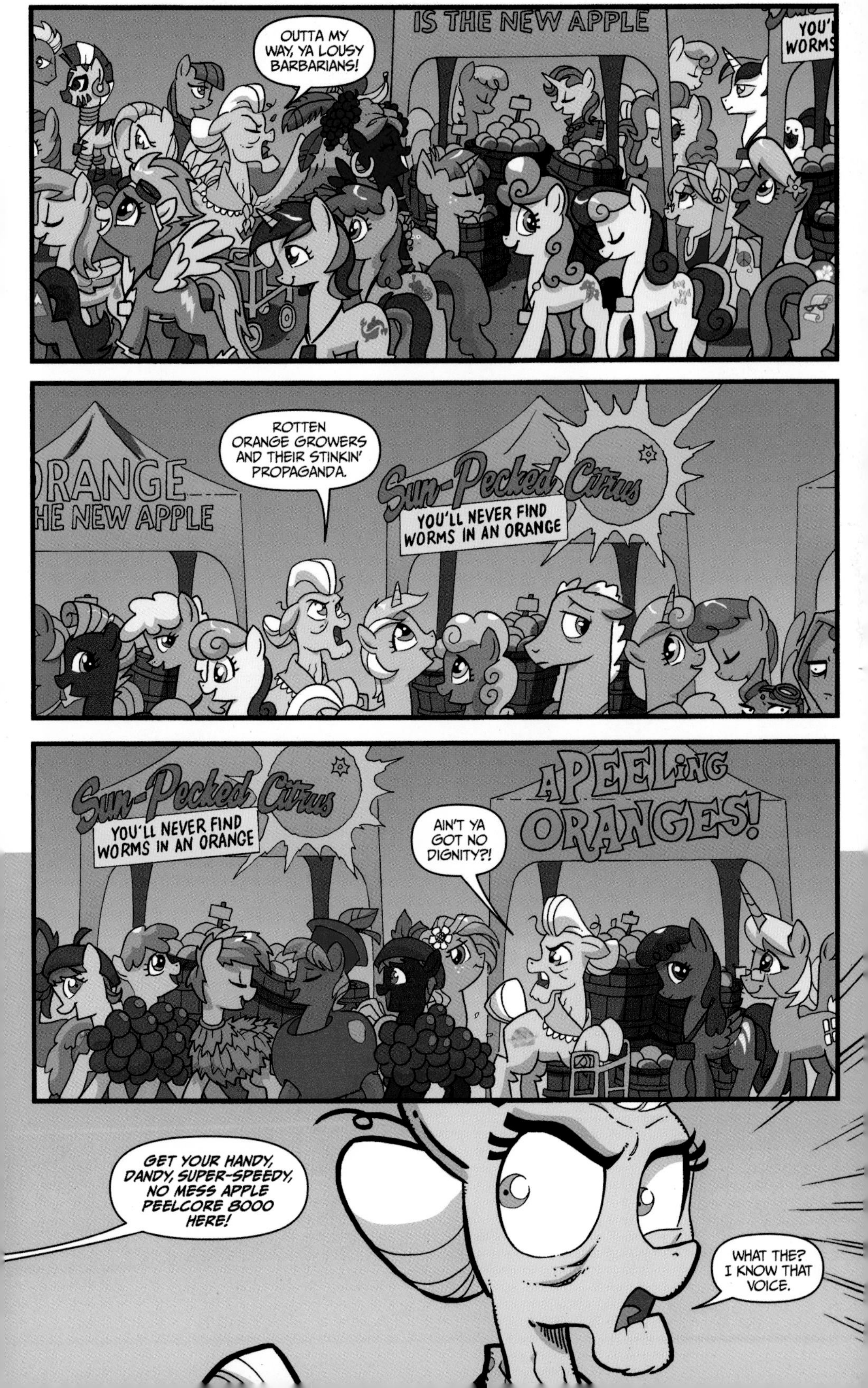
IS THE NEW APPLE
YOU'L
WORMS
OUTTA MY WAY, YA LOUSY BARBARIANS!
ORANGE
HE NEW APPLE
ROTTEN ORANGE GROWERS AND THEIR STINKIN' PROPAGANDA.
Sun-Pecked Citrus
YOU'LL NEVER FIND WORMS IN AN ORANGE
Sun-Pecked Citrus
YOU'LL NEVER FIND WORMS IN AN ORANGE
APEELing ORANGES!
AIN'T YA GOT NO DIGNITY?!
GET YOUR HANDY, DANDY, SUPER-SPEEDY, NO MESS APPLE PEELCORE 8000 HERE!
WHAT THE? I KNOW THAT VOICE.

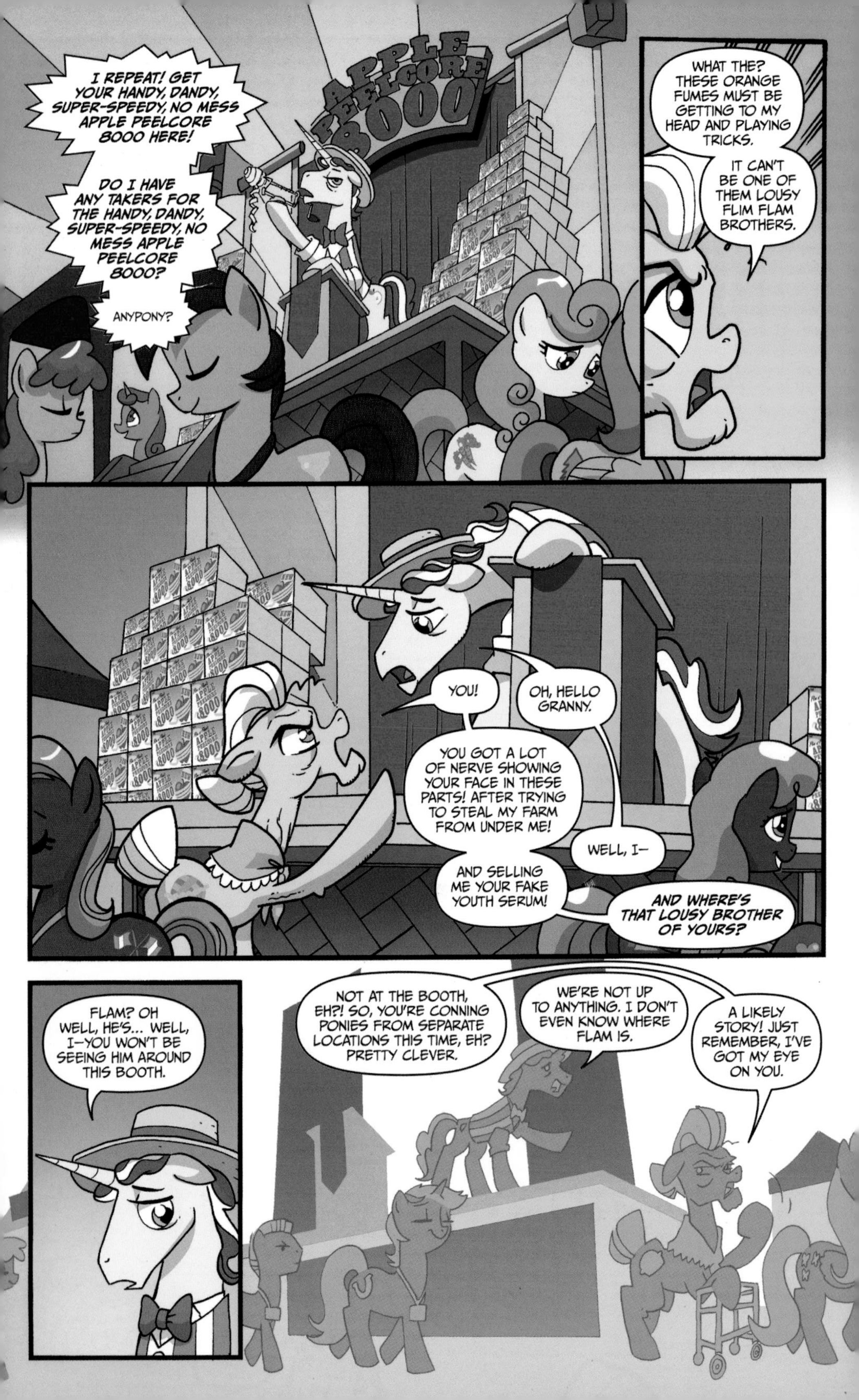
I REPEAT! GET YOUR HANDY, DANDY, SUPER-SPEEDY, NO MESS APPLE PEELCORE 8000 HERE!
DO I HAVE ANY TAKERS FOR THE HANDY, DANDY, SUPER-SPEEDY, NO MESS APPLE PEELCORE 8000?
ANYPONY?
APPLE PEELCORE 8000
WHAT THE? THESE ORANGE FUMES MUST BE GETTING TO MY HEAD AND PLAYING TRICKS.
IT CAN'T BE ONE OF THEM LOUSY FLIM FLAM BROTHERS.
YOU!
OH, HELLO GRANNY.
YOU GOT A LOT OF NERVE SHOWING YOUR FACE IN THESE PARTS! AFTER TRYING TO STEAL MY FARM FROM UNDER ME!
WELL, I—
AND SELLING ME YOUR FAKE YOUTH SERUM!
AND WHERE'S THAT LOUSY BROTHER OF YOURS?
FLAM? OH WELL, HE'S... WELL, I—YOU WON'T BE SEEING HIM AROUND THIS BOOTH.
NOT AT THE BOOTH, EH?! SO, YOU'RE CONNING PONIES FROM SEPARATE LOCATIONS THIS TIME, EH? PRETTY CLEVER.
WE'RE NOT UP TO ANYTHING. I DON'T EVEN KNOW WHERE FLAM IS.
A LIKELY STORY! JUST REMEMBER, I'VE GOT MY EYE ON YOU.

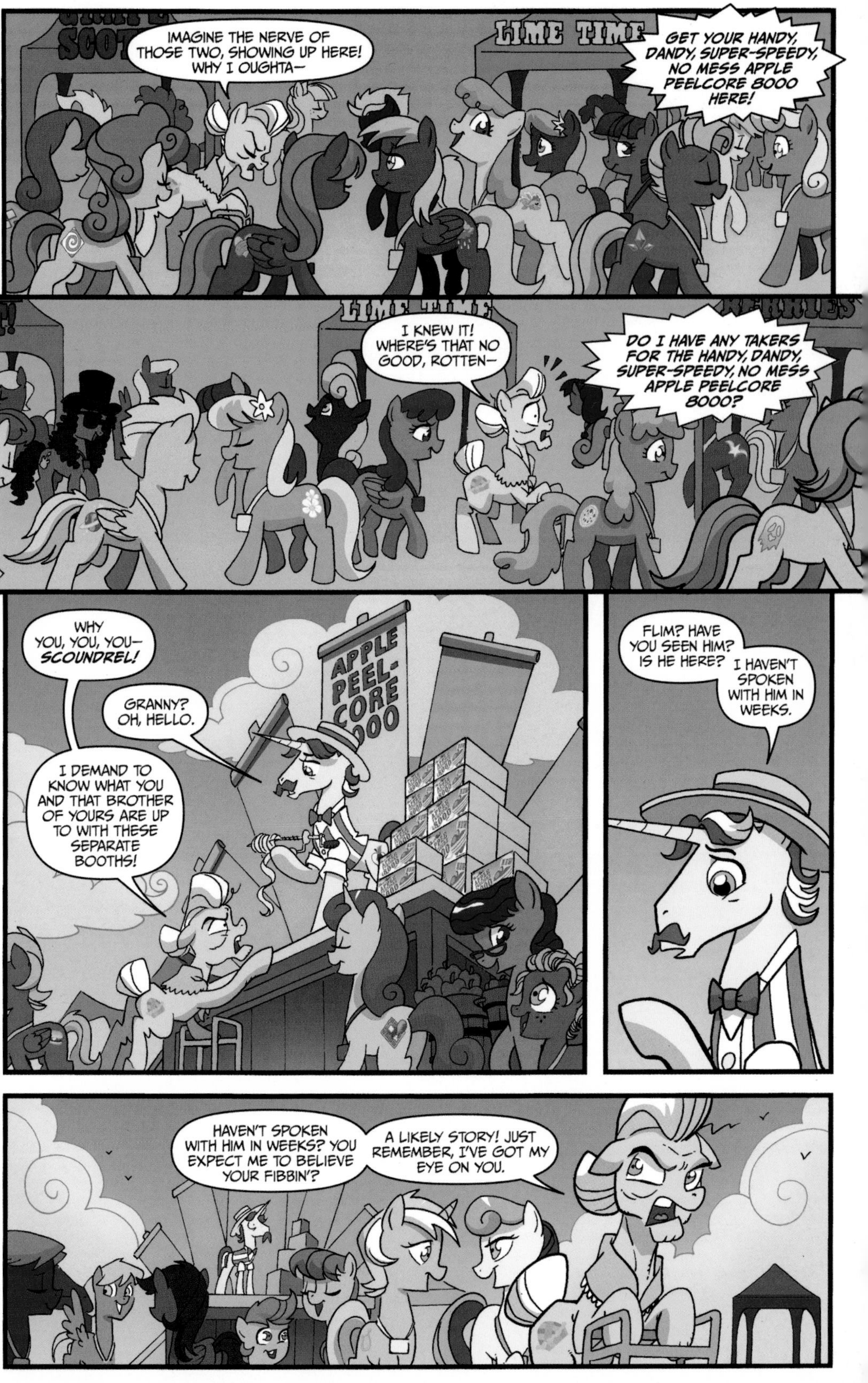
SCOT
LIME TIME
IMAGINE THE NERVE OF THOSE TWO, SHOWING UP HERE! WHY I OUGHTA—
GET YOUR HANDY, DANDY, SUPER-SPEEDY, NO MESS APPLE PEELCORE 8000 HERE!
LIME TIME
I KNEW IT! WHERE'S THAT NO GOOD, ROTTEN—
DO I HAVE ANY TAKERS FOR THE HANDY, DANDY, SUPER-SPEEDY, NO MESS APPLE PEELCORE 8000?
WHY YOU, YOU, YOU— SCOUNDREL!
GRANNY? OH, HELLO.
APPLE PEEL-CORE 8000
I DEMAND TO KNOW WHAT YOU AND THAT BROTHER OF YOURS ARE UP TO WITH THESE SEPARATE BOOTHS!
FLIM? HAVE YOU SEEN HIM? IS HE HERE?
I HAVEN'T SPOKEN WITH HIM IN WEEKS.
HAVEN'T SPOKEN WITH HIM IN WEEKS? YOU EXPECT ME TO BELIEVE YOUR FIBBIN'?
A LIKELY STORY! JUST REMEMBER, I'VE GOT MY EYE ON YOU.

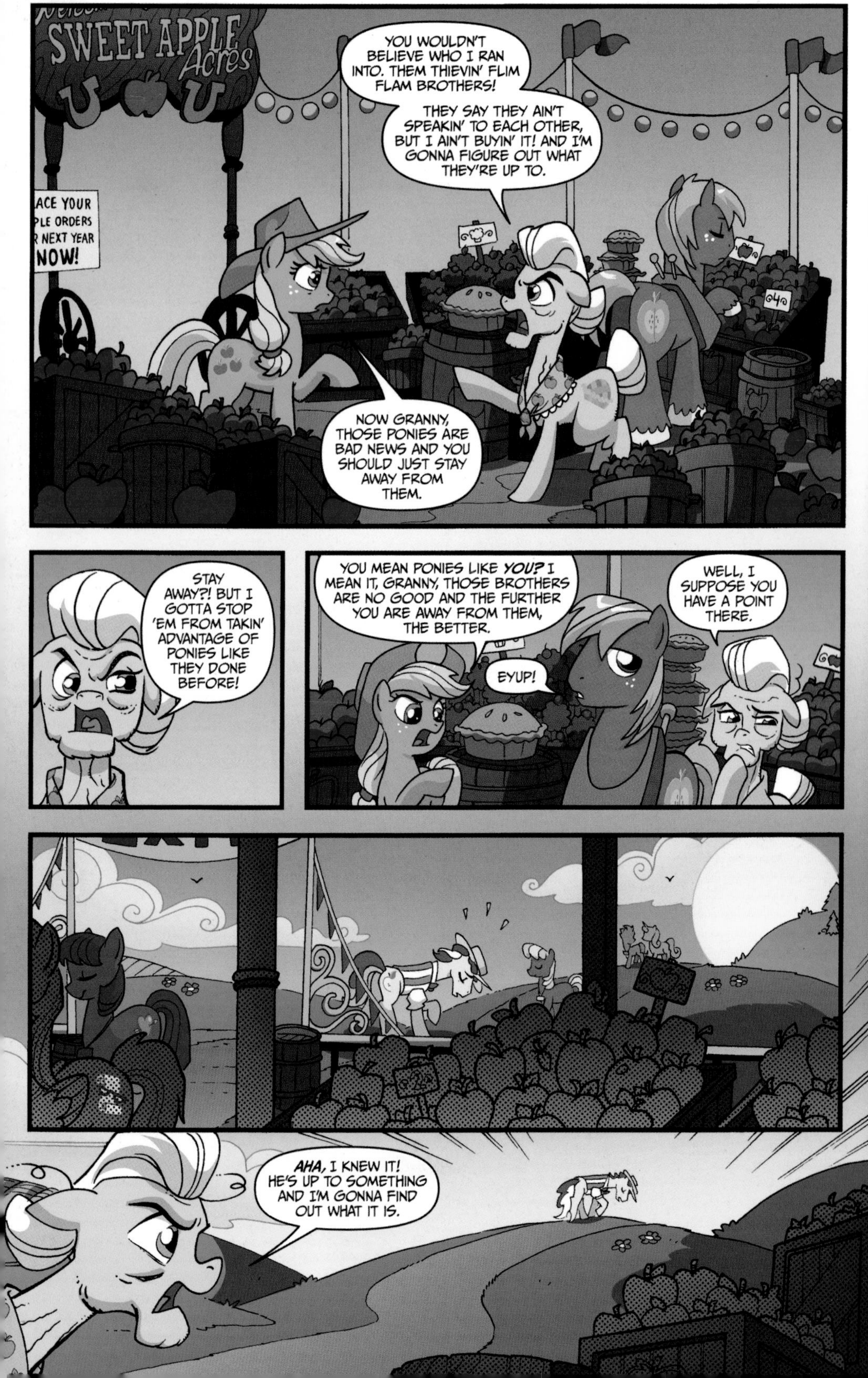
SWEET APPLE Acres
NOW!
YOU WOULDN'T BELIEVE WHO I RAN INTO. THEM THIEVIN' FLIM FLAM BROTHERS!
THEY SAY THEY AIN'T SPEAKIN' TO EACH OTHER, BUT I AIN'T BUYIN' IT! AND I'M GONNA FIGURE OUT WHAT THEY'RE UP TO.
NOW GRANNY, THOSE PONIES ARE BAD NEWS AND YOU SHOULD JUST STAY AWAY FROM THEM.
STAY AWAY?! BUT I GOTTA STOP 'EM FROM TAKIN' ADVANTAGE OF PONIES LIKE THEY DONE BEFORE!
YOU MEAN PONIES LIKE *YOU?* I MEAN IT, GRANNY, THOSE BROTHERS ARE NO GOOD AND THE FURTHER YOU ARE AWAY FROM THEM, THE BETTER.
EYUP!
WELL, I SUPPOSE YOU HAVE A POINT THERE.
AHA, I KNEW IT! HE'S UP TO SOMETHING AND I'M GONNA FIND OUT WHAT IT IS.

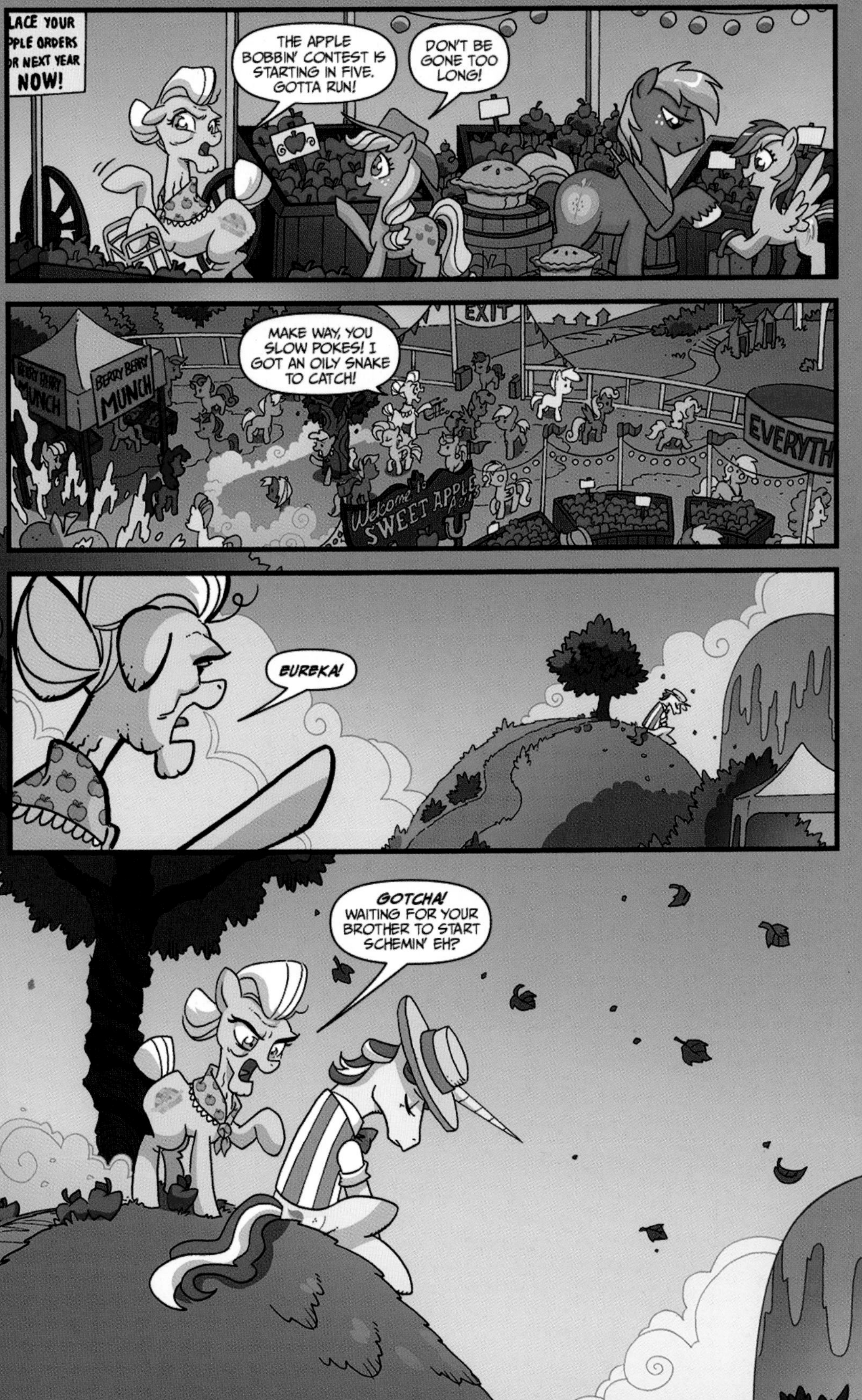

LACE YOUR
PPLE ORDERS
R NEXT YEAR
NOW!
THE APPLE BOBBIN' CONTEST IS STARTING IN FIVE. GOTTA RUN!
DON'T BE GONE TOO LONG!
EXIT
BERRY BERRY MUNCH
BERRY BERRY MUNCH
MAKE WAY, YOU SLOW POKES! I GOT AN OILY SNAKE TO CATCH!
EVERYTH
Welcome to SWEET APPLE
EUREKA!
GOTCHA! WAITING FOR YOUR BROTHER TO START SCHEMIN' EH?

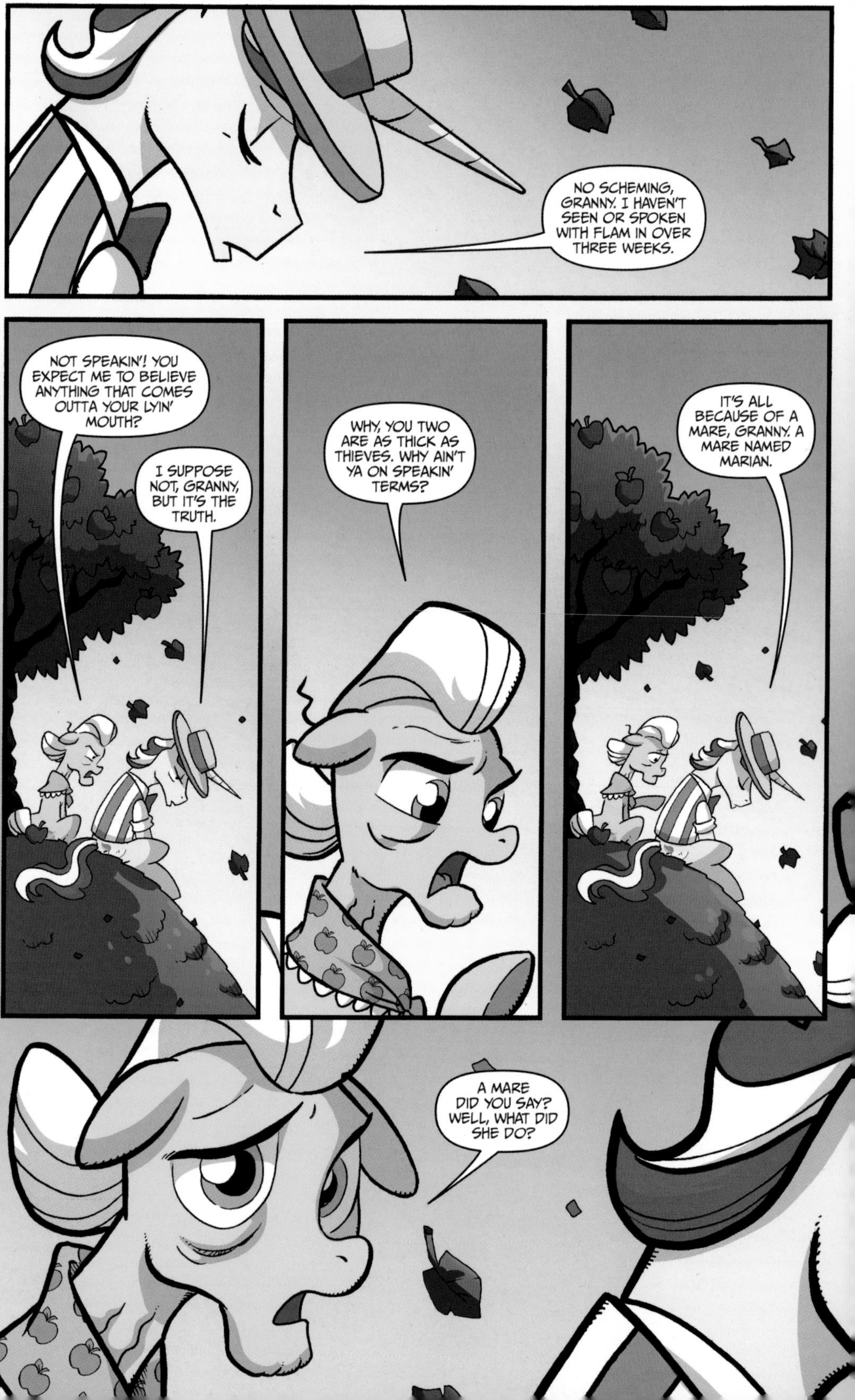
NO SCHEMING, GRANNY. I HAVEN'T SEEN OR SPOKEN WITH FLAM IN OVER THREE WEEKS.
NOT SPEAKIN'! YOU EXPECT ME TO BELIEVE ANYTHING THAT COMES OUTTA YOUR LYIN' MOUTH?
I SUPPOSE NOT, GRANNY, BUT IT'S THE TRUTH.
WHY, YOU TWO ARE AS THICK AS THIEVES. WHY AIN'T YA ON SPEAKIN' TERMS?
IT'S ALL BECAUSE OF A MARE, GRANNY. A MARE NAMED MARIAN.
A MARE DID YOU SAY? WELL, WHAT DID SHE DO?

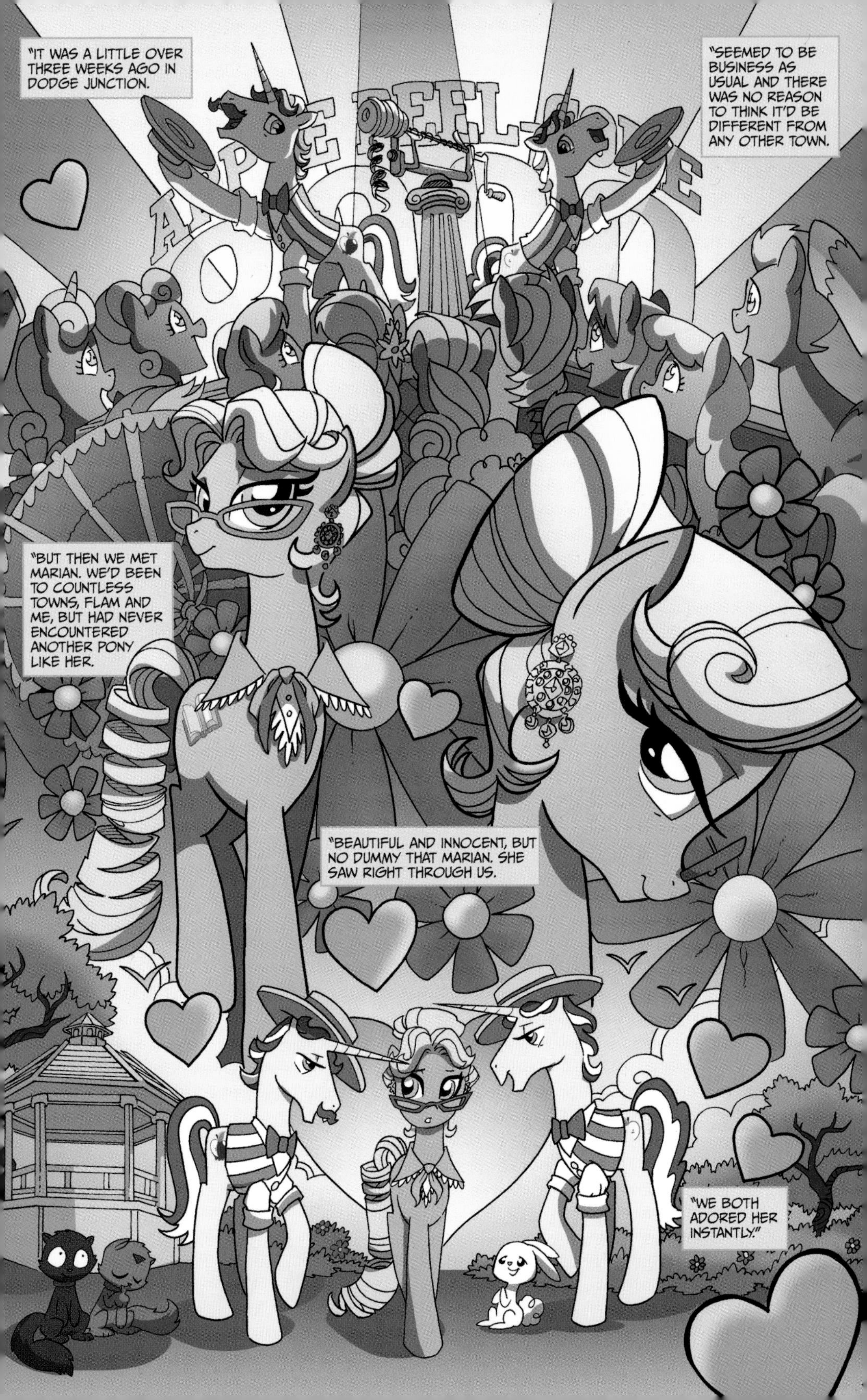
"IT WAS A LITTLE OVER THREE WEEKS AGO IN DODGE JUNCTION.
"SEEMED TO BE BUSINESS AS USUAL AND THERE WAS NO REASON TO THINK IT'D BE DIFFERENT FROM ANY OTHER TOWN.
"BUT THEN WE MET MARIAN. WE'D BEEN TO COUNTLESS TOWNS, FLAM AND ME, BUT HAD NEVER ENCOUNTERED ANOTHER PONY LIKE HER.
"BEAUTIFUL AND INNOCENT, BUT NO DUMMY THAT MARIAN. SHE SAW RIGHT THROUGH US.
"WE BOTH ADORED HER INSTANTLY."

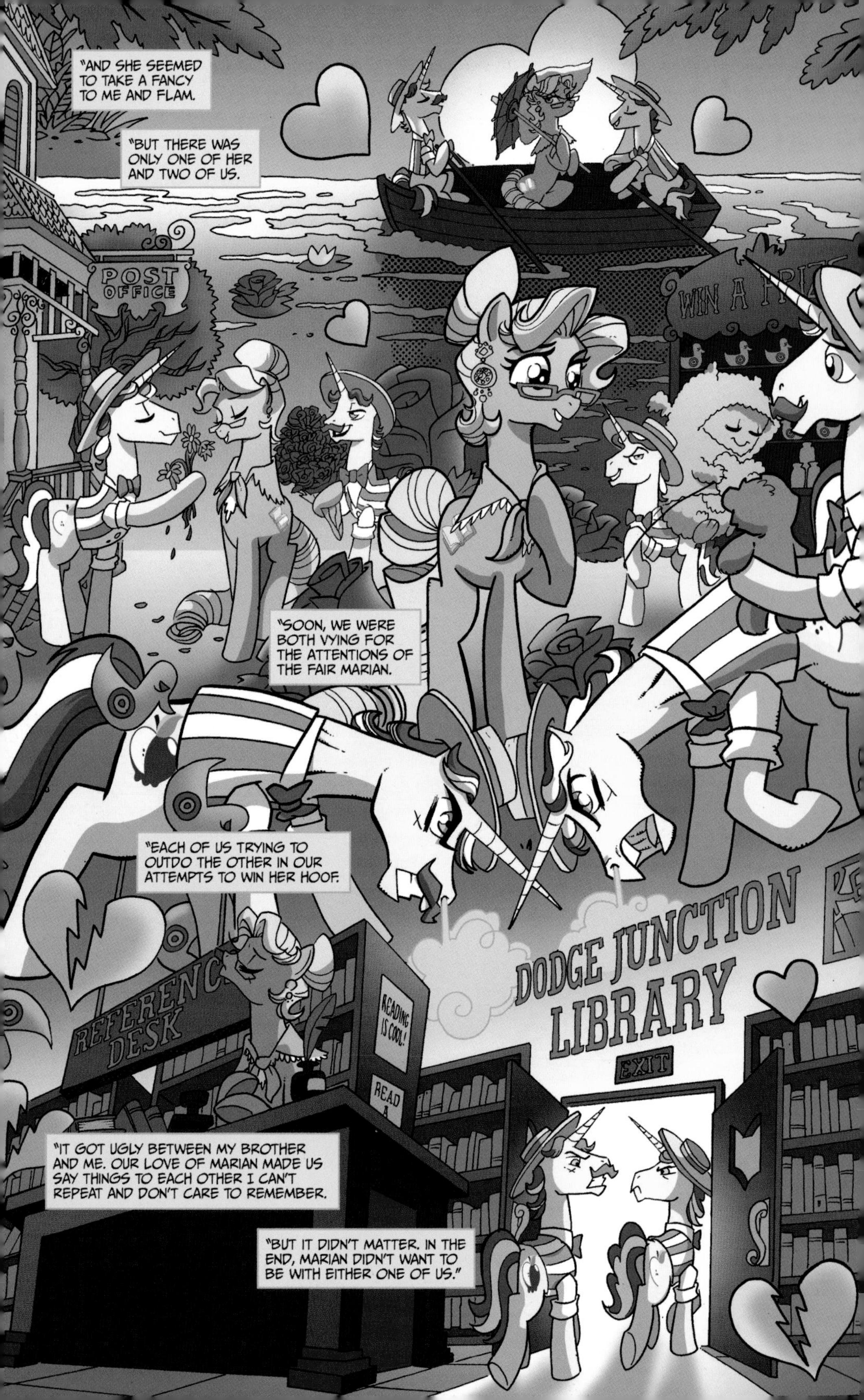
"AND SHE SEEMED TO TAKE A FANCY TO ME AND FLAM.
"BUT THERE WAS ONLY ONE OF HER AND TWO OF US.
POST OFFICE
WIN A PRIZE
"SOON, WE WERE BOTH VYING FOR THE ATTENTIONS OF THE FAIR MARIAN.
"EACH OF US TRYING TO OUTDO THE OTHER IN OUR ATTEMPTS TO WIN HER HOOF.
DODGE JUNCTION LIBRARY
REFERENCE DESK
READING IS COOL!
EXIT
"IT GOT UGLY BETWEEN MY BROTHER AND ME. OUR LOVE OF MARIAN MADE US SAY THINGS TO EACH OTHER I CAN'T REPEAT AND DON'T CARE TO REMEMBER.
"BUT IT DIDN'T MATTER. IN THE END, MARIAN DIDN'T WANT TO BE WITH EITHER ONE OF US."

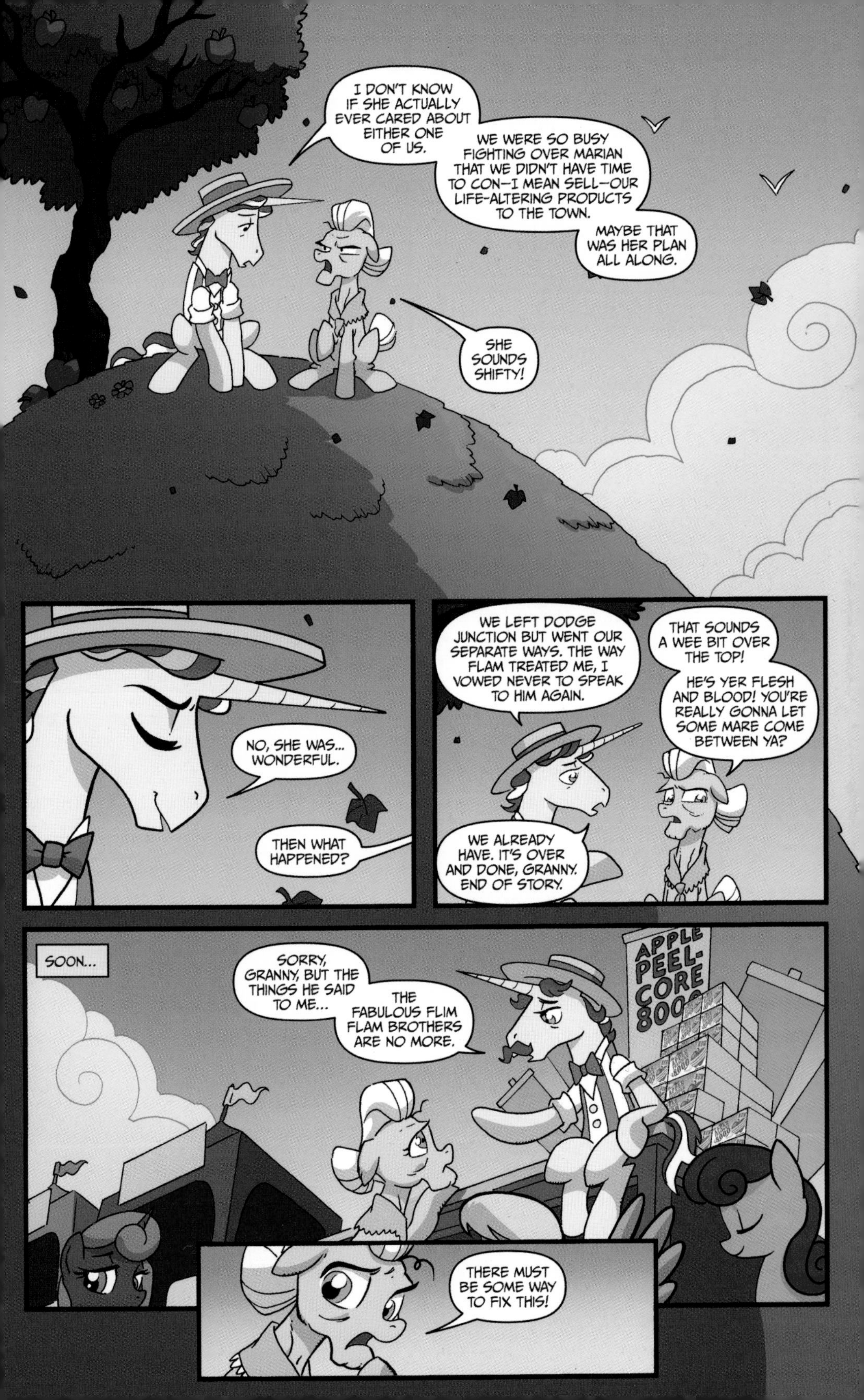
I DON'T KNOW IF SHE ACTUALLY EVER CARED ABOUT EITHER ONE OF US.
WE WERE SO BUSY FIGHTING OVER MARIAN THAT WE DIDN'T HAVE TIME TO CON—I MEAN SELL—OUR LIFE-ALTERING PRODUCTS TO THE TOWN.
MAYBE THAT WAS HER PLAN ALL ALONG.
SHE SOUNDS SHIFTY!
NO, SHE WAS... WONDERFUL.
THEN WHAT HAPPENED?
WE LEFT DODGE JUNCTION BUT WENT OUR SEPARATE WAYS. THE WAY FLAM TREATED ME, I VOWED NEVER TO SPEAK TO HIM AGAIN.
THAT SOUNDS A WEE BIT OVER THE TOP!
HE'S YER FLESH AND BLOOD! YOU'RE REALLY GONNA LET SOME MARE COME BETWEEN YA?
WE ALREADY HAVE. IT'S OVER AND DONE, GRANNY. END OF STORY.
SOON...
SORRY, GRANNY, BUT THE THINGS HE SAID TO ME...
THE FABULOUS FLIM FLAM BROTHERS ARE NO MORE.
APPLE PEEL-CORE 800
THERE MUST BE SOME WAY TO FIX THIS!

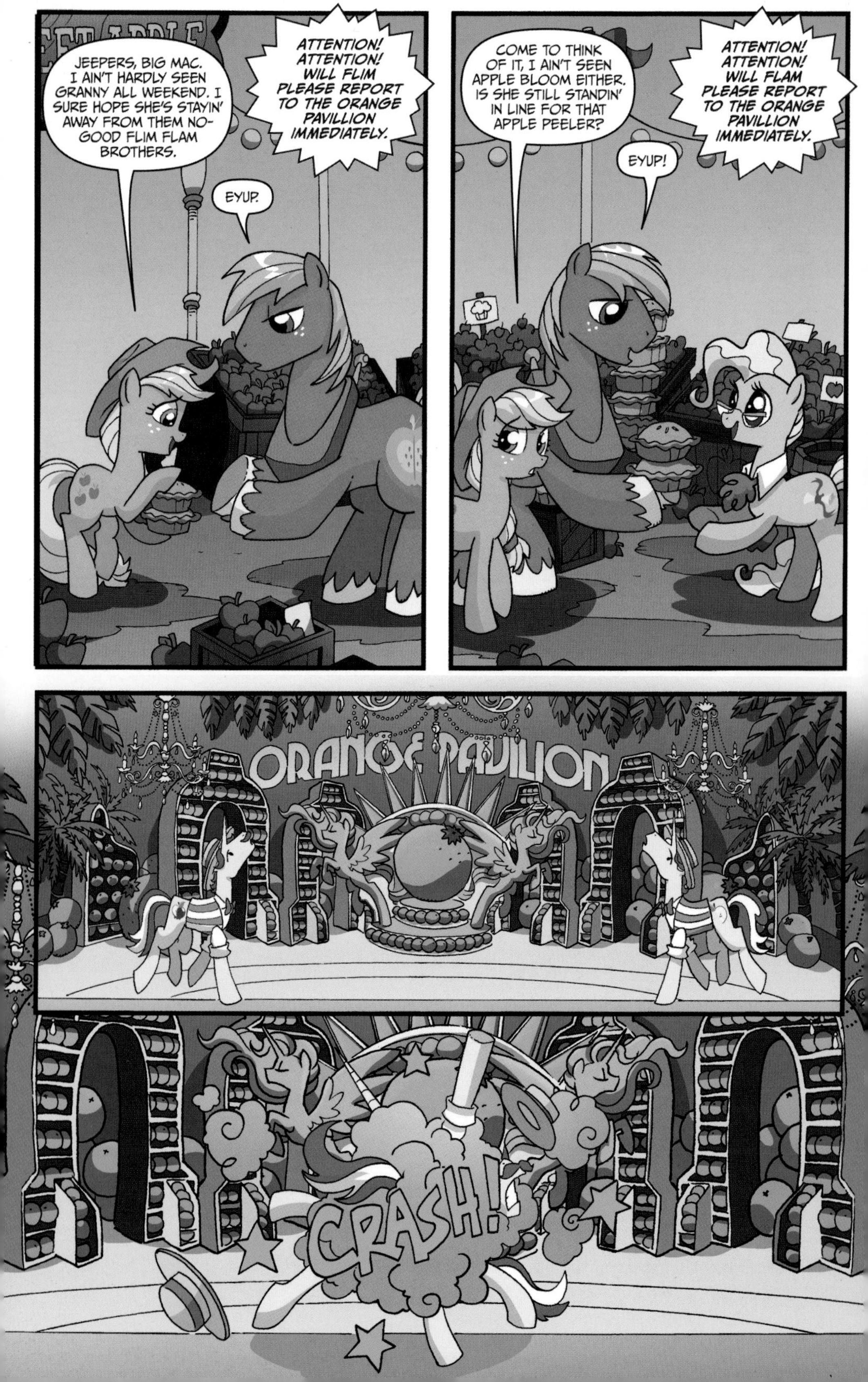
JEEPERS, BIG MAC. I AIN'T HARDLY SEEN GRANNY ALL WEEKEND. I SURE HOPE SHE'S STAYIN' AWAY FROM THEM NO-GOOD FLIM FLAM BROTHERS.
ATTENTION! ATTENTION! WILL FLIM PLEASE REPORT TO THE ORANGE PAVILLION IMMEDIATELY.
EYUP.
COME TO THINK OF IT, I AIN'T SEEN APPLE BLOOM EITHER. IS SHE STILL STANDIN' IN LINE FOR THAT APPLE PEELER?
EYUP!
ATTENTION! ATTENTION! WILL FLAM PLEASE REPORT TO THE ORANGE PAVILLION IMMEDIATELY.
ORANGE PAVILION
CRASH!

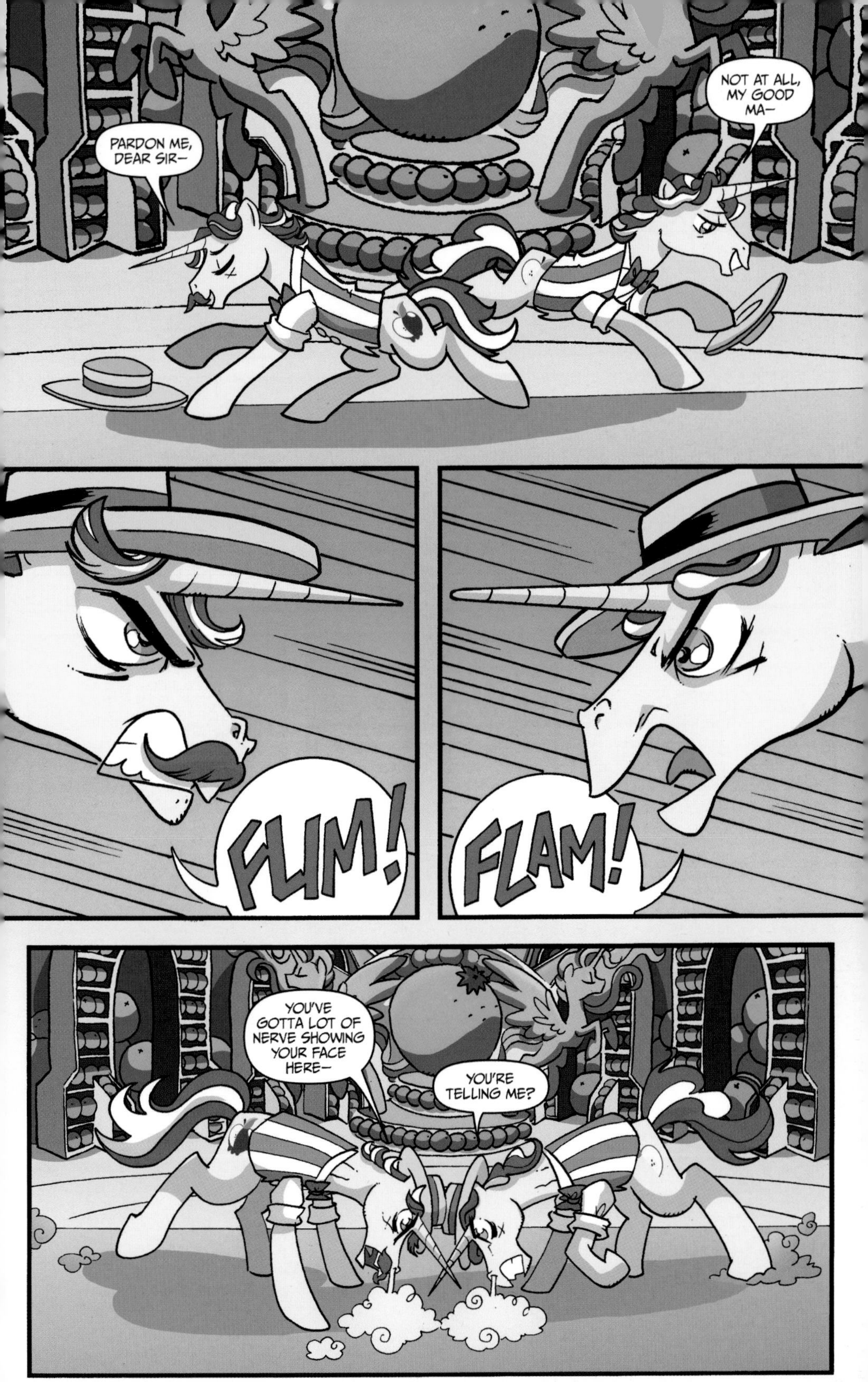
PARDON ME, DEAR SIR—
NOT AT ALL, MY GOOD MA—
FLIM!
FLAM!
YOU'VE GOTTA LOT OF NERVE SHOWING YOUR FACE HERE—
YOU'RE TELLING ME?

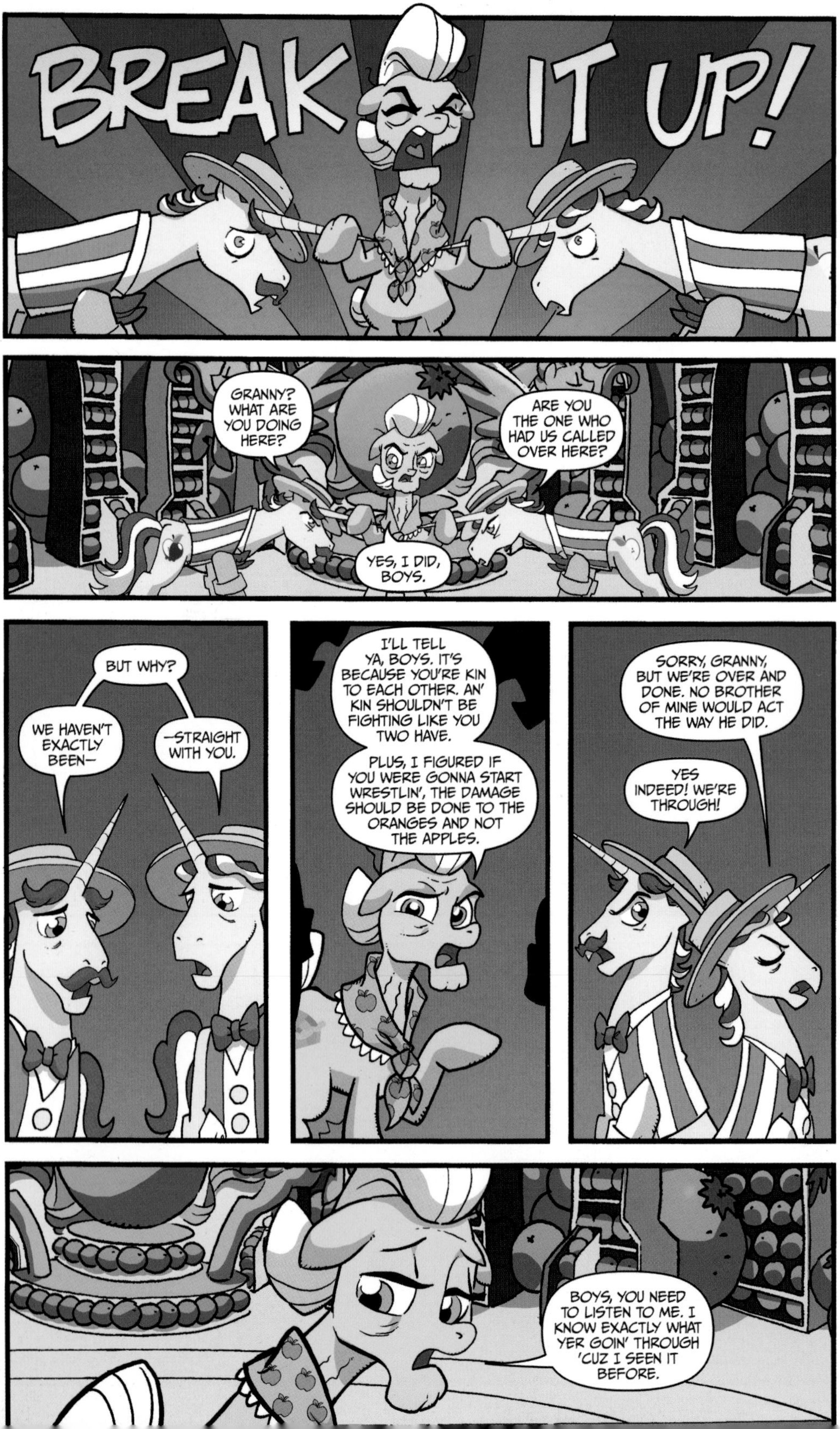
BREAK IT UP!
GRANNY? WHAT ARE YOU DOING HERE?
ARE YOU THE ONE WHO HAD US CALLED OVER HERE?
YES, I DID, BOYS.
BUT WHY?
WE HAVEN'T EXACTLY BEEN—
—STRAIGHT WITH YOU.
I'LL TELL YA, BOYS. IT'S BECAUSE YOU'RE KIN TO EACH OTHER. AN' KIN SHOULDN'T BE FIGHTING LIKE YOU TWO HAVE.
PLUS, I FIGURED IF YOU WERE GONNA START WRESTLIN', THE DAMAGE SHOULD BE DONE TO THE ORANGES AND NOT THE APPLES.
SORRY, GRANNY, BUT WE'RE OVER AND DONE. NO BROTHER OF MINE WOULD ACT THE WAY HE DID.
YES INDEED! WE'RE THROUGH!
BOYS, YOU NEED TO LISTEN TO ME. I KNOW EXACTLY WHAT YER GOIN' THROUGH 'CUZ I SEEN IT BEFORE.

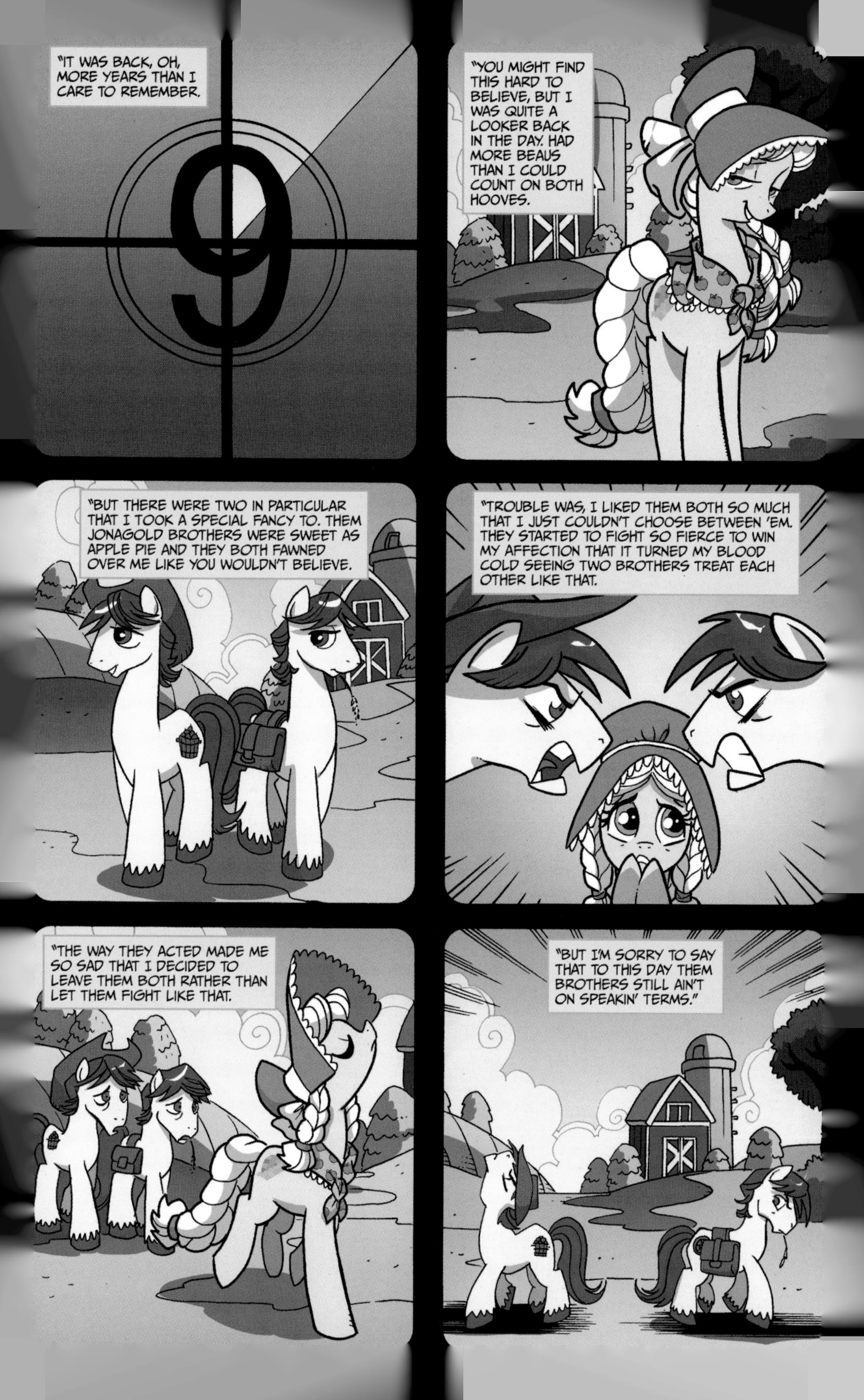
"IT WAS BACK, OH, MORE YEARS THAN I CARE TO REMEMBER.
9
"YOU MIGHT FIND THIS HARD TO BELIEVE, BUT I WAS QUITE A LOOKER BACK IN THE DAY. HAD MORE BEAUS THAN I COULD COUNT ON BOTH HOOVES.
"BUT THERE WERE TWO IN PARTICULAR THAT I TOOK A SPECIAL FANCY TO. THEM JONAGOLD BROTHERS WERE SWEET AS APPLE PIE AND THEY BOTH FAWNED OVER ME LIKE YOU WOULDN'T BELIEVE.
"TROUBLE WAS, I LIKED THEM BOTH SO MUCH THAT I JUST COULDN'T CHOOSE BETWEEN 'EM. THEY STARTED TO FIGHT SO FIERCE TO WIN MY AFFECTION THAT IT TURNED MY BLOOD COLD SEEING TWO BROTHERS TREAT EACH OTHER LIKE THAT.
"THE WAY THEY ACTED MADE ME SO SAD THAT I DECIDED TO LEAVE THEM BOTH RATHER THAN LET THEM FIGHT LIKE THAT.
"BUT I'M SORRY TO SAY THAT TO THIS DAY THEM BROTHERS STILL AIN'T ON SPEAKIN' TERMS."

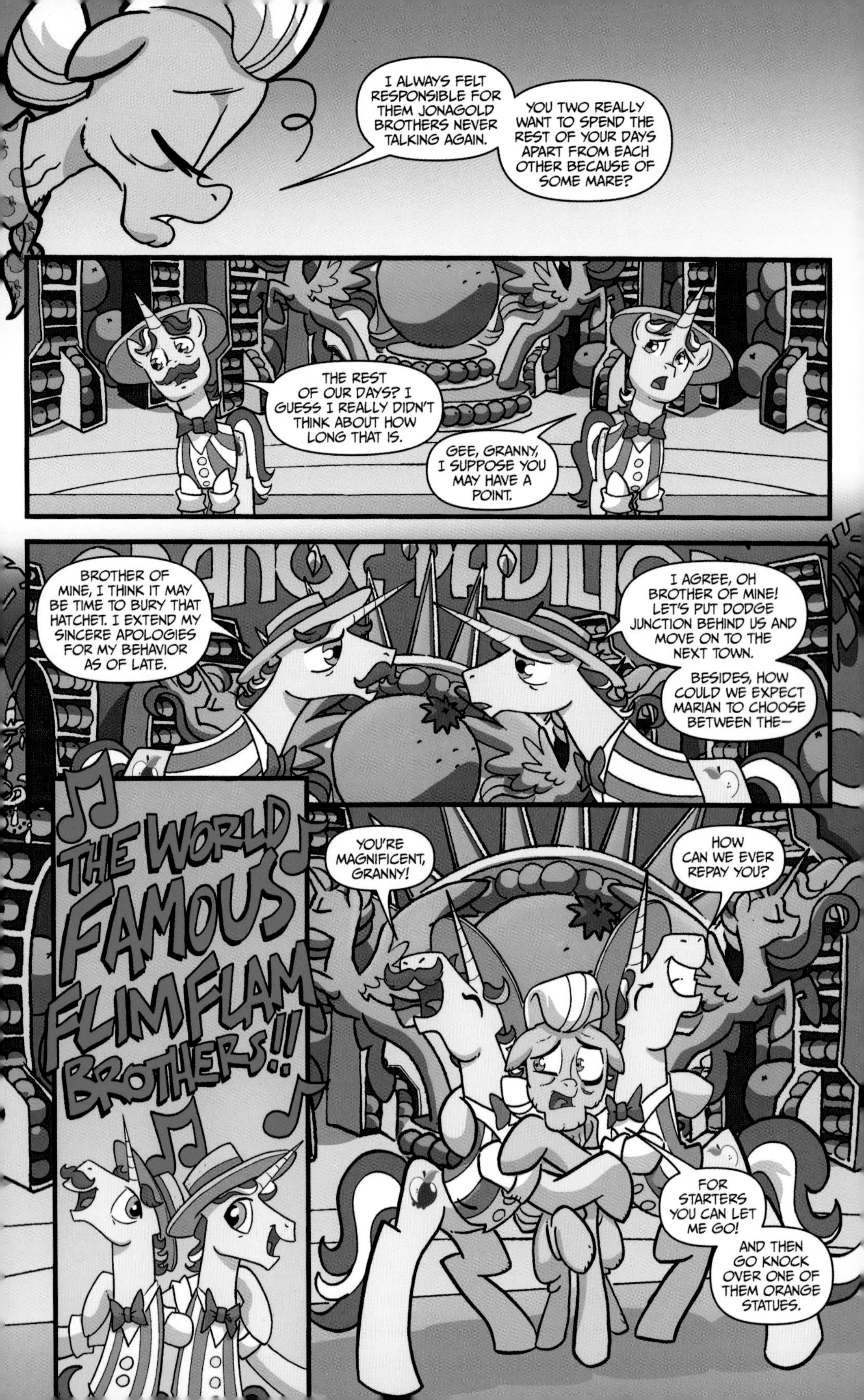
I ALWAYS FELT RESPONSIBLE FOR THEM JONAGOLD BROTHERS NEVER TALKING AGAIN.
YOU TWO REALLY WANT TO SPEND THE REST OF YOUR DAYS APART FROM EACH OTHER BECAUSE OF SOME MARE?
THE REST OF OUR DAYS? I GUESS I REALLY DIDN'T THINK ABOUT HOW LONG THAT IS.
GEE, GRANNY, I SUPPOSE YOU MAY HAVE A POINT.
BROTHER OF MINE, I THINK IT MAY BE TIME TO BURY THAT HATCHET. I EXTEND MY SINCERE APOLOGIES FOR MY BEHAVIOR AS OF LATE.
I AGREE, OH BROTHER OF MINE! LET'S PUT DODGE JUNCTION BEHIND US AND MOVE ON TO THE NEXT TOWN.
BESIDES, HOW COULD WE EXPECT MARIAN TO CHOOSE BETWEEN THE—
THE WORLD FAMOUS FLIM FLAM BROTHERS!!
YOU'RE MAGNIFICENT, GRANNY!
HOW CAN WE EVER REPAY YOU?
FOR STARTERS YOU CAN LET ME GO!
AND THEN GO KNOCK OVER ONE OF THEM ORANGE STATUES.

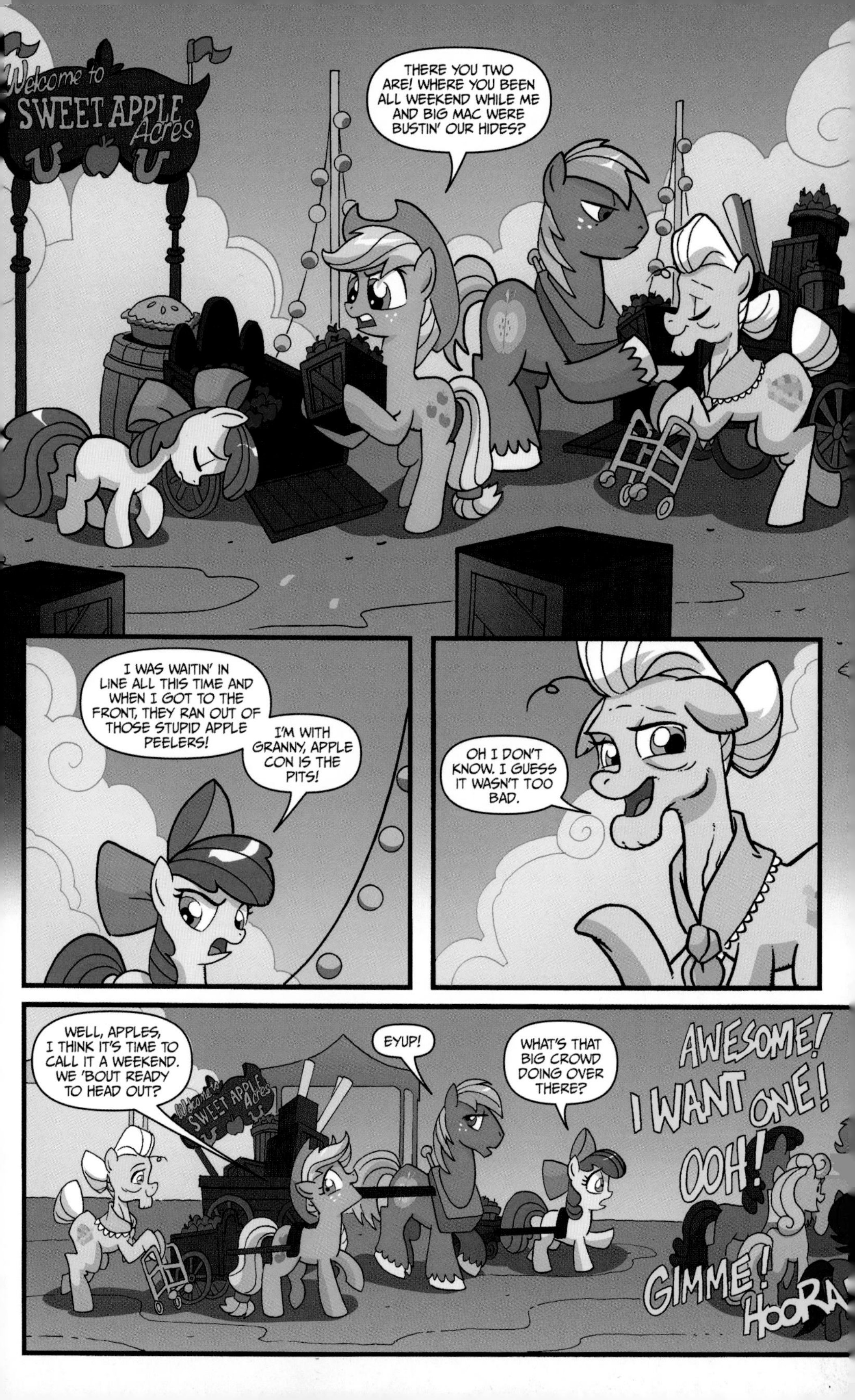
Welcome to SWEET APPLE Acres
THERE YOU TWO ARE! WHERE YOU BEEN ALL WEEKEND WHILE ME AND BIG MAC WERE BUSTIN' OUR HIDES?
I WAS WAITIN' IN LINE ALL THIS TIME AND WHEN I GOT TO THE FRONT, THEY RAN OUT OF THOSE STUPID APPLE PEELERS!
I'M WITH GRANNY, APPLE CON IS THE PITS!
OH I DON'T KNOW. I GUESS IT WASN'T TOO BAD.
WELL, APPLES, I THINK IT'S TIME TO CALL IT A WEEKEND. WE 'BOUT READY TO HEAD OUT?
EYUP!
WHAT'S THAT BIG CROWD DOING OVER THERE?
Welcome to SWEET APPLE Acres
AWESOME!
I WANT ONE!
OOH!
GIMME!
HOORA

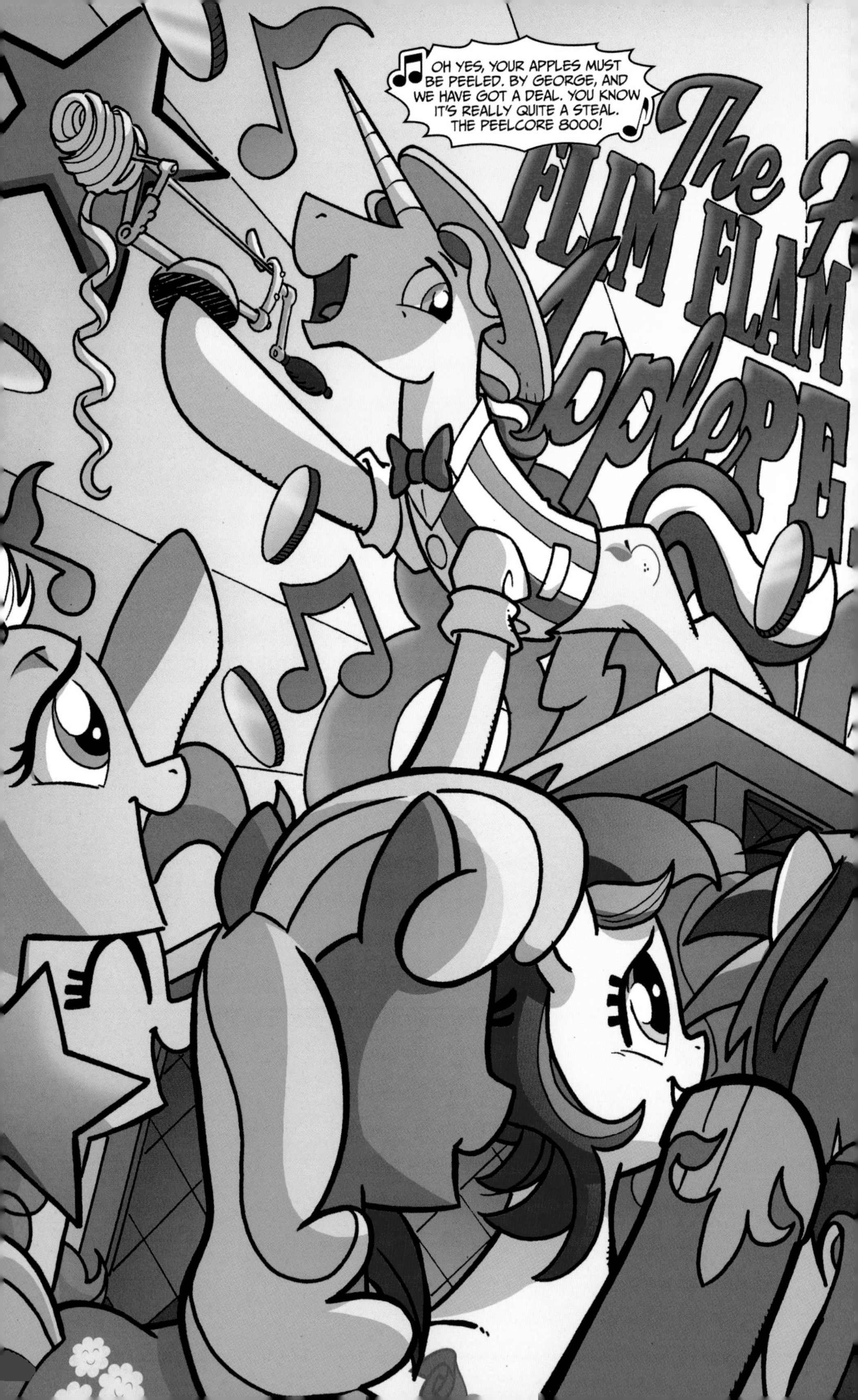
OH YES, YOUR APPLES MUST BE PEELED. BY GEORGE, AND WE HAVE GOT A DEAL. YOU KNOW IT'S REALLY QUITE A STEAL. THE PEELCORE 8000!
FLIM FLAM

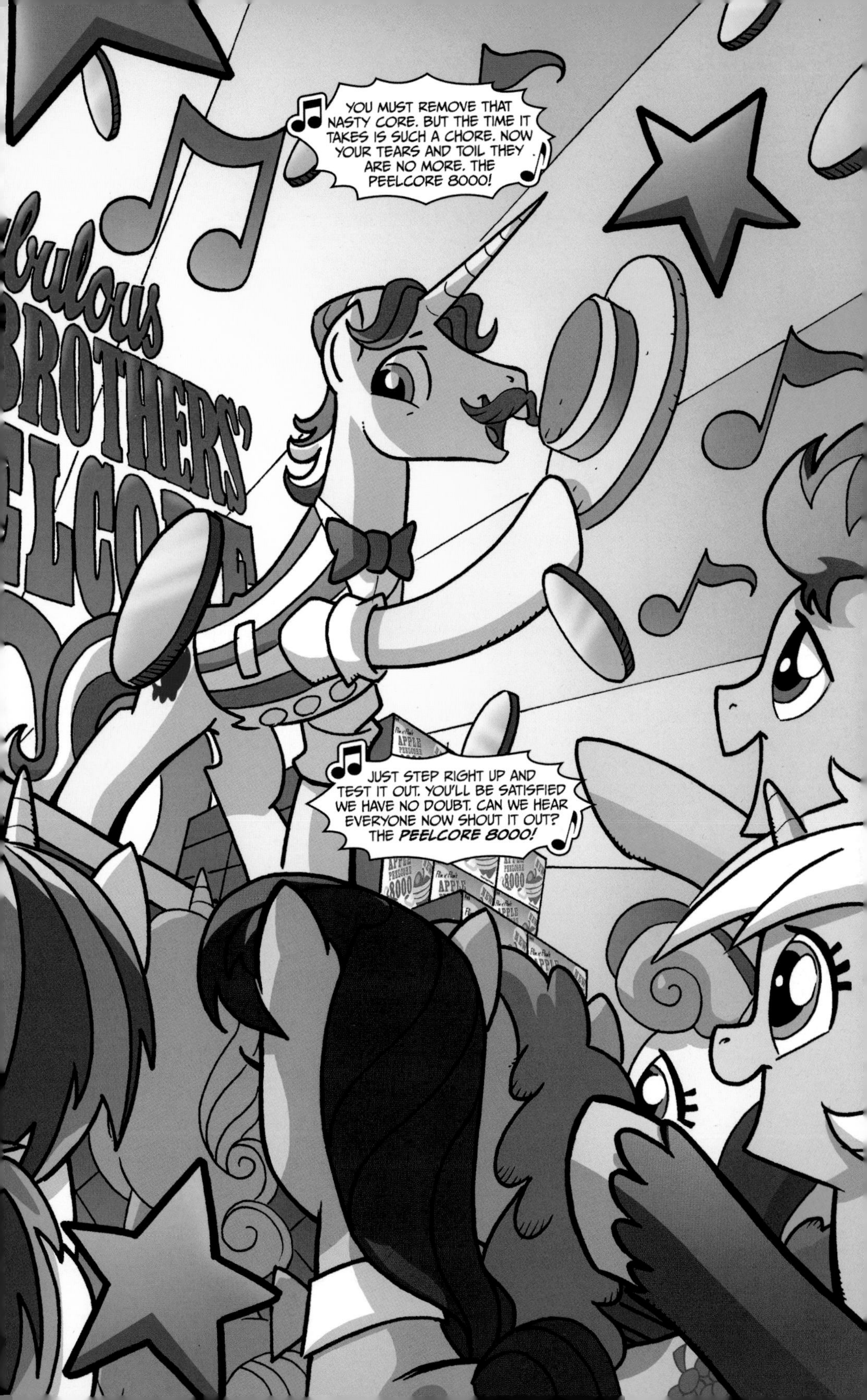
YOU MUST REMOVE THAT NASTY CORE. BUT THE TIME IT TAKES IS SUCH A CHORE. NOW YOUR TEARS AND TOIL THEY ARE NO MORE. THE PEELCORE 8000!
JUST STEP RIGHT UP AND TEST IT OUT. YOU'LL BE SATISFIED WE HAVE NO DOUBT. CAN WE HEAR EVERYONE NOW SHOUT IT OUT? THE *PEELCORE 8000!*

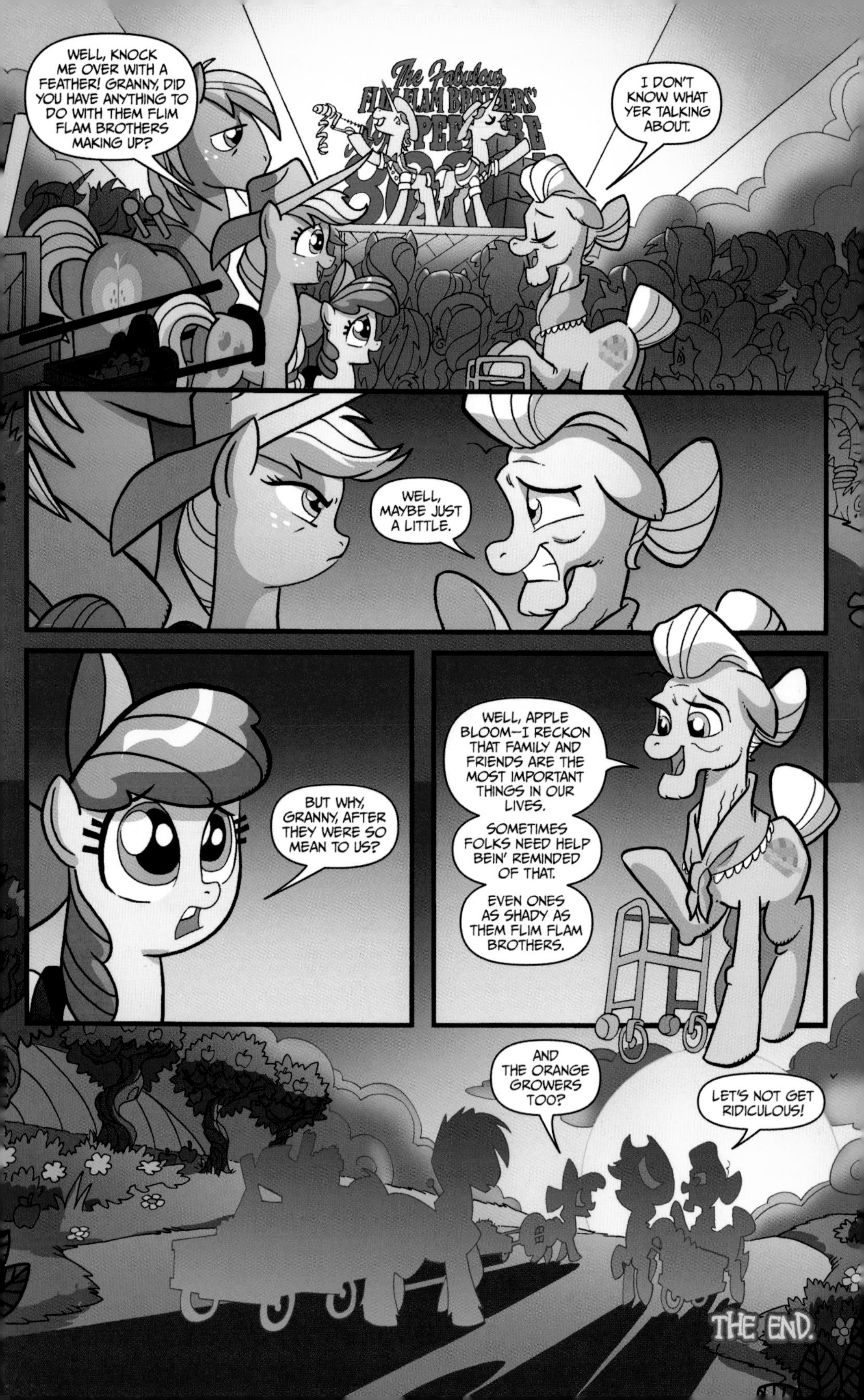
WELL, KNOCK ME OVER WITH A FEATHER! GRANNY, DID YOU HAVE ANYTHING TO DO WITH THEM FLIM FLAM BROTHERS MAKING UP?
The Fabulous FLIM FLAM BROTHERS'
I DON'T KNOW WHAT YER TALKING ABOUT.
WELL, MAYBE JUST A LITTLE.
BUT WHY, GRANNY, AFTER THEY WERE SO MEAN TO US?
WELL, APPLE BLOOM—I RECKON THAT FAMILY AND FRIENDS ARE THE MOST IMPORTANT THINGS IN OUR LIVES.
SOMETIMES FOLKS NEED HELP BEIN' REMINDED OF THAT.
EVEN ONES AS SHADY AS THEM FLIM FLAM BROTHERS.
AND THE ORANGE GROWERS TOO?
LET'S NOT GET RIDICULOUS!
THE END.

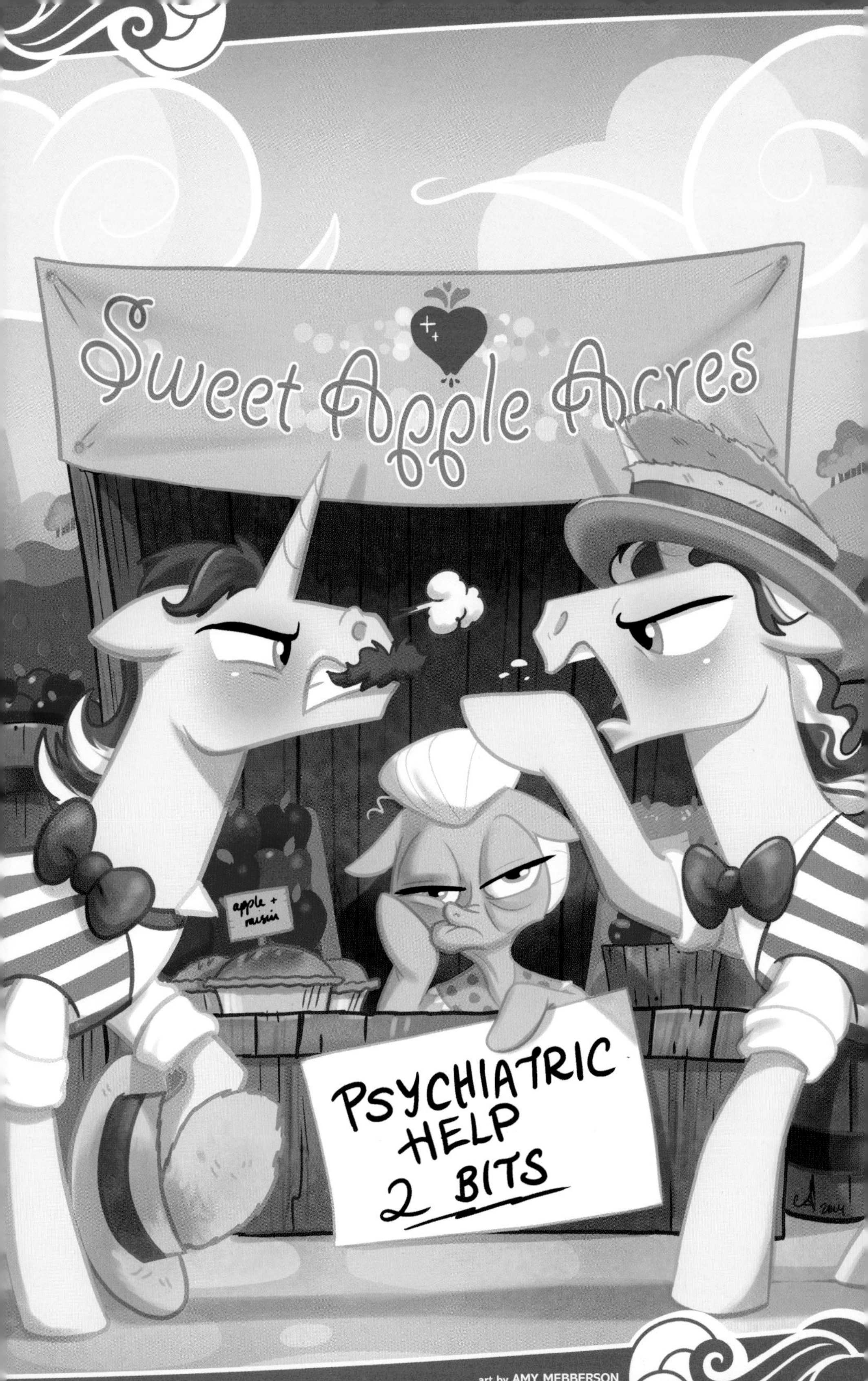
Sweet Apple Acres
apple + raisin
PSYCHIATRIC HELP 2 BITS
art by AMY MEBBERSON

Fluttershy & Iron Will

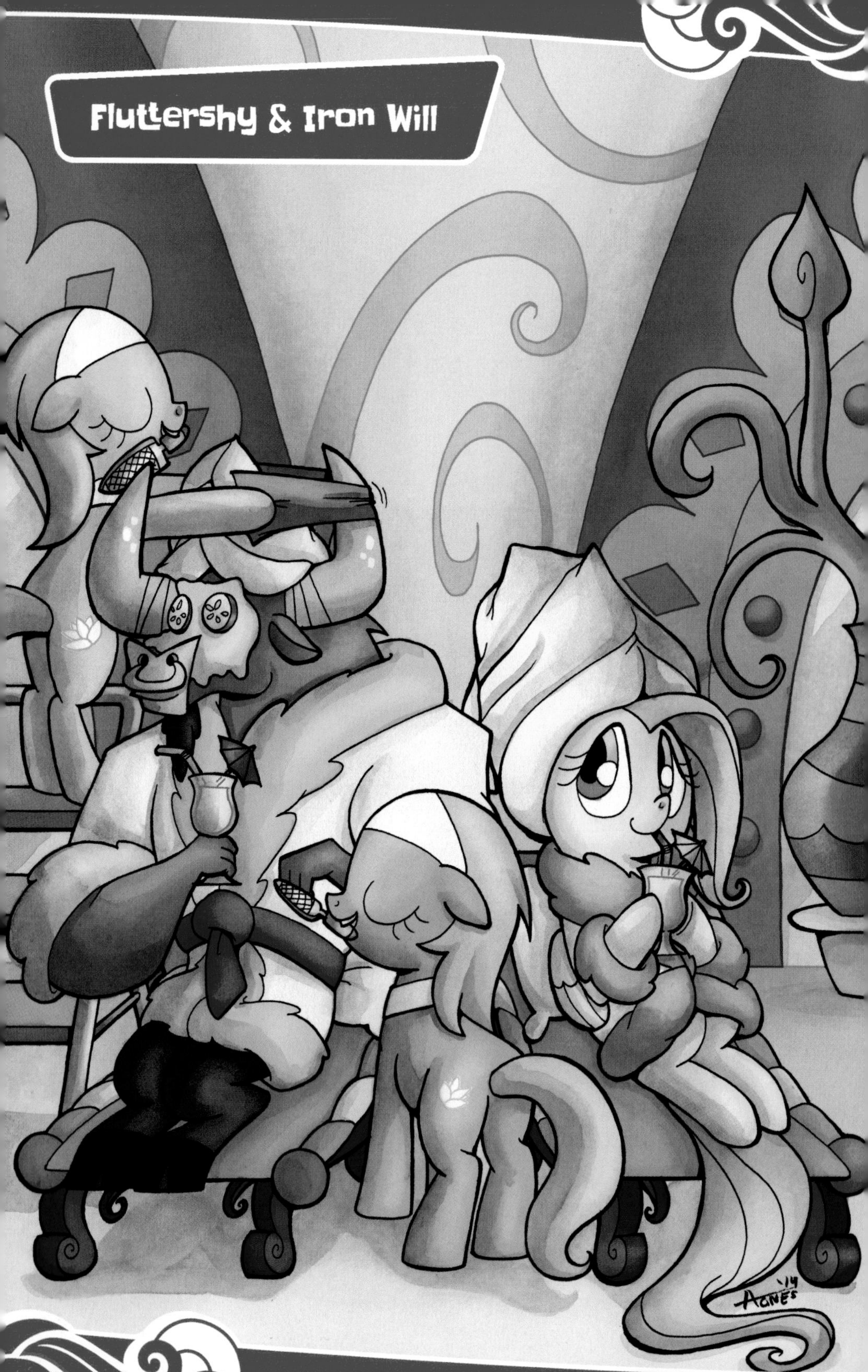

art by AGNES GARBOWSKA

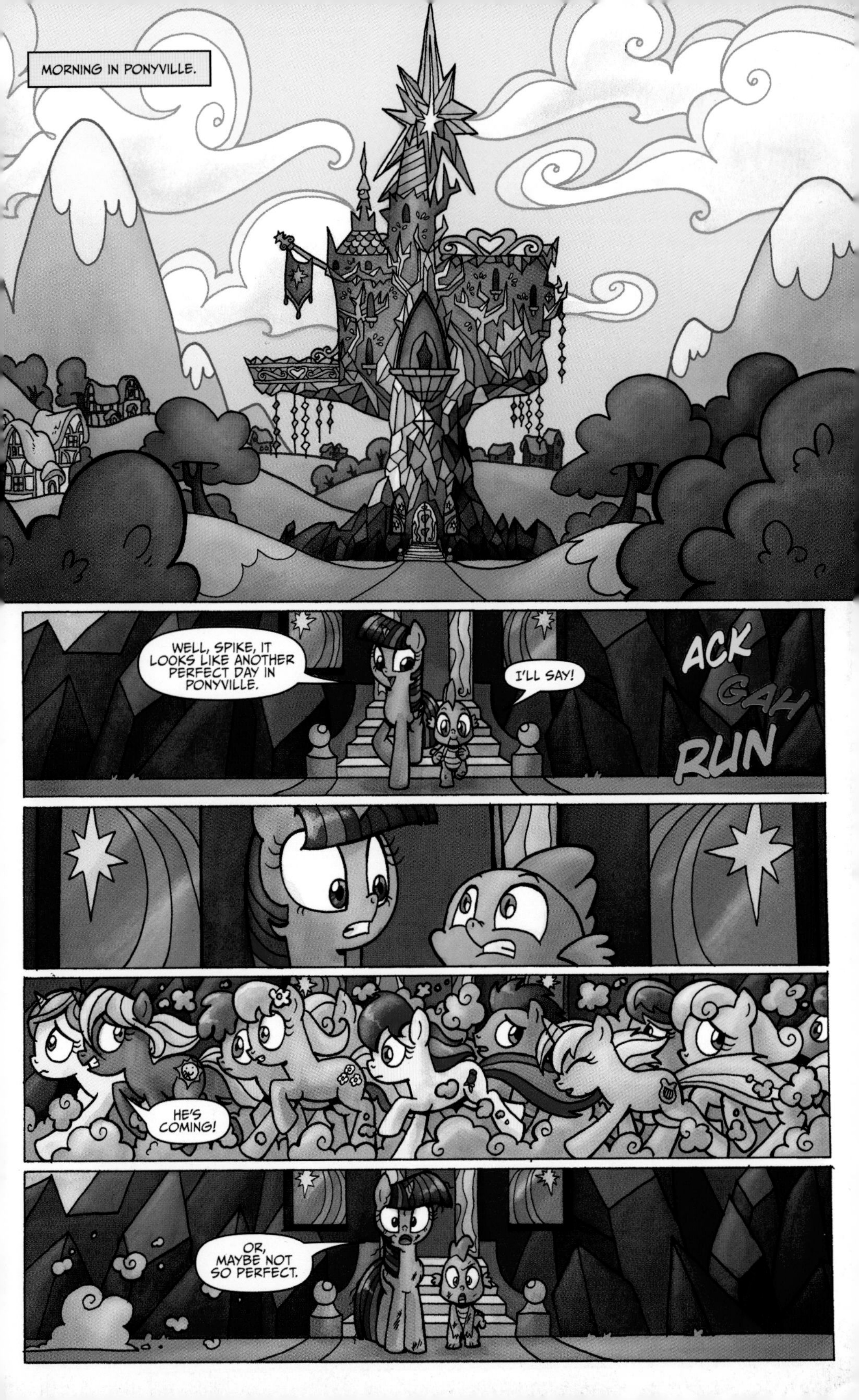
MORNING IN PONYVILLE.
WELL, SPIKE, IT LOOKS LIKE ANOTHER PERFECT DAY IN PONYVILLE.
I'LL SAY!
ACK
GAH
RUN
HE'S COMING!
OR, MAYBE NOT SO PERFECT.

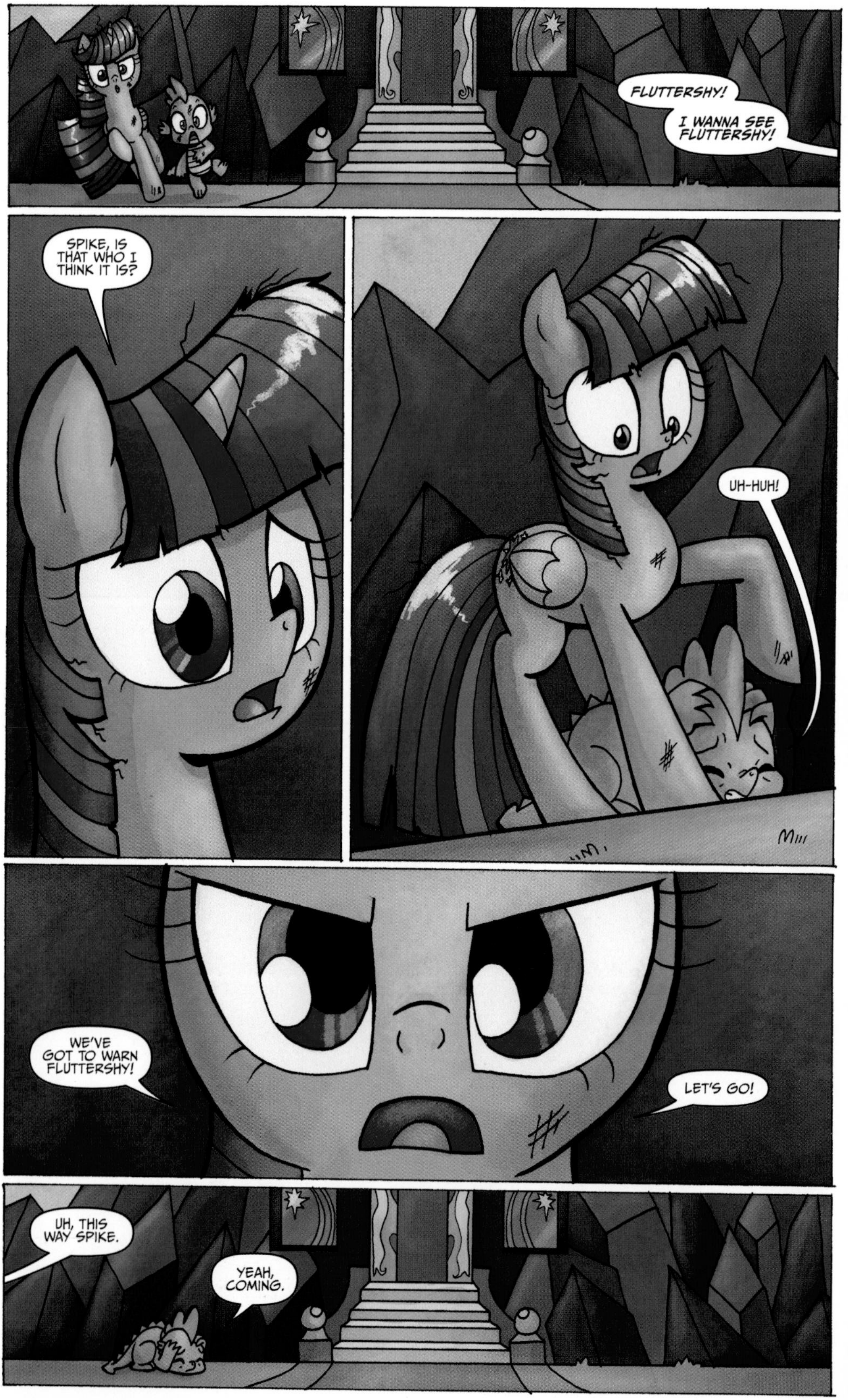
FLUTTERSHY!
I WANNA SEE FLUTTERSHY!
SPIKE, IS THAT WHO I THINK IT IS?
UH-HUH!
MIII
WE'VE GOT TO WARN FLUTTERSHY!
LET'S GO!
UH, THIS WAY SPIKE.
YEAH, COMING.

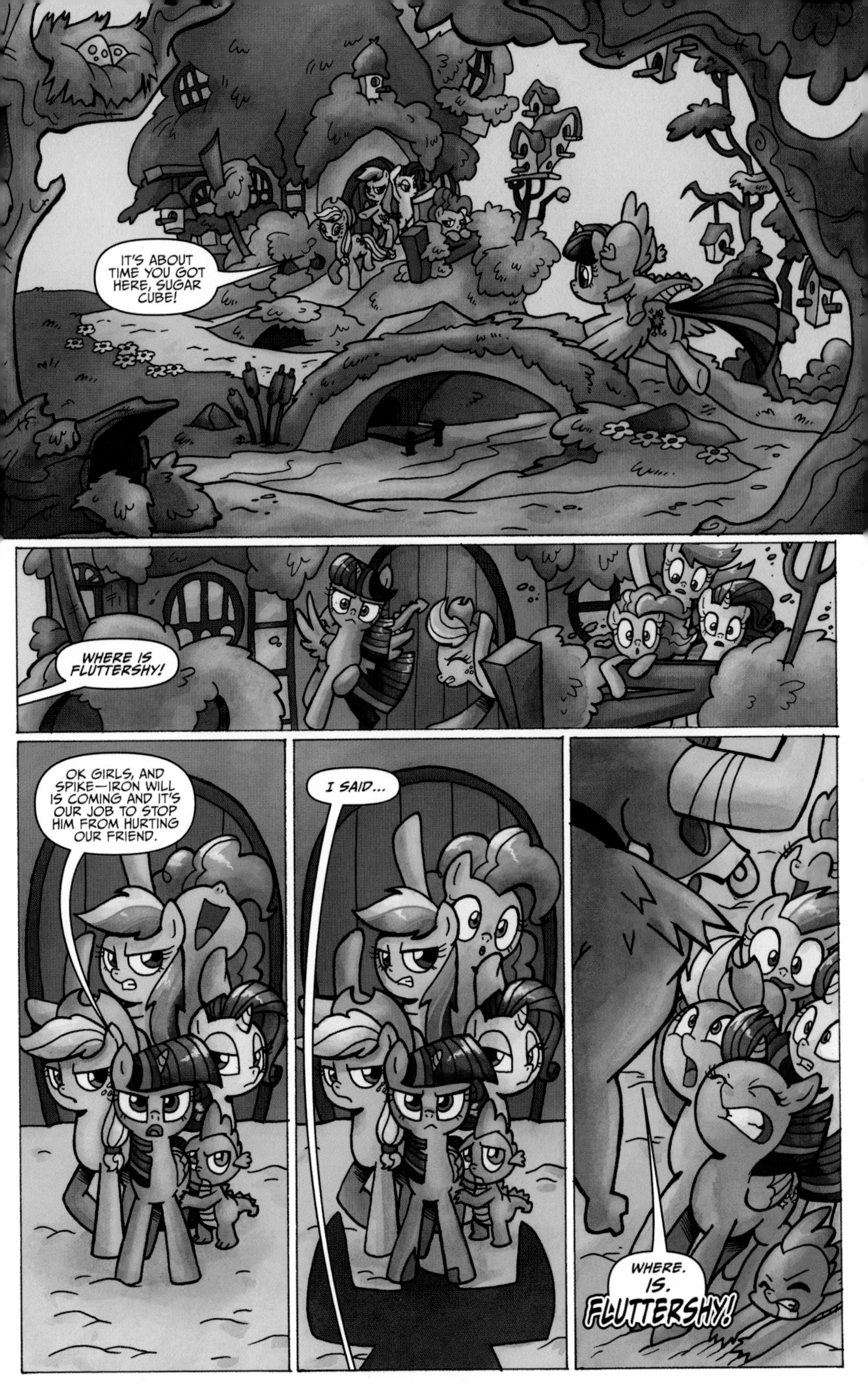
IT'S ABOUT TIME YOU GOT HERE, SUGAR CUBE!
WHERE IS FLUTTERSHY!
OK GIRLS, AND SPIKE—IRON WILL IS COMING AND IT'S OUR JOB TO STOP HIM FROM HURTING OUR FRIEND.
I SAID...
WHERE. IS. FLUTTERSHY!

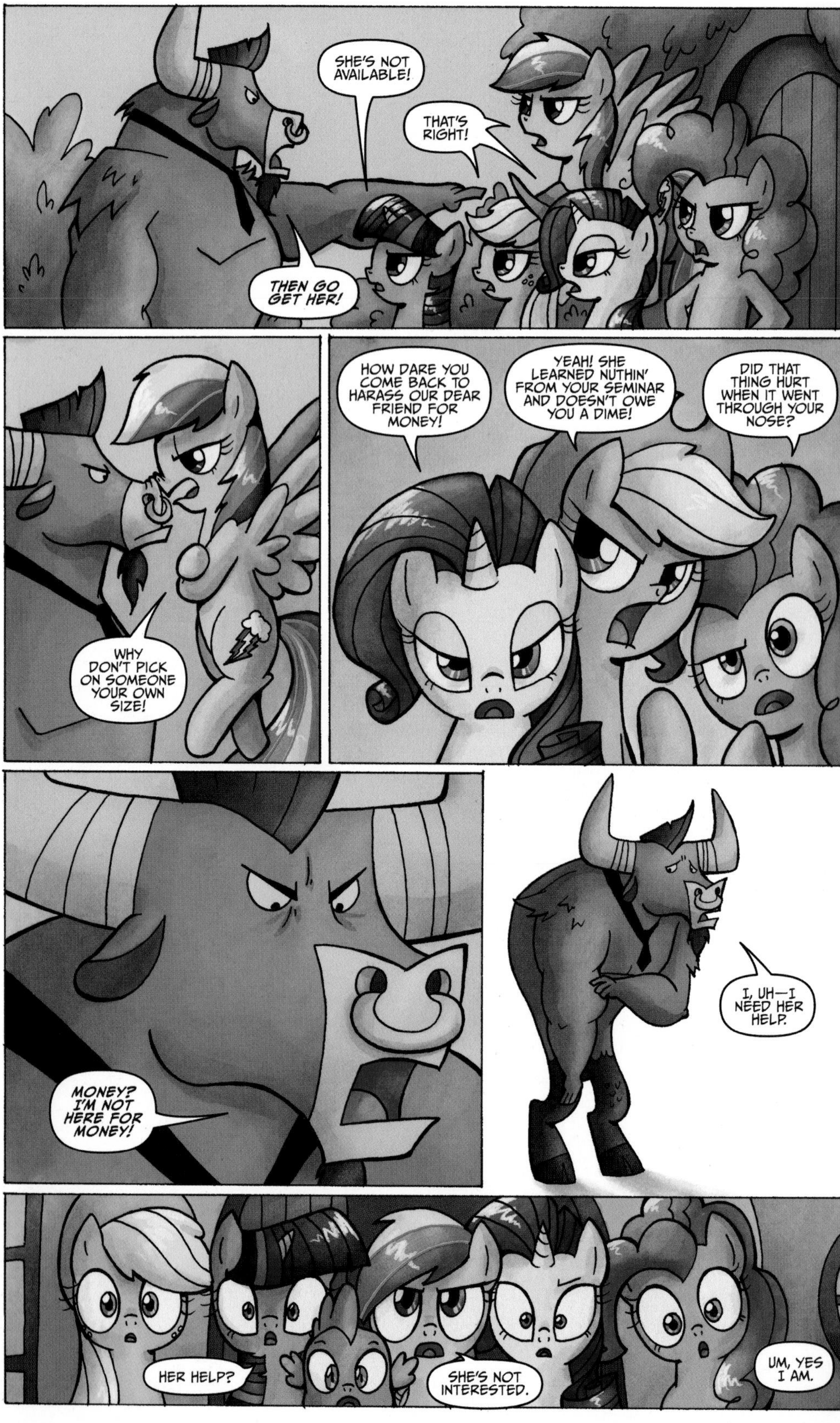
SHE'S NOT AVAILABLE!
THAT'S RIGHT!
THEN GO GET HER!
WHY DON'T PICK ON SOMEONE YOUR OWN SIZE!
HOW DARE YOU COME BACK TO HARASS OUR DEAR FRIEND FOR MONEY!
YEAH! SHE LEARNED NUTHIN' FROM YOUR SEMINAR AND DOESN'T OWE YOU A DIME!
DID THAT THING HURT WHEN IT WENT THROUGH YOUR NOSE?
MONEY? I'M NOT HERE FOR MONEY!
I, UH—I NEED HER HELP.
HER HELP?
SHE'S NOT INTERESTED.
UM, YES I AM.

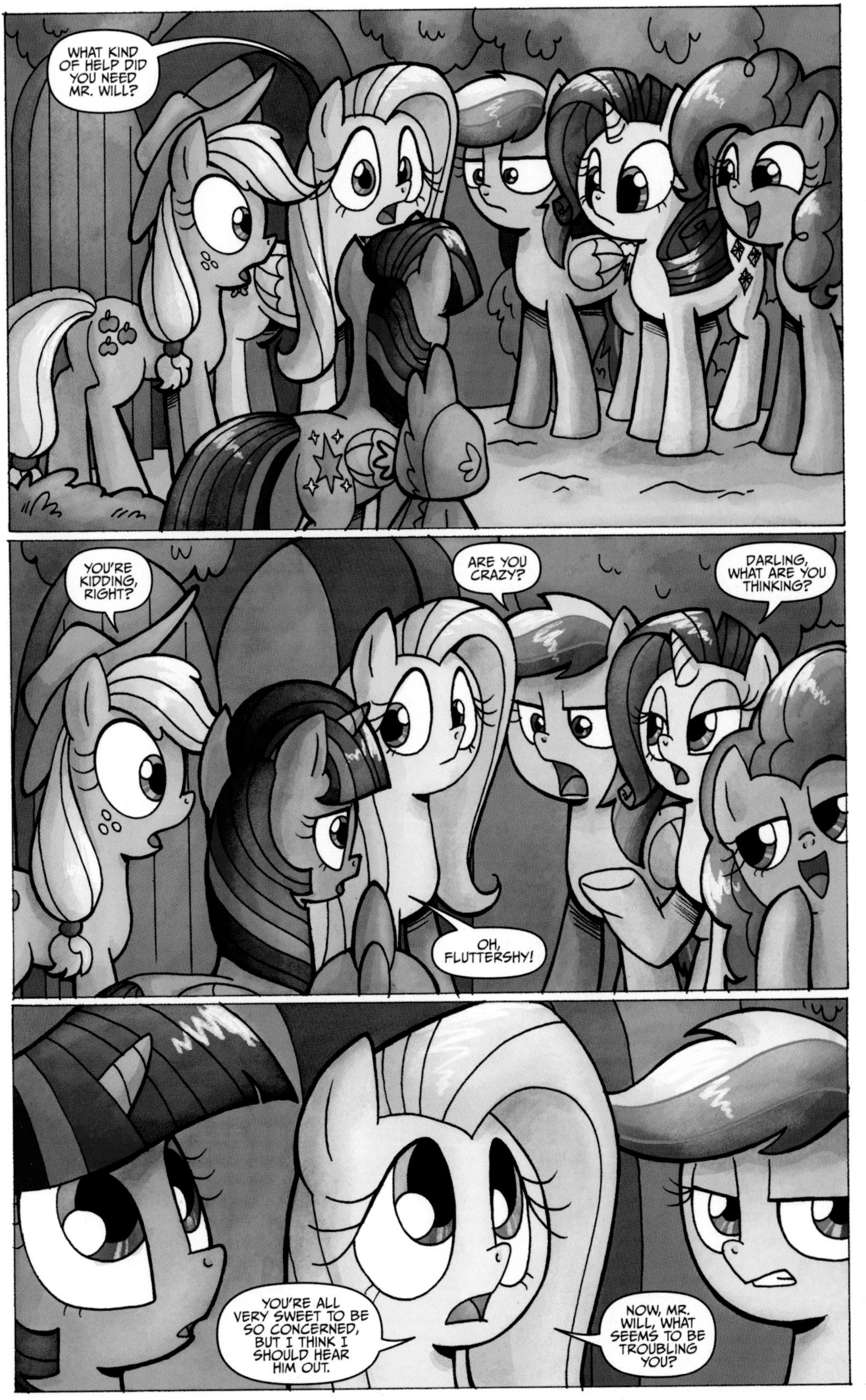
WHAT KIND OF HELP DID YOU NEED MR. WILL?
YOU'RE KIDDING, RIGHT?
ARE YOU CRAZY?
DARLING, WHAT ARE YOU THINKING?
OH, FLUTTERSHY!
YOU'RE ALL VERY SWEET TO BE SO CONCERNED, BUT I THINK I SHOULD HEAR HIM OUT.
NOW, MR. WILL, WHAT SEEMS TO BE TROUBLING YOU?

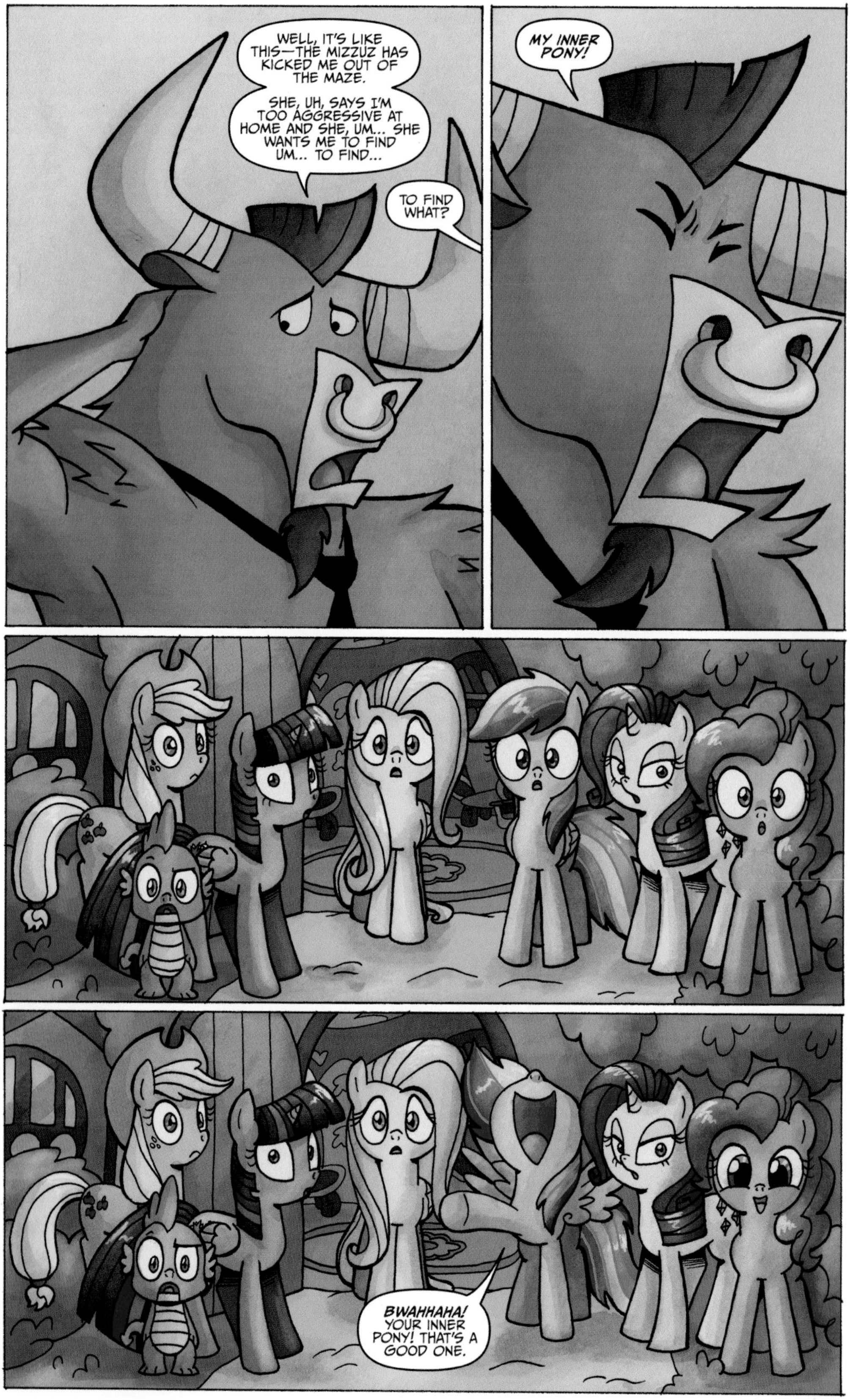
WELL, IT'S LIKE THIS—THE MIZZUZ HAS KICKED ME OUT OF THE MAZE.
SHE, UH, SAYS I'M TOO AGGRESSIVE AT HOME AND SHE, UM... SHE WANTS ME TO FIND UM... TO FIND...
TO FIND WHAT?
MY INNER PONY!
BWAHHAHA! YOUR INNER PONY! THAT'S A GOOD ONE.

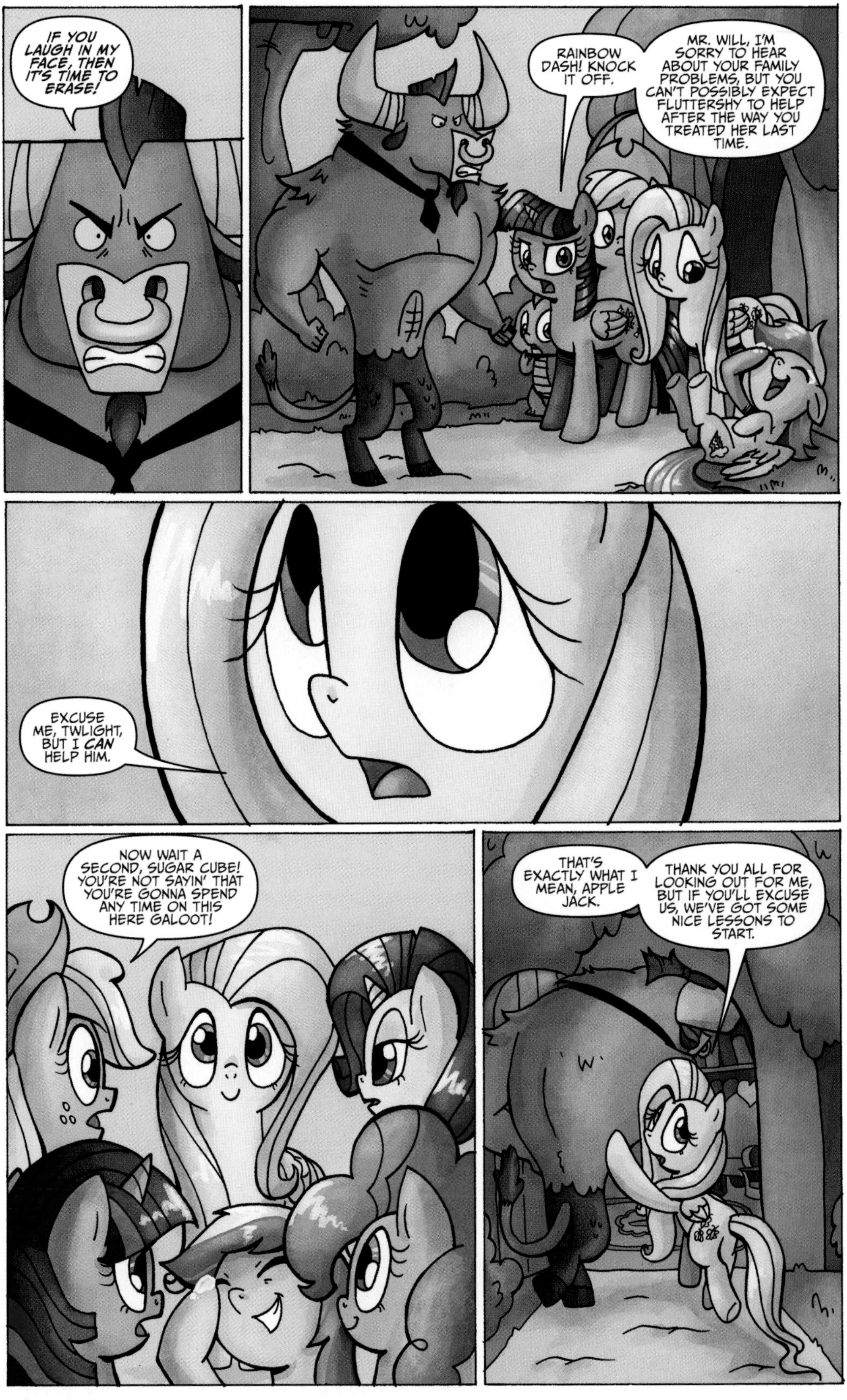
IF YOU LAUGH IN MY FACE, THEN IT'S TIME TO ERASE!
RAINBOW DASH! KNOCK IT OFF.
MR. WILL, I'M SORRY TO HEAR ABOUT YOUR FAMILY PROBLEMS, BUT YOU CAN'T POSSIBLY EXPECT FLUTTERSHY TO HELP AFTER THE WAY YOU TREATED HER LAST TIME.
EXCUSE ME, TWLIGHT, BUT I CAN HELP HIM.
NOW WAIT A SECOND, SUGAR CUBE! YOU'RE NOT SAYIN' THAT YOU'RE GONNA SPEND ANY TIME ON THIS HERE GALOOT!
THAT'S EXACTLY WHAT I MEAN, APPLE JACK.
THANK YOU ALL FOR LOOKING OUT FOR ME, BUT IF YOU'LL EXCUSE US, WE'VE GOT SOME NICE LESSONS TO START.

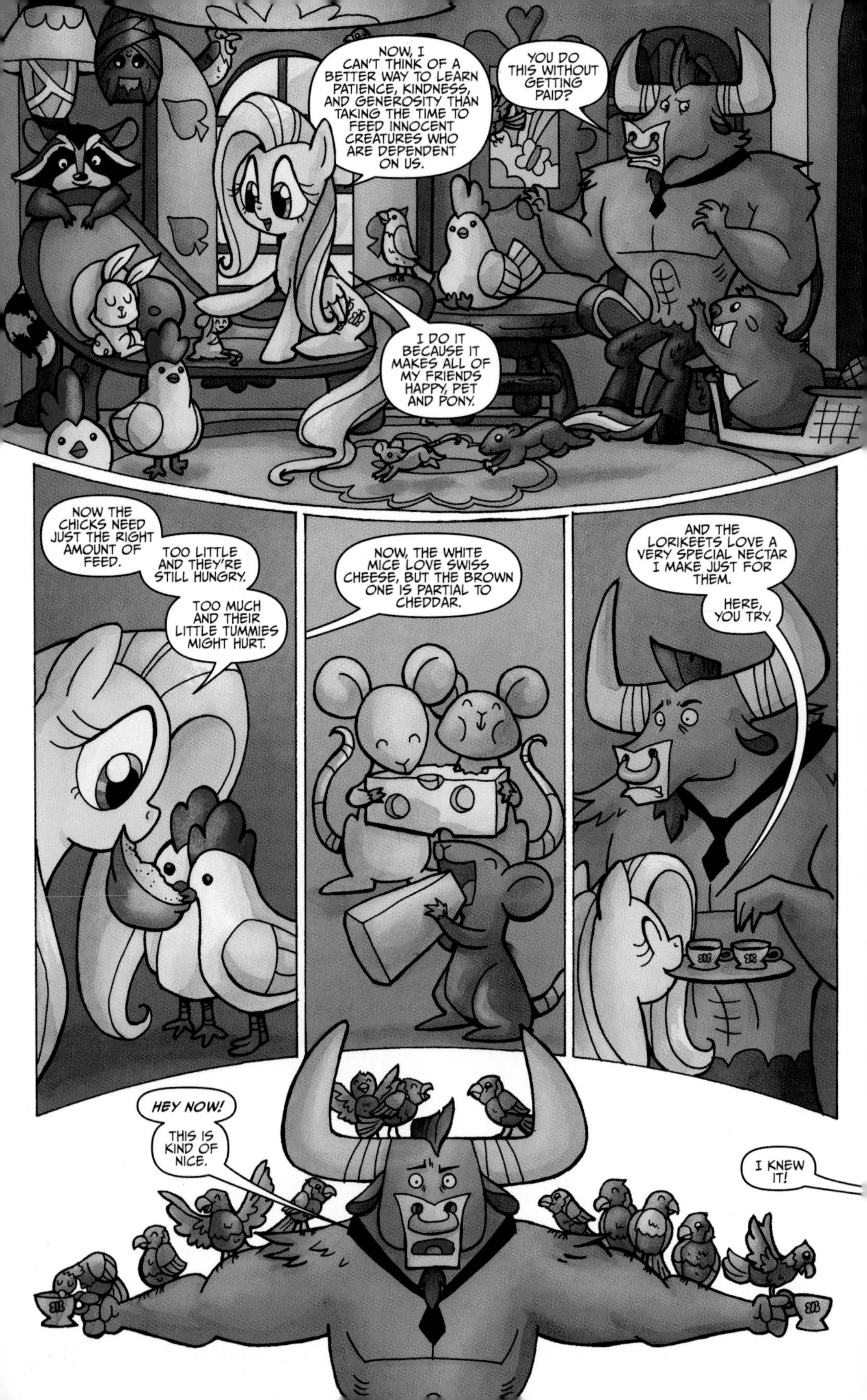
NOW, I CAN'T THINK OF A BETTER WAY TO LEARN PATIENCE, KINDNESS, AND GENEROSITY THAN TAKING THE TIME TO FEED INNOCENT CREATURES WHO ARE DEPENDENT ON US.
YOU DO THIS WITHOUT GETTING PAID?
I DO IT BECAUSE IT MAKES ALL OF MY FRIENDS HAPPY, PET AND PONY.
NOW THE CHICKS NEED JUST THE RIGHT AMOUNT OF FEED.
TOO LITTLE AND THEY'RE STILL HUNGRY.
TOO MUCH AND THEIR LITTLE TUMMIES MIGHT HURT.
NOW, THE WHITE MICE LOVE SWISS CHEESE, BUT THE BROWN ONE IS PARTIAL TO CHEDDAR.
AND THE LORIKEETS LOVE A VERY SPECIAL NECTAR I MAKE JUST FOR THEM.
HERE, YOU TRY.
HEY NOW!
THIS IS KIND OF NICE.
I KNEW IT!

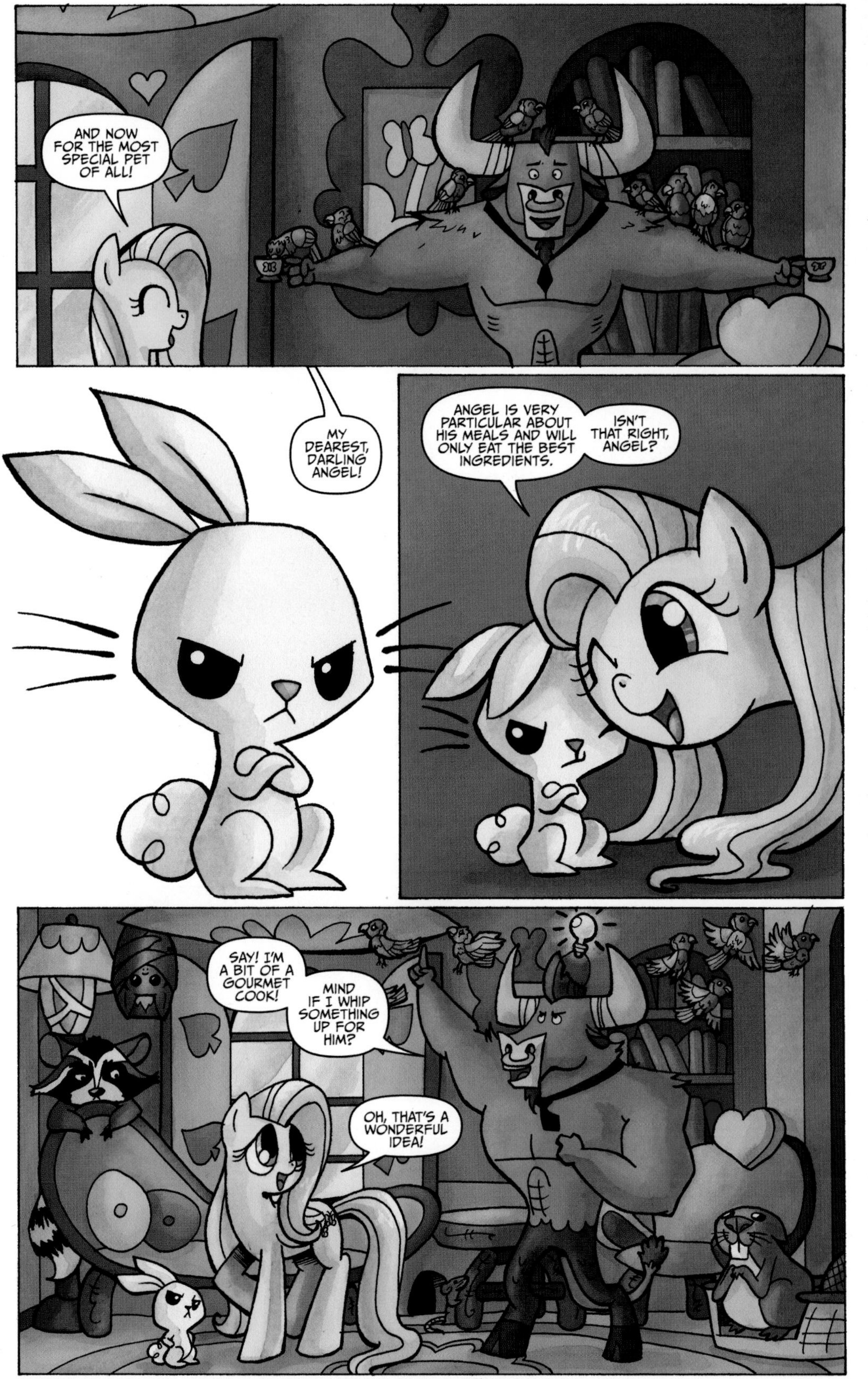
AND NOW FOR THE MOST SPECIAL PET OF ALL!
MY DEAREST, DARLING ANGEL!
ANGEL IS VERY PARTICULAR ABOUT HIS MEALS AND WILL ONLY EAT THE BEST INGREDIENTS.
ISN'T THAT RIGHT, ANGEL?
SAY! I'M A BIT OF A GOURMET COOK!
MIND IF I WHIP SOMETHING UP FOR HIM?
OH, THAT'S A WONDERFUL IDEA!

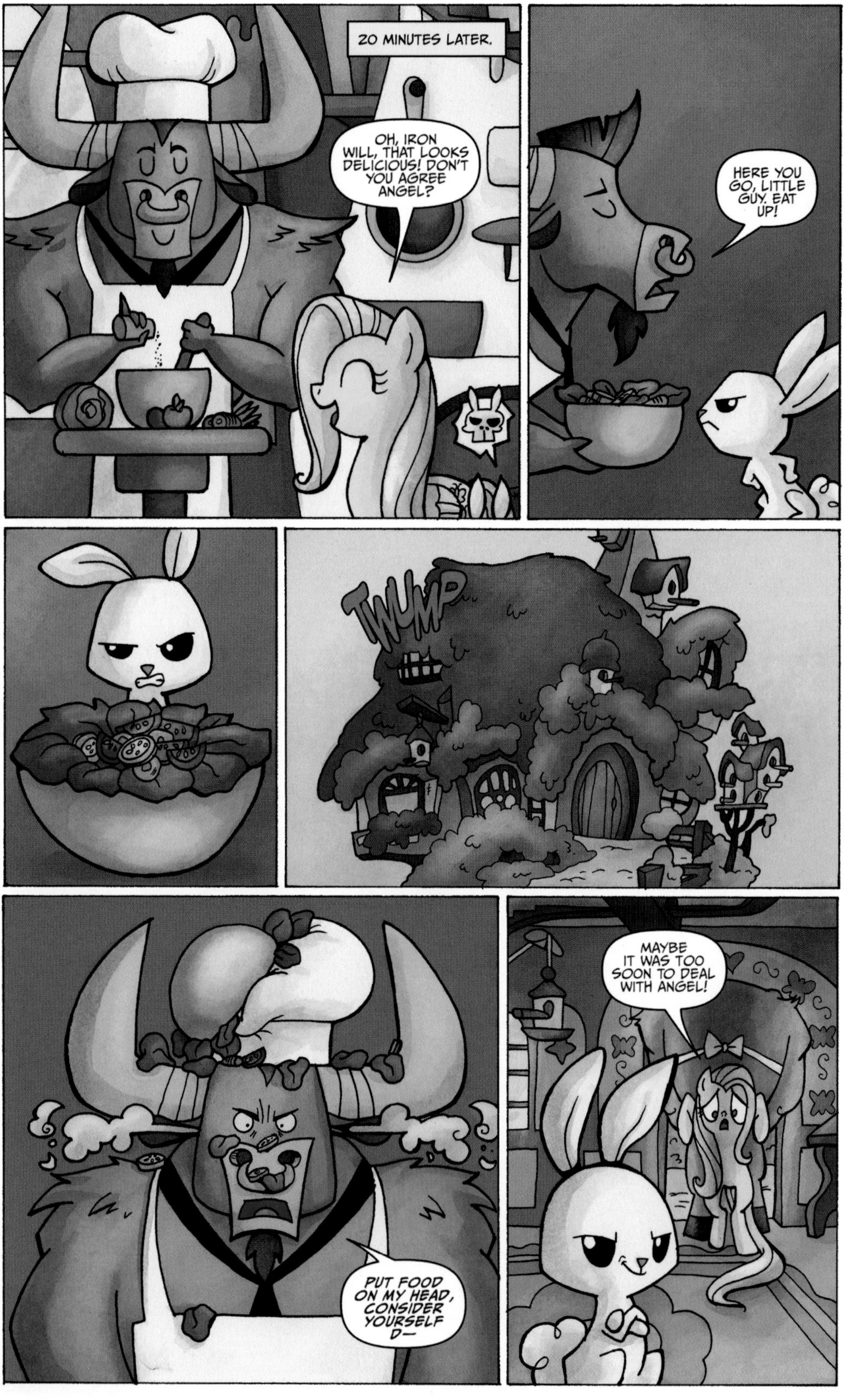

20 MINUTES LATER.
OH, IRON WILL, THAT LOOKS DELICIOUS! DON'T YOU AGREE ANGEL?
HERE YOU GO, LITTLE GUY. EAT UP!
TWUMP
PUT FOOD ON MY HEAD, CONSIDER YOURSELF D—
MAYBE IT WAS TOO SOON TO DEAL WITH ANGEL!

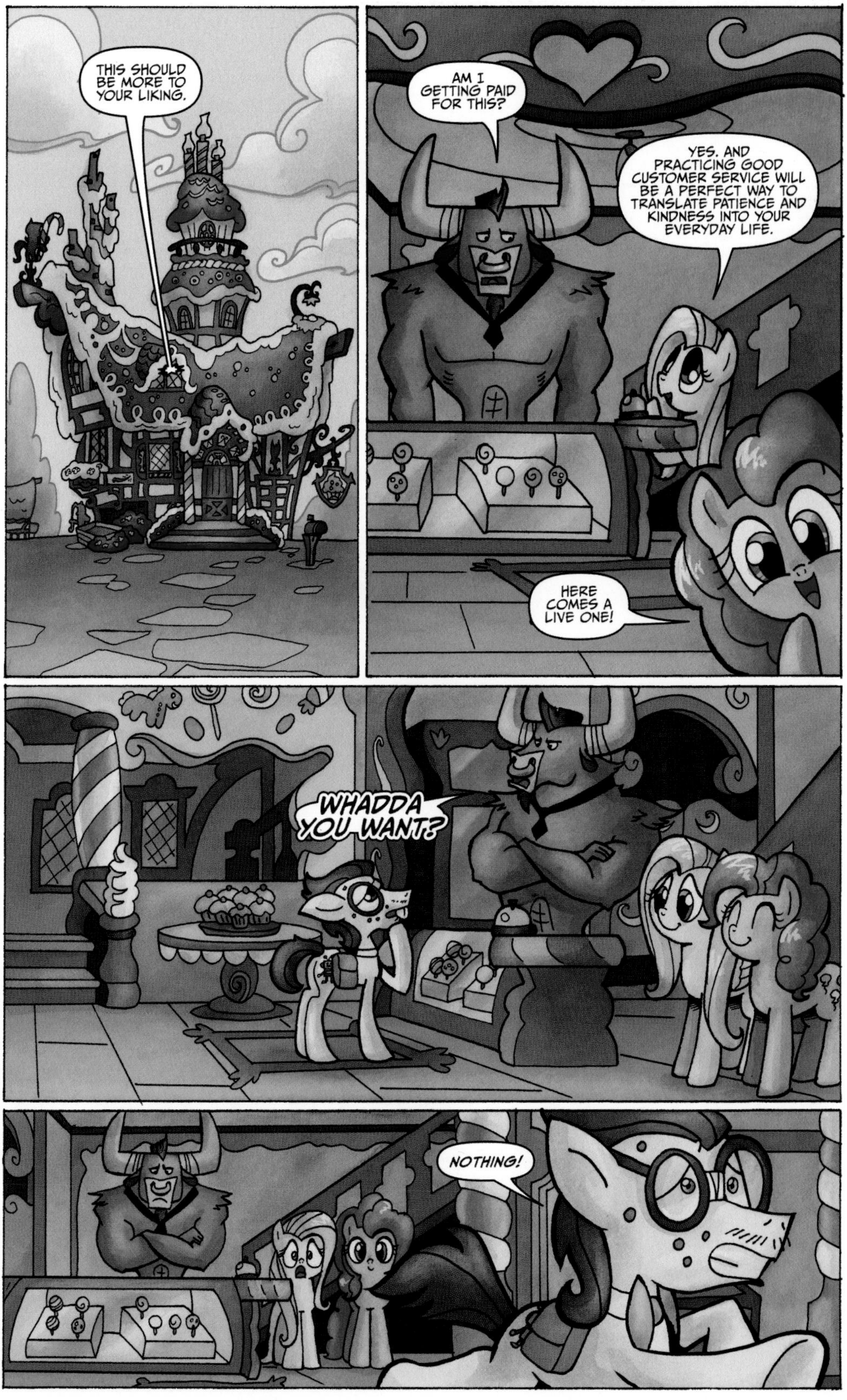
THIS SHOULD BE MORE TO YOUR LIKING.
AM I GETTING PAID FOR THIS?
YES. AND PRACTICING GOOD CUSTOMER SERVICE WILL BE A PERFECT WAY TO TRANSLATE PATIENCE AND KINDNESS INTO YOUR EVERYDAY LIFE.
HERE COMES A LIVE ONE!
WHADDA YOU WANT?
NOTHING!

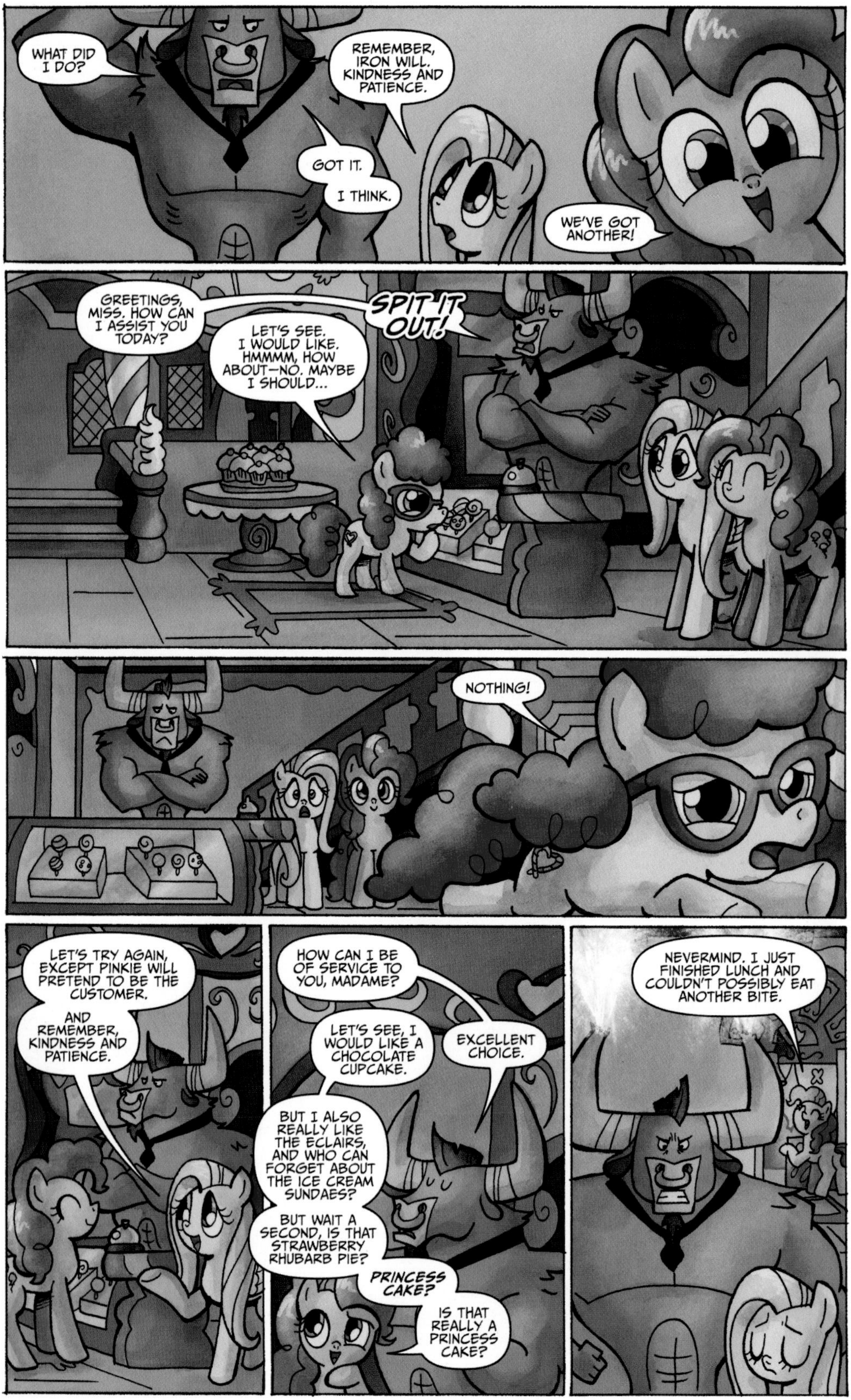
WHAT DID I DO?
REMEMBER, IRON WILL. KINDNESS AND PATIENCE.
GOT IT.
I THINK.
WE'VE GOT ANOTHER!
GREETINGS, MISS. HOW CAN I ASSIST YOU TODAY?
LET'S SEE. I WOULD LIKE. HMMMM, HOW ABOUT—NO. MAYBE I SHOULD...
SPIT IT OUT!
NOTHING!
LET'S TRY AGAIN, EXCEPT PINKIE WILL PRETEND TO BE THE CUSTOMER.
AND REMEMBER, KINDNESS AND PATIENCE.
HOW CAN I BE OF SERVICE TO YOU, MADAME?
LET'S SEE, I WOULD LIKE A CHOCOLATE CUPCAKE.
EXCELLENT CHOICE.
BUT I ALSO REALLY LIKE THE ECLAIRS, AND WHO CAN FORGET ABOUT THE ICE CREAM SUNDAES?
BUT WAIT A SECOND, IS THAT STRAWBERRY RHUBARB PIE?
PRINCESS CAKE?
IS THAT REALLY A PRINCESS CAKE?
NEVERMIND. I JUST FINISHED LUNCH AND COULDN'T POSSIBLY EAT ANOTHER BITE.

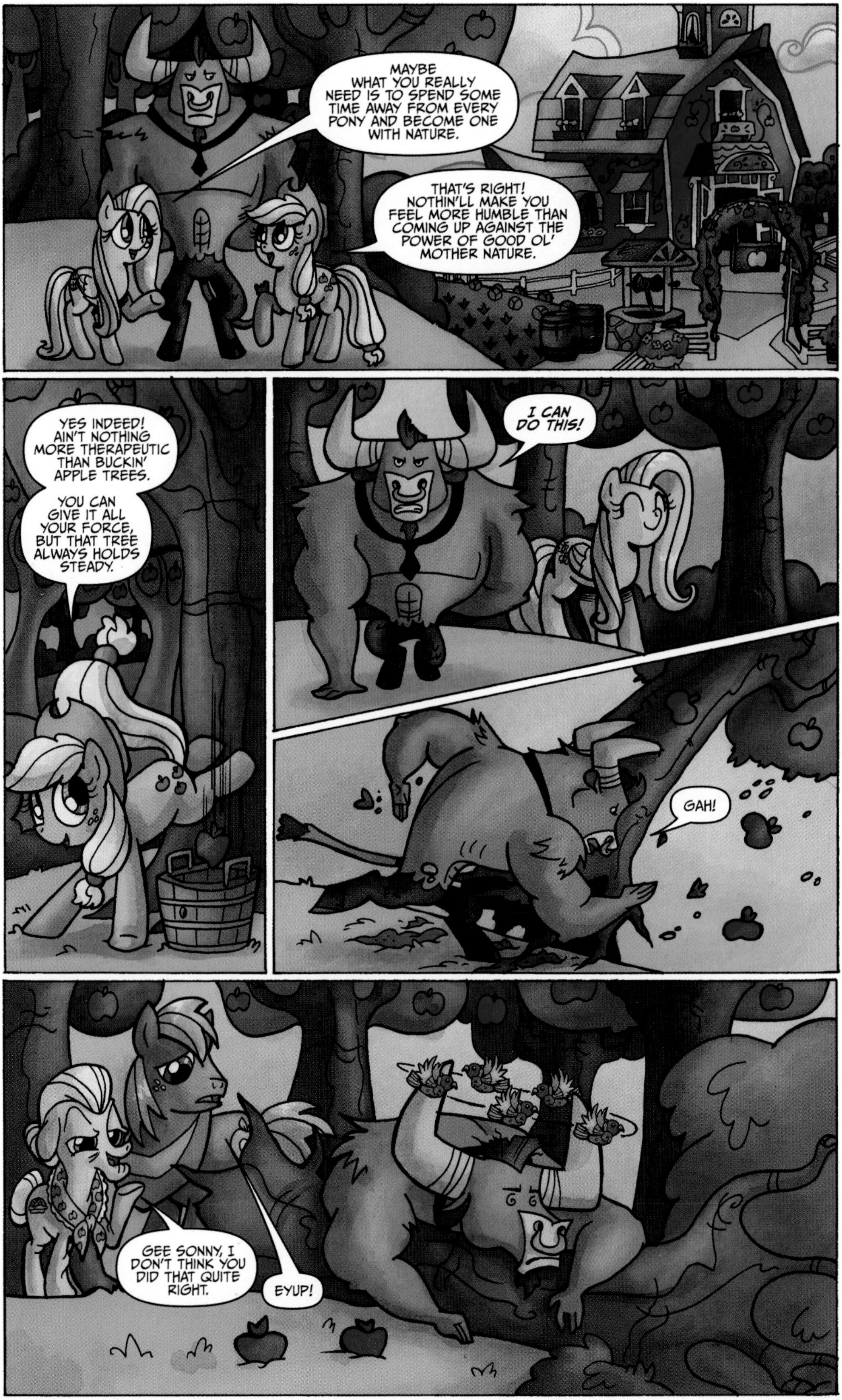
MAYBE WHAT YOU REALLY NEED IS TO SPEND SOME TIME AWAY FROM EVERY PONY AND BECOME ONE WITH NATURE.
THAT'S RIGHT! NOTHIN'LL MAKE YOU FEEL MORE HUMBLE THAN COMING UP AGAINST THE POWER OF GOOD OL' MOTHER NATURE.
YES INDEED! AIN'T NOTHING MORE THERAPEUTIC THAN BUCKIN' APPLE TREES.
YOU CAN GIVE IT ALL YOUR FORCE, BUT THAT TREE ALWAYS HOLDS STEADY.
I CAN DO THIS!
GAH!
GEE SONNY, I DON'T THINK YOU DID THAT QUITE RIGHT.
EYUP!

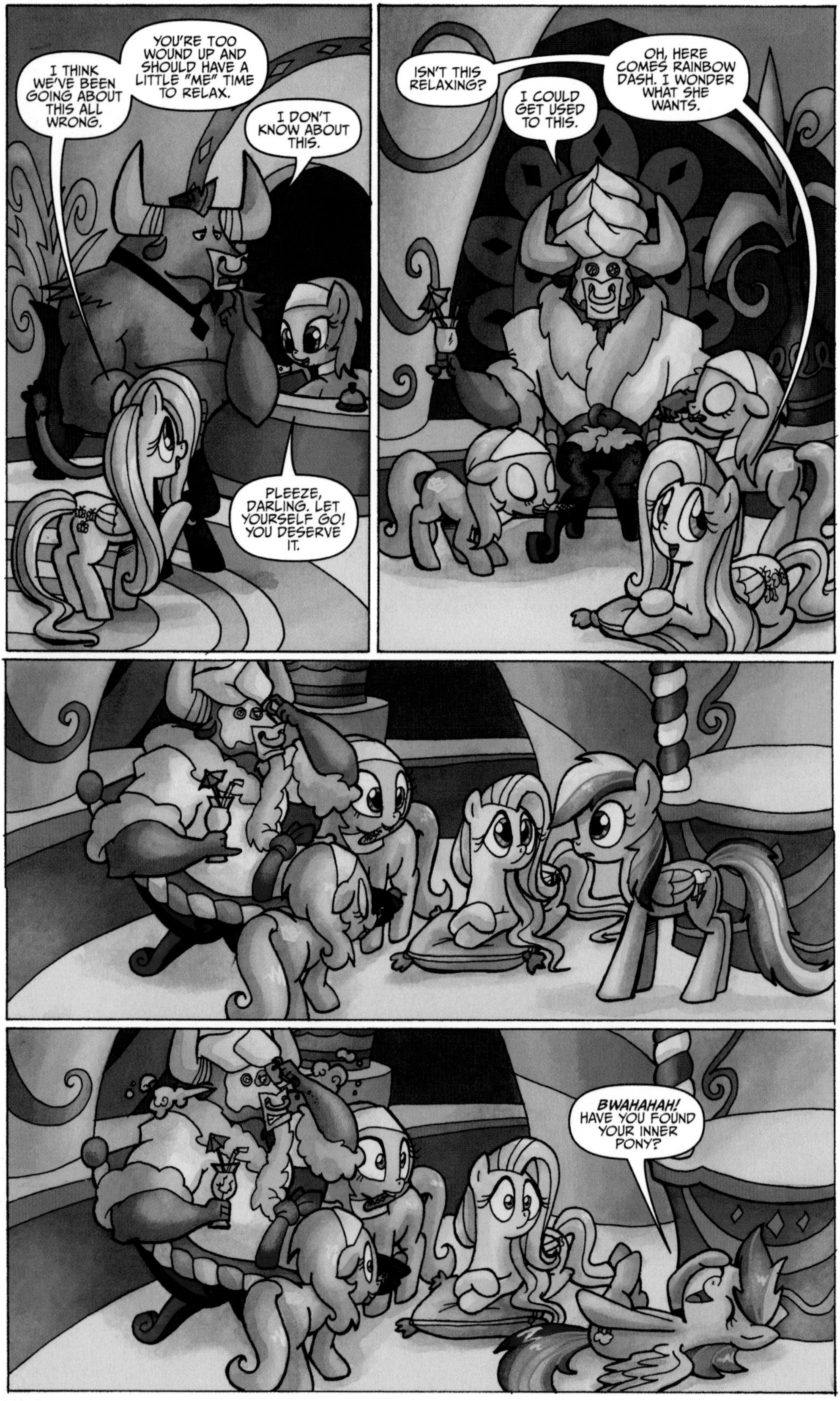
I THINK WE'VE BEEN GOING ABOUT THIS ALL WRONG.
YOU'RE TOO WOUND UP AND SHOULD HAVE A LITTLE "ME" TIME TO RELAX.
I DON'T KNOW ABOUT THIS.
PLEEZE, DARLING. LET YOURSELF GO! YOU DESERVE IT.
ISN'T THIS RELAXING?
I COULD GET USED TO THIS.
OH, HERE COMES RAINBOW DASH. I WONDER WHAT SHE WANTS.
BWAHAHAH! HAVE YOU FOUND YOUR INNER PONY?

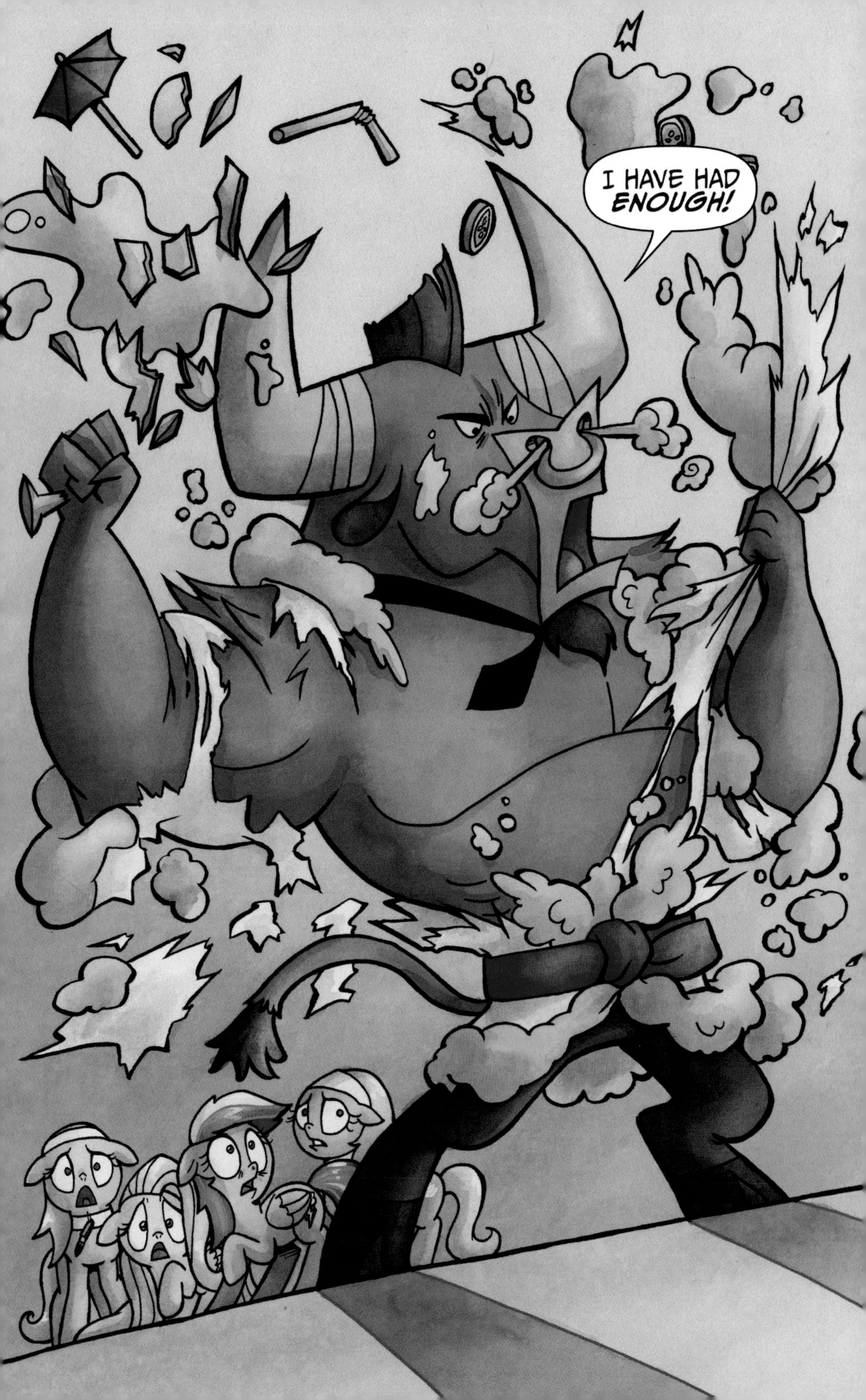
I HAVE HAD *ENOUGH!*

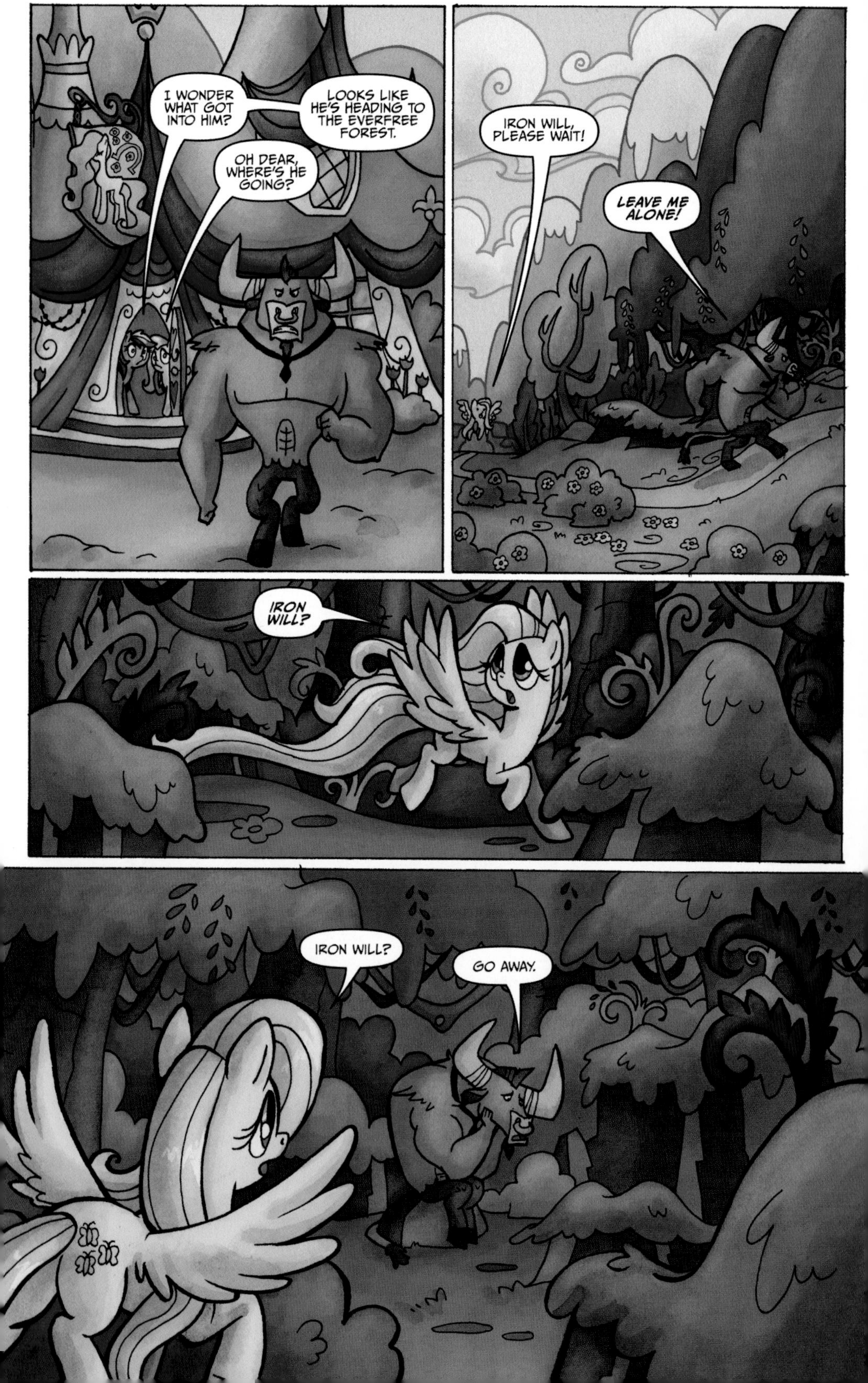
I WONDER WHAT GOT INTO HIM?
LOOKS LIKE HE'S HEADING TO THE EVERFREE FOREST.
OH DEAR, WHERE'S HE GOING?
IRON WILL, PLEASE WAIT!
LEAVE ME ALONE!
IRON WILL?
IRON WILL?
GO AWAY.

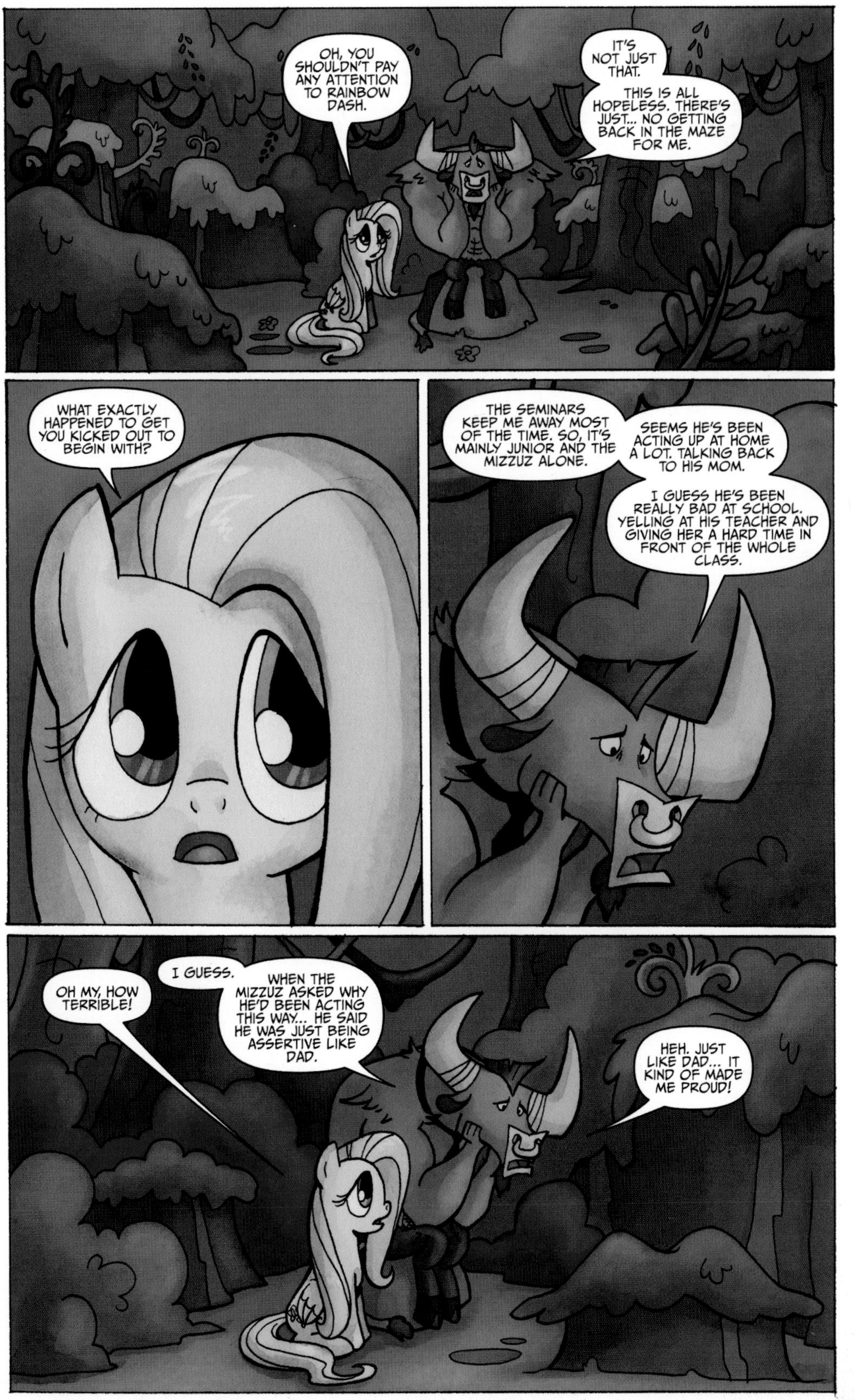
OH, YOU SHOULDN'T PAY ANY ATTENTION TO RAINBOW DASH.
IT'S NOT JUST THAT.
THIS IS ALL HOPELESS. THERE'S JUST... NO GETTING BACK IN THE MAZE FOR ME.
WHAT EXACTLY HAPPENED TO GET YOU KICKED OUT TO BEGIN WITH?
THE SEMINARS KEEP ME AWAY MOST OF THE TIME. SO, IT'S MAINLY JUNIOR AND THE MIZZUZ ALONE.
SEEMS HE'S BEEN ACTING UP AT HOME A LOT. TALKING BACK TO HIS MOM.
I GUESS HE'S BEEN REALLY BAD AT SCHOOL. YELLING AT HIS TEACHER AND GIVING HER A HARD TIME IN FRONT OF THE WHOLE CLASS.
OH MY, HOW TERRIBLE!
I GUESS.
WHEN THE MIZZUZ ASKED WHY HE'D BEEN ACTING THIS WAY... HE SAID HE WAS JUST BEING ASSERTIVE LIKE DAD.
HEH. JUST LIKE DAD... IT KIND OF MADE ME PROUD!

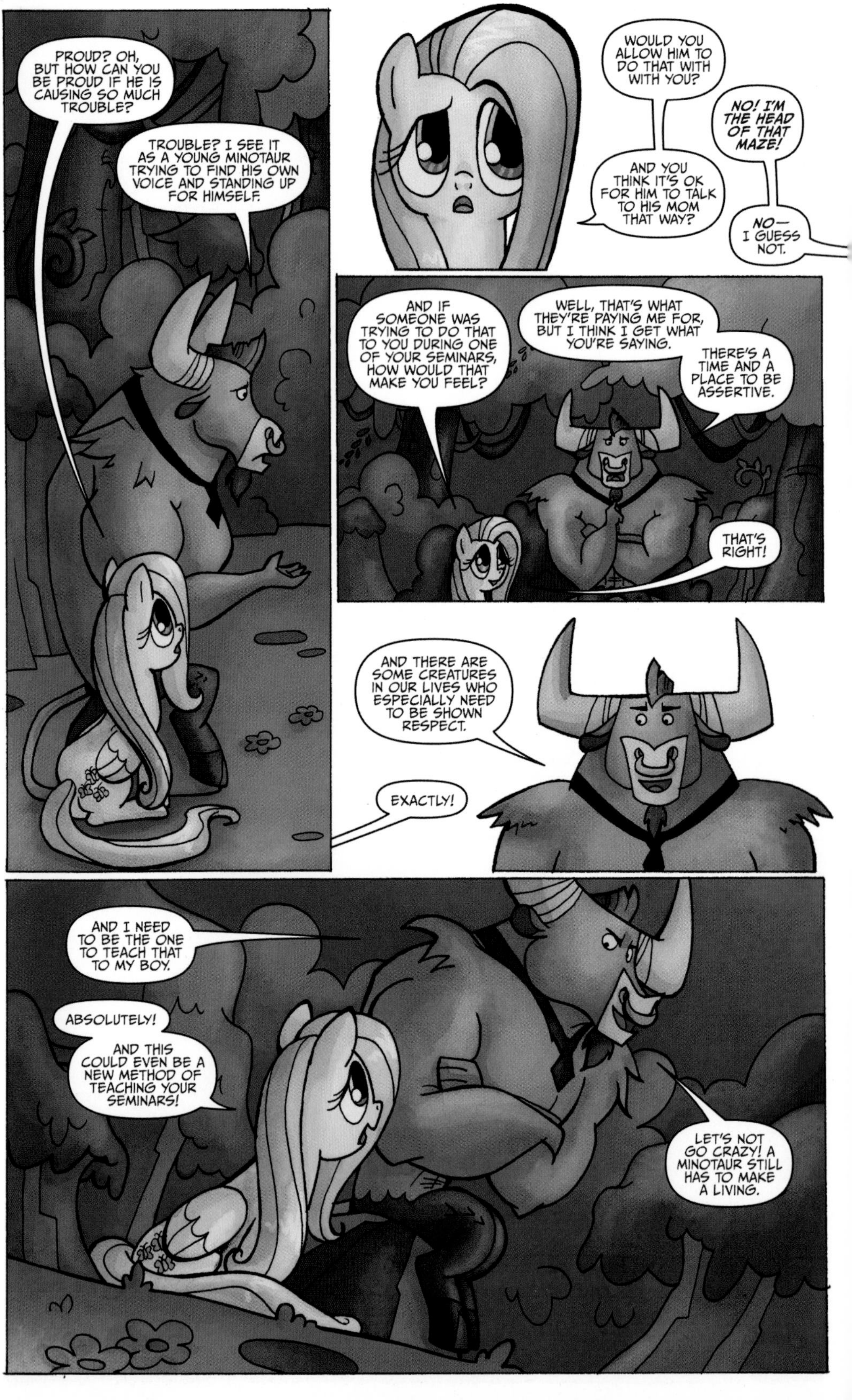
PROUD? OH, BUT HOW CAN YOU BE PROUD IF HE IS CAUSING SO MUCH TROUBLE?
TROUBLE? I SEE IT AS A YOUNG MINOTAUR TRYING TO FIND HIS OWN VOICE AND STANDING UP FOR HIMSELF.
WOULD YOU ALLOW HIM TO DO THAT WITH WITH YOU?
NO! I'M THE HEAD OF THAT MAZE!
AND YOU THINK IT'S OK FOR HIM TO TALK TO HIS MOM THAT WAY?
NO— I GUESS NOT.
AND IF SOMEONE WAS TRYING TO DO THAT TO YOU DURING ONE OF YOUR SEMINARS, HOW WOULD THAT MAKE YOU FEEL?
WELL, THAT'S WHAT THEY'RE PAYING ME FOR, BUT I THINK I GET WHAT YOU'RE SAYING.
THERE'S A TIME AND A PLACE TO BE ASSERTIVE.
THAT'S RIGHT!
AND THERE ARE SOME CREATURES IN OUR LIVES WHO ESPECIALLY NEED TO BE SHOWN RESPECT.
EXACTLY!
AND I NEED TO BE THE ONE TO TEACH THAT TO MY BOY.
ABSOLUTELY!
AND THIS COULD EVEN BE A NEW METHOD OF TEACHING YOUR SEMINARS!
LET'S NOT GO CRAZY! A MINOTAUR STILL HAS TO MAKE A LIVING.

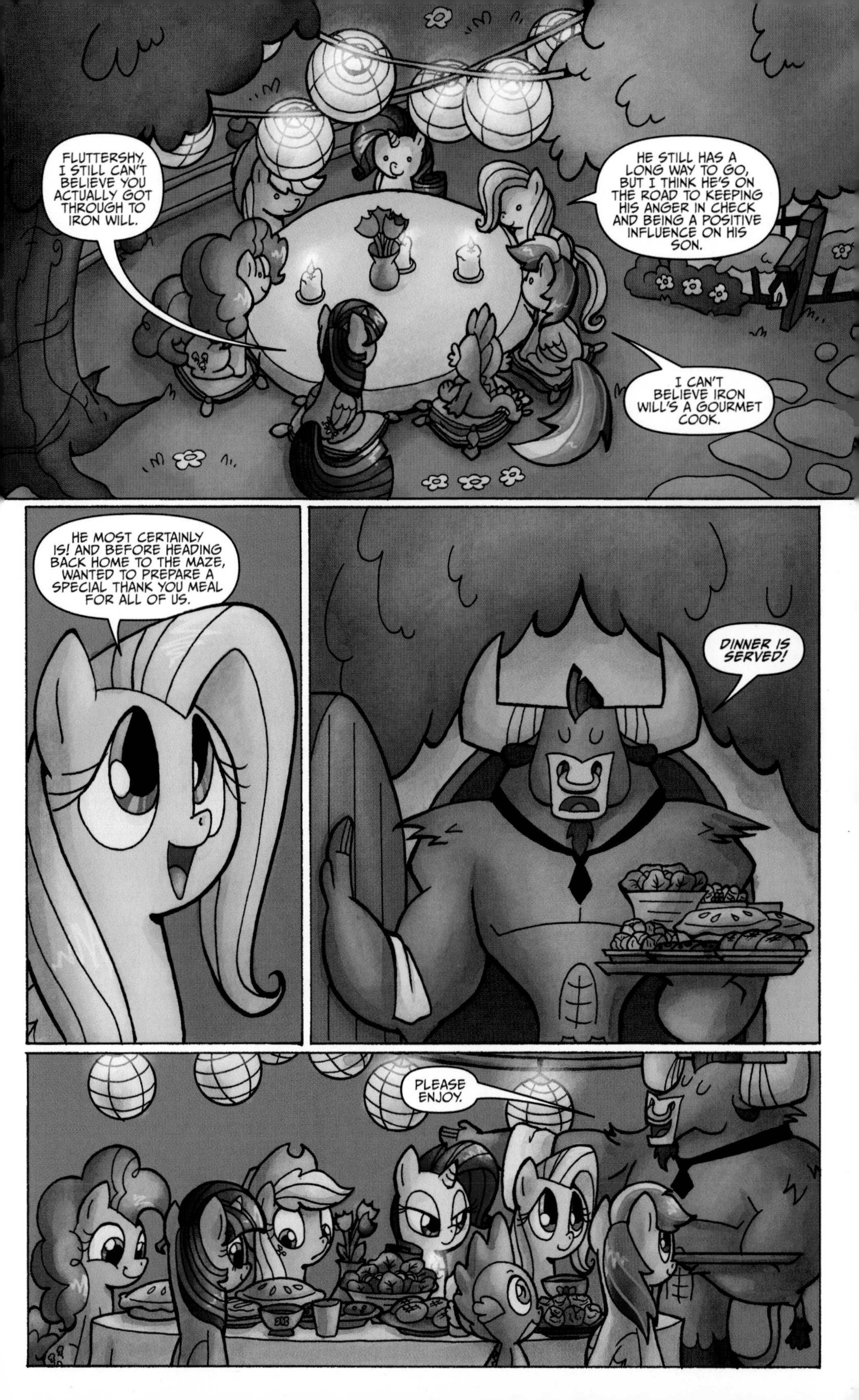
FLUTTERSHY, I STILL CAN'T BELIEVE YOU ACTUALLY GOT THROUGH TO IRON WILL.
HE STILL HAS A LONG WAY TO GO, BUT I THINK HE'S ON THE ROAD TO KEEPING HIS ANGER IN CHECK AND BEING A POSITIVE INFLUENCE ON HIS SON.
I CAN'T BELIEVE IRON WILL'S A GOURMET COOK.
HE MOST CERTAINLY IS! AND BEFORE HEADING BACK HOME TO THE MAZE, WANTED TO PREPARE A SPECIAL THANK YOU MEAL FOR ALL OF US.
DINNER IS SERVED!
PLEASE ENJOY.

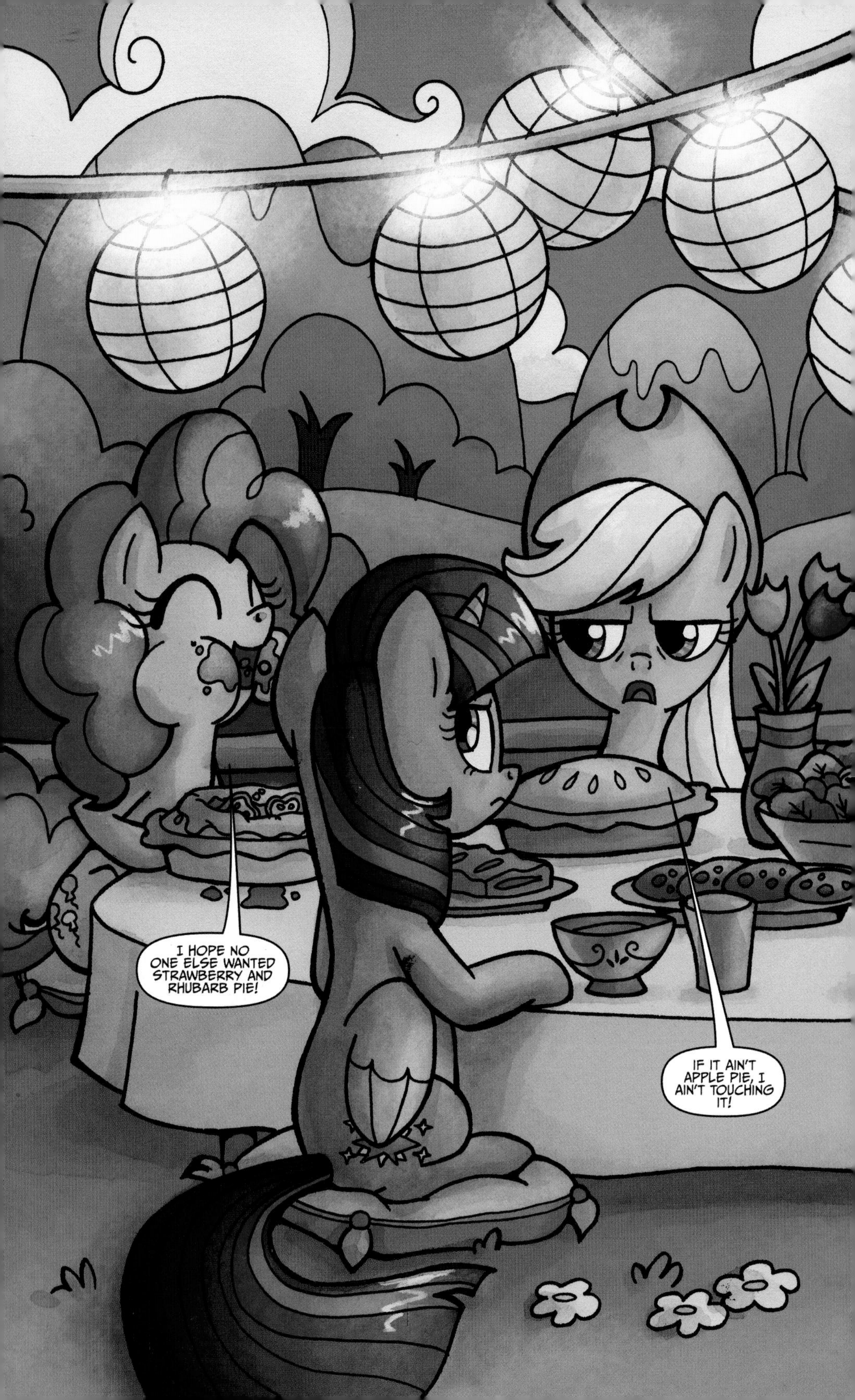
I HOPE NO ONE ELSE WANTED STRAWBERRY AND RHUBARB PIE!
IF IT AIN'T APPLE PIE, I AIN'T TOUCHING IT!

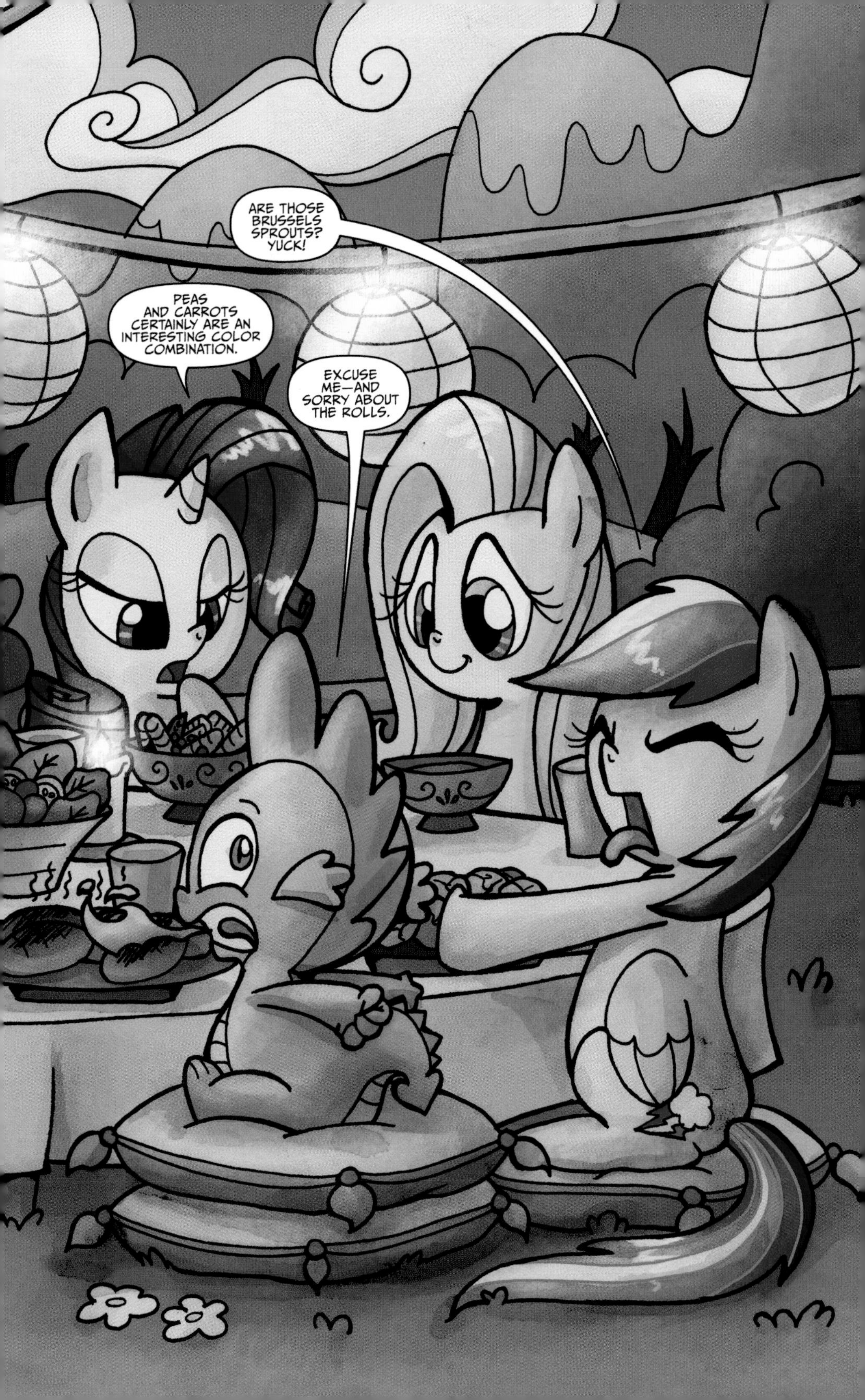
PEAS AND CARROTS CERTAINLY ARE AN INTERESTING COLOR COMBINATION.
ARE THOSE BRUSSELS SPROUTS? YUCK!
EXCUSE ME—AND SORRY ABOUT THE ROLLS.

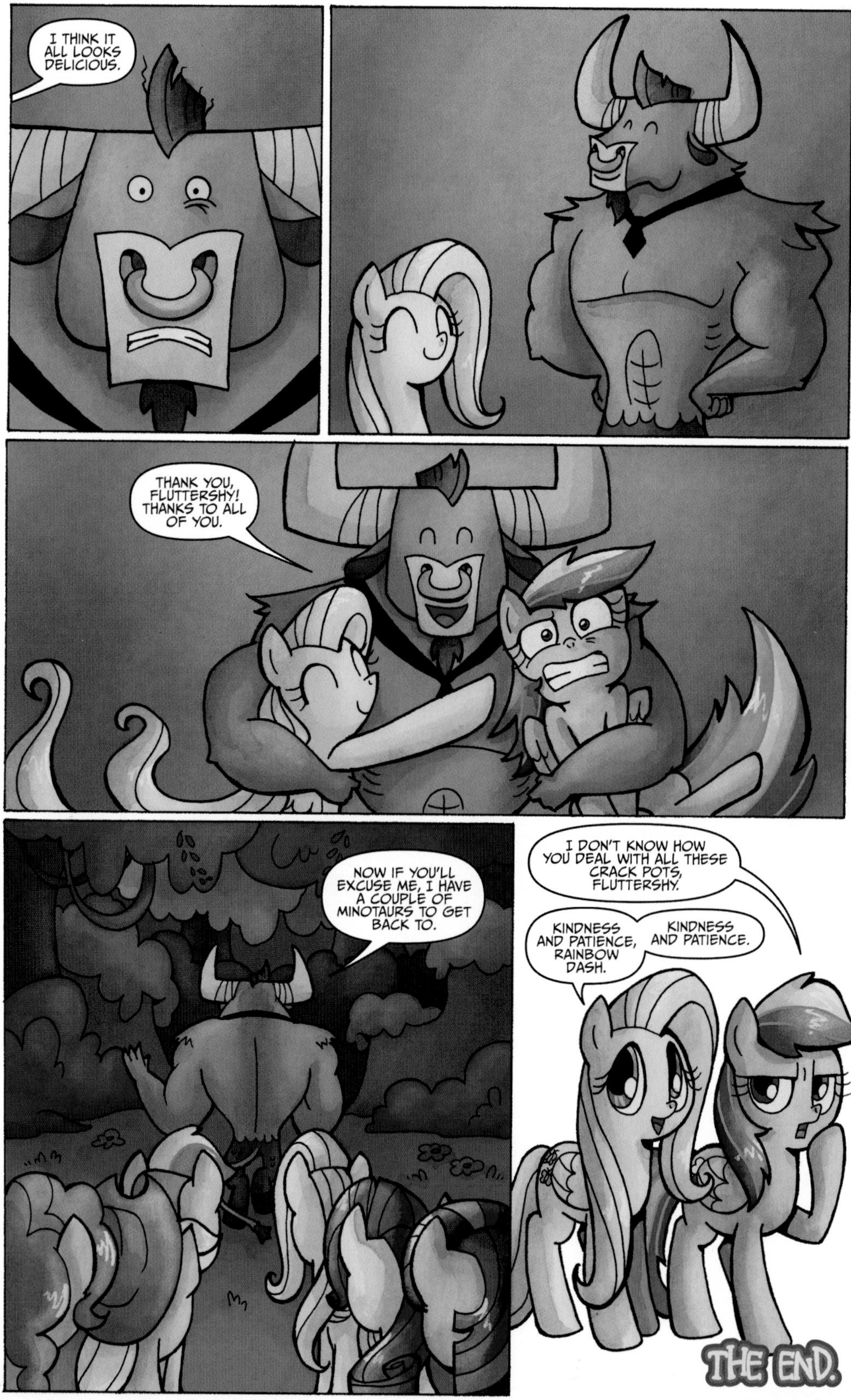
I THINK IT ALL LOOKS DELICIOUS.
THANK YOU, FLUTTERSHY! THANKS TO ALL OF YOU.
NOW IF YOU'LL EXCUSE ME, I HAVE A COUPLE OF MINOTAURS TO GET BACK TO.
I DON'T KNOW HOW YOU DEAL WITH ALL THESE CRACK POTS, FLUTTERSHY.
KINDNESS AND PATIENCE, RAINBOW DASH.
KINDNESS AND PATIENCE.
THE END.

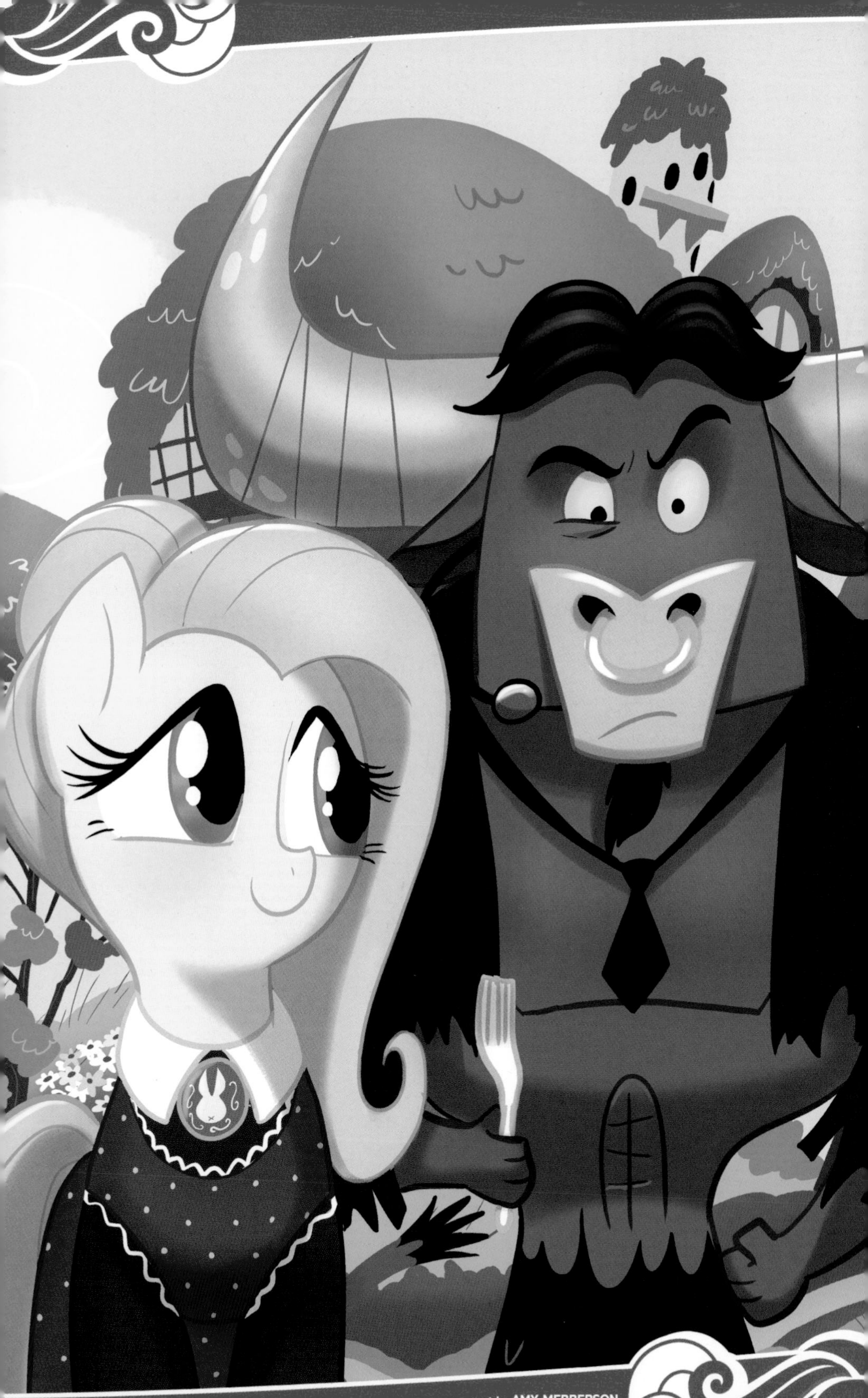

art by AMY MEBBERSON

Rainbow Dash & Spitfire

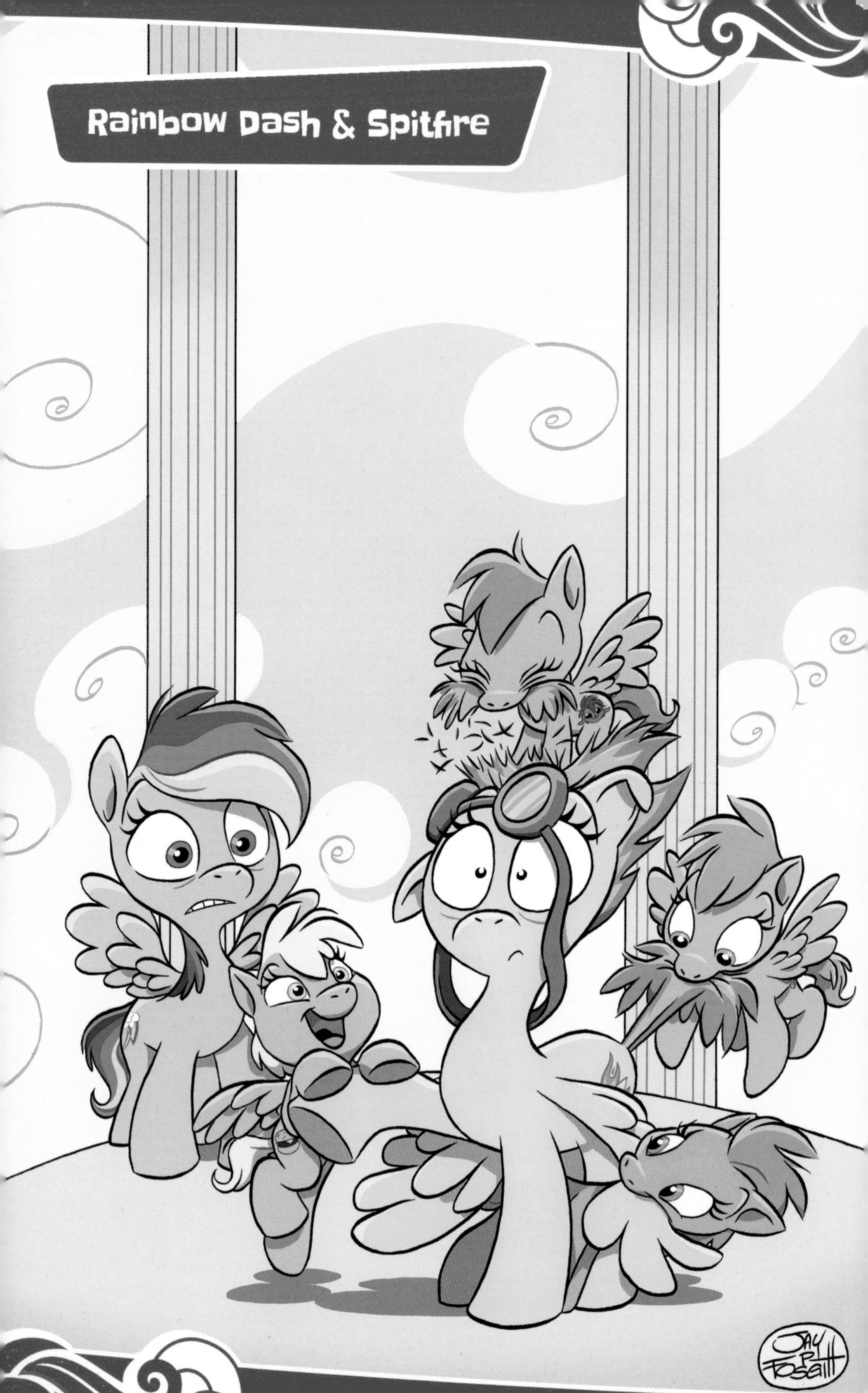

art by JAY FOSGITT

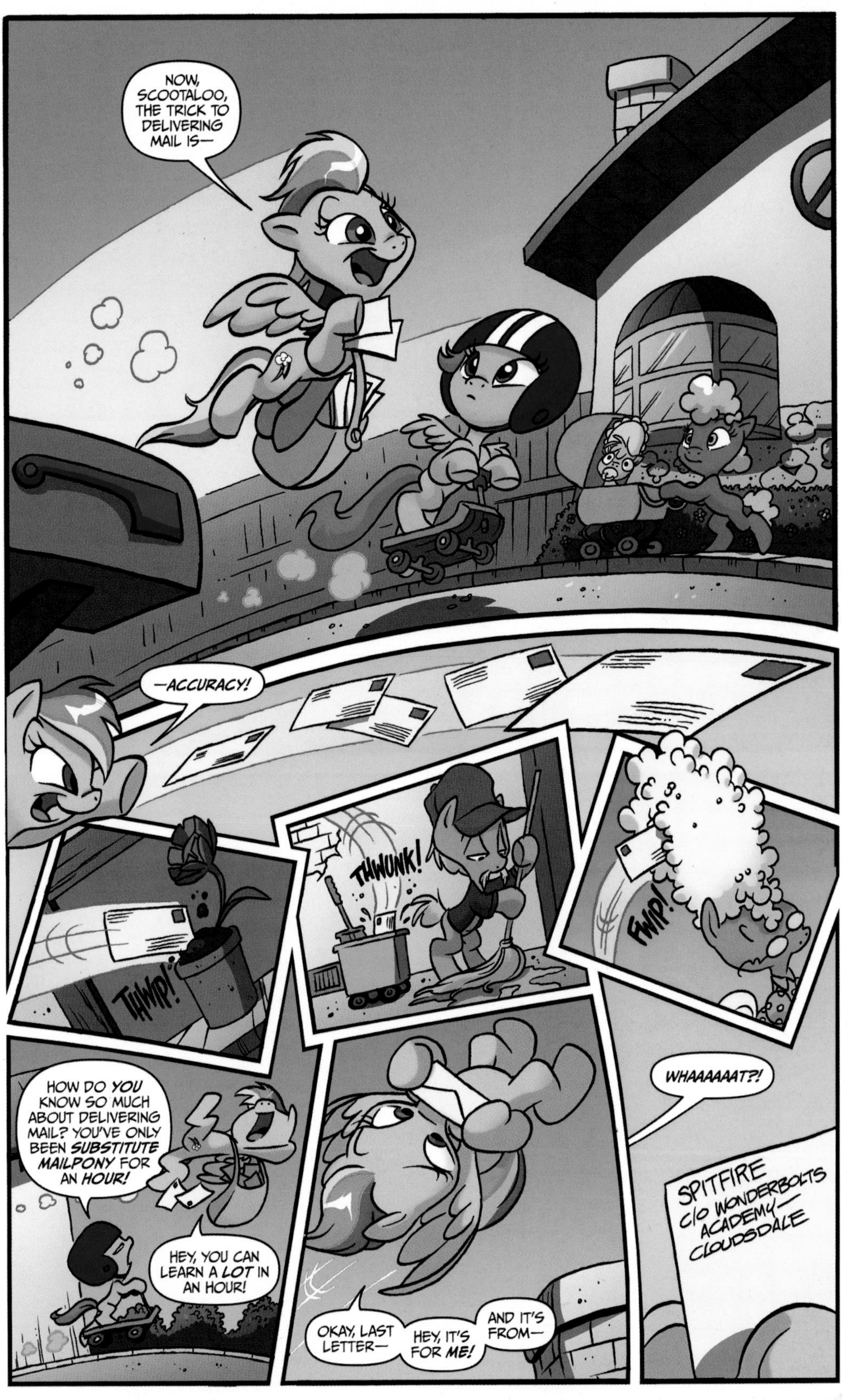

NOW, SCOOTALOO, THE TRICK TO DELIVERING MAIL IS—
—ACCURACY!
THWIP!
THWUNK!
FWIP!
HOW DO YOU KNOW SO MUCH ABOUT DELIVERING MAIL? YOU'VE ONLY BEEN SUBSTITUTE MAILPONY FOR AN HOUR!
HEY, YOU CAN LEARN A LOT IN AN HOUR!
OKAY, LAST LETTER—
HEY, IT'S FOR ME!
AND IT'S FROM—
WHAAAAAAT?!
SPITFIRE
C/O WONDERBOLTS ACADEMY—
CLOUDSDALE

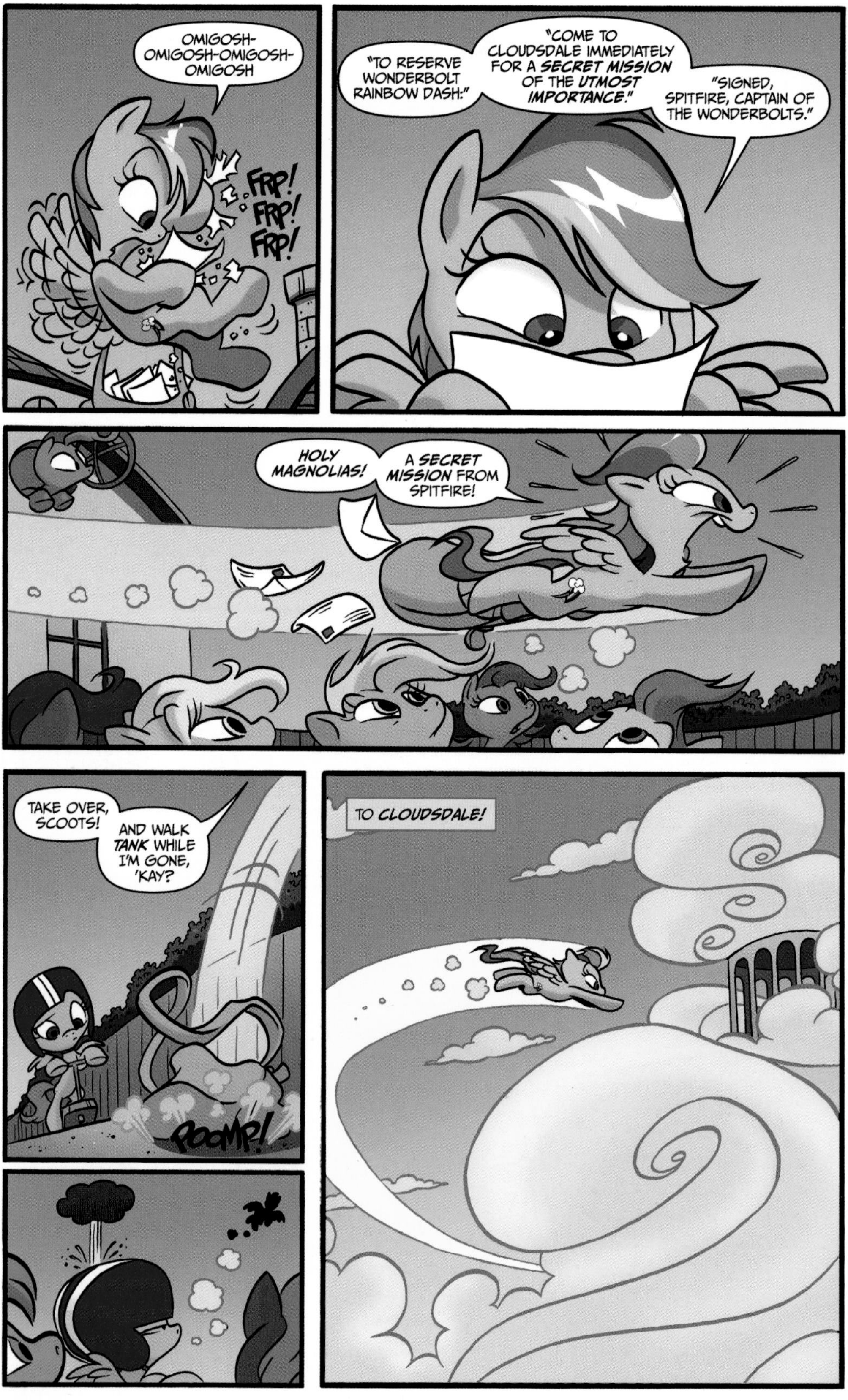
OMIGOSH-OMIGOSH-OMIGOSH-OMIGOSH
FRP! FRP! FRP!
"TO RESERVE WONDERBOLT RAINBOW DASH:"
"COME TO CLOUDSDALE IMMEDIATELY FOR A SECRET MISSION OF THE UTMOST IMPORTANCE."
"SIGNED, SPITFIRE, CAPTAIN OF THE WONDERBOLTS."
HOLY MAGNOLIAS!
A SECRET MISSION FROM SPITFIRE!
TAKE OVER, SCOOTS!
AND WALK TANK WHILE I'M GONE, 'KAY?
POOMP!
TO CLOUDSDALE!

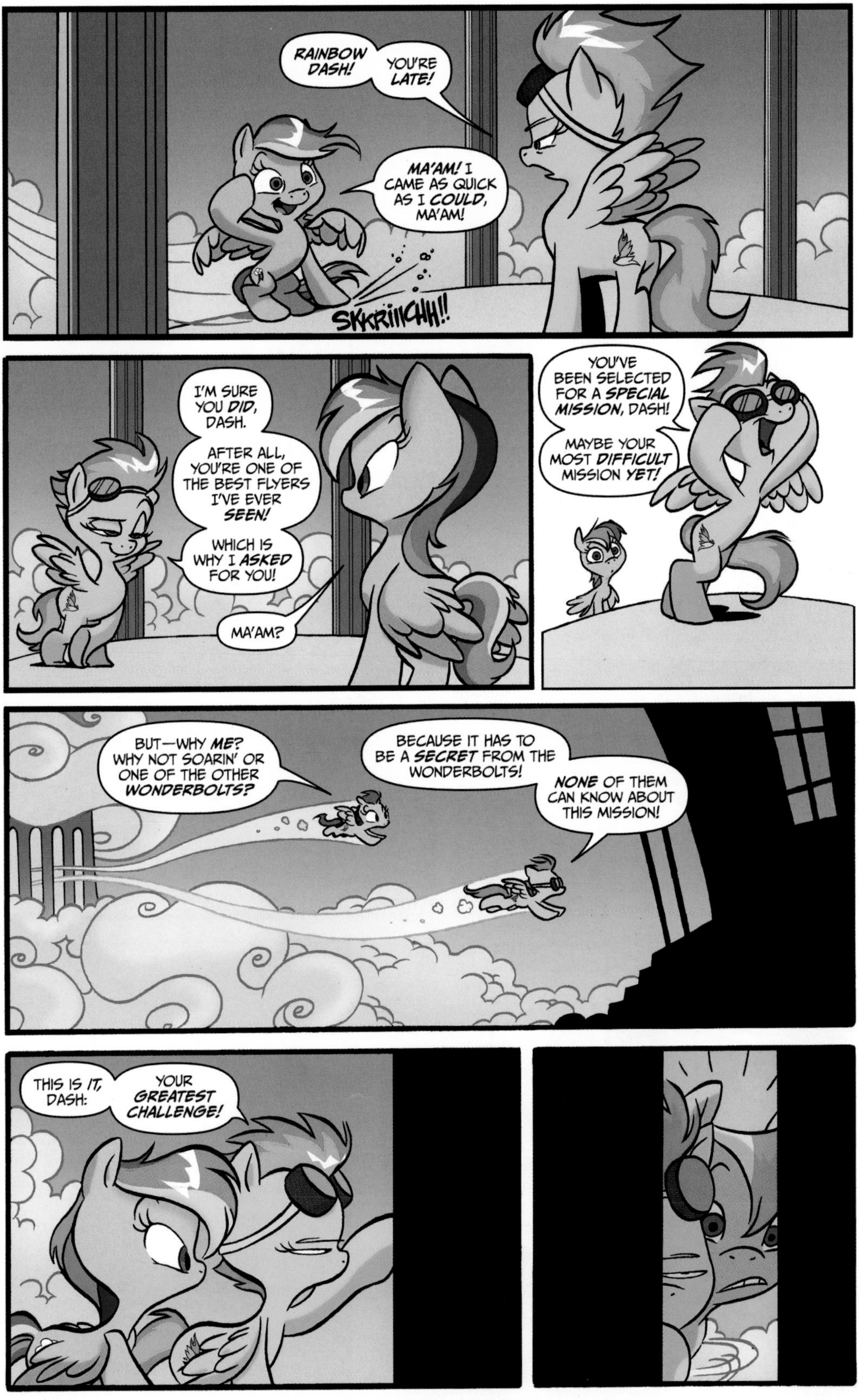
RAINBOW DASH!
YOU'RE LATE!
MA'AM! I CAME AS QUICK AS I COULD, MA'AM!
SKKRIIICHH!!
I'M SURE YOU DID, DASH.
AFTER ALL, YOU'RE ONE OF THE BEST FLYERS I'VE EVER SEEN!
WHICH IS WHY I ASKED FOR YOU!
MA'AM?
YOU'VE BEEN SELECTED FOR A SPECIAL MISSION, DASH!
MAYBE YOUR MOST DIFFICULT MISSION YET!
BUT—WHY ME? WHY NOT SOARIN' OR ONE OF THE OTHER WONDERBOLTS?
BECAUSE IT HAS TO BE A SECRET FROM THE WONDERBOLTS!
NONE OF THEM CAN KNOW ABOUT THIS MISSION!
THIS IS IT, DASH:
YOUR GREATEST CHALLENGE!

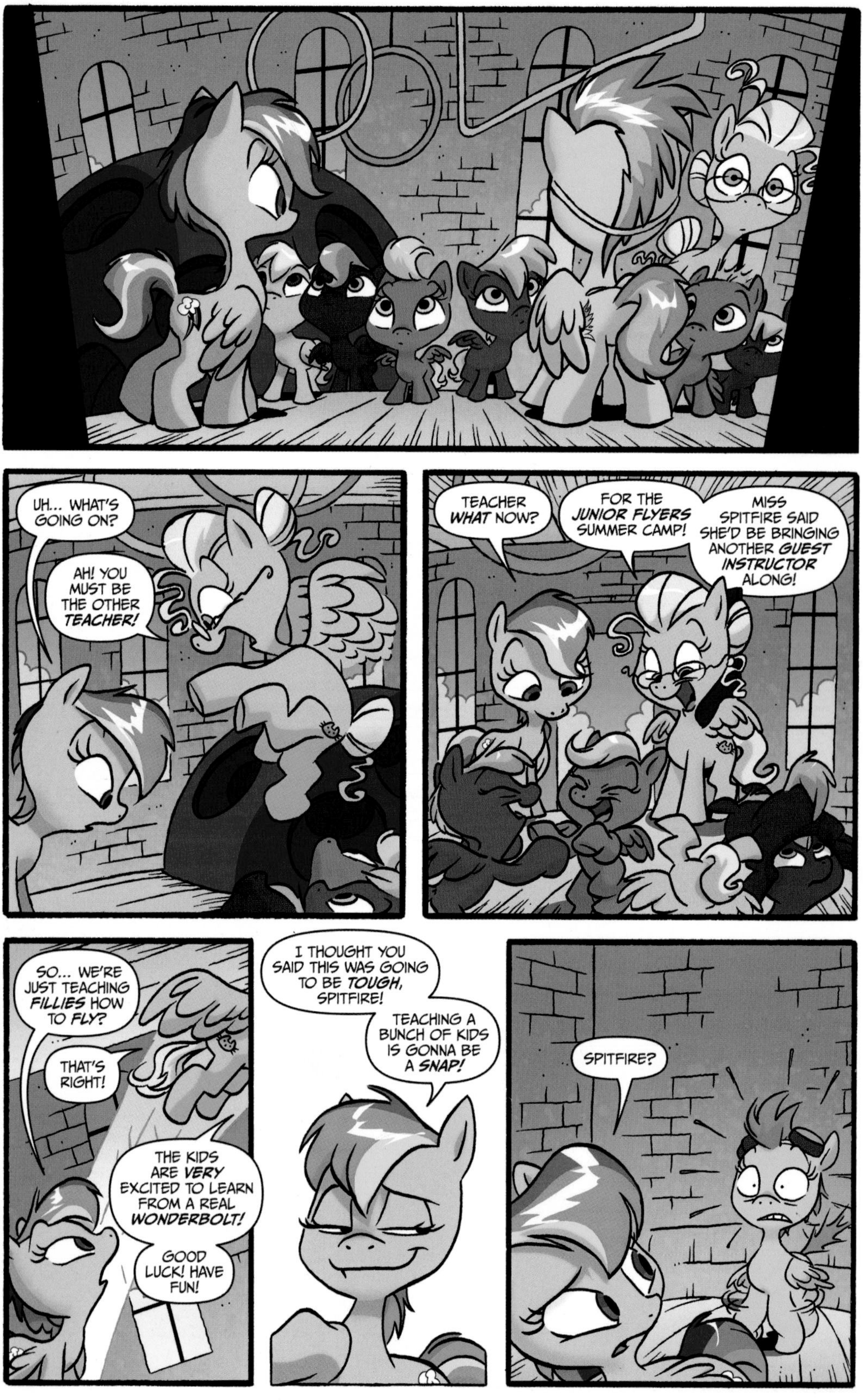
UH... WHAT'S GOING ON?
AH! YOU MUST BE THE OTHER TEACHER!
TEACHER WHAT NOW?
FOR THE JUNIOR FLYERS SUMMER CAMP!
MISS SPITFIRE SAID SHE'D BE BRINGING ANOTHER GUEST INSTRUCTOR ALONG!
SO... WE'RE JUST TEACHING FILLIES HOW TO FLY?
THAT'S RIGHT!
THE KIDS ARE VERY EXCITED TO LEARN FROM A REAL WONDERBOLT!
GOOD LUCK! HAVE FUN!
I THOUGHT YOU SAID THIS WAS GOING TO BE TOUGH, SPITFIRE!
TEACHING A BUNCH OF KIDS IS GONNA BE A SNAP!
SPITFIRE?

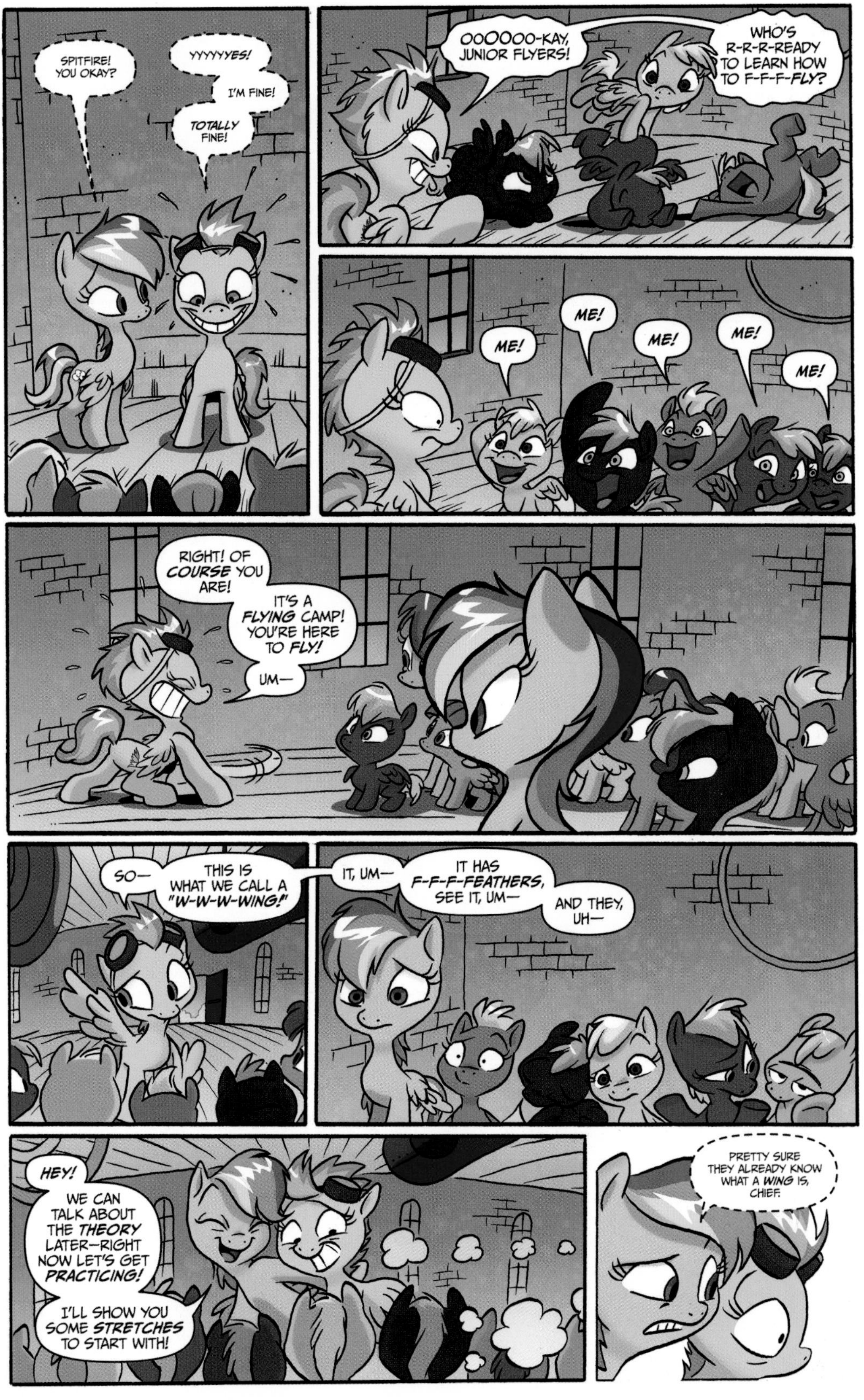
SPITFIRE! YOU OKAY?
YYYYYYES!
I'M FINE!
TOTALLY FINE!
OOOOOO-KAY, JUNIOR FLYERS!
WHO'S R-R-R-READY TO LEARN HOW TO F-F-F-FLY?
ME!
ME!
ME!
ME!
ME!
RIGHT! OF COURSE YOU ARE!
IT'S A FLYING CAMP! YOU'RE HERE TO FLY!
UM—
SO—
THIS IS WHAT WE CALL A "W-W-W-WING!"
IT, UM—
IT HAS F-F-F-FEATHERS, SEE IT, UM—
AND THEY, UH—
HEY!
WE CAN TALK ABOUT THE THEORY LATER—RIGHT NOW LET'S GET PRACTICING!
I'LL SHOW YOU SOME STRETCHES TO START WITH!
PRETTY SURE THEY ALREADY KNOW WHAT A WING IS, CHIEF.

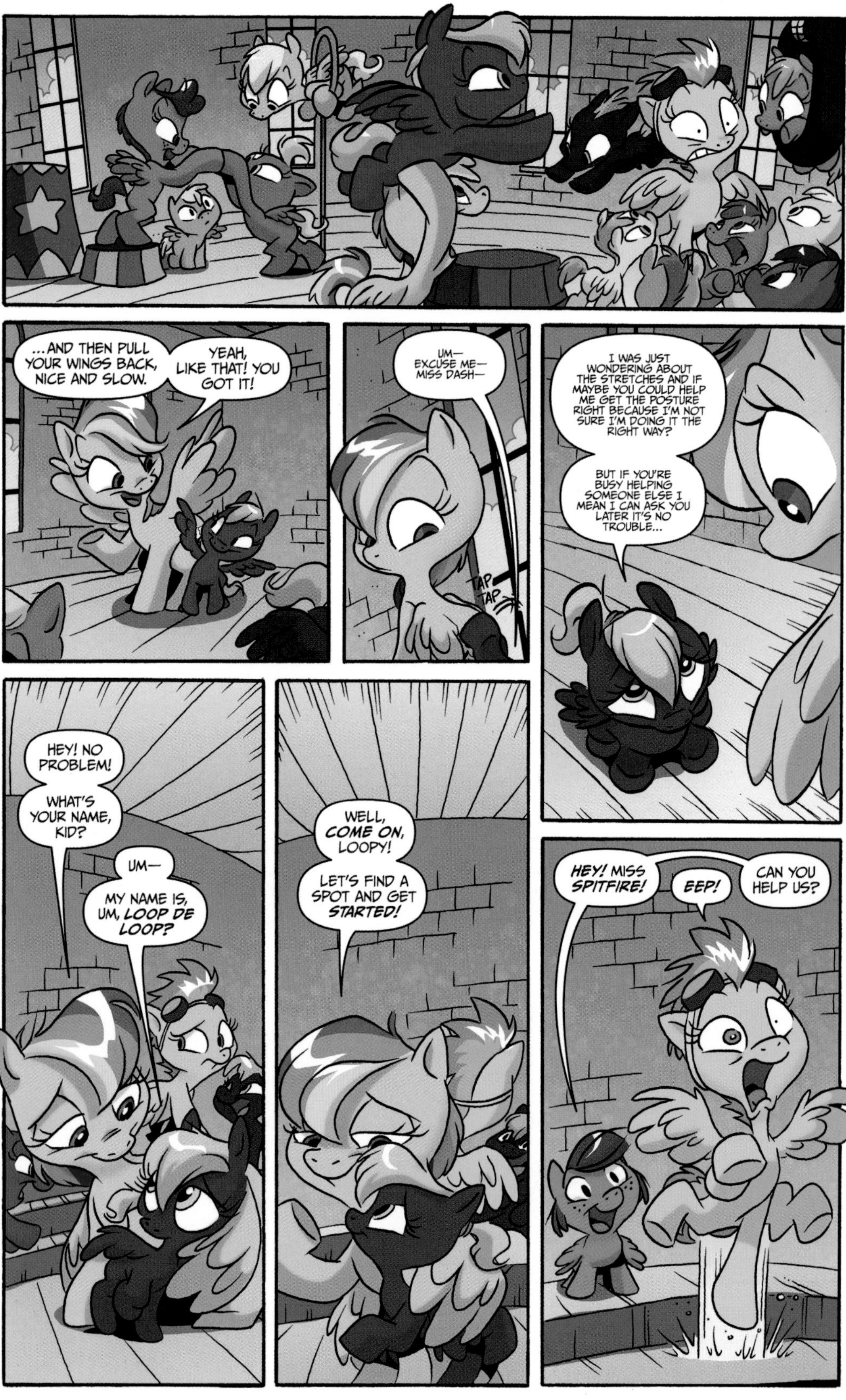
...AND THEN PULL YOUR WINGS BACK, NICE AND SLOW.
YEAH, LIKE THAT! YOU GOT IT!
UM— EXCUSE ME— MISS DASH—
TAP TAP
I WAS JUST WONDERING ABOUT THE STRETCHES AND IF MAYBE YOU COULD HELP ME GET THE POSTURE RIGHT BECAUSE I'M NOT SURE I'M DOING IT THE RIGHT WAY?
BUT IF YOU'RE BUSY HELPING SOMEONE ELSE I MEAN LATER I CAN ASK YOU LATER IT'S NO TROUBLE...
HEY! NO PROBLEM!
WHAT'S YOUR NAME, KID?
UM—
MY NAME IS, UM, LOOP DE LOOP?
WELL, COME ON, LOOPY!
LET'S FIND A SPOT AND GET STARTED!
HEY! MISS SPITFIRE!
EEP!
CAN YOU HELP US?

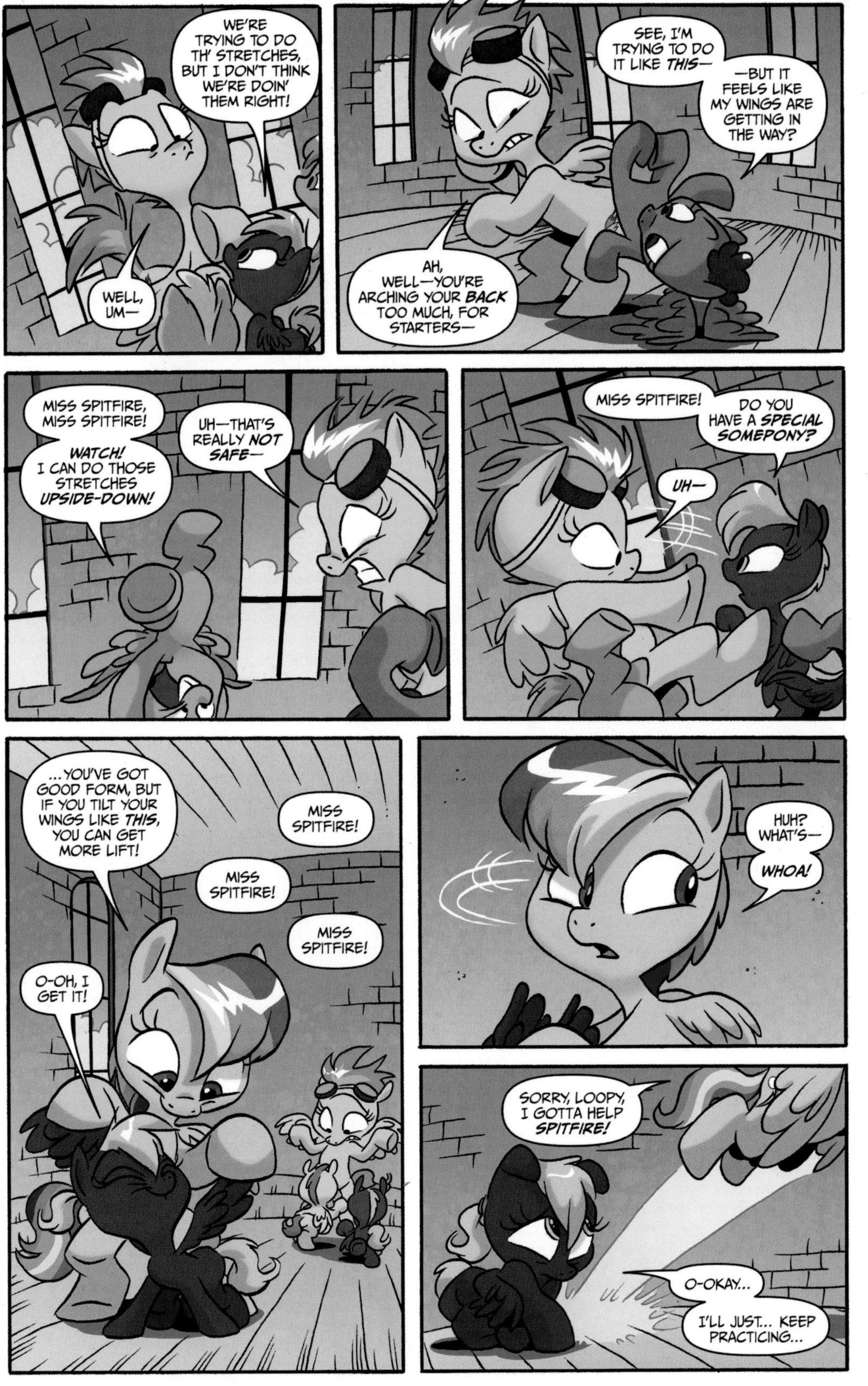

WE'RE TRYING TO DO TH' STRETCHES, BUT I DON'T THINK WE'RE DOIN' THEM RIGHT!
WELL, UM—
SEE, I'M TRYING TO DO IT LIKE THIS—
—BUT IT FEELS LIKE MY WINGS ARE GETTING IN THE WAY?
AH, WELL—YOU'RE ARCHING YOUR BACK TOO MUCH, FOR STARTERS—
MISS SPITFIRE, MISS SPITFIRE!
WATCH! I CAN DO THOSE STRETCHES UPSIDE-DOWN!
UH—THAT'S REALLY NOT SAFE—
MISS SPITFIRE!
DO YOU HAVE A SPECIAL SOMEPONY?
UH—
...YOU'VE GOT GOOD FORM, BUT IF YOU TILT YOUR WINGS LIKE THIS, YOU CAN GET MORE LIFT!
MISS SPITFIRE!
MISS SPITFIRE!
MISS SPITFIRE!
O-OH, I GET IT!
HUH? WHAT'S—
WHOA!
SORRY, LOOPY, I GOTTA HELP SPITFIRE!
O-OKAY...
I'LL JUST... KEEP PRACTICING...

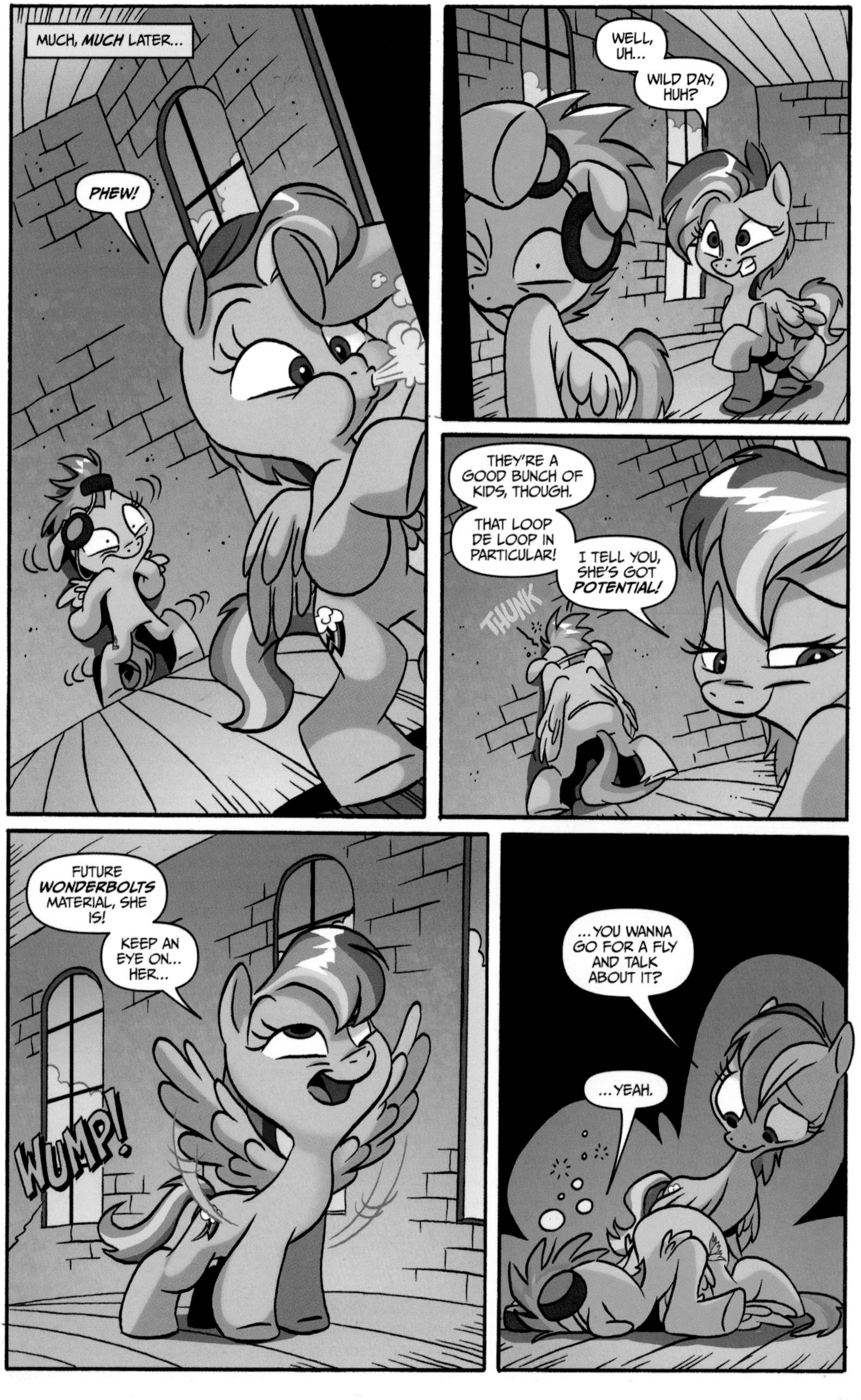
MUCH, *MUCH* LATER...
PHEW!
WELL, UH...
WILD DAY, HUH?
THEY'RE A GOOD BUNCH OF KIDS, THOUGH.
THAT LOOP DE LOOP IN PARTICULAR!
I TELL YOU, SHE'S GOT *POTENTIAL!*
THUNK
FUTURE *WONDERBOLTS* MATERIAL, SHE IS!
KEEP AN EYE ON... HER...
WUMP!
...YOU WANNA GO FOR A FLY AND TALK ABOUT IT?
...YEAH.

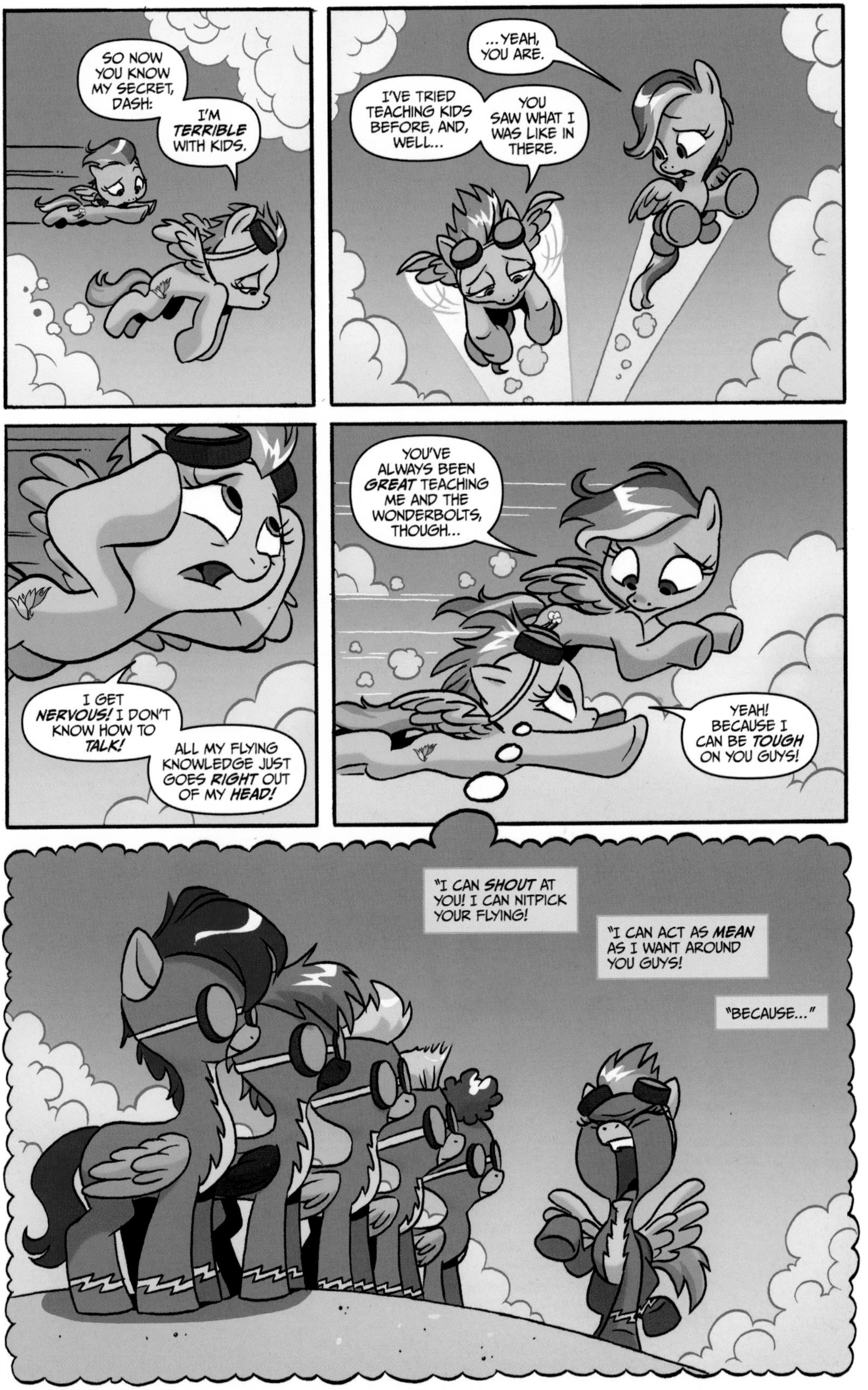
SO NOW YOU KNOW MY SECRET, DASH:
I'M *TERRIBLE* WITH KIDS.
...YEAH, YOU ARE.
I'VE TRIED TEACHING KIDS BEFORE, AND, WELL...
YOU SAW WHAT I WAS LIKE IN THERE.
I GET *NERVOUS!* I DON'T KNOW HOW TO *TALK!*
ALL MY FLYING KNOWLEDGE JUST GOES *RIGHT* OUT OF MY *HEAD!*
YOU'VE ALWAYS BEEN *GREAT* TEACHING ME AND THE WONDERBOLTS, THOUGH...
YEAH! BECAUSE I CAN BE *TOUGH* ON YOU GUYS!
"I CAN *SHOUT* AT YOU! I CAN NITPICK YOUR FLYING!
"I CAN ACT AS *MEAN* AS I WANT AROUND YOU GUYS!
"BECAUSE..."

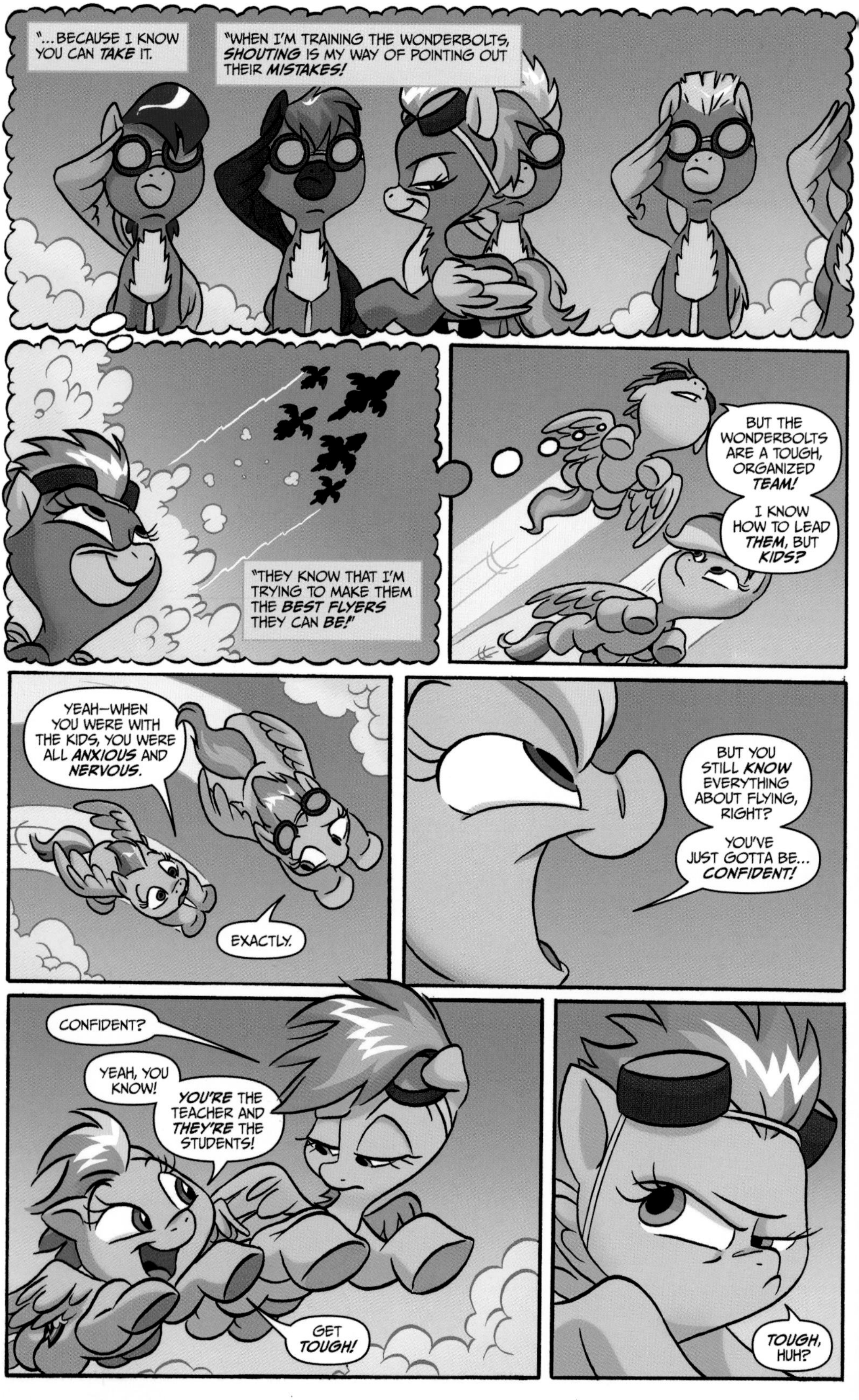
"...BECAUSE I KNOW YOU CAN TAKE IT.
"WHEN I'M TRAINING THE WONDERBOLTS, SHOUTING IS MY WAY OF POINTING OUT THEIR MISTAKES!
"THEY KNOW THAT I'M TRYING TO MAKE THEM THE BEST FLYERS THEY CAN BE!"
BUT THE WONDERBOLTS ARE A TOUGH, ORGANIZED TEAM!
I KNOW HOW TO LEAD THEM, BUT KIDS?
YEAH—WHEN YOU WERE WITH THE KIDS, YOU WERE ALL ANXIOUS AND NERVOUS.
EXACTLY.
BUT YOU STILL KNOW EVERYTHING ABOUT FLYING, RIGHT?
YOU'VE JUST GOTTA BE... CONFIDENT!
CONFIDENT?
YEAH, YOU KNOW!
YOU'RE THE TEACHER AND THEY'RE THE STUDENTS!
GET TOUGH!
TOUGH, HUH?

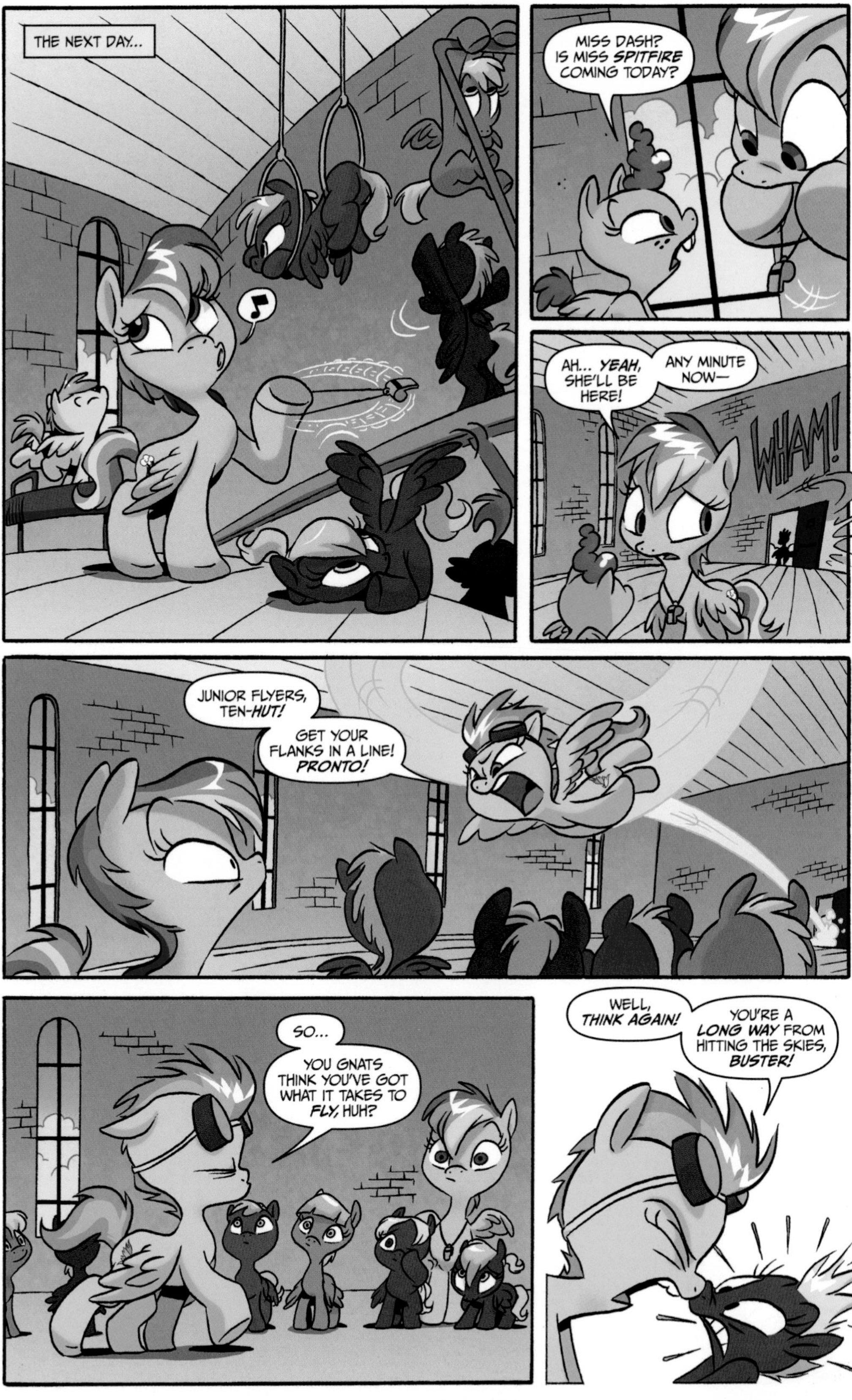
THE NEXT DAY...
MISS DASH? IS MISS SPITFIRE COMING TODAY?
AH... YEAH, SHE'LL BE HERE!
ANY MINUTE NOW—
WHAM!
JUNIOR FLYERS, TEN-HUT!
GET YOUR FLANKS IN A LINE! PRONTO!
SO...
YOU GNATS THINK YOU'VE GOT WHAT IT TAKES TO FLY, HUH?
WELL, THINK AGAIN!
YOU'RE A LONG WAY FROM HITTING THE SKIES, BUSTER!

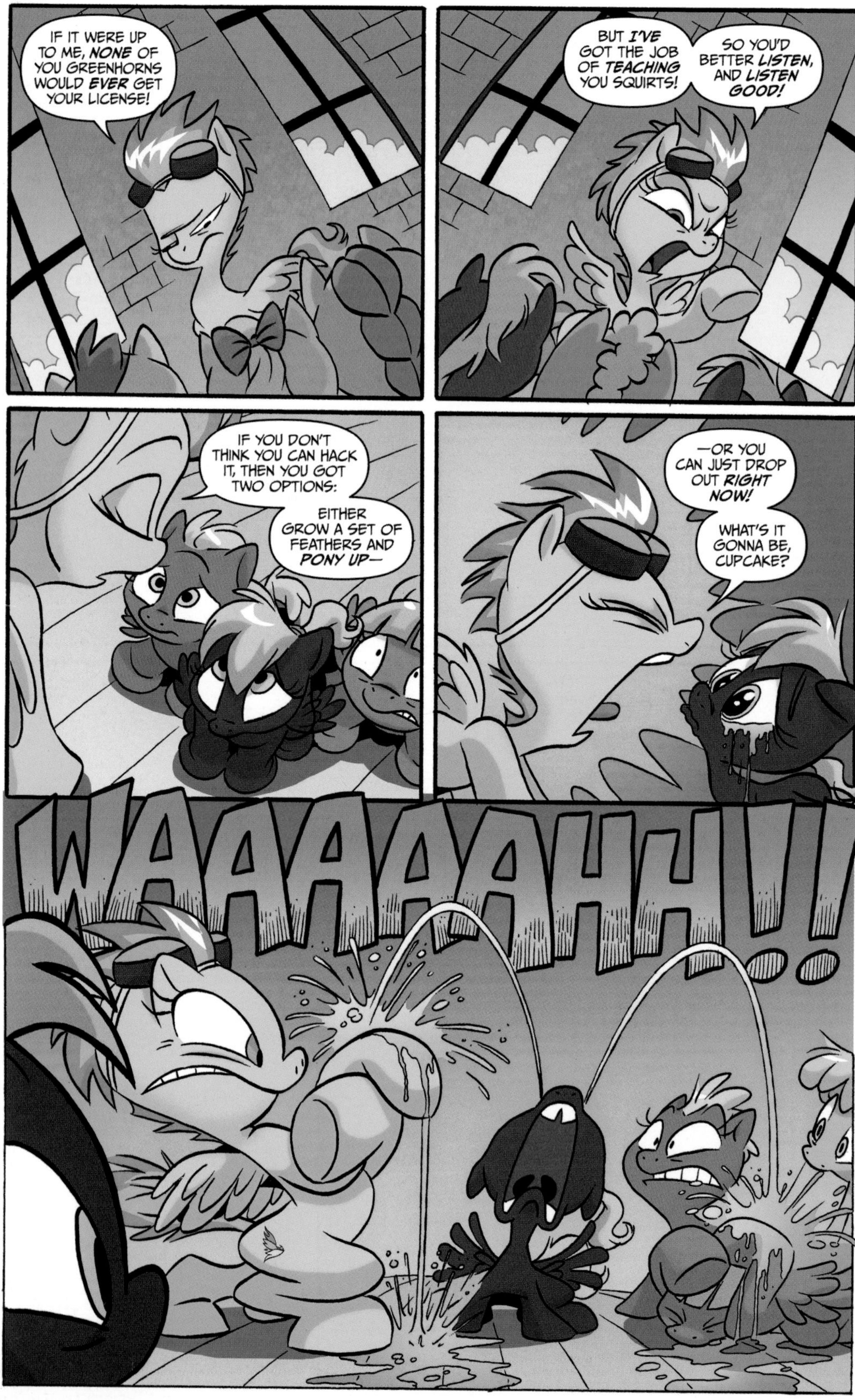
IF IT WERE UP TO ME, NONE OF YOU GREENHORNS WOULD EVER GET YOUR LICENSE!
BUT I'VE GOT THE JOB OF TEACHING YOU SQUIRTS!
SO YOU'D BETTER LISTEN, AND LISTEN GOOD!
IF YOU DON'T THINK YOU CAN HACK IT, THEN YOU GOT TWO OPTIONS:
EITHER GROW A SET OF FEATHERS AND PONY UP—
—OR YOU CAN JUST DROP OUT RIGHT NOW!
WHAT'S IT GONNA BE, CUPCAKE?
WAAAAAHH!!

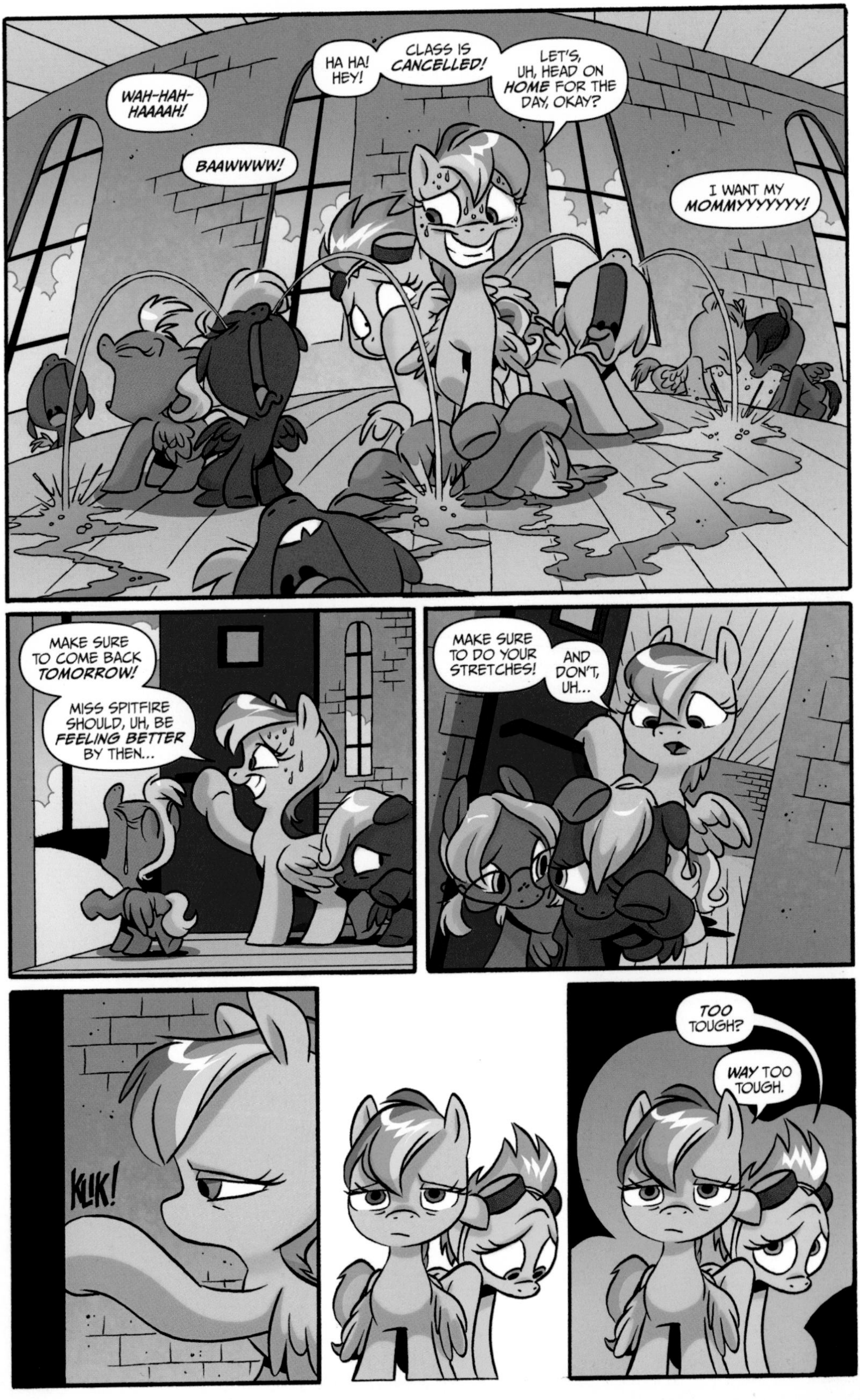
WAH-HAH-HAAAAH!
BAAWWWW!
HA HA! HEY!
CLASS IS CANCELLED!
LET'S, UH, HEAD ON HOME FOR THE DAY, OKAY?
I WANT MY MOMMYYYYYYY!
MAKE SURE TO COME BACK TOMORROW!
MISS SPITFIRE SHOULD, UH, BE FEELING BETTER BY THEN...
MAKE SURE TO DO YOUR STRETCHES!
AND DON'T, UH...
KLIK!
TOO TOUGH?
WAY TOO TOUGH.

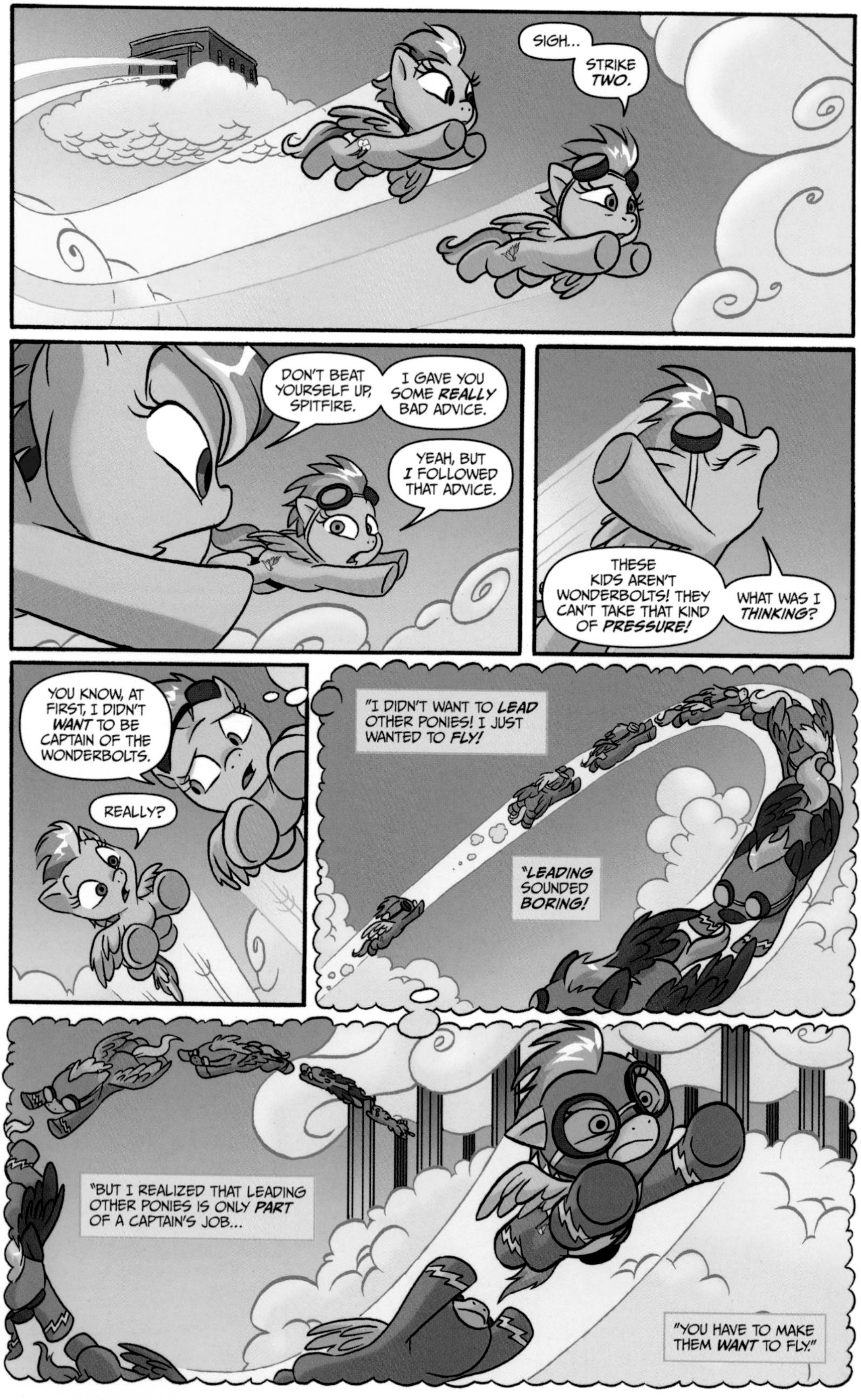
SIGH...
STRIKE TWO.
DON'T BEAT YOURSELF UP, SPITFIRE.
I GAVE YOU SOME REALLY BAD ADVICE.
YEAH, BUT I FOLLOWED THAT ADVICE.
THESE KIDS AREN'T WONDERBOLTS! THEY CAN'T TAKE THAT KIND OF PRESSURE!
WHAT WAS I THINKING?
YOU KNOW, AT FIRST, I DIDN'T WANT TO BE CAPTAIN OF THE WONDERBOLTS.
REALLY?
"I DIDN'T WANT TO LEAD OTHER PONIES! I JUST WANTED TO FLY!
"LEADING SOUNDED BORING!
"BUT I REALIZED THAT LEADING OTHER PONIES IS ONLY PART OF A CAPTAIN'S JOB...
"YOU HAVE TO MAKE THEM WANT TO FLY."

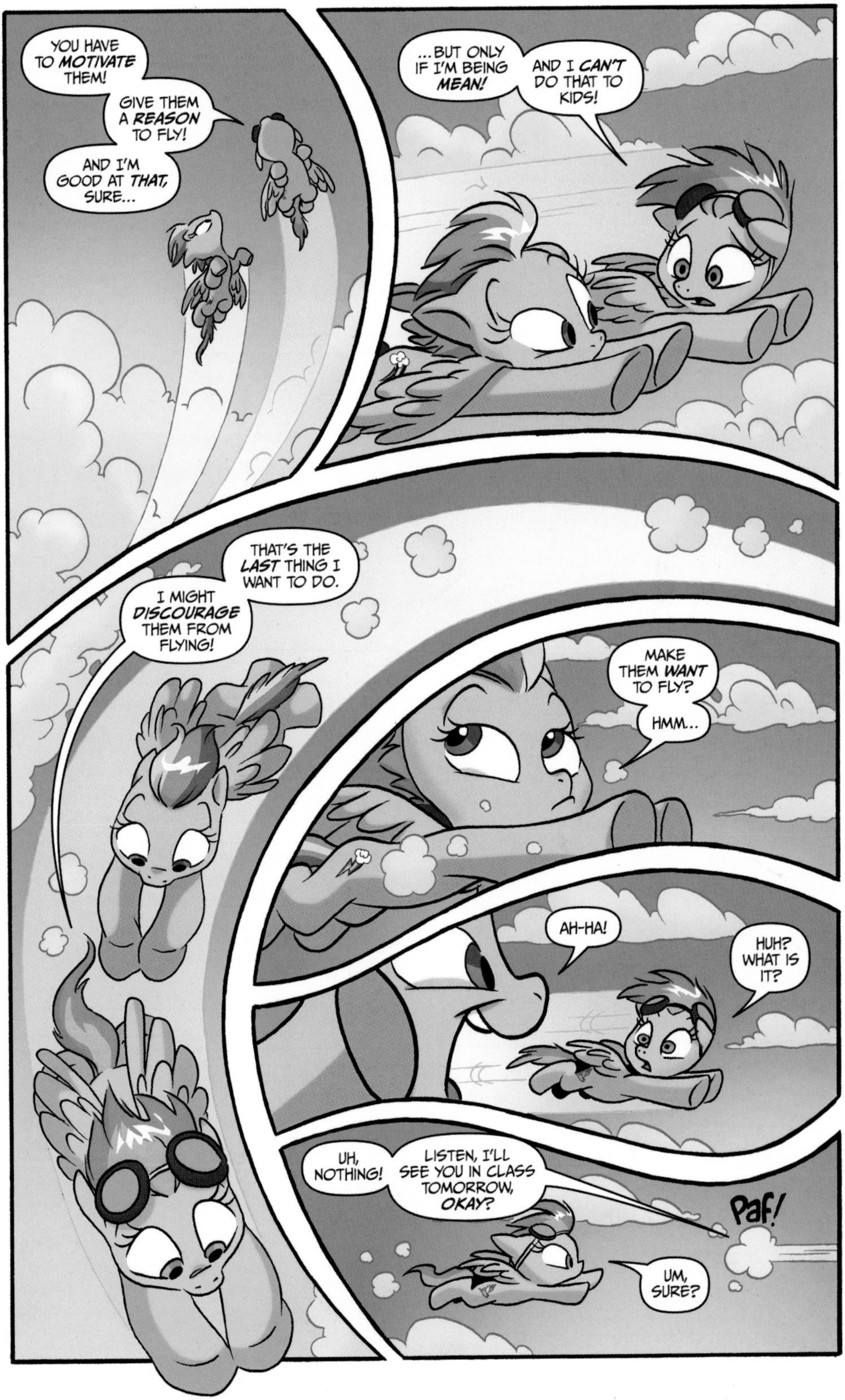
YOU HAVE TO MOTIVATE THEM!
GIVE THEM A REASON TO FLY!
AND I'M GOOD AT THAT, SURE...
...BUT ONLY IF I'M BEING MEAN!
AND I CAN'T DO THAT TO KIDS!
I MIGHT DISCOURAGE THEM FROM FLYING!
THAT'S THE LAST THING I WANT TO DO.
MAKE THEM WANT TO FLY?
HMM...
AH-HA!
HUH? WHAT IS IT?
UH, NOTHING!
LISTEN, I'LL SEE YOU IN CLASS TOMORROW, OKAY?
PAF!
UM, SURE?

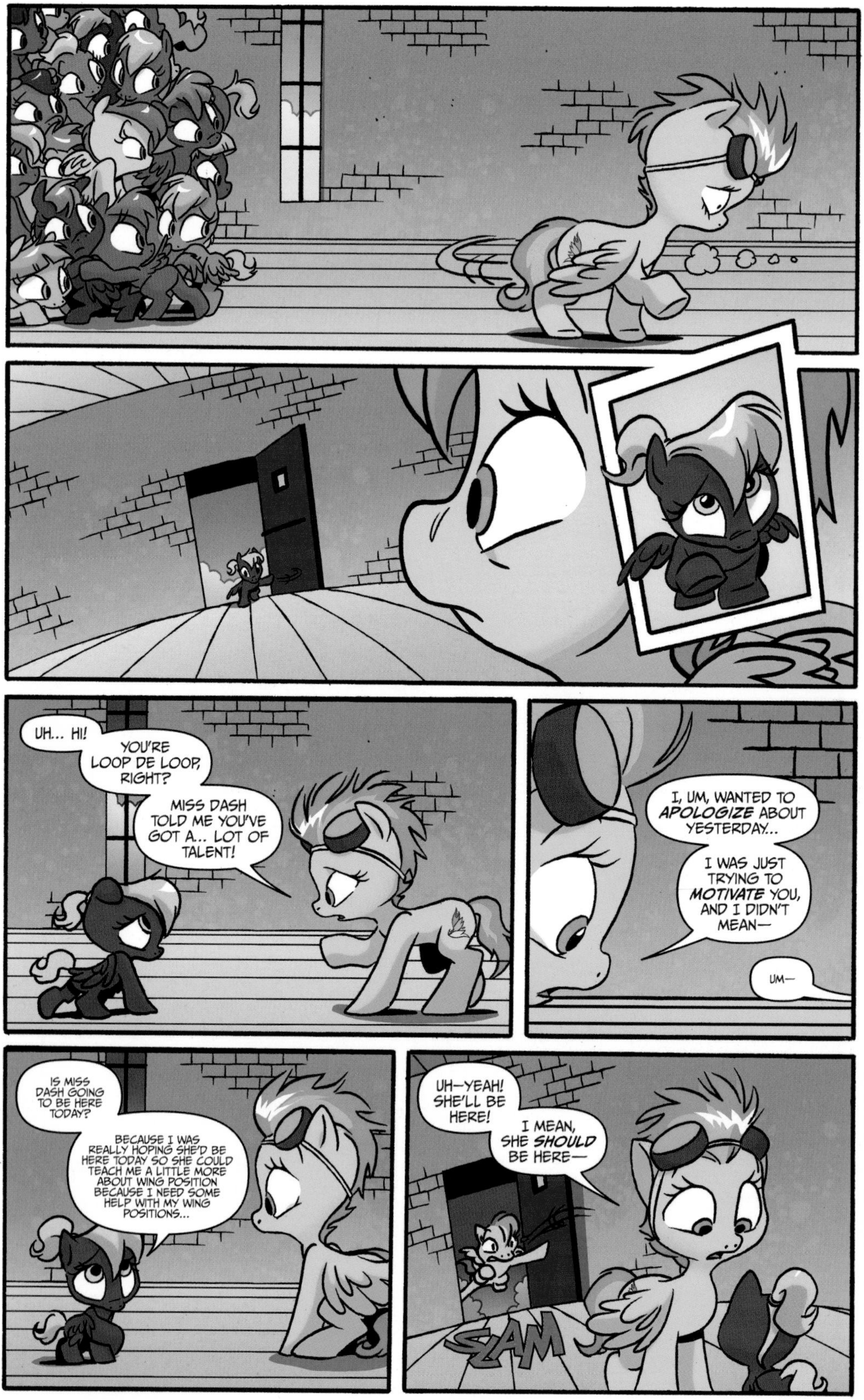

UH... HI!
YOU'RE LOOP DE LOOP, RIGHT?
MISS DASH TOLD ME YOU'VE GOT A... LOT OF TALENT!
I, UM, WANTED TO APOLOGIZE ABOUT YESTERDAY...
I WAS JUST TRYING TO MOTIVATE YOU, AND I DIDN'T MEAN—
UM—
IS MISS DASH GOING TO BE HERE TODAY?
BECAUSE I WAS REALLY HOPING SHE'D BE HERE TODAY SO SHE COULD TEACH ME A LITTLE MORE ABOUT WING POSITION BECAUSE I NEED SOME HELP WITH MY WING POSITIONS...
UH—YEAH! SHE'LL BE HERE!
I MEAN, SHE SHOULD BE HERE—
SLAM

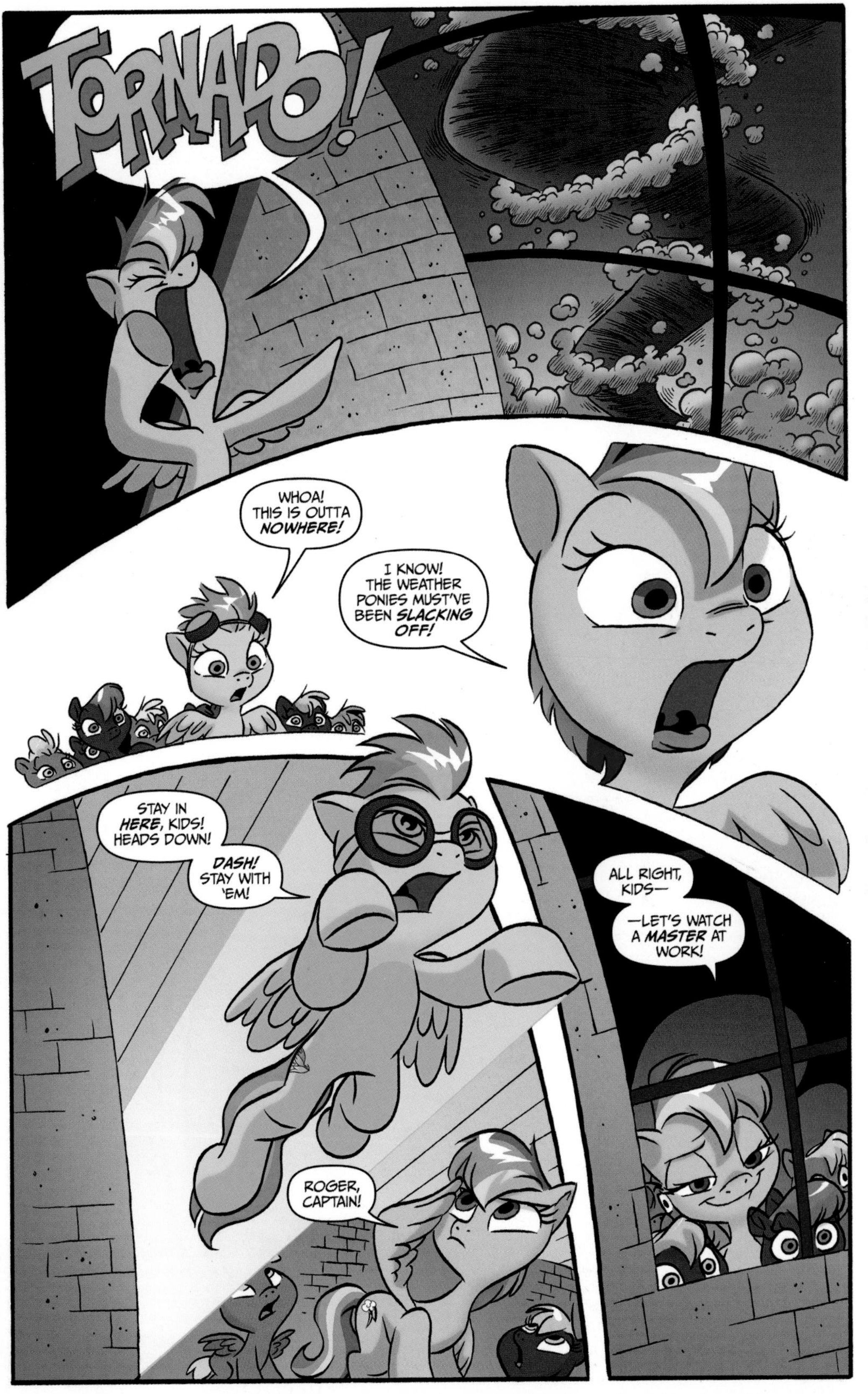
TORNADO!
WHOA! THIS IS OUTTA NOWHERE!
I KNOW! THE WEATHER PONIES MUST'VE BEEN SLACKING OFF!
STAY IN HERE, KIDS! HEADS DOWN!
DASH! STAY WITH 'EM!
ROGER, CAPTAIN!
ALL RIGHT, KIDS—
—LET'S WATCH A MASTER AT WORK!

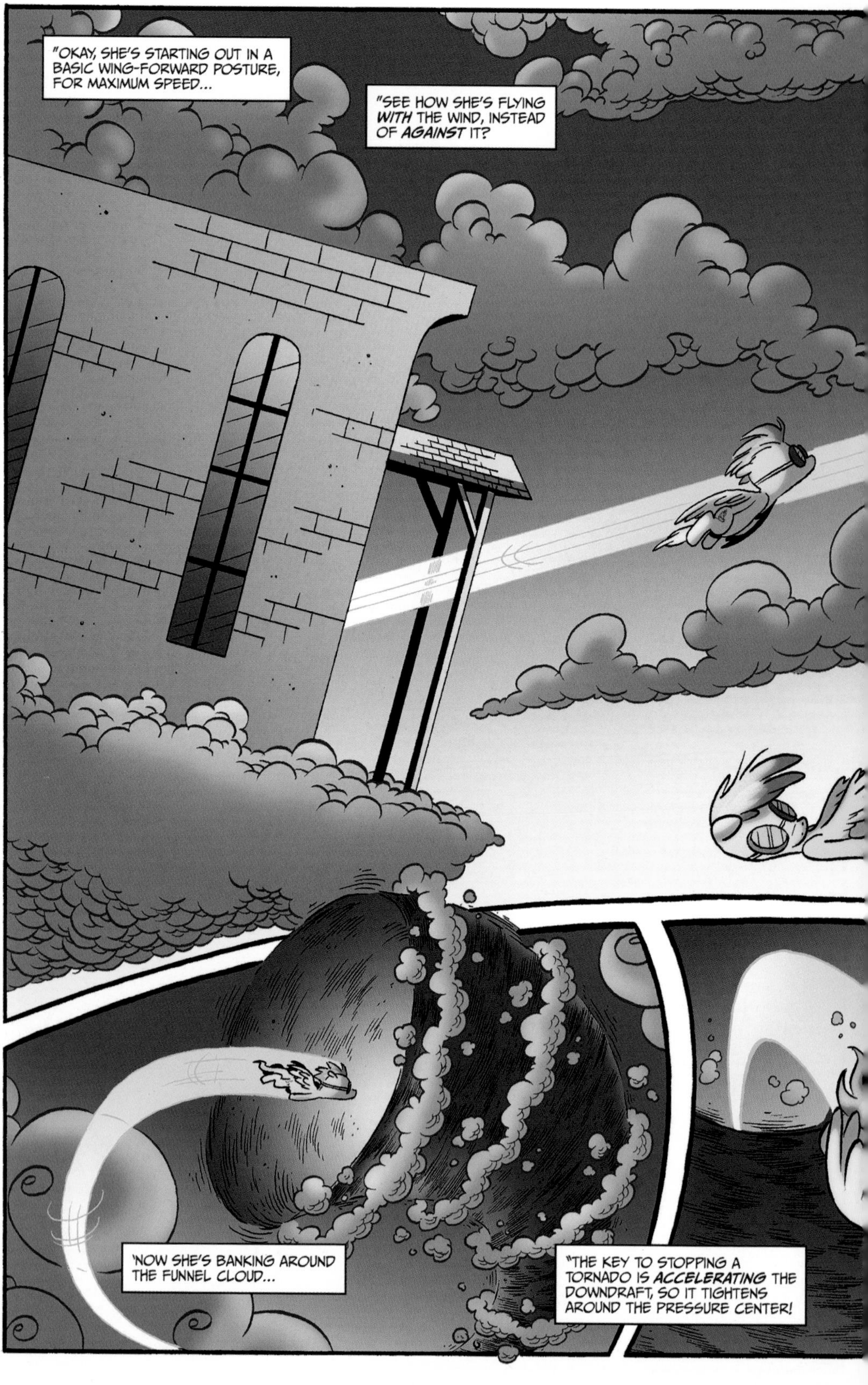
"OKAY, SHE'S STARTING OUT IN A BASIC WING-FORWARD POSTURE, FOR MAXIMUM SPEED...
"SEE HOW SHE'S FLYING *WITH* THE WIND, INSTEAD OF *AGAINST* IT?
'NOW SHE'S BANKING AROUND THE FUNNEL CLOUD...
"THE KEY TO STOPPING A TORNADO IS *ACCELERATING* THE DOWNDRAFT, SO IT TIGHTENS AROUND THE PRESSURE CENTER!

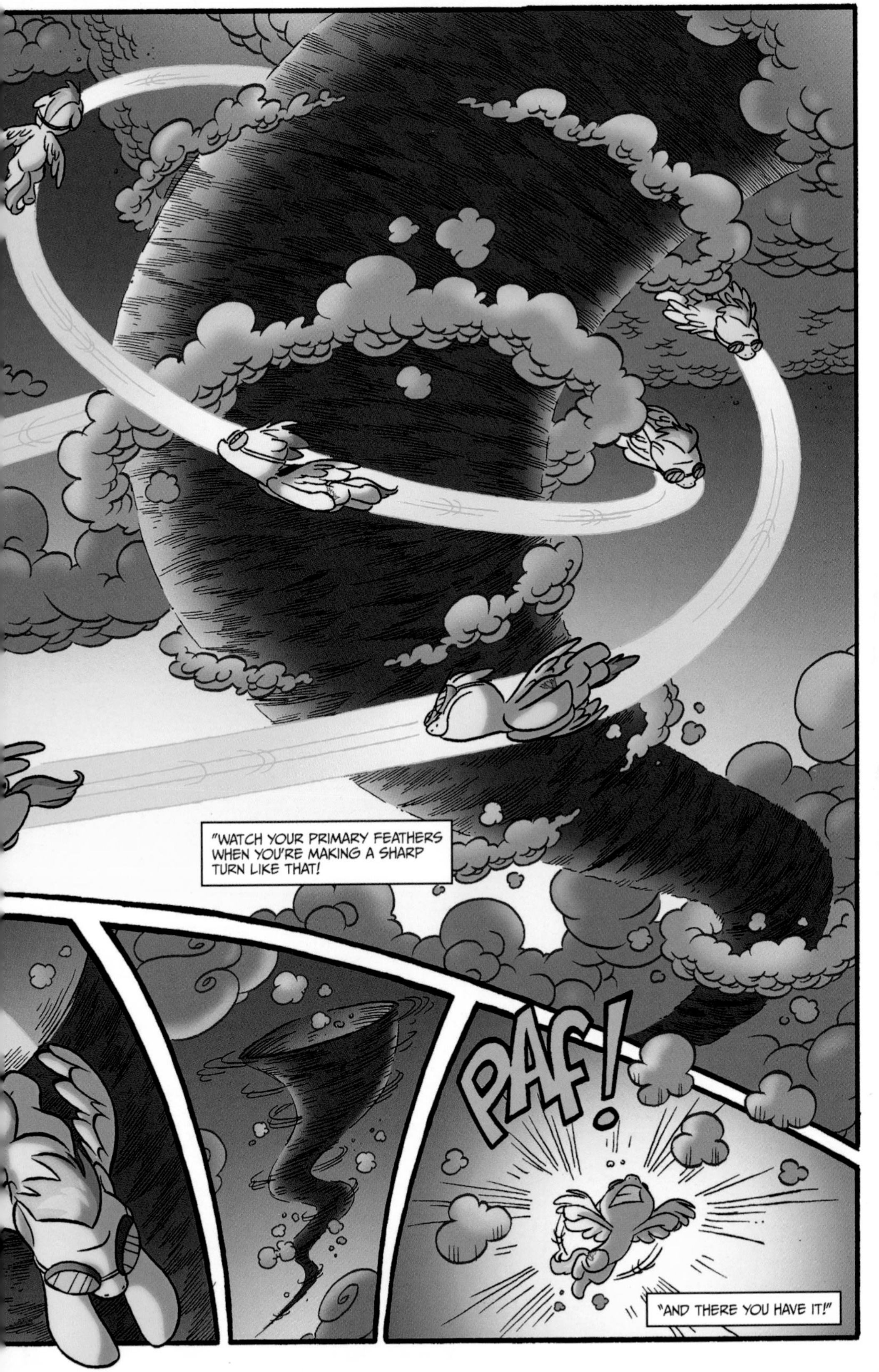
"WATCH YOUR PRIMARY FEATHERS WHEN YOU'RE MAKING A SHARP TURN LIKE THAT!
PAF!
"AND THERE YOU HAVE IT!"

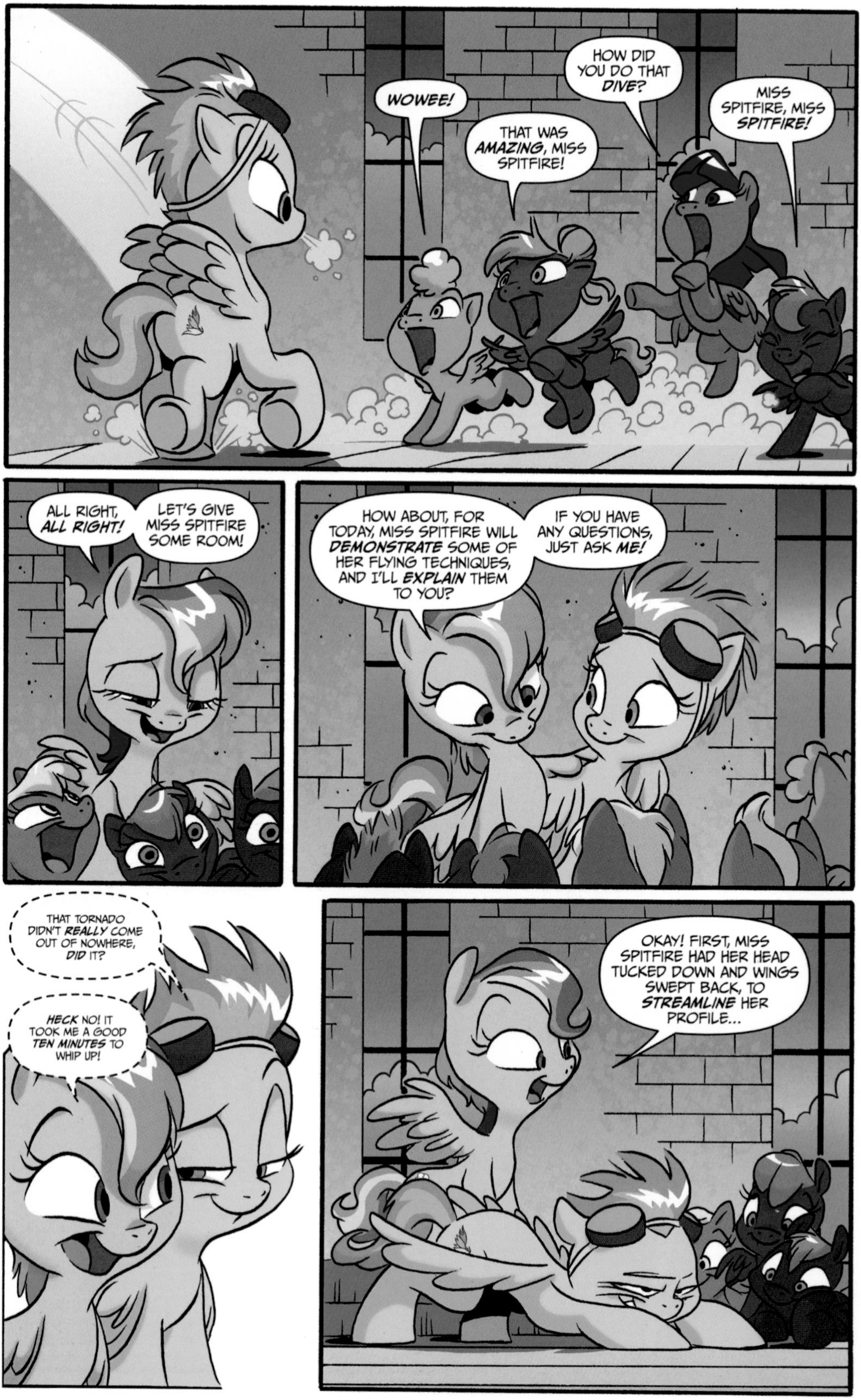
WOWEE!
THAT WAS AMAZING, MISS SPITFIRE!
HOW DID YOU DO THAT DIVE?
MISS SPITFIRE, MISS SPITFIRE!
ALL RIGHT, ALL RIGHT!
LET'S GIVE MISS SPITFIRE SOME ROOM!
HOW ABOUT, FOR TODAY, MISS SPITFIRE WILL DEMONSTRATE SOME OF HER FLYING TECHNIQUES, AND I'LL EXPLAIN THEM TO YOU?
IF YOU HAVE ANY QUESTIONS, JUST ASK ME!
THAT TORNADO DIDN'T REALLY COME OUT OF NOWHERE, DID IT?
HECK NO! IT TOOK ME A GOOD TEN MINUTES TO WHIP UP!
OKAY! FIRST, MISS SPITFIRE HAD HER HEAD TUCKED DOWN AND WINGS SWEPT BACK, TO STREAMLINE HER PROFILE...

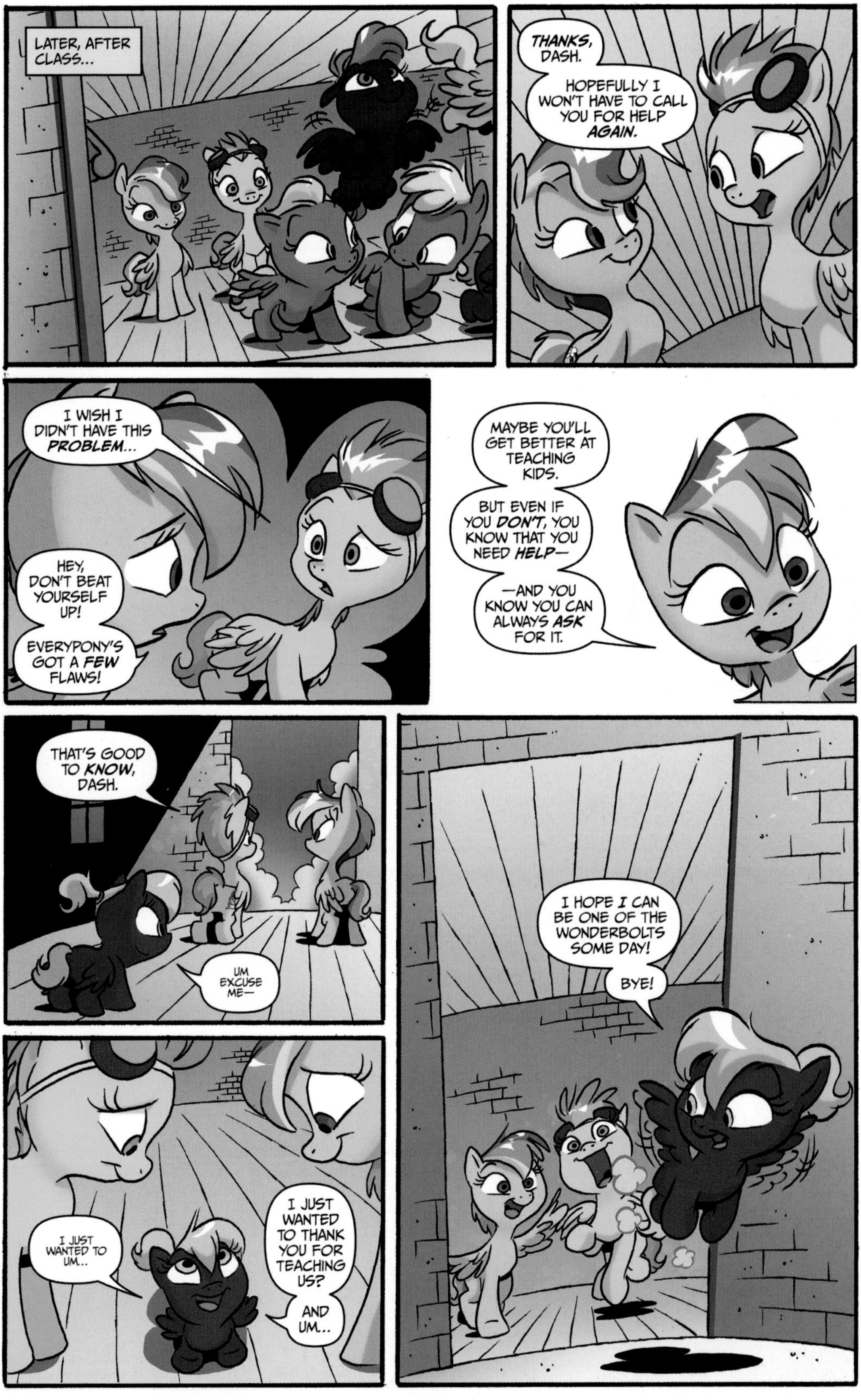
LATER, AFTER CLASS...
THANKS, DASH.
HOPEFULLY I WON'T HAVE TO CALL YOU FOR HELP AGAIN.
I WISH I DIDN'T HAVE THIS PROBLEM...
HEY, DON'T BEAT YOURSELF UP!
EVERYPONY'S GOT A FEW FLAWS!
MAYBE YOU'LL GET BETTER AT TEACHING KIDS.
BUT EVEN IF YOU DON'T, YOU KNOW THAT YOU NEED HELP—
—AND YOU KNOW YOU CAN ALWAYS ASK FOR IT.
THAT'S GOOD TO KNOW, DASH.
UM EXCUSE ME—
I JUST WANTED TO UM...
I JUST WANTED TO THANK YOU FOR TEACHING US?
AND UM...
I HOPE I CAN BE ONE OF THE WONDERBOLTS SOME DAY!
BYE!

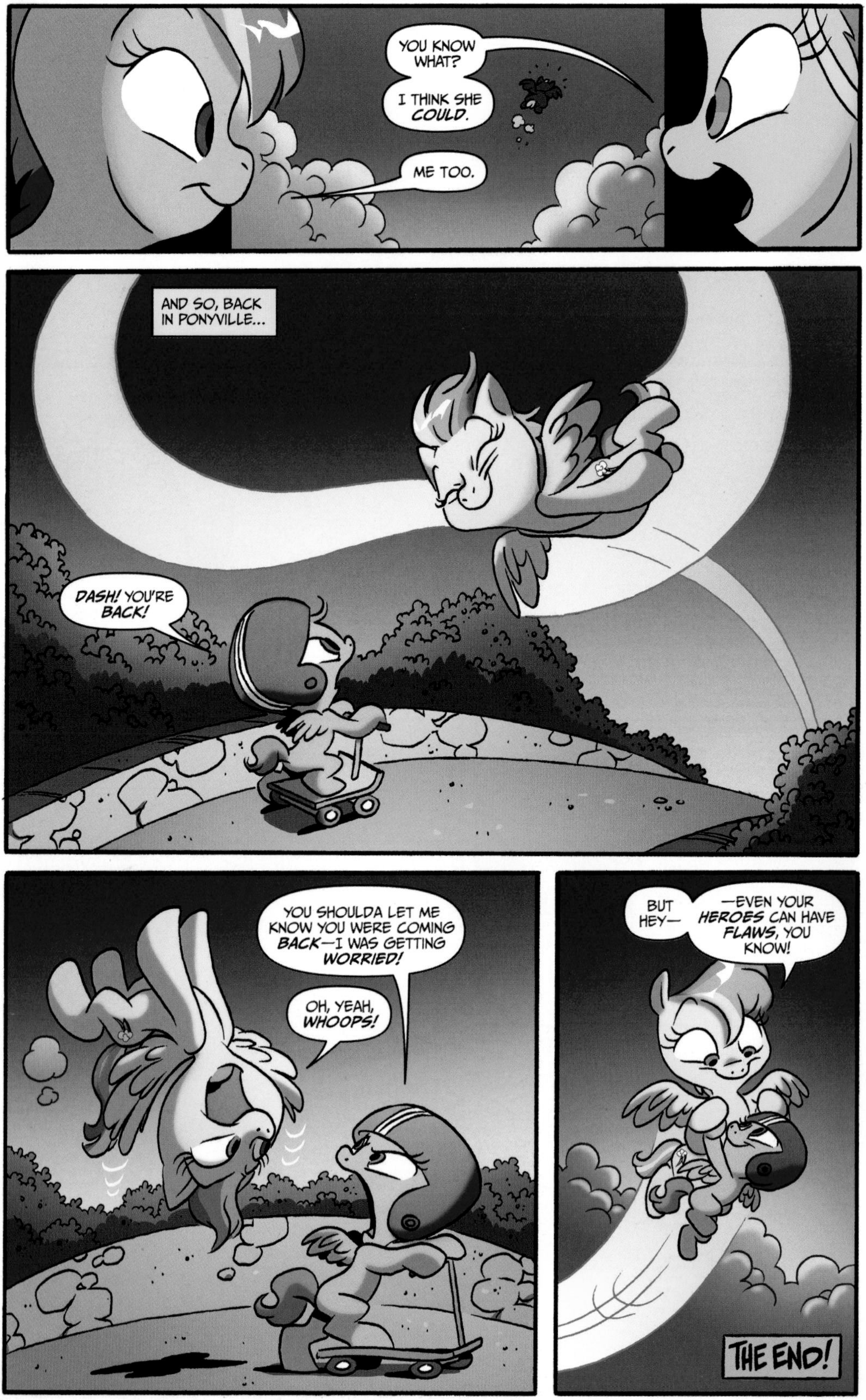
YOU KNOW WHAT?
I THINK SHE COULD.
ME TOO.
AND SO, BACK IN PONYVILLE...
DASH! YOU'RE BACK!
YOU SHOULDA LET ME KNOW YOU WERE COMING BACK—I WAS GETTING WORRIED!
OH, YEAH, WHOOPS!
BUT HEY—
—EVEN YOUR HEROES CAN HAVE FLAWS, YOU KNOW!
THE END!

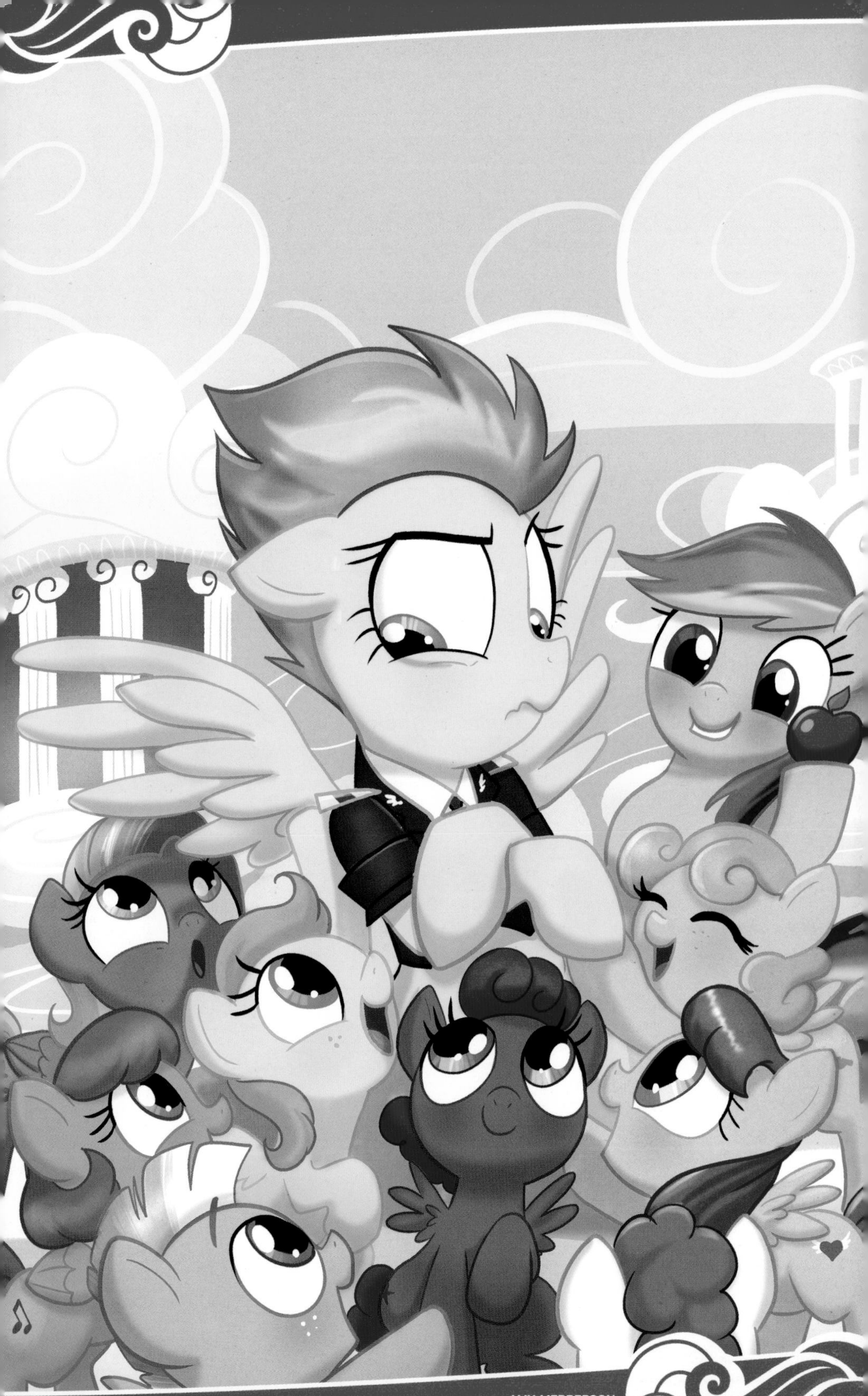

art by AMY MEBBERSON

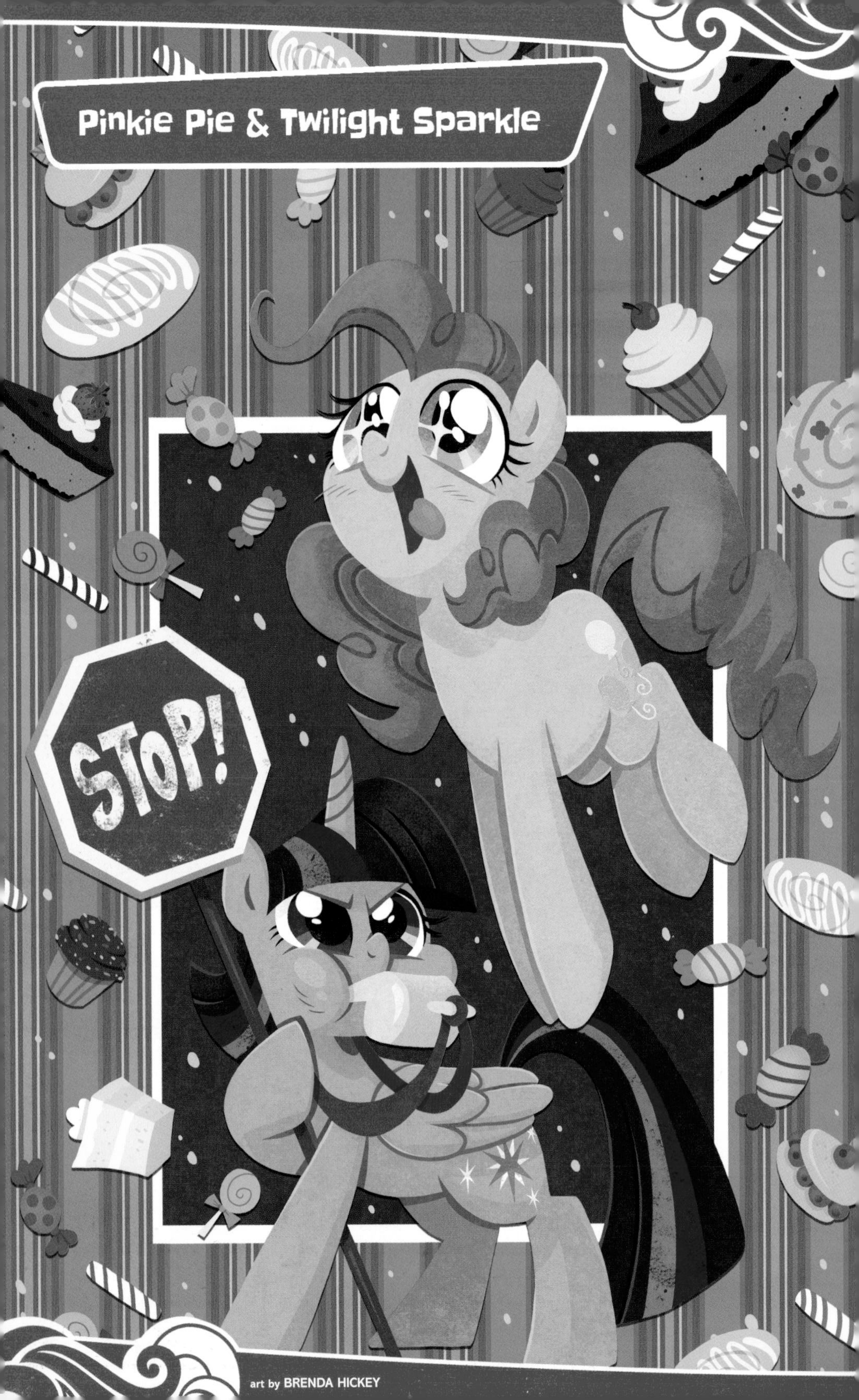
Pinkie Pie & Twilight Sparkle
STOP!
art by BRENDA HICKEY

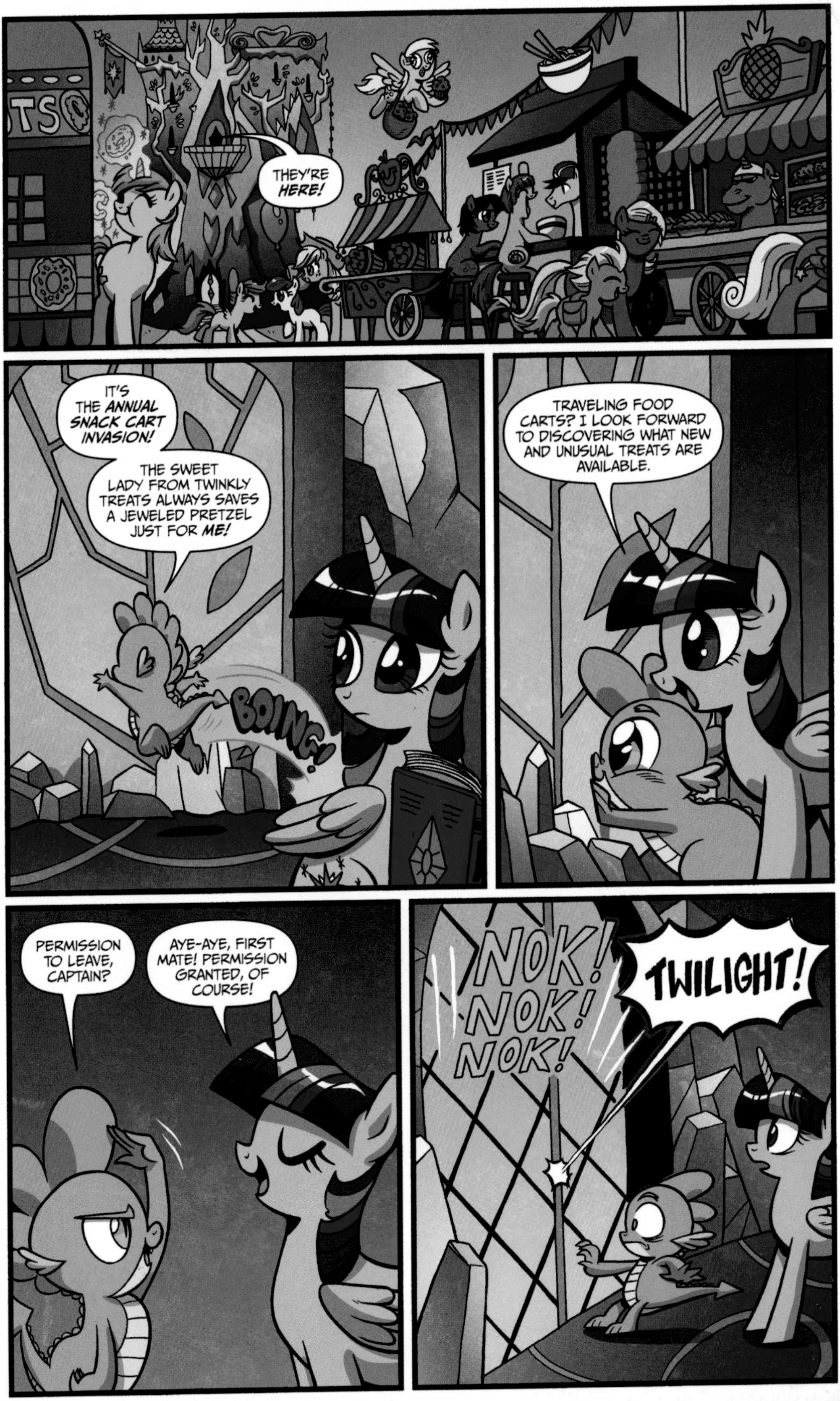

OTS
THEY'RE HERE!
IT'S THE ANNUAL SNACK CART INVASION!
THE SWEET LADY FROM TWINKLY TREATS ALWAYS SAVES A JEWELED PRETZEL JUST FOR ME!
BOING!
TRAVELING FOOD CARTS? I LOOK FORWARD TO DISCOVERING WHAT NEW AND UNUSUAL TREATS ARE AVAILABLE.
PERMISSION TO LEAVE, CAPTAIN?
AYE-AYE, FIRST MATE! PERMISSION GRANTED, OF COURSE!
NOK! NOK! NOK!
TWILIGHT!

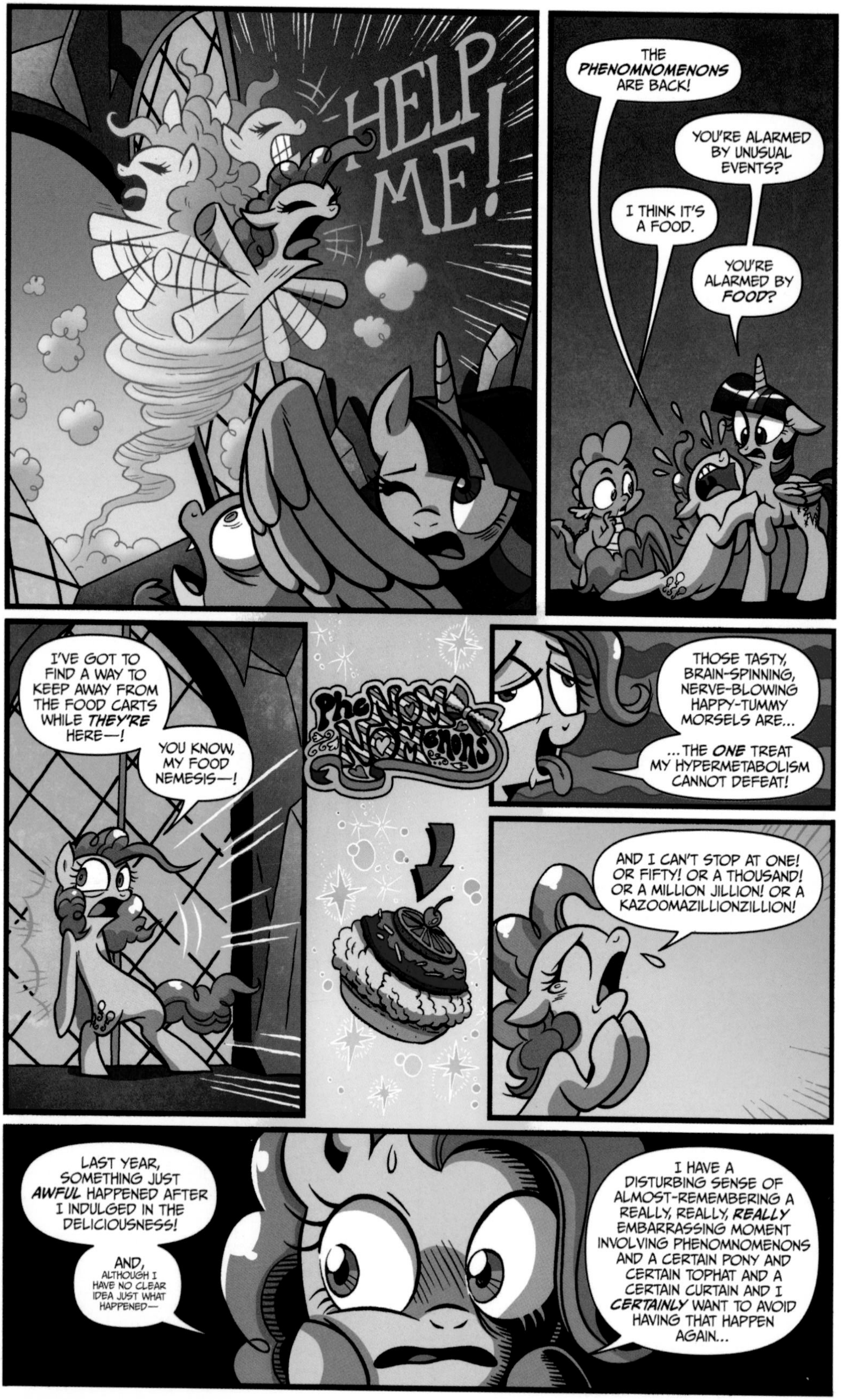
HELP ME!
THE PHENOMNOMENONS ARE BACK!
YOU'RE ALARMED BY UNUSUAL EVENTS?
I THINK IT'S A FOOD.
YOU'RE ALARMED BY FOOD?
I'VE GOT TO FIND A WAY TO KEEP AWAY FROM THE FOOD CARTS WHILE THEY'RE HERE—!
YOU KNOW, MY FOOD NEMESIS—!
THOSE TASTY, BRAIN-SPINNING, NERVE-BLOWING HAPPY-TUMMY MORSELS ARE...
...THE ONE TREAT MY HYPERMETABOLISM CANNOT DEFEAT!
AND I CAN'T STOP AT ONE! OR FIFTY! OR A THOUSAND! OR A MILLION JILLION! OR A KAZOOMAZILLIONZILLION!
LAST YEAR, SOMETHING JUST AWFUL HAPPENED AFTER I INDULGED IN THE DELICIOUSNESS!
AND, ALTHOUGH I HAVE NO CLEAR IDEA JUST WHAT HAPPENED—
I HAVE A DISTURBING SENSE OF ALMOST-REMEMBERING A REALLY, REALLY, REALLY EMBARRASSING MOMENT INVOLVING PHENOMNOMENONS AND A CERTAIN PONY AND CERTAIN TOPHAT AND A CERTAIN CURTAIN AND I CERTAINLY WANT TO AVOID HAVING THAT HAPPEN AGAIN...

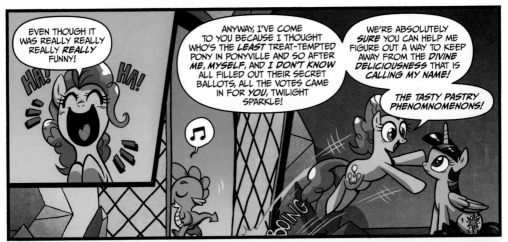

EVEN THOUGH IT WAS REALLY REALLY REALLY *REALLY* FUNNY!

HA! HA!

ANYWAY, I'VE COME TO YOU BECAUSE I THOUGHT WHO'S THE *LEAST* TREAT-TEMPTED PONY IN PONYVILLE AND SO AFTER *ME, MYSELF,* AND *I DON'T KNOW* ALL FILLED OUT THEIR SECRET BALLOTS, ALL THE VOTES CAME IN FOR *YOU,* TWILIGHT SPARKLE!

WE'RE ABSOLUTELY *SURE* YOU CAN HELP ME FIGURE OUT A WAY TO KEEP AWAY FROM THE *DIVINE DELICIOUSNESS* THAT IS CALLING MY NAME!

THE TASTY PASTRY PHENOMNOMENONS!

BOING

PINKIE PIE, YOU'VE COME TO THE RIGHT PLACE!

THERE'S *NO* PROBLEM I CAN'T RESEARCH AND FIND THE SOLUTION TO!

WE ARE *ON* THE JOB!

SO IT LOOKS LIKE TREATS ARE *OFF* THE AGENDA...

IT'S *JUST* ABOUT BREAKING A HABIT! HOW HARD CAN *THAT* BE?

PRETZELS...

BOUNCE!

WE JUST HAVE TO TURN TASTY TO DISTASTE!

HMMM...

PERHAPS A FORM OF AVERSION THERAPY?

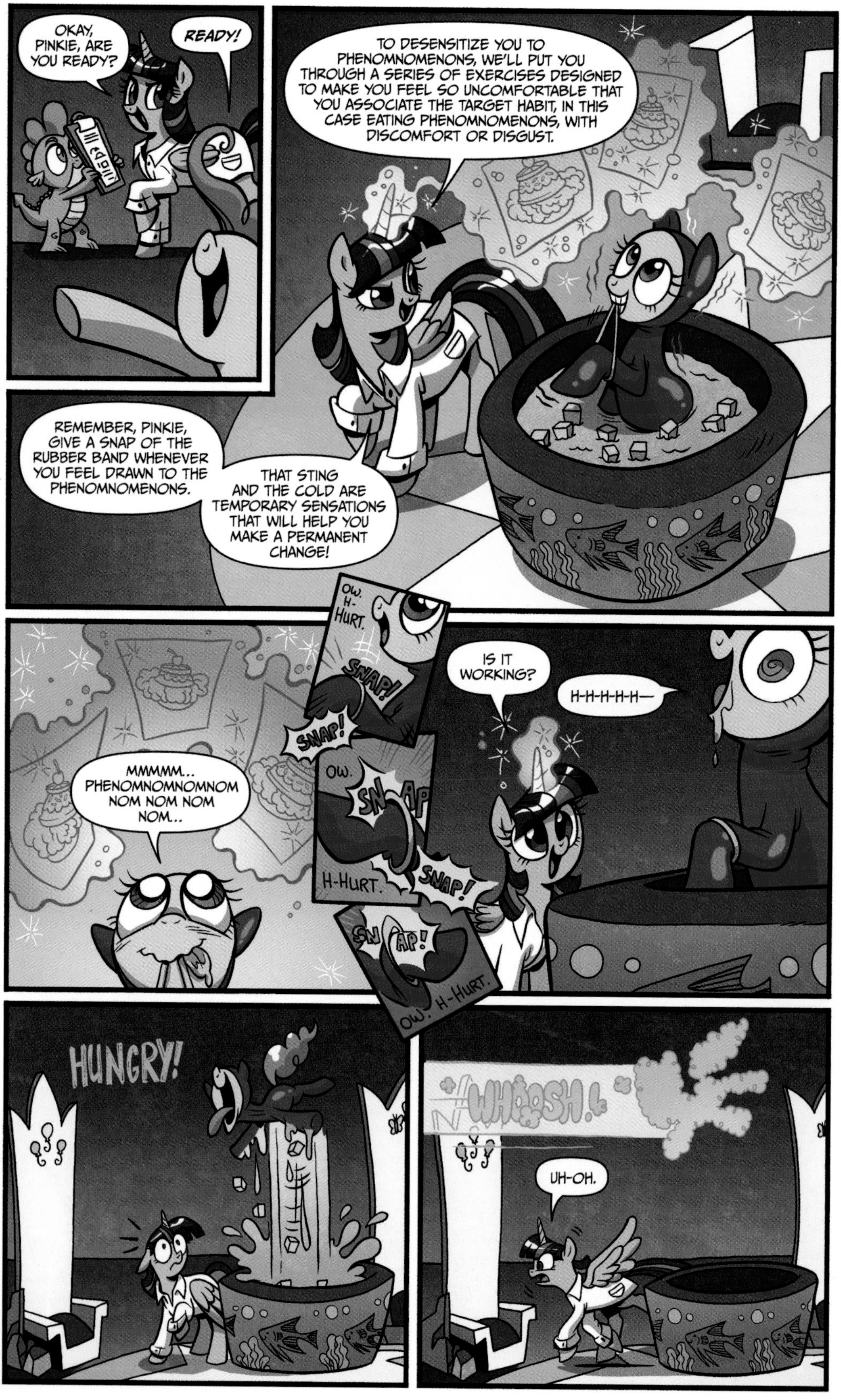
OKAY, PINKIE, ARE YOU READY?
READY!
TO DESENSITIZE YOU TO PHENOMNOMENONS, WE'LL PUT YOU THROUGH A SERIES OF EXERCISES DESIGNED TO MAKE YOU FEEL SO UNCOMFORTABLE THAT YOU ASSOCIATE THE TARGET HABIT, IN THIS CASE EATING PHENOMNOMENONS, WITH DISCOMFORT OR DISGUST.
REMEMBER, PINKIE, GIVE A SNAP OF THE RUBBER BAND WHENEVER YOU FEEL DRAWN TO THE PHENOMNOMENONS.
THAT STING AND THE COLD ARE TEMPORARY SENSATIONS THAT WILL HELP YOU MAKE A PERMANENT CHANGE!
MMMMM... PHENOMNOMNOMNOM NOM NOM NOM NOM...
OW. H-HURT.
SNAP!
SNAP!
OW.
SNAP!
H-HURT.
SNAP!
SNAP!
OW. H-HURT.
IS IT WORKING?
H-H-H-H-H—
HUNGRY!
WHOOSH!
UH-OH.

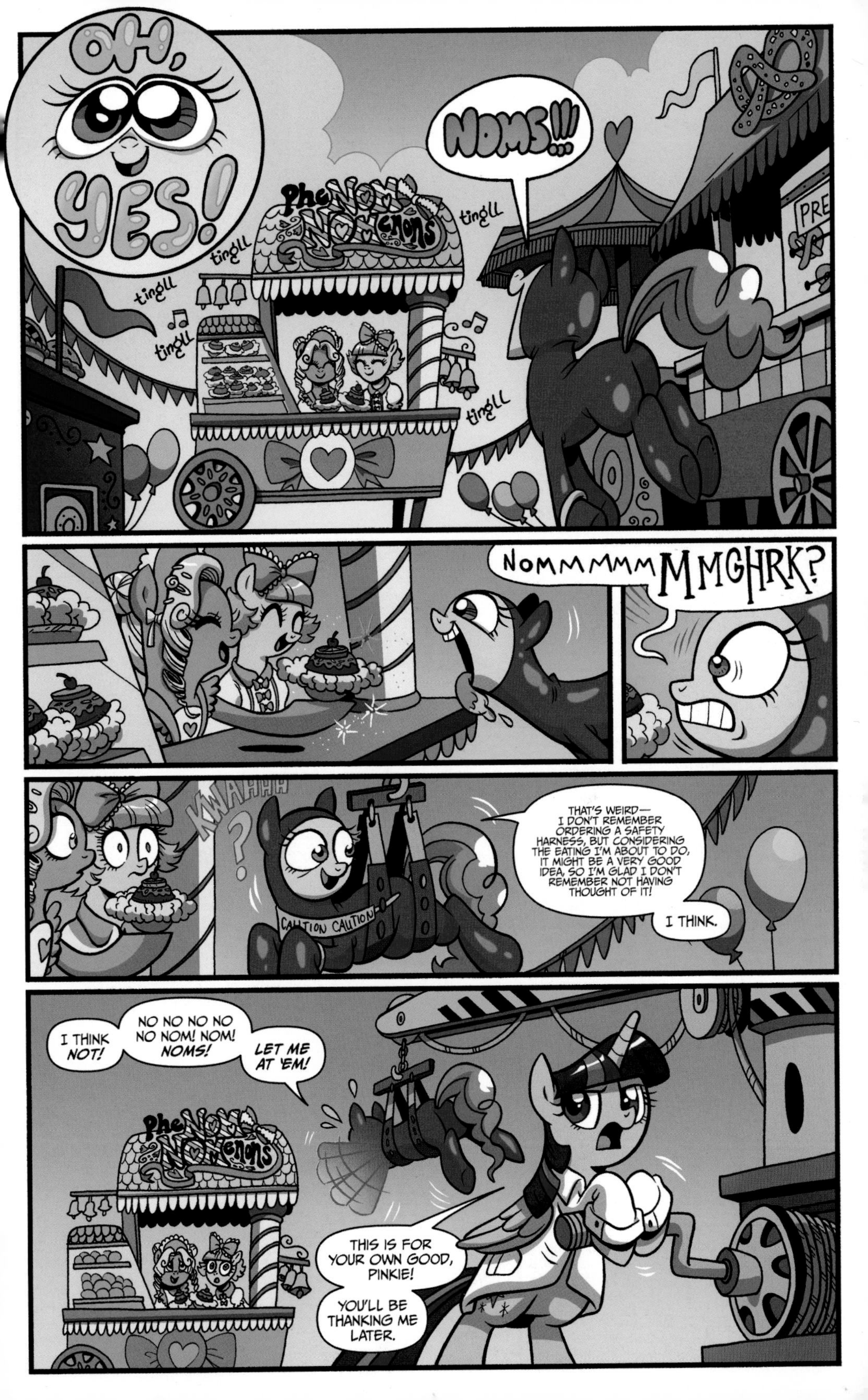
OH, YES!
tingLL
tingLL
tingLL
tingLL
tingLL
PheNOMNOMenons
NOMS!!!
NOMMMMMMMMGHRK?
KWAHHH
?
THAT'S WEIRD— I DON'T REMEMBER ORDERING A SAFETY HARNESS, BUT CONSIDERING THE EATING I'M ABOUT TO DO, IT MIGHT BE A VERY GOOD IDEA, SO I'M GLAD I DON'T REMEMBER NOT HAVING THOUGHT OF IT!
I THINK.
CAUTION CAUTION
I THINK *NOT!*
NO NO NO NO NO NOM! NOM! *NOMS!*
LET ME AT 'EM!
PheNOMNOMenons
THIS IS FOR YOUR OWN GOOD, PINKIE!
YOU'LL BE THANKING ME LATER.

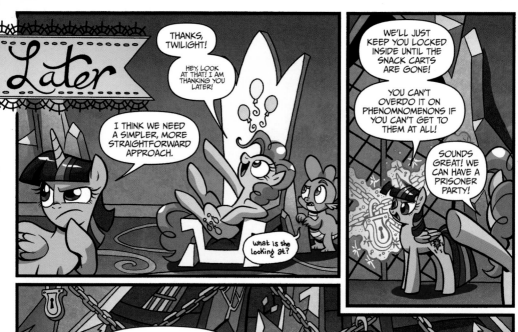

THANKS, TWILIGHT!

HEY, LOOK AT THAT! I AM THANKING YOU LATER!

I THINK WE NEED A SIMPLER, MORE STRAIGHTFORWARD APPROACH.

What is she looking at?

WE'LL JUST KEEP YOU LOCKED INSIDE UNTIL THE SNACK CARTS ARE GONE!

YOU CAN'T OVERDO IT ON PHENOMNOMENONS IF YOU CAN'T GET TO THEM AT ALL!

SOUNDS GREAT! WE CAN HAVE A PRISONER PARTY!

WE'VE ALREADY GOT LOCKS, SO WE'LL WEAR STRIPED PAJAMAS AND GET BAD HAIRCUTS AND EAT TERRIBLE LITTLE PRISON SNACK CAKES! IT'LL BE FIFTY-ELEVEN FLAVORS OF AWESOME AWFULNESS!

AND THERE'S THE SOUND OF THE PHENOMNOMENONS CART!

IT'S CALLING MY NAME, AND I CAN'T GET TO IT! SO FAR, SO GOOD, TWILIGHT!

tingll tingll tingll tingll tingll tingll tingll tingll

SO... SO... GOOD....

NOMSS

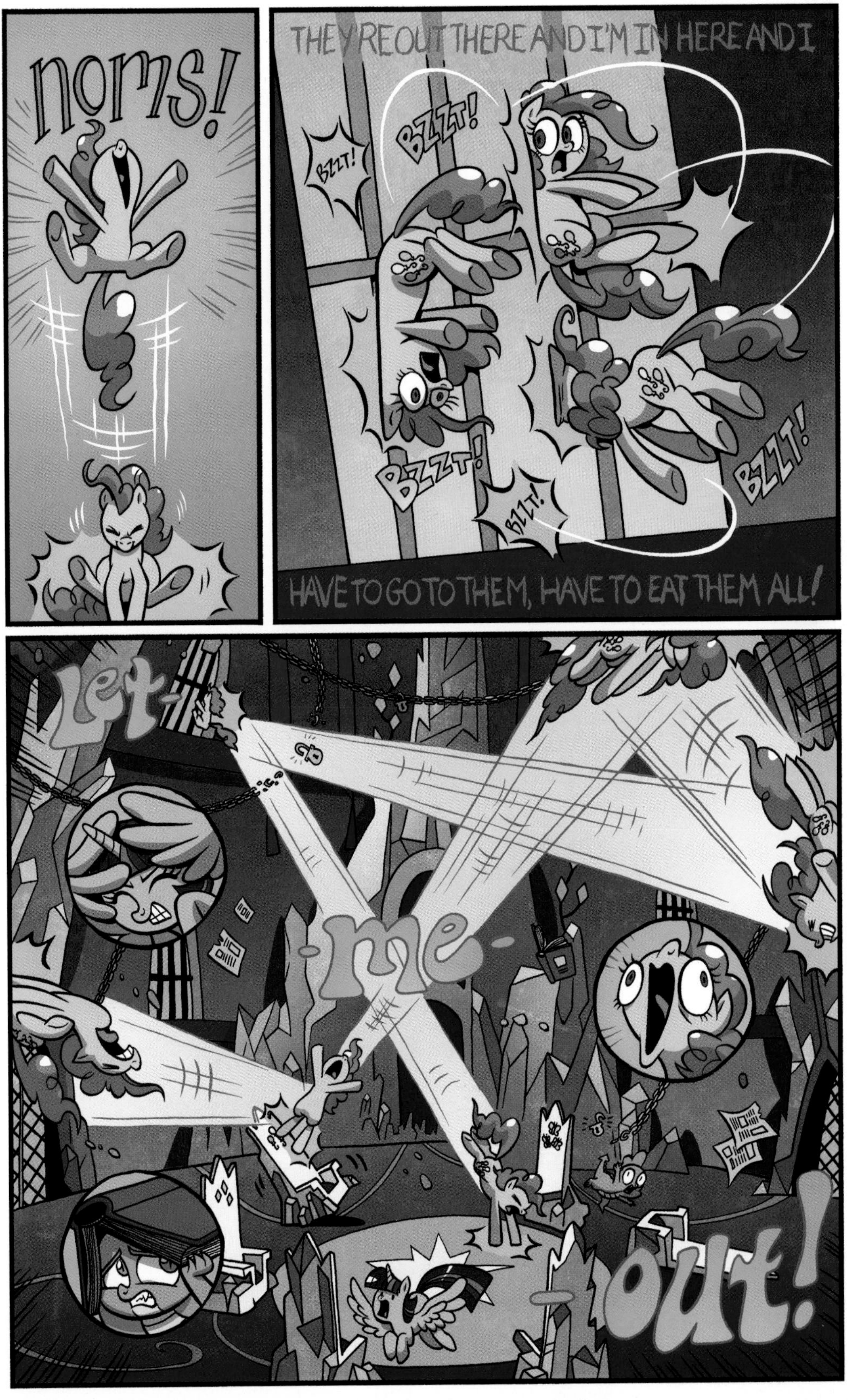
noms!
THEY'RE OUT THERE AND I'M IN HERE AND I
BZZT!
BZZT!
BZZT!
BZZT!
BZZT!
HAVE TO GO TO THEM, HAVE TO EAT THEM ALL!
Let-
-me-
-out!

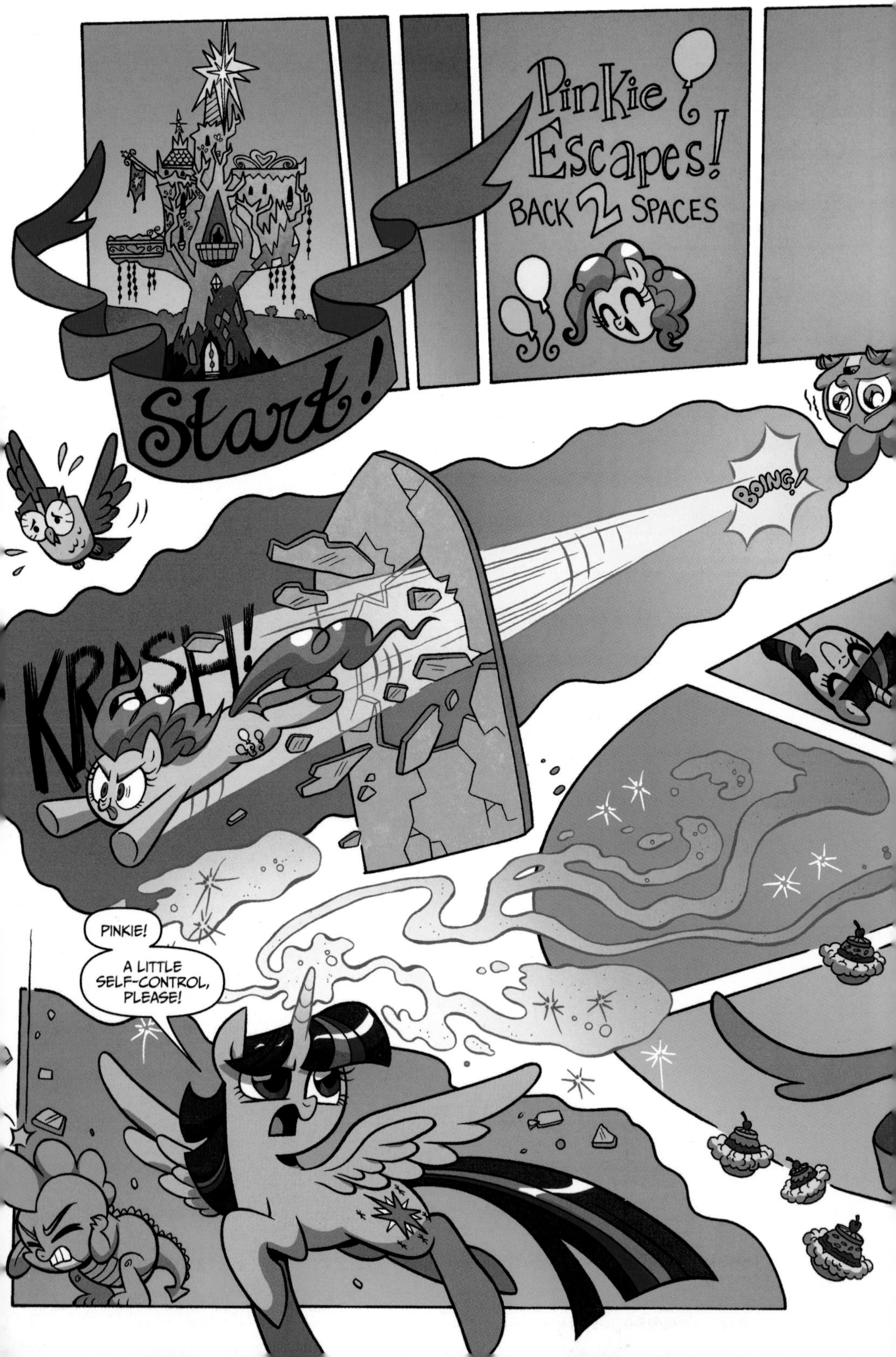
Start!
Pinkie Escapes!
BACK 2 SPACES
BOING!
KRASH!
PINKIE!
A LITTLE SELF-CONTROL, PLEASE!

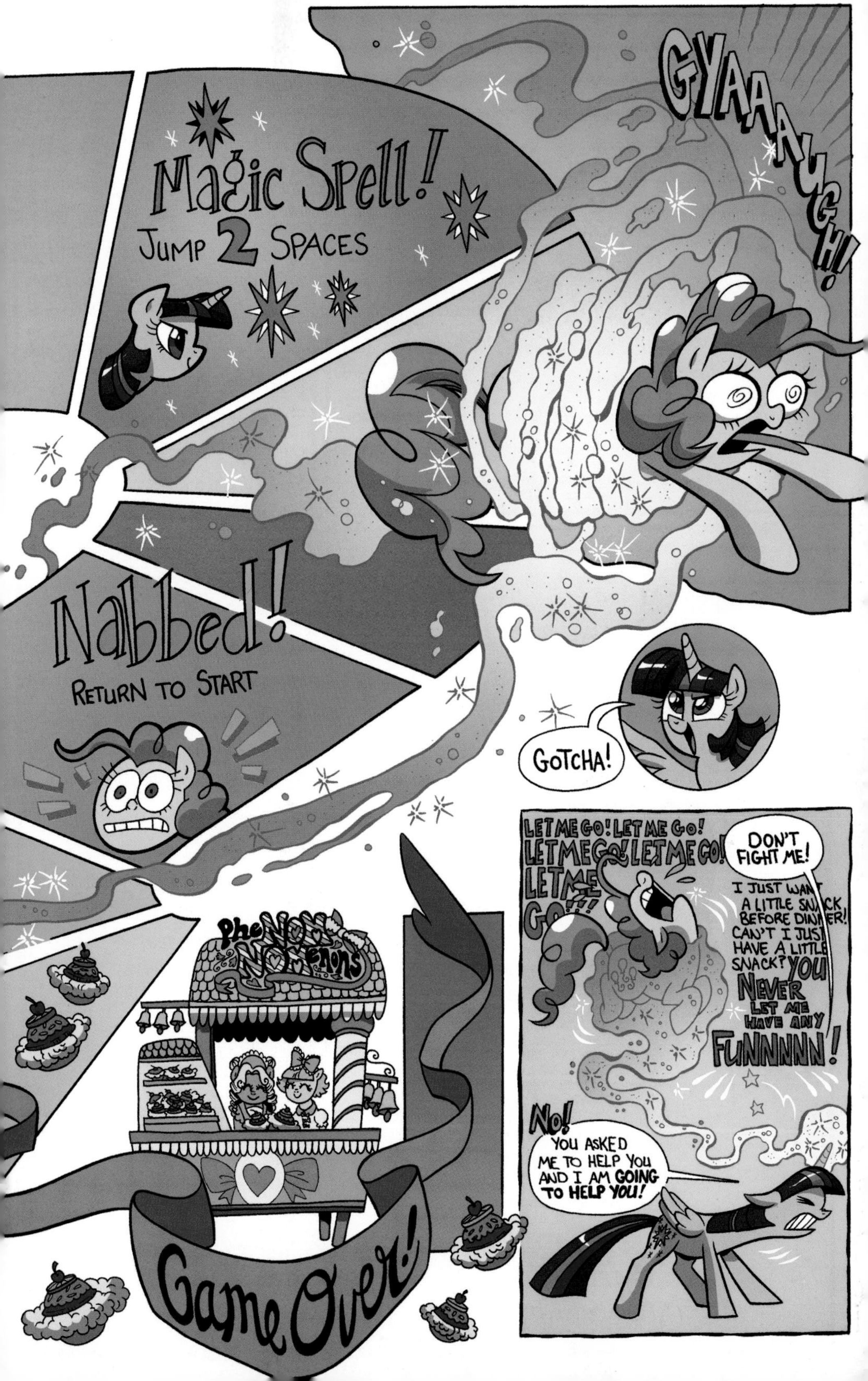
Magic Spell!
JUMP 2 SPACES
GYAAAAUGH!
Nabbed!
RETURN TO START
GOTCHA!
PheNOMNOMenons
Game Over!
LET ME GO! LET ME GO! LET ME GO! LET ME GO! LET ME GO!!!
DON'T FIGHT ME!
I JUST WANT A LITTLE SNACK BEFORE DINNER! CAN'T I JUST HAVE A LITTLE SNACK? YOU NEVER LET ME HAVE ANY FUNNNNN!
NO!
YOU ASKED ME TO HELP YOU AND I AM GOING TO HELP YOU!

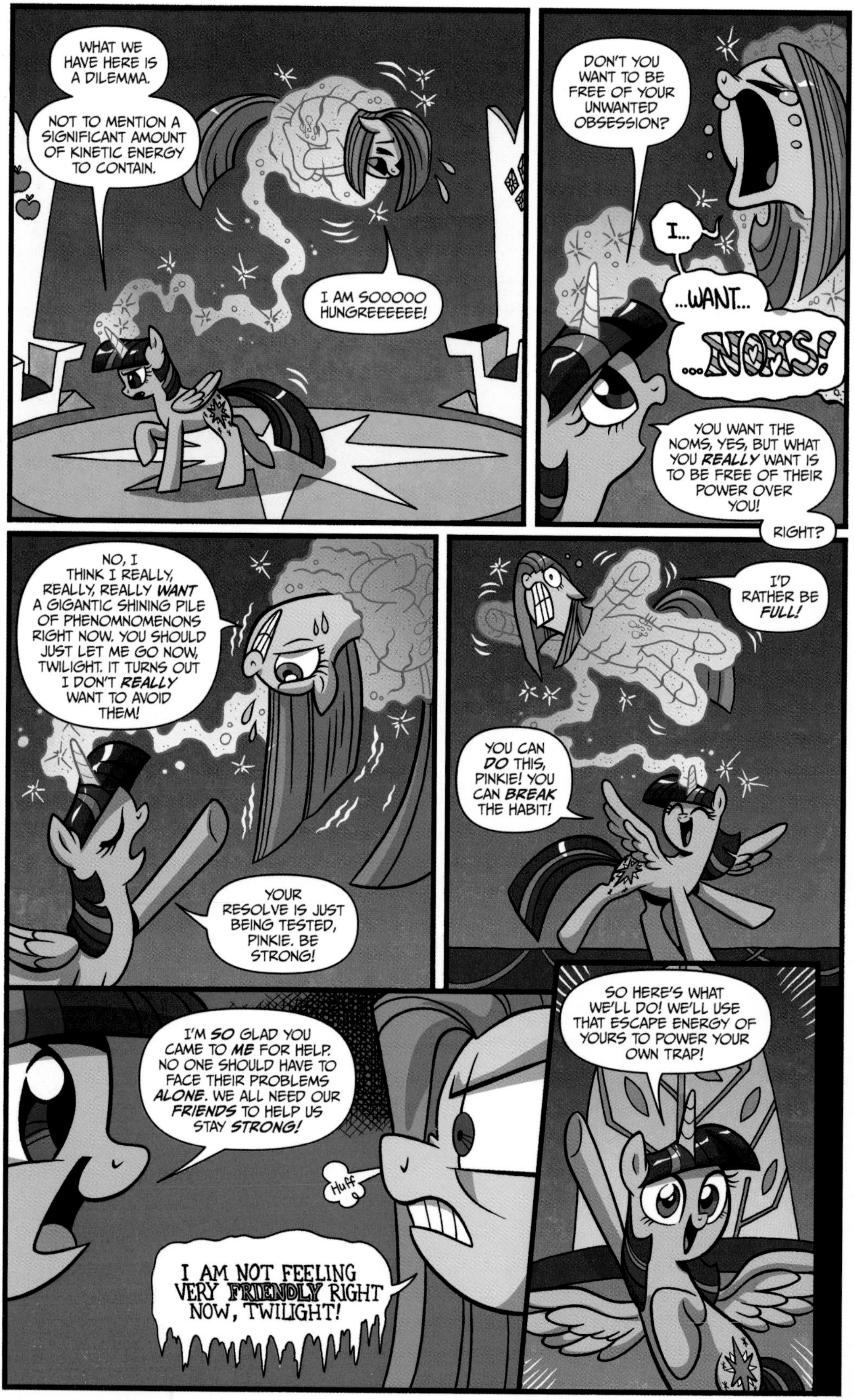

WHAT WE HAVE HERE IS A DILEMMA.
NOT TO MENTION A SIGNIFICANT AMOUNT OF KINETIC ENERGY TO CONTAIN.
I AM SOOOOO HUNGREEEEEE!
DON'T YOU WANT TO BE FREE OF YOUR UNWANTED OBSESSION?
I...
...WANT...
...NOMS!
YOU WANT THE NOMS, YES, BUT WHAT YOU REALLY WANT IS TO BE FREE OF THEIR POWER OVER YOU!
RIGHT?
NO, I THINK I REALLY, REALLY, REALLY WANT A GIGANTIC SHINING PILE OF PHENOMNOMENONS RIGHT NOW. YOU SHOULD JUST LET ME GO NOW, TWILIGHT. IT TURNS OUT I DON'T REALLY WANT TO AVOID THEM!
YOUR RESOLVE IS JUST BEING TESTED, PINKIE. BE STRONG!
I'D RATHER BE FULL!
YOU CAN DO THIS, PINKIE! YOU CAN BREAK THE HABIT!
I'M SO GLAD YOU CAME TO ME FOR HELP. NO ONE SHOULD HAVE TO FACE THEIR PROBLEMS ALONE. WE ALL NEED OUR FRIENDS TO HELP US STAY STRONG!
Huff
I AM NOT FEELING VERY FRIENDLY RIGHT NOW, TWILIGHT!
SO HERE'S WHAT WE'LL DO! WE'LL USE THAT ESCAPE ENERGY OF YOURS TO POWER YOUR OWN TRAP!

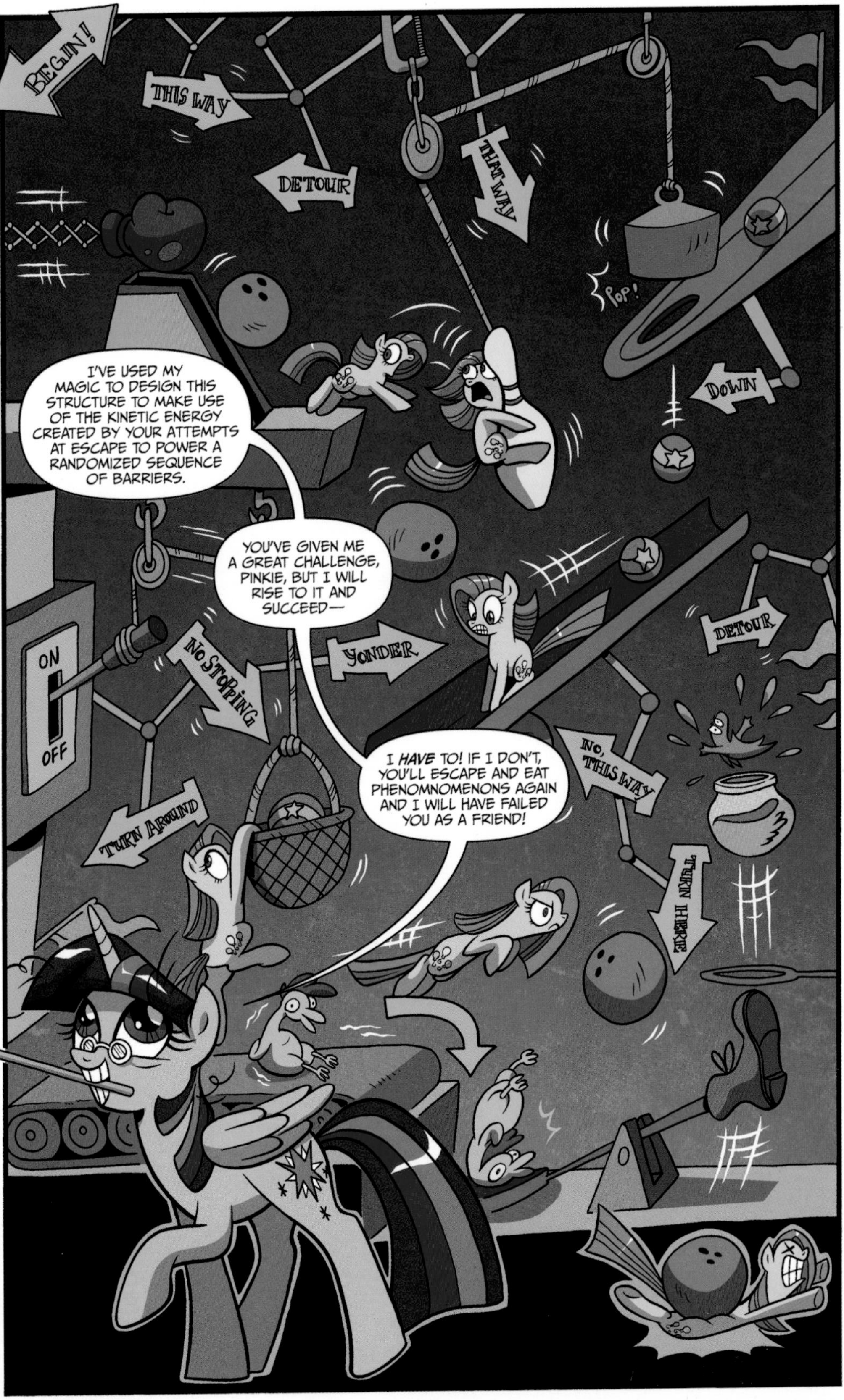
BEGIN!
THIS WAY
DETOUR
THAT WAY
POP!
DOWN
I'VE USED MY MAGIC TO DESIGN THIS STRUCTURE TO MAKE USE OF THE KINETIC ENERGY CREATED BY YOUR ATTEMPTS AT ESCAPE TO POWER A RANDOMIZED SEQUENCE OF BARRIERS.
YOU'VE GIVEN ME A GREAT CHALLENGE, PINKIE, BUT I WILL RISE TO IT AND SUCCEED—
ON
OFF
NO STOPPING
YONDER
DETOUR
NO, THIS WAY
I ***HAVE*** TO! IF I DON'T, YOU'LL ESCAPE AND EAT PHENOMNOMENONS AGAIN AND I WILL HAVE FAILED YOU AS A FRIEND!
TURN AROUND
TURN HERE

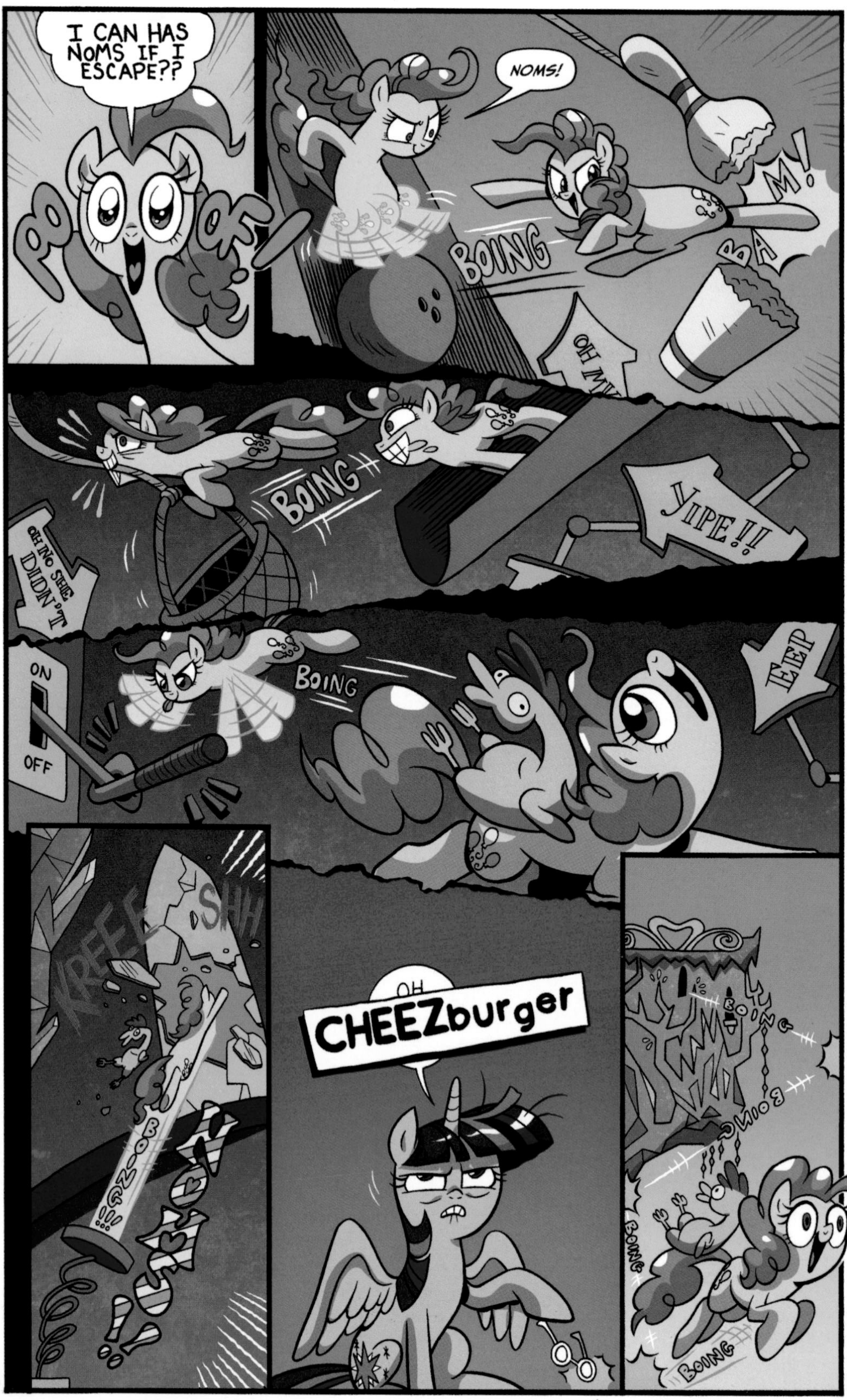

I CAN HAS NOMS IF I ESCAPE??
POOF
NOMS!
BOING
BAM!
BOING
YIPE!!
OH NO SHE DIDN'T
ON
OFF
BOING
EEP
KREEE
SHH!
BOING!!!
OH
CHEEZburger
BOING
BOING
BOING

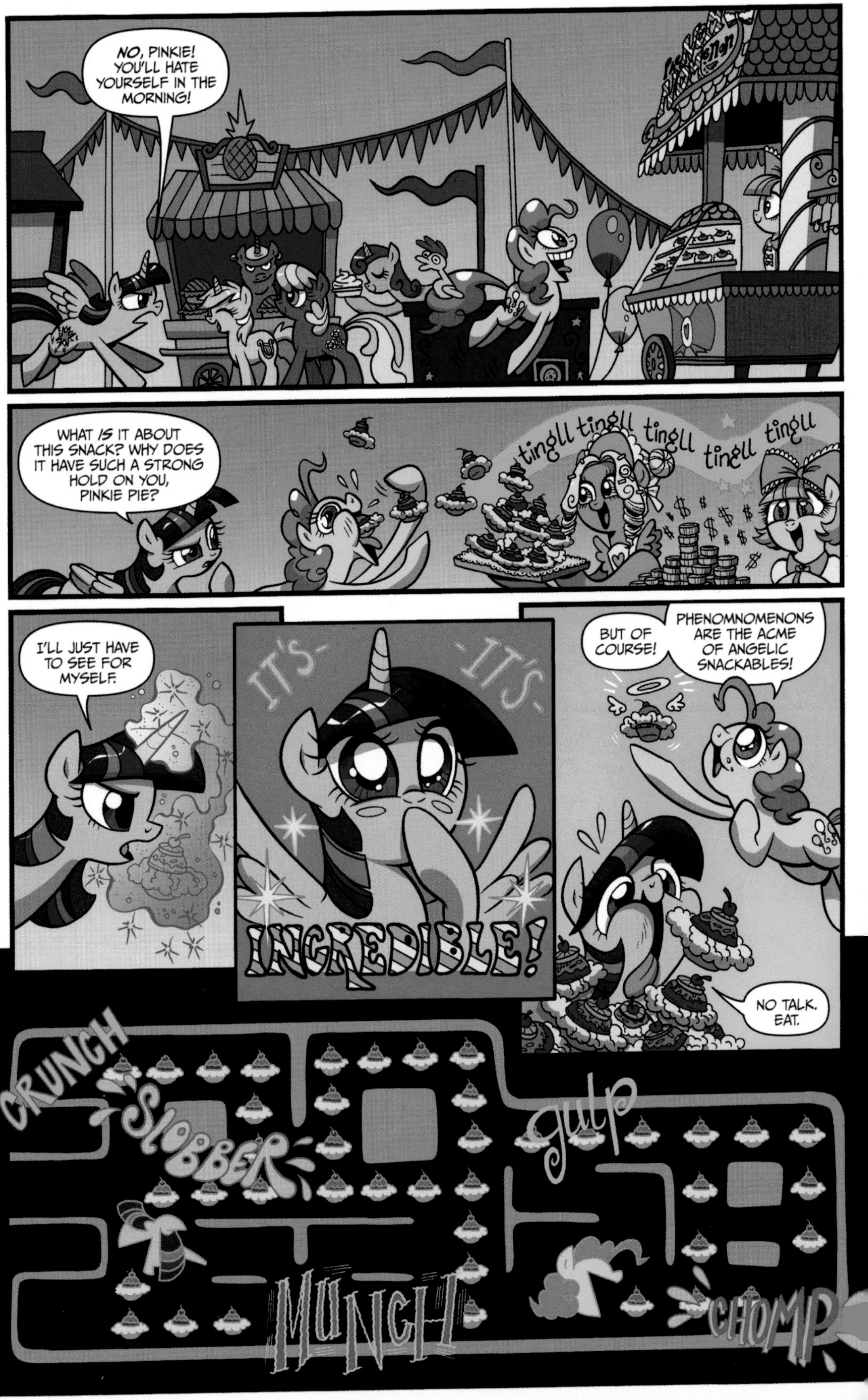

NO, PINKIE! YOU'LL HATE YOURSELF IN THE MORNING!
WHAT IS IT ABOUT THIS SNACK? WHY DOES IT HAVE SUCH A STRONG HOLD ON YOU, PINKIE PIE?
tingll tingll tingll tingll tingll
I'LL JUST HAVE TO SEE FOR MYSELF.
IT'S- -IT'S-
INCREDIBLE!
BUT OF COURSE!
PHENOMNOMENONS ARE THE ACME OF ANGELIC SNACKABLES!
NO TALK. EAT.
CRUNCH
SLOBBER
gulp
MUNCH
CHOMP

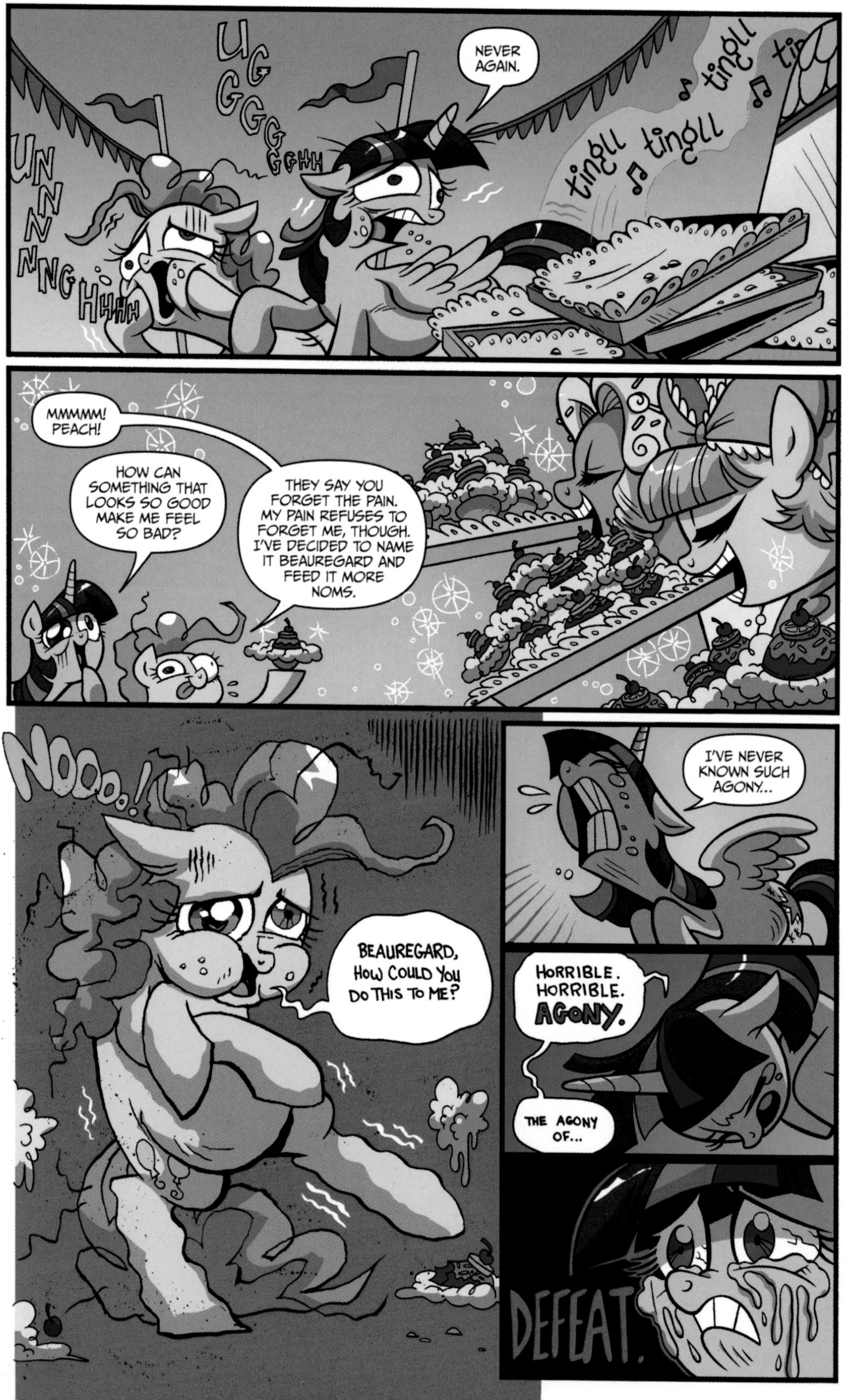
UNNNNNNGHHHHH
UGGGGGGHH
NEVER AGAIN.
tingll tingll tingll tin
MMMMM! PEACH!
HOW CAN SOMETHING THAT LOOKS SO GOOD MAKE ME FEEL SO BAD?
THEY SAY YOU FORGET THE PAIN. MY PAIN REFUSES TO FORGET ME, THOUGH. I'VE DECIDED TO NAME IT BEAUREGARD AND FEED IT MORE NOMS.
NOOo..!
BEAUREGARD, HOW COULD YOU DO THIS TO ME?
I'VE NEVER KNOWN SUCH AGONY...
HORRIBLE. HORRIBLE. AGONY.
THE AGONY OF...
DEFEAT.

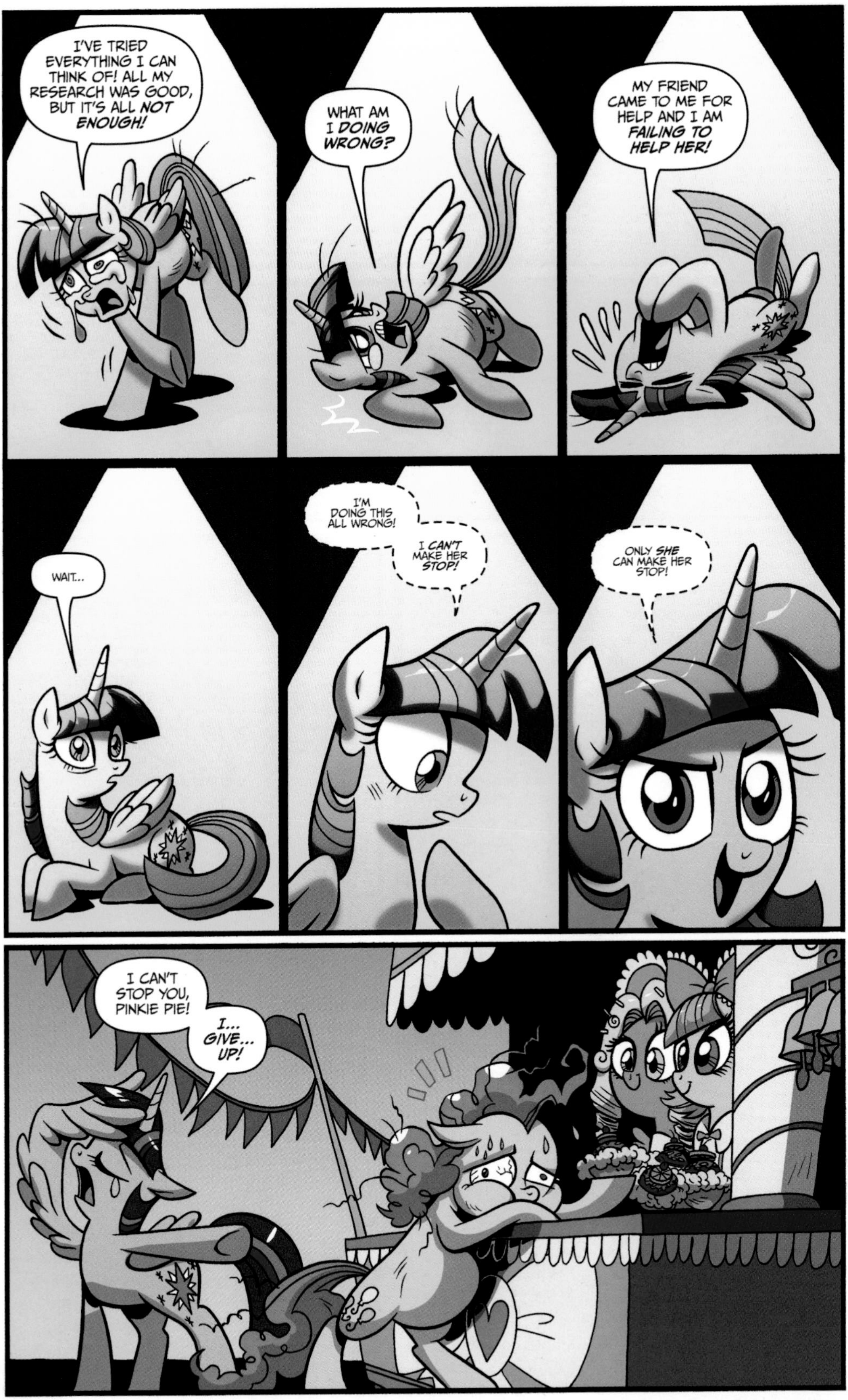
I'VE TRIED EVERYTHING I CAN THINK OF! ALL MY RESEARCH WAS GOOD, BUT IT'S ALL NOT ENOUGH!
WHAT AM I DOING WRONG?
MY FRIEND CAME TO ME FOR HELP AND I AM FAILING TO HELP HER!
WAIT...
I'M DOING THIS ALL WRONG!
I CAN'T MAKE HER STOP!
ONLY SHE CAN MAKE HER STOP!
I CAN'T STOP YOU, PINKIE PIE!
I... GIVE... UP!

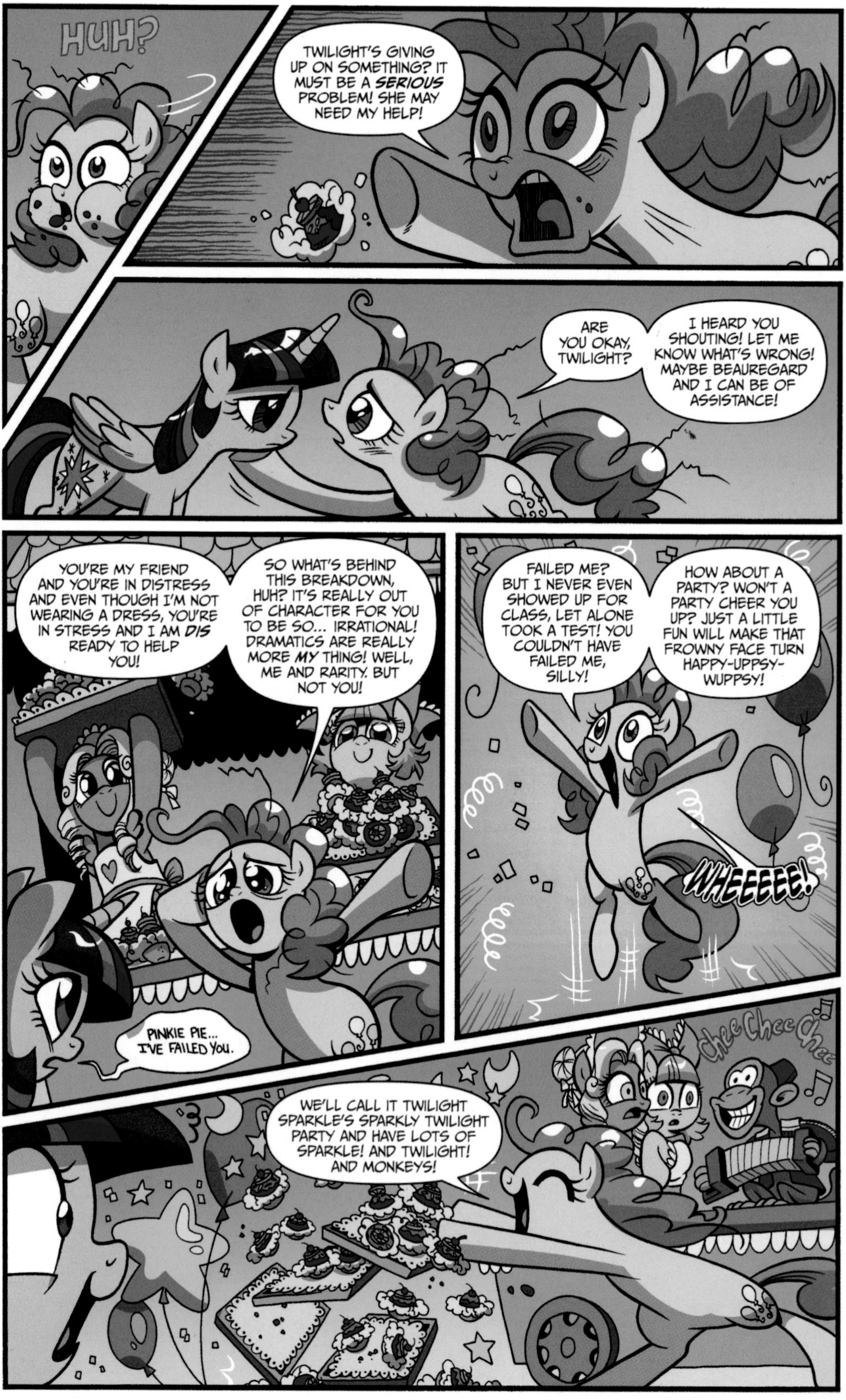
HUH?
TWILIGHT'S GIVING UP ON SOMETHING? IT MUST BE A *SERIOUS* PROBLEM! SHE MAY NEED MY HELP!
ARE YOU OKAY, TWILIGHT?
I HEARD YOU SHOUTING! LET ME KNOW WHAT'S WRONG! MAYBE BEAUREGARD AND I CAN BE OF ASSISTANCE!
YOU'RE MY FRIEND AND YOU'RE IN DISTRESS AND EVEN THOUGH I'M NOT WEARING A DRESS, YOU'RE IN STRESS AND I AM *DIS* READY TO HELP YOU!
SO WHAT'S BEHIND THIS BREAKDOWN, HUH? IT'S REALLY OUT OF CHARACTER FOR YOU TO BE SO... IRRATIONAL! DRAMATICS ARE REALLY MORE *MY* THING! WELL, ME AND RARITY. BUT NOT YOU!
PINKIE PIE... I'VE FAILED YOU.
FAILED ME? BUT I NEVER EVEN SHOWED UP FOR CLASS, LET ALONE TOOK A TEST! YOU COULDN'T HAVE FAILED ME, SILLY!
HOW ABOUT A PARTY? WON'T A PARTY CHEER YOU UP? JUST A LITTLE FUN WILL MAKE THAT FROWNY FACE TURN HAPPY-UPPSY-WUPPSY!
WHEEEEEE!
Chee Chee Chee
WE'LL CALL IT TWILIGHT SPARKLE'S SPARKLY TWILIGHT PARTY AND HAVE LOTS OF SPARKLE! AND TWILIGHT! AND MONKEYS!

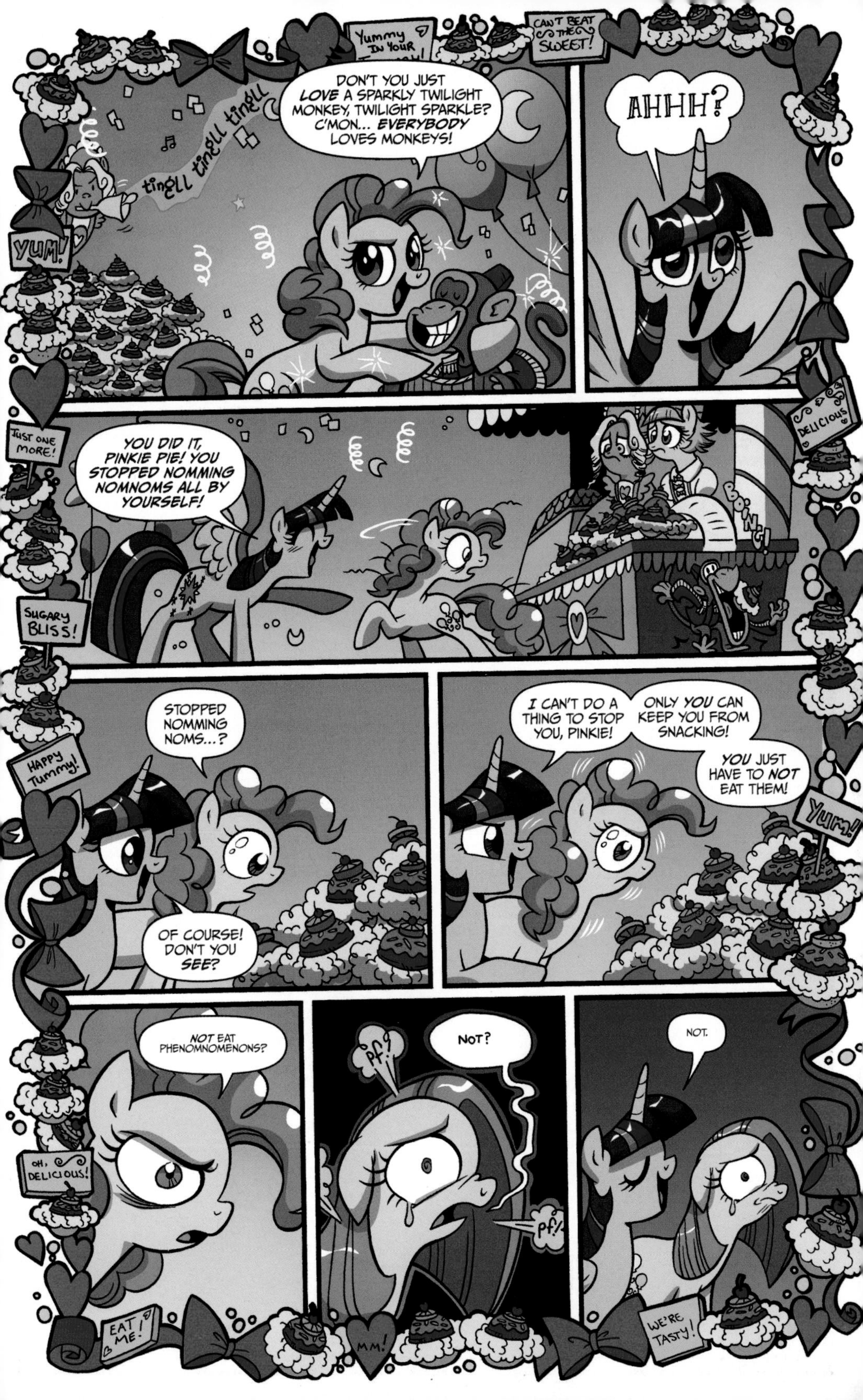

Yummy IN YOUR
CAN'T BEAT THE SWEET!
tingLL tingLL tingLL tingLL
DON'T YOU JUST *LOVE* A SPARKLY TWILIGHT MONKEY, TWILIGHT SPARKLE? C'MON... *EVERYBODY* LOVES MONKEYS!
YUM!
AHHH?
JUST ONE MORE!
YOU DID IT, PINKIE PIE! YOU STOPPED NOMMING NOMNOMS ALL BY YOURSELF!
DELICIOUS
BOING!
SUGARY BLISS!
STOPPED NOMMING NOMS...?
OF COURSE! DON'T YOU *SEE*?
HAPPY TUMMY!
I CAN'T DO A THING TO STOP YOU, PINKIE!
ONLY *YOU* CAN KEEP YOU FROM SNACKING!
YOU JUST HAVE TO *NOT* EAT THEM!
Yum!
NOT EAT PHENOMNOMENONS?
pf!?
NOT?
pf!
NOT.
OH, DELICIOUS!
EAT ME!
MM!
WE'RE TASTY!

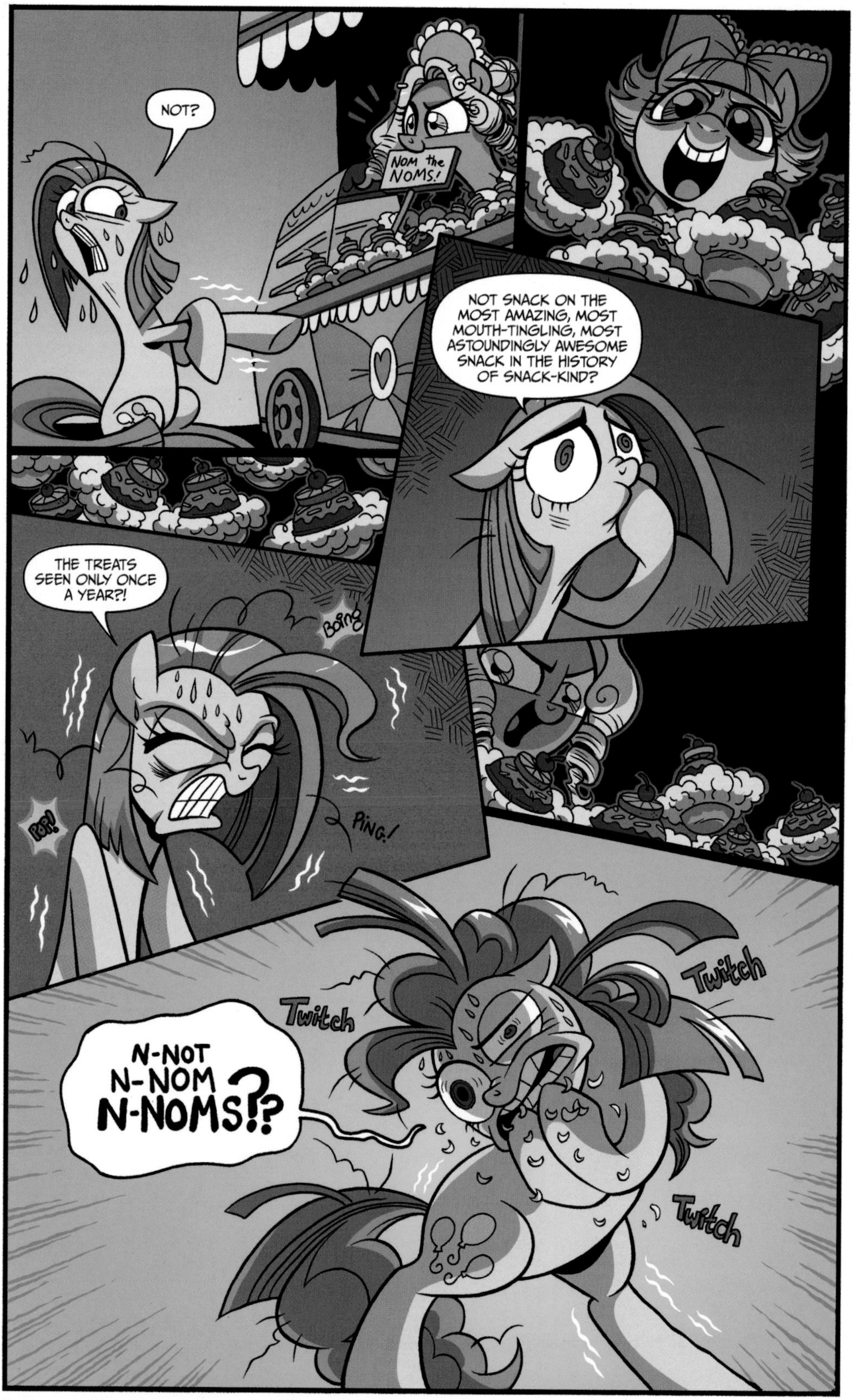
NOT?
Nom the NOMS!
NOT SNACK ON THE MOST AMAZING, MOST MOUTH-TINGLING, MOST ASTOUNDINGLY AWESOME SNACK IN THE HISTORY OF SNACK-KIND?
THE TREATS SEEN ONLY ONCE A YEAR?!
Boing
POP!
PING!
Twitch
Twitch
N-NOT N-NOM N-NOMS!?
Twitch

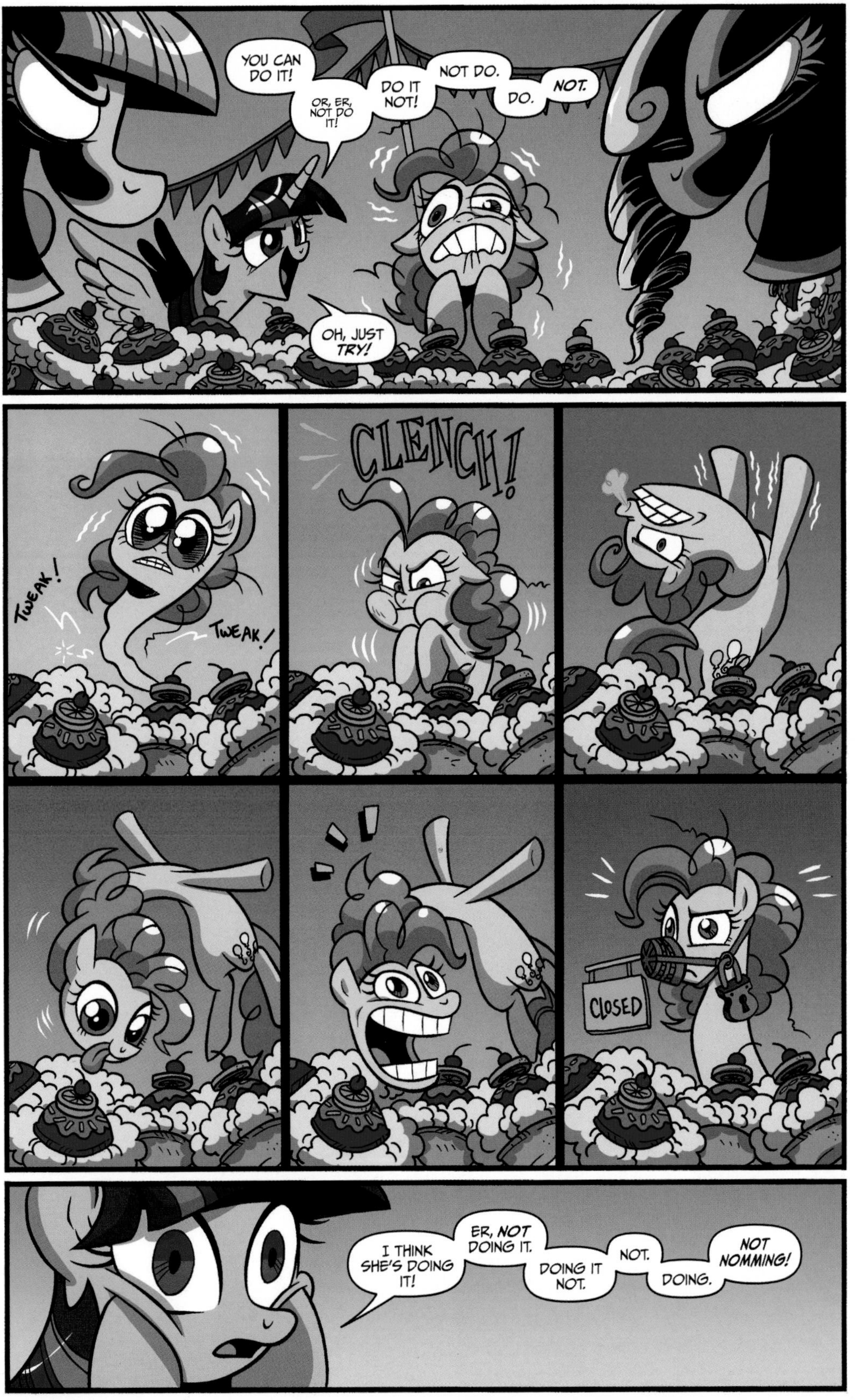

YOU CAN DO IT!
OR, ER, NOT DO IT!
DO IT NOT!
NOT DO.
DO.
NOT.
OH, JUST TRY!
TWEAK!
TWEAK!
CLENCH!
CLOSED
I THINK SHE'S DOING IT!
ER, NOT DOING IT.
DOING IT NOT.
NOT.
DOING.
NOT NOMMING!

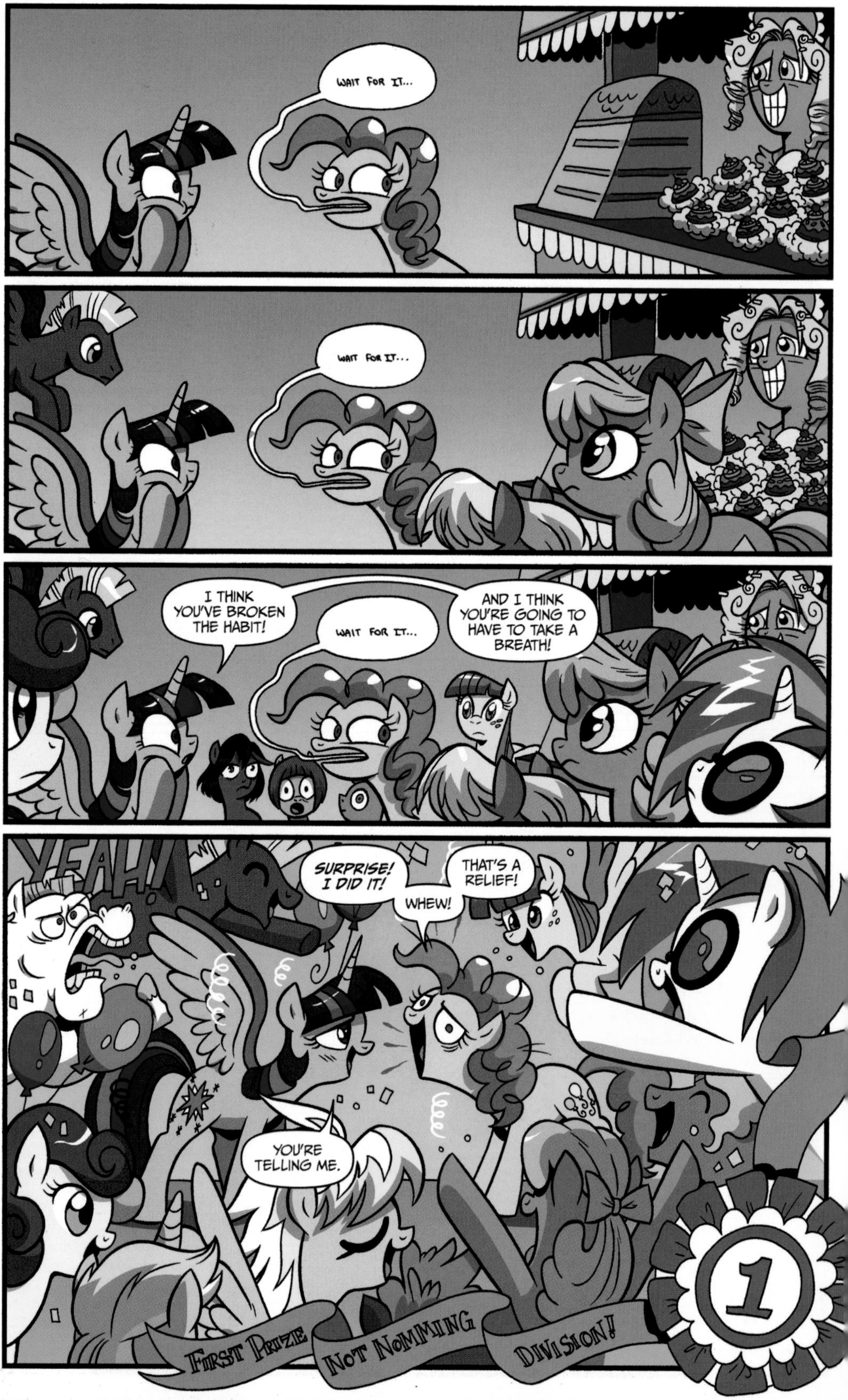

WAIT FOR IT...
WAIT FOR IT...
I THINK YOU'VE BROKEN THE HABIT!
WAIT FOR IT...
AND I THINK YOU'RE GOING TO HAVE TO TAKE A BREATH!
YEAH!!
SURPRISE! I DID IT!
WHEW!
THAT'S A RELIEF!
YOU'RE TELLING ME.
FIRST PRIZE NOT NOMMING DIVISION!
1

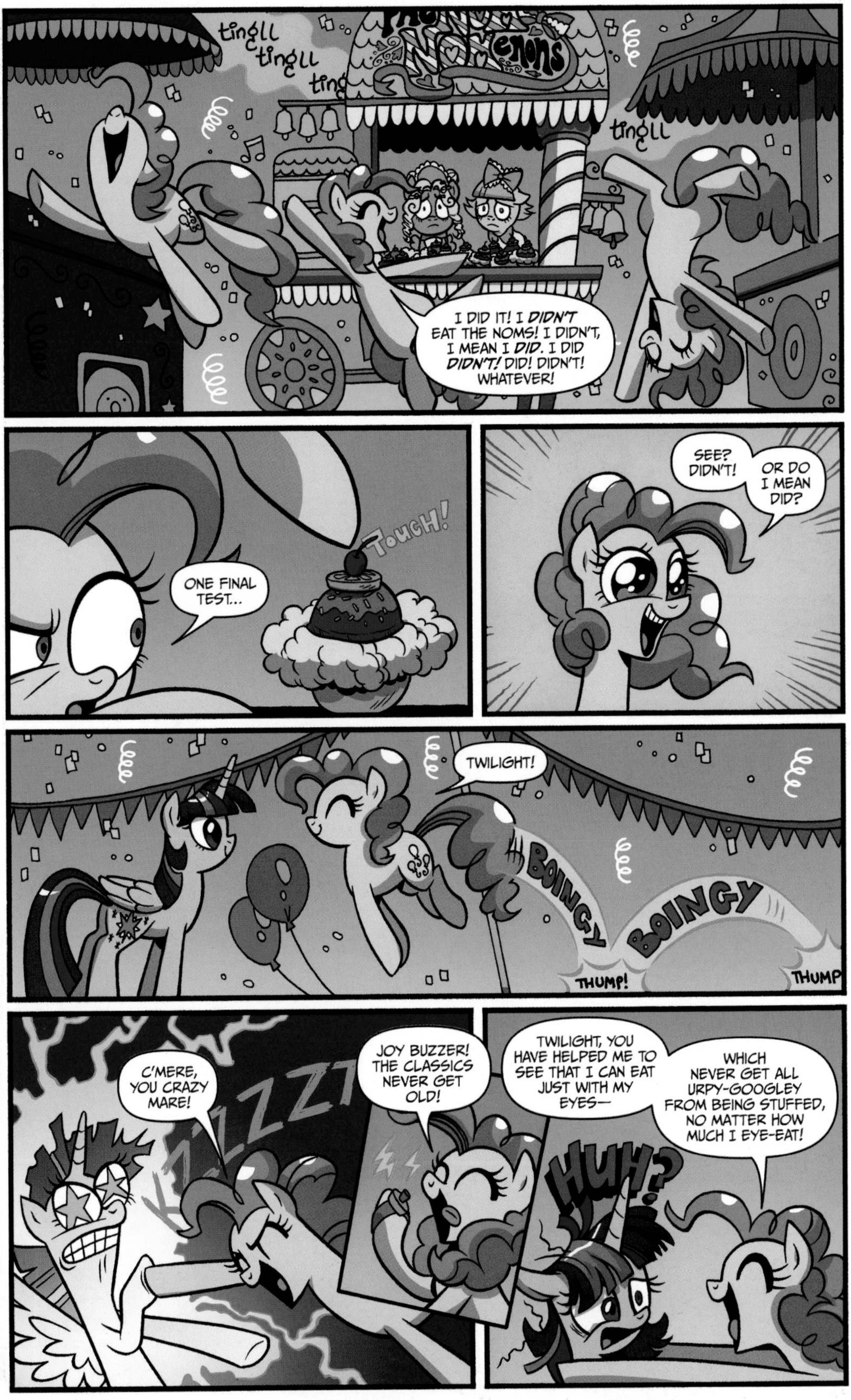

tingLL
tingLL
ting
tingLL
I DID IT! I *DIDN'T* EAT THE NOMS! I DIDN'T, I MEAN I *DID*. I DID *DIDN'T!* DID! DIDN'T! WHATEVER!
ONE FINAL TEST...
TOUCH!
SEE? DIDN'T!
OR DO I MEAN DID?
TWILIGHT!
BOINGY
BOINGY
THUMP!
THUMP
C'MERE, YOU CRAZY MARE!
JOY BUZZER! THE CLASSICS NEVER GET OLD!
TWILIGHT, YOU HAVE HELPED ME TO SEE THAT I CAN EAT JUST WITH MY EYES—
WHICH NEVER GET ALL URPY-GOOGLEY FROM BEING STUFFED, NO MATTER HOW MUCH I EYE-EAT!
HUH?

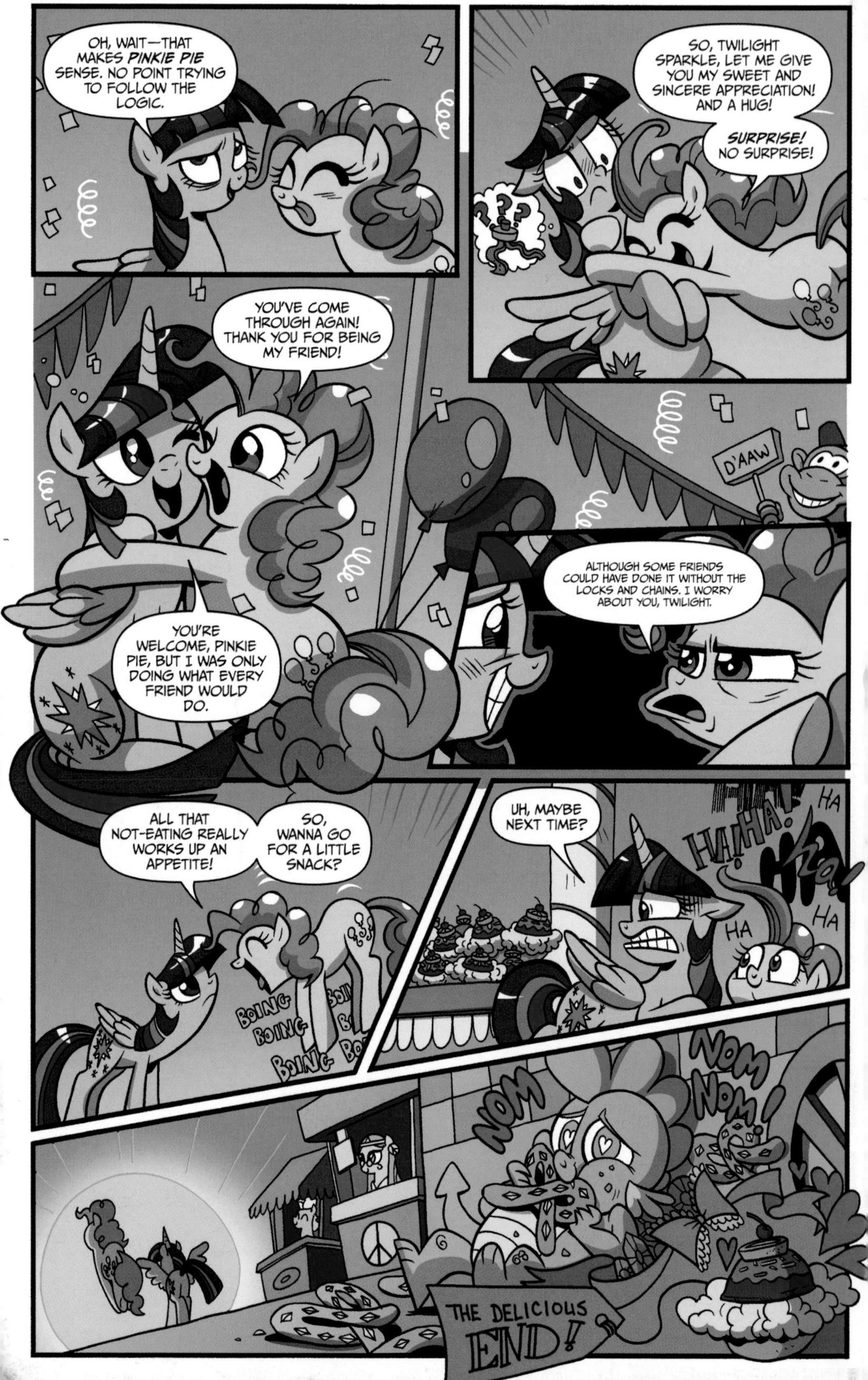
OH, WAIT—THAT MAKES PINKIE PIE SENSE. NO POINT TRYING TO FOLLOW THE LOGIC.
SO, TWILIGHT SPARKLE, LET ME GIVE YOU MY SWEET AND SINCERE APPRECIATION! AND A HUG!
SURPRISE! NO SURPRISE!
YOU'VE COME THROUGH AGAIN! THANK YOU FOR BEING MY FRIEND!
YOU'RE WELCOME, PINKIE PIE, BUT I WAS ONLY DOING WHAT EVERY FRIEND WOULD DO.
D'AAW
ALTHOUGH SOME FRIENDS COULD HAVE DONE IT WITHOUT THE LOCKS AND CHAINS. I WORRY ABOUT YOU, TWILIGHT.
ALL THAT NOT-EATING REALLY WORKS UP AN APPETITE!
SO, WANNA GO FOR A LITTLE SNACK?
BOING BOING BOING
UH, MAYBE NEXT TIME?
HA HA! HA HA
NOM NOM NOM!
THE DELICIOUS END!

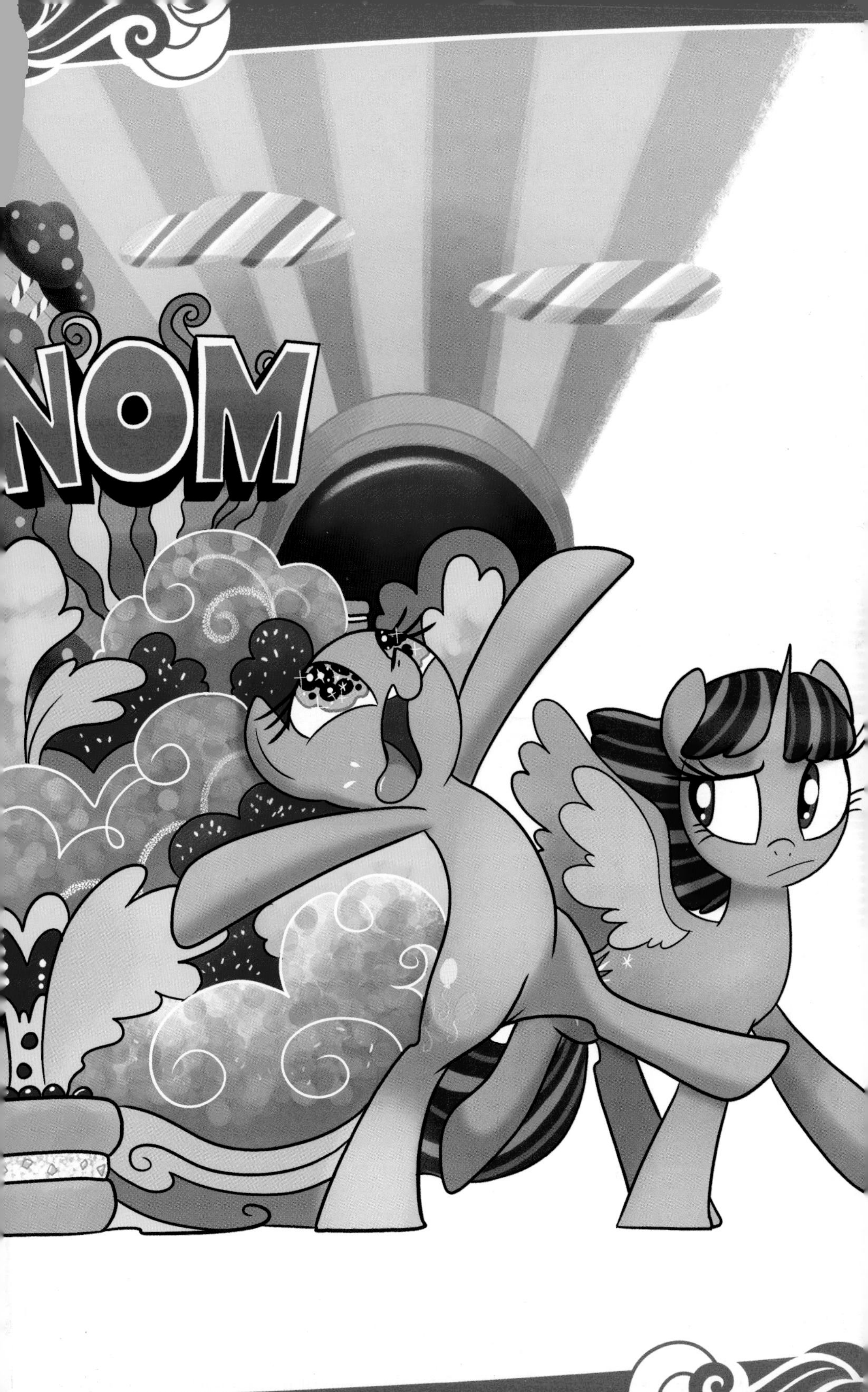
NOM

art by AMY MEBBERSON

MY LITTLE PONY